KU-739-133

A COURT OF SILVER FLAMES

BOOKS BY SARAH J. MAAS

THE COURT OF THORNS AND ROSES SERIES

A Court of Thorns and Roses

A Court of Mist and Fury

A Court of Wings and Ruin

A Court of Frost and Starlight

A Court of Silver Flames

A Court of Thorns and Roses Coloring Book

THE CRESCENT CITY SERIES

House of Earth and Blood

THE THRONE OF GLASS SERIES

The Assassin's Blade

Throne of Glass

Crown of Midnight

Heir of Fire

Queen of Shadows

Empire of Storms

Tower of Dawn

Kingdom of Ash

The Throne of Glass Coloring Book

A COURT OF SILVER FLAMES

SARAH J. MAAS

BLOOMSBURY PUBLISHING
LONDON • OXFORD • NEW YORK • NEW DELHI • SYDNEY

BLOOMSBURY PUBLISHING
Bloomsbury Publishing Plc
50 Bedford Square, London, WC1B 3DP, UK
29 Earlsfort Terrace, Dublin 2, Ireland

BLOOMSBURY, BLOOMSBURY PUBLISHING and the Diana logo are
trademarks of Bloomsbury Publishing Plc

First published in Great Britain 2021

Copyright © Sarah J. Maas, 2021
Map by Virginia Allyn, 2019

Sarah J. Maas has asserted her right under the Copyright, Designs and Patents Act, 1988,
to be identified as Author of this work

All rights reserved. No part of this publication may be reproduced or transmitted in any form or by any means, electronic or mechanical, including photocopying, recording, or any information storage or retrieval system, without prior permission in writing from the publishers

A catalogue record for this book is available from the British Library

ISBN: HB: 978-1-5266-0231-2; TPB: 978-1-5266-2064-4; eBook: 978-1-5266-0230-5;
ePDF: 978-1-5266-3469-6; UK exclusive: 978-1-5266-3475-7;
UK exclusive signed: 978-1-5266-3468-9; UK standard signed: 978-1-5266-3390-3;
UK tour: 978-1-5266-3476-4

2 4 6 8 10 9 7 5 3

Typeset by Westchester Publishing Services
Printed and bound in Great Britain by CPI Group (UK) Ltd, Croydon CR0 4YY

To find out more about our authors and books visit www.bloomsbury.com
and sign up for our newsletters, including news about Sarah J. Maas.

For every Nesta out there—
climb the mountain

And for Josh, Taran, and Annie,
who are the reason I keep climbing my own

The Faerie Lands of
Prythian
North
Illyrian Mountains
The Prison
Illyrian Steppes
Velaris
Night Court
Court of Nightmares
Hybern
Palace
Day Court
Dawn Court
Under the Mountain
Winter Court
Weaver's Cottage
Autumn Court
Adriata
Summer Court
The Forest House
Spring Court
The Wall
Feyre's Village
Mortal Lands

Vallahan
Montesere
Rask
Faerie Realms
The Wall
Scythia
Mortal Lands

The black water nipping at her thrashing heels was freezing.

Not the bite of winter chill, or even the burn of solid ice, but something colder. Deeper.

The cold of the gaps between stars, the cold of a world before light.

The cold of hell—true hell, she realized as she bucked against the strong hands trying to shove her into that Cauldron.

True hell, because that was Elain lying on the stone floor with the red-haired, one-eyed Fae male hovering over her. Because those were pointed ears poking through her sister's sodden gold-brown hair, and an immortal glow radiating from Elain's fair skin.

True hell—worse than the inky depths mere inches from her toes.

Put her under, the hard-faced Fae king ordered.

And the sound of that voice, the voice of the male who had done this to Elain . . .

She knew she was going into the Cauldron. Knew she would lose this fight.

Knew no one was coming to save her: not sobbing Feyre, not Feyre's gagged former lover, not her devastated new mate.

Not Cassian, broken and bleeding on the floor. The warrior was still trying to rise on trembling arms. To reach her.

The King of Hybern—he had done this. To Elain. To Cassian.

And to her.

The icy water bit into the soles of her feet.

It was a kiss of venom, a death so permanent that every inch of her roared in defiance.

She was going in—but she would not go gently.

The water gripped her ankles with phantom talons, tugging her down. She twisted, wrenching her arm free from the guard who held it.

And Nesta Archeron pointed. One finger—at the King of Hybern.

A death-promise. A target marked.

Hands shoved her into the water's waiting claws.

Nesta laughed at the fear that crept into the king's eyes just before the water devoured her whole.

In the beginning

And in the end

There was Darkness

And nothing more

She did not feel the cold as she sank into a sea that had no bottom, no horizon, no surface. But she felt the burning.

Immortality was not a serene youth.

It was fire.

It was molten ore poured into her veins, boiling her human blood until it was nothing but steam, forging her brittle bones until they were fresh steel.

And when she opened her mouth to scream, when the pain ripped her very self in two, there was no sound. There was nothing in this place but darkness and agony and power—

They would pay. All of them.

Starting with this Cauldron.

Starting *now*.

She tore into the darkness with talons and teeth. Rent and cleaved and shredded.

And the dark eternity around her shuddered. Bucked. Thrashed.

She laughed as it recoiled. Laughed around the mouthful of raw power she ripped out and swallowed whole; laughed at the fistfuls of eternity she shoved into her heart, her veins.

The Cauldron struggled like a bird under a cat's paw. She refused to relent.

Everything it had stolen from her, from Elain, she would take from it.

Wrapped in black eternity, Nesta and the Cauldron twined, burning through the darkness like a newborn star.

PART ONE

NOVICE

CHAPTER 1

Cassian raised his fist to the green door in the dim hallway—and hesitated.

He'd cut down more enemies than he cared to tally, had stood knee-deep in gore on countless battlefields and kept swinging, had made choices that cost him the lives of skilled warriors, had been a general and a grunt and an assassin, and yet . . . here he was, lowering his fist.

Balking.

The building on the north side of the Sidra River was in need of new paint. And new floors, if the creaking boards beneath his boots as he'd climbed the two flights had been any indication. But at least it was clean. Definitely grim by Velaris's standards, but when the city itself had no slums, that wasn't saying much. He'd seen and stayed in far worse.

He'd never understood, though, why Nesta insisted on dwelling here. He got why she wouldn't take up rooms in the House of Wind—it was too far from the city, and she couldn't fly or winnow in. Which meant dealing with the ten thousand steps up and down. But why live in this dump, when the town house was sitting empty? Since construction had finished on Feyre and Rhys's sprawling home on the river, the town house had been left open to any of their friends who needed or wanted it. He knew for a fact that Feyre had offered Nesta a room there—and had been rejected.

He frowned at the door's peeling paint. No sounds trickled through the sizable gap between the door and the floor, wide enough for even the fattest of rats to meander through; no fresh scents lingered in the cramped hallway.

Maybe he'd get lucky and she'd be out—perhaps sleeping under the bar of whatever seedy tavern she'd frequented last night. Though that might be worse, since he'd need to track her down there instead.

Cassian lifted his fist again, the red of his Siphon flickering in the ancient faelights tucked into the ceiling.

Coward. Grow some damned balls.

Cassian knocked once. Twice.

Silence.

Cassian almost sighed his relief aloud. Thank the fucking Mother—

Clipped, precise footsteps sounded from the other side of the door. Each more pissed off than the last.

He tucked his wings in tight, squaring his shoulders as he braced his feet apart. A traditional fighting stance, beaten into him during his training years, now mere muscle memory. He didn't dare consider why the sound of those footsteps sent his body falling into it.

The snap as she unlatched each of her four locks might as well have been the beating of a war-drum.

Cassian ran through the list of things he was to say, how Feyre had suggested he say them.

The door was yanked open, the knob twisting so hard Cassian wondered if she was imagining it as his neck.

Nesta Archeron already wore a scowl. But there she was.

She looked like hell.

"What do you want?" She didn't open the door wider than a hand's breadth.

When had he last seen her? The end-of-summer party on that barge in the Sidra last month? She hadn't looked this bad. Though he supposed a night trying to drown oneself in wine and liquor never left anyone looking particularly good the next morning. Especially at—

"It's seven in the morning," she went on, raking him over with that gray-blue stare that always kindled his temper.

She wore a male's shirt. Worse, she wore *only* a male's shirt.

Cassian propped a hand on the doorjamb and gave her a half grin he knew brought out her claws. "Rough night?"

Rough year, really. Her beautiful face was pale, far thinner than it had been before the war with Hybern, her lips bloodless, and those eyes . . . Cold and sharp, like a winter morning in the mountains.

No joy, no laughter, in any plane of it. Of her.

She made to shut the door on his hand.

He shoved a booted foot into the gap before she could break his fingers. Her nostrils flared slightly.

"Feyre wants you at the house."

"Which one?" Nesta said, frowning at the foot he'd wedged in the door. "She has five."

He bit back his retort. This wasn't the battlefield—and he wasn't her opponent. His job was to transport her to the assigned spot. And then pray that the lovely home Feyre and Rhys had just moved into wouldn't be reduced to rubble.

"The new one."

"Why didn't my sister fetch me herself?" He knew that suspicious gleam in her eye, the slight stiffening of her back. His own instincts surged to meet her defiance, to push and push and discover what might happen.

Since Winter Solstice, they'd exchanged only a handful of words. Most had been at the barge party last month. They'd consisted of:

Move.

Hello, Nes.

Move.

Gladly.

After months and months of nothing, of barely seeing her at all, that had been it.

He hadn't even understood why she'd shown up to the party, especially when she knew she'd be stuck on the water with them for hours. Amren likely deserved the credit for the rare appearance, due to whatever bit of sway the female held over Nesta. But by the end of that night, Nesta had been at the front of the line to get off the boat, arms tight around herself, and Amren had been brooding at the other end of it, nearly shaking with rage and disgust.

No one had asked what had happened between them, not even Feyre. The boat had docked, and Nesta had practically run off, and no one had spoken to her since. Until today. Until this conversation, which felt like the longest they'd had since the battles against Hybern.

Cassian said at last, "Feyre is High Lady. She's busy running the Night Court."

Nesta cocked her head, gold-brown hair sliding over a bony shoulder. On anyone else, the movement would have been contemplative. On her, it was the warning of a predator, sizing up prey.

"And my sister," she said in that flat voice that refused to yield any sign of emotion, "deemed my *immediate presence* necessary?"

"She knew you'd likely need to clean yourself up, and wanted to give you a head start. You're expected at nine."

He waited for the explosion as she did the math.

Her eyes flared. "Do I look like I need *two hours* to become presentable?"

He took the invitation to survey her: long bare legs, an elegant sweep of hips, tapered waist—too damn thin—and full, inviting breasts that were at odds with the new, sharp angles of her body.

On any other female, those magnificent breasts might have been enough cause for him to begin courting her the moment he met her. But from the instant he'd met Nesta, the cold fire in her eyes had been a temptation of a different sort.

And now that she was High Fae, all inherent dominance and aggression—and piss-poor attitude—he avoided her as much as possible. Especially with what had happened during and after the war against Hybern. She'd made her feelings about him more than clear.

Cassian said at last, "You look like you could use a few big meals, a bath, and some real clothes."

Nesta rolled her eyes, but fingered the hem of her shirt.

Cassian added, "Kick out the sorry bastard, get washed, and I'll bring you some tea."

Her brows rose a fraction of an inch.

He gave her a crooked smile. "You think I can't hear that male in your bedroom, trying to quietly put on his clothes and sneak out the window?"

As if in answer, a muffled thud came from the bedroom. Nesta hissed.

"I'll be back in an hour to see how things are proceeding." Cassian put enough bite behind the words that his soldiers would know not to push him—they'd remember that he required seven Siphons to keep his magic under control for good reason. But Nesta did not fly in his legions, did not fight under his command, and certainly did not seem to recall that he was over five hundred years old and—

"Don't bother. I'll be there on time."

He pushed off the doorjamb, wings flaring slightly as he backed away a few steps. "That's not what I was asked to do. I'm to see you from door to door."

Her face tightened. "Go perch on a chimney."

He sketched a bow, not daring to take his eyes off her. She'd emerged from the Cauldron with . . . gifts. Considerable gifts—dark ones. But no one had seen nor felt any sign of them since that last battle with Hybern, since Amren had shattered the Cauldron and Feyre and Rhys had managed to heal it. Elain, too, had revealed no indication of her seer's abilities since then.

But if Nesta's power remained, still capable of leveling battlefields . . . Cassian knew better than to make himself vulnerable to another predator. "Do you want your tea with milk or lemon?"

She slammed the door in his face.

Then locked each of those four locks.

Whistling to himself and wondering if that poor bastard inside the apartment would indeed flee out the window—mostly to escape *her*—Cassian strode down the dim hallway and went to find some food.

He'd need the sustenance today. Especially once Nesta learned precisely why her sister had summoned her.

⁜

Nesta Archeron didn't know the name of the male in her apartment.

She ransacked her wine-soaked memory as she returned to the bedroom, dodging piles of books and lumps of clothing, recalling heated glances at the tavern, the wet, hot meeting of their mouths, the sweat coating her as she rode him until pleasure and drink sent her into blessed oblivion, but not his name.

The male had already leaned out the window, with Cassian no doubt lurking on the street below to witness his spectacularly pathetic exit, when Nesta reached the dim, cramped bedroom. The brass-poster bed was rumpled, the sheets half-spilled on the creaky, uneven wood floor, and the cracked window banged against the wall on its loose hinges. The male twisted toward her.

He was handsome, in the way most High Fae males were handsome. A bit thinner than she liked them—practically a boy compared to the towering mass of muscle that had just filled her doorway. He winced as she padded in, his expression turning pained as he noted what she wore. "I . . . That's . . ."

Nesta tugged off his shirt, leaving nothing but bare skin in its wake.

His eyes widened, but the scent of his fear remained—not fear of her, but of the male he'd heard at the front door. As he remembered who her sister was. Who her sister's mate was. Who her sister's friends were. As if any of that meant something.

What would his fear smell like if he learned she'd used him, slept with him, to keep herself at bay? To settle that writhing darkness that had simmered inside her from the moment she'd emerged from the Cauldron? Sex, music, and drink, she'd learned this past year—all of it helped. Not entirely, but it kept the power from boiling over. Even if she could still feel it streaming through her blood, coiled tight around her bones.

She chucked the white shirt at him. "You can use the front door now."

He slung the shirt over his head. "I— Is he still—" His gaze kept snagging on her breasts, peaked against the chill morning; her bare skin. The apex of her thighs.

"Good-bye." Nesta entered the rusty, leaky bathroom attached to her bedroom. At least the place had hot running water.

Sometimes.

Feyre and Elain had tried to convince her to move. She'd always ignored their advice. Just as she'd ignore whatever was said today. She knew Feyre planned a scolding. Perhaps something to do with the fact that Nesta had signed last night's outrageous tab at the tavern to her sister's bank account.

Nesta snorted, twisting the handle in the bath. It groaned, the metal icy to the touch, and water sputtered, then sprayed into the cracked, stained tub.

This was her residence. No servants, no eyes monitoring and judging every move, no company unless she invited them. Or unless prying, swaggering warriors made it their business to stop by.

It took five minutes for the water to actually heat enough to start filling the tub. There had been some days in the past year when she hadn't even bothered to take the time. Some days when she'd climbed into the icy water, not feeling its bite but that of the Cauldron's dark depths as it devoured her whole. As it ripped away her humanity, her mortality, and made her into *this*.

It had taken her months of battling it—the body-tensing panic that made her very bones tremble to be submerged. But she'd forced herself to face it down. Had learned to sit in the icy water, nauseated and shaking, teeth gritted; had refused to move until her body recognized that she was in a tub and not the Cauldron, that she was in her apartment and not the stone castle across the sea, that she was alive, immortal. Even though her father was not.

No, her father was ashes in the wind, his existence marked only by a headstone on a hill outside this city. Or so her sisters had told her.

I loved you from the first moment I held you in my arms, her father had said to her in those last moments together.

Don't you lay your filthy hands on my daughter. Those had been his final words, spat at the King of Hybern. Her father had squandered those final words on that worm of a king.

Her father. The man who had never fought for his children, not until the end. When he had come to save them—to save the humans and the Fae, yes, but most of all, his daughters. Her.

A grand, stupid waste.

Unholy dark power flowed through her, and it had not been enough to stop the King of Hybern from snapping his neck.

She had hated her father, hated him deeply, and yet he had loved her, for some inexplicable reason. Not enough to try to spare them from poverty or keep them from starving. But somehow it had been enough for him to raise an army on the continent. To sail a ship named for her into battle.

She had still hated her father in those last moments. And then his neck had cracked, his eyes not full of fear as he died, but of that foolish love for her.

That was what had lingered—the look in his eyes. The resentment in her heart as he died for her. It had festered, gnawing at her like the power she buried deep, running rampant through her head until no icy baths could numb it away.

She could have saved him.

It was the King of Hybern's fault. She knew that. But it was hers, too. Just as it was her fault that Elain had been captured by the Cauldron after Nesta spied on it with that scrying, her fault that Hybern had done such terrible things to hunt her and her sister down like a deer.

Some days, the sheer dread and panic locked Nesta's body up so thoroughly that nothing could get her to breathe. Nothing could stop the awful power from beginning to rise, rise, rise in her. Nothing beyond the music at those taverns, the card games with strangers, the endless bottles of wine, and the sex that made her feel nothing—but offered a moment of release amid the roaring inside her.

Nesta finished washing away the sweat and other remnants of last night. The sex hadn't been bad—she'd had better, but also much worse. Even immortality wasn't enough time for some males to master the art of the bedroom.

So she'd taught herself what she liked. She'd obtained a monthly contraceptive tea from her local apothecary, and then she'd brought that first male here. He had no idea that her maidenhead had been intact until he'd spied the smeared blood on the sheets. His face had tightened with distaste—then a glimmer of fear that she might report an unsatisfactory first bedding to her sister. To her sister's insufferable mate. Nesta hadn't bothered to tell him that she avoided both of them at all costs. Especially the latter. These days, Rhysand seemed content to do the same.

After the war with Hybern, Rhysand had offered her jobs. Positions in his court.

She didn't want them. They were pity offerings, thin attempts to get her to be a part of Feyre's life, to be gainfully employed. But the High Lord had never liked her. Their conversations were coldly civil at best.

She'd never told him that the reasons he hated her were the same reasons she lived here. Took cold baths some days. Forgot to eat on others. Couldn't stand the crack and snap of a fireplace. And drowned herself in wine and music and pleasure each night. Every damning thing Rhysand thought about her was true—and she'd known it long before he had ever shadowed her doorstep.

Any offering Rhysand threw her way was made solely out of love for Feyre. Better to spend her time the way she wished. They kept paying for it, after all.

The knock on the door rattled the entire apartment.

She glared toward the front room, debating whether to pretend she'd left, but Cassian could hear her, smell her. And if he broke down the door, which he was likely to do, she'd just have the headache of explaining it to her stingy landlord.

So Nesta donned the dress she'd left on the floor last night, and then again freed all four locks. She'd installed them the first day she'd arrived. Locking them each night was practically a ritual. Even when the nameless male had been here, even out of her mind on wine, she'd remembered to lock them all.

As if that would keep the monsters of this world at bay.

Nesta tugged open the door enough to see Cassian's cocky grin, and left it ajar as she stormed away to search for her shoes.

He strode in after her, a mug of tea in his hand—the cup probably borrowed from the shop at the corner. Or outright given to him, considering how people tended to worship the ground his muddy boots walked on. He'd already been adored in this city before the Hybern conflict. His heroism and sacrifice—the feats he'd performed on the battlefields—had won him even more awe after its end.

She didn't blame his admirers. She'd experienced the pleasure and sheer terror of watching him on those battlefields. Still woke with sweat coating her at the memories: how she couldn't breathe while she'd witnessed him fight, enemies swarming him; how it had felt when the Cauldron's power had surged and she'd known it was going to strike where their army was strongest—him.

She hadn't been able to save the one thousand Illyrians who had fallen in the moment after she'd summoned him to safety. She turned away from that memory, too.

Cassian surveyed her apartment and let out a low whistle. "Ever thought of hiring a cleaner?"

Nesta scanned the small living area—a sagging crimson couch, a soot-stained brick hearth, a moth-eaten floral armchair, then the ancient kitchenette, piled with leaning columns of dirty dishes. Where had she thrown her shoes last night? She shifted her search to her bedroom.

"Some fresh air would be a good start," Cassian added from the other room. The window groaned as he cracked it open.

She found her brown shoes in opposite corners of the bedroom. One reeked of spilled wine.

Nesta perched on the edge of the mattress to slide them on, tugging at the laces. She didn't bother to look up as Cassian's steady steps approached, then halted at the threshold.

He sniffed once. Loudly.

"I'd hoped you at least changed the sheets between visitors, but apparently that doesn't bother you."

Nesta tied the laces on the first shoe. "What business is it of yours?"

He shrugged, though the tightness on his face didn't reflect such nonchalance. "If I can smell a few different males in here, then surely your companions can, too."

"Hasn't stopped them yet." She tied the other shoe, Cassian's hazel eyes tracking the movement.

"Your tea is getting cold." His teeth flashed.

Nesta ignored him and searched the bedroom again. Her coat . . .

"Your coat is on the ground by the front door," he said. "And it's going to be brisk out, so bring a scarf."

She ignored that, too, but breezed by him, careful to avoid touching him, and found her dark blue overcoat exactly where he'd claimed it was. She opened the front door, pointing for him to leave first.

Cassian held her gaze as he stalked for her, then reached out an arm—

And plucked the cerulean-and-cream scarf Elain had given her for her birthday this spring off the hook on the wall. He gripped it in his fist, dangling it like a strangled snake as he brushed past her.

Something was eating at him. Usually, Cassian held out a bit longer before yielding to his temper. Perhaps it had to do with whatever Feyre wanted to say up at the house.

Nesta's gut twisted as she set each lock.

She wasn't stupid. She knew there had been unrest since the war had ended, both in these lands and on the continent. Knew that without the barrier of the wall, some Fae territories were pushing the limits on what they could get away with in terms of border claims and how they treated humans. And she knew that those four human queens still squatted in their shared palace, their armies unused and intact.

They were monsters, all of them. They'd killed the golden-haired queen who'd betrayed them and sold another—Vassa—to a sorcerer-lord. It seemed only fitting that the youngest of the four remaining queens had been transformed into a crone by the Cauldron. Made into a long-lived Fae, yes, but aged into a withered shell as punishment for the power Nesta had taken from the Cauldron. How she'd ripped it apart while it had torn her mortal body into something new.

That wizened queen blamed her. Had wanted to kill her, if Hybern's Ravens had been correct before Bryaxis and Rhysand had destroyed them for infiltrating the House of Wind's library.

There had been no whisper of that queen in the fourteen months since the war.

But if some new threat had arisen . . .

The four locks seemed to laugh at her before Nesta followed Cassian out of the building and into the bustling city beyond.

✢

The riverfront "house" was actually an estate, and so new and clean and beautiful that Nesta remembered her shoes were covered in stale wine precisely as she strode through the towering marble archway and into the shining front hall, tastefully decorated in shades of ivory and sand.

A mighty staircase bisected the enormous space, a chandelier of handblown glass—made by Velaris artisans—drooping from the carved ceiling above it. The faelights in each nest-shaped orb cast shimmering reflections on the polished pale wood floors, interrupted only by potted ferns, wood furniture also made in Velaris, and an outrageous array of art. She didn't bother to remark on any of it. Plush blue rugs broke up the pristine floors, a long runner flowing along the cavernous halls on either side, and one ran beneath the arch of the stairs, straight to a wall of windows on its other side, which looked out onto the sloping lawn and gleaming river at its feet.

Cassian headed to the left—toward the formal rooms for business, Feyre had informed Nesta during that first and only tour two months ago. Nesta had been half-drunk at the time, and had hated every second of it, each perfect room.

Most males bought their wives and mates jewelry for an outrageous Winter Solstice present.

Rhys had bought Feyre a palace.

No—he'd purchased the war-decimated land, and then given his mate free rein to design the residence of their dreams.

And somehow, Nesta thought as she silently followed an unnaturally quiet Cassian down the hall toward one of the studies whose doors were cracked open, Feyre and Rhys *had* managed to make this place seem cozy, welcoming. A behemoth of a building, but still a home. Even the formal furniture seemed designed for comfort and lounging, for long conversations over hearty food. Every piece of art had been picked by Feyre herself, or painted by her, many of them portraits and depictions of *them*—her friends, her . . . new family.

There were none of Nesta, naturally.

Even their gods-damned father had a portrait on the wall along one side of the grand staircase: him and Elain, smiling and happy, as they'd been before the world went to shit. Sitting on a stone bench amid bushes bursting with pink and blue hydrangea. The formal gardens of their first home, that lovely manor near the sea. Nesta and their mother were nowhere in sight.

That was how it had been, after all: Elain and Feyre doted on by their father. Nesta prized and trained by their mother.

During that first tour, Nesta had noted the lack of herself here. The lack of their mother. She said nothing, of course, but it was a pointed absence.

It was enough to now set her teeth on edge, to make her grab the invisible, internal leash that kept the horrible power within her at bay and pull tight, as Cassian slipped into the study and said to whoever awaited them, "She's here."

Nesta braced herself, but Feyre merely chuckled. "You're five minutes early. I'm impressed."

"Seems like a good omen for gambling. We should head to Rita's," Cassian drawled just as Nesta stepped into the wood-paneled room.

The study opened into a lush garden courtyard. The space was warm and rich, and she might have admitted she liked the floor-to-ceiling bookshelves, the sapphire velvet furniture before the black marble hearth, had she not seen who was sitting inside.

Feyre perched on the rolled arm of the couch, clad in a heavy white sweater and dark leggings.

Rhys, in his usual black, leaned against the mantel, arms crossed. No wings today.

And Amren, in her preferred gray, sat cross-legged in the leather armchair by the roaring hearth, those muted silver eyes sweeping over Nesta with distaste.

So much had changed between her and the female.

Nesta had seen to that—the destruction. She didn't let herself think about that argument at the end-of-summer party on the river barge. Or the silence between herself and Amren since then.

No more visits to Amren's apartment. No more chats over jigsaw puzzles. Certainly no more lessons in magic. She'd made sure of that last part, too.

Feyre, at least, smiled at her. "I heard you had quite the night."

Nesta glanced between where Cassian had claimed the armchair across from Amren, the empty spot on the couch beside Feyre, and where Rhys stood by the hearth.

She kept her spine straight, her chin high, hating that they all eyed her as she opted to sit on the couch beside her sister. Hating that Rhys and Amren noted her filthy shoes, and probably still smelled that male on her despite the bath.

"You look atrocious," Amren said.

Nesta wasn't stupid enough to glare at the . . . whatever Amren was. She was High Fae now, yes, but she'd once been something different. Not of this world. Her tongue was still sharp enough to wound.

Like Nesta, Amren did not possess court-specific magic related to the High Fae. It didn't make her influence in this court any less mighty. Nesta's own High Fae powers had never materialized—she had only what she'd taken from the Cauldron, rather than letting it deign to gift her with power, as it had with Elain. She had no idea what she'd ripped from the Cauldron while it had stolen her humanity from her—but she knew they were things she did not and would never wish to understand, to master. The very thought had her stomach churning.

"Though I bet it's hard to look good," Amren went on, "when you're out until the darkest hours of the night, drinking yourself stupid and fucking anything that comes your way."

Feyre whipped her head to the High Lord's Second. Rhys seemed inclined to agree with Amren. Cassian kept his mouth shut. Nesta said smoothly, "I wasn't aware that my activities were under your jurisdiction."

Cassian loosed a murmur that sounded like a warning. To which one of them, she didn't know. Or care.

Amren's eyes glowed, a remnant of the power that had once burned inside her. All that was left now. Nesta knew her own power could shine like that, too—but while Amren's had revealed itself to be light and heat, Nesta knew that her silver flame came from a colder, darker place. A place that was old—and yet wholly new.

Amren challenged, "They are when you spend that much of our gold on wine."

Perhaps she had pushed them too far with last night's tab.

Nesta looked to Feyre, who winced. "So you really did make me come all the way here for a scolding?"

Feyre's eyes—mirror images of her own—softened slightly. "No, it's not a scolding." She cut a sharp glance at Rhys, still icily silent against the mantel, and then to Amren, seething in her chair. "Think of this as a discussion."

Nesta shot to her feet. "My life is not your concern, or up for any sort of *discussion*."

"*Sit down*," Rhys snarled.

The raw command in that voice, the utter dominance and power . . .

Nesta froze, fighting it, hating that Fae part of her that bowed to such things. Cassian leaned forward in his chair, as if he'd leap between them. She could have sworn something like pain had etched itself across his face.

But Nesta held Rhysand's gaze. Threw every ounce of defiance she could into it, even as his order made her knees *want* to bend, to sit.

Rhys said, "You are going to stay. You are going to listen."

She let out a low laugh. "You're not my High Lord. You don't give me orders." But she knew how powerful he was. Had seen it, felt it. Still trembled to be near him.

Rhys scented that fear. One side of his mouth curled up in a cruel smile. "You want to go head-to-head, Nesta Archeron?" he purred. The High Lord of the Night Court gestured to the sloping lawn beyond the windows. "We've got plenty of space out there for a brawl."

Nesta bared her teeth, silently roaring at her body to obey *her* orders. She'd sooner die than bow to him. To any of them.

Rhys's smile grew, well aware of that fact.

"That's enough," Feyre snapped at Rhys. "I told you to keep out of it."

He dragged his star-flecked eyes to his mate, and it was all Nesta could do to keep from collapsing onto the couch as her knees gave out at last. Feyre angled her head, nostrils flaring, and said to Rhysand, "You can either *leave*, or you can stay and keep your mouth shut."

Rhys again crossed his arms, but said nothing.

"You too," Feyre spat to Amren. The female harrumphed and nestled into her chair.

Nesta didn't bother to look pleasant as Feyre twisted to face her, taking a proper seat on the couch, the velvet cushions sighing beneath her. Her sister swallowed. "We need to make some changes, Nesta," Feyre said hoarsely. "You do—and *we* do."

Where the hell was Elain?

"I'll take the blame," Feyre went on, "for allowing things to get this far, and this bad. After the war with Hybern, with everything else that was going on, it . . . You . . . I should have been there to help you, but I wasn't, and I am ready to admit that this is partially my fault."

"That *what* is your fault?" Nesta hissed.

"You," Cassian said. "This bullshit behavior."

He'd said that at the Winter Solstice. And just as it had then, her spine locked at the insult, the *arrogance*—

"Look," Cassian went on, holding up his hands, "it's not some moral failing, but—"

"I understand how you're feeling," Feyre cut in.

"You know *nothing* about how I'm feeling."

Feyre plowed ahead. "It's time for some changes. Starting now."

"Keep your self-righteous do-gooder nonsense out of my life."

"You don't have a life," Feyre retorted. "And I'm not going to sit by for another moment and watch you destroy yourself." She put a tattooed hand on her heart, like it meant something. "I decided after the war to give you time, but it seems that was wrong. *I* was wrong."

"Oh?" The word was a dagger thrown between them.

Rhys tensed at the sneer, but still said nothing.

"You're done," Feyre breathed, voice shaking. "This behavior, that apartment, all of it—you are *done*, Nesta."

"And where," Nesta said, her tone mercifully icy, "am I supposed to go?"

Feyre looked to Cassian.

For once, Cassian wasn't grinning. "You're coming with me," he said. "To train."

CHAPTER 2

Cassian felt as if he'd loosed an arrow at a sleeping firedrake. Nesta, bundled in that worn blue coat, with her stained shoes and her wrinkled gray dress, looked him over and demanded, "*What?*"

"As of this meeting," Feyre clarified, "you're moving into the House of Wind." She nodded eastward, toward the palace carved into the mountains at the far end of the city. "Rhys and I have decided that each morning, you will train with Cassian in Windhaven, in the Illyrian Mountains. After lunch, for the rest of the afternoon, you will be assigned work in the library beneath the House of Wind. But the apartment, the seedy taverns—all of that is *over*, Nesta."

Nesta's fingers curled into fists in her lap. But she said nothing.

He should have positioned himself beside her, instead of allowing his High Lady to sit on that couch within arm's reach of her. No matter that Feyre already had a shield around herself courtesy of Rhys—it had been there at breakfast, too. *Part of my ongoing training*, Feyre had muttered when Cassian asked about the ironclad defenses, so strong they even masked her scent. *Rhys is having Helion teach him about truly impenetrable shields, so of course I have the pleasure of being the test subject.*

I'm supposed to try to break this one to see if Rhys is following Helion's instructions correctly. It's a new kind of insanity.

But one that had proved fortuitous. Even if they didn't know *what* Nesta's power could do against ordinary magic.

Rhys seemed to be thinking the same thing, and Cassian poised himself to jump between the two sisters. His Siphons flared in warning as Rhys's power rumbled.

Cassian had no doubt Feyre could defend herself against most opponents, but Nesta . . .

He wasn't entirely sure Feyre would hit back, even if Nesta launched that terrible power at her. And he hated that he didn't know if Nesta would sink low enough to do it. That things had become so bad that he even considered the possibility.

"I'm not moving to the House of Wind," Nesta said. "And I'm not training at that miserable village. Certainly not with *him*." She threw him a look that was nothing short of venomous.

"It's not up for negotiation," Amren said, breaking her vow to keep out of the discussion as much as possible for the second time in so many minutes. The eldest of the Archeron sisters had a talent for getting under everyone's skin. Yet Nesta and Amren had always shared a bond—an understanding.

Until their fight on the barge.

"Like hell it isn't," Nesta challenged, but didn't attempt to stand as Rhys's eyes flickered with cold warning.

"Your apartment is being packed as we speak," Amren said, picking at a speck of lint on her silk blouse. "By the time you return, it will be empty. Your clothes are already being sent to the House, though I doubt they will be suitable for training at Windhaven." A pointed glance at Nesta's gray dress, baggier on her than it had once been. Did Nesta notice the faint glimmer of worry in Amren's smoky eyes—understand how rare it was?

More than that, did Nesta understand that this meeting wasn't to condemn her, but instead came from a place of concern? Her simmering stare told him she considered this purely an attack.

"You can't do this," Nesta said. "I'm not a member of this court."

"You seem to have no qualms about spending this court's money," Amren countered. "During the war with Hybern, you accepted the position as our human emissary. You never resigned from the role, so formal law still considers you an official member of this court." A wave of her small fingers and a book floated toward Nesta before thumping onto the cushions beside her. That was about the extent of the magic Amren now possessed—ordinary, unremarkable High Fae magic. "Page two hundred thirty-six, if you want to check."

Amren had combed through their *laws* for this? Cassian didn't even know such a rule existed—he'd accepted the position Rhys had offered him without question, not caring what he was agreeing to, only that he and Rhys and Azriel would be together. That they'd have a home that no one could ever take from them. Until Amarantha.

He'd never stop being grateful for it: for the High Lady mere feet from him, who had saved them all from Amarantha's rule, who had returned his brother to him and then brought Rhys out of the darkness that lingered.

"So here are your options, girl," Amren said, delicate chin rising. Cassian didn't miss the look between Feyre and Rhys: the utter agony in his High Lady's face at the ultimatum he knew was to be presented to Nesta, and the half-restrained rage in Rhys's that his mate was in such pain because of it. He'd already seen that exchanged look once today—had hoped he wouldn't see it again.

Cassian had been eating an early breakfast with them this morning when Rhys had gotten the bill for Nesta's night out. When Rhys had read each item aloud. Bottles of rare wine, exotic foods, gambling debts . . .

Feyre had stared at her plate until silent tears dripped into her scrambled eggs.

Cassian knew there'd been previous conversations—fights—about Nesta. About whether to give her time to heal herself, as they'd all believed would happen at first, or to step in. But as Feyre wept at the table, he knew it was a breaking of some sort. An acceptance of a hope failed.

It had required all of Cassian's training, every horror he'd endured on and off the battlefield, to keep that same crushing sorrow from his own face.

Rhys had laid a comforting hand on Feyre's, squeezing gently before he looked at Azriel, and then Cassian, and laid out his plan. As if he'd had it waiting a long, long while.

Elain had walked in halfway through. She'd been toiling in the estate gardens since dawn, and had been solemn as Rhys filled her in. Feyre had been unable to say a word. But Elain's gaze remained steady as she listened to Rhys.

Then Rhys summoned Amren from her attic apartment across the river. Feyre had insisted that the order come through Amren, not Rhys, to preserve any sort of familial bond between Rhys and her sister.

Cassian didn't think there was one to begin with, but Rhys had agreed, moving to kneel at Feyre's side, wiping away the remnants of her tears, kissing her temple. They'd all left the table then, giving their High Lord and Lady privacy.

Cassian took to the skies moments later, letting the roaring wind drown out every thought in his head, letting its briskness cool his pounding heart. This meeting, what was to come—none of it would be easy.

Amren, they'd agreed, had always been one of the few people who could get through to Nesta. Whom Nesta seemed to fear, if only slightly. Who understood, somehow, what Nesta was, deep down.

She'd been the only one Nesta had truly spoken to after the war.

It didn't seem like a coincidence that in the past month, since they'd argued on that boat, Nesta's behavior had deteriorated further. That she now looked like . . . this.

"One," Amren said, raising a slender finger, "you can move up to the House of Wind, train with Cassian in the mornings, and work in the library in the afternoons. You will not be a prisoner. But there will be no one to fly or winnow you down to the city. If you want to venture into the city proper, by all means, go ahead. That is, if you can brave the ten thousand steps down from the House." Amren's eyes glittered with the challenge. "And if you can somehow find two coppers to rub together to buy yourself a drink. But if you follow this plan, we will reevaluate where and how you live in a few months."

"And my other option?" Nesta spat.

Mother above, this woman—female. She was no longer human. Cassian could think of very, very few people who would defy Amren and Rhys. Certainly not in the same room. Certainly not with such venom.

"You go back to the human lands."

Amren had suggested a few days in a dungeon in the Hewn City, but Feyre had simply said that the human world would be more than enough of a prison for someone like Nesta.

Someone like Feyre, too. And Elain.

All three sisters were now High Fae with considerable powers, though only Feyre's were let loose. Even Amren had no idea whether Elain's and Nesta's powers remained. The Cauldron had granted them unique powers, different from other High Fae: the gift of sight to the former, and the gift of . . . Cassian didn't know what to call Nesta's gift. Didn't know whether it was a gift at all—or something she had taken. The silver fire, that sense of death looming, the raw power he'd witnessed as it blasted into the King of Hybern. Whatever it was, it existed beyond the usual array of High Fae gifts.

The human world was behind them. They could never return. Even though all three of them were war heroes, each in their own right, the humans wouldn't care. Would stay far, far away, if they weren't provoked to violence. So, yes: Nesta might technically be able to return to the human lands, but she would find no companionship there, no warm welcome or town that would accept her. Wherever she was able to find a place to live, she would be essentially housebound, confined to the grounds of her home for fear of human prejudices.

Nesta turned to Feyre, lips pulling back from her teeth. "And these are my only options?"

"I—" Feyre caught herself before she could say the rest—*I'm sorry*—and squared her shoulders. Became the High Lady of the Night Court, even without her black crown, even in Rhys's old sweater. "Yes."

"You have no right."

"I—"

Nesta erupted. "*You* dragged me into this mess, this horrible place. *You* are why I am like this, why I am *stuck* here—"

Feyre flinched. Rhys's rage became palpable, a pulse of night-kissed power that tightened Cassian's gut, every warrior's instinct beaten into him coming to attention.

"That's enough," Feyre breathed.

Nesta blinked.

Feyre swallowed, but didn't balk. "That is *enough*. You're moving up to the House, you're going to train and work, and I don't care what vitriol you spew my way. You're doing it."

"Elain needs to be able to see me—"

"Elain agreed to this hours ago. She's currently packing your things. They'll be waiting for you when you arrive."

Nesta recoiled.

Feyre didn't relent. "Elain knows how to contact you. If she wishes to visit you at the House of Wind, she is free to do so. One of us will gladly take her up there."

The words hung between them, so heavy and awkward that Cassian said, "I promise not to bite."

Nesta's upper lip curled back as she faced him. "I suppose this was *your* idea—"

"It was," he lied with a grin. "We're going to have a wonderful time together."

They'd likely kill each other.

"I want to speak to my sister. Alone," Nesta ordered.

Cassian glanced at Rhys, who leveled an assessing stare at Nesta. Cassian had been on the receiving end of that same stare a few times over the centuries and did not envy Nesta one bit. But the High Lord of the Night Court nodded. "We'll be in the hall."

Cassian's fist tightened at the implied insult that they didn't trust her enough to go farther than that, despite the shield on Feyre. Even if the rational, warrior-minded part of him agreed. Nesta's eyes flared, and he knew she'd understood it, too.

From the way Feyre's jaw tightened, he suspected she wasn't pleased at the subtle jab—it wouldn't help convince Nesta that they were doing this to help her. Rhys would be getting the verbal beating he deserved later.

Cassian waited until Rhys and Amren rose before following them out. True to his word, Rhys walked three steps down the hall, away from the wood doors spelled against eavesdroppers, and leaned against the wall.

Doing the same, Cassian said to Amren, "I didn't even know we had laws like that about court membership."

"We don't." Amren picked at her red-painted nails.

He swore under his breath.

Rhys smiled wryly. But Cassian frowned toward the shut double doors and prayed Nesta didn't do anything stupid.

⸸

Nesta held her spine ramrod straight, back aching with the effort. She had never hated anyone so much as she hated all of them now. Save for the King of Hybern, she supposed.

They'd all been discussing her, deeming her unfit and unchecked, and—

"You didn't care before," Nesta said. "Why now?"

Feyre toyed with her silver-and-star-sapphire wedding ring. "I told you: it wasn't that I didn't care. We—everyone, I mean—had multiple conversations about this. About you. We— *I* decided that giving you time and space would be best."

"And what did Elain have to say about it?" Part of her didn't want to know.

Feyre's mouth tightened. "This isn't about Elain. And last I checked, you barely saw her, either."

Nesta hadn't realized they were paying such close attention.

She'd never explained to Feyre—had never found the words to explain—why she'd put such distance between them all. Elain had been stolen by the Cauldron and saved by Azriel and Feyre. Yet the terror still gripped Nesta, waking and asleep: the memory of how it had felt in those moments after hearing the Cauldron's seductive call and realizing it had been for Elain, not for her or Feyre. How it had felt to find Elain's tent empty, to see that blue cloak discarded.

Things had only gotten worse from there.

You have your lives, and I have mine, she'd said to Elain last Winter Solstice. She'd known how deeply it would wound her sister. But she couldn't bear it—the bone-deep horror that lingered. The flashes of that discarded cloak or the Cauldron's chill waters or Cassian crawling toward her or her father's neck snapping—

Feyre said carefully, "For what it's worth, I was hoping you'd turn yourself around. I wanted to give you space to do it, since you seem to lash out at everyone who comes close enough, but you didn't even *try*."

Perhaps you can find it in yourself to try a little harder this year. Cassian's words from nine months ago still rang fresh in Nesta's mind, uttered on an ice-slick street blocks from here.

Try? It was all she could think to say.

I know that's a foreign word to you.

Then her rage had ruptured from her. *Why should I have to* try *to do anything? I was dragged into this world of yours, this court.*

Then go somewhere else.

She'd swallowed her own response: *I have nowhere to go.*

It was the truth. She had no desire to return to the human realm. Had never felt at home there, not really. And this strange, new Fae world . . . She might have accepted her different, altered body, that she was now permanently changed and her humanity gone, but she didn't know where she belonged in this world, either. The thought was one she tried to drown in liquor and music and cards, as often as she used those things to quell that writhing power deep inside.

Feyre continued, "All you have done is help yourself to our money."

"Your mate's money." Another flash of hurt. Nesta's blood sang at the direct blow. "Thank you so much for taking time out of your home-making and shopping to remember me."

"I built a room in this house for you. I *asked* you to help me decorate it. You told me to piss off."

"Why would I ever want to stay in this house?" Where she could see precisely how happy they were, where none of them seemed remotely as decimated as she'd been by the war. She'd come so close to being a part of it—of that circle. Had held their hands as they'd stood together on the morning of the final battle and believed they might all make it.

Then she'd learned precisely how mercilessly it might be ripped away. What the cost of hope and joy and love truly was. She never wanted to face it again. Never wanted to endure what she'd felt in that forest clearing, with the King of Hybern chuckling, blood everywhere.

Her power hadn't been enough to save them that day. She supposed she'd been punishing it for failing her ever since, keeping it locked up tight inside her.

Feyre said, "Because you're my sister."

"Yes, and you're always sacrificing for us, your sad little human family—"

"You spent *five hundred gold marks* last night!" Feyre exploded, shooting to her feet to pace in front of the hearth. "Do you know how much money that is? Do you know how *embarrassed* I was when we got the bill this morning and my friends—my *family*—had to hear all about it?"

Nesta hated that word. The term Feyre used to describe her court. As if things had been so miserable with the Archeron family that Feyre had needed to find another one. Had chosen her own. Nesta's nails bit into her palms, the pain overriding that of her tightening chest.

Feyre went on, "And to hear not just the amount of the bill, but what you *spent* it on—"

"Oh, so it's about you saving face—"

"It is about how it reflects upon me, upon Rhys, and upon my court when my damned sister spends our money on wine and gambling and does *nothing* to contribute to this city! If my sister cannot be controlled, then why should we have the right to rule over anyone else?"

"I am not a thing to be controlled by you," Nesta said icily. Everything in her life, from the moment she was born, had been controlled by other people. Things happened *to* her; anytime she tried to exert control, she'd been thwarted at every turn—and she hated that even more than the King of Hybern.

"That's why you're going to train at Windhaven. You will learn to control *yourself*."

"I won't go."

"You're going, even if you have to be tied up and hauled there. You will follow Cassian's lessons, and you will do whatever work Clotho requires in the library." Nesta blocked out the memory—of the dark depths of that library, the ancient monster that had dwelled there. It had saved them from Hybern's cronies, yes, but . . . She refused to think of it. "You will respect her, and the other priestesses in the library," Feyre said, "and you will *never* give them a moment's trouble. Any free time is yours to spend as you wish. In the House."

Hot rage pumped through her, so loud Nesta could barely hear the real fire before which her sister paced. Was glad of the roaring in her head when the sound of wood cracking as it burned was so much like her father's breaking neck that she couldn't stand to light a fire in her own home.

"You had no right to close up my apartment, to take my things—"

"What things? A few clothes and some rotten food." Nesta didn't have the chance to wonder how Feyre knew that. Not as her sister said, "I'm having that entire building condemned."

"You wouldn't dare."

"It's done. Rhys already visited the landlord. It will be torn down and rebuilt as a shelter for families still displaced by the war."

Nesta tried to master her uneven breathing. One of the few choices she'd made for herself, stripped away. Feyre didn't seem to care. Feyre had always been her own master. Always got whatever she wished. And now, it seemed, Feyre would be granted this wish, too. Nesta seethed, "I never want to speak to you again."

"That's fine. You can talk to Cassian and the priestesses instead."

There was no insulting her way out of it. "I won't be your prisoner—"

"No. You can go wherever you wish. As Amren said, you are free to leave the House. If you can manage those ten thousand steps." Feyre's eyes blazed. "But I'm done paying for you to destroy yourself."

Destroy herself. The silence hummed in Nesta's ears, rippled across her flames, suffocating them, stilling the unbearable wrath. Utter, frozen silence.

She'd learned to live with the silence that had started the moment her father had died, the silence that had begun crushing her when she'd gone to his study at their half-wrecked manor days later and found one of his pathetic little wood carvings. She'd wanted to scream and scream, but there had been so many people around. She'd held herself together until the meeting with all those war heroes had ended. Then she'd let herself fall. Straight into this silent pit.

"The others are waiting," Feyre said. "Elain should be done by now."

"I want to talk to her."

"She'll come visit when she's ready."

Nesta held her sister's stare.

Feyre's eyes gleamed. "You think I don't know why you've pushed even Elain away?"

Nesta didn't want to talk about it. About the fact that it had *always* been her and Elain. And, somehow, now it had become Feyre and Elain instead. Elain had chosen Feyre and these people, and left her behind. Amren had done the same. She'd made it clear on the barge.

Nesta didn't care that during the war with Hybern, her own tentative bond had formed with Feyre, forged over common goals: protect Elain, save the human lands. They were excuses, Nesta had realized, to paper over what now boiled and raged in her heart.

Nesta didn't bother replying, and Feyre didn't speak again as she departed.

There was nothing to bind them together anymore.

CHAPTER 3

Cassian watched Rhysand carefully stir his tea.

He'd seen Rhys slice up their enemies with the same cold precision that he was now using with that spoon.

They sat in the High Lord's study, illuminated by the light of green glass lamps and a heavy iron chandelier. The two-level atrium occupied the northern end of the business wing, as Feyre called it.

There was the main floor of the study—bedecked in the hand-knotted blue carpets that Feyre had gone to Cesere to select from its artisans—with its two sitting areas, Rhys's desk, and twin long tables near the bookshelves. At the far end of the room, a little dais led into a broad raised alcove flanked by more books—and in its center, a massive, working model of their world, the stars and planets around it, and some other fancy things that had been explained to Cassian once before he deemed them boring and proceeded to ignore them completely.

Az, of course, had been fascinated. Rhys had built the model himself centuries ago. It could not only track the sun, but also tell time, and it somehow allowed Rhys to ponder the existence of life beyond their own world and other things Cassian had, again, instantly forgotten.

On the mezzanine, accessible by an ornate wrought-iron spiral staircase just to the left when one walked in, were more books—thousands in this space alone—a few glass cabinets full of delicate objects that Cassian stayed away from (for fear of breaking them with his "bear paws," as Mor described his hands), and several of Feyre's paintings.

There were plenty of those on the bottom level, too, some in shadow and meant to stay that way, some revealed by the streaming light reflecting off the river at the foot of the sloping lawn. Cassian's High Lady had a way of capturing the world that always made him pause. Her paintings sometimes unsettled him. The truths she portrayed weren't always pleasant ones.

He'd gone to her studio a few times to watch her paint. Surprisingly, she had let him.

The first time he'd visited, he'd found Feyre tense at her easel. She was painting what he realized was an emaciated rib cage, so thin he could count most of the bones.

When he spotted a familiar birthmark on the too-thin left arm beside it, he eyed the same mark amid the tattoo on her own extended arm, brush in hand. He merely nodded to her, an acknowledgment that he understood.

He had never been as thin as Feyre during his own years of poverty, but he understood the hunger in each brushstroke. The desperation. The hollow, empty feeling that *felt* like those grays and blues and pale, sickly white. The despair of the black pit behind that torso and arm. Death, hovering close like a crow awaiting carrion.

He'd thought about that painting a great deal in the days afterward—how it had made him feel, how close they'd all come to losing their High Lady before they'd ever met her.

Rhys finished stirring his tea and set down his spoon with terrible gentleness.

Cassian raised his eyes to the portrait behind his High Lord's mammoth desk. The golden faelight orbs in the room were positioned to make it seem alive, glowing.

Feyre's face—a self-portrait—seemed to laugh at him. At the mate whose back was to her. So she could watch over him, Rhys said.

Cassian prayed that the gods were watching over *him* as Rhys sipped from his tea and said, "You're ready?"

He leaned back in his seat. "I've gotten young warriors in line before."

Rhys's violet eyes glowed. "Nesta's not some young buck pushing the boundaries."

"I can handle her."

Rhys stared at his tea.

Cassian recognized that face. That serious, unnervingly calm face.

"You did good work getting the Illyrians back in order this spring, you know."

He braced himself. He'd been anticipating this talk since he'd spent four months with the Illyrians, soothing the jagged edges amongst the war-bands, making sure the families who'd lost fathers and sons and brothers and husbands were taken care of, that they knew he was there to help and to listen, and generally making it very fucking clear that if they rose up against Rhys, there would be hell to pay.

The Blood Rite last spring had taken care of the worst of them, including the troublemaker Kallon, whose arrogance hadn't been enough to compensate for his shoddy training when he'd been slain just miles from the slopes of Ramiel. That Cassian had heaved a sigh of relief at the news of the young male's demise had lingered with him, but the Illyrians had stopped their grumbling soon after. And Cassian had spent the time since then rebuilding their ranks, overseeing the training of promising new warriors and making sure the seasoned ones were still in good enough shape to fight again. Replenishing their depleted numbers had at least given the Illyrians something to focus on—and

Cassian knew there was little he could add anymore beyond the occasional inspection and council meeting.

So the Illyrians were at peace—or as peaceful as a warrior society could be, with their constant training. Which was what Rhys wanted. Not just because a rebellion would be a disaster, but because of this. What he knew Rhys was about to say.

"I think it's time for you to take on bigger responsibilities."

Cassian grimaced. There it was.

Rhys chuckled. "You can't honestly mean to tell me you didn't know the Illyrian situation was a test?"

"I'd hoped not," he grumbled, tucking in his wings.

Rhys smirked, though he quickly sobered. "Nesta is not a test, though. She's . . . different."

"I know." Even before she'd been Made, he'd seen it. And after that terrible day in Hybern . . . He'd never forgotten the Bone Carver's whispered words in the Prison.

What if I tell you what the rock and darkness and sea beyond whispered to me, Lord of Bloodshed? How they shuddered in fear, on that island across the sea. How they trembled when she *emerged. She took something—something precious. She ripped it out with her teeth.*

What did you wake that day in Hybern, Prince of Bastards?

That final question had chased him from slumber more nights than he cared to admit.

Cassian made himself say, "We haven't seen a hint of her power since the war. For all we know, it vanished with the Cauldron's breaking."

"Or maybe it's dormant, as the Cauldron is now asleep and safely hidden in Cretea with Drakon and Miryam. Her power could rise at any moment."

A chill skittered down Cassian's spine. He trusted the Seraphim prince and the half-human woman to keep the Cauldron concealed, but there would be nothing they or anyone could do to control its power if awoken.

Rhys said, "Be on your guard."

"You sound like you're afraid of her."

"I am."

Cassian blinked.

Rhys lifted a brow. "Why do you think I sent you to get her this morning?"

Cassian shook his head, unable to help his laugh. Rhys smiled, lacing his fingers behind his head and leaning back in his seat.

"You need to get out in the practice ring more, brother," Cassian told him, surveying his friend's powerful body. "Don't want that mate of yours to find any soft bits."

"She never finds any soft bits when I'm around her," Rhys said, and Cassian laughed again.

"Is Feyre going to kick your ass for what you said earlier?"

"I already told the servants to clear out for the rest of the day as soon as you take Nesta up to the House."

"I think the servants hear you fighting plenty." Indeed, Feyre had no hesitation when it came to telling Rhys that he'd stepped out of line.

Rhys threw him a wicked smile. "It's not the fighting I don't want them hearing."

Cassian grinned right back, even as something like jealousy tugged on his gut. He didn't begrudge them their happiness—not at all. There were plenty of times when he'd see the joy on Rhys's face and have to walk away to keep from weeping, because his brother had waited for that love, earned it. Rhys had gone to the mat again and again to fight for that future with Feyre. For *this*.

But sometimes, Cassian saw that mating ring, and the portrait behind the desk, and this house, and just . . . wanted.

The clock chimed ten thirty, and Cassian rose. "Enjoy your not-fighting."

"Cassian."

The tone stopped him.

Rhys's face was carefully calm. "You didn't ask what bigger responsibilities I have in mind for you."

"I assumed Nesta was big enough," he hedged.

Rhys gave him a knowing look. "You could be more."

"I'm your general. Isn't that enough?"

"Is it enough for you?"

Yes, he almost said. But found himself hesitating.

"Oh, you're certainly hesitating," Rhys said. Cassian tried to snap up his mental shields, but found they were intact. Rhys was smiling like a cat. "You still reveal everything on that face of yours, brother," Rhys crooned. But his amusement swiftly faded. "Az and I have good reason to believe that the human queens are scheming again. I need you to look into it. Deal with it."

"What, we're doing some role reversal? Az gets to lead the Illyrians now?"

"Don't play stupid," Rhys said coolly.

Cassian rolled his eyes. But they both knew Azriel would sooner disband and destroy Illyria than help it. Convincing their brother that the Illyrians were a people worth saving was still a battle amongst the three of them.

Rhys went on, "Azriel is juggling more than he'll admit right now. I'm not dumping another responsibility on him. This task of yours will help him." Rhys flashed a challenging smile. "And let us all see what you're really made of."

"You want me to play spy?"

"There are other ways to glean information, Cass, besides peeking through keyholes. Az isn't a courtier. He works from the shadows. But I need someone—I need you—standing in the open. Mor can fill you in on the details. She'll be back from Vallahan at some point today."

"I'm no courtier, either. You know that." The thought made his stomach churn.

"Scared?"

Cassian let the Siphons atop the backs of his hands shimmer with inner fire. "So I'm to deal with these queens as well as train Nesta?"

Rhys leaned back, his silence confirmation.

Cassian strode toward the shut double doors, reining in a string of curses. "We're in for a long few months, then."

He was almost to the door when Rhys said quietly, "You certainly are."

✠

"Did you keep those fighting leathers from the war?" Cassian said to Nesta by way of greeting as he stalked into the entry hall. "You'll need them tomorrow."

"I made sure Elain packed them for her," Feyre replied from her perch on the stairs, not looking at her stiff-backed sister standing at their base. He wondered if his High Lady had noticed the disappearing servants yet.

The secret smile in Feyre's eyes told him she knew plenty about it. And what was coming for her in a few minutes.

Thank the gods he was getting out of here. He'd probably have to fly to the sea itself *not* to hear Rhys. Or feel his power when he . . . Cassian stopped himself before he could finish the thought. He and his brothers had put a good deal of distance between the stupid youths they'd been—fucking any female who showed interest, often in the same room as each other—and the males they were now. He wanted to keep it that way.

Nesta just crossed her arms.

"Are you winnowing us up to the House?" he asked Feyre.

As if in answer, Mor said from behind him, "I am." She winked at Feyre. "She's got a special meeting with Rhysie."

Cassian grinned as Mor strode in from the residential wing. "I thought you wouldn't be back until later today." He threw open his arms, folding her against his chest and squeezing tight. Mor's waist-length golden hair smelled of cold seas.

She squeezed him back. "I didn't feel like waiting until the afternoon. Vallahan is already knee-deep in snow. I needed some sunshine."

Cassian pulled away to scan her beautiful face, as familiar to him as his own. Her brown eyes were shadowed despite her words. "What's wrong?"

Feyre rose from her seat, noting the strain as well. "Nothing," Mor said, flipping her hair over a shoulder.

"Liar."

"I'll tell you all later," Mor conceded, and looked toward Nesta. "You should wear the leathers tomorrow. When you train up at Windhaven, you'll want them against the cold."

Nesta leveled a bored, icy look at Mor.

Mor just beamed at her in return.

Feyre took that as a good moment to casually step between them, Rhys's shield still hard as steel around her. Never mind that they'd all be real damn close in about a minute. "Today we'll let you get settled at the House—you can unpack your things. Get some rest, if you want."

Nesta said nothing.

Cassian dragged a hand through his hair. Cauldron spare them. Rhys expected him to play politics when he couldn't even navigate *this*?

Mor smirked, as if reading the thought on his face. "Congratulations on your promotion." She shook her head. "Cassian the courtier. I never thought I'd see the day."

Feyre snickered. But Nesta's eyes slid to him, surprised and wary. He said to her, if only to beat her to it, "Still a bastard-born nobody, don't worry."

Nesta's lips thinned.

Feyre said carefully to Nesta, "We'll talk soon."

Nesta again didn't reply.

It seemed she had stopped speaking to Feyre at all. But at least she was going willingly.

Semi-willingly.

"Shall we?" Mor said, offering up either elbow.

Nesta gazed at the floor, her face pale and gaunt, eyes blazing.

Feyre met his stare. The look alone conveyed everything she was begging of him.

Nesta stepped past her, grabbed Mor's forearm, and watched a spot on the wall.

Mor cringed at him, but Cassian didn't dare share the look. Nesta might not be gazing at them, but he knew she saw and heard and assessed everything.

So he merely took Mor's other arm and winked at Feyre before they all vanished into wind and darkness.

✠

Mor winnowed them into the sky right above the House of Wind.

Before the stomach-dropping plunge could register, Nesta was in Cassian's arms, his wings spread, as he flew toward the stone veranda. It had been a long while since she'd been held by him, since she'd seen the city so small below.

He could have flown them both up here, Nesta realized as he alighted and Morrigan vanished from her deadly plummet with a wave. The rules of the House were simple: no one could winnow directly inside thanks to its heavy wards, so it was a choice to either walk up the ten thousand steps, winnow and drop a terrifying distance to the veranda—likely breaking bones—or winnow to the edge of the wards with someone who had wings to fly the rest of the way in. But being in Cassian's arms . . . She'd rather have risked breaking every bone in her body from the plunge to the veranda. Thankfully, the flight was over in a matter of seconds.

Nesta shoved out of his grip the moment her feet hit the worn stones. Cassian let her, folding his wings and lingering by the rail, all of Velaris glittering below and beyond him.

She'd spent weeks here last year—during that terrible period after being turned Fae, begging Elain to demonstrate any sign of wanting to live. She'd barely slept for fear of Elain walking off this veranda, or leaning too far out of one of the countless windows, or simply throwing herself down those ten thousand stairs.

Her throat closed at the surge of memories and at the sprawling view—the glimmering ribbon of the Sidra far below, the red-stoned palace built into the side of the flat-topped mountain itself.

Nesta dug her hands into her pockets, wishing she'd opted for the warm gloves Feyre had coaxed her to take. She'd refused. Or silently refused, since she had not uttered a word to her sister after they'd left the study.

Partially because she was afraid of what would come out.

For a long moment, Nesta and Cassian watched each other.

The wind ripped at his shoulder-length dark hair, but he might have been standing in a summer field for all the reaction he yielded to the cold—so much sharper up here, high above the city. It was all she could do to keep her teeth from clattering their way out of her skull.

Cassian finally said, "You'll be staying in your old room."

As if she had any sort of claim on this place. On anywhere at all.

He went on, "My room's a level above that."

"Why would I need to know that?" The words snapped out of her.

He began walking toward the glass doors that led into the mountain's interior. "In case you have a bad dream and need someone to read you a story," he drawled, a half smile dancing on his face. "Maybe one of those smutty books you like so much."

Her nostrils flared. But she walked through the door he held open for her, nearly sighing at the cozy warmth filling the red stone halls. Her new residence. Sleeping site.

It wasn't a home, this place. Just as her apartment hadn't been a home. Neither had her father's fancy new house, before Hybern had half-destroyed it. And neither had the cottage, or the glorious manor before that. *Home* was a foreign word.

But she knew this level of the House of Wind well: the dining room to the left, and the stairway to her right that would take her down two levels to her floor, and the kitchens a level below that. The library far, far beneath it.

She wouldn't have cared where she stayed, except for the convenience of the small, private library also on her level. Which had been the place where she'd discovered those smutty books, as Cassian called them. She'd devoured a few dozen of them during those weeks she'd first been here, desperate for any lifeline to keep her from falling apart, from bellowing at what had been done to her body, her life—to Elain. Elain, who would not eat, or speak, or do anything at all.

Elain, who had somehow become the *adjusted* one.

In the months leading to and during the war, Nesta had managed. Had stepped into this world, with these people, and started to see it—a future.

Until she'd been hunted by the King of Hybern and the Cauldron. Until she'd realized that everyone she cared for would be used to hurt her, break her, trap her. Until that last battle when she couldn't stop one thousand Illyrians from dying, and had instead been able to save only one.

Him. She would do it again, if forced to. And knowing that . . . She couldn't bear that truth, either.

Cassian aimed for the downward stairs, his every movement brimming with unfaltering arrogance.

"I don't need an escort to my room." No matter that his rooms were that way, too. "I know how to get there."

He threw a smirk over a muscled shoulder and strode down the stairs anyway. "I just want to make sure you arrive in one piece before I settle in." He nodded to the landing they passed, the open archway that led into the hall with his bedroom. She knew it only because she'd had little more to do during those initial weeks as High Fae than wander this palace like a ghost.

Cassian added, "Az is in the room two doors down from mine." They reached the level of her bedroom and he swaggered along the hall. "You probably won't see him, though."

"He's here to spy on me?" Her words bounced off the red stone.

Cassian said tightly, "He says he'd rather stay up here than at the river house."

That made two of them. "Why?"

"I don't know. He's Az. He likes his space." He shrugged, the faelight filtering through the golden sconces gilding the taloned apex of his wings. "He'll keep to himself, so most of the time it'll be only you and me."

She didn't dare reply. Not to all that statement implied. Alone—with Cassian. Here.

Cassian stopped in front of a familiar, arched wood door. He leaned against the jamb, hazel eyes monitoring her every step.

She knew the House belonged to Rhys. Knew Cassian's entire existence was paid for by Rhys, just as the High Lord bankrolled all of his Inner Circle. Knew that the fastest and deepest way to annoy Cassian, hurt him right now would be to strike for that, to make him doubt the work he did and whether he deserved to be here. The instinct crept up, a rising wave, each word selected to slice and wound. She'd always had the gift, if it could be called that. Yet it wasn't a curse, not entirely. It had served her well.

He scanned her face as she stopped in front of the bedroom door. "Let's hear it, Nes."

"Don't call me that." She dangled the words like bait. Let him think her vulnerable.

But he pushed off the door, wings tucking in. "You need a hot meal."

"I don't want one."

"Why?"

"Because I'm not hungry."

It was true. Her appetite had been the first thing to go after that battle. Only instinct and the occasional social requirement to appear like she gave a shit about anything kept her eating.

"You won't last through an hour of training tomorrow without food in your belly."

"I'm not training at that horrible place." She'd hated Windhaven from the first time she'd seen it, cold and bleak and full of humorless, harsh-faced people.

The Siphon strapped atop Cassian's left hand gleamed, a red band of light twining from the stone to wrap around the door handle. It yanked the iron downward, the door swinging open with a creak, then vanished like smoke. "You were given an order, as well as the alternative to following it. You want to go back to the human lands, be my guest."

Then go somewhere else.

He'd likely have that preening Morrigan dump her over the border like so much baggage.

And Nesta would have called the bluff, except . . . she knew what she'd face down south. The war had done little to warm human sentiments toward the Fae.

She had nowhere to go. Elain, mourn as she might for the life she would have had with Graysen, had found a place, a role here. Tending to the gardens of Feyre's veritable palace on the river, helping other residents of Velaris restore their own destroyed gardens—she had purpose, and joy, and *friends*: those two half-wraiths who worked in Rhysand's household. But those things had always come easily to her sister. Had always made Elain special.

Had made Nesta fight like hell to keep Elain safe at all costs.

The Cauldron had learned that. The King of Hybern had learned it, too.

An old, heavy weight tugged her down, oblivion beckoning. "I'm tired." Her words came out mercifully flat.

"Take the day to rest, then," Cassian said, his voice a shade quiet. "Mor or Rhys will winnow us up to Windhaven after breakfast tomorrow."

She said nothing. He went on, "We'll start easy: two hours of training, then lunch, then you'll be brought back here to meet with Clotho."

She didn't have the energy to ask further about the training, or the work in the library with its high priestess. She didn't really care. Let Rhysand and Feyre and Amren and Cassian make her do this bullshit. Let them think it could somehow make a lick of difference.

Nesta didn't bother to reply before she strode through the archway and into her bedroom. But she felt his stare on her, assessing every step over the threshold, the way her hand gripped the side of the door, the way she flexed her fingers before she slammed it shut.

Nesta waited mere feet inside the bedroom, blinking at the glaring light through the wall of windows at its other end. A scuff of boots on stone informed her that he'd left.

It wasn't until the sound faded completely that she took in the room before her, unchanged since she'd last been in it, the connecting door to Elain's old suite now sealed shut.

The wide space easily accommodated a mammoth four-poster bed against the wall to her left, as well as a small sitting area to her right, complete with a sofa and two chairs. A carved marble fireplace occupied the wall before the sitting area, mercifully dark, and multiple rugs lay scattered throughout, offering reprieve from the chilly stone floors.

But that wasn't what she'd liked about this room. No, it was what she now faced: the wall of windows that overlooked the city, the river, the flatlands and distant sparkle of sea beyond. All that land, all those people, so far away. As if this palace floated in the clouds. There had been some days up here when the mist had been thick enough to block the view below, swirling so close to the window that she'd been able to trail her fingers through it.

No tendrils of mist drifted by now, though. The windows revealed nothing but a clear early-autumn day, the sunlight near-blinding.

Seconds ticked by. Minutes.

A familiar roaring built in her ears. That heavy hollowness tugged her down, as surely as some faerie creature wrapping its bony hands around her ankle and yanking her beneath a dark surface. As surely as she had been shoved under that eternal, icy water in the Cauldron.

Nesta's body became distant, foreign, as she shut the heavy gray velvet curtains against the light. Shrouding the room in darkness bit by bit. She ignored the three bags and two trunks set beside the dresser as she approached the bed.

She barely managed to toe off her shoes before she slid beneath the layers of white down blankets and quilts, closed her eyes, and breathed.

And breathed.

And breathed.

CHAPTER 4

Mor had already commandeered a table at the riverfront café, an arm slung across the back of a wrought-iron chair, the other elegantly draped over her crossed knees. Cassian halted a few feet from the maze of tables along the walkway, smiling to himself at the sight of her: head tipped toward the sun, unbound hair gleaming and rippling around her like liquid gold, her full lips curled upward, basking in the light.

She never stopped appreciating the sunshine. Even five hundred years after leaving that veritable prison she'd called home and the monsters who claimed her as kin, his friend—his sister, honestly—still savored every moment in the sun. As if the first seventeen years of her life, spent in the darkness of the Hewn City, still lurked around her like Az's shadows.

Cassian cleared his throat as he approached the table, offering pleasant smiles to the other patrons and people along the walkway who either gawked or waved at him, and by the time he sat, Mor was already smirking, her brown eyes lit with amusement.

"Don't start," he warned, settling his wings around the chair's back and motioning to the owner of the café, who knew him well enough to understand that meant he wanted water—no tea or sweets, both of which Mor had before her.

Mor grinned, so beautiful it took his breath away. "Can't I enjoy the sight of my friend being fawned over by the public?"

He rolled his eyes, and murmured his thanks to the owner as a pitcher of water and a glass appeared before him.

Mor said when the owner had gone to tend to other tables, "I seem to remember a time when you enjoyed that sort of thing, too."

"I was a young, arrogant idiot." He cringed to recall how he'd strutted around after successful battles or missions, believing he deserved the praise of strangers. For too damn long, he'd indulged in that bullshit. It had taken walking these same streets after Rhys had been imprisoned by Amarantha—after Rhys sacrificed so much to shield this city, and seeing the disappointment and fear in so many faces—to make Cassian realize what a fool he'd been.

Mor cleared her throat, as if sensing the direction of his thoughts. She didn't possess Rhys's skill set, but having survived in the Court of Nightmares, she'd learned to read the subtlest of expressions. A mere blink, she'd once told him, might mean the difference between life and death in that miserable court. "She's settled, then?"

Cassian knew who she meant. "Taking a nap."

Mor snorted.

"Don't." His attention drifting to the glittering Sidra mere feet away. "Please don't."

Mor sipped her tea, the portrait of elegant innocence. "We'd be better off throwing Nesta into the Court of Nightmares. She'd thrive there."

Cassian clenched his jaw, both at the insult and the truth. "That's exactly the sort of existence we're trying to steer her away from."

Mor assessed him with a bob of her thick lashes. "It pains you seeing her like this."

"All of it pains me." He and Mor had always had this kind of relationship: truth at all costs, however harsh. Ever since that first and only time they'd slept together, when he'd learned too late that she'd hidden from him the terrible repercussions. When he'd seen her broken body and known that even if she'd lied to him, he'd still played a part.

Cassian blew out a breath, shaking away the blood-soaked memory still staining his mind five centuries later. "It pains me that Nesta has become . . . this. It pains me that she and Feyre are always at each other's throats. It pains me that Feyre hurts over it, and I know Nesta does, too. It pains me that . . ." He drummed his fingers on the table, then sipped from his water. "I really don't want to talk about it."

"All right." The breeze ruffled the gauzy fabric of Mor's twilight-blue dress.

He again let himself admire her perfect face. Beyond the disastrous consequences for Mor after their night together, the fallout with Rhys afterward had been awful, and Azriel had been so furious in his own quiet way that Cassian had quelled any further desire for Mor. Had let lust turn into affection, and all romantic feelings turn into familial bonds. But he could still admire her sheer beauty—as he'd admire any work of art. Even though he knew well that what lay inside Mor was far more lovely and perfect than her exterior.

He wondered if she knew that.

Drinking again, he said, "Tell me what happened in Vallahan." The ancient, mountainous Fae territory across the northern sea had been stirring since before the war with Hybern, and had been both enemy and ally to Prythian in different historical eras. What role Vallahan's hot-tempered king and proud people would play in this new world of theirs was yet to be decided, though much of its fate seemed to depend upon Mor's now-frequent presence at their court as Rhys's emissary.

Indeed, Mor's eyes shuttered. "They don't want to sign the new treaty."

"Fuck." Rhys, Feyre, and Amren had spent months working on that treaty, with input from their allies in other courts and territories. Helion,

High Lord of the Day Court and Rhys's closest ally, had been the most involved. Helion Spell-Cleaver was unrivaled in sheer, swaggering arrogance—he'd probably made up the moniker himself. But the male had one thousand libraries at his disposal, and had put them all to good use for the treaty.

"I've spent weeks in that blasted court," Mor said, poking at the flaky pastry beside her teacup, "freezing my ass off, trying to kiss *their* cold asses, and their king and queen refused the treaty. I came home on the earlier side today because I knew any more last-minute pushing from me would be unwelcome. My time there was supposed to be a friendly visit, after all."

"Why won't they sign it?"

"Because those stupid human queens are stirring—their army still isn't disbanded. The Queen of Vallahan even asked me what the point of a peace treaty would be when another war, this time against the humans, might redraw the territory lines far below the wall. I don't think Vallahan is interested in peace. Or allying with us."

"So Vallahan wants another war in order to add to their territory?" They'd already seized more than their fair share after the War five hundred years ago.

"They're bored," Mor said, frowning with distaste. "And the humans, despite those queens, are far weaker than we are. Pushing into human lands is low-hanging fruit. Montesere and Rask are likely thinking the same thing."

Cassian groaned skyward. That had been the fear during the recent war: that those three territories across the sea might ally with Hybern. Had they, there would have been no chance at all of survival. Now, even with Hybern's king dead, its people remained angry. An army might be raised again in Hybern. And if it united with Vallahan, if Montesere and Rask joined with the goal of claiming more territory from the humans . . . "You already told Rhys this."

It wasn't a question, but Mor nodded. "That's why he's asking you to look into what's going on with the human queens. I'm taking a few days off before I head back to Vallahan—but Rhys needs to know where the human queens stand in all of this."

"So you're supposed to convince Vallahan not to start another war, and I'm supposed to convince the human queens not to do so, either?"

"You won't get near the human queens," Mor said frankly. "But from what I observed in Vallahan, I know they're up to something. Planning something. We just can't figure out what, or why the humans would be stupid enough to start a war they cannot win."

"They'd need something in their arsenal that could grant them the advantage."

"That's what you have to find out."

Cassian tapped his booted foot on the stones of the walkway. "No pressure."

Mor drained her tea. "Playing courtier isn't all nice clothes and fancy parties."

He scowled. Long moments passed in amiable silence, though Cassian half-heard the wind whispering over the Sidra, the merry chatter of the people around them, the clink of silverware against plates. Content to let him think, Mor returned to her sunning.

Cassian straightened. "There's one person who knows those queens inside and out. Who can offer some insight."

Mor opened an eye, then slowly sat forward, hair falling around her like a rippling golden river. "Oh?"

"Vassa." Cassian hadn't dealt much with the ousted human queen—the only good one out of the surviving group, who had been betrayed by her fellow queens when they'd sold her to a sorcerer-lord who'd cursed her to be a firebird by day, woman by night. She'd been lucky: they'd given the other rebellious queen in their midst to the Attor. Who had then impaled her on a lamppost a few bridges away from where Cassian and Mor now sat.

Mor nodded. "She might be able to help."

He leaned his arms on the table. "Lucien is living with Vassa. And Jurian. He's supposed to be our emissary to the human lands. Let him deal with it."

Mor took another bite from her pastry. "Lucien can't be entirely trusted anymore."

Cassian started. "What?"

"Even with Elain here, he's become close with Jurian and Vassa. He's voluntarily living with them these days, and not just as an emissary. As their friend."

Cassian went over all he'd heard and observed from his encounters with Lucien since the war, trying to contemplate it like Rhys and Mor would. "He's spent months helping them sort out the politics of who rules Prythian's slice of the human lands," Cassian said slowly. "So Lucien can't be unbiased in reporting to us on Vassa."

Mor nodded gravely. "Lucien might mean well, but any reports would be skewed—even if he isn't aware of it—in their favor. We need someone outside of their little bubble to collect information and report." She finished off her pastry. "Which would be you."

Fine. That made sense. "Why haven't we already contacted Vassa about this?"

Mor waved a hand, though her shadowed eyes belied her casual gesture. "Because we're just now piecing it all together. But you should definitely speak with her, when you can. As soon as you can, actually."

Cassian nodded. He didn't dislike Vassa, though meeting her would also entail talking with Lucien and Jurian. The former he'd learned to live with, but the latter . . . It didn't matter that it turned out that Jurian had been fighting on their side. That the human general who'd been Amarantha's tortured prisoner for five centuries had played Hybern after being rebirthed by the Cauldron, and had helped Cassian and his family win the war. Cassian still didn't like the man.

He rose, leaning to ruffle Mor's shining hair. "I miss you these days." She'd been away frequently lately, and each time she returned, a shadow he couldn't place dimmed her eyes. "You know we'd warn you if Keir ever came here." Her asshole of a father still hadn't called in his favor with Rhys: to visit Velaris.

"Eris bought me time." Her words were laced with acid.

Cassian had tried not to believe it, but he knew Eris had done it as a gesture of good faith. He'd invited Rhysand into his mind to see exactly why he'd convinced Keir to indefinitely delay his visit to Velaris. Only Eris had that sort of sway with the power-hungry Keir, and whatever Eris had offered Keir in exchange for not coming here was still a mystery. At least to Cassian. Rhys probably knew. From Mor's pale face, he wondered if she knew, too. Eris must have sacrificed something big to spare Mor from her father's visit, which would have likely been timed for a moment that would maximize tormenting her.

"It doesn't matter to me." Mor waved off the conversation with a flip of her hand. He could tell something else was eating at her. But she'd let him in when she was ready.

Cassian walked around the table and pressed a kiss to the top of her head. "Get some rest." He shot skyward before she could answer.

⁜

Nesta woke to pure darkness.

Darkness that she had not witnessed in years now. Since that ramshackle cottage that had become a prison and a hell.

Jolting upright, hands clutching at her chest, she gasped for air. Had it been some fever dream on a winter's night? She was still in that cottage, still starving and poor and desperate—

No. The air in the room was toasty, and she was the lone person in the bed, not clinging to her sisters for warmth, always squabbling over who got the coveted middle place in the bed on the coldest nights, or the edges on the hottest summer ones.

And though she'd become as bony as she'd been during those long winters . . . this body was new, too. Fae. Powerful. Or it had once been.

Scrubbing at her face, Nesta slid from the bed. The floors were warmed. Not the icy wooden planks in the cottage.

Padding to the window, she drew back the drapes and peered out at the darkened city below. Golden lights shone along the streets, dancing on the twining band of the Sidra. Beyond that, only starlight silvered the lowlands before the cold and empty sea.

A scan of the sky revealed nothing regarding how far off dawn might be, and a long moment of listening suggested the household remained asleep. All three of them who occupied it.

How long had she slept? They'd arrived by eleven in the morning, and she'd fallen asleep soon after that. She'd consumed absolutely nothing all day. Her stomach grumbled.

But she ignored it, leaning her brow against the cool glass of the window. She let the starlight gently brush her head, her face, her neck. Imagined it running its shimmering fingers down her cheek, as her mother had done for her and her alone.

My Nesta. Elain shall wed for love and beauty, but you, my cunning little queen . . . You shall wed for conquest.

Her mother would thrash in her grave to know that, years later, her Nesta had come dangerously close to marrying a weak-willed woodcutter's son who had sat idly by while his father beat his mother. Who had put his hands on her when she called things off between them. Who had then attempted to take what she hadn't offered.

Nesta had tried to forget Tomas. She often found herself wishing the Cauldron had ripped those memories away just as it had her humanity, but his face sometimes sullied her dreams. Her waking thoughts. Sometimes, she could still feel his rough hands pawing at her, bruising her. Sometimes, the coppery tang of his blood still coated her tongue.

Pulling back from the window, Nesta studied those distant stars again. Half-wondered if they might speak.

My Nesta, her mother had always called her, even on her deathbed, so wasted and pale from typhus. *My little queen.*

Nesta had once delighted in the title. Had done her best to fulfill its promise, indulging in a dazzling life that had melted away as soon as the debtors swept in and all her so-called friends had revealed themselves to be nothing more than envious cowards wearing smiling masks. Not one of them had offered to help save the Archeron family from poverty.

They had thrown them all, mere children and a crumbling man, to the wolves.

So Nesta had become a wolf. Armed herself with invisible teeth and claws, and learned to strike faster, deeper, more lethally. Had relished it. But when the time came to put away the wolf, she'd found it had devoured her, too.

The stars flickered above the city, as if blinking their agreement.

Nesta curled her hands into fists and climbed back into bed.

✢

Cauldron damn him, maybe he shouldn't have agreed to bring her here.

Cassian lay awake in his behemoth of a bed—large enough for three Illyrian warriors to sleep side by side, wings and all. Little in the room itself had changed in the past five hundred years. Mor occasionally groused about wanting to redecorate the House of Wind, but he liked this room how it was.

He'd awoken at the sound of a door shutting and been instantly alert, heart hammering as he pulled free the knife he kept on the nightstand. Two more were hidden under his mattress, another set above the doorway, and two swords lay beneath the bed and in a dresser drawer, respectively. That was just his collection. The Mother knew what Az had stored in his own room.

He supposed that between him, Az, Mor, and Rhys, in the five centuries they'd used the House of Wind, they had filled it with enough weapons to arm a small legion. They'd hidden and stashed and forgotten about so many of them that there was always a good chance of sitting on a couch and being poked in the ass by something. And a good chance that most of the weapons were now little more than rust in their sheaths.

But the ones in this bedroom, those he kept oiled and clean. Ready.

The knife gleamed in the starlight, his Siphons fluttering with red light as his power scanned the hall beyond the door.

But no threat emerged, no enemy breaching the new wards. Hybern's soldiers had broken through more than a year ago, nearly getting their hands on Feyre and Nesta in the library. He hadn't forgotten it—that terror on Nesta's face as she'd raced for him, arms outstretched.

But the sound in the hall . . . Azriel, he'd realized a heartbeat later.

That he'd heard the door at all told him Az wanted him aware of his return. Hadn't wanted to talk, but had wanted Cassian to know that he was around.

Which had left Cassian here, staring at the ceiling, his Siphons slumbering once more and knife again sheathed and set on the nightstand. From the stars' position, he knew it was past three—dawn was still far off. He should get some sleep. Tomorrow would be hard enough.

As if his silent plea had gone out into the world, a smooth male voice purred into his mind. *Why are you up so late?*

Cassian scanned the sky beyond the wall of windows, as if he'd see Rhys flying there. *I have the same question for you.*

Rhys chuckled. *I told you: I had some apologizing to do with my mate.* A long, wicked pause. *We're taking a break.*

Cassian laughed. *Let the poor female sleep.*

She was the one who initiated this round. Pure male satisfaction edged every word. *You still didn't answer my question.*

Why are you snooping on me at this hour?

I wanted to make sure all was well. It's not my fault you were already up.

Cassian let out a soft groan. *It's fine. Nesta went to sleep right after we got here and stayed in bed. I'm assuming she's still asleep.*

You got there before eleven.

I know.

It's three fifteen in the morning.

I know.

The silence was pointed enough that Cassian added, *Don't butt in.*

I wouldn't dream of it.

Cassian didn't particularly want to have this conversation, not at three in the morning and certainly not twice in one day. *I'll check in tomorrow night with an update on the first lesson.*

Rhys's pause was again too pointed to ignore. But his brother said, *Mor will bring you up to Windhaven. Good night, Cass.*

The dark presence in his mind faded, leaving him hollow and chilled.

Tomorrow would be a battlefield unlike any other he'd walked onto.

Cassian wondered how much of him would be left intact by the end of it.

CHAPTER 5

"If you don't eat that, you're going to regret it in about thirty minutes."

Seated at the long table in the House of Wind's dining room, Nesta looked up from the plate of scrambled eggs and steaming bowl of porridge. Sleep still weighed her bones, sharpening her temper as she said, "I'm not eating this."

Cassian dug into his own portion—nearly double what lay before her. "It's either that or nothing."

Nesta kept perfectly still in her chair, keenly aware of every movement in the fighting leathers she'd donned. She'd forgotten how it felt to wear pants—the nakedness of having her thighs and ass on display.

Mercifully, Cassian had been too busy reading some report to see her slink in and slide into her seat. She glanced toward the doorway, hoping a servant might appear. "I'll eat toast."

"You'll burn through that in ten minutes and be tired." Cassian nodded toward the porridge. "Put some milk in it if you need to make it more palatable." He added before she could demand it, "There's no sugar."

She clenched the spoon. "As punishment?"

"Again, it'll give you energy for a short blast, and then make you crash." He shoveled eggs into his mouth. "You need to keep your energy level constant throughout the day—foods full of sugar or flimsy bread give you a temporary high. Lean meats, whole grains, and fruits and vegetables keep you relatively steady and full."

She drummed her nails on the smooth table. She'd sat here several times before with the members of Rhysand's court. Today, with only the two of them, it felt obscenely large. "Are there any other areas of my daily life that you're going to be presiding over?"

He shrugged, not pausing his eating. "Don't give me a reason to add any more to the list."

Arrogant asshole.

Cassian nodded toward the food again. "Eat."

She shoved the spoon into the bowl but didn't lift it.

"Have it your way, then." He finished his porridge and returned to the eggs.

"How long will today's session be?" The dawn had revealed clear skies, though she knew the Illyrian Mountains had their own weather. Might already be crusted in the first snows.

"As I said yesterday: the lesson is two hours. Right until lunch." He set his bowl on his plate, piling the silverware within. They vanished a heartbeat later, taken by the magic of the House. "Which will be the next time we eat." He glanced pointedly at her food.

Nesta leaned back in her chair. "One: I'm not participating in this *lesson*. Two: I'm not hungry."

His hazel eyes guttered. "Not eating won't bring your father back."

"That has *nothing* to do with this," she hissed. "*Nothing*."

He braced his forearms on the table. "We're going to cut the bullshit. You think I haven't gone through what you're dealing with? You think I haven't seen and done and felt all that before? And seen those I love deal with it, too? You aren't the first, and you won't be the last. What happened to your father was terrible, Nesta, but—"

She shot to her feet. "You don't know *anything*." She couldn't stop the shaking that overtook her. From rage or something else, she didn't know. She balled her hands into fists. "Keep your fucking opinions to yourself."

He blinked at the profanity, at what she guessed was the white-hot rage crinkling her face. And then he said, "Who taught you to curse?"

She squeezed her fists harder. "You lot. You have the filthiest mouths I've ever heard."

Cassian's eyes narrowed with amusement, but his mouth remained a thin line. "I'll keep my fucking opinions to myself if you eat."

She threw every bit of venom she could muster into her gaze.

He only waited. Unmovable as the mountain into which the House had been built.

Nesta sat down, grabbed the bowl of porridge, shoved a lumpy spoonful into her mouth, and nearly gagged at the taste. But she forced it down. Then another spoonful. Another. Until the bowl was clean and she started on the eggs.

Cassian monitored each bite.

And when there was nothing left, she scooped up her plate and bowl and held his stare as she dumped her dishes atop each other, the sound of the rattling silverware filling the room.

She again rose, stalking toward him. The doorway beyond him. He stood as well.

Nesta could have sworn he wasn't breathing as she passed, close enough that a shift of her elbow would have had it brushing his stomach. She said sweetly, "I look forward to your silence."

Unable to help the smirk blooming on her mouth, she aimed for the door. But a hand on her arm stopped her.

Cassian's eyes blazed, the red Siphon tethered on the back of the hand that gripped her fluttering with color. A wicked, taunting smile curved his lips.

"Glad to see you woke up ready to play, Nesta." His voice dropped to a low rumble.

She couldn't help the thundering of her heart at that voice, the challenge in his eyes, the nearness and size of him. Had never been able to help it. Had once let him nuzzle and lick at her throat because of it.

Had let him kiss her during the final battle because of it. Barely a kiss—about all he could manage in his injured state—and yet it had shattered her entirely.

I have no regrets in my life, but this. That we did not have time. That I did not have time with you, *Nesta. I will find you again in the next world—the next life. And we will have that time. I promise.*

She relived those moments more often than she cared to admit. The press of his fingers as he'd cupped her face, the way his mouth had felt and tasted, tinged with blood but still tender.

She couldn't bear it.

Cassian didn't so much as blink, though his grip on her arm gentled.

She willed herself not to swallow. Willed her surging blood to chill to ice.

His eyes again narrowed with amusement, but he let go. "You have five minutes until we leave."

Nesta managed to step away. "You're a brute."

He winked. "Born and raised."

She managed another step. If she refused to leave the House, Cassian or Morrigan or Rhys could just haul her to Windhaven. And if she flat-out refused to do anything, they'd drop her in the human lands without a second thought. The realization was enough to steel her further. "Don't ever put your hands on me again."

"Noted." His eyes still blazed.

Her fingers curled once more. She selected her next words like throwing knives. "If you think this training nonsense is going to result in you climbing into my bed, you're delusional." She added with a slice of a smile, "I'd sooner let in a mangy street dog."

"Oh, it's not going to result in me climbing into your bed."

Nesta snickered, victory achieved, and had reached the stairs when he crooned, "You'll climb into *mine*."

She whirled toward him, foot still suspended midair. "I'd rather rot."

Cassian threw her a mocking smile. "We'll see."

She fumbled for more of those sharp-edged words, for a sneer or a snarl or anything, but his smile grew. "You have three minutes to get ready now."

Nesta debated chucking the nearest thing at him—a vase on a little pedestal beside the doorway. But demonstrating that he'd gotten under her skin would be too satisfying for him.

So she merely shrugged and walked through the doorway. Slowly. Utterly unaffected by him and his swaggering, insufferable boasts.

Climb into his bed, indeed.

✢

Those pants were going to kill him.

Brutally, thoroughly kill him.

Cassian hadn't forgotten the sight of Nesta in Illyrian fighting leathers during the war—not at all. But compared to the memory . . . Mother above.

Every word, every language he knew had vanished at the sight of her striding past, straight-backed and unhurried as any noble lady presiding over her household.

Cassian knew he'd let her win that round, that he'd lost the upper hand the moment she threw him that little shrug and continued into the hall, unaware of the view it presented. How it made every thought beyond the most primal eddy out of his mind.

Settling himself required the entire three minutes she was downstairs.

The Mother knew he had enough to deal with today, both with Nesta's lesson and beyond it, without descending into thoughts of peeling those pants off her and worshipping every inch of that spectacular backside.

He couldn't afford distractions like that. Not for a million reasons.

But fuck—when had he last had a satisfying roll in the sheets? Certainly not since the war. Maybe since before Feyre had freed them all from Amarantha's grip. Cauldron boil him, it had been the month before Amarantha had fallen, hadn't it? With that female he'd met at Rita's. In an alley outside the pleasure hall. Against a brick wall. Quick and dirty and over within minutes, neither he nor the female wanting anything more than swift release.

That had been more than two years ago. It had been his hand ever since.

He should have scratched that particular itch before deciding that living in the House with Nesta was a good idea. She was hurting and adrift and the *last* thing she needed was him panting after her. Grabbing her arm like an animal, unable to stop himself from drawing near.

She wanted nothing to do with him. She'd said as much at Winter Solstice.

I've made my thoughts clear enough on what I want from you.

A whole lot of nothing.

It had cracked an intrinsic piece of him, some final resistance and shred of hope that everything they'd endured during the war might amount to something. That when he spilled his heart to her as he lay dying, that when she'd covered him with her body and chosen to die alongside him, she'd chosen *him*, too.

A stupid fucking hope, and one he should have known better than to harbor. So that Winter Solstice night on the icy streets, when he knew she'd only shown up at the town house to get the money Feyre had dangled in exchange for making an appearance, when she'd asserted that she wanted nothing to do with him . . . he'd thrown the present he'd spent months hunting down into the frozen Sidra and then busied himself with quelling the growing dissent amongst the Illyrians.

And he'd stayed away from her for the intervening nine months. Far, far away. He'd come so close to making a stupid mistake that night, to laying his heart bare for her to rip out of his chest. He'd hardly managed to walk away with some semblance of pride. Over his cold, dead body would she do that to him again.

Nesta emerged, her braided hair now coiled across the crown of her head like a woven tiara. He made a point not to look beneath her neck. At the body left on display. She needed to gain back the weight she'd lost, and pack on some muscle, but . . . those fucking leathers.

"Let's go," he said, his voice rough and cold. Thank the Cauldron for that.

On the veranda beyond the dining room's glass doors, Mor landed, as if plunging from the thirty feet above the wards was nothing. For her, Cassian supposed it was.

Mor hopped from foot to foot, rubbing her arms and gritting her teeth, and gave him a look that said, *You owe me so big for this, asshole.*

Nesta scowled, but slung on her cloak, each movement graceful and unhurried, then aimed for where Mor waited. Cassian would fly them both out beyond the wards' reach, then Mor would winnow them to Windhaven.

Where he'd somehow find a way to convince Nesta to train.

But thankfully, Nesta knew that she had to do the bare minimum today, which meant going to Windhaven. She'd always known how to wage this kind of emotional, mental warfare. She'd have made a fine general. Might still be one, someday.

Cassian couldn't tell if it would be a good thing. To turn Nesta into that sort of a weapon.

She'd pointed at the King of Hybern in a death-promise before she'd been turned High Fae against her will. Months later, she'd held up his severed head like a trophy and stared into his dead eyes.

And if the Bone Carver had spoken true about her emerging from the Cauldron as something to fear . . . Fuck.

He didn't bother with his cloak as he yanked open the glass doors, breathing in a face full of crisp autumn air, and stalked toward Mor's opening arms.

✢

No ice or snow crusted the mountain hold of Windhaven, but it didn't stop the bitter cold from slamming into Nesta the moment they appeared. Morrigan vanished with a wink at Cassian and a warning glower thrown at Nesta, leaving them assessing the field stretching ahead.

A few small stone houses rose to the right, and beyond them stood some new residences made of fresh pine. A village—that was what this place had become recently. But immediately before them lay the fighting rings, right along the edge of the flat mountaintop, fully stocked with various weapons, weights, and training supplies. Nesta had no idea what any of the impressive varieties were, beyond their basic names: sword, dagger, arrow, shield, spear, bow, brutal-looking round-spiky-ball-on-a-chain . . .

On their other side smoldered fire pits, clouds of smoke drifting to a fenced-in array of livestock, sheep and pigs and goats, all shaggy but well fed. And, of course, the Illyrians themselves. Females tended to steaming pots and pans around those fires—and all of them halted when Cassian and Nesta appeared. So did the dozens of males in those sparring rings. None smiled.

A broad-shouldered, stocky male whom Nesta vaguely recognized sauntered their way, flanked two deep by younger males. They all had their wings tucked in tight, perhaps to walk as a unit, but as they stopped in front of Cassian, those wings spread slightly.

Cassian kept his in what Nesta called his casual spread—not wide, but not tucked in close. The position conveyed the perfect amount of ease and arrogance, readiness and power.

The familiar male's gaze snagged on her. "What's *her* business here?"

Nesta gave him a secretive smile. "Witchcraft."

She could have sworn Cassian muttered a plea to the Mother before he cut in, "I will remind you, Devlon, that Nesta Archeron is our High Lady's sister, and will be treated with respect." The words held enough of a bite that even Nesta glanced at Cassian's stone-cold face. She had not heard that unyielding tone since the war. "She will be training here."

Nesta wanted nothing more than to shove him off the nearby cliff edge.

Devlon's face curdled. "Any weapons she touches must be buried afterward. Leave them in a pile."

Nesta blinked.

Cassian's nostrils flared. "We will do no such thing."

Devlon sniffed at her, his cronies snickering. "Are you bleeding, witch? If you are, you will not be allowed to touch the weapons at all."

Nesta made herself pause. Contemplate the best way to knock the bastard down a few pegs.

Cassian said with remarkable steadiness, "Those are outdated superstitions. She can touch the weapons whether she has her cycle or not."

"She can," Devlon said, "but they will still be buried."

Silence fell. Nesta didn't fail to note that Cassian's expression had darkened as he stared down Devlon. But he said abruptly, "How are the new recruits faring?"

Devlon opened his mouth, then shut it, irritation flashing there at a fight denied. "Fine," he spat, and turned away, his soldiers following.

Cassian's face tightened with each breath, and Nesta braced herself, a thrill slowly building in her blood, for him to rip into Devlon.

But Cassian growled, "Let's go," and began walking toward an empty training area.

Devlon glared over a shoulder, and Nesta threw him a cool look before striding after Cassian. The Illyrian's gaze lingered like a burning brand on her spine.

Cassian didn't go for one of the countless weapons racks stationed throughout the training area. He just halted in the farthest ring, hands on his hips, and waited for her.

Like hell would she join him. She spied a weatherworn rock near the rack of weapons, its smoothness either from the harsh climate or the untold number of warriors who'd taken a seat on it as she did then. Its frigid surface bit into her skin even through the thickness of the leathers.

"What are you doing?" Cassian's handsome face was nearly predatory.

She crossed her legs at the ankles and arranged the fall of her cape like the train of a gown. "I told you: I'm not training."

"Get up." He'd never ordered her like that.

Get up, she'd sobbed that day before the King of Hybern. *Get up*.

Nesta met his stare. Willed hers to be distant and unruffled. "I am officially attending training, Cassian, but you can't make me *do* a lick of it." She motioned to the mud. "Drag me through it, if you want, but I won't lift a finger."

The Illyrians' stares pelted them like stones. Cassian bristled.

Good. Let him see what a waste of life, what an utter wretch, she'd become.

"Get *the hell* up." His words were a soft snarl.

Devlon and his group had returned, attracted by their argument, and gathered beyond the edge of the circle. Cassian's hazel eyes remained fixed on her, though.

A slight pleading note flickered in them.

Get up, a small voice whispered in her head, her bones. *Don't humiliate him like this. Don't give these assholes the satisfaction of seeing him made a fool.*

But her body refused to move. She'd drawn her line, and to yield—to him, to anyone—

Something like disgust filled his face. Disappointment. Anger.

Good. Even as something crumpled inside her, she couldn't stop the relief.

Cassian turned away from her, drawing the sword sheathed down his back. And without another word, without a glance, he began his morning exercises.

Let him hate her. It was better that way.

CHAPTER 6

Each series of steps and movements Cassian went through was beautiful and lethal and precise, and it was all Nesta could do to not gawk.

She'd never been able to look away from him. From the moment they'd met, she'd developed a keen awareness of his presence in any space, any room. She hadn't been able to stop it, to block it out, no matter how much she suggested otherwise.

Go! he had begged her as he lay dying.

I can't, she'd wept. *I* can't.

She didn't know where the person she'd been in that moment had gone. Couldn't find her way back to her.

But even as she sat on that rock and stared at the swaying pines covering the mountains, she watched Cassian from the corner of her eye, aware of every graceful movement, the rasp of his steady breathing, the flow of his dark hair in the wind.

"Hard at work, I see."

Morrigan's voice drew Nesta's gaze from the mountains and the warrior who seemed so much a part of them. The stunning female stood beside her, brown eyes fixed on Cassian, admiration shining in them. There was no sign of Devlon or his followers, as if they'd drifted away long ago. Had it been two hours already? Mor said mildly, "He is pretty, isn't he?"

Nesta's spine stiffened at the warmth in her tone. "Just ask him."

No amusement lit Morrigan's face as she shifted her attention down to Nesta. "Why aren't you out there?"

"I'm taking a break."

Morrigan's gaze swept over Nesta's face, noting the lack of sweat or flushed skin, the hair barely out of place. The female said quietly, "My vote would have been to dump you right back in the human lands, you know."

"Oh, I know." Nesta refused to stand, to meet the challenge. "Good thing being Feyre's sister has its advantages."

Morrigan's lip curled. Beyond her, Cassian had halted his smooth movements.

Dark fire simmered in Morrigan's eyes. "I knew plenty of people like you once." Her hand drifted to her abdomen. "You never deserve the benefit of the doubt that good people like him give you."

Nesta was well aware of that. And knew what manner of people Morrigan referred to—those who dwelled in the Court of Nightmares in the Hewn City. Feyre had never told her the full story, but Nesta knew the bare details: the monsters who had tormented and brutalized Morrigan until she was thrown to the wolves.

Nesta leaned back on her hands, the cold rock biting through her gloves. She opened her mouth, but Cassian had reached them, breathless and gleaming with sweat. "You're early."

"I wanted to see how things were coming along." Morrigan pulled her burning gaze from Nesta. "Seems like today was a slow start."

Cassian raked his fingers through his hair. "You could say that."

Nesta clenched her jaw hard enough to hurt.

Morrigan extended a hand to him, and then threw one toward Nesta without so much as a glance. "Shall we?"

✣

Morrigan was a self-righteous busybody.

The thought raged through Nesta as she stood in the subterranean library beneath the House of Wind. A vain, self-righteous busybody.

Cassian hadn't spoken to her upon their return. She hadn't waited to see if he'd offer lunch, either, before going to her room and taking a bath to warm her bones.

When she'd emerged, she found that a note had been slipped beneath her door. In tight, bold lettering, it told her to be in the library at one. No threats, no promises to ship her off to the human lands. As if he didn't care whether she obeyed.

Well, at least breaking him had been accomplished faster than she'd anticipated.

She'd ventured to the library not because of any desire to obey his or Rhysand's commands, but because the alternative was equally unbearable: sitting in her silent bedroom, nothing but the roaring in her head to fill the quiet.

It had been more than a year since she'd last been down here. Since those terrifying moments when Hybern's assassins had snuck in, chasing her and Feyre into the dark heart of the library. She peered over the edge of the landing's stone railing, straight into the black pit far below. No ancient creature slumbered in that darkness anymore, but the dimness remained. And at its bottom lay the ground where Cassian had landed, reaching for her. There had been such rage on his face at the sight of her terror—

She sliced off the thought. Pushed back the tremor that went through her, and focused on the female sitting at the desk, nearly hidden by columns of books stacked there.

The female's hands were wrecked. There was no polite way of

describing them beyond that. Bones bent and knobbed, fingers at the wrong angles . . . Feyre had once mentioned that the priestesses in this library had difficult pasts. To say the least.

Nesta didn't want to know what had been done to Clotho, the library's high priestess, to render her thus. To have her tongue cut out and then deliberately healed that way so the damage might never be undone. Males had hurt her, and—

Hands shoving her down, down, down into freezing water, voices laughing and sneering.

A brutish male face grinning as he anticipated the trophy that would be pulled forth—

She couldn't stop it. Couldn't save Elain, sobbing on the floor. Couldn't save herself. No one was coming to rescue her, and these males would do what they wanted, and her body was not her own, not human—not for much longer—

Nesta wrenched her thoughts back to the present, blasting back the memory.

Her face veiled in the shadows beneath her pale hood, Clotho sat in silence, as if she'd seen the thoughts blare through Nesta, as if she knew how often the memory of that day in Hybern woke her. The limpid blue stone crowning the hood of Clotho's robe flickered like a Siphon in the dim light as she slid a piece of parchment across the desk.

You can begin today by shelving books on Level Three. Take the ramp behind me to reach it. There will be a cart with the books, which are organized alphabetically by author. If there is no author, set them aside and ask for help at the end of your shift.

Nesta nodded. "When is the end of my shift?"

Using her wrists and the backs of her hands, Clotho pulled a small clock to herself. Pointed with a bulging knuckle to the six o'clock marker.

Five hours of work. Nesta could do that. "Fine."

Clotho considered her again. Like she could see the churning, roaring sea inside her, that refused to leave her alone for so much as a moment, that refused to grant her a second of peace.

Nesta lowered her eyes to the desk. Forced herself to release a breath. But with its escape past her lips, that familiar weight swept in.

I am worthless and I am nothing, Nesta nearly said. She wasn't sure why the words bubbled up, pressing on her lips to voice them. *I hate everything that I am. And I am so, so tired. I am tired of wanting to be anywhere but in my own head.*

She waited for Clotho to gesture, to do anything to say she'd heard the thoughts.

The priestess motioned to the library above and below. A silent dismissal.

Feet heavy, Nesta made her way to the sloping ramp.

⁜

The task was menial, but required enough concentration that time slipped away, her mind quieting to a blissful nothing.

No one approached Nesta as she hunted down sections and shelves, fingers skimming over the spines of books as she searched for the right place. There were at least three dozen priestesses who worked and researched and healed here, though it was nearly impossible to count them when they all wore the same pale robes and so many kept the hoods over their faces. The ones who'd left their hoods down had offered her tentative smiles.

This was their sanctuary, gifted to them by Rhysand. No one could enter without their permission.

Which meant they'd approved her presence, for whatever reason.

Nesta's hands were near-withered with dust by the time a bell chimed six silvery peals throughout the cavernous library, ringing from its top levels down to the black pit. Some priestesses rose from where they worked at the desks and chairs on each level; some remained.

She found Clotho at the same desk. Did she ever lift her hood? She must, in order to bathe, but did she ever show anyone her face?

"I'm done for the day," Nesta announced.

Clotho slid another note across the desk.

Thank you for your assistance. We will see you tomorrow.

"All right." Nesta pocketed the note.

But Clotho held up a broken hand. Nesta watched with no shortage of awe as a fountain pen lifted above a piece of paper and began to write.

Wear clothes you don't mind getting dusty. You'll wreck that beautiful dress down here.

Nesta glanced to the gray gown she'd thrown on. "All right," she repeated.

The pen began moving again, somehow spelled to connect with Clotho's thoughts. *It was nice to meet you, Nesta. Feyre speaks highly of you.*

Nesta turned away. "No one likes a liar, Priestess."

She could have sworn a breath of amusement fluttered from beneath the female's hood.

✢

Cassian didn't come to dinner.

Nesta had stopped in her room only long enough to wash the dust from her hands and face, and then nearly sprinted upstairs, stomach growling.

The dining room had been empty. The place setting for one confirmed that she was in for a solitary meal.

She'd stared at the sunset-bathed city far below, the sole sounds her rustling dress and creaking chair.

Why was she surprised? She'd humiliated him at Windhaven. He was probably with his friends at the river house, ranting at them to find some other way to deal with her.

A plate of food appeared, dumped unceremoniously onto the place mat. Even the House hated her.

Nesta scowled at the red-stoned room. "Wine."

None appeared. She lifted the glass before her. "*Wine.*"

Nothing. She tapped her nails on the table's smooth surface. "Were you told to *not* give me wine?"

Talking to a house: a new low.

But as if in answer, the glass filled with water.

Nesta snarled toward the open archway at her back. "Funny."

She surveyed the food: half a roast chicken seasoned with what smelled like rosemary and thyme; mashed potatoes swimming in butter; and green beans sautéed with garlic.

That silence roared in her head, in the room.

She drummed her fingers again.

Ridiculous. This whole thing, this high-handed interference was *ridiculous.*

Nesta stood and aimed for the doorway. "Keep your wine. I'll get my own."

CHAPTER 7

Without the wall's magic blocking access to the human lands, Mor winnowed Cassian after sundown directly to the manor that had become home and headquarters to Jurian, Vassa, and—apparently—Lucien. Even more than a year later, the ravages of war lay evident around the estate: trees felled, barren patches of earth where greenery had not yet returned, and a general bleak openness that made the gray-stoned house seem like an accidental survivor. In the moonlight, that starkness was even emptier, the remnants of trees silvered, the shadows in the pock-marked earth deeper.

Cassian didn't know to whom the home had once belonged, and apparently neither did its new occupants. Feyre had told him that they called themselves the Band of Exiles. Cassian snorted to himself at the thought. Mor didn't linger upon dropping him at the house's arched wooden door, smirking in a way that told him even if he begged her to help, she wouldn't. No, she wanted to see him play courtier, precisely as Rhys had asked.

He hadn't planned on starting this mission today, but after that disastrous attempt at a lesson with Nesta, he'd needed to do something. Anything.

Nesta had known exactly what bullshit she was pulling by refusing to get off that rock. How it would appear to Devlon and the other preening assholes. She'd known, and done it anyway.

So as soon as he'd dumped Nesta at the House, he'd headed to a deserted cliff by the sea where the roar of the surf drowned the raging heat in his bones.

He'd stopped by the river house to admit to his failure, but Feyre had only simmered with annoyance at Nesta's behavior, and Rhys had given him a wary, amused look.

It was Amren who had said, *Let her dig her own grave, boy. Then offer her a hand.*

I thought that's what this past year has been, he'd countered.

Keep reaching out your hand, had been Amren's only reply.

He'd found Mor soon after that, explained that he needed to be transported, and here he was. He raised his fist to the door, but the wooden slab pulled away before he could touch it.

Lucien's scarred, handsome face appeared, his golden eye whirring. "I thought I sensed someone else arriving."

Cassian stepped into the house, floorboards creaking beneath his boots. "You just got here?"

"No," Lucien said, and Cassian marked the tightness of his shoulders beneath the dark gray jacket he wore, the taut silence emanating from every stone of the house. He marked its layout, in case he needed to fight his way to an exit. Which, given the displeasure that Lucien radiated as he strode for an archway to their left, seemed a distinct possibility.

Without turning, Lucien said, "Eris is here."

Cassian didn't falter. Didn't reach for the knife strapped to his thigh, though it was an effort to block the memory of Mor's battered face. The note nailed to her abdomen, her naked body dumped like garbage at the border of the Autumn Court. The fucking bastard had found her there and *left* her. She had been on death's threshold and—

Cassian's plans for what he'd one day do to him went far beyond the pain inflicted by a knife. Eris's suffering would last weeks. Months. Years.

Cassian didn't care that Eris had convinced Keir to delay his visit to Velaris, had apparently done so out of whatever shred of kindness remained in him. Didn't care that Rhys had noted something in Eris that had earned his trust. None of that mattered to Cassian one fucking bit. His attention focused on the red-haired male seated near the roaring fire in the surprisingly fancy parlor. He knew enough to keep tabs on an enemy.

Eris lounged in a golden chair, legs crossed, his pale face the portrait of courtly arrogance.

Cassian's fingers curled. Every time he'd seen the prick these past five centuries, he'd struggled with it. This blinding rage at the mere sight of him.

Eris smiled, well aware of it. "Cassian."

Lucien's gold eye clicked, reading Cassian's rage while warning flashed in his remaining russet eye.

The male had grown up alongside Eris. Had dealt with Eris's and Beron's cruelty. Had his lover slaughtered by his own father. But Lucien had learned to keep his cool.

Right. Rhys had asked Cassian to do this. He should think like Rhys, like Mor. Push aside the rage.

Cassian gave himself a second to do so, vaguely aware of Vassa saying something. He had noted and half-dismissed the two humans in the room: the brown-haired warrior—Jurian—and the red-haired young queen.

If Rhys and Mor were here . . . They wouldn't say a word about anything in front of Eris. Would pretend this was a friendly visit, to check on how the human lands were holding together. Even if Eris was most likely their ally.

No, Eris *was* their ally. Rhys had bargained with him, worked with him. Eris had held up his end at every turn. Rhys trusted him. Mor, despite all that had happened, trusted him. Sort of. So Cassian supposed he should do so as well.

His head hurt. So many things to calculate. He'd done it on battlefields, but these mind games and webs of lies . . . *Why* had Rhys asked him to do this? He'd been direct in dealing with the Illyrians: he'd laid out the hell that would be brought down upon them if they rebelled, and shown up to help with whatever they needed. That was in no way comparable to this.

Cassian blinked, and registered what Vassa had said: *General Cassian. A pleasure.*

He gave the queen a swift, perfunctory bow. "Your Majesty."

Jurian coughed, and Cassian glanced to the human warrior. Once human? Partially human? He didn't know. Jurian had been sliced apart by Amarantha, his consciousness somehow trapped within his eye, which she'd mounted on a ring and worn for five hundred years. Until his lingering bones had been used by Hybern to resurrect his body and return that essence into this form, the same one that had led armies on those long-ago battlefields during the War. Who was Jurian now? *What* was he?

From his spot on a ridiculous pink sofa by the far wall, Jurian said, "It only goes to her head when you call her that."

Vassa straightened, her cobalt jacket a sharp contrast to the red-gold of her hair. Of the three redheaded people in this room, Cassian liked her coloring the best: the golden hue of her skin, the large, uptilted blue eyes framed by dark lashes and brows, and the silken red hair, which she'd cut to her shoulders since he'd last seen her.

Vassa said to Jurian, "I *am* a queen, you know."

A queen by night, and firebird by day, sold by her fellow human queens to a sorcerer-lord who had enchanted her. Damned her into transforming each dawn into a bird of fire and ash. Cassian had waited until sundown to visit, so as to find her in her human form. He needed her to be able to speak.

Jurian crossed an ankle over a knee, his muddy boots dull in the firelight. "Last I heard, your kingdom was no longer yours. Are you still a queen?"

Vassa rolled her eyes, then looked to Lucien, who sank onto the sofa beside Jurian. Like the Fae male had settled similar arguments between them before. But Lucien's attention was upon Cassian. "Did you come with news or orders?"

Keenly aware of Eris's presence near the fire, Cassian kept his gaze upon Lucien. "We give you orders as our emissary." He nodded to Jurian and Vassa. "But when you are with your friends, we only give suggestions."

Eris snorted. Cassian ignored him, and asked Lucien, "How's the Spring Court?"

He had to give Lucien credit: the male was somehow able to move between his three roles—an emissary for the Night Court, ally to Jurian and Vassa, and liaison to Tamlin—and still dress immaculately.

Lucien's face revealed nothing of how Tamlin and his court fared. "It's fine."

Cassian didn't know why he'd expected an update regarding the High Lord of Spring. Lucien only gave those in private to Rhys.

Eris snorted again at Cassian's fumbling, and, unable to help himself, Cassian at last turned toward him. "What are you doing here?"

Eris didn't so much as shift in his seat. "Several dozen of my soldiers were out on patrol in my lands several days ago and have not reported back. We found no sign of battle. Even my hounds couldn't track them beyond their last known location."

Cassian's brows lowered. He knew he shouldn't let anything show, but . . . Those hounds were the best in Prythian. Canines blessed with magic of their own. Gray and sleek like smoke, they could race fast as the wind, sniff out any prey. They were so highly prized that the Autumn Court forbade them from being given or sold beyond its borders, and so expensive that only its nobility owned them. And they were bred rarely enough that even one was extremely difficult to come by. Eris, Cassian knew, had twelve.

"None of them could winnow?" Cassian asked.

"No. While the unit is one of my most skilled in combat, none of its soldiers are remarkable in magic or breeding."

Breeding was tossed at Cassian with a smirk. Asshole.

Vassa said, "Eris came to see if I could think of any reason why his soldiers might have gotten into trouble with humans. His hounds detected strange scents at the site of the abduction. Ones that seemed human, but were . . . odd, somehow."

Cassian lifted a brow at Eris. "You believe a group of humans could kill your soldiers? They can't be *that* skilled, then."

"Depends on the human," Jurian said, the male's face dark. Vassa's was a mirror.

Cassian grimaced. "Sorry. I— Sorry."

Some courtier.

But Eris shrugged a shoulder. "I think plenty of parties are interested in triggering another war, and this would be the start of it. Though perhaps your court did it. I wouldn't put it past Rhysand to winnow my soldiers away and plant some mysterious scents to throw us off."

Cassian flashed him a savage grin. "We're allies, remember?"

Eris gave him an identical smile. "Always."

Cassian couldn't stop himself. "Maybe you made your own soldiers vanish—if they even vanished at all—and are just making this up for the same bullshit reason you just spewed out."

Eris chuckled, but Jurian cut in, "There have been tensions amongst the humans regarding your kind. But as far as we know, as far as we've heard from Lord Graysen's forces, the humans here have kept to the old demarcation lines, and have no interest in starting trouble."

Yet was left unsaid.

Would asking about the human queens on the continent reveal Rhys's hand? The conversation had shifted toward it, so he could bring it up as idle talk, rather than as the reason he'd come here . . . Fuck, his head hurt. "What about your—your sisters?" He nodded to Vassa. "Would they have anything to do with this?"

Eris's gaze shot to him, and Cassian reined in his curse. Perhaps he'd said too much. He wished Mor were here. Even if putting her and Eris in a room together . . . No, he'd save her that misery.

Vassa's cerulean eyes darkened. "We were just getting to that, actually." She gestured to Cassian. "You've heard the same rumors we have: they're stirring again across the sea, and are poised to start trouble."

"Are they stupid enough to do it is the real question," Jurian said.

"They're anything but stupid," Lucien said, shaking his head. "But leaving a human scent at the site is so obvious a clue that it seems unlikely it was one of them."

"Any move they make is heavily weighed," Vassa said, glancing to the wall of windows overlooking the destroyed lands beyond. "Though I cannot think why any of them would capture your soldiers," she said to Eris, who seemed to be monitoring each word out of their mouths. "There are other Fae on the continent itself, so why bother to cross the sea to take yours? And why not the Spring Court's? Tamlin wouldn't notice anyone missing at this point."

Lucien cringed, and Cassian, while inclined to smirk at the thought of the asshole suffering, found himself frowning. If war was coming, they needed Tamlin and his forces in fighting shape. Needed Tamlin ready. Rhys had been visiting him regularly, making sure he'd be both on their side and capable of leading.

How Rhys had managed not to kill the High Lord of Spring was something Cassian still couldn't understand.

But that was why Rhys was High Lord, and Cassian his blade.

He knew if he ever got the name of the human bastard who'd put his hands on Nesta, nothing would stop him from finding the man. A conversation he'd had with Nesta years ago, when she'd still been human, forever lurked in the back of his mind. How she'd stiffened at his touch, and he'd known—scented and seen the fear in her eyes and *known*—that a man had hurt her. Or tried to. She'd never told him the details, but she'd confirmed it enough by refusing to share the man's name. He'd often contemplated how he'd kill the man, if Nesta gave him the go-ahead. Peeling his skin from his bones would be a good start.

His friends would understand the wound it pressed. How far the pain of that ancient wound would push him to go. A razed Illyrian camp was all that remained of the first and last time he'd let himself sink to that level of rage.

And Rhys had appointed him to play courtier. To put aside the blade and use his words. It was a joke.

Eris uncrossed his legs. "I suppose this could be to sow tensions amongst us. To make us eye each other with suspicion. Weaken our bonds."

"Hybern would have done that," Jurian agreed. "He might have taught them a thing or two." Before Nesta had beheaded him.

But Vassa said, "The queens require no teaching. They were well versed in treachery before they ever contacted Hybern. And have dealt with greater monsters than him."

Cassian could have sworn flames rippled across her blue eyes.

Both Jurian and Lucien stared at her, the former's face utterly unreadable, and the latter's pained. Cassian suppressed his jolt. He should have asked someone before coming here how much time remained before Vassa would be forced to return to the continent—to the sorcerer-lord at a remote lake who held her leash, and had allowed her to leave only temporarily, as part of a bargain Feyre's father had struck.

Feyre's father . . . and Nesta's father. Cassian blocked out the memory of the man's neck being snapped. Of Nesta's face as it had happened. And deciding to damn caution to hell, he asked, "Which of the queens would do something this bold?"

Vassa's golden face tightened. "Briallyn."

The once-young, once-human queen who had been turned High Fae by the Cauldron. But in its rage at whatever Nesta had taken from it, the Cauldron had punished Briallyn. She was Made immortal Fae, yes—but she was withered into a crone. Doomed to be old for millennia.

She'd made no secret of her hatred for Nesta. Her desire for revenge.

If Briallyn made a move against Nesta, he'd kill the queen himself.

Cassian tried to think over the bellowing beast in his head that tightened every muscle of his body until only bloody violence would appease it.

"Easy," Lucien said.

Cassian snarled.

"*Easy*," Lucien repeated, and flame sizzled in his russet eye.

The flame, the surprising dominance within it, hit Cassian like a stone to the head, knocking him from his need to kill and kill and kill whatever might threaten—

They were all staring. Cassian rolled his tensed shoulders, stretching out his wings. He'd revealed too much. Like a stupid brute, he'd let them all see too much, learn too much.

"Send that shadowsinger of yours to track Briallyn," Jurian ordered, his face grave. "If she's somehow capable of capturing a unit of Fae soldiers, we need to know how. Swiftly." Spoken like the general Jurian had once been.

Cassian said to Vassa, "You really think Briallyn would do something like this? Be that blatant? Someone has to be trying to fool us into going after her."

Lucien asked, "How would she even get here and vanish that quickly? Crossing the sea takes weeks. She'd need to winnow to pull it off."

"The queens *can* winnow," Jurian corrected. "They did so during the war, remember?"

But Vassa said, "Only when several of us are together. And it is not winnowing as the Fae do, but a different power. It's akin to the way all seven High Lords can combine their powers to perform miracles."

Well, fuck.

Eris said, "I have it on good authority that the other three queens have scattered to the winds." Cassian tucked away the information and the questions it raised. How did Eris know that? "Briallyn has been residing alone in their palace for weeks now. Long before my soldiers vanished."

"So she can't winnow, then," Cassian concluded. "And again—would she really be foolish enough to do something like this if the other queens have left?"

Vassa's eyes darkened. "Yes. The others' departure would serve to remove obstacles to her ambitions. But she'd only do this if she had someone of immense power behind her. Perhaps pulling her strings."

Even the fire seemed to quiet.

Lucien's eye clicked. "Who?"

"You wonder who is capable of making a unit of Fae soldiers across the sea vanish? Who could give Briallyn the power to winnow—or do it for her? Who could aid Briallyn so she'd be bold enough to do such a thing? Look to Koschei."

Cassian froze as memories clicked into place, as surely as one of Amren's jigsaw puzzles. "The sorcerer who imprisoned you is named Koschei? Is he . . . is he the Bone Carver's brother?" Everyone gaped at him. Cassian clarified, "The Bone Carver mentioned a brother to me once, a fellow true immortal and a death-lord. That was his name."

"Yes," Vassa breathed. "Koschei is—was—the Bone Carver's older brother."

Lucien and Jurian looked at her in surprise. But Vassa's gaze lay upon him. Fear and hatred filled it, as if speaking the male's name were abhorrent.

Her voice hoarsened. "Koschei is no mere sorcerer. He's confined to the lake only due to an ancient spell. Because he was outsmarted once. Everything he does is to free himself."

"Why was he imprisoned?" Cassian asked.

"The story is too long to tell," she hedged. "But know that Briallyn and the others sold me to him not through their devices, but his. By words he planted in their courts, whispered on the winds."

"He's still at the lake," Lucien said carefully. Lucien had been there, Cassian recalled. Had gone with Nesta's father to the lake where Vassa was held captive.

"Yes," Vassa said, relief in her eyes. "But Koschei is as old as the sea—older."

"Some say he is Death itself," Eris murmured.

"I do not know if that is true," Vassa said, "but they call him Koschei the Deathless, for he has no death awaiting him. He is truly immortal. And would know of anything that might give Briallyn an edge against us."

"And you think Koschei would do all of this," Cassian pressed, "not out of sympathy for the human queens, but with the goal of freeing himself?"

"Certainly." Vassa peered at her hands, fingers flexing. "I fear what may happen if he ever gets free of the lake. If he sees this world on the cusp of disaster and knows he could strike, and strike hard, and make himself its master. As he once tried to do, long ago."

"Those are legends that predate our courts," Eris said.

Vassa nodded. "It is all I have gleaned from my time enslaved to him."

Lucien stared out the window—as if he could see the lake across a sea and a continent. As if he were setting his target.

But Cassian had heard enough. He didn't wait for their good-byes before heading for the archway, and the front hall behind it.

He'd made it two steps beyond the front door, breathing in the crisp night air, when Eris said behind him, "You make a terrible courtier." Cassian turned to find Eris shutting the front door and leaning against it. His face was pale and stony in the moonlight. "What do you know?"

"As little as you," Cassian said, offering a truth that he hoped Eris would deem a deception.

Eris sniffed the night breeze. Then smiled. "She couldn't be bothered to come inside to say hello?"

How he'd detected Mor's lingering scent, Cassian didn't know. Perhaps Eris and his smokehounds had more in common than he realized. "She didn't know you were here."

A lie. Mor had probably sensed it. He'd spare her the pain of coming back here, and have Rhys retrieve him. He'd fly north for a few hours—until he was in range of Rhys's power—and then shoot a thought toward him.

Eris's long red hair ruffled in the wind. "Whatever it is you're doing, whatever it is you're looking into, I want in."

"Why? And no."

"Because I need the edge Briallyn has, what Koschei has told her or shown her."

"To overthrow your father."

"Because my father has already pledged his forces to Briallyn and the war she wishes to incite."

Cassian started. "What?"

Eris's face filled with cool amusement. "I wanted to feel out Vassa and Jurian." He didn't mention his brother, oddly enough. "But they clearly know little about this."

"Explain what the fuck you mean by Beron *pledging* his forces to Briallyn."

"It's exactly what it sounds like. He caught wind of her ambitions, and went to her palace a month ago to meet with her. I stayed here, but I sent my best soldiers with him." Cassian refrained from sniping about Eris opting out, especially as the last words settled.

"Those wouldn't happen to be the same soldiers who went missing, would they?"

Eris nodded gravely. "They returned with my father, but they were . . . off. Aloof and strange. They vanished soon after—and my hounds confirmed that the scents at the scene are the same as those on gifts Briallyn sent to curry my father's favor."

"You knew it was her this entire time?" Cassian motioned to the house and the three people inside it.

"You didn't think I'd just spill all that information, did you? I needed Vassa to confirm that Briallyn could do something like that."

"Why would Briallyn ally with your father only to abduct your soldiers?"

"That's what I'd like to find out."

"What does Beron say?"

"He is unaware of it. You know where I stand with my father. And this unholy alliance he's struck with Briallyn will only hurt us. *All* of us. It will turn into a Fae war for control. So I want to find answers on my own—rather than what my father tries to feed me."

Cassian surveyed the male, his grim face. "So we take out your father."

Eris snorted, and Cassian bristled. "I am the only person my father has told of his new allegiance. If the Night Court moves, it will expose me."

"So your worry about Briallyn's alliance with Beron is about what it means for you, rather than the rest of us."

"I only wish to defend the Autumn Court against its worst enemies."

"Why would I work with you on this?"

"Because we are indeed allies." Eris's smile became lupine. "And because I do not believe your High Lord would wish me to go to other territories and ask *them* to help with Briallyn and Koschei. To help them remember that all it might take to secure Briallyn's alliance would be to hand over a certain Archeron sister. Don't be stupid enough to believe my father hasn't thought of that, too."

Cassian's rage flashed red before his eyes. He'd revealed that weakness earlier. Let Eris see how much Nesta meant, what he'd do to defend her.

Fool, he cursed himself. *Stupid, useless fool.*

"I could kill you now and not worry about this at all," Cassian mused. He'd enjoyed beating the shit out of the male that night on the ice with Feyre and Lucien. And he'd waited centuries to kill him, anyway.

"Then you would certainly have a war on your hands. My father would go straight to Briallyn—and Koschei, I suppose—and then go to the other discontent territories, and you would be wiped off the proverbial map. Perhaps literally, since the Night Court would be divvied up between the other territories if Rhysand and Feyre die without an heir."

Cassian clenched his jaw. "So you're to be my ally whether I wish it or not?"

"The brute understands at last." Cassian ignored the barb. "Yes. What you know, *I* want to know. I will notify you of any movement on my father's part regarding Briallyn. So send out your shadowsinger. And when he returns, find me."

Cassian stared at him from under lowered brows. Eris's mouth curled upward, and before he winnowed into the night like a ghost, he said, "Stick to fighting battles, General. Leave the ruling to those capable of playing the game."

CHAPTER 8

Nesta didn't bother to go to the wine cellar. Or to the kitchen. They'd be locked.

But she knew where the stairs lay. Knew that particular door, at least, would not be locked.

Still snarling, Nesta yanked open the heavy oak door and peered down the steep, narrow stairwell. Spiral stairs. Each a foot high.

Ten thousand steps, around and around and around. Only the occasional slitted window to offer a breath of air and a glimpse of progress.

Ten thousand steps between her and the city—and then a half-mile walk at least from the bottom of the mountain to the nearest tavern. And awaiting, blessed oblivion.

Ten thousand steps.

She was no longer human. This High Fae body could do it.

She could do it.

⸸

She couldn't do it.

The dizziness hit her first. Winding around, over and over, eyes trained downward to avoid a slip that would kill her, caused her head to spin.

Her empty stomach churned.

But she focused, counting each step. *Seventy. Seventy-one. Seventy-two.*

The city below barely drew any closer through the occasional slitted windows she passed.

Her legs started to shake; her knees groaned with the effort of keeping her upright, balancing on the steep drop of each step.

Nothing but her own breathing and the sound of her scuffing steps filled the narrow space. All she could see was the endlessly curving, perfect arc of the wall ahead. It never altered, save for those tiny, too-rare windows.

Around and around and around and around and around—

Eighty-six, eighty-seven—

Down and down and down and down—

One hundred.

She halted, no window in sight, and the walls pushed, the floor kept moving—

Nesta leaned into the red stone wall, let its coolness sink into her brow. Breathed.

Nine thousand nine hundred steps to go.

Bracing a hand on the wall, she renewed her descent.

Her head spun again. Her legs wobbled.

She got in eleven more steps before her knees buckled so suddenly she nearly slid. Only her hand grappling at the uneven wall kept her from wiping out.

The stairwell spun and spun and spun, and she shut her eyes against it.

Her jagged panting bounced off the stones. And in the stillness, she had no defenses against what her mind whispered. She couldn't shut out her father's final words to her.

I loved you from the first moment I held you in my arms.

Please, she'd begged the King of Hybern. *Please*.

He'd snapped her father's neck anyway.

Nesta gritted her teeth, blowing out breath after breath. She opened her eyes and stretched out her leg to take another step.

It trembled so badly that she didn't dare.

She didn't let herself dwell on it, rage about it, as she turned around. Didn't even let herself feel the defeat. Her legs protested, but she forced them upward. Away.

Around and around again.

Up and up, one hundred and eleven steps.

She was nearly crawling by the last thirty, unable to get a breath down, sweat pooling in the bodice of her dress, her hair sticking to her damp neck. What the hell were the benefits of becoming High Fae if she couldn't endure this? The pointed ears, she'd learned to like. The infrequent cycle, which Feyre had warned would be painful, had actually been a boon, something Nesta was happy to worry about only twice a year. But what was the point of it—of any of it—if she couldn't conquer these stairs?

She kept her eyes on each step, rather than the twisting wall and the dizzying sensation it brought.

This hateful House. This horrible place.

She grunted as the oak door at the top of the stairwell became visible at last.

Fingers digging into the steps hard enough for the tips to bark in pain, she dragged herself up the last few, slithering on her belly onto the hallway floor.

And arrived face-first in front of Cassian, smirking as he leaned against the adjacent wall.

✢

Cassian had needed some time before seeing her again.

He'd updated Rhys and the others immediately upon returning;

they'd received his information with dour, somber faces. By the end of it, Azriel was preparing for some reconnaissance on Briallyn as Amren pondered what powers or resources the queen and Koschei might possess, if they had indeed captured Eris's soldiers so easily.

And then Cassian had been slapped with a new order: keep an eye on Eris. *Beyond the fact that he approached you*, Rhys had said, *you are my general. Eris commands Beron's forces. Be in communication with him.* Cassian had started to object, but Rhys had directed a pointed look at Azriel, and Cassian had caved. Az had too much on his plate already. Cassian could deal with that piece of shit Eris on his own.

Eris wants to avoid a war that would expose him, Feyre had guessed. *If Beron sides with Briallyn, Eris would be forced to choose between his father and Prythian. The careful balance he's struck by playing both sides would crumble. He wants to act when it's convenient for his plans. This threatens that.*

But no one had been able to decide which was the bigger threat for *them*: Briallyn and Koschei, or Beron's willingness to ally with them. While the Night Court had been trying to make the peace permanent, the bastard had been doing his best to start another war.

After an unusually quiet dinner, Cassian had flown back up to the House. And found the oak door to the stairs open, Nesta's scent lingering.

So he'd waited. Counted the minutes.

It had been worth it.

Seeing her claw her way onto the landing, panting, hair curling with the sweat sliding down her face—completely worth his generally shit day.

Nesta was still sprawled on the hall floor when she hissed, "Whoever designed those stairs was a monster."

"Would you believe that Rhys, Az, and I had to climb up and down them as punishment when we were boys?"

Her eyes shimmered with temper—good. Better than the vacant ice. "Why?"

"Because we were young and stupid and testing boundaries with a High Lord who didn't understand practical jokes regarding public nudity." He nodded toward the stairs. "I got so dizzy on the hike down that I puked on Az. He then puked on Rhys, and Rhys puked all over himself. It was the height of summer, and by the time we made the trek back up, the heat was unbearable, we all reeked, and the scent of the vomit on the stairs had become horrific. We all puked again as we walked through it."

He could have sworn the corners of her mouth were trying to twitch upward.

He didn't hold back his own grin at the memory. Even if they'd still had to hike back down and mop it all up.

Cassian asked, "What stair did you make it to?"

"One hundred eleven." Nesta didn't rise.

"Pathetic."

Her fingers pushed into the floor, but her body didn't move. "This stupid House wouldn't give me wine."

"I figured that would be the only motivator to make you risk ten thousand stairs."

Her fingers dug into the stone floor once more.

He threw her a crooked smile, glad for the distraction. "You can't get up, can you."

Her arms strained, elbows buckling. "Go fly into a boulder."

Cassian pushed off the wall and reached her in three strides. He wrapped his hands under her arms and hauled her up.

She scowled at him the entire time. Glared at him some more when she swayed and he gripped her tighter, keeping her upright.

"I knew you were out of shape," he observed, stepping away when she'd proved she wasn't about to collapse, "but a hundred steps? Really?"

"Two hundred, counting the ones up," she grumbled.

"Still pathetic."

She straightened her spine and raised her chin.

Keep reaching out your hand.

Cassian shrugged, turning toward the hall and the stairwell that would take him up to his rooms. "If you get tired of being weak as a mewling kitten, come to training." He glanced over a shoulder. Nesta still panted, her face flushed and furious. "And participate."

✠

Nesta sat at the breakfast table, grateful she'd left her room soon after sunrise to make the trek up to the dining room.

It had taken her double the time it normally would, thanks to her stiff, throbbing legs.

Getting out of bed had required gritted teeth and a litany of cursing. Everything afterward had only gotten worse. Bending to put her legs into her pants, going to the bathroom, even just heaving open the door. There wasn't one part of her legs that didn't ache.

So she'd left her room early, not wanting to give Cassian the satisfaction of seeing her limp and grimace into the dining room.

The problem, of course, was that now she wasn't entirely certain she could stand.

So she'd taken a good, long while eating her meal. Was choking down the porridge when Cassian prowled through the dining room doors, took one look at her, and smirked.

He knew. Somehow, the swaggering asshole knew.

She might have snapped something, but Azriel stalked into the room on his heels. Nesta straightened at the shadowsinger's appearance, the darkness clinging to his shoulders as he offered her a grim smile.

Azriel was nothing short of beautiful. Even with those scarred hands and the shadows that flowed from him like smoke, she'd always found him to be the prettiest of the three males who called themselves brothers.

Cassian slid into the chair opposite hers, his food instantly appearing before him, and said with grating cheer, "Morning, Nesta."

She threw him an equally saccharine smile. "Good morning, Cassian."

Azriel's hazel eyes danced, but he said nothing as he gracefully took his place beside Cassian, a plate of his own food appearing.

"I haven't seen you in a while," Nesta said to him. She couldn't remember the last time, actually.

Azriel took a bite of his eggs before replying. "Likewise." The shadowsinger nodded toward her clothes. "How's training?" Cassian cut him a sharp look.

Nesta glanced between them. There was no way Azriel didn't know about yesterday. Cassian had probably gloated about the incident with the stairs, too.

She sipped from her tea. "Training is fantastic. Absolutely riveting."

Azriel's mouth curled up at the corner. "I hope you're not giving my brother a hard time."

She set down her teacup. "Is that a threat, Shadowsinger?"

Cassian took a long drink from his own tea. Drained it to the dregs.

Azriel said coolly, "I don't need to resort to threats." The shadows coiled around him, snakes ready to strike.

Nesta gave him a smile, holding his stare. "Neither do I."

She leaned back in her chair and said to Cassian, who was frowning at both of them, "I want to train with him instead."

She could have sworn Cassian went still. Interesting.

Azriel coughed into his tea.

Cassian drummed his fingers on the table. "I think you'll find that Az is even less forgiving than I am."

"With that pretty face?" she crooned. "I have a hard time believing that."

Azriel ducked his head, focusing on his food.

"You want to train with Az," Cassian said tightly, "then go ahead." He appeared thoughtful for a moment, his eyes lighting before he added, "Though I doubt that you'll survive a lesson with him, when you can't manage to walk down a hundred stairs without being so sore the next morning that you're unable to get out of your chair."

She braced her feet on the floor. He'd read every tinge of pain on her face if she stood, but letting him see he was right—

Azriel studied the two of them as she planted her hands on the table, bit down on her yelp, and stood in a great rush.

Cassian shoveled more eggs into his mouth and said around them, "Doesn't count when you use your hands to do most of the work."

Nesta schooled her face into utter disdain, even as a hiss rose inside her. "I bet that isn't what you've been telling yourself at night."

Azriel's shoulders shook with silent laughter as Cassian set down his fork, his eyes gleaming with challenge.

Cassian's voice dropped an octave. "Is that what those smutty books teach you? That it's only at night?"

It took a heartbeat for the words to settle. And she couldn't stop it, the heat that sprang to her face, her glance at his powerful hands. Even with Azriel now biting his lip to keep from laughing, she couldn't stop herself.

Cassian said with a wicked smile, "It could be anytime—dawn's first light, or when I'm bathing, or even after a long, hard day of practice."

She didn't miss the slight emphasis he put on *long, hard*.

Nesta couldn't stop her toes from curling in her boots. But she said with a slight smile, striding for the doorway, refusing to let one bit of the discomfort in her sore legs show, "Sounds like you have a lot of time on your hands, Cassian."

✣

"You're in deep shit," Azriel said mildly to him on the chilly veranda as Nesta donned her cloak inside.

"I know," Cassian muttered. He had no idea how it had happened: how he'd gone from mocking Nesta to taunting her with his own bedroom habits. Then imagining *her* hand wrapped around him, pumping him, until he was a heartbeat away from exploding out of his chair and leaping into the skies.

He knew Az had been well aware of the shift in his scent. How his skin had become too tight at the way she said his name, his cock an insistent ache rubbing against the buttons of his pants.

He could count on one hand the number of times she'd addressed him by name.

The thought of that one hand led him back to her hand, squeezing him rough and hard, just the way he liked it—

Cassian gritted his teeth and breathed in the crisp morning air. Willed it to settle him. Made himself focus on the morning wind's sweet song. The wind around Velaris had always been lovely, gentle. Not like the vicious, unforgiving mistress that ruled the peaks of Illyria.

Az chuckled, the wind shifting the strands of his dark hair. "You two need a chaperone up here?"

Yes. No. Yes. "I thought you were the chaperone."

Az threw him a wicked smile. "I'm not entirely sure I'm enough."

Cassian flipped him off. "Good luck today."

Az would leave soon to begin his spying on Briallyn—Feyre had decided it last night. Though Rhys had asked Cassian to look into the human queens, the subterfuge would fall to Az.

Azriel's hazel eyes glimmered. He squeezed Cassian's shoulder, his hand a warm weight against the chill. "Good luck to you, too."

✥

Cassian didn't know why he'd thought Nesta would enter the sparring ring with him today. She sat her ass right on the same rock as the day before and did not move.

By the time Mor had appeared to winnow them to the camp, he'd managed to get enough control over himself that he'd stopped thinking about what Nesta's hands would feel like and started considering what they'd cover today. He'd planned to keep the lesson to an hour, then leave her at Rhys's mother's old house while he did a standard check of the Illyrian war-bands' state of rebuilding their ranks.

He wouldn't mention that they might be flying into battle soon, depending on what Az learned.

He didn't tell Nesta any of this information, either. Especially about Eris. She'd made her contempt of the Fae realms perfectly clear. And he'd be damned if he gave her one more verbal weapon to wield against him, since she'd likely see right through him and realize he knew all of this political scheming and planning was far beyond his abilities.

He also didn't let himself consider whether it was wise to leave her alone up here even for an hour.

"So we're back to this?" Cassian asked, ignoring how every single asshole in the camp watched him. Them. Her.

Nesta picked at her nails, wisps of her braided hair drifting free in the wind. She'd hunched over her knees, keeping her body as compact as possible.

He said, "You'd stop being so cold if you got up and moved."

She only folded one ankle over another.

"If you want to sit on that rock and freeze for the next two hours, go ahead."

"Fine."

"Fine."

"Fine."

"Good one, Nes." He threw her a mocking grin that he knew made her see red, and strode to the center of the practice area. He halted in its heart, allowing his breathing to take over.

When she didn't reply, he let himself fall into that calm, steady place within his mind, let his body begin the series of motions he'd performed for five centuries straight.

The initial steps were to remind his body that it was about to start working. Stretching and breathing, concentrating on everything from his toes to the tips of his wings. Waking everything up.

It got harder from there.

Cassian yielded to instinct and movement and breath, only dimly aware of the female watching from that rock.

Keep reaching out your hand.

Cassian was breathless by the time he finished an hour later. Nesta, to his satisfaction, had become rigid with cold.

But she hadn't moved. Hadn't even shifted during his exercises.

Wiping the sweat from his brow, he noted that her lips had taken on a blue tinge. Unacceptable.

He indicated Rhys's mother's house. "Go wait in there. I have business to attend to."

She didn't move.

Cassian rolled his eyes. "Either you sit out here for the next hour, or you can go inside and warm up."

She wasn't that stubborn—was she?

Thankfully, a blast of icy wind hit the camp at that exact moment, and Nesta began moving toward the house.

Its interior was indeed warm, with a fire crackling in the sooty hearth that occupied much of the main room. Feyre or Rhys must have woken the house for them. He held the door for Nesta as she walked in, already rubbing her hands.

Slowly, Nesta surveyed the space: the kitchen table before the windows, the little sitting area that occupied the other half of the room, the narrow staircase that led to the exposed upstairs hallway and the two bedrooms beyond. One of those rooms had been his since childhood—the first bedroom, the first night indoors, he'd ever experienced.

This house was the first true home he'd ever had. He knew every scratch and splinter, every dent and burn mark, all of it preserved with magic. There, the gouged-out spot by the base of the railing—that was where he'd cracked his head when Rhys had tackled him during one of their countless brawls. There, that stain on the old red couch: that was when he'd spilled his ale while the three of them were drunk out of their minds on their first solo night in this house at age sixteen—Rhys's mother had been off in Velaris for a rare visit to her mate—and Cassian had been too stupid drunk to know how to clean it. Even Rhys, swaying with the combination of ale and liquor, had failed to lift the stain, his magic accidentally setting it instead of wiping it away. They'd rearranged the throw pillows to hide it from his mother when she returned the next morning, but she'd spied it immediately.

Perhaps it had something to do with the fact that they'd still been drunk, given away by Az's relentless hiccupping.

Cassian nodded to the kitchen table. "Since you're so good at sitting, why don't you make yourself comfortable?"

When she didn't answer, he turned to find Nesta standing in front of the hearth, arms tightly crossed, the flickering light dancing in her beautiful hair. She didn't look up at him.

She'd always stood with that stillness. Even as a human. It had only amplified when she'd become High Fae.

Nesta stared at the fire as if it murmured to that burning soul of hers.

"What are you looking at?" he asked.

She blinked, seeming to realize he was still there.

A log on the fire popped, and she flinched.

Not in surprise, he noted, but in dread. Fear.

He glanced between her and the fire. Where had she gone, for those few moments? What horror had she been reliving?

Her face had blanched. And shadows dimmed her blue-gray eyes.

He knew that expression. Had seen it and felt it so many times he'd lost track.

"There are some shops in the village," he offered, suddenly desperate for anything to remove that hollowness from her. "If you don't feel like sitting in here, you could visit them."

Nesta still said nothing. So he let it drop, and left the house in silence.

CHAPTER 9

Nesta stepped into the warmth of the small shop. The bell above the door jangled as she entered.

The floors were fresh pine, all polished and gleaming, a matching counter occupying the back, an open door beyond it revealing a rear room. Clothes for both males and females occupied the space, some displayed on dummies, others folded neatly along display tables.

A dark-haired female appeared on the other side of the counter, her braided-back hair shining in the lights. Her face was striking—elegant and sharp, contrasting with her full mouth. Her angular eyes and light brown skin suggested a heritage from another region, perhaps a recent ancestor from the Dawn Court. The light in those eyes was direct. Clear.

"Good morning," the female said, her voice solid and frank. "Can I help you?"

If she recognized Nesta, she didn't let on. Nesta gestured down at her fighting leathers. "I was looking for something warmer than this. The cold leaks through."

"Ah," the female said, glancing toward the door and the empty street beyond. Worried that someone might see her in here? Or waiting for another customer? "The warriors are all such proud fools that they never complain about the leathers being cold. They claim they keep them perfectly warm."

"They're decently warm," Nesta confessed, part of her smiling at the way the female had said *proud fools*. As if she shared Nesta's instinct to be unimpressed by the males in the camp. "But the cold still hits me."

"Hmmm." The woman folded back the partition on the counter, entering the showroom proper. She surveyed Nesta from head to toe. "I don't sell fighting gear, but I wonder if we could get fleece-lined leathers made." She nodded toward the street. "How often do you train?"

"I'm not training. I'm . . ." Nesta struggled for the right words. Honestly, what she was doing was being a wretched asshole. "I'm watching," she said a shade pathetically.

"Ah." The female's eyes glinted. "Brought here against your will?"

It was none of her business. But Nesta said, "Part of my duties to the Night Court."

She wanted to see if the female would pry, to see if she really did not know her. If she would judge her for being a miserable waste of life.

The female angled her head, her braid slipping over the shoulder of her simple, homespun gown. Her wings twitched, the motion drawing Nesta's eye. Scars ran down them—unusual for the Fae. Azriel and Lucien were two of the few who bore scars, both from traumas so terrible Nesta had never dared ask for details. For this female to bear them as well—

"My wings were clipped," the female said. "My father was a . . . traditional male. He believed females should serve their families and be confined to their homes. I disagreed. He won, in the end."

Sharp, short words. Rhys's mother, Feyre had once told her, had nearly been doomed to such a fate. Only the arrival of his father had stopped the clipping from occurring. She'd been revealed as his mate, and endured the miserable union mostly from gratitude for her unharmed wings.

No one, it seemed, had been there to save this female.

"I'm sorry." Nesta shifted on her feet.

The female waved a slim hand. "It's of no consequence now. This shop keeps me busy enough that some days I forget I could ever fly in the first place."

"No healer can repair them?"

Her face tightened, and Nesta regretted her question. "It is extremely complex—all the connecting muscles and nerves and senses. Short of the High Lord of Dawn, I'm not certain anyone could handle it." Thesan, Nesta recalled, was a master of healing—Feyre bore his power in her veins. Had offered to use it to heal Elain from her stupor after being turned High Fae.

Nesta blocked out the memory of that pale face, the empty brown eyes.

"Anyway," the female said quickly, "I can make inquiries to my suppliers about whether the leathers could be made warmer. It might take a few weeks, possibly a month, but I'll send word as soon as I hear."

"That's fine. Thank you." A thought clanged through Nesta. "I— How much will it cost?" She had no money.

"You work for the High Lord, do you not?" The female angled her head again. "I can send the bill to Velaris."

"They . . ." Nesta didn't want to admit how low she'd fallen—not to this stranger. "I actually don't need the warmer clothes."

"I thought Rhysand paid you all well."

"He does, but I am . . ." Fine. If the female could be blunt, so could she. "I'm cut off."

Curiosity flooded the female's eyes. "Why?"

Nesta stiffened. "I don't know you well enough to tell you that."

The female shrugged. "All right. I can still make inquiries. Get a price for you. If you're cold out there, you shouldn't suffer." She added pointedly, "No matter what the High Lord may think."

"I think he'd rather Cassian threw me off the edge of that cliff over there."

The female snorted. But she held out a hand toward Nesta. "I'm Emerie."

Nesta took her hand, surprised to find her grip like iron. "Nesta Archeron."

"I know," Emerie said, releasing Nesta's hand. "You killed the King of Hybern."

"Yes." There was no denying that fact. And she couldn't bring herself to lie that she wasn't the least bit smug about it.

"Good." Emerie's smile was a thing of dangerous beauty. She said again, "Good." There was steel in this female. Not just in her straight spine and chin, but in her eyes.

Nesta turned toward the door and waiting cold, unsure what to do with the naked approval of what so many others had regarded either with awe or fear or doubt. "Thank you for your help."

So strange, to speak polite, normal words. Strange to wish to offer them, and to a stranger no less.

Males and females, children darting amongst them, gawked at Nesta as she exited onto the street. A few hurried their children along. She met their stares with cool indifference.

You're right to hide your children from me, she wanted to say. *I am the monster you fear.*

✠

"Same task as yesterday?" Nesta asked Clotho by way of greeting, still half-chilled from the camp she'd departed only ten minutes earlier.

Cassian had barely spoken upon returning to Rhysand's mother's house, his face taut with whatever he'd dealt with at the other Illyrian villages, and Morrigan had been just as sour-faced when she'd appeared to winnow them back to the House of Wind. Cassian had dumped Nesta on the landing veranda without so much as a farewell before he pivoted to where Mor dusted herself off. Within seconds, he was carrying the blond beauty into the brisk wind.

It shouldn't have bothered her—seeing him flying away with another female in his arms. Some small part of her knew it wasn't remotely fair to feel that body-tightening irritation at the sight. She had pushed him away again and again, and he had no reason to believe she'd wish it differently. And she knew he had a history with Morrigan, that they'd been lovers long ago.

She'd turned from the sight, entering the House through its dining room, where she found a bowl of some sort of pork-and-bean soup waiting. A silent, thoughtful offering.

She'd just said to the House, "I'm not hungry," before striding down to the library.

Now she waited as Clotho wrote out an answer and handed over a piece of paper.

Nesta read, *There are books to be shelved on Level Five.*

Nesta peered over the railing beside Clotho's desk, silently counting. Five was . . . very far down. Not within the first ring of true darkness, but hovering in the dimness above it. "Nothing lives down there anymore, right? Bryaxis hasn't come back?"

Clotho's enchanted pen moved. The second note read, *Bryaxis never harmed any of us.*

"Why?"

The pen scratched along the paper. *I think Bryaxis took pity on us. We saw our nightmares come true before we came here.*

It was an effort not to look at Clotho's gnarled hands or try to pierce the shadows beneath her hood.

The priestess added to the note, *I can reassign you to a higher level.*

"No," Nesta said hoarsely. "I'll manage."

And that was that. An hour later, her leathers covered in dust, Nesta slumped at an empty wooden table, in need of a pause.

That same bowl of pork-and-bean soup appeared on the table.

She peered at the distant ceiling. "I *said* I'm not hungry."

A spoon appeared alongside the bowl. And a napkin.

"This is absolutely none of your business."

A glass of water thudded down next to the soup.

Nesta crossed her arms, leaning back in the chair.

"Who are you talking to?"

The light female voice had Nesta twisting around, stiffening as she found a priestess in the robes of an acolyte standing between the two nearest shelves. Her hood was thrown back, and faelight danced in the rich coppery chestnut of her pin-straight hair. Her large teal eyes were as clear and depthless as the stone usually atop a priestess's hood, and a scattering of freckles lay across her nose and cheeks, as if someone had tossed them with a careless hand. She was young—almost coltish, with her slender, elegant limbs. High Fae, and yet . . . Nesta couldn't explain the way she sensed that there was something else mixed into her. Some secret beneath the pretty face.

Nesta gestured to the soup and water, but they were gone. She scowled at the ceiling, at the House that had the nerve to pester her and then make her look like a lunatic. But she said to the priestess, "I wasn't talking to anyone."

The priestess hefted the five tomes in her arms. "Are you finished for today?"

Nesta glanced at the cart of books she'd left unsorted. "No. I was taking a break."

"You've only been working for an hour."

"I didn't realize anyone was timing me." Nesta allowed every bit of unpleasantness to show in her face. She'd already conversed with one stranger today, fulfilling her quota of basic decency. Being kind to a second one was beyond her.

The acolyte remained unimpressed. "It's not every day we have someone new in our library." She dumped the books onto Nesta's cart. "These can be shelved."

"I don't answer to acolytes."

The priestess drew up to her full height, which was slightly taller than average for Fae females. A crackling sort of energy buzzed around her, and Nesta's power grumbled in answer. "You're here to work," the acolyte said, her voice unruffled. "And not only for Clotho."

"You speak rather informally of your high priestess."

"Clotho does not enforce rank. She encourages us to use her name."

"And what is your name?" She would certainly be complaining to Clotho about this impertinent acolyte's attitude.

The priestess's eyes glittered with amusement, as if aware of Nesta's plan. "Gwyneth Berdara." Unusual, for these Fae to use family names. Even Rhys didn't use one, as far as Nesta knew. "But most call me Gwyn."

A level above, two priestesses walked by the railing in silence, hooded heads bowed and books in their arms. Nesta could have sworn one of them watched, though.

Gwyn tracked the focus of her attention. "That's Roslin and Deirdre."

"How can you tell?" With their hoods on, they appeared nearly identical save for their hands.

"Their scents," Gwyn said simply, and turned to the books she'd left on the cart. "Do you plan to shelve these, or do I need to take them elsewhere?"

Nesta leveled a flat look at her. Living down here, there was a good chance the priestesses didn't know who she was. What she'd done. What power she bore. "I'll do it," Nesta said through clenched teeth.

Gwyn hooked her hair behind her arched ears. Freckles dotted her hands, too, like splattered bits of rust. If marks of trauma lingered, any evidence was hidden by her robe.

But Nesta knew well how invisible wounds could be. How they could scar as deeply and badly as any physical breaking.

And it was for that reminder alone that Nesta said more gently, "I'll do it right now." Perhaps she had a little bit of her decency quota left.

Gwyn marked the change. "I don't need your pity." The words were sharp, as clear as her teal eyes.

"It wasn't pity."

"I've been here for nearly two years, but I haven't become so disconnected from others that I can't tell when someone remembers *why* I am here and alters their behavior." Gwyn's mouth flattened to a line. "I don't need to be coddled. Only spoken to like a person."

"I doubt you'll enjoy the way I speak to most people," Nesta said.

Gwyn snorted. "Try me."

Nesta looked at her from under lowered brows again. "Get out of my sight."

Gwyn grinned, a broad, bright thing that showed most of her teeth and made her eyes sparkle in a way Nesta knew her own never had. "Oh, you're good." Gwyn turned back to the stacks. "Really good." She vanished into the gloom.

Nesta stared after her for a long moment, wondering if she'd imagined the whole thing. Two friendly conversations in one day. She had no idea when such a thing had last occurred.

Another hooded priestess drifted by, and offered Nesta a bob of the chin in greeting.

Quiet settled around her, as if Gwyn had been a summer storm that blew in and evaporated within a moment. Sighing, Nesta gathered the books Gwyn had left on the cart.

✠

Hours later, dusty and exhausted and finally hungry, Nesta stood before Clotho's desk and said, "Same story tomorrow?"

Clotho wrote, *Are you not pleased by your work?*

"I would be if your acolytes didn't boss me around like a servant."

Gwyneth mentioned she had run into you earlier. She works for Merrill, my right hand, who is a fiercely demanding scholar. If Gwyneth's requests were abrupt, it was due to the pressing nature of the work she does.

"She wanted me to shelve her books, not find more."

Other scholars need them. But I am not in the business of explaining my acolytes' behavior. If you did not like Gwyneth's request, you should have said so. To her.

Nesta bristled. "I did. She's a piece of work."

Some might say the same of you.

Nesta crossed her arms. "Some might."

She'd have bet that Clotho was smiling beneath her hood, but the priestess wrote, *Gwyneth, like you, has her own history of bravery and survival. I would ask that you give her the benefit of the doubt.*

Acid that felt an awful lot like regret burned in Nesta's veins. She shoved it aside. "Noted. And the work is fine."

Clotho only wrote, *Good night, Nesta.*

Nesta trudged up the steps, and entered the House proper. The wind seemed to moan through the halls, answered only by her grumbling stomach.

The private library was mercifully empty when she strode through the double doors, instantly relaxing at the sight of all those books crammed close, the sunset on the city below, the Sidra a living band of gold. Sitting at the desk before the wall of windows, she said to the House, "I'm sure you won't do it now, but I would like that soup."

Nothing. She sighed up at the ceiling. Fantastic.

Her stomach twisted, as if it'd devour her organs if she didn't eat soon. She added tightly, "Please."

The soup appeared, a glass of water beside it. A napkin and silverware followed. A fire roared to life in the hearth, but she said quickly, "No fire. No need."

It banked to nothing, but the faelights in the room flared brighter.

Nesta was reaching for her spoon when a plate of fresh, crusty bread appeared. As if the House were a fussing mother hen.

"Thank you," she said into the quiet, and dug in.

The faelights flickered once, as if to say, *You're welcome.*

CHAPTER 10

Nesta ate until she couldn't fit another morsel into her body, helping herself to thirds of the soup. The House seemed more than happy to oblige her, and had even offered her a slice of double-chocolate cake to finish.

"Is this Cassian-approved?" She picked up the fork and smiled at the moist, gleaming cake.

"It certainly isn't," he said from the doorway, and Nesta whirled, scowling. He nodded toward the cake. "But eat up."

She put down the fork. "What do you want?"

Cassian surveyed the family library. "Why are you eating in here?"

"Isn't it obvious?"

His grin was a slash of white. "The only thing that's obvious is that you're talking to yourself."

"I'm talking to the House. Which is a considerable step up from talking to you."

"It doesn't talk back."

"Exactly."

He snorted. "I walked into that one." He stalked across the room, eyeing the cake she still didn't touch. "Are you really . . . talking to the House?"

"Don't you talk to it?"

"No."

"It listens to me," she insisted.

"Of course it does. It's enchanted."

"It even brought food down to the library unasked."

His brows rose. "Why?"

"I don't know how your faerie magic works."

"Did you . . . *do* anything to make it act that way?"

"If you're taking a page from Devlon's book and asking if I did any witchcraft, the answer is no."

Cassian chuckled. "That's not what I meant, but fine. The House likes you. Congratulations." She growled, and he leaned over her to pick up the fork. She went stiff at his closeness, but he said nothing as he took a bite of the cake. He let out a hum of pleasure that traveled along her bones. And then took another bite.

"That's supposed to be mine," she groused, peering up at him as he continued to eat.

"Then take it from me," he said. "A simple disarming maneuver would do, considering my center of gravity is off balance and I'm distracted by this delicious cake."

She glowered at him.

He took a third bite. "These are the things, Nes, that you'd learn in lessons with me. Your threats would be a hell of a lot more impressive if you could back them up."

She drummed her fingers on the desk. Eyed the fork in his hands and pictured stabbing him in the thigh with it.

"You could do that, too," he said, reading the direction of her stare. "I could teach you how to turn anything into a weapon. Even a fork."

She bared her teeth, but Cassian only set down the fork with grating precision and walked out, leaving her the half-eaten cake.

⸸

Nesta read the deliciously erotic romance she'd found on a shelf of the private library until her eyelids grew so heavy only iron will could hold them open. It was then that she trudged down the hall to her bedroom and collapsed into bed, not bothering to change out of her clothes before she sprawled on the mattress.

She woke freezing in the dark of night, roused herself enough to strip off the leathers, and climbed under the sheets, teeth clattering.

A moment later, a fire blazed in the hearth.

"No fire," she ordered, and it vanished again.

She could have sworn a tentative curiosity curled around her. Shivering, she waited for the sheets to warm to her body temperature.

Long minutes passed, and then the bed heated. Not from her own naked body, but some manner of spell. The very air warmed, too, as if someone had blown a great breath into the space.

Her shaking stopped, and she nestled into the warmth. "Thank you," she murmured.

The House's only answer was to slide the still-open drapes shut. By the time they'd finished swaying, she was again asleep.

⸸

Elain had been stolen. By Hybern. By the Cauldron, which had seen Nesta watching it and watched her in turn. Had noted her scrying with bones and stones and made her regret it.

She had done this. Brought this upon them. Touching her power, wielding it, had done this, and she would never forgive herself, never—

Elain would surely be tormented, ripped apart body and soul.

A crack cleaved the world.

Her father stood before her, neck twisted. Her father, with his soft brown eyes, the love for her still shining in them as their light faded—

Nesta jolted awake, nausea rippling through her as she grasped at the sheets.

Deep in her gut, her soul, something writhed and twined around itself, seeking a way out, seeking a way into the world—

Nesta shoved it down. Stomped on her power. Slammed every mental door she could on it.

Dream, she told it. *Dream and memory. Go away.*

Her power grumbled in her veins, but obeyed.

The bed had become hot enough that Nesta kicked off the sheets before rubbing her hands over her sweat-soaked face.

She needed a drink. Needed anything to wash this away.

She dressed swiftly, not quite feeling her body. Not quite caring what time it was or where she was, thinking only of the obstacle between her and that pleasure hall.

The door to the ten thousand steps was already open, the faelights in the hall dimmed to near darkness. Her boots scuffed on the stones as she approached, glancing behind her to make sure no one followed.

Hands shaking, she began the descent.

Around and around and around.

I loved you from the first moment I held you in my arms.

Down and down and down.

That ancient Cauldron opening an eye to stare at her. To pin her in place.

The Cauldron dragging her into itself, into the pit of Creation, taking and taking from her, merciless despite her screaming—

Around and down, exactly as she had been pulled in by the Cauldron, crushed beneath its terrible power—

Nausea swelled, her power with it, and her foot slipped.

She had only a heartbeat to grab for the wall, but too late. Her knees banged into the steps, her face hitting a second later, and then she was twisting and careening down, blasting into the wall, ricocheting off and tumbling down step after step after step.

She flung out a hand blindly, nails biting into stone. Sparks exploded as she cried out and held on.

The world stopped moving. Her body halted its plunge.

Sprawled across the steps, hand clutching the stone, she panted, great sawing breaths that cut with each inhale. She shut her eyes, savoring the stillness, the utter lack of motion.

And in the quiet, pain set in. Barking, bleating pain across every part of her body.

The coppery tang of blood filled her mouth. Something wet and warm slid down her neck. A sniff told her it was blood, too.

And her fingernails, the ones gripping the stone steps—

Nesta blinked at her hand. She *had* seen sparks.

Her fingers were embedded in the stone, the rock glowing as if lit with an inner flame.

Gasping, she snatched back her hand, and the stone went dark.

But the fingerprints remained, four furrows buried in the top of the step, a single hole in the riser where her thumb had pressed.

Icy dread sluiced through her. Sent her to her battered legs, knees groaning as she sprinted upward. Away from that handprint, forever etched in stone.

⁜

"So, who won the fight?" Cassian asked the next morning as she sat on her rock and watched him go through his exercises.

He hadn't asked at breakfast about the black eye and cut chin or how stiffly she'd moved. Neither had Mor upon her arrival. That the bruising and cuts remained at all told Nesta how bad the fall had been, but as High Fae, with her improved healing, they were already on the mend.

As a human, she supposed, the fall might have killed her. Perhaps this Fae body had its advantages. Being human, being weak in this world of monsters, was a death sentence. Her High Fae body was her best chance at survival.

Cassian's reticence had only lasted an hour into his routine. He stood in the center of the sparring ring, panting, sweat running down his face and neck.

"What fight?" She examined her mangled nails. Even with the . . . whatever it was she'd flung out to catch herself, her nails had cracked. She didn't let herself name what had come from within her, didn't let herself acknowledge it. By dawn, it had been strangled into submission.

"The one between you and the stairs."

Nesta cut him a glare. "I don't know what you're talking about."

Cassian began moving once more, drawing his sword and running through a series of movements that all seemed designed to hack a person in two. "You know: three in the morning, you leave your room to get shitfaced-drunk in town, and you're in such a rush to conquer the steps that you fall down a good thirty of them before you can stop yourself."

Had he seen the step? The handprint?

She demanded, "How do you know that?"

He shrugged.

"Are you *watching* me?" Before he could answer, she spat, "You were watching and didn't come to help?"

Cassian shrugged again. "You stopped falling. If you'd kept at it, someone would have eventually come to catch you before you hit the bottom."

She hissed at him.

He only grinned and beckoned with a hand. "Want to join me?"

"I should push *you* down those stairs."

Cassian sheathed his sword down his back in one elegant movement. Five hundred years of training—he must have drawn and sheathed that sword so many times it was muscle memory.

"Well?" he demanded, an edge creeping into his voice. "If you've got those glorious bruises, you might as well claim it came from training and not a pathetic tumble." He added, "How many stairs did you manage this time?"

Sixty-six. But Nesta said, "I'm not training."

At the edge of the ring, males were watching them again. They'd been watching Cassian first, partially with awe and partially with what she could only assume was envy. No one moved like he did. No one even came close. But now their stares turned amused—mocking him.

Once, last year, she might have gone up to those males and ripped them apart. Might have let a bit of that terrible power within her show so they truly believed she was a witch and would curse them and a thousand generations of their offspring if they insulted Cassian again.

Nesta stretched out her legs, leaning her bruised palms on the stone. "Enjoy your exercises."

Cassian bristled. But he held out his hand again. "Please."

She'd never heard him say that word. It was a rope thrown between them. He'd meet her halfway—let her win the power battle, admit defeat, if she would just get off the rock.

She told herself to get up, to take that outstretched hand.

But she couldn't. Couldn't bring her body to rise.

His hazel eyes were bright with pleading in the morning sun, the wind dancing in his dark hair. Like he was made from these mountains, crafted from wind and stone. He was so beautiful. Not in the way that Azriel and Rhys were beautiful, but in an uncut way. Savage and unrelenting.

The first time she'd seen Cassian, she couldn't take her eyes off him. She felt like she'd spent her life surrounded by boys, and then a man—a male, she supposed—had suddenly appeared. Everything about him had radiated that confident, arrogant masculinity. It had been heady and overwhelming, and all she'd wanted, all she'd wanted for so many months, was to touch him, smell him, taste him. Get close to that strength and throw everything she was against it because she knew he'd never break, never falter, never balk.

But the light in his eyes dimmed as he lowered his hand.

She deserved his disappointment. Deserved his resentment and disgust. Even if it carved something vital from her.

"Tomorrow, then," Cassian said. He didn't speak to her again for the rest of the day.

CHAPTER 11

The private library's doors were locked. Nesta jangled the handle, but it refused to open.

She said quietly, "Open this door."

The House ignored her.

She tried the handle again, shoving a shoulder into the door. "*Open* this door."

Nothing.

She continued slamming her shoulder into the door. "*Open this door right now.*"

The House declined to obey.

She gritted her teeth, panting. She'd had more books than yesterday to shelve, as the priestesses had apparently heard from Gwyn that Nesta was to be their errand girl.

So they began dumping their tomes on her cart—and a few asked her to retrieve books as well. Nesta had heeded them, if only because finding the requested books took her to new places in the library and occupied her thoughts, but by the time the clock had struck six, she was exhausted and dusty and hungry. She'd ignored the sandwich the House had laid out for her in the afternoon, and this had apparently pissed off the House enough that it now refused to allow her entry into the private library.

"All I want," Nesta ground out, "is a nice, hot meal and a good book." She tried the handle again. "Please."

Nothing. Nothing at all.

"*Fine.*" She stormed down the hall. Hunger alone carried her up to the dining room, where she found Cassian mid-meal, Azriel across from him.

The shadowsinger's face was solemn, his eyes wary. Cassian, his back to her, only stiffened, no doubt alerted either by her scent or the cadence of her steps.

She didn't speak as she aimed for a chair halfway down the table. A place setting and spread of food appeared as she reached her seat. She had a feeling that if she took the plate and left, it'd vanish from her hands before she reached the door.

Nesta maintained her silence as she slid into her chair, picked up her fork, and dug into the fillet of beef and roasted asparagus.

Cassian cleared his throat and said to Azriel, "How long will you be gone?"

"I'm not sure." The shadowsinger's eyes bore into her before he added, "Vassa was right to suspect something deadly amiss. Things are dangerous enough over there that it would be wiser for me to keep my base here at the House and winnow back and forth."

Curiosity bit deep, but Nesta said nothing. Vassa—she hadn't seen the enchanted human queen since the war had ended. Since the young woman had tried to speak to her about how *wonderful* Nesta's father had been, how he had been a true father to her, helped her and won her this temporary freedom, and on and on until Nesta's bones were screaming to get away, her blood boiling to think that her father had found his courage for someone other than her and her sisters. That he'd been the father she had needed—but for someone else. He had let their mother die in his refusal to send his merchant fleet hunting for a cure for her, had fallen into poverty and let them starve, but had decided to fight for this stranger? This nobody queen peddling a sad tale of betrayal and loss?

That thing deep in Nesta stirred, but she ignored it, pushed it down as best she could without the distraction of music or sex or wine. She took a sip of her water, letting it cool her throat, her belly, and supposed that would have to be enough.

"What'd Rhys say about it?" Cassian asked around a mouthful of food.

"Who do you think insisted I not risk a base over there?"

"Protective bastard." A note of affection rang in Cassian's words, though.

Silence fell again. Azriel nodded at her. "What happened to you?"

She knew what he meant: the black eye that was finally fading. Her hands and chin had healed, along with the bruising on her body, but the black eye had turned greenish. By tomorrow morning, it'd be gone entirely. "Nothing," she said without looking at Cassian.

"She fell down the stairs," Cassian said, not looking at her, either.

Azriel's silence was pointed before he asked, "Did someone . . . push you?"

"Asshole," Cassian growled.

Nesta lifted her eyes from her plate enough to note the amusement in Azriel's gaze, even though no smile graced his sensuous mouth.

Cassian went on, "I told her earlier today: if she'd bother to train, she'd at least have bragging rights for the bruises."

Azriel took a calm sip of his water. "Why aren't you training, Nesta?"

"I don't want to."

"Why not?"

Cassian muttered, "Don't waste your breath, Az."

She glared at him. "I'm not training in that miserable village."

Cassian glared right back. "You've been given an *order*. You know the consequences. If you don't get off that fucking rock by the end of this week, what happens next is out of my hands."

"So you'll tattle to your precious High Lord?" she crooned. "Big, tough warrior needs oh-so-powerful Rhysand to fight his battles?"

"Don't you fucking talk about Rhys with that tone," Cassian snarled.

"Rhys is an asshole," Nesta snapped. "He is an arrogant, preening *asshole.*"

Azriel sat back in his seat, eyes simmering with anger, but said nothing.

"That's bullshit," Cassian spat, the Siphons on the backs of his hands burning like ruby flames. "You know that is *bullshit*, Nesta."

"I hate him," she seethed.

"Good. He hates you, too," Cassian shot back. "Everyone fucking hates you. Is that what you want? Because congratulations, it's happened."

Azriel let out a long, long breath.

Cassian's words pelted her, one after another. Hit her somewhere low and soft, and hit hard. Her fingers curled into claws, scraping along the table as she flung back at him, "And I suppose now you'll tell me that *you* are the only person who doesn't hate me, and I'm supposed to feel something like gratitude, and agree to train with you."

"Now I tell you I'm *done.*"

The words rumbled between them. Nesta blinked, the only sign of surprise she'd allow.

Azriel tensed, as if surprised as well.

But she sliced into Cassian before he could go on. "Does that mean you're done panting after me as well? Because what a *relief* that will be, to know you've finally taken the hint."

Cassian's muscled chest heaved, his throat working. "You want to rip yourself apart, go right ahead. Implode all you like." He stood, meal half-finished. "The training was supposed to help you. Not punish you. I don't know why you don't fucking *get that.*"

"I told you: I'm not training in that miserable village."

"Fine." Cassian stalked out, his pounding steps fading down the hall.

Alone with Azriel, Nesta bared her teeth at him.

Azriel watched her with that cool quiet, keeping utterly still. Like he saw everything in her head. Her bruised heart.

She couldn't bear it. So she stood, only two bites taken from her food, and left the room as well.

She returned to the library. The lights blazed as brightly as they had during the day, and a few lingering priestesses wandered the levels. She found her cart, filled again with books needing to be shelved.

No one spoke to her, and she spoke to no one as she began to work, with only the roaring silence in her head for company.

Amren had been wrong. *Keep reaching out your hand* was utter bullshit when the person it was extended to could bite hard enough to rip off fingers.

Cassian sat on the flat top of the mountain in which the House of Wind had been built, peering down into the open-air training ring beneath him. The stars glinted overhead, and a brisk autumn breeze that whispered of changing leaves and crisp nights flowed past him. Below, Velaris was a golden sparkle, accented along the Sidra with a rainbow of color.

He had never failed at anything. Not like this.

And he'd been so stupidly desperate, so stupidly hopeful, that he hadn't believed she'd truly refuse. Until today, when he'd seen her on that rock and known she'd wanted to get up, but watched her shut down the instinct. Watched her clamp that steel will over herself.

"You're not the brooding type."

Cassian started, whipping his head to find Feyre sitting beside him.

She dangled her feet into the emptiness, her golden-brown hair ruffled by the wind as she peered into the training pit. "Did you fly in?"

"Winnowed. Rhys said you were 'thinking loudly.' " Feyre's mouth quirked to the side. "I figured I'd see what was happening."

A fine skin of power remained wrapped around his High Lady, invisible to the naked eye but glittering with strength. Cassian nodded toward her. "Why's Rhysie still got that ironclad shield on you?" It was mighty enough to guard all of Velaris.

"Because he's a pain in the ass," Feyre said, but smiled softly. "He's still learning how it works, and I still haven't figured out how to break free of it. But with the queens a renewed threat, and Beron in the mix, especially if Koschei is their puppet master, Rhys is perfectly happy to leave it on."

"Everything with those queens is a fucking headache," Cassian grumbled. "Hopefully, Az will figure out what they're really up to. Or at least what Briallyn and Koschei are up to."

Rhys was still contemplating what to do about Eris's demands. Cassian supposed he'd get his orders on that front soon. And would then have to deal with the asshole. General to general.

"Part of me dreads what Azriel will find," Feyre said, leaning back on her hands. "Mor's heading off to Vallahan again tomorrow. I worry about that, too. That she'll come back with worse news about their intentions."

"We'll deal with it."

"Spoken like a true general."

Cassian knocked Feyre's shoulder with his wing, a casual, affectionate gesture. One he never dared make with the females of any Illyrian community. Illyrians were psychotic on a good day about who touched their wings and how, and wing-touching outside of the bedroom, training, or mortal combat was an enormous taboo. But Rhys never cared, and Cassian had needed the contact. Always needed physical contact, he'd learned. Probably thanks to a childhood spent with precious little of it.

Feyre seemed to understand his need for a reassuring touch, because she said, "How bad is it?"

"Bad." It was all he could bring himself to admit.

"But she's going to the library?"

"She went back to the library tonight. She's still down there for all I know."

Feyre gave a *hmm* of contemplation, gazing at the city. His High Lady looked so young—he always forgot how young she truly was, considering what she'd already faced and achieved in her life. At twenty-one, he'd still been drinking and brawling and fucking, unconcerned with anything and anybody except his ambition to be the most skilled of Illyrian warriors since Enalius himself. At twenty-one, Feyre had saved their world, mated, and found true happiness.

Feyre asked, "Did Nesta say why she won't train?"

"Because she hates me."

Feyre snorted. "Cassian, Nesta does not hate you. Believe me."

"She sure as shit acts like it."

Feyre shook her head. "No, she doesn't." Her words were pained enough that he frowned.

"She doesn't hate you, either," he said quietly.

Feyre shrugged. The gesture made his chest ache. "For a while, I thought she didn't. But now I don't know."

"I don't understand why you two can't just . . ." He struggled for the right word.

"Get along? Be civil? Smile at each other?" Feyre's laugh was hollow. "It's always been that way."

"Why?"

"I have no idea. I mean, it was always that way with us, and our mother. She only had an interest in Nesta. She ignored me, and saw Elain as barely more than a doll to dress up, but Nesta was *hers*. Our mother made sure we knew it. Or she just cared so little what we thought or did that she didn't bother to hide it from us." Resentment and long-held pain laced every word. That a mother would do such a thing to her children . . . "But when we fell into poverty, when I started hunting, it got worse. Our mother was gone, and our father wasn't exactly present. He wasn't fully *there*. So it was me and Nesta, always at each other's throats." Feyre rubbed her face. "I'm too exhausted to go over every detail. It's all just a tangled mess."

Cassian refrained from observing that both sisters seemed to need each other—that Nesta perhaps needed Feyre more than she realized. And from mentioning that this mess between the two females hurt him more than he could express.

Feyre sighed. "That's my long way of saying that if Nesta hated you . . . I know what it looks like, and she doesn't hate you."

"She might after what I said to her tonight."

"Azriel filled me in." Feyre rubbed her face again. "I don't know what to do. How to help her."

"Three days in and I'm already at my wits' end," he said.

They sat in silence, the wind drifting past them. Mist gathered on the Sidra far below, and white plumes of smoke from countless chimneys rose to meet it.

Feyre asked, "So what do we do?"

He didn't know. "Maybe the library work will be enough to pull her out of this." But even as he spoke the words, they rang false.

Feyre apparently agreed. "No, in the library she can hide in the silence and amongst the shelves. The library was meant to balance what the training does."

He rolled his shoulders. "Well, she said she's not training in that *miserable* village, so we're at an impasse."

Feyre sighed again. "Seems like it."

But Cassian paused. Blinked once, and peered down at the training ring before him.

"What?"

He snorted, shaking his head. "I should have known."

A tentative smile bloomed on Feyre's mouth, and Cassian leaned in to kiss her cheek. He only got within an inch of her face before his lips met night-kissed steel.

Right—the shield. "That level of protection is insane."

She smoothed her thick cream sweater. "So is Rhys."

Cassian sniffed, trying and failing to detect her scent. "He's got your scent shielded, too?"

Feyre grinned. "It's all part of the same shield. Helion wasn't joking about it being impenetrable."

And despite everything, Cassian grinned back. Memory washed over him from when he'd met her in the dining room several levels below, this girl who would become his High Lady. She'd been so horribly thin then, so dead-eyed and withdrawn that it had taken all his self-control not to fly to the Spring Court and rip Tamlin limb from limb.

Cassian shook the thought away, focusing instead on the revelation before him.

One last time. He'd try one last time.

CHAPTER 12

Nesta stood in the training ring atop the House of Wind and scowled. "I thought we were going up to Windhaven."

Cassian strode over to the rope ladder laid out on the ground and straightened a rung. "Change of plans." No trace of that red-hot anger had remained on his face this morning when she'd walked into the breakfast room. Azriel was already gone, and Cassian hadn't said a word about why he'd left. Something about the queens, presumably, judging by what she'd heard the previous night.

When she'd finished her porridge, she'd looked for any sign of Morrigan, but the female had never appeared. And Cassian had led her here, not speaking on the walk up.

Everyone hates you. The words had lingered, like a bell that wouldn't stop ringing.

He finally clarified, "Mor's gone back to Vallahan, and Rhys and Feyre are busy. So there's no one to winnow us to Windhaven. We'll be training here today." He gestured to the empty ring. Free of any watching eyes. He added with a sharp grin that made her swallow, "Just you and me, Nes."

⸭

Nesta had said last night she wasn't training at the village. She'd said it multiple times, Cassian had realized. She wasn't training at *that miserable village*.

He should have realized it days ago. He knew her better than that, after all.

Nesta might be willing to face down the King of Hybern himself, but she was proud as all hell. Appearing foolish, making herself vulnerable—she'd rather die. Would rather sit on a freezing rock in the icy wind for hours than look like a fool in front of anyone, especially arrogant warriors predisposed to mock any female who attempted to fight like them.

It didn't matter to him where she trained. So long as she began the training.

If she refused today, he didn't know what he'd do.

The morning sun beat down, promising a warm day, and Cassian removed his leather jacket before rolling up a shirtsleeve. "Well?" he asked, lifting his eyes to her face.

"I . . ."

The hesitation made his chest tighten unbearably. But he stomped on that hope, slowly folding his other sleeve. He wondered if she noticed his fingers trembling slightly.

Pretend everything is normal. Don't scare her off.

There was nowhere for her to plant that beautiful ass here. He'd already moved the lounge chairs that Amren—and sometimes Mor—liked to use for sunbathing while he and the others trained.

When Nesta remained by the doorway, Cassian found himself saying, "I'll make a bargain with you."

Her eyes flashed. Fae bargains were no idle thing. He knew Feyre had already versed Nesta in them, when her sister had first come here. As a precaution. From Nesta's wary gaze, he knew she remembered Feyre's warnings well: Fae bargains were bound by magic and marked in ink upon one's body. The ink would not fade until the bargain had been fulfilled. And if the bargain was broken . . . the magic could exact terrible vengeance.

Cassian maintained a casual stance. "If you do an hour of exercises right now, I'll owe you a favor."

"I don't need any favors from you."

"Then name your price." He struggled to calm his racing heart. "An hour of training for whatever you want."

"That's a fool's bargain for you." Her eyes narrowed. "I thought you were a general. Aren't you supposed to be good at negotiating?"

His mouth quirked upward. She wasn't fighting him. "For you, I have no strategies."

She studied him with unflinching focus. "Anything I want?"

"Anything." He added wryly, "Anything short of you ordering me to fall out of the sky and smash my head on the earth."

She didn't smile the way he'd hoped. Her eyes turned to chips of ice. "You truly believe me capable of such a thing?"

"No," he said without hesitation.

Her mouth tightened. Like she didn't believe him. And—those were purple smudges under her eyes. How long had she worked in the library last night? Demanding to know why she'd stayed up so late wouldn't be wise. He'd save that battle for another time. In an hour, perhaps.

She surveyed him again, and Cassian willed himself to stand still, to appear open and nonthreatening and not like his very heart was in his bloody, outstretched hands.

She said at last, "Fine. Let's just say it will be a favor. Of whatever size I wish."

It was dangerous to allow this. Deadly. Stupid. But he said, "Yes."

He extended his hand. One last time.

Keep reaching out your hand.

"A bargain." He met her steely expression with his own. "You train with me for an hour, and I'll owe you one favor of whatever size you wish."

"Agreed." She slid her hand into his and shook firmly.

Magic zapped between them, and she gasped, recoiling.

Cassian let it thunder into him, like a stampede of galloping horses. He rode it out. Whatever her power was, it had made the bargain more intense. Demanding.

He scanned his hands, his bare forearms, seeking any hint of a tattoo beyond the Illyrian ones he bore for luck and glory. Nothing.

It had to be somewhere.

He peeled off his shirt and scanned the muscled planes of his torso. Nothing.

He approached the narrow mirror leaned against one end of the ring, left there for them to study their technique while exercising alone. Stopping before it, Cassian twisted, staring over a shoulder at his tattooed back.

There, dead in the center of the Illyrian tattoo snaking down his spine, a new tattoo had appeared. An eight-pointed star, whose compass points radiated in sharp lines across and up the groove of his back, twining with the Illyrian markings long inked there. The eastern and western points of the star shot right onto his wings, black blending into black. A matching one, he knew, would be on Nesta's spine. He tried not to think about her bare expanse of skin, now marked in black ink, as he faced her.

Nesta's eyes weren't on the mirror, though.

No, they'd fixed on his torso. On his chest, on his abdominal muscles, on his bare arms. Her pulse fluttered in her throat.

He didn't dare move, not as her gaze fixed on the vee of muscles that sloped beneath the waist of his pants. Not as her eyes darkened, her lashes bobbing as color crept over her pale skin.

His blood heated, skin tightening over bone and muscle, as if it could feel the touch of her blue-gray eyes, as if it were her fingers running over his stomach. Lower.

He knew better than to throw out a teasing remark. Rile her, and she'd not only refuse to train, bargain or no, but she'd stop looking at him like that.

Slowly, her eyes trailed up his body, lingering on his carved pectorals and the Illyrian tattoo that swirled over one of them before flowing down his left arm. He might have flexed. Slightly. His voice thick, he managed to say, "Ready?"

Cauldron boil him, he knew the question held more meanings than he cared to unravel.

From the glimmer in her eyes, he knew she got it. But she squared her shoulders. "All right. I owe you one hour of training."

"You sure as hell do." Cassian mastered his breathing, shoving aside that roaring desire. He strode to the center of the ring, but opted to keep his shirt off. Because of the warm day. Because his skin was now burning hot.

He gestured to the space beside him, and flashed her his broadest grin. "Let's see what you've got, Archeron."

A bargain—with Cassian. Nesta didn't know how she'd allowed herself to agree to it, to let that magic pass between them and mark her, but . . .

Everyone hates you.

Maybe it was that fact alone that had her agreeing to this insanity. She had no idea what favor she'd call in from him, but . . . Fine. This training ring, with its high walls, the sky her only witness—here, she supposed, she could let him do his worst.

No matter that Cassian without a shirt bordered on obscene, even with the collection of scars peppering his golden-brown skin. The one on his left pectoral was especially horrific—and one she knew he hadn't received during the war with Hybern. She didn't want to know what had been bad enough to leave a scar on his quick-healing body. Especially when all evidence of the devastating wound he'd gotten during the war was gone. Only rippling muscle and skin remained.

Honestly, there were so many muscles she couldn't count them all. Muscles on his damned ribs. She didn't know people could have them there. And those ones that flowed into his pants, like a golden arrow pointing to exactly what she wanted—

Nesta shook the thought out of her head as she approached Cassian in the center of the ring. He grinned like a fiend.

She stopped a good three feet away, the morning sun warm on her hair, her cheeks. It was the closest she'd stood to him without arguing or bickering in . . . a long time.

Cassian rolled his powerful shoulders, his sprawling tattoo shifting with the movement. "All right. We start with the basics."

"Swords?" She indicated the rack of weapons against the wall to the left of the archway into the stairwell.

His mouth curled upward. "You won't be getting to swords yet. You need to learn to control your movements, your balance. You'll develop basic strength and awareness of your body before you'll pick up even a wooden practice sword." He glanced at her laced-up boots. "Feet and breathing."

She blinked. "Feet?"

"Your toes especially."

He was completely serious. "What about my toes?"

"Learning how to grip the ground, to balance your weight—it builds a foundation for everything else."

"I'm going to be exercising my toes."

He chuckled. "You thought it'd be swords and arrows on day one?"

Arrogant ass. "You threw my sister into the training ring and did just that."

"Your sister already possessed a skill set you don't have, and also lacked the luxury of time."

Hunting to keep them fed had taught Feyre that skill set. Hunting, while Nesta had stayed home, safe and warm, and let Feyre venture into that forest alone. Those skills Feyre had honed had allowed her to survive against the High Fae and all their terrors, but . . . Feyre only had them because of what she'd been forced to do. Because Nesta hadn't been the one to do it. To step up.

She found Cassian watching carefully. As if he heard those thoughts, felt their weight on her.

"Feyre taught me how to use a bow." Only a few lessons, and long ago, but Nesta remembered. It was one of the few times she and Feyre had been allies.

"Not an Illyrian bow." Cassian gestured to a rack of massive bows and quivers beside the mirror. The bows were nearly as tall as a grown woman. "It took me until I was a mature adult to have the strength to even string one of those."

Nesta crossed her arms, drumming her fingers on her biceps. "So I'm going to spend an hour out here, wiggling my toes?"

Cassian's grin bloomed again. "Yes."

⁂

At some point, Nesta began sweating. Her feet ached, her legs turned to jelly.

She'd taken off her boots and gone through a few stances with Cassian, focusing on clenching her toes, finding her balance, and generally looking like a fool. At least no one was around to see her standing on one leg while hinging at the hip, the other leg rising behind her. Or using two wooden poles to steady herself while she swung her foot from pole to pole, working her way up each stick. Or doing a basic squat—that it turned out was all wrong, her weight misplaced and back too arched.

All basic, stupid things. And all things she failed utterly at.

Cassian didn't seem even remotely impressed as she rose from the squat he'd made her hold while supporting a wooden stick above her head. "Stand straight up, head first."

Nesta obeyed.

"No." He motioned for her to sink back down. "Head first. Don't curl your back or lean forward. Shoot straight up."

"I'm doing that."

"You're hunching. Push your feet into the ground. Grip with your toes as you bring your head right— Yes." She glared as she stood. Cassian just said, "Do another good one, then our hour's up."

She did so, panting hard, knees trembling and thighs bleating in burning pain. When she'd finished, she propped herself up with the pole she'd lifted over her head. "That's it?"

"Unless you want to bargain with me for a second hour."

"You really want to owe me two favors?"

"If it'll keep you here to finish the lesson, sure."

"I'm not sure I can take any more of these stretches."

"Then we'll do some breathing work and then a cooldown."

"What's a cooldown?"

"More stretching." He grinned. When she opened her mouth, he explained, "It's designed to help bring your body back to a normal pace and limit any soreness you'll have later."

His tone held no condescension. So she asked, "And what's breathing work?"

"Exactly what it sounds like." He put a hand on his stomach, right on those rippling muscles, and took a big, inhaling breath before slowly releasing it. "Your power when you fight comes from many places, but your breathing is one of the big ones." He nodded toward the stick in her hands. "Thrust it forward like you're skewering someone with a spear."

Brows rising, she did so, the motion awkward and inelegant.

He only nodded. "Now do it again, and as you do, *inhale*."

She did, the motion markedly weaker.

"And now do it again, but *exhale* with the thrust."

It took her a second or two to orient her breathing, but she obeyed, shoving the stick forward as she blew out a breath. Power rippled down her arms, her body.

Nesta blinked at the stick. "I could feel the difference."

"It's all linked. Breath and balance and movement. Bulky muscle like this"—he tapped that absurdly contoured stomach of his—"means shit when you don't know how to utilize it."

"So how do you learn to control your breathing?"

He smiled again, hazel eyes bright in the sun. "Like this."

So began another series of movements, all so damned simple when he demonstrated, but nearly impossible to coordinate in her own body when she went to replicate them. But she focused on her breathing, on the power of it, as if her lungs were the bellows of some great forge.

The sun arced higher, crossing the training space, dragging the shadows with it.

Inhale. Exhale. Breaths accented by a deep lunge, or a squat, or balancing on one leg. All exercises she'd done in the first hour, but now revealed anew with the added layer of breathing.

Breathing in and out, out and in, body and mind flowing, her concentration unwavering.

Cassian's commands were firm, but gentle, encouraging without being irksome. *Hold it, hold it, hold it—and release. Good. Again. Again. Again.*

There wasn't a part of her body that wasn't sliding with sweat, wasn't one part that wasn't shaking as he bade her lie down on a black mat at the far end of the ring. "Cooldown," he said, kneeling and patting the mat.

She was too tired to object, practically flinging herself onto it and staring at the sky.

The blue bowl arched into forever, the sun stinging against the sweat on her face. Wisps of clouds drifted through the dazzling blue, unconcerned with her entirely.

Her mind had become as clear as that sky, the fog and pressing shadows gone. "Do you like flying?" She didn't know where the question came from.

He peered down at her. "I love it." The truth rang out in those words. "It's freedom and joy and challenge."

"I met a female shop owner at Windhaven who'd had her wings clipped." She turned her head from the sky to look over at him. His face had tightened. "Why do Illyrians do that?"

"To control their women," Cassian said with quiet anger. "It's an old tradition. Rhys and I tried to stamp it out by making it illegal, but change takes a while amongst the High Fae. For stubborn asses like the Illyrians, it takes even longer. Emerie—I'm assuming that's who you met, since she's the only female shop owner—was one who slipped through the cracks. It was during Amarantha's reign, and . . . a lot of shit slipped through the cracks."

His eyes turned haunted, not only from what had been done to Emerie by her father, Nesta could tell, but at the memories of those fifty years. The guilt.

And perhaps it was to save him from reliving those memories, to banish that unwarranted guilt in his eyes, that she nestled against the mat and said, "Cooldown."

"You sound eager."

She met his stare. "I . . ." She swallowed. Hated herself for balking, and forced herself to say, "The breathing makes my head stop being so . . ." Horrible. Awful. Miserable. "Loud."

"Ah." Understanding washed over his face. "Mine too."

For a moment, she held his gaze, watched the wind tug at the strands of his shoulder-length hair. The instinct to touch the sable locks had her pressing her palms to the mat, as if physically restraining herself.

"Right." Cassian cleared his throat. "Cooldown."

✣

She'd done well. Really damn well.

Nesta finished the cooldown and sprawled on the black mat, as if needing to piece herself together. Rally her strength.

Cassian let her, rising to his feet and walking to the water station to the right of the archway. "You need to drink as much water as you can," he said, taking two glasses and filling them from the ewer on the small table. He returned to her side, sipping from his own.

Nesta remained prone, limbs loose, eyes closed, the sunlight making her hair, her sweaty skin, shine. He couldn't stop the image from rising: of her lying in his bed like this, sated, her body limp with pleasure.

He swallowed hard. She cracked open an eye, sitting up slowly, and took the water he extended. Chugged it, realized how thirsty she was, and eased to her feet. He watched as she aimed for the ewer, filling her glass and draining it twice more before she finally set it down.

"You never told me what you wanted for the second hour of training," he said eventually.

She looked over a shoulder. Her skin was rosy in a way he hadn't seen for a long, long time, her eyes bright. The breathing, she'd said, had helped her. Settled her. Looking at the slight change on her face, he believed it.

What would happen when the high wore off remained to be seen. Small steps, he assured himself. Small, small steps.

Nesta said, "The second hour was on the house."

She didn't smile, didn't so much as wink, but Cassian grinned. "Generous of you."

She rolled her eyes, but without her usual venom. "I have to change before I go to the library."

As Nesta entered the archway, the gloom of the stairwell beyond it, Cassian blurted, "I didn't mean what I said last night—about everyone hating you."

She halted, her blue-gray eyes frosting. "It's true."

"It's not." He dared one step closer. "You're here because we *don't* hate you." He cleared his throat, running a hand through his hair. "I wanted you to know that. That we don't—that *I* don't hate you."

She weighed whatever the hell lay in his stare. Likely more than was wise to let her see. But she said quietly, "And I have never hated you, Cassian."

With that, she walked through the doorway into the House, as if she hadn't hit him right in the gut, first with the words, then by using his name.

It wasn't until she'd vanished down the stairs that he released the breath he'd been holding.

CHAPTER 13

She was starving. It was the only thought that occupied Nesta as she shelved book after book. That, and how sore her body was. Her thighs burned with each foot she walked up and down the ramp of the library, her arms unbearably stiff with each book she lifted to its resting place.

That much soreness, just from stretches and balance exercises. She didn't want to consider what a workout like the ones she'd seen Cassian go through would do to her.

She was pathetic for being so weak. Pathetic for now being unable to walk so much as a step without grimacing.

"Cooldown, my ass," she grumbled, heaving a tome into her hands. She peered at the title and groaned. It belonged on the other side of this level—a good five-minute walk across the central atrium and down the endless hall. Her throbbing legs might very well give out halfway there.

Her stomach gurgled. "I'll deal with you later," she told the book, and scanned the other titles remaining in her cart. None, fortunately or unfortunately, needed to be shelved in the section that book belonged in. To lug the cart all the way over there would be exhausting—better to just carry the tome, even if it was an essentially meaningless trip to deposit one book.

Not that she had anything better to do with her time. Her day. Her life.

Whatever clarity she'd felt in the training ring levels and levels above fogged up again. Whatever calm and quiet she'd managed to capture in her head had dissipated like smoke. Only moving would keep it at bay.

Nesta found the next shelf required—quite a ways above her head, with no stool in sight. She rose onto her toes, legs shrieking in protest, but it was too high. Nesta was on the taller side for a female, standing a good two inches above Feyre, but this shelf was out of reach. Grunting, she attempted to shelve the book with her fingertips, arms straining.

"Oh, good. It's you," a familiar female voice said from down the row. Nesta pivoted to discover Gwyn striding swiftly toward her, arms laden with books and coppery hair shimmering in the dim light.

Nesta didn't bother to look pleasant as she lowered herself fully onto her feet.

Gwyn angled her head, as if finally realizing what she'd been doing. "Can't you use magic to put it up on the shelf?"

"No." The word was cool and sullen.

Gwyn's brows twitched toward each other. "You don't mean to tell me you've been shelving everything *by hand*?"

"How else would I do it?"

Gwyn's teal eyes narrowed. "You have power, though, don't you?"

"It's none of your concern." It was no one's concern. She had none of the High Fae's usual gifts. Her power—that *thing*—was utterly alien. Grotesque.

But Gwyn shrugged. "Very well." She dumped her books right into Nesta's arms. "These can go back."

Nesta staggered under the books' weight and glared.

Gwyn ignored the look, instead glancing around before lowering her voice. "Have you seen volume seven of Lavinia's *The Great War*?"

Nesta scanned her memory. "No. I haven't come across that one."

Gwyn frowned. "It's not on its shelf."

"So someone else has it."

"That's what I was afraid of." She released a dramatic breath.

"Why?"

Gwyn's voice quieted into a conspiratorial whisper. "I work for someone who is very . . . demanding."

Memory tugged at Nesta. Someone named Merrill, Clotho had told her the other day. Her right hand. "I take it you're not fond of the person?"

Gwyn leaned against one of the shelves, crossing her arms with a casualness that belied her priestess's robes. Again, she wore no hood and no blue stone atop her head. "Honestly, while I consider many of the females here to be my sisters, there are a few who are not what I would consider nice."

Nesta snorted.

Gwyn again peered down the row. "You know why we're all here." Shadows swarmed her eyes—the first Nesta had seen there. "We all have endured . . ." She rubbed her temple. "So I hate, I *hate* to even speak ill of any one of my sisters here. But Merrill is unpleasant. To everyone. Even Clotho."

"Because of her experiences?"

"I don't know," Gwyn said. "All I know is that I was assigned to work with Merrill and aid in her research, and I might have made a teensy mistake." She grimaced.

"What manner of mistake?"

Gwyn blew out a sigh toward the darkened ceiling. "I was supposed to deliver volume seven of *The Great War* to Merrill yesterday, along with a stack of other books, and I could have *sworn* I did, but this morning, while I was in her office, I looked at the stack and saw I'd given her volume eight instead."

Nesta reined in her eye rolling. "And this is a bad thing?"

"She'll kill me when it's not there for her to read today." Gwyn hopped from foot to foot. "Which could be any moment. I got away the instant I could, but the book isn't on the shelf." She halted her fidgeting. "Even if I found the book, she'd spot me swapping it into the pile."

"And you can't tell her?" Gwyn couldn't be serious about the killing thing. Though with the faeries, Nesta supposed it might be a possibility. Despite this place being one of peace.

"Gods, no. Merrill doesn't accept mistakes. The book is supposed to be there, I *told* her it was there, and . . . I messed up." The priestess's face paled. She looked almost ill.

"Why does it matter?"

Emotion stirred in those remarkable eyes. "Because I don't like to fail. I *can't* . . ." Gwyn shook her head. "I don't want to make any more mistakes."

Nesta didn't know how to unpack that statement. So she just said, "Ah."

Gwyn went on, "These females took me in. Gave me shelter and healing and family." Again, her large eyes darkened. "I cannot stand to fail them in anything. Especially someone as demanding as Merrill. Even when it might seem trivial."

Admirable, though Nesta was loath to admit it. "Have you left this mountain since you arrived?"

"No. Once we come in, we do not leave unless it is time for us to depart—back to the world at large. Though some of us remain forever."

"And never see daylight again? Never feel fresh air?"

"We have windows, in our dormitories." At Nesta's confused expression, she clarified, "They're glamoured from sight on the mountainside. Only the High Lord knows about them, since they're his spells. And you now, I suppose."

"But you don't leave?"

"No," Gwyn said. "We don't."

Nesta knew she could let the conversation end there, but she asked,

"And what do you do with the time you're not in the library? Practice your . . . religious things?"

Gwyn huffed a soft laugh. "In part. We honor the Mother, and the Cauldron, and the Forces That Be. We have a service at dawn and at dusk, and on every holy day."

Nesta must have made a face of distaste because Gwyn snorted. "It's not so dull as all that. The services are beautiful, the songs as fair as any you'd hear in a music hall."

That *did* sound rather interesting.

"I enjoy the dusk services," Gwyn continued. "The music was always my favorite part of it, you know. I mean, not here. I was a priestess—an acolyte still—before I came here." She added a shade quietly, "In Sangravah."

The name sounded familiar to Nesta, but she couldn't place it.

Gwyn shook her head, her face pale enough that her freckles stood out in stark relief. "I need to return to Merrill before she starts wondering where I am. And come up with some way to save my hide when she can't find that book in the pile." She jerked her chin to the books in Nesta's hands. "Thanks for that."

Nesta only nodded, and the priestess was gone, coppery-brown hair fading from sight.

She made it back to her cart with minimal wincing and grunting, though standing still for so long with Gwyn had made it nearly impossible for her to start walking again.

A few priestesses drifted by, either directly past her or on one of the levels above or below, utterly silent. This whole place was utterly silent. The only bit of color and sound came from Gwyn.

Would she remain here, locked beneath the earth, for the rest of her immortal life?

It seemed a shame. Understandable for what Gwyn must have endured, yes—what all these females had endured and survived. But a shame as well.

Nesta didn't know why she did it. Why she waited until no one was around before she said into the hushed air of the library, "Can you do me a favor?"

She could have sworn she sensed a pause in the dust and dimness, a piqued interest. So she asked, "Can you get me volume seven of *The Great War*? By someone named Lavinia." The House had no problem sending her food—perhaps it could find the tome for her.

Again, Nesta could have sworn she felt that pause of interest, then a sudden vacancy.

And then a thump sounded on her cart as a gray leather-bound book with silver lettering landed atop her pile. Nesta's lips curved upward. "Thank you." A soft, warm breeze brushed past her legs, like a cat wending between them in warm greeting and farewell.

When the next priestess passed, Nesta approached her. "Excuse me."

The female halted so swiftly her pale robes swayed with her, the blue stone on her hood gleaming in the soft faelight. "Yes?" Her voice was soft, breathy. Curly black hair peeked out from her robe, and rich brown skin gleamed on her lovely, delicate hands. Like Clotho, she wore her hood over her face.

"Merrill's office—where is it?" Nesta gestured to the cart behind her. "I have a few books for her but don't know where she works."

The priestess pointed. "Three levels up—Level Two—at the end of the hall on your right."

"Thank you."

The priestess hurried along, as if even that moment of social interaction had been too much.

But Nesta gazed toward the level three stories above.

⁜

Her aching body did not make for easy stealth work, but Nesta mercifully didn't encounter anyone on her way up. She knocked on the shut wood door.

"Enter."

Nesta opened the door to a rectangular cell of a room, occupied by a desk on the far side and two bookshelves lining both long walls. A small pallet lay to the left of the desk, a blanket and pillow neatly aligned. As if the hooded priestess with her back to Nesta sometimes couldn't be bothered to return to the dormitory to sleep.

No sign of Gwyn. Nesta wondered if she'd already been dismissed for her so-called failure.

But Nesta took a few steps into the room, surveying the shelf to her right before she said, "I brought the books you requested."

The female hunched over her work, the scratching of her pen filling the room. "Fine." She didn't so much as turn. Nesta scanned the other shelf.

There—volume eight of *The Great War*. Nesta had taken a silent step toward it when the priestess's head snapped up. "I didn't ask for any more books. And where's Gwyneth? She should have returned half an hour ago."

Nesta asked as blandly and stupidly as she could, "Who's Gwyneth?"

Merrill turned at that, and Nesta was greeted with a surprisingly young face—and a stunningly beautiful one. All the High Fae were beautiful, but Merrill made even Mor look drab.

Hair white as fresh snow contrasted against the light brown of her skin, and eyes the color of a twilight sky blinked once, twice. As if focusing on the here and now and not whatever work she'd been doing. She noted Nesta's leathers, the lack of any robes or stone atop her braided hair, and demanded, "Who are you?"

"Nesta." She hefted the books in her arms. "I was told to bring these to you."

Volume eight of *The Great War* lay mere inches away. If she just stuck out a hand to her left, she could snatch it off the shelf. Swap it out with volume seven from the stack in her arms.

Merrill's remarkable eyes narrowed. She looked as young as Nesta, yet an ornery sort of energy buzzed around her. "Who gave you those orders?"

Nesta blinked, the portrait of stupidity. "A priestess."

Merrill's full mouth tightened. "*Which* priestess?"

Gwyn was right in her assessment of this female. Being assigned to work with her seemed more like a punishment than an honor. "I don't know. You all wear those hoods."

"These are the sacred clothes of our order, girl. Not *those hoods*." Merrill returned to her papers.

Nesta asked, because it would piss off the female, "So you didn't ask for these books, Roslin?"

Merrill threw down her pen and bared her teeth. "You think I'm *Roslin*?"

"I was told to bring these books to Roslin, and someone said your—her office was here."

"Roslin is on Level *Four*. I am on Level *Two*." She said it as if it implied some sort of hierarchy.

Nesta shrugged again. And might have enjoyed the hell out of it.

Merrill seethed, but returned to her work. "Roslin," she muttered. "Insufferable, inane Roslin. *Endless* prattling."

Nesta reached a stealthy hand toward the shelf to her left.

Merrill whipped her head around, and Nesta snapped her arm down to her side. "Never disturb me again." Merrill pointed to the door. "Get out and shut the door behind you. If you see that silly Gwyneth, tell her she's expected here *immediately*."

"Apologies," Nesta said, unable to keep the glimmer of annoyance out of her eyes, but Merrill was already twisting back to her desk.

It had to be now.

One eye on the priestess, Nesta moved.

She coughed to cover the whisper of books moving. And by the time Merrill whipped her head around again, Nesta made sure she wasn't so much as looking toward the shelf. Where volume seven of *The Great*

War stood in place of volume eight, which now sat atop the other books in Nesta's arms.

Nesta's heart pounded in her entire body.

Merrill hissed, "What are you lingering for? *Get out.*"

"Apologies," Nesta repeated, bowing at the waist, and left. Shut the door behind her.

And only when she stood in the silent hall did she allow herself to smile.

✠

She found Gwyn the same way she'd found Merrill: by asking a priestess, this one more quiet and withdrawn than the other. So trembling and nervous that even Nesta had used her most gentle voice. And been unable to shake the heaviness in her heart as she'd walked to the first-level reading area. Across the hushed, cavernous space, it was easy to hear Gwyn's soft singing as she flitted from table to table, looking at the piles of discarded books. Trying desperately to find the missing tome.

The words of Gwyn's merry song were in a language Nesta didn't know, but for a heartbeat, Nesta allowed herself to listen—to savor the pure, sweet voice that rose and fell with sinuous ease.

Gwyn's hair seemed to glow brighter with her song, skin radiating a beckoning light. Drawing any listener in.

But Merrill's warning clanged through the beauty of Gwyn's voice, and Nesta cleared her throat. Gwyn whirled toward her, glow fading even as her freckled face lit with surprise. "Hello again," she said.

Nesta only extended volume eight of *The Great War*. Gwyn gasped.

Nesta threw her a wicked smile. "This was shelved improperly. I swapped it with the right book."

Gwyn didn't seem to need more than that, thankfully, and clutched the book to her chest like a treasure. "Thank you. You've just saved me from a terrible tongue-lashing."

Nesta arched a brow at the book. "What's Merrill researching, anyway?"

Gwyn frowned. "Lots of things. Merrill's brilliant. Horrible, but brilliant. When she first came here, she was obsessed with theories regarding the existence of different realms—different worlds. Living on top of each other without even knowing it. Whether there is merely one existence, our existence, or if it might be possible for worlds to overlap, occupying the same space but separated by time and a whole bunch of other things I can't even begin to explain to you because I barely understand them myself."

Nesta's brows rose. "Really?"

"Some philosophers believe there are eleven worlds like that. And some believe there are as many as *twenty-six*, the last one being Time itself, which . . ." Gwyn's voice dropped to a whisper. "Honestly, I looked at some of her early research and my eyes bled just reading her theorizing and formulas."

Nesta chuckled. "I can imagine. But she's researching something else now?"

"Yes, thank the Cauldron. She's writing a comprehensive history of the Valkyries."

"The who?"

"A clan of female warriors from another territory. They were better fighters than the Illyrians, even. The Valkyrie name was just a title, though—they weren't a race like the Illyrians. They hailed from every type of Fae, usually recruited from birth or early childhood. They had three stages of training: Novice, Blade, and finally Valkyrie. To become one was the highest honor in their land. Their territory is gone now, subsumed into others."

"And the Valkyries are gone, too?"

"Yes." Gwyn sighed. "Valkyries existed for millennia. But the War—the one five hundred years ago—wiped out most of them, and the few survivors were elderly enough to quickly fade into old age and die afterward. From the shame, legend claims. They *let* themselves die, rather than face the shame of their lost battle and surviving when their sisters had not."

"I've never heard of them." She knew little about any of the Fae history, both by choice and because of the human world's utter lack of education on it.

"The Valkyrie history and training were mostly oral, so any accounts we have are through whatever passing historians or philosophers or tradespeople wrote down. It's just bits and pieces, scattered in various books. No primary sources beyond a few precious scrolls. Merrill got it into her head years ago to begin compiling all of it into one volume. Their history, their training techniques."

Nesta opened her mouth to ask more, but a clock chimed somewhere behind them. Gwyn stiffened. "I've been gone too long. She'll be furious." Merrill would indeed. Gwyn twisted toward the ramp beyond the reading area. But she paused, looking over her shoulder. "But not as mad as she would have been with the wrong book." She flashed Nesta a grin. "Thank you. I am in your debt."

Nesta shifted on her feet. "It was nothing."

Gwyn's eyes sparkled, and before Nesta could avoid the emotion shining there, the priestess sprinted toward Merrill's chambers, robes flying behind her.

⁜

Nesta made it to her room without collapsing from sheer exhaustion or Merrill realizing she'd been duped and coming to kill her, both of which she considered to be great accomplishments.

She found a hot meal waiting on the desk of her bedroom, and she'd barely sat down before she tore into the meat and bread and medley of roasted vegetables. Standing again was an effort, but she made it to her bathroom, where a hot bath was already steaming away.

Getting into the tub required all her concentration, hefting one leg at a time, and she moaned with relief as the delicious heat soaked through her. She lay there until her body had loosened enough to move, and fell into the warmed sheets without bothering to put on a nightgown.

There would be no trying the stairs tonight. No dreams chased her awake, either.

Nesta slept and slept and slept, though she could have sworn that her door opened at one point. Could have sworn a familiar, beckoning scent filled her room. She reached toward it with a sleep-heavy hand, but it was already gone.

CHAPTER 14

Cassian stood in the training ring, trying not to stare at the empty doorway.

Nesta hadn't come to breakfast. He'd let it slide because she hadn't come to dinner, either, but that had been because she'd been passed out cold in her bed. Naked. Or close to it.

He hadn't seen anything when he'd poked his head into her room—at least, nothing that might have scrambled his mind to the point of uselessness—but her bare shoulder had suggested enough. He'd debated waking her and insisting that she eat, but the House had stepped in.

A tray had appeared beside her doorway, full of empty plates.

As if the House was showing him precisely how much she'd eaten. As if the House was *proud* of what it had gotten her to eat.

"Good work," he'd muttered into the air, and the tray vanished. He made a mental note to ask Rhys about it later—whether the House was sentient. He'd never heard his High Lord mention it in five centuries.

Considering the filthy things he'd done in his bedroom, his bathroom—fuck, in so many of the rooms here—the idea of the House *watching* him . . . Cauldron boil him alive.

So Cassian had let Nesta sleep through breakfast, hoping the House had at least brought the meal to her room. But it meant he had no idea if she'd show up. She'd made a bargain with him yesterday, and he'd come here today to see if she'd at least meet him. Prove yesterday hadn't been a fluke.

Minutes dripped by.

Maybe he'd been a fool to hope. To think one lesson might be enough—

Muffled cursing filled the stairwell beyond the archway. Each scrape of boots seemed to move slowly.

He didn't dare to breathe, not as her cursing grew nearer. Inch by inch. As if it was taking her a long, long time to climb the stairs.

And then she was there, hand braced on the wall, a grimace of such misery on her face that Cassian laughed.

Nesta scowled, but he only said, relief wobbling his knees, "I should have realized."

"Realized *what?*" She stopped five feet from him.

"That you'd be late because you're so sore you can't climb the stairs."

She pointed to the archway. "I got up here, didn't I?"

"True." He winked. "I'll let that count as part of your warm-up. To get the muscles in your legs loose."

"I need to sit down."

"And risk not being able to get back up?" He grinned. "Not a chance." He nodded to the space beside him. "Stretches."

She grumbled. But she got into position.

And when Cassian began to instruct her through the movements, she listened.

✠

Two hours later, sweat poured down Nesta's body, but the aching had at least ceased. *You need to get the lactic acid out of your muscles—that's what's hurting you*, Cassian had said when she'd complained nonstop for the first thirty minutes. Whatever the hell that meant.

She lay on the black mat, panting again, taking in the cloudy sky. It was a good deal crisper than yesterday, with tendrils of mist wandering past the ring every now and then.

"When do I stop being sore?" she asked Cassian breathlessly.

"Never."

She turned her head toward him, about as much movement as she could manage. "*Never?*"

"Well, it gets better," he amended, and moved down to her feet. "May I?"

She had no idea what he was asking, but she nodded.

Cassian lightly wrapped his hands around her ankle, his skin warm against her foot, and lifted her leg upward. She hissed as a muscle along the back of her thigh shrieked in protest, drawing so tight she gritted her teeth. "Breathe into it when I push the leg toward you," he ordered.

He waited until she exhaled before he lifted her leg higher. The tightness in her thigh was considerable enough that she stopped thinking about his callused, warm hands against her bare ankle, about how he knelt between her legs, so close she turned her head away to stare at the red rock of the wall.

"Again," he told her, and she exhaled, winning another inch. "Again. Cauldron, your hamstrings are tight enough to snap."

Nesta obeyed, and he kept stretching her leg upward, gaining inch after inch.

"The soreness does get easier," Cassian said after a moment, as if he weren't holding her leg flush to his chest. "Though I have plenty of days when I can barely walk at the end. And after a battle? I need a week to recover from that alone."

"I know." His eyes found hers, and she clarified, "I mean—I saw you. In the war."

Saw him hauled in unconscious, his guts hanging out. Saw him in the sky, death racing at him until she screamed for him, saved him. Saw him on the ground, broken and bleeding, the King of Hybern about to kill them both—

Cassian's face gentled. As if he knew what memories pelted her. "I'm a soldier, Nesta. It's part of my duties. Part of who I am."

She looked back toward the wall, and he lowered her leg before starting on the other. The tightness in that hamstring was unbearable.

"The more stretching you do," he explained when she squeezed her eyes shut against the pain, "the more mobility you'll gain." He nodded toward the rope ladder laid out on the floor of the training ring, where he'd had her run it up and down, knees to chest, keeping within each of the boxes, for five minutes straight. "You're nimble on your feet."

"I took dancing lessons as a girl."

"Really?"

"We weren't always poor. Until I was fourteen, my father was as rich as a king. They called him the Prince of Merchants."

He gave her a tentative smile. "And you were his princess?"

Ice cracked through her. "No. Elain was his princess. Even Feyre was more his princess than I ever was."

"And what were you?"

"I was my mother's creature." She said it with such cold it nearly froze her tongue.

Cassian said carefully, "What was she like?"

"A worse version of me."

His brows twitched together. "I . . ."

She didn't want to have this conversation. Even the sunlight failed to warm her. She pulled her leg from his hands and sat up, needing the distance between them.

And because it looked like he'd speak again, Nesta said the only thing she could think of. "What happened to the priestesses in Sangravah two years ago?"

He went wholly still.

It was terrifying. The stillness of a male ready to kill, to defend, to bloody himself. But his voice was terribly calm as he asked, "Why?"

"What happened?"

His mouth tightened, and he swallowed once before he said, "Hybern was looking for the Cauldron back then—for the pieces of its feet. One was hidden at the temple in Sangravah, its power used to fuel its priestesses' gifts for millennia. Hybern found out, and sent a unit of their deadliest and cruelest warriors to retrieve it." Cold rage filled his face. "They slaughtered most of the priestesses for sport. And raped any they found to their liking."

Horror, icy and deep, sluiced through her. Gwyn had—

"You met one of them," he asked, "in the library?"

She nodded, unable to find the words.

He closed his eyes, as if reeling his rage back into himself. "I heard that Mor had brought one in. Azriel was the one who made it out there first, and he killed any of the Hybern soldiers left, but by that point . . ." He shuddered. "I don't know what became of the other survivors. But I'm glad one wound up here. Safe, I mean. With people who understand, and wish to help."

"So am I," Nesta said quietly.

She rose on surprisingly loose legs and blinked down at them. "They don't hurt as much."

"Stretching," Cassian said, as if that were answer enough. "Never forget the stretching."

⸸

The Spring Court made Cassian itch. It had little to do with the bastard who ruled it, he'd realized, but rather the fact that the lands lay in perpetual spring. Which meant plumes of pollen drifting by, setting his nose to running and skin to itching, until he was certain that at least a dozen insects were slithering all over him.

"Stop scratching," Rhys said without looking at him as they strode through a blooming apple orchard. No wings to be seen today.

Cassian lowered his hand from his chest. "I can't help it if this place makes my skin crawl."

Rhys snorted, gesturing to one of the blossoming trees above them, petals falling thick as snow. "The feared general, felled by seasonal allergies."

Cassian gave an unnecessarily loud sniffle, earning a full chuckle from Rhys. Good. When he'd met his brother half an hour ago, Rhys's eyes had been distant, his face solemn.

Rhys halted in the middle of the orchard, located to the north of Tamlin's once-lovely estate.

The afternoon sun warmed Cassian's head, and if his entire body weren't itching so damned much, he might have lain on the velvety grass and sunned his wings. "I'd peel my skin off right now, if it'd stop the itching."

"There's a sight I'd like to see," a voice said behind them, and Cassian didn't bother to look pleasant as they found Eris standing at the base of a tree five feet away. Amid the pink and white blossoms, the cold-faced Autumn Court heir looked truly faerie—as if he'd stepped out of the tree, and his one and only master was the earth itself.

"Eris," Rhys purred, sliding his hands into his pockets. "A pleasure."

Eris nodded at Rhys, red hair dappled in the sunlight leaking through the blossom-heavy branches. "I only have a few minutes."

"You asked for this meeting," Cassian said, crossing his arms. "So out with it."

Eris shot him a look laced with distaste. "I'm sure you've reported my offer to Rhysand."

"He did," Rhys said, dark hair ruffled by a soft, sighing breeze. As if even the wind itself loved to touch him. "I didn't appreciate the threats."

Eris shrugged. "I merely wanted to make myself clear."

"Spit it out, Eris," Cassian said. One more minute here, and the itching would drive him mad.

He wished anyone else could have come in his stead. But he'd been appointed by Rhys to deal with the bastard. General to general. Eris had asked for the meeting this morning, naming this location as neutral ground. Thankfully, its lord had no interest in patrolling who entered these lands.

Eris kept his eyes on Rhys. "I assume your shadowsinger is off doing what he does best."

Rhys said nothing, revealed nothing. Cassian followed his lead.

Eris went on with a shrug, "We are wasting our time, gathering information rather than acting." His amber eyes gleamed in the shade of the apple tree. "Regardless of the death-lord pulling their strings, if the human queens intend to be a thorn in our sides, we could simply deal with them now. All of them. My father would be forced to abandon his plans. And I'm sure you could invent some reason that has nothing to do with me or what I've told you to excuse their . . . removal."

Cassian blurted, "You want us to take out the queens?"

It was Eris's turn to say nothing.

Rhys, too, remained silent.

Cassian threw them an incredulous look. "We kill those queens and we'll be in a greater mess than ever. Wars have been started for less. Killing even one queen, let alone four, would be a catastrophe. Everyone would know who'd done it, regardless of the reasons we'd invent to justify it."

Rhys angled his head. "Only if we're sloppy."

"You're kidding," Cassian said to his brother.

"Half-kidding," Rhys said, throwing him a dry smile. It didn't quite meet his eyes, though. A grave distance lurked there. But Rhys turned to Eris. "Tempting as it may be to take the easy way out, I agree with my brother. It's a simple solution to our current problems, and to thwarting your father, but it would create a conflict far greater than any we're anticipating." Rhys surveyed Eris. "You know that already."

Eris still said nothing.

Cassian glanced between them, watching Rhys piece it together.

Rhys asked solemnly, "Why does your father want to start a war so badly?"

"Why does anyone go to war?" Eris reached out a long, slender hand, letting the falling petals gather there. "Why does Vallahan not sign the treaty? The borders of this new world have not yet been set."

"Beron doesn't have the military strength to control the Autumn Court and a territory on the continent," Cassian countered.

Eris's fingers closed around the petals. "Who says he wants land on the continent?" He surveyed the orchard—as if to make a point.

Silence fell.

Rhys murmured, "Beron knows another war that pits Fae against Fae would be catastrophic. Many of us would be wiped out entirely. Especially . . ." Rhys tilted his head back to take in the apple blossoms. "Especially those of us who are weakened. And when the dust settles, there would be at least one court left vacant, its lands bare for the taking."

Eris looked toward the hills beyond the orchard, green and gold and glowing in the sunlight. "They say a beast prowls these lands now. A beast with keen green eyes and golden fur. Some people think the beast has forgotten his other shape, so long has he spent in his monstrous form. And though he roams these lands, he does not see or care for the neglect he passes, the lawlessness, the vulnerability. Even his manor has fallen into disrepair, half-eaten by thorns, though rumors fly that he himself destroyed it."

"Enough with the double-talk," Cassian said. "Tamlin's staying in his beast form and is finally getting the punishment he deserves. So what?"

Eris and Rhys held each other's gaze. Eris said, "You've been trying to bring Tamlin back for a while. But he isn't getting better, is he?"

Rhys's jaw tightened, his only sign of displeasure.

Eris nodded knowingly. "I can delay my father from allying with Briallyn and starting this war for a little while. But not forever. A few months, perhaps. So I'd suggest your shadowsinger hurry. Find a way to deal with Briallyn, find out what she wants and why. Discover whether Koschei is indeed involved. At best, we'll stop them all. At worst, we'll have proof to justify any conflict and hopefully win allies to our side, avoiding the bloodshed that would carve up these lands once more. My father would think twice before standing against an army of superior strength and size."

"You've turned into quite the little traitor," Rhys said, stars winking out in his eyes.

"I told you years ago what I wanted, High Lord," Eris said.

To seize his father's throne. "Why?" Cassian asked.

Eris grasped what he meant, apparently, because flame sizzled in his eyes. "For the same reason I left Morrigan untouched at the border."

"You left her there to suffer and die," Cassian spat. His Siphons flickered, and all he could see was the male's pretty face, all he could feel was his own fist, aching to make contact.

Eris sneered. "Did I? Perhaps you should ask Morrigan whether that is true. I think she finally knows the answer." Cassian's head spun, and the relentless itching resumed, like fingers trailing along his spine, his legs, his scalp. Eris added before winnowing away, "Tell me when the shadowsinger returns."

Petals streamed past, thick as a mountain blizzard, and Cassian turned to Rhys.

But Rhys's gaze had gone distant—once again distracted. He stared toward the faraway hills, as if he could see the beast that roamed there.

Cassian had witnessed Rhys going deep into his own head often enough. Knew his brother was prone to withdrawing while appearing perfectly fine. But this level of distraction . . .

"What's the matter with you?" Cassian scratched his scalp. This fucking place.

Rhys blinked, as if he'd forgotten Cassian stood beside him. "Nothing." He flicked a petal off the gauntlet of his leathers. "Nothing."

"Liar." Cassian tucked in his wings.

But Rhys wasn't listening again. He didn't say a word before he winnowed them home.

⸸

Nesta stared into the reddish gloom of the staircase.

She'd been just as sore as yesterday while working in the library, but thankfully Merrill hadn't come to rip into her about the swapped book. She spoke to no one but Clotho, who had given her only perfunctory greetings. So Nesta had shelved in the dimness, surrounded by whispers of rustling paper, only pausing to wipe the dust from her hands. Priestesses drifted by like ghosts, but Nesta had no glimpse of coppery-brown hair and large teal eyes.

She honestly didn't know why she wished to see Gwyn. What Cassian had told her about the attack on the temple wasn't the sort of thing she had any right to bring up.

But Gwyn didn't seek her out, and Nesta didn't dare go up to the second level to knock on Merrill's door to see if Gwyn was there.

So it was silence and soreness, and the roaring in her head. Maybe it was the roaring that had brought her to the stairwell, instead of to her bedroom to wash up. The gloom beckoned, challenging her like the open maw of some great beast. A wyrm, poised to devour her whole.

Her legs moved of their own accord, and her foot landed upon the first step.

Down and down, around and around. Nesta ignored the step with the five holes embedded in it. Made a point not to look down as she carefully stepped over it.

Silence and roaring and nothing nothing nothing—

Nesta made it to step one hundred fifty before her legs nearly gave out again. Sparing herself another tumble, she panted on the steps, leaning her head against the stone.

In that roaring silence, she waited for the stairs to stop twisting around her. And when the world was again still, she made the long, horrible climb back up.

The House had dinner waiting on her desk, along with a book. Apparently, it had noted her request for a book the other day and deemed *The Great War* too dull. The title of this one was suitably smutty. "I didn't know you had dirty taste," Nesta said wryly.

The House only responded by running a bath.

"Dinner, bath, and a book," Nesta said aloud, shaking her head in something close to awe. "It's perfect. Thank you."

The House said nothing, but when she stepped into her bathroom, she found that it wasn't an ordinary bath. The House had added an assortment of oils that smelled of rosemary and lavender. She breathed in the heady, beautiful scent, and sighed.

"I think you might be my only friend," Nesta said, then groaned her way into the tub's welcoming warmth.

The House was apparently so pleased by her words that as soon as she lay back, a tray appeared across the width of the tub. Laden with a massive piece of chocolate cake.

CHAPTER 15

The seventh level of the library was unnerving.

Standing at the stone railing on Level Six, clutching a book to be shelved, Nesta stared into the darkness mere feet from her, so thick that it hovered like a layer of fog, veiling the levels below.

Books dwelled down there. She knew that, but she'd never been sent down to those dark levels. Had never seen one of the priestesses venture past the spot where she now stood, peering over the railing. Ahead of her, the darkness beckoned down the ramp. Like it was an entry into some dark pit of hell.

Hybern's twin Ravens were dead. Did their blood still stain the ground far below? Or had Rhysand and Bryaxis wiped even that trace of them away?

The darkness seemed to rise and fall. Like it was breathing.

The hair on her arms rose.

Bryaxis was gone. Set loose into the world. Even Feyre and Rhysand's hunting hadn't retrieved the thing that was Fear itself.

And yet the darkness remained. It pulsed, tendrils of shadow drifting upward.

She'd stared too long into its depths. It might gaze back.

But she didn't move from the rail. Couldn't remember how she'd come down this far, or which book she still held in her hands.

There was night, and there was the darkness of extinguishing a candle, and then there was this. Not only the true absence of light, but . . . a womb. The womb from which all life had come and would return, neither good nor evil, only dark, dark, dark.

Nesta.

Her name drifted to her as if rising from the depths of some black ocean.

Nesta.

It slid along her bones, her blood. She had to pull back. Pull away.

The darkness pulsed, beckoning.

"Nesta."

She whirled, nearly dropping the book over the edge.

Gwyn was standing there, eyeing her. "What are you doing?"

Heart thundering, Nesta twisted toward the darkness, but—it was only that. Murky darkness, through which she could now barely make out the sublevels beneath. As if the thick, impenetrable black had vanished. "It . . . I . . ."

Gwyn, arms laden with books, strode to her side and surveyed the dark. Nesta waited for the chiding, the ridicule and disbelief, but Gwyn only asked gravely, "What did you see?"

"Why?" Nesta asked. "Do you see things in that darkness?" Her voice was thin.

"No, but some of the others do. They say the dark has trailed them. Right to their doors." Gwyn shivered.

"I saw darkness," Nesta managed to say. Her heart would not calm. "Pure darkness."

The likes of which she had not seen since she'd been inside the Cauldron.

Gwyn glanced between Nesta and the chasm below. "We should go higher."

Nesta lifted the book still in her shaking arms. "I need to shelve this."

"Leave it," Gwyn said, enough authority lacing her words that Nesta dropped the book onto a dark wood table. The priestess put a hand to Nesta's back, escorting her up the sloping ramp. "Don't look behind," Gwyn muttered out of the corner of her mouth. "What level is your cart on?"

"Four." She began to twist her head to gaze over her shoulder, but Gwyn pinched her.

"Don't look behind," Gwyn murmured again.

"Is it following?"

"No, but . . ." Gwyn's swallow was audible. "I can feel something. Like a cat. Small and clever and curious. It's watching."

"If you're joking—"

Gwyn reached into the pocket of her pale robe and pulled out the blue stone of the priestesses. It fluttered with light, like the sun on a shallow sea. "Hurry now," she whispered, and they increased their pace, reaching the fifth level. No other priestesses approached, and there was no one to witness Gwyn urging, "Keep going."

The stone in her hand glimmered.

They made another loop upward, and just as they reached the fourth level, that presence—that sensation of something at their backs—eased.

They waited until they'd reached Nesta's cart before Gwyn dumped her books on the ground and flung herself into the nearest tufted armchair. Her hands trembled, but the blue stone had gone dormant again.

Nesta had to swallow twice before she could say, "What *is* that?"

"It's an Invoking Stone." Gwyn unfurled her fingers, revealing the gem within her hand. "Similar to the Siphons of the Illyrians, except that the power of the Mother flows through it. We cannot use it for harm, only healing and protection. It was shielding us."

"No—I mean, that darkness."

Gwyn's eyes matched her stone almost perfectly, right down to the shadows that now veiled her expression. "They say the being that dwelled down there is gone. But I believe some piece of it might have lingered. Or at the very least altered the darkness itself."

"It didn't feel like that. It felt . . . older."

Gwyn's brows rose. "Are you an adept in such things?" There was no condescension in the words, only curiosity.

"I . . ." Nesta blinked. "Do you not know who I am?"

"I know you are the High Lady's sister. That you slew the King of Hybern." Gwyn's face grew solemn, haunted. "That you, like Lady Feyre, were once mortal. Human."

"I was Made by the Cauldron. At the King of Hybern's order."

Gwyn traced her fingers over the smooth dome of the Invoking Stone. It rippled with light at the touch. "I didn't know such a thing was possible."

"My other sister, Elain—we were forced into the Cauldron and turned High Fae." Nesta swallowed again. "It . . . imparted some of itself to me."

Gwyn considered the railing, the open drop into the darkness beyond it. "Like calls to like."

"Yes."

Gwyn shook her head, hair swaying. "Well, perhaps don't go down to Level Six again."

"It's my job to shelve the books."

"Make it known to Clotho and she'll ensure those books are given to others."

"It seems cowardly."

"I don't wish to learn what might come crawling out of that darkness if you, Cauldron-Made, fear it. Especially if it's . . . drawn to you."

Nesta sank into the chair beside Gwyn's. "I'm not a warrior."

"You slew the King of Hybern," Gwyn repeated. "With the shadow-singer's knife."

"Luck and rage," Nesta admitted. "And I had made a promise to kill him for what he did to me and my sister."

A priestess walked by, beheld them lounging there, and scurried off. Her fear left a tang in the air like burned food.

Gwyn sighed after her. "That's Riven. She's still uncomfortable with any manner of contact with strangers."

"When did she arrive?"

"Eighty years ago."

Nesta started. But sorrow filled Gwyn's eyes as she explained, "We do not gossip about each other here. Our stories remain our own to tell or to keep. Only Riven, Clotho, and the High Lord know what happened to her. She will not speak of it."

"And there has been no help for her?"

"I am not privy to that information. I know of the resources available to us, but it is not my business whether Riven has utilized them." From the worry that now etched Gwyn's face, Nesta knew she had used those services. Or had at least tried.

Gwyn tucked her hair behind her arched ears. "I meant to find you yesterday to thank you again for switching out that book, but I got tied up with Merrill's work." She inclined her head. "I'm in your debt."

Nesta rubbed at a persistent cramp in her thigh. "It was nothing."

Gwyn noted the movement. "What's wrong with your leg?"

Nesta gritted her teeth. "Nothing. I'm training every morning with Cassian." She had no idea if Gwyn knew of him, so she clarified, "The High Lord's general—"

"I know who he is. Everyone knows who he is." It was impossible to read Gwyn's face. "Why do you train with him?"

Nesta brushed a clump of dust off her knee. "Let's just say that I was presented with several options, all designed to . . . curb my behavior.

Training with Cassian in the morning and working here in the afternoon was the most palatable."

"Why do you need to curb your behavior?"

Gwyn truly didn't know—about what a horrible, wretched waste she'd become. "It's a long story."

Gwyn seemed to read her reluctance. "What manner of training is it? Combat?"

"Right now, it's a whole lot of balancing and stretching."

She nodded toward Nesta's leg. "Such things are painful?"

"They are when you're as out of shape as I am." A pathetic weakling.

Two more priestesses passed by, and apparently the presence of one of them was enough to send Gwyn launching to her feet. "Well, I should be getting back to Merrill," she declared, any trace of solemnity gone. She nodded to the drop into the pit. "Don't go looking for trouble."

Gwyn turned on her heel, blue flashing in her hand.

The sight of that blue made Nesta blurt, "Why don't you wear that stone on your head like the others?"

Gwyn pocketed the gem. "Because I don't deserve to."

⁜

"Is this really all we'll be doing?" Nesta demanded the next morning in the training ring as she rose from what Cassian had called a curtsy-squat. "Balance and stretching?"

Cassian crossed his arms. "So long as you keep having shit balance, yes."

"I don't fall *that* often." Only every few minutes.

He motioned for her to do another squat. "You still keep your weight on your right leg when you stand. It opens up your hip, and your right foot rolls slightly to the side. Your entire center is off. Until we correct that, you're not starting anything more intense, no matter how nimble you are on your feet. You'd only injure yourself."

Nesta puffed out a breath as she did another squat, her right leg sweeping out behind her left as she ducked low. Fire quivered along her left thigh and knee. How many curtsies had she practiced under her mother's sharp eye? She'd forgotten they were this demanding. "Like you stand so perfectly."

"I do." Unflinching arrogance laced every word. "I've been training since I was a child. I was never given the chance to learn how to stand incorrectly. You have twenty-five years of bad habits to break."

She rose from the squat, legs shaking. She had half a mind to call in their bargain and order him to never make her do another squat again. "And you truly enjoy this endless exercising and training?"

"Two more, and then I'll tell you."

Grumbling, Nesta obeyed. Only because she was tired of being as weak as a mewling kitten, as he'd called her several nights ago.

When she was done, Cassian said, "Get some water." The midmorning sun beat down on them relentlessly.

"I don't need you to tell me when to drink," she snapped.

"Then go ahead and faint."

Nesta met his hazel stare, the no-nonsense face, and drank the water. To stop her head spinning, she told herself. When she'd gulped down a glass, Cassian said, "I was born to an unwed female in a settlement that makes Windhaven look like a tolerant, welcoming paradise. She was shunned for bearing a child out of wedlock, and forced to give birth to me alone in a tent in the dead of winter."

Horror lurched through her. She'd known Cassian was low-born, but that level of cruelty because of it . . . "What of your father?"

"You mean the piece of shit who forced himself on her and then went back to his wife and family?" Cassian let out a cold laugh that she rarely heard. "There were no consequences for him."

"There never are," Nesta said coolly. She blocked out the image of Tomas's face.

"There are here," Cassian growled, as if he sensed the direction of her thoughts. Cassian gestured to the city below, hidden by the mountain and the House blocking the view. "Rhys changed the laws. Here in the Night Court, and in Illyria." His face hardened further. "But it still requires the survivor to come forward. And in places like Illyria, they make life a living hell for any female who does. They deem it a betrayal."

"That's outrageous."

"We're all Fae. Forget the High Fae or lesser Fae bullshit. We're all immortal or close to it. Change comes slowly for us. What humans accomplish in decades takes us centuries. Longer, if you live in Illyria."

"Then why do you bother with the Illyrians?"

"Because I fought like hell to prove my worth to them." His eyes glittered. "To prove that my mother brought some good into this world."

"Where is she now?" He'd never spoken of her.

His eyes shuttered in a way she had not witnessed before. "I was taken away from her when I was three. Thrown out into the snow. And in her so-called disgraced state, she became prey to other monsters." Nesta's stomach twisted with each word. "She did their backbreaking labor until she died, alone and . . ." His throat worked. "I was at Windhaven by then. I wasn't strong enough to return to help her. To bring her somewhere safe. Rhys wasn't yet High Lord, and none of us could do anything."

Nesta wasn't entirely certain how they'd wound up speaking of this.

Apparently, Cassian realized it as well. "It's a story for another time. But what I meant to try to explain is that through it all, through every awful thing, the training centered me. Guided me. When I had a shit day, when I was spat on or pummeled or shunned, when I led armies and lost good warriors, when Rhys was taken by Amarantha—through *all* of that, the training remained. You said the other day the breathing helped you. It helps me, too. It helped Feyre." She watched the wall rise in his eyes, word after word. As if he waited for her to rip it down. Rip him down. "Make of that what you will, but it's true."

Oily shame slithered through her. She'd done that—brought this level of defensiveness to him.

Heaviness weighed on her. Started gnawing on her insides.

So Nesta said, "Show me another set of movements."

Cassian scanned her face for a heartbeat, his gaze still shuttered, and began his next demonstration.

✣

The House had a taste for romance novels. Nesta stayed up later than she should have to finish the one it had left the day before, and when she returned to her room that evening, another was waiting.

"Don't tell me you somehow read these." She leafed through the volume on her nightstand.

In answer, two more books thumped on the surface. Each one utterly filthy.

Nesta let out a small chuckle. "It must get awfully dull up here."

A third book plopped atop the others.

Nesta laughed again, a rusty, hoarse sound. She couldn't remember the last time she'd laughed. A true, belly-deep laugh.

Maybe before her mother had died. She'd certainly had nothing to laugh about once they'd fallen into poverty.

Nesta nodded toward the desk. "No dinner tonight?"

Her bedroom door only swung open to reveal the dimly lit hallway.

"I've had enough of him for one day." She'd barely been able to speak to Cassian for the rest of their lesson, unable to stop thinking of how he'd put up a wall without her so much as saying a word, anticipating that she would go after him, assuming that she was so awful she couldn't have a normal conversation. That she'd mock him about his mother and their pain.

"I'd rather stay here."

The door opened wider.

Nesta sighed. Her stomach ached with hunger. "You're as much a busybody as the rest of them," she muttered, and aimed for the dining room.

Cassian sat alone at the table, the setting sun gilding his black hair in golds and reds, shining through his beautiful wings. For a heartbeat, she understood Feyre's urge to paint things—to capture sights like this, preserve them forever.

"How was the library?" he asked as she claimed the seat across from him.

"Nothing tried to eat me today, so it was fine."

A plate of roast pork and green beans appeared with a glass of water before her.

He'd gone still, though. "Something tried to eat you on *another* day?"

"Well, it didn't get close enough to try, but that was the general impression I received."

He blinked, his Siphons glowing. "Tell me."

Nesta wondered if she'd said something wrong, but she related the incident with the darkness and finished with Gwyn's assistance. She hadn't seen the priestess after that, but at the end of the day there had been a note on her cart that said, *Just a friendly reminder to stay away from the lowest levels!*

Nesta had snorted, balling up the note, but she'd kept it in her pocket.

Across from her, Cassian's face was pale.

"You saw Bryaxis once," Nesta said into the silence.

"A few times," he breathed. His skin had turned greenish. "I know we should keep hunting for Bryaxis. It's not a good thing that it's out in the world. But I don't think I could endure encountering it again."

"What was it like?"

His eyes met hers. "My worst nightmares. And I'm not talking about petty phobias. I mean my deepest, most primal fears. I've put some of the worst, most vile monsters into the Prison, but these were monsters in every sense of the word. It's . . . I don't think anyone can understand unless they've seen it."

He glanced at her again, and she could tell he was bracing for her venom.

Monster—*she* was a monster. The knowledge cut and sliced deep. But she said, hoping to let him see she wouldn't pry into his business just to hurt him, "What manner of creatures did you put in the Prison?"

Cassian took a bite of food. A good sign that this, at least, was acceptable territory. "When you lived in the human world, you had legends of the dread beasts and faeries who would slaughter you if they ever breached the wall, didn't you? Things that slithered through open windows to drink the blood of children? Things that were so wicked, so cruel there was no hope against their evil?"

The hair on her neck rose. "Yes." Those stories had always unnerved and petrified her.

"They were based on truth. Based on ancient, near-primordial beings who existed here before the High Fae split into courts, before the High Lords. Some call them the First Gods. They were beings with almost no physical form, but a keen, vicious intelligence. Humans and Fae alike were their prey. Most were hunted and driven into hiding or imprisonment ages ago. But some remained, lurking in forgotten corners of the land." He swallowed another mouthful.

"When I was nearing three hundred years old, one of them appeared again, crawling out of the roots of a mountain. Before he went into the Prison and confinement weakened him, Lanthys could turn into wind and rip the air from your lungs, or turn into rain and drown you on dry land; he could peel your skin from your body with a few movements. He never revealed his true form, but when I faced him, he chose to appear as swirling mist. He fathered a race of faeries that still plague us, who thrived under Amarantha's reign—the Bogge. But the Bogge are lesser, mere shadows compared to Lanthys. If there is such a thing as evil incarnate, it is him. He has no mercy, no sense of right or wrong. There is him, and there is everyone else, and we are all his prey. His methods of killing are creative and slow. He feasts on fear and pain as much as the flesh itself."

Her blood chilled. "How did you trap such a thing?"

Cassian tapped a spot on his neck where a scar slashed beneath his ear. "I quickly learned I could never beat him in combat or magic. Still have the scar here to prove it." Cassian smiled faintly. "So I used his arrogance against him. Flattered and taunted him into trapping himself in a mirror bound with ash wood. I bet him the mirror would contain him—and Lanthys bet wrong. He got out of the mirror, of course, but by that time, I'd dumped his miserable self into the Prison."

Nesta lifted a brow. He cut her a sharp smile that didn't meet his eyes and said, "Not just a brute after all."

No, he wasn't, even though she'd said as much to him, but she'd never once believed it—

Cassian went on, "Of all the occupants of the Prison, Lanthys is the one I dread finding a way out."

"Would such a thing ever happen?"

"I don't think so, thank the Cauldron. That Prison is inescapable. Unless you're Amren."

Nesta didn't want to talk about Amren. Or think about her. "You said you put others in." Half of her didn't want to know.

He shrugged, as if it were of no consequence that he had done such remarkable things. "Seven-headed Lubia, who made the mistake of surfacing from the caves of the deep ocean to prey on girls along the western coast. Blue Annis, who was a terror to behold—cobalt skin and iron claws and, like Lubia, a taste for female flesh. Lubia, at least, swallowed her prey swiftly. Annis . . . she took longer. Annis was like Lanthys in that regard." His throat bobbed, and he tugged back the collar of his shirt to reveal another scar: the horrific, thick one above his left pectoral. She'd spied it the other day in the training ring. "That's all that remains of it now, but Annis had shredded through my chest with those iron claws and was nearly at my heart when Azriel intervened. So I suppose her capture is shared between the two of us." He drummed his fingers on the table. "And then there was—"

"I've heard enough." Her words were breathless. "I'll never sleep tonight." She shook her head, taking another bite of food. "I don't know how you can, having faced all that."

He leaned back in his seat. "You learn to live with it. How to block the horrors from your present thoughts." He added a touch quietly, "But they still lurk there. In the back of your mind."

She wished she knew how to do such things: to push all the thoughts that devoured her behind some wall, or into a hole within her, so she could bury them deep.

Cassian asked her, voice still quiet, "The darkness in the library—do you think it reacted to you specifically?" When she said nothing, he pressed, "Because of your powers?"

"I don't have any powers," she lied. Training with Amren hadn't done a lick to help her understand them, anyway.

"Then who left that handprint on the stairs?"

She didn't bother to look pleasant. "Maybe Lucien. He's got fire in his veins."

"He said your fire was different from his. That it burned cold, somehow."

"Perhaps you should lock me up in that Prison, then."

He set down his fork. "I'm just asking you a question."

"Does it matter if I have powers?"

Cassian shook his head in what seemed to be a mixture of admiration and disgust. "You might have been born human, but you're pure faerie. Answering questions with questions, evading an honest answer."

"I can't tell if that's a compliment or not."

"It's not." His teeth flashed. "The kind of powers you have aren't the sort that should sit idly by. They need an outlet, and training—"

"Balancing and stretching?"

His jaw clenched. "What happened with you and Amren?"

"Why so many questions tonight?"

"Because we're talking like normal people, and I want to know. About all of it."

Nesta rose from the table, aiming for the door. "What does it matter to you?"

"Let's not retread old territory, Nes."

She threw over a shoulder, "I hadn't realized we'd moved beyond it."

"Bullshit."

"Here's the part where you remind me everyone hates me, and I leave."

Cassian shot from his seat, blocking her path to the door in three strides. She'd forgotten how fast he was, how graceful despite his size. He glowered down at her. "It never mattered to me whether you took half the Cauldron's power or a drop. It still doesn't matter."

"Why?" Nesta couldn't stop herself from asking. "Why do you even *bother*?"

His features turned stark. "Why did you stay at my side when we went up against the King of Hybern during that last battle?"

As if that were an answer. She couldn't bear it, this talk, the expression on his face. "Because I was a stupid fool." She shoved past him.

"What is it you're afraid of?" he asked, following her into the hall.

She drew up short. "I'm not afraid of anything."

"Liar."

Nesta turned slowly. Let him see every bit of anger rippling through her.

Cassian's eyes gleamed in savage satisfaction.

His Siphons flared, casting red light upon the stones, like watery blood had been spilled. His mouth twisted to the side in a crooked, mocking grin. "Do you know how your eyes glow when your power rises to the surface? Like molten steel. Like silver fire."

He'd done it on purpose—riled her like this. To get her to show her hand.

Nesta's fingers curled into claws at her sides. She took a step toward him. Cassian held his ground. So she took another step. Another.

Until they were close enough that a heaving breath would have had her chest brushing his. Until she was baring her teeth at his still-smirking face.

Cassian surveyed her. Gazed into her eyes and breathed, "Beautiful."

He didn't halt the hand she laid on his muscled chest. Or when she pushed against that chest, backing him into the wall, his wings splaying on impact. He just stared and stared at her, marveling—hungry.

Nesta didn't, couldn't, move as Cassian leaned to whisper in her ear, "The first time I saw that look on your face, you were still human. Still human, and I nearly went to my knees before you." His breath caressed the shell of her ear and she couldn't stop her eyes from fluttering shut. His smile brushed against her temple. "Your power is a song, and one I've waited a very, very long time to hear, Nesta." Her back arched slightly at the way he said her name, the way he bit out the second syllable. Like he was imagining clamping his teeth down on other parts of her. But only her hand bridged their bodies. Only her hand, now bunching up his shirt, his thundering heartbeat pulsing beneath it.

Until Cassian lowered his face an inch, and grazed the tip of his nose along her neck. Beneath her hand, his chest heaved upward as he inhaled a great, greedy breath of her scent.

Too far. She shouldn't have let herself go this far with him, let him this close.

Yet she couldn't withdraw. Couldn't do anything but let him brush his nose over her neck again. The urge to press her body into his, to feel his warmth and hardness grinding into her, nearly overrode every rational thought.

Cassian's hands remained at his sides, though. As if waiting for her to give permission.

Nesta pulled her head back, away—just enough to see his features.

Her knees nearly wobbled at the desire blazing in them. Liquid, unrelenting desire, all fixed upon her.

She couldn't get a breath down as she drowned in that stare. As low, sensitive parts of her tightened and began throbbing, her breasts becoming heavy and aching. His nostrils flared, scenting that, too.

She couldn't. She couldn't do this to him. To herself.

Couldn't, couldn't, couldn't—

Nesta began to withdraw her hand from his chest, but he slid his own atop it. Rubbed his thumb over the back of her hand, and just that graze of callused flesh had her grinding her teeth, unable to think, to breathe—

Cassian whispered in her ear, "Do you know what I'm going to think of tonight?"

A small sound must have come out of her, because he grinned as he stepped to the side. Let go of her hand.

The absence of his warmth, his scent, was like a bucket of ice water.

He smiled, nothing but wickedness and challenge. "I'm going to think of that look on your face." He took another step down the hall. "I'm always thinking of that look on your face."

✢

She couldn't sleep. The sheets chafed, strangled her, smothered her with their heat until sweat ran down her body.

I'm always thinking of that look on your face.

Nesta lay in the darkness, her breathing uneven, her body flushed and aching.

She'd barely been able to focus on reading when she'd returned to her room. And she'd been tossing and turning in bed for what had felt like hours now.

I'm always thinking of that look on your face.

She could see it: Cassian in his own bed, sprawled out like a dark king, gripping himself, pumping hard—

She managed to whisper into the room, "Come back at dawn."

She didn't know if the House obeyed. Didn't find out if it understood why she wanted privacy as she traced her hand up her nightgown, the slide of silk against her skin nearly unbearable.

She moaned into her pillow as her fingers slid between her legs, instantly slippery with the wetness pooled there, which hadn't gone away since she'd been left standing in that hallway. Her hips arched into the touch, and she gritted her teeth, letting out a long hiss as she dragged her fingers down her aching, throbbing center.

I'm always thinking of that look on your face.

She slid her fingers in deep, writhing at the intrusion, unable to stop seeing Cassian's face, that half smile, that light in his eyes. The powerful body and beautiful wings. She withdrew her fingers nearly to their tips, and as she plunged them back in, it was Cassian's hand she pictured there, felt there. Cassian's other hand that rose to clasp her breast, squeezing hard, just the way she liked it, a sharp, slight edge of pain to heighten the pleasure.

It was Cassian's hand she rode, biting her lip to keep her moaning contained. It was Cassian's hand that brought her over the edge and into a release so intense she nearly cried out. It was Cassian's hand that slid into her, over and over again, release after release, until Nesta lay wrung out and panting upon the bed, with only the darkness to hold her.

CHAPTER 16

Cassian hadn't slept well.

It was hard to sleep well when he'd been so aroused he'd had to pleasure himself not once but *three times* just to calm the hell down enough to close his eyes. But he awoke before dawn aching for her, her scent still in his nose, and another release had barely taken the edge off.

He'd told her exactly what he planned to do last night, but meeting Nesta's stare over the breakfast table the next morning was more uncomfortable than he'd anticipated.

She'd beaten him to the table, and had been reading a book while she ate. It lay closed now, but from the spine, he gleaned that it was one of the romances she favored so much.

To break the silence, Cassian asked, "What are you reading?"

Color stained Nesta's pale cheeks. And he could have sworn it took an effort of will for her to meet his eyes, too. "A romance."

"I gathered that. What's this one about?"

She dropped her gaze quickly. But the blush remained.

He knew it had nothing to do with the novel.

But she lifted her eyes to him again, spine stiffening. Like she was working hard as hell to make herself meet his stare. Her fingers clenched her fork. And when he looked at them, she pulled her hand under the table.

As if it were blazing with proof.

His blood heated as he realized the blush, her embarrassment . . . He made himself take deep, steadying breaths. They had to train together for the next two hours. Being at attention wasn't only unhelpful, but inappropriate in the training ring.

It didn't make him stop picturing it: that hand between her legs, her body as aching for release as his had been. The way she'd probably bitten her lip, just as he had, to keep from crying out. His cock grew hard, pushing at his pants to the point of pain.

Cassian shifted in his seat, trying to free up any space for himself. It only succeeded in making the hard seam rub against his cock, the friction enough to make him grit his teeth.

Training. They had training.

"The book," Nesta said, a bit breathlessly, "is about . . ." Her nostrils flared and her eyes went a bit unfocused. "A book."

"Interesting," Cassian murmured. "Sounds great."

He had to get out of this room. Had to sort his shit out before he went upstairs. The heat between them didn't belong in the training ring. Where the fuck was Az when he needed him? Cassian had played buffer for Mor for years—where the fuck was *she* when he needed her?

But he couldn't rise from his chair. If he did, Nesta would see precisely how she'd affected him. That is, if she hadn't already scented it—and understood the shift in his smell. And if she looked at the bulge in his pants with that heat she'd had in her eyes last night, the heat he'd come to just picturing her, he might very well make a fool of himself.

It was a risk he was willing to take. Had to take, before he laid her flat on the table and removed their clothing piece by piece.

Cassian shot out of his chair, muttering, "I'll see you there," and left.

⁜

"The book," Nesta repeated to herself, staring at her porridge, "is about a book." She cupped her forehead in her hands. "Idiot."

At least Cassian hadn't seemed to be listening. But whatever willingness had been in his eyes last night seemed reluctant today, as if he couldn't help—didn't *want* that heat between them, that tension. He'd practically run out of the room to avoid her.

Training would be awful.

He was waiting in the ring, the portrait of a swaggering warrior. Nesta didn't dare look at his pants. To what she could have sworn she'd glimpsed straining at the stays and buttons when he'd fled the room.

But if he appeared unruffled, then fine. She'd match him in it.

Nesta rolled her shoulders, approaching him. "More stretching and balance?"

"No."

Their eyes met, and there was only clear, determined calm—and a challenge. "We'll do the warm-up, and then we're moving into some core work."

She gaped. Her . . . *core?*

"Abdominals," he clarified, and pink washed across his face. He cleared his throat. "Filthy mind." He flicked her cheek. "Too much smut."

She batted him away and gestured to the muscles hidden beneath his shirt. "You're going to make me look like that?"

His low laugh rippled over her body. "No one can look like this but me, Nes."

Arrogant ass.

"Rhysand and Azriel do," she said sweetly.

"I've got one or two muscles on them."

"I don't see it."

He winked. "Maybe they're in other places."

She couldn't help it. Couldn't stop it. Not the flash of desire, but the smile that overtook her face. She huffed a laugh.

Cassian stared like he hadn't seen her before.

His shock was enough that Nesta dropped her smile. "All right," she said. "Warm-up, then abdominals."

⁜

She hated abdominal exercises.

Mostly because she couldn't *do* them.

"I knew you didn't have much muscle," Cassian observed as Nesta lay belly-down on the ground, having collapsed onto her front after trying to hold a full-body plank, "but this is absolutely pathetic."

"Aren't you supposed to be my inspirational teacher?"

"You can't do more than five seconds."

She spat, "And how long can you do?"

"Five minutes."

Nesta pushed herself onto her elbows. "I'm sorry if I haven't had five hundred years of *core* work."

"I asked you to hold that plank for thirty seconds."

She shoved onto her knees, stomach aching. He'd had her doing curls upward, then leg extensions while lying on her back, and then lifting a smooth five-pound rock over her head while she'd tried to raise herself from lying prone into a sitting position using only her stomach muscles. She hadn't been able to do more than one or two of any of them before her body gave out. No amount of will or grit could make it move.

"This is torture." Bracing her hands on her knees, Nesta pointed to the ring. "If you're so perfect, do everything you just ordered me to do."

Cassian snorted. "A ten-year-old Illyrian boy could do it in the span of a few minutes."

"Then do *your* big, tough male routine."

He smirked. "All right. You want to mouth off, then I'll show you my big, tough male routine."

He slung his shirt off. Tied back his hair.

And this was a different sort of torture. To watch him go through the same exercises, only harder, heavier, faster. To watch the muscles of his stomach ripple, muscles *everywhere* ripple. To watch sweat glisten and then run down his golden body, over his tattoos, along the eight-pointed star of their bargain on his spine before sliding into the waist of his pants.

But he'd been professional during their lesson. Utterly professional and distant, as if this training ring was sacred to him.

Nesta couldn't tear her eyes away as he completed his exercises, panting softly. She tried not to wonder if that panting was how he'd sounded last night when he'd pleasured himself.

But Cassian's hazel eyes were clear. Triumphant.

In another age, another world, he might have been deemed a warrior-god by mortals. After what he'd told her about the monsters he'd put in the Prison, he might very well be considered a great hero in *this* age. The kind that would one day be whispered about around a fire. People would name their children after him. Warriors would want to *be* him. A fine warrior would be known as *Cassian reborn*.

She'd called him a brute.

"What?" Cassian wiped the sweat from his face.

She asked, to distract herself from her thoughts, "Are there truly no female fighting units amongst the Illyrians?" She hadn't seen any during the war.

His smile faded. "We tried once and it failed spectacularly. So, no. There aren't."

"Because Illyrians are backward and horrible."

He winced. "Have you been talking to Az?"

"Just my observations."

He untied his hair, the thick, straight locks falling around his face. "The Illyrians . . . I told you. Progress is slow. It's an ongoing goal of ours—me and Rhys, I mean."

"It's that hard for the females to become warriors?"

"It's not just the training. It's running the social gauntlet, too. And then there's the Blood Rite, which they'd also have to complete."

"What's the Blood Rite?"

"What it sounds like." He rubbed his neck. "When an Illyrian warrior comes into his full power, usually in his twenties, he has to go through the Blood Rite before he can qualify as a full warrior and adult. Would-be warriors from every clan and village get sent in, usually three or four from each—all of them scattered across an area in the Illyrian Mountains. We're left there for a week with two goals: survival, and making it to Ramiel."

"What's Ramiel?" She felt like a child with these questions, but her curiosity got the better of her.

"Our sacred mountain." He drew a familiar symbol in the dirt: an upward-pointing triangle with three dots above it. A mountain, she realized. And three stars. "It's the symbol of the Night Court. The Blood Rite always takes place when Arktos, Carynth, and Oristes, our three holy stars, shine above it for one week a year. On the final day of the Rite, they're directly above its peak."

"So you hike to the mountain?"

"We kill our way to the mountain." His eyes had turned hard. "We're drugged and dumped into the wilderness, with nothing but our clothes."

"And you have to participate?"

"Once you're in, you can't leave. At least until the Rite is over, or you reach the peak of Ramiel. If anyone breaks into the Rite to extract or save you, the law declares that both of you will be hunted down and killed for the transgression. Even Rhys isn't exempt from those laws."

Nesta shivered. "It sounds barbaric."

"That's not the half of it. A spell is in place so our wings are rendered useless and no magic may be used." He held up a hand, displaying the red Siphon on its back. "Magic is rare amongst Illyrians, but when it does manifest, it requires Siphons to be controlled, filtered into something usable. But it gives us an advantage over the other Illyrians without it—so the spell levels the playing field. Illyrians do possess magic on one night a year, though: the night before the Blood Rite, when the war-band leaders can winnow the drugged novices into the wilds. Don't even ask me why that is. No one knows."

"Azriel can winnow all the time, though."

"Az is different. In a lot of ways." His tone didn't invite further questioning.

"So without the use of magic in the Rite, you kill each other the normal way? Swords and daggers?"

"Weapons are banned, too. At least ones that are brought in from the outside. But you can build your own. You *need* to build your own. Or else you'll be slaughtered."

"By the other warriors?"

"Yes. Rival clans, enemies, assholes seeking notoriety—all of it. In some villages, the higher the kill count, the more glory you bring. The most backward clans claim the slaughter is to thin out the weaker warriors, but I always thought it was a grand waste of any potential talent." Cassian dragged a hand through his hair. "And then there are the creatures that roam the mountains—ones that can easily bring down an Illyrian warrior with claws and fangs."

A murky memory surfaced, of Feyre telling her about the horrible beasts she'd once encountered in the region. Cassian went on, "So you're facing all of that while trying to make your way to Ramiel's slopes. The majority of the males forget to save enough strength for the end of the week to make the climb. It's a full day and night of brutal climbing, where one fall can kill you. Most don't even make it to the base of the mountain. But if they do, the opponent changes. You're not facing other warriors—you're pitting yourself, your very soul, against the mountain. It's usually that fact that breaks anyone who tries to scale it."

"And what—you make it to the top and get a trophy?"

Cassian snorted, but his words were serious. "There's a sacred stone atop it. Touch the stone first, and you win. It will transport you out immediately."

"And everyone else when the week is done?"

"Whoever is left standing is considered a warrior. Where you are when it ends sorts you into one of the three echelons of warrior, named after our holy stars: Arktosian, the ones who don't make it to the mountain but survive; Oristian, the ones who make it to the mountain but don't reach the top; and Carynthian, the ones who scale the summit and are considered elite warriors. Touching the stone atop Ramiel is to win the Rite. Only a dozen warriors in the past five centuries have reached the mountain."

"You touched the stone, I take it."

"Rhys, Az, and I touched it together, even though we were deliberately separated from each other at the beginning."

"Why?"

"The leaders feared us and what we'd become. They thought the warriors or beasts would handle us, if we didn't have each other to lean against. They were wrong." His eyes glittered fiercely. "What they learned was that we love each other as true brothers. And there was nothing that we wouldn't do, no one we wouldn't kill, to reach each other. To save each other. We killed our way across the mountains, and made it through the Breaking—the worst of Ramiel's three routes to the top—and we won the damn thing. We touched the stone in the same moment, the same breath, and entered the Carynthian tier of warriors."

Nesta failed to keep the shock off her face. "And you say only twelve have become Carynthian . . . in five hundred years?"

"No. Twelve made it to the mountain and became Oristian. Only three others, besides us, won the Blood Rite and became Carynthian." His throat bobbed. "They were fine warriors, and led exemplary units. We lost two of them against Hybern."

Likely in that blast that had decimated a thousand of them. The blast she'd shielded him from. Him, and only him.

Nesta's stomach clenched, nausea sliding through her. She forced herself to take a long breath. "So you think females can't participate in the Rite?"

"Mor would likely win the damn thing in record time, but no. I wouldn't want even her participating in the Rite." The unspoken part of his reasoning lay coldly in his eyes. There would be a different, worse kind of violence to defend against, even if the females were as highly trained as the males.

Nesta shivered. "Could you have a female unit without them taking the Blood Rite?"

"They would never be honored as true warriors without it—without one of those three titles. Well, I would consider them warriors, but not the rest of the Illyrians. No other units would fly with them. They'd consider it a disgrace and an insult." She frowned and he held up his hands. "Like I said: change comes slowly. You heard the bullshit Devlon spewed about your cycle. *That's* considered progress. In the past, they'd kill a female for picking up a weapon. Now they 'decontaminate' the blade and call themselves modern thinkers." Disgust contorted his features.

Nesta eased to her feet and scanned the sky. Her head had cleared—only slightly. She didn't relish the prospect of shelving books when her body was already aching . . . But perhaps she'd see Gwyn.

"Training the Illyrian females," Cassian went on, "wouldn't be about fighting in our wars. It would be about proving they're equally as capable and strong as the males. It would be about mastering their fear, honing the strength they already have."

"What do they fear?"

"Becoming my mother," he said softly. "Going through what she endured."

What the priestesses beneath the mountain had endured.

Nesta thought of the quiet priestesses who did not leave the mountain, who dwelled in the dimness. Riven flashed through her memory, hurrying past, unable to stomach a stranger's presence. Gwyn, with her bright eyes that sometimes darkened with shadows.

Cassian tilted his head to the side at her silence. "What is it?"

"Would you train non-Illyrian females?"

"I'm training you, aren't I?"

"I mean, would you consider . . ." She didn't know how to elegantly phrase it, not like silver-tongued Rhysand. "The priestesses in the library. If I invited them to train with us here, where it's private and safe. Would you train them?"

Cassian blinked slowly. "Yes. I mean, of course, but . . ." He winced. "Nesta, many of the females in the library do not want to be—*cannot* stand to be—around males again."

"Then we'll ask one of your female friends to join. Mor or anyone else you can think of."

"The priestesses might not even be able to stomach having me present."

"You'd never hurt anyone like that."

His eyes softened slightly. "It's not about that for them. It's about the fear—the trauma they bear. Even if they know I'd never do that to them, I might still drag up memories that are incredibly difficult for them to face."

"You said this training would help me with my . . . problems.

Perhaps it could help them. At the very least give them a reason to get outside for a bit."

Cassian watched her for a long moment. Then he said, "Whoever you can get up here with us, I'll gladly train. Mor's away, but I can ask Feyre—"

"Not Feyre." Nesta hated the words. The way his back stiffened. She couldn't look at him as she said, "I just . . ." How could she explain the tangle between her and her sister? The self-loathing that threatened to consume her every time she looked at her sister's face?

"All right," Cassian repeated. "Not Feyre. But I need to give her and Rhys a heads-up. You should probably ask Clotho for permission, too." A warm hand clasped her shoulder and squeezed. "I like this idea, Nes." His hazel eyes shone bright. "I like it a lot."

And for some reason, the words meant everything.

CHAPTER 17

"I have a proposition for you."

Stomach muscles throbbing, legs aching, Nesta stood before Clotho's desk as the priestess finished writing on whatever manuscript she was annotating, her enchanted pen scratching along.

Clotho lifted her head when the pen dotted its last mark and wrote on a scrap of paper, *Yes?*

"Would you allow your priestesses to train with me every morning in the ring at the top of the House? Not all of them—just whoever might be interested."

Clotho sat perfectly still. Then the pen moved. *Train for what?*

"To strengthen their bodies, to defend themselves, to attack, if they wish. But also to clear their minds. Help steady them."

Who will oversee this training? You?

"No. I'm not qualified for that. I'll be training with them." Her heart pounded. She wasn't sure why. "Cassian will be overseeing it. He's not handsy— I mean, he's respectful and . . ." Nesta shook her head. She sounded a proper fool.

Beneath the shadows of her hood, Nesta could sense Clotho's gaze lingering upon her. The pen moved again.

Not many will come, I am afraid.

"I know. But even one or two . . . I'd like to offer." Nesta gestured to a pillar beyond Clotho. "I'll put a sign-up sheet there. Whoever wants to join is welcome."

Again, that long stare from beneath the hood, its weight like a phantom touch.

Then Clotho wrote, *Whoever wants to join has my blessing.*

✠

Nesta pasted the sign-up sheet onto the pillar that day.

No one had inked their name on it by the time she departed.

She awoke early, made the trek to the library to check the list, and found it still empty.

"It'll take time," Cassian consoled her when he read whatever lay etched on her face as she stepped into the training ring. He added a shade softly, "Keep reaching out your hand."

So Nesta did.

Every afternoon when she arrived at the library, she checked the list. Every evening when she left, she checked it as well. It was always empty.

At training, Cassian began to instruct her on basic footwork and body positioning in hand-to-hand combat. No punches or kicks, not yet. Nesta held that infernal plank for ten seconds. Then fifteen. Then twenty. Thirty.

Cassian added weights to her exercises, in order to build up her flimsy arms. Heavy stones with carved handles to carry while she did her lunges and squats.

All while she breathed and breathed and breathed.

She tried the stairs again. Made it to step five hundred before her muscles demanded she turn around. The next night, she halted on six hundred ten. Then seven hundred fifty.

She didn't know what she'd do at the bottom: find a tavern or a pleasure hall and drink herself stupid, she supposed. If she made it, she'd deserve it, she told herself with each step.

At night, exhaustion weighed so heavily she could barely eat and bathe before tumbling into bed. Barely read a chapter of a book before her eyelids drooped. She'd found a smutty novel she'd already read and loved in one of the trunks Elain had packed, and had laid it on the desk.

She'd said to the air, "I found this for you. It's a present." The book had vanished into nothing. But in the morning, she'd found a bouquet of autumnal flowers upon her desk, the glass vase bursting with asters and chrysanthemums of every color.

A week passed, during which she barely saw Gwyn, though she learned through Clotho that Merrill had been pushing her hard with the Valkyrie research. But Nesta had so many books to shelve that the hours passed swiftly.

Especially once she began using the books to train. While striding up the ramp, she'd hold a heavy stack and execute an assortment of lunges. Several times, she caught passing priestesses a level above peering at her while she did so.

Every day, she checked the sign-up sheet on the pillar beyond Clotho's desk. Empty.

Day after day after day.

Keep reaching out your hand, Cassian had told her.

But what would it matter, she began to wonder, if no one bothered to reach back?

✠

"You hold your fist like that when you punch someone and you'll shatter your thumb."

Panting, with sweat running down her back in great rivers, Nesta scowled at Cassian. She held up the fist he'd ordered her to make, her thumb inside her folded fingers. "What's wrong with my fist?"

"Keep your thumb atop the knuckles on your pointer and middle finger." He made a fist to demonstrate and wiggled the thumb tucked against his fingers. "If your thumb makes the hit, it's going to hurt like hell."

Studying the fist Cassian extended, Nesta mimicked the positioning on her own hand. "What then?"

He jerked his chin. "Get into the position we went over yesterday. Feet parallel, rooting your strength into the ground . . ."

"I know, I know," Nesta muttered, and took up the stance he'd spent three days making her practice. She observed her feet as they shuffled into position, then she bent her knees slightly, bobbing twice to make sure she'd secured her center of power.

Cassian circled her. "Good. Any punch you make should be swift and precise, not a wild swing that'll knock you off balance and deprive your arm of strength. Your body and breath will power the punch more than your actual arm." He took up a similar stance—and struck at the air.

He moved so smoothly, so brutally, that the blow was done before she could blink.

He held out his arm when he'd finished, muscles shifting. He'd rolled up his sleeves against the warm autumn day, but hadn't taken his shirt off entirely. In the stark sunlight, the tattoo along his left arm seemed to drink down the brightness. "Line up the first two knuckles with your forearm. That's what you want to hit with, and the strength in your arm will carry right through to them. If you hit with your ring finger and pinky, you'll break your hand."

"I had no idea punching was so fraught with peril."

"Apparently, it takes brains to be a brute."

Nesta flattened her brows, but focused on aligning her forearm and the knuckles he'd indicated. "That's it?"

"To hit with the proper knuckles, you need to angle your wrist downward just a fraction."

"Why?"

"So your wrist doesn't snap."

She lowered her arm. "Considering how many ways there are to break my own hand when punching someone, it doesn't seem worth it."

"That's why a good warrior knows when to pick his battles." He lowered his fist. "You have to ask yourself if the risk is worth it each time."

"And do you always throw a punch with perfect form?"

"Yes," Cassian said without one ounce of doubt. He shook his hair from his eyes. "Well, most of the time. There have been some brawls when I didn't have the right angle and balance, but a punch, even one that could break my hand, was the best way out of a bind. I've shattered my hand . . ." He squinted at the sky, as if doing a mental tally. "Oh, probably ten times."

"In five hundred years."

"I can't be perfect every moment of every day, Nes." His eyes flickered.

There had been no repeats of that madness in the hallway last week. And she'd been too tired at night to even make it up to the dining room, let alone to pleasure herself in bed.

"Right," he said. "Now shift your hips into the punch." He struck at the air again. He moved more slowly this time, letting her see how his body flowed into the blow. "It will engage your core and your shoulder, both of which add extra power." Another jab.

"So those abdominal exercises are useful beyond wanting to show off your muscles?"

He threw her a wry grin. "You really think this is just for show?"

"I think I've caught you looking at yourself in that mirror at least a dozen times each lesson." Nesta nodded to the slender mirror across the ring.

He chuckled. "Liar. You use that mirror to watch me when you think I'm not paying attention."

She refused to let him see the truth on her face. Refused to so much as lower her head. She focused again on her stance.

"All business today, huh?"

"You want me to train," Nesta said coolly, "so train me."

Even if no priestesses showed up, even if she was a stupid fool for hoping that they would, she didn't mind this training. It cleared her head, required so much thinking and breathing that the roaring thoughts had little chance to devour her whole. Only in the quiet moments did those thoughts pounce again, usually if she lost focus while working in the library or bathing. And when that happened, the stairwell always beckoned. The infernal ten thousand steps.

But would it do anything—the training, the work, the stairs—beyond keeping her busy? The thoughts still waited like wolves to swarm her. To rip her apart.

I loved you from the first moment I held you in my arms.

The wolves prowled closer, claws clicking.

"Where'd you go?" Cassian asked, hazel eyes dim with worry.

Nesta took up her stance again. It sent the wolves retreating a step. "Nowhere."

✢

Elain was in the private library.

Nesta knew it before she'd cleared the stairs, covered in dust from the library.

Her sister's delicate scent of jasmine and honey lingered in the red-stoned hall like a promise of spring, a sparkling river that she followed to the open doors of the chamber.

Elain stood at the wall of windows, clad in a lilac gown whose close-fitting bodice showed how well her sister had filled out since those initial days in the Night Court. Gone were the sharp angles, replaced by softness and elegant curves. Nesta knew she herself had looked like that at one point, even if Elain's breasts had always been smaller.

She peered down at herself, bony and gangly. Her sister turned toward her, glowing with health.

Elain's smile was as bright as the setting sun beyond the windows. "I thought I'd drop by to see how you were doing."

Someone had brought Elain here, since there was no way in hell she had climbed those ten thousand steps.

Nesta didn't return her sister's smile, but rather gestured to her body, the leathers, the dust. "I've been busy."

"You look a little better than you did a few weeks ago."

The last time she'd seen Elain—a week before she'd come to the House. She'd passed her sister in the bustling market square they called the Palace of Bone and Salt, and though Elain had halted, no doubt intending to speak to her, Nesta had kept walking. Hadn't looked back before vanishing into the throng. Nesta didn't wish to consider how poorly she'd looked then, if the picture she presented now was better.

"You've got good coloring, I mean," Elain clarified, striding from the windows to cross the room. She stopped a few feet away. As if holding herself back from the embrace she might have given.

Like Nesta was some sort of disease-ridden leper.

How many times had they been in this room during those initial months? How many times had it been this way, only with their positions switched? Elain had been the ghost then, too thin, with her thoughts turned inward.

Somehow, Nesta had become the ghost.

Worse than a ghost. A wraith, whose rage and hunger were bottomless, eternal.

Elain had only needed time to adjust. But Nesta knew she herself needed more than that.

"Are you enjoying your time up here?"

Nesta met her sister's warm brown eyes. When human, Elain had easily been the prettiest of the three of them, and when she'd been turned High Fae, that beauty had been amplified. Nesta couldn't put her finger on what changes had been wrought beyond the pointed ears, but Elain had gone from lovely to devastatingly beautiful. Elain never seemed to realize it.

It was always that way between them: Elain, sweet and oblivious, and Nesta, the snarling wolf at her side, poised to shred anyone who threatened her.

Elain is pleasant to look at, her mother had once mused while Nesta sat beside her dressing table, a servant silently brushing her mother's gold-brown hair, *but she has no ambition. She does not dream beyond her garden and pretty clothes. She will be an asset on the marriage market for us one day, if that beauty holds, but it will be our own maneuverings, Nesta, not hers, that win us an advantageous match.*

Nesta had been twelve at the time. Elain barely eleven.

She'd absorbed every word of her mother's scheming, plans for futures that had never come to pass.

We shall have to petition your father to go to the continent when the time is right, her mother had often said. *There are no men here worthy of either of you.* Feyre hadn't even been considered at that point, a sullen, strange child whom her mother ignored. *Human royalty rules there still—lords and dukes and princes—but their wealth is tapped out, many of their estates nearing ruin. Two beautiful ladies with a king's fortune could go far.*

I might marry a prince? Nesta had asked. Her mother had only smiled.

Nesta shook her head clear of the memories and said at last, "I don't have any choice but to be here, so I don't see how I could be enjoying myself."

Elain wrung her slender fingers, nails kept trimmed short for her work in the gardens. "I know the circumstances for your coming here were awful, Nesta, but it doesn't mean you need to be so miserable about it."

"I sat by your side for weeks," Nesta said flatly. "Weeks, while you wasted away, refusing food and drink. While you appeared to hope you'd just wither and die."

Elain flinched. But Nesta couldn't stop the words from pouring out. "No one suggested *you* either shape up or be shipped back to the human lands."

Elain, surprisingly, held her ground. "I wasn't drinking myself into oblivion and—and doing those other things."

"Fucking strangers?"

Elain flinched again, her face coloring.

Nesta snorted. "You're living amongst beings who have none of our human primness, you know." Elain squared her shoulders again, just as Nesta added, "It's not like you and Graysen didn't act on your feelings."

It was a low blow, but Nesta didn't care. She knew Elain had given her maidenhead to Graysen a month before they'd been turned Fae. Elain had been glowing the next morning.

Elain cocked her head. Didn't dissolve into the crying mess she usually became when Graysen came up. Instead she said, "You're angry with me."

Fine, then. She could be direct, too. Nesta shot back, "For packing my things while Rhysand and Feyre told me I'm a worthless pile of shit? Yes."

Elain crossed her arms and said calmly, sadly, "Feyre warned me this might happen."

The words struck Nesta like a slap. They'd spoken of her, her *behavior*, her attitude. Elain and Feyre—that was the new status of things. The bond Elain had chosen.

It was inevitable, Nesta supposed, stomach churning. She was the monster. Why shouldn't the two of them band together and shove her out? Even if she'd foolishly believed that Elain had always seen every horrible part of her and decided to stick by her anyway.

"I still wanted to come," Elain went on with that focused calm, the quiet steel building in her voice. "I wanted to see you, to explain."

Elain had chosen Feyre, chosen her perfect little world. Amren hadn't been any different. Nesta's spine stiffened. "There is nothing to explain."

Elain held up her hands. "We did this because we *love* you."

"Spare me the bullshit, please."

Elain stepped closer, brown eyes wide. Undoubtedly wholly convinced of her own innocence, her innate goodness. "It's the truth. We did this because we love you, and worry for you, and if Father were here—"

"Don't *ever* mention him." Nesta bared her teeth, but kept her voice low. "*Never fucking mention him again.*"

She forbade her leash to slip completely. But she felt it—the stirring of that terrible beast inside her. Felt its power surge, blazing yet cold. She lunged for it, shoving it down, down, down, but it was too late. Elain's gasp confirmed that Nesta's eyes had gone to silver fire, as Cassian had described it.

But Nesta smothered the fire in her darkness, until she was cold and empty and still once more.

Pain slowly washed over Elain's face. And understanding. "Is that what this is all about? Father?"

Nesta pointed to the door, finger shaking with the effort of keeping that writhing power at bay. Each word from Elain's mouth threatened to undo her restraint. "*Get out.*"

Silver lined Elain's eyes, but her voice remained steady, sure. "There was nothing that could have been done to save him, Nesta."

The words were kindling. Elain had accepted his death as inevitable. She hadn't bothered to fight for him, as if he hadn't been worth the effort, precisely as Nesta knew she herself wasn't worth the effort.

This time, Nesta didn't stop the power from shining in her eyes; she shook so violently she had to fist her hands. "You tell yourself there's nothing that could have been done because it's unbearable to think that *you* could have saved him, if you'd only deigned to show up a few minutes earlier." The lie was bitter in her mouth.

It wasn't Elain's fault their father had died. No, that was entirely Nesta's own fault. But if Elain was so determined to root out the good in her, then she'd show her sister how ugly she could be. Let a fraction of this agony rip into her.

This was why Elain had chosen Feyre. *This*.

Feyre had rescued Elain time and again. But Nesta had sat by, armed only with her viper's tongue. Sat by while they starved. Sat by when Hybern stole them away and shoved them into the Cauldron. Sat by when Elain had been kidnapped. And when their father had been in Hybern's grip, she had done nothing, *nothing* to save him, either. Fear had frozen her, blanketing her mind, and she'd let it do so, let it master her, so that by the time her father's neck had snapped, it had been too late. And entirely her fault.

Why *wouldn't* Elain choose Feyre?

Elain stiffened, but refused to balk from whatever she beheld in Nesta's gaze. "You think *I'm* to blame for his death?" Challenge filled each word. Challenge—from Elain, of all people. "No one but the King of Hybern is to blame for that." The quaver in her voice belied her firm words.

Nesta knew she'd hit her mark. She opened her mouth, but couldn't continue. Enough. She had said enough.

That fast, the power in her receded, vanishing into smoke on the wind. Leaving only exhaustion weighing her bones, her breath. "It doesn't matter what I think. Go back to Feyre and your little garden."

Even during their squabbles in the cottage, fighting over who got clothes or boots or ribbons, it had never been like this. Those fights had been petty, born of misery and discomfort. This was a different beast entirely, from a place as dark as the gloom at the base of the library.

Elain headed for the doors, purple dress sweeping behind her. "Cassian said he thought the training was helping," she murmured, more to herself than to Nesta.

"Sorry to disappoint you." Nesta slammed the doors so hard they rattled.

Silence filled the room.

She didn't twist toward the windows to see who might fly past with Elain, who'd be witness to the tears Elain would likely shed.

Nesta slid into one of the armchairs before the unlit fireplace and stared at nothing.

She didn't stop the wolves when they gathered around her again, hateful, razor-sharp truths on their red tongues. She didn't stop them as they began to rend her apart.

⁜

When Elain burst into the dining room of the House, Cassian and Rhys were shaking off the frigid air that had been howling through Windhaven.

Her brown eyes were bright with tears, but she kept her chin high.

"I want to go home," she said, voice wobbling slightly.

Cassian looked at Rhys, who'd dropped off the middle Archeron sister before retrieving Cassian from Windhaven. He'd wanted to see for himself how ready the Illyrians were to fight. That Rhys had found nothing lacking both elated Cassian and filled him with dread. If war began once more, how many would die? It was a soldier's lot in life to fight, to march with Death beside him, and he had led males into battle multiple times. Yet how many promises had he foolishly made to the families of those who'd fallen in the recent war that the peace would last for a while? How many more families would he have to comfort? He didn't know why it was different this time, why it weighed so heavily. But while Rhys and Devlon had been speaking, Cassian had been staring at the children of Windhaven, wondering how many would lose their fathers.

Cassian cast the memory aside as Rhys surveyed Elain, his violet-blue eyes missing nothing. "What happened."

When Rhys spoke like that, it was more of a command than a question.

Elain waved a hand in dismissal before flinging open the veranda doors and striding into the open air.

"Elain," Rhys said as he and Cassian trailed her into the dying light.

Elain stood by the rail, the breeze caressing her hair. "She's not getting any better. She's not even trying." She wrapped her arms around herself and stared toward the distant sea.

Rhys turned to him, his face grave. *Feyre warned her.*

Cassian swore softly. *Nesta is making progress—I know she is. Something set her off.* He added, because Rhys was still looking like cold death personified, *It'll take time. Maybe no more visits from her sisters, for the time being. At least not without her permission.* He didn't want to isolate Nesta. Not at all. *If Elain wants to see her again, let me ask Nesta first.*

Rhys's voice slithered like liquid night. *What about Feyre?*

She doesn't want Feyre here.

Power rumbled through Rhys, guttering the stars in his eyes.

Calm the fuck down, Cassian snapped. *They have their own shit to sort out. You threatening to obliterate Nesta every time it comes up doesn't help.*

Rhys held his stare, the inherent dominance in it like the force of a tidal wave. But Cassian weathered it. Let it wash past him. Then Rhys shook his head and said to Elain, "I'll fly you home."

Elain didn't object when Rhys scooped her up and launched into the red-and-pink-stained sky.

When they were a speck of black and purple over the rooftops, Rhys sweeping along the gilded river as if giving Elain a scenic tour, then and only then did Cassian enter the House.

He stormed across the dining room and into the hallway; he charged down the stairs, his feet eating every inch of distance until he flung open the family library's doors.

"What the fuck happened?"

Nesta was sitting in an armchair before the dark fireplace, fingers digging into the rolled arms of the seat. A queen on a quilted throne.

"I don't want to talk to you," was all she said.

His heart thundered, his chest heaving as if he'd run a mile. "What did you say to Elain?"

She leaned forward to peer at him. Then rose to her feet, a pillar of steel and flame, her lips curling back from her teeth. "Of course you'd assume I'm the one at fault." She prowled closer, her eyes burning with cold fire. "Always defending sweet, innocent Elain."

He crossed his arms, letting her get as close to him as she wanted. Like hell would he yield one step to her. "I'll remind you that you've been the chief defender of sweet, innocent Elain until recently." He'd witnessed her go toe to toe with Fae capable of slaughtering her without giving it a thought, all for her sister.

Nesta only simmered, near-shaking with rage. Or cold. Cauldron, it was cold in here. Only the heated floors offered any reprieve. "Fire," he said, and the House obeyed. A great blaze flared to life in the hearth behind him.

"No fire," she said, focused upon Cassian, though her words were not to him.

The House seemed to ignore her.

"*No* fire," she ordered. He could have sworn she blanched slightly.

For a heartbeat, he was again in Rhys's mother's house in Windhaven. She'd been staring and staring into the fire, as if speaking to it, as if unaware that even he was there.

The fire crackled and popped. Nesta seethed to the open air, "I *said*—"

A log cracked, as if the House were merrily ignoring her, adding heat to the flame.

But Nesta flinched. Barely a blink and half a shudder, but her entire body went rigid. Fear and dread flashed over her features, then vanished.

Strange.

Whatever curiosity Nesta noted on his face had her bristling again before launching toward the open doors of the library.

"Where are you going?" he demanded, unable to keep the temper from his voice.

"Out." She hit the hall and aimed for the stairwell.

Cassian stalked after her, a snarl ripping from his throat. He quickly closed the distance between them.

"Leave me alone," she bit out.

"What's the plan, Nes?" He trailed her to the lowest level of the House and the stairwell halfway down the corridor. "You tear into the people who love you until they eventually give up and leave you alone? Is that what you want?"

She yanked on the handle of the ancient door and threw him a withering glare over a shoulder. She opened her mouth, then shut it against whatever had been about to come out.

As if she'd bank herself for him. Pity him. *Spare him.* Like he needed shielding from her.

"Say it," he hissed. "Just fucking *say it.*"

Nesta's gaze lit with that silver fire. Her nose crinkled with animalistic rage.

The Siphons atop his hands warmed, readying for an enemy he refused to acknowledge.

Her eyes slid down to the red stones. And when they again lifted to his face, the unholy fire in her stare was gone. Replaced by something so dead and vacant it was like gazing into the unseeing eyes of a fallen soldier on a battlefield. He'd seen crows pick at eyes that dead.

Nesta said nothing as she turned back to the stairwell and began her descent.

CHAPTER 18

There was only the red stone of the stairwell, and her jagged breathing, and the knives that had turned inward and sliced and sliced, the walls pushing in, her legs burning with each step downward.

She didn't want to be in her head, didn't want to be in her body. Wanted the beating of drums and the riotous song of a fiddle to fill her with sound, to silence any thought. Wanted to find a bottle of wine and drink deep, let the wine pull her out of herself, set her mind drifting and numb.

Down and down and down.

Around and around and around.

Nesta passed the step with her burning handprint. Passed step two hundred fifty. Three hundred. Five hundred. Eight hundred.

It was on step eight hundred and three that her legs began to wobble.

The roaring in her head dulled as she focused upon keeping upright.

By step one thousand, she had stopped entirely.

There was only the spinning silence.

Nesta closed her eyes and leaned her brow into the cool stone to her right, bringing up an arm to rest against it, as if she were clinging tight to a lover. She could have sworn a heartbeat thumped within the stone, as surely as if it beat within a chest beneath her ear.

It was her own pounding blood, she told herself. Even as she clung to the wall, that heartbeat.

She let her breathing saw in and out of her. Let the trembling of her body ease.

The heartbeat in the stone faded. The wall turned icy beneath her flushed cheek. Rough against her fingertips.

She began the walk upward. One step after another after another. Thighs straining, knees groaning, chest on fire.

Her head had emptied by the time she half-crawled up the last twenty steps. She'd had to stop five times to rest. Five times, only for as long as it took to catch her breath and steady herself—just until the roaring threatened to press in again.

She was wrung out, utterly empty, by the time she arrived back at the landing. Cassian leaned against the opposite wall, his face grave.

"I don't feel like sparring with you," she said flatly, too drained to be angry. She knew she could call in their bargain to order him to fly her down to the city, but she didn't possess the energy to even bother. "Good night."

He moved into her path, wings blocking her. "What step did you reach this time?"

As if it mattered. "One thousand." Her legs throbbed and throbbed.

"Impressive."

Nesta lifted her stare to his face, and found him earnest. She didn't bother to hide the weariness weighing on every part of her.

She made to walk past him, but he didn't lower his wings. Short of punching her way through, she wasn't getting by. "What?"

"What set you off today?"

"Everything." She didn't want to say more.

"What did Elain say to you?"

She couldn't revisit that conversation, couldn't talk about her father or his death or any of it. So she shut her heavy eyes. "Why don't they sign up for training?"

He knew who she meant. "Maybe they're not ready."

"I thought they'd sign up."

"Is that what you're upset about?" His question was so gentle, so sad.

Nesta opened her eyes. "Some of them have been here for hundreds of years and still haven't been able to come back from what they endured. So what hope do I have?"

He rubbed at his shoulder, as if it were sore. "We've been working for barely two weeks, Nesta. Physically, you might be seeing changes, but what's happening in your mind, your heart, will take far longer than that. Fuck, it took Feyre months—"

"I don't want to hear about Feyre and her special journey. I don't want to hear about Rhys's journey, or Morrigan's, or anyone's."

"Why?"

The words, the rage, built again. She refused to speak, instead focusing on tamping down that power inside her until it didn't so much as murmur.

"Why?" he pushed.

"Because I don't," she snapped. "Put those bat wings away."

Cassian obeyed, but stepped closer, towering over her. "Then I'll tell you about my special journey, Nes." His tone was icy in a way she'd never heard.

"No."

"I slaughtered every person who hurt my mother."

She blinked up at him, the weight in her vanishing at the vicious words.

Cassian's face held only ancient rage. "When I was old and strong enough, I went back to the village where I was born, where I'd been ripped from her arms, and I learned that she was dead. And there was no one I could fight to change that. They refused to tell me where they'd buried her. One of the females hinted that they'd dumped her off the cliff."

Horror and something like pain went through her.

His eyes flared with cold light. "So I destroyed them. Anyone who wasn't responsible—children and some females and the elderly—I let them leave. But anyone who had played a role in her suffering . . . I made them suffer in return. Rhys and Azriel helped me. Found the piece of shit who'd sired me. I let my brothers tear him apart before I finished him."

The words hung between them.

He said with soft fury, "It took me ten years before I was able to face it. What I'd done to those people, and what I'd lost. Ten years." He was trembling, but not with fear. "So if you want to take ten years to face whatever is eating you alive from the inside out, go ahead. You want to take twenty years, go ahead."

Silence fell, interrupted only by their uneven panting.

Nesta breathed, "Do you regret what you did?"

"No." Such unflinching honesty. The same honesty that now assessed her, marking every roaring, sharp piece of her.

Nesta dipped her head, as if it'd stop him from seeing everything.

Warm, strong fingers cupped her chin, calluses scraping against her skin.

She let him lift her head. She hadn't realized he'd come closer. That only inches separated them. Unless she'd been the one to drift toward him, drawn by each brutal word.

Cassian kept his light grip on her chin. "Whatever you need to throw at me, I can take it. I won't break." No challenge laced the words. Only a plea.

"You don't understand," she said, voice rasping. "I am not *like* you and the others."

"That's never bothered me one bit." He lowered his hand from her chin.

She straightened. "It should."

"You say that like you want it to bother me."

"It bothers everyone. Even oh-so-special *Rhysand*."

His teeth flashed, any semblance of softness gone. "I told you once, and I'll say it again: don't take that snide fucking tone when you speak about him."

"He's not my High Lord. I may speak of him as I wish." She made to step away, but he gripped her wrist, holding her in place. "Let go."

"Make me. Use that training and *make* me."

Hot temper poured in. "You're an arrogant bastard."

"And you're a haughty witch. We're evenly matched."

She snarled. "Let *go*."

Cassian snorted, but obeyed, turning his face as he backed a step away. And it was the light of victory in his eyes, the clear sense that he believed he'd somehow unnerved her and *won* this fight that had her grabbing the front of his leather jacket.

Nesta told herself it was to knock that smirk off his face that she curled her fingers in the leather and hauled her mouth to his.

CHAPTER 19

For a heartbeat, there was only the warmth of Cassian's mouth, the press of his body, the stiffness in his every trembling muscle as Nesta slanted her lips over his, rising onto her toes.

She'd kissed him with her eyes open, so she could see precisely how his own widened.

Nesta pulled away a moment later and found his eyes still wide, his breathing harsh.

She laughed softly, making to unhook her fingers from his jacket and strut down the hall.

She only got as far as lowering her right hand before he surged forward to kiss her back.

The force of that kiss knocked them toward the wall, the stone slamming into her shoulders as all of him lined up against all of her, a hand sliding into her hair while the other gripped her hip.

The moment Nesta hit that wall, the moment Cassian enveloped her, it destroyed any illusion of restraint. She opened her mouth, and his tongue swept in, the kiss punishing and savage.

And the taste of him, like snow-kissed wind and crackling embers—

She moaned, unable to help herself.

It seemed that sound was his undoing, for the fingers in her hair dug into her scalp, angling her head so he could better taste her, claim her.

Her hands roved over his muscled chest, desperate for any skin, anything to touch as their tongues met and parted, as he licked the roof of her mouth, as he slid his tongue over her teeth.

She met him stroke for stroke, and all sense of self went flying from her. She plunged her fingers into his hair, and it was as soft as she'd imagined, the strands like silk against her skin.

Every hateful thought eddied from her mind. She gave herself to the distraction, welcomed it with open arms, let the kiss burn through all of it. There was only his mouth and his tongue and his teeth, licking and tasting and biting; there was only the strength of his body, pressing against hers, but not nearly close enough—

He slid his hands around her, grasping her ass, and lifted her into the air. She wrapped her legs around his middle, and moaned again as he pressed himself between her thighs.

She needed this temporary reprieve from her mind, that *thing* burning deep inside her, the memories that hounded her. She needed this. Needed him.

Cassian ground into her, and groaned into her mouth at the first push of his hips. She arched her back at that deep-throated sound, baring her neck to him. He seized on it, dragging his mouth from hers.

His tongue traced a line up the column of her neck, dragging heat in its wake, and reached that spot just below her ear that had her clenching, had her whimpering. He let out a laugh against her skin. "Like that?" he murmured, and licked it again.

Her breasts ached, and she moved against him, seeking any contact with his chest, any bit of friction. But Cassian buried his face against her neck, teeth clamping down lightly atop her fluttering pulse. The slight hurt set her panting; the scrape of his tongue over the spot had her eyes rolling back in her head.

He pulled his head from her neck, though. And Nesta had never been laid so bare as she was while he ground his hips into her again and watched her writhe.

A dark smile graced his mouth. "So responsive," he purred in a voice she'd never heard but knew she'd crawl to hear again. He drove his hips between hers, a lazy, thorough push of the hardness of him into the throbbing ache of her. She scrambled to regain any sense of control, of sanity—found herself wanting to hand it all over to him, to let him touch and touch and touch her, lick and suckle and fill her—

Cassian growled, as if he read that in her stare, and kissed her again.

Their tongues tangled, their bodies pressed so tightly she could feel his heartbeat against her chest. He tasted her thoroughly, withdrew, and tasted her again. Like he was learning every place in her mouth.

She had to feel his skin. Had to feel the hardness pushing into her with her hands, her mouth, her body. She'd go mad if she didn't, go mad if she couldn't get these clothes off, go mad if he stopped kissing her—

Nesta wedged her hand between their bodies, seeking him out. Cassian groaned again, long and low, as her hand cupped him through the leather of his pants. The breath stole out of her. The sheer size of him—

Her mouth watered. She was aching, so wet that every stitch of the seam down the center of her pants was torture.

His kiss turned deeper, wilder, and she grappled with the laces and buttons of his pants. There were so many she didn't know where to find the ones to undo them, her fingertips ripping at every loop, nearly clawing to get him free.

Cassian's panting caressed her skin as he nipped at her bottom lip, her ear, her jaw. Her own staccato breathing echoed it, fire roaring in her blood, and he captured her mouth again, moaning into her as she gave up on the laces and buttons and laid her hand flat against him. He bucked as she rubbed the heel of her palm down his length, marveling at each inch.

He tore his mouth from hers. "If you keep doing that, I'll—"

Nesta did it again, dragging the heel of her palm upward, toward the tip she knew pressed against his lower abdomen. His hips arced toward her, and he tilted back his head, exposing the strong column of his throat. She learned the shape of him through his pants, and pressed her hand harder, working him. He gritted his teeth, chest heaving like a bellows, and the sight of him coming undone had her leaning forward. Had her clamping her teeth onto his neck. Just as she rubbed him again, harder and rougher.

He hissed. With her name on his lips, his hips thrust into her hand with a strength that made her core throb to the point of pain, imagining that force, that size and heat, buried deep in her. Another punishing rub of her palm, a scrape of teeth at his neck, and Cassian erupted.

His wings tucked in tight as he came, and each spurt of his cock shuddered through his pants, echoing along her hand as she stroked and stroked him.

When Cassian had stilled, when he was shaking—only then did Nesta remove her face from his neck. His hazel eyes were wide enough that the whites shone around them. A blush stained his golden cheeks, so enticing that she nearly leaned forward to lick that, too.

But he remained gaping. Like he'd realized what he'd done and regretted it.

Every bit of desire, of blessed distraction within her winked out.

Nesta shoved at his chest, and he immediately let go, almost dropping her to the floor as their bodies pulled apart.

She didn't wait to hear his words of regret, that this had been a mistake. She wouldn't let him hold that power over her. So Nesta curled her lips in a cold, cruel smile and said as she left, "Someone's quick off the mark."

✢

Cassian couldn't look Azriel in the face at breakfast the next morning.

His brother had returned late last night, refused to say anything about what he'd found regarding Briallyn, and only insisted that today they'd all meet at the river house and learn of it together. Cassian hadn't cared. He'd barely listened to Azriel asking about training.

He'd come in his pants after a few touches from Nesta, soaking himself like he was no better than he'd been in his youth.

But the moment she had kissed him in the hall, he'd lost all semblance of sanity. He'd turned into something just short of an animal, licking and biting at her neck, unable to think clearly beyond the base instinct to claim.

The taste of her had been like fire and steel and a winter sunrise. That had just been her mouth, her neck. If he got his tongue between her legs . . . He shifted in his seat.

"Did something happen that I, as your chaperone, should know about?" Azriel's dry question dragged Cassian from his rising arousal. From the amusement on his brother's face, he knew Az could not only scent that arousal but see it on his face.

"No," Cassian grumbled. He'd never hear the end of it if he admitted what he'd done.

He'd found his pleasure, and Nesta had not. He'd never allowed such a thing to happen.

But he'd come hard enough to see stars, and only then realized she had not. That he'd embarrassed himself, that he'd left her unsatisfied, and if it was the only taste of her he'd ever get, he'd monumentally fucked it all to hell.

And then there'd been her parting shot, blasting what was left of his pride into shards.

Quick off the mark, she'd purred, like what they'd done hadn't meant anything.

He knew it was bullshit. He'd felt her frantic need, heard her moans and wanted to devour them whole. But that kernel of doubt took root.

He had to make it even, somehow. Had to get the upper hand again.

Azriel cleared his throat, and Cassian blinked. "What?"

"I said, are you two ready to head down to the river house?"

"Two?" He blinked through the cloud of arousal.

Azriel chuckled, shadows skittering. "Did you listen at all last night?"

"No."

"At least you're honest." Azriel smirked. "You and Nesta are wanted down there."

"Because of the shit with Elain?"

Azriel stilled. "What happened to Elain?"

Cassian waved a hand. "A fight with Nesta. Don't bring it up," he warned when Azriel's eyes darkened. Cassian blew out a breath. "I take that as a no regarding the meeting topic, then."

"It's about what I discovered. Rhys said he requires you both there."

"It's bad, then." Cassian surveyed the shadows gathered around Az. "You all right?"

His brother nodded. "Fine." But shadows still swarmed him.

Cassian knew it was a lie, but didn't push it. Az would speak when he was ready, and Cassian would have better success convincing a mountain to move than getting Az to open up.

So he said, "All right. We'll meet you there."

CHAPTER
20

Nesta could barely stand to be near Cassian as they flew over Velaris. Every glance, every scent of him, every touch while he carried her down to the river house grated along her skin, threatening to bring her back to last night, when she'd been starved for any taste of him.

Thankfully, Cassian didn't speak to her. Barely looked at her. And by the time the sprawling manor along the river appeared, she'd forgotten to be annoyed by his silence. Two weeks up at the House, and the city suddenly loomed large, too loud, too full of people.

"This meeting will be fast," Cassian promised as they landed on the front lawn, as if he'd read the tension in her body.

Nesta said nothing, unable to speak with the churning in her stomach. Who would be here? Which of them would she have to face, to endure them judging her so-called progress? They'd probably all heard of her fight with Elain—gods, would Elain be present?

She followed Cassian into the beautiful house, barely noting the round table in the heart of the entry, crowned with a massive vase full of freshly cut flowers. Barely noting the silence of the house, not a servant to be seen.

But Cassian paused before a landscape painting of a towering, barren mountain, void of life yet somehow thrumming with presence. Snow and pines crusted the smaller peaks around it, but this strange, bald mountain . . . Only a black stone jutted from its top. A monolith, Nesta realized, stepping closer.

Cassian murmured, "I didn't realize Feyre had painted Ramiel."

The sacred mountain from the Blood Rite. Indeed, three stars faintly glowed in the twilight skies above the peak. It was a near-perfect, real-life rendering of the Night Court's insignia.

"I wonder when she saw it," Cassian mused, smiling faintly.

Nesta didn't bother to suggest Feyre might have simply peered into Rhysand's mind. Cassian continued onward, leading her down the hall without another word.

Nesta steeled herself as he stopped before the study doors—the same room where she'd sat and received a public lashing—and then flung one open.

Rhys and Feyre sat on the sapphire couch before the window. Azriel leaned against the mantel. Amren had curled herself into an armchair, bundled in a gray fur coat, as if the nip in the air today were a blast of winter. No Elain, no Morrigan.

Feyre's gaze was wary. Cold. But it warmed as she smiled at Cassian, who strode to her and kissed her cheek—or tried to. He said to Rhys, "Really? She's shielded even in here?"

Rhys stretched out his long legs, crossing one ankle over the other. "Even in here."

Cassian rolled his eyes and plopped into the armchair beside Amren's, surveying her fur coat and saying, "It's *barely* cold today."

Amren's teeth flashed. "Keep talking like that and it'll be your pelt I wear tomorrow."

Nesta might have smiled had Amren not turned toward her.

Tension, thick and painful, stretched between them. Nesta refused to look away.

Amren's red lips curled, her bob of black hair gleaming.

Feyre cleared her throat. "All right, Az. Let's hear it."

Azriel folded his wings, shadows writhing around his ankles and neck. "Queen Briallyn has been busier than we thought, but not in the way we expected."

Nesta's blood went cold. The queen who had leaped into the Cauldron of her own free will, desperate to be turned young and immortal. She'd emerged a withered crone—and immortal. Doomed to be old and bent forever.

Azriel went on, "In the week I've been watching her, I . . . learned what her next steps are." The way he hesitated before he said *learned* said enough: he'd tortured it out of someone. Many people.

Nesta glanced at his scarred hands, and Azriel tucked them behind his back, as if he noted her attention.

"Get on with it," Amren snapped, rustling in her chair.

"The other queens indeed fled from Briallyn weeks ago, as Eris said. She alone sits in the throne room of their shared palace. And what Eris revealed about Beron was true, too: the High Lord visited Briallyn on the continent, pledging his forces to her cause." A muscle ticked in Azriel's jaw. "But Briallyn's gathering of armies, the alliance with Beron, is only the auxiliary force to what she has planned." He shook his head, shadows slithering over his wings. "Briallyn wishes to find the Cauldron again. In order to retrieve her youth."

"She'll never attain the Cauldron," Amren said, waving a hand gleaming with rings. "No one but us, Miryam, and Drakon know where it's hidden. Even if Briallyn did uncover its location, there are enough wards and spells on it that no one could ever break through."

"Briallyn knows this," Azriel said gravely. Nesta's stomach churned.

Azriel nodded to Cassian. "What Vassa suspected is true. The death-lord Koschei has been whispering in Briallyn's ear. He remains trapped at his lake, but his words carry on the wind to her. He is ancient, his depth of knowledge fathomless. He pointed Briallyn toward the Dread Trove—not for her sake, but for his own ends. He wishes to use it to free himself from his lake. And Briallyn is not the puppet we believed her to be—she and Koschei are allies." He added to Cassian, "You need to ask Eris whether Beron knows about this. And the Trove."

Cassian nodded into the ensuing silence. Nesta found herself asking, "What's the Dread Trove?"

Amren's eyes glowed with a remnant of her power. "The Cauldron Made many objects of power, long ago, forging weapons of unrivaled might. Most were lost to history and war, and when I went into the Prison, only three remained. At the time, some claimed there were four, or that the fourth had been Unmade, but today's legends only tell of three."

"The Mask," Rhys murmured, "the Harp, and the Crown."

Nesta had a feeling none of them were good.

Feyre frowned at her mate. "They're different from the objects of power in the Hewn City? What can they do?"

Nesta had tried her best to forget that night she and Amren had gone to test her so-called gift against the hoard within those unhallowed catacombs. The objects had been half-imprisoned in the stone itself: knives and necklaces and orbs and books, all shimmering with power. None of it pleasant. For the Dread Trove to be worse than what she'd witnessed . . .

"The Mask can raise the dead," Amren answered for Rhys. "It is a death mask, molded from the face of a long-forgotten king. Wear it and you may summon the dead to you, command them to march at your will. The Harp can open any door, physical or otherwise. Some say between worlds. And the Crown . . ." Amren shook her head.

"The Crown can influence anyone, even piercing through the mightiest of mental shields. Its only flaw is that it requires close physical proximity to initially sink its claws into a victim's mind. But wear the Crown, and you could make your enemies do your bidding. Could make a parent slaughter their child, aware of the horror but unable to stop themselves."

"And these things were *lost*?" Nesta demanded.

Rhys threw her a frown. "Those who possessed them grew careless. They were lost in ancient wars, or to treachery, or simply because they were misplaced and forgotten."

"What does it have to do with the Cauldron?" Nesta pushed.

"Like calls to like," Feyre murmured, looking to Amren, who nodded. "Because the Trove was Made by the Cauldron, so might the Trove find its Maker." She angled her head. "Briallyn was Made, though. Can't she track the Cauldron herself?"

Amren drummed her fingers on the arm of her chair. "The Cauldron aged Briallyn to punish her." A glance at Nesta. "Or punish you, I suppose." Nesta kept her face carefully blank. Amren went on, "But I think you took something from it when you seized your power, girl."

Feyre looked toward Nesta, her voice soft as she asked, "What exactly happened in the Cauldron?"

Every image, thought, feeling pelted Nesta. Smothered her, exactly as she had to smother the rising power in her at her sister's question. No one spoke. They all just stared.

Cassian cleared his throat. "Does it matter?" Everyone faced him, and Nesta nearly sagged with relief at the shift of their attention. Even as something kindled in her chest at his words. His defense of her.

"It'd help us gain insight," Feyre said.

"We can discuss it later . . . ," Cassian began, but Nesta straightened.

"I . . ." They all halted. Twisted toward her. Her mouth went dry. Nesta swallowed against it, praying they didn't see the shaking hands she tucked under her thighs. Her thoughts swarmed her, each memory screaming, and she didn't know where to start, how to explain it—

Breathe. It calmed her mind whenever Cassian led her through their exercises. So she let herself inhale—then slowly exhale. Again. A third time.

And into the silence, Nesta said, "I wasn't aware of what I took. Just that I was taking things the Cauldron did not want me to have. It seemed fitting, given what it was doing to me."

There. That was all she could say, would say.

But Feyre nodded, eyes shining bright with something Nesta could not place. Feyre said to Amren, "So it's highly possible that the Cauldron *couldn't* imbue Briallyn with the ability to track it. All it could do was give Briallyn the ability to track anything it Made, a sorry shadow of the original gift."

The others nodded, and Nesta dared a look at Cassian, who gave her a soft smile. Like in saying the few words she'd managed to get out, she'd somehow done something . . . worthy. Her chest tightened.

Had she done so many *un*worthy things that her scant contribution earned that much praise?

Nesta forced herself to ignore the nauseating thought as Amren continued, "If you were to gather all three objects, you could use the potency of their combined Made essence to track down the Cauldron, no matter where it is."

"Not to mention gain three objects of terrible power," Azriel added grimly. "Capable of granting even a human army an advantage against the Fae."

"Raise the dead," Cassian mused, his face tightening, any trace of that approving smile gone, "and you'd have an unstoppable force, able to march without rest or food. Open any door, and you could move that army of the dead wherever you wished. And with unrestrained influence, you could make any enemy territory and its people bow to you."

Silence again filled the room. Nesta's heart thundered.

"And all Koschei wants is to be free from his lake?" Rhys asked Azriel.

But Amren answered. "No one really knows the full scope of the Trove's powers. Beyond freeing him from his lake, Koschei may very well know something about the Trove that we don't—some greater power that manifests when all three are united."

Rhys looked at Azriel, who nodded grimly.

"What is a death-lord?" Nesta asked into the silence.

Their stares struck her like stones. Cassian answered, tapping the scar on the side of his neck. "I told you of Lanthys—the wound he gave me. He is literally deathless. Nothing can kill him. Koschei, too, cannot be killed. He is the master of his own death." He lowered his hand from the horrible scar. The gleam in his eye suggested that his thoughts had turned toward her own powers. She ignored the *thing* that writhed within her in answer and confirmation, cold fire licking up her spine. Mercifully, Cassian went on, "They are death-lords."

The words hung in the air. Rhys cursed. "I'd forgotten about Lanthys."

Cassian threw him a dry look, again tapping that scar. "I haven't."

To Nesta's horror, Amren shuddered. *Amren.*

Feyre cleared her throat. "So they are trying to find this Dread Trove in order to track down the Cauldron for Briallyn, and likely free Koschei in the process. And launch a war, with Beron as her ally, that would grant them whatever territories they wish. Or give some to Koschei, depending on what bargain he strikes with Briallyn—probably one to his advantage."

"Again, Briallyn is well aware of Koschei's insidious influence," Azriel said. "If her strings are being pulled, it is only because she's allowing it to achieve her own ends."

Cassian said, "So we've got them on one front, and Beron here, ready and eager to go into war with Briallyn so he might expand his own territory after the carnage halts."

Nesta's head spun. She'd had no idea any of this was occurring.

She'd picked up hints, but nothing that had confronted her with the knowledge of the danger that faced them. To be on the brink of such disaster again . . . She shifted in her seat.

Feyre asked Azriel, "Briallyn has not found the Dread Trove yet?"

Azriel shook his head. "Not as far as I could tell. The Dread Trove was last rumored to be here in Prythian. That's all Koschei knows, apparently. We have that on our side at least. Briallyn won't risk coming over here—not yet. Even with Beron as an ally. And Koschei is bound to his lake. But they are readying Briallyn to come, gathering her realm's greatest spies and warriors. There was already a host of them at the queens' palace. Why Briallyn and Koschei took Eris's soldiers is something I still haven't figured out." He gestured to Cassian. "You need to meet with Eris."

Cassian nodded. "I will. But we'll have to shore up the borders. Warn the courts. Tell them of Beron's plan. To hell with secrecy."

"We'd expose Eris in doing that," Rhys countered. "And lose a valuable ally," he added when Cassian rolled his eyes. "Eris is a snake, but he's useful. His motives might be selfish and power-hungry, but he can offer us a great deal." He frowned, and said carefully, "I agree with Az. I want you to update Eris on this, as you promised."

"Fine," Cassian agreed. "But what of warning the courts about the Trove?"

"No," Rhys said. "We'd only risk one of them going after it. Beron would send out every warrior and spy of his to find it first. That he hasn't done so already suggests he doesn't know about the Trove, but we need Eris to confirm."

Feyre asked, "Why didn't we look for the Trove when we were hunting for the Cauldron ourselves?"

"The Book was easier to find," Amren said. "And it has been ten thousand years since anyone used the Trove. I assumed it was all at the bottom of an ocean."

"So we find it," Cassian declared. "Any ideas?"

"Made objects tend to not wish to be found by just anyone," Amren cautioned. "That they have faded from memory, that even *I* didn't think of them immediately in the fight against Hybern, suggests that perhaps they willed it that way. Wanted to stay hidden. True things of power have such gifts."

"You say that as if the objects have a sentience," Cassian said.

"They do," Amren said, storms drifting across her eyes. "They were Made in a time when wild magic still roamed the earth, and the Fae were not masters of all. Made objects back then tended to gain their own self-awareness and desires. It was not a good thing." Amren's face clouded with memory, and a chill whispered over Nesta's spine.

Rhys mused, "Just as I'm able to alter a mind to forget, perhaps they have a similar gift."

"But Briallyn is Made," Amren said. Nesta's mouth again went dry. "When Briallyn was Made, it likely removed from her the Dread Trove's glamour, for lack of a better term. Recognized her as kin. Where she might have glanced over a mention of the items before and never thought twice, now it stuck. Or perhaps called to her, presented itself in a dream."

All of them, all at once, looked at Nesta.

"You," Amren said quietly, "are the same. So is Elain."

Nesta stiffened. "If they're all enchanting you to forget, how is it that Azriel was able to remember and bear the information here?"

"Perhaps once you learn of it, recognize it, the spell is broken," Amren said. "Or perhaps the Dread Trove wants us to know of it now, for some dark reason of its own."

The hair on Nesta's arms rose.

Cassian shifted in his seat. "So we track down the Dread Trove—how?"

Elain spoke from the doorway, having appeared so silently that they all twisted toward her, "Using me."

CHAPTER 21

Nesta's head went silent as Elain's words finished sounding in the room. Feyre had twisted in her seat, face white with alarm.

Nesta shot to her feet. "No."

Elain remained in the doorway, her face pale but her expression harder than Nesta had ever seen it. "You do not decide what I can and cannot do, Nesta."

"The last time we involved ourselves with the Cauldron, it abducted you," Nesta countered, fighting her shaking. She found the words, the weapons she sought. "I thought you didn't have powers anymore."

Elain pursed her lips. "I thought you didn't, either."

Nesta's spine straightened. No one spoke, but their attention lingered on her like a film on her skin. "You will not go looking for it."

Amren said coolly, "So you look for it, girl."

Nesta turned to the small female. "I don't know how to find anything."

"Like calls to like," Amren countered. "You were Made by the Cauldron. You may track other objects Made by it as well, as Briallyn can. And because you are Made by it, you are immune to the influence and power of the Trove. You might use them, yes, but they cannot be used upon you." A glance to Elain. "Either of you."

Nesta swallowed. "I can't." But to let Elain involve herself, jeopardize her safety—

Amren said, "You tracked the Cauldron—"

"It nearly *killed* me. It trapped me like a bird in a cage."

Elain said, "Then I will find it. I might require some time to . . . reacquaint myself with my powers, but I could start today."

"Absolutely not," Nesta spat, fingers curling at her sides. "*Absolutely not.*"

"Why?" Elain demanded. "Shall I tend to my *little garden* forever?" When Nesta flinched, Elain said, "You can't have it both ways. You cannot resent my decision to lead a small, quiet life while also refusing to let me do anything greater."

"Then go off on adventures," Nesta said. "Go drink and fuck strangers. But stay *away* from the Cauldron."

Feyre said, "It is Elain's choice, Nesta."

Nesta whirled on her, ignoring the warning flicker of primal wrath in Rhys's stare. "Keep out of this," she hissed at her youngest sister. "I have no doubt *you* put these thoughts in her head, probably *encouraging* her to throw herself into harm's way—"

Elain cut in sharply, "I am not a child to be fought over."

Nesta's pulse pounded throughout her body. "Do you not remember the war? What we encountered? Do you not *remember* the Cauldron kidnapping you, bringing you into the heart of Hybern's camp?"

"I do," Elain said coldly. "And I remember Feyre rescuing me."

Roaring erupted in Nesta's head.

For a heartbeat, it appeared that Elain might say something to soften the words. But Nesta cut her off, seething at the pity about to be thrown her way. "Look who decided to grow claws after all," she crooned. "Maybe you'll become interesting at last, Elain."

Nesta saw the blow land, like a physical impact, in Elain's face, her posture. No one spoke, though shadows gathered in the corners of the room, like snakes preparing to strike.

Elain's eyes brightened with pain. Something imploded in Nesta's chest at that expression. She opened her mouth, as if it could somehow be undone. But Elain said, "I went into the Cauldron, too, you know. And it captured *me*. And yet somehow all you think of is what *my* trauma did to *you*."

Nesta blinked, everything inside her hollowing out.

But Elain turned on her heel. "Find me when you wish to begin." The doors shut behind her.

Every awful word Nesta had spoken hung in the air, echoing.

Feyre said to her, gratingly gentle, "It wasn't an easy choice for me to ask Elain to endanger herself like this."

Nesta twisted to Feyre. "Can't *you* find the Trove?" She hated each cowardly word, hated the fear in her heart, hated that in merely asking, she'd exposed her preference for Elain. "You've got all that magic, and you were Made yourself, even if it wasn't by the Cauldron. You trained—you are a *warrior*. Can't you find it?"

Again, that silence. But a different kind. Like a thunderhead about to break.

"No," Feyre said quietly. "I can't." She looked to Rhys, who nodded, his eyes shining.

Everyone watched Feyre now. But Feyre's attention remained fixed upon Nesta. "I can't risk it."

"Why?" Nesta snapped.

"Because I'm pregnant."

Silence fell. Silence, and then Cassian let out a whoop of such joy that it shattered the fraught silence into smithereens, leaping from his chair to tackle Rhys.

They went down in a tangle of wings and dark hair, and then Amren was saying to Feyre, light dancing in her eyes, "Congratulations, girl."

Azriel stooped to press a kiss to Feyre's head—or an inch from it.

"I *knew* that stupid shield wasn't just to practice something Helion taught you," Cassian was saying, giving Rhys a smacking kiss on the cheek before turning to Feyre and grabbing her to him. Rhysand relented on the shield enough that Cassian could wrap his arms around her, still laughing.

And as Rhys dropped the shield, Feyre's scent filled the room.

It was Feyre's usual scent, only—only something new. A smaller, softer scent, like a budding rose, lay within it.

Cassian laughed. "No wonder you've been a moody bastard, Rhys. I suppose we're about to learn a whole new level of overprotective."

Feyre glowered at him, then up at her mate. "We've already had discussions about this. The shield is a compromise."

Amren smiled broadly. "What was his starting offer?"

Feyre scowled. "That he never leave my side for the next ten months." The Fae took longer to grow children, Nesta had learned from poring over the books in the House's library during her initial weeks here. A month longer than a human pregnancy.

"How far along are you?" Azriel asked, gazing at Feyre's still-flat stomach.

She slid her fingers over it, as if anyone's attention there made her wish to protect the child inside. "Two months."

Cassian pivoted toward Rhys. "You've been hiding this for two *months*?"

Rhys threw him an arrogant smile. "We thought you'd all guess it by now, to be honest."

Cassian laughed again. "How can we guess when you've got her bundled in that shield?"

"Moody bastard, remember?"

Cassian grinned, and said to Azriel, "We're going to be uncles."

Feyre groaned. "Mother help this child."

Azriel's own grin bloomed at that, but Feyre's gaze slid to Nesta.

Nesta said quietly to her sister, "Congratulations."

For she'd said nothing, had only been able to stand and watch them all, their joy and closeness, as if she were looking in through a window.

But Feyre offered her a tentative smile. "Thank you. You'll be an aunt, you know."

"Gods help this child indeed," Cassian muttered, and Nesta glared at him.

She turned to Rhys and Feyre and found the former watching her carefully, the epitome of ease with his arm around his mate's shoulders—the gleam in his eye one of pure threat.

Nesta let him see it then. That she bore no ill will toward Feyre or the babe. Some primal part of her understood that Rhys was not only male, but a Fae male, and he would eliminate any threats to his mate and child. That he'd do it slowly and painfully and then walk away from her shredded corpse without an ounce of regret.

It was self-preservation, perhaps some new Fae instinct of her own, that had Nesta bowing her chin slightly, letting him see she meant no harm, would never hurt them.

Rhys's own chin dipped, and that was that.

Nesta said to Feyre, "Did you tell Elain?"

Before Feyre could reply, Azriel said, "What about Mor?"

Feyre smiled. "Elain was the only one who guessed. She caught me vomiting two mornings in a row." She nodded toward Azriel. "I think she's got you beat for secret-keeping."

"I'll tell Mor when she returns from Vallahan," Rhys said. "Given your reaction, Cass, I don't trust that she can keep her excitement to herself if I tell her while she's there, even if she doesn't say anything to them. And I don't want a potential enemy knowing. Not yet."

"Varian?" Amren asked. Nesta had never learned the story of how the female and the Summer Court's Prince of Adriata had become entwined. She supposed now she never would.

"Not yet," Rhys repeated, shaking his head. "Not until Feyre's farther along."

Nesta angled her head at her sister. "So you can't do magic while pregnant?"

Feyre winced. "I can, but given my unusual set of gifts, I'm not sure how it might impact the baby. Winnowing is fine, but some other powers, when we're still so early in the pregnancy, could strain my body dangerously." Rhys's hand tightened on her shoulder. "It's a pain in the ass." Feyre flicked at the hand gripping her arm. "As much of a pain in the ass as he's become."

Rhys winked at her. Feyre rolled her eyes. But then she said to Nesta, "Elain will need time to dust off her powers to try to See the Trove. But you, Nesta . . . You could scry again."

Rhys added, "As swiftly as possible. Time is not our ally."

Nesta asked Amren, "You're not Made?"

"Not as you were," Amren said. She gave Nesta a wicked grin. "Afraid?"

Nesta ignored the taunt. Even Cassian's bright happiness had faded.

"What choice do I have?" Nesta asked.

If it was between her and Elain, there was no choice at all. She would always go first if it meant keeping Elain from harm. Even if she'd just hurt her sister more than she could stomach.

"You do have a choice," Rhys said firmly. "You will always have a choice here."

Nesta threw him a cool look. "I'll search for it." She glanced at her sister's stomach, the hand idly resting atop it. "Of course I'll search for it."

⸸

Cassian wanted to have a word with Rhys about the Illyrian legions, so Nesta found herself walking to the front entry of the river house alone.

She'd made it halfway down the hall when Feyre called her name, and Nesta paused, right in front of the painting of Ramiel.

Feyre's smile was tentative. "I'll wait with you until he's done."

Don't bother, Nesta almost said, but reined it in. They walked in silence to the main entry, all those paintings and portraits of everyone but her and their mother watching them.

The quiet tightened, becoming nearly unbearable as they halted in the sprawling foyer. Nesta could think of nothing to say, nothing to *do* with herself.

Until Feyre said, "It's a boy."

Nesta whipped her head toward her sister. "The baby?"

Feyre smiled. "I wanted you to know first. I told Rhys to wait until I'd told you, but . . ." Feyre chuckled as renewed shouts of joy echoed down the hall. "I suppose he's telling Az and Cassian now."

But Nesta needed a breath to sort through it: the offering of kindness Feyre had extended, what she had revealed—"How can you possibly know its sex?"

The smile faded from Feyre's face. "During the conflict with Hybern, the Bone Carver showed me a vision of the child I'd have with Rhys."

"How did *he* know?"

"I don't know," Feyre admitted, her hand again drifting to her stomach. "But I didn't realize how much I wanted a boy until I knew I'd bear one."

"Likely because having sisters was so horrible for you."

Feyre sighed. "That's not what I meant."

Nesta shrugged. Feyre might say that, but the feeling was no doubt there. Everything that had just happened with Elain—

Feyre seemed to sense the direction of her thoughts. "Elain was right. We've become so focused on how her trauma impacted *us* that we forget she was the one who experienced it."

"It was directed at me, not you."

"I've been guilty of the same things, Nesta." Sorrow dimmed Feyre's eyes. "It was unfair for Elain to level that truth only at you."

Nesta didn't have an answer to that, didn't know where to start. "Why not tell Elain about the baby's sex first?"

"She discovered the pregnancy. I wanted you to know this part before anyone else."

"I hadn't realized you were keeping score."

Feyre gave her an exasperated look. "I'm not, Nesta. I just . . . Do I need an excuse to share things with you? You're my sister. I wanted to tell you before anyone else. That's it."

Nesta didn't have an answer to that, either. Thankfully, Cassian's voice filled the hallway as he bid his farewell to Rhys.

"Good luck," Feyre said softly before rushing to meet a jubilant Cassian, and Nesta knew her sister didn't only mean with the Dread Trove.

CHAPTER 22

"Do you think Nesta can find the Trove?" Azriel asked Cassian as they relaxed in the sitting room that separated their bedchambers, flames crackling in the hearth before them. The night had turned chill enough that they needed the fire, and Cassian, who'd always loved fall despite the pricks in the Autumn Court, savored the warmth.

"I hope so," Cassian hedged. He couldn't stomach the thought of Nesta putting herself in danger, but he understood her motivations entirely. If he'd had to pick between sending one of his brothers into danger or doing it himself, he would always—*always*—choose himself. Though he'd winced at every harsh word that had come out of Nesta's mouth to Elain, he couldn't fault the fear and love behind her decision. Could only admire that she had stepped up—if not for the good of the world, then to keep her sister safe.

Azriel said, "Nesta really should do a scrying."

Cassian gazed across the space between their two armchairs. They'd sat in them, before this fire, so many times that it was an unspoken rule that Azriel's was the one on the left, closer to the window, and Cassian's the one to the right, closer to the door. A third sat to Azriel's left, usually for Rhys, and a fourth to Cassian's right, always for Mor. A lace-lined golden throw pillow adorned the fourth chair, a permanent mark of her ownership. Amren, for whatever reason, rarely stayed here long enough to see this room, so no chair had ever been held for her.

"Nesta isn't up for a scrying," Cassian said. "We don't even know what power she has left."

But Elain had confirmed it for everyone: both sisters still possessed their Cauldron-gifted powers. Whether they were as powerful as before, he had no idea.

"You do know, though," Azriel countered. "You've seen it—even beyond when it glows in her eyes."

Cassian hadn't told anyone about the step he'd found with the clear finger holes burned into it. He wondered if Azriel had somehow learned of them, the news brought to him on his shadows' whispers. "She's volatile right now. The last time she did a scrying, it ended badly. The Cauldron *looked* at her. And then took Elain." He'd seen every horrific memory flash before Nesta's eyes today. And though he understood that Elain had spoken true, claiming the trauma of that memory, Cassian knew firsthand the lingering horror and pain of a loved one stolen and hurt.

Azriel stiffened. "I know. I helped rescue Elain, after all."

Az hadn't so much as hesitated before going into the heart of Hybern's war-camp.

Cassian leaned his head against the back of the chair, rustling his wings through the gaps crafted to accommodate them. "Nesta will scry on her own, eventually, if she's capable."

"If Briallyn and Koschei find just one of the Dread Trove items—"

"Let Nesta try it her way first." Cassian held Az's stare. "If we go in and order her to do it, it'll backfire. Let her exhaust her other options before she realizes only one is viable."

Azriel studied his face, then nodded solemnly.

Cassian blew out a breath, watching the flames leap and flutter. "We're going to be uncles," he said after a moment, unable to keep the wonder from his voice.

Azriel's face filled with pride and joy. "A boy."

It wasn't a guarantee that a High Lord's firstborn would be his heir. The magic sometimes took a while to decide, and often jumped around the birth order completely. Sometimes it found a cousin instead. Sometimes it abandoned the bloodline entirely. Or chose the heir in that moment of birth, in the echoes of a newborn's first cries. It wouldn't matter to Cassian, though, if Rhys's son inherited his world-shaking power, or barely a drop.

It wouldn't matter to Rhys, either. To any of them. That boy was already loved. "I'm happy for Rhys," Cassian said quietly.

"So am I."

Cassian looked over at Az. "You think you'll ever be ready for one?" *Ever be ready to confess to Mor what's in your heart?*

"I don't know," Azriel said.

"Do you want a child?"

"It doesn't matter what I want." Distant words—ones that prevented Cassian from prying further. He was still happy to be Mor's buffer with Azriel, but there'd been a change lately. In both of them. Mor no longer sat beside Cassian, draped herself over him, and Azriel . . . those longing glances toward her had become few and far between. As if he'd given up. After five hundred years, he'd somehow given up. Cassian couldn't think why.

Az asked, "Do *you* want a child?"

Cassian couldn't stop the thought that flashed: of him and Nesta against the wall a level below, her hand rubbing him exactly the way he liked it, her moans like sweet music.

He'd left her unsatisfied—she'd run off before he could make it even between the two of them. He'd gone up to Windhaven after the meeting earlier, and hadn't seen her at dinner. Wasn't even sure what the hell he'd say to her, how they'd have a conversation.

It was like the unfinished bargain inked across their backs, that imbalance of pleasure. And a matter of what he unashamedly could call male pride. She had the upper hand now. Had looked so damned smug when she'd cut him: *quick off the mark*.

His knee bounced, and he glowered at the flame.

"Cassian?"

He realized Azriel had asked him a question. Right—about children.

"Of course I want children." He'd contemplated it often, what manner of family he'd build for himself, how he'd make sure his children never spent a moment thinking they were unloved and unwanted; never, ever spent a moment hungry or scared or cold or in pain.

But no female had ever come along who'd tempted him enough to fight for that future.

He supposed, deep down, that was what he was holding out for: the mating bond. What he'd seen between Feyre and Rhys.

Cassian blew out another breath and got to his feet. Azriel lifted a silent brow.

Cassian aimed for the door. He wouldn't be able to rest, to focus, until he evened the playing field. As he entered the hall, he muttered without looking back, "Turn a blind eye, chaperone."

✢

Curled up in bed, a book propped on the thick down comforter, Nesta was just getting to the sizzling first kiss in her latest novel when a knock thudded on her door.

She slammed the book shut and sat up against the pillows. "Yes?"

The handle turned, and there he was.

Cassian still wore his leathers, the overlapping scales of them full of shadows that made him look like some great, writhing beast as he shut the door.

He leaned against the carved oak, his wings rising high above his head like twin mountain peaks.

"What?" She slid the book onto the nightstand, sitting up further. His eyes dipped to her sleeveless silk nightgown, then quickly returned to her face. "What?" she demanded again, angling her head. Her unbound hair slid over a shoulder, and she saw him mark that, too.

His voice was rough as he said, "I've never seen you with your hair down."

She always wore it braided across her head or pinned up. She frowned at the locks that flowed to her waist, the gold amongst the brown glimmering in the dim light. "It's a nuisance when it's down."

"It's beautiful."

Nesta couldn't stop her swallow as she lifted her gaze. His eyes were blazing, yet he remained leaning against the door, hands trapped behind his body. As if he were physically restraining himself.

His scent drifted to her, darker, muskier than usual. She'd bet all the money she didn't have that it was the scent of his arousal.

It set her pulse hammering, careening so far off the path of sanity that she scrambled after its vanishing leash. To let him affect her so easily, so greatly—unacceptable.

She didn't dare look below his waist, not as she shaped her lips into a cool smile. "Here for more?"

"I'm here to settle the debt between us."

His words were guttural. Her toes curled beneath the blanket.

But her voice remained surprisingly calm. "What debt?"

"The one I owe you for last night."

He spoke as if there was no room in him for teasing, for humor. His eyes drifted lower than her face, noting the hammering of her pulse. "We have unfinished business."

She grappled for anything to guard against him. "Male pride is a thing of wonder." When he didn't respond, she threw another wall his way: "Why are you even here? You made it clear enough that last night was a mistake."

He was having none of it. "I never said that." His attention remained fixed on her hammering pulse.

"You didn't need to. I saw it in your eyes."

His gaze snapped to hers. "The only mistake was that I came before I could taste you."

Nesta knew he didn't mean her mouth. Or her skin.

Cassian went on, "The only mistake was that you ran off before I could get on my knees."

Breathing became difficult. "Won't your friends tell you *this* is a mistake?" She gestured to the air between them.

"My friends have nothing to do with this. With what I want from you."

He said it with such intent that her breasts pebbled. His eyes dipped again, and when he saw her nipples hard against the silk of her nightgown . . .

His entire being seemed to focus on it. On her. All five hundred years of being a trained warrior, an apex predator. All of it, narrowing on her.

His appraisal enveloped her like a rush of wind, of fire. "What about training?" she breathed.

"This stays out of training." His eyes had turned wholly dark.

Her skin tightened, becoming almost painful as she went molten and throbbing between her legs.

"Nesta."

A note of pleading had entered his voice. He was trembling—the door behind him rattling with the force of his deteriorating self-control.

She looked then. Below his waist. At what strained against his pants.

Her head emptied out, and there was only him and her and the space between them.

Cassian let out a growl, the sound a plea as well.

She made herself say, "This stays out of training—and everything else. This is just sex."

Something shifted in his expression, but he said, "Just sex."

This was sure to be a mistake, sure to be something she paid for, suffered for. But she couldn't bring herself to deny him. Deny herself. Just for tonight, she'd allow it.

So Nesta met his eyes again, took in every trembling, restrained inch, and said, "Yes."

Cassian lunged for her, a beast freed of its cage, and she barely had time to twist toward the edge of the bed before his lips were on hers, devouring and claiming.

Deep purring sounds vibrated from his chest through her fingers as she clawed off his jacket, his shirt, ripping through the fabric. He tore his lips from hers only long enough to pull his shirt away, the fabric snaring on his wings before falling to the floor. Then he was on her again, climbing onto the bed, and she spread her legs for him, letting his body fall into the cradle between her thighs.

She couldn't stop her moan as he drove his hips into hers, the leather of his pants sliding against her. He plunged his tongue into her mouth, the kiss like a brand, one hand sliding up her bare thigh, tugging her nightgown with it. When he reached her hip and still had found no underwear, he hissed. Looked to where he pressed his hardness against her and realized that only the leather of his pants separated him from her wetness.

She was shaking, and not from fear, as he took a trembling hand and slid her nightgown higher. Pulled it up to her navel and then stared at her, bare and gleaming, pressed against the bulge in his pants. His chest heaved, and she waited for that brutal, demanding touch, but he only leaned down and pressed a kiss to her throat.

Tender, coaxing. Cassian pressed another to her shoulder, and she shivered. Shivered more as he dragged his tongue over the spot. He kissed the hollow of her throat. Licked it.

He slipped the straps of her nightgown down her arms. Kissed her collarbones. With each kiss, he pulled down the neck of her nightgown further. Until his breath warmed her bare breasts.

Cassian let out a sound from the back of his throat, from his gut. Like some sort of starved, tormented creature. He stared at her breasts, and she couldn't breathe under that burning gaze. Couldn't breathe as his head dipped and he wrapped his lips around her nipple.

Nesta arced off the bed, a breathless sound rupturing from her.

Cassian only repeated the movement on her other breast.

And then raked his teeth across the sensitive peak before clamping down lightly.

She moaned then, tipping her head back, thrusting her chest up toward him in silent plea.

Cassian let out that dark laugh and returned to her other breast, teeth grazing, teasing, biting.

She strained her hands toward him, toward where he'd gone still between her legs. She needed him—now. In her hand or her body, she didn't care.

But Cassian only pulled away. Pulled up, and knelt before her. Surveyed her spread beneath him, her nightgown a bunch of silk around her middle, everything else bared to him. His own feast to devour.

"I owe you a debt," he said in that guttural voice that made her writhe. He watched her hips undulate, and braced his large, powerful hands on either thigh. He waited for her to signal that she understood what he intended. What she'd dreamed of for so long, in the darkest hours of the night.

In a choked whisper, she said, "Yes."

Cassian gave her a feral, purely male smile. And then his hands tightened on her bare thighs, spreading them wider. His head lowered, and all she could see was his dark hair, gilded by the lamps, and his exquisite wings, rising above them both.

He didn't waste time with gentle touches and tastes.

Parting her with one hand, he dragged his tongue clear up her center.

The world fractured, re-formed, and fractured again. He cursed against her wetness, and he reached down with his other hand to adjust himself in his pants.

He licked her again, lingering at the spot atop the apex of her legs. Sucking it into his mouth, teeth nipping, before he withdrew.

She arched, unable to stop the moan breaking from her throat.

Cassian's tongue ran downward in an unhurried sweep, and he pressed a hand to her abdomen, stilling her, as he slid his tongue straight into her core. It curled into her, driving deeper than she'd expected, and she couldn't think, couldn't do anything but luxuriate in it, in him—

"You taste," he growled against her, making his way up again toward the bundle of nerves in short, teasing licks, "even more delicious than I dreamed."

Nesta whimpered, and he flicked his tongue there. Her whimper turned to a cry, and he laughed against her and flicked his tongue again.

Release became a shimmering veil, just beyond her grasp but drifting closer.

"So wet," he breathed, and licked at her entrance, as if determined to consume every drop of her. "Are you always this wet for me, Nesta?"

She wouldn't allow him the satisfaction of the truth. But she couldn't think of a lie, not with his tongue pumping in and out of her, coaxing her toward but still denying her the pressure and relentless pounding she so badly needed.

Cassian snickered, as if he knew the answer anyway. He licked her, his silken hair brushing over her belly, and looked up to meet her gaze.

As their eyes locked, he slid a finger into her.

She cried out, and he trailed a hand from her thigh to hold her open again as he licked at that spot while his finger pumped in and out of her in a teasingly slow rhythm.

More—she wanted more. She undulated her hips against him, hard enough to drive his finger deeper.

"Greedy," he murmured onto her, and withdrew his finger nearly to its tip. Only to add a second finger as he plunged back in.

Nesta let go entirely then. Let go of sanity and any pride as he filled her with those two fingers. He sucked and nibbled, and release gathered around her like an iridescent mist.

Cassian growled again, given over to whatever need drove him, and the reverberations of the sound echoed into places of her that had never been touched. In and out his fingers slid, stretching and filling, all while he tasted and savored.

Nesta rode his hand, his face, grinding into him with abandon.

"Holy gods." Cassian's teeth grazed against her. "Nesta."

The sound of her name on his lips against her most sensitive place sent her mind scattering into eternity.

She bowed off the bed with the force of her climax, and he became ravenous, fingers pumping and pumping, tongue and lips moving against her, like he'd devour her pleasure whole. He didn't stop until she'd collapsed against the mattress, until she was limp and reeling and trying to piece her mind back together.

The slide of his fingers out of her left her empty and aching, the removal of his tongue and mouth from between her legs like a cold kiss.

Cassian was panting, still hard as he rose up and stared at her.

She couldn't move—couldn't remember how to move. No one had ever done that to her. Made her feel like that.

It had knocked the breath from her, the thoroughness of her pleasure. Like the world could be remade in the force of what had erupted from her.

She just watched the carved, heaving muscle of his chest, his wings, his handsome face.

Nesta reached for the cock she was dying to feel, to taste, but he backed off the bed.

Cassian grabbed his shirt and aimed for the door. "We're even now."

CHAPTER 23

Watching Nesta climax had been as close to a religious experience as Cassian had ever had. It had rocked him to his very core, and only pure will and pride had kept him from spilling in his pants again. Only pure will and pride had made him back off the bed when she'd reached for him. Only pure will and pride had made him leave the room, when all he'd wanted was to plunge his cock into that sweet, tight warmth and ride her until they were both screaming.

He couldn't get her perfect taste out of his mouth. Not as he washed for bed. Not as he pumped himself dry, soaking his sheets. Not as he ate breakfast. Couldn't stop feeling the clamp of her around his fingers, like a burning, silken fist. He'd washed his hands a dozen times by the time he faced Nesta in the training ring, and he could still smell her there, could still feel her, taste her.

Cassian banished the thought from his mind. Along with the knowledge that Nesta might have felt good on his fingers, on his tongue, but it would be nothing compared to how she'd feel on his cock. She'd been tight enough that he knew it'd be paradise and madness—his undoing.

And she'd been so drenched for him that he knew he'd do deplorable things to be allowed to taste that wetness again.

The Nesta who emerged into the training pit was the one he saw every morning, though.

No hint of a blush, or a sparkle in her eye to tell him she'd enjoyed herself.

But maybe that was because Azriel walked in behind her.

His brother took one look at him and smirked. Az knew. Could either scent Cassian on Nesta, or could already scent Nesta on Cassian, even from across the ring.

Cassian didn't regret what he'd done with her. Not at all. And maybe it was the fact that it had been two years since he'd had any sort of sex, but he couldn't remember the last time he'd been so ridden by his own base need.

Some small, quiet part of his brain whispered otherwise. He ignored it. Had ignored it for a long time now.

"Morning, Az," Cassian said cheerfully. He nodded to Nesta. "Nes. How'd you sleep?"

Her eyes flashed with the anger that was like kindling to his own, but then she smiled coolly. "Like a babe."

It was to be a game, then. Which one of them could pretend that nothing had happened the longest. Which one of them might seem the least affected.

Cassian threw her a grin that declared he was in. And he'd make her crawl before the end.

Nesta merely began to unlace her boots.

He jerked his chin toward Azriel. "Why are you up here?"

"I thought I'd do some training myself before heading out for the day," Az said, his shadows lingering in the archway, as if fearful of the bright sunlight in the ring. "I'm not interrupting anything, am I?"

Cassian could have sworn Nesta's fingers stalled on the laces of her boots. He drawled, "Nothing at all. We're starting on hand-to-hand combat."

"My least favorite," Azriel said.

Toeing off her boots, Nesta asked, "Why?"

Az observed her, striding barefoot into the ring. "I like swordplay better. Hand-to-hand is too close for my tastes."

"He doesn't like getting a face full of someone's armpit sweat," Cassian said, chuckling.

Azriel rolled his eyes but didn't deny it.

Nesta watched the shadowsinger with a frankness that most people shied from. Azriel returned the look with a stillness that most people ran from.

Even Feyre had been hesitant around Az initially, but Nesta considered him with the same unflinching assessment she laid upon everyone.

Maybe that was why Azriel had never said a bad word about Nesta. Never seemed inclined to start a fight with her. She saw him, and was not afraid of him. There weren't many people who fit that bill.

Nesta said, "Show me how you two fight." Azriel blinked, but she added, "I want to know what I'm up against." When neither of them said anything, she asked, "What I saw in battle was different, wasn't it?"

"Yes," Cassian said. "A variation of what we do here, but it requires a different sort of fighting." Shadows clouded her eyes, as if the memory of those battlefields haunted her. He said, "We won't start battle training for a while yet." Years, probably. Az was watching her as if he, too, had marked the shadows in her eyes. Cassian asked him, "You want to do a little sparring? It's been a while since I wiped the floor with you."

He needed to get the energy out—the lingering, addling desire from last night. Needed to burn it from his body through movement and breath.

Az rolled a shoulder, unruffled and calm, eyes glittering as if he marked Cassian's need to expel that coiled-up energy. But Az peeled off his jacket and his shirt, leaving the Siphons atop the backs of his hands, anchored in place around the wrist and through a loop on his middle finger. Cassian did the same as he removed his own shirt.

Nesta's stare seared him from across the ring. Cassian might have flexed his stomach muscles as he approached the chalk-lined circle. Az shook his head and muttered, "Pathetic, Cass."

Cassian winked, nodding to his brother's equally muscled stomach. "Where have you been exercising these days?"

"Here," Azriel said. "At night." After he returned from spying on their enemies.

"Can't sleep?" Cassian took up a fighting stance.

A shadow curled around Azriel's neck, the only one brave enough to face the sunlight. "Something like that," he said, and settled into his own stance across from Cassian.

Cassian let it drop, knowing Az would have told him already if he'd wanted to share what had been hounding him enough to exercise at night, rather than in the morning with them. Cassian explained to Nesta, who stood a few feet outside the chalk ring, "We'll go full speed, then stop, and I'll break it down for you. All right?"

He needed to expunge this energy before he'd dare let himself be that close to her.

Nesta crossed her arms, face so neutral he wondered for a moment if he'd dreamed some wild fantasy last night of his head between her legs.

Shaking off the thought, he again looked to Az. Their eyes met, Az's face as unreadable as Nesta's, and Cassian gave a nod. *Begin.*

It started with footwork: a slow circling, an assessment, waiting for the other to reveal his first move.

Cassian knew Az's tricks. Knew which side Az favored and how he liked to strike.

The problem was, Az knew all of his techniques and shortcomings, too.

They circled each other again, Cassian's feet pounding a steady beat on the dry ground.

"Well?" he asked Az. "Why don't you show me what all that nighttime brooding has resulted in?"

Az's mouth curved. He refused to take the bait.

The sun beat down on them, warming Cassian's bare skin and hair.

"Is this really all it is?" Nesta asked. "Circling and taunting?"

Cassian didn't dare look her way. Not even for an instant. As soon as he so much as blinked at her, Azriel would strike, and strike hard. But—

Cassian grinned. And glanced toward Nesta.

Az fell for his deception, launching toward him at last.

Cassian, waiting for it, met the fist Az sent flying for his face, blocking and deflecting and counterstriking. Az caught the blow, ducked the second Cassian had waiting, and aimed one for Cassian's exposed ribs.

Cassian blocked, counterpunched, and then the sparring unfolded.

Fists and feet and wings, punch and block, kick and stomp, breath sawing out of them as he and Az tried to break past each other's defenses. Neither of them put the full force of their bodies into the blows—not the way they'd do in a real brawl, when one punch could shatter a jaw. But they used enough power to make Cassian's ribs bleat at the impact, to make Az whoosh out a breath as Cassian landed a lucky hit to his stomach. Az was spared from having the air knocked out of him by twisting, otherwise the fight would have ended right then and there.

Around and around the ring, fists flying, teeth bared in fierce grins, they lost themselves to sweat and sun and breathing. They'd been born for such things, endured centuries of training that had honed their bodies into instruments of violence. To allow their bodies to do just what they wished was its own sort of freedom.

Faster and faster they fought, and even Cassian's breathing became labored. Though Cassian had more bulk, Azriel was quick as hell—they were evenly matched. They might be at this for hours, if they were truly facing each other as enemies. Might have been at it for days, if they'd been opponents in one of the old wars, where entire battles had come to a standstill to watch great heroes go head-to-head.

But time wasn't unlimited, and he did have a lesson to get through with Nesta.

"Right," Cassian panted through gritted teeth as he blocked Az's kick and bounced a step back, circling again. "Whoever lands the next blow wins."

"That's ridiculous," Az panted back. "We go until one of us eats dirt."

Az had a vicious competitive streak. It wasn't boastful and arrogant, the way Cassian knew he himself was prone to be, or possessive and terrifying like Amren's. No, it was quiet and cruel and utterly lethal. Cassian had lost track of how many games they'd played over the centuries, with one of them certain of a win, only for Az to reveal some master strategy. Or how many games had been reduced to only Rhys and Az left standing, battling it out over cards or chess until the middle of the night, when Cassian and Mor had given up and started drinking.

They circled again, but Az snapped his head toward Nesta, eyes wide.

Cassian looked, heart leaping into his throat—

Azriel struck, a punch to the jaw hard enough that Cassian staggered.

Reeling, steadying himself, he cursed.

Az let out a soft laugh, eyes flickering. He'd wielded the same deception that Cassian had used at the start of this, played the one card that would get Cassian to remove his focus from an opponent.

It had happened before—against Hybern. Nesta had screamed his name, and even in the midst of the battlefield, he'd abandoned his soldiers and rushed for her, not caring about anything other than reaching her, saving her.

Only, Nesta had saved him. And she had screamed his name to get him out of the Cauldron's range.

His soldiers had been blasted apart a moment later. And when he'd looked at her face, he'd understood something—something that the past year and a half had shredded apart and turned cold.

Cassian rolled his shoulder, hand at his jaw as he said to Az, "Bastard."

Az laughed again, and they turned toward Nesta.

She remained a pillar of cool calm, but a line of color stained her cheeks.

There was no wind to blow her scent to him, but from the way her throat bobbed as she glanced between them . . .

Azriel let out a cough and walked toward the water station.

"You're drooling," Cassian said to her, and Nesta went rigid.

"If there was anything enticing," she hissed, entering the ring, "it was seeing Azriel punch your face."

Cassian motioned for her to get into her fighting stance. "Keep telling yourself that, Nes."

✠

"What do you know of the Dread Trove?"

"The what?" Gwyn turned from the desk where Nesta had found the priestess singing softly to herself, situated just outside Merrill's shut office door.

"The Dread Trove," Nesta said, wincing at her sore body's protestations as she took a seat on the edge of Gwyn's desk. "Three ancient artifacts . . ."

Gwyn shook her head. "I've never heard of such a thing."

Nesta was still sweaty from the lesson with Cassian and Azriel. They'd walked her through the punches and kicks and steps they'd done with ease, though neither had laughed when she was clumsy or ungraceful.

Seeing them spar had been overwhelming. Their beautiful forms, tattooed and scarred and carved with muscle, gleaming with sweat as they fought with a viciousness and intelligence she'd never seen . . . She'd been sweating herself when they'd finished, wondering what it'd be like to be between those two male bodies, letting them turn all that lethal attention on worshipping her.

Elain would faint to hear such thoughts. And to hear that Nesta had already had two males in her bed not once but twice, and had enjoyed every second of it. But the males Nesta had shared herself with hadn't looked like Cassian and Azriel. Hadn't *been* Cassian and Azriel.

Nesta had made herself focus during the lesson, but as soon as she'd left them in the training ring, filthy thoughts had poured in, leaving her half-distracted while she'd walked down to the library. The thought of Cassian pumping into her mouth while Azriel pounded into her from behind, the two of them working her in tandem—

Talking to Gwyn about the Dread Trove had sobered her up fast enough.

"It seems like the Trove has a glamour to make people forget that it exists," Nesta said to Gwyn, and succinctly explained what it was, along with vague details about why it was wanted. She didn't mention Queen Briallyn, or Koschei, or the Cauldron. Only that the Trove must be found quickly. And that Gwyn should not mention it to anyone.

Nesta supposed that in doing so, she directly disobeyed Rhys's order for silence, but . . . to hell with him.

When she was done, Gwyn was wide-eyed, her face so pale that her freckles stood out in stark relief. "And you must find it?"

"I don't have the faintest idea where to begin looking. Which one to find first."

Gwyn chewed on her bottom lip. "We do have an extensive card-cataloging system," she mused idly, but peered toward the stacks beyond them, to the open pit at the bottom of the library. "But they don't list what's below Level Seven."

"I know."

Gwyn angled her head. "So why come to me?"

"You're clearly good at what you do, if you're working with someone as demanding as Merrill. If you have a spare moment, any help would be appreciated. Or just point me in a direction."

"Let me finish proofing this chapter and then I'll see what I can discover."

Nesta offered a tight smile. "Thank you."

Gwyn waved a hand. "Finding objects to help our court protect the world is rather exciting. About as exciting as I'm willing to get these days, but it shall be an adventure."

"You could come to training if you want another sort of adventure," Nesta said carefully.

Gwyn offered her a tight smile. "That's not for me, I'm afraid."

"Why not?"

Gwyn gestured to Nesta's fighting leathers, the overlapping scales. "I'm not a warrior."

"Neither am I. But you could be."

Gwyn shook her head. "I don't think so. If I wished to be a warrior, I would have gone that route as a child. Instead I offered myself as an acolyte—and that is what I am."

"You don't have to give up one thing to be the other. Training is exercise. Learning to breathe and stretch and fight. Aren't you researching Valkyries for Merrill? That might even give you further insight." Nesta patted a thigh. "And I already have muscle building up. Two weeks, and I can tell the difference."

"Why would a priestess need muscular thighs?"

Nesta narrowed her eyes as Gwyn went back to her work. "Is it Cassian?"

"Cassian is a good and honorable male."

"I know he is." She'd always known it. She pressed, "But is it Cassian's presence that makes you hesitate?"

There had been no hint this morning as to what had gone on between them last night. As if the debt between them had been paid, and he had no further interest in touching her. Like she was an itch scratched, and that was it. Or perhaps he had not enjoyed it as she had.

It unsettled her, that she spent so much time thinking about it.

Gwyn didn't answer, and Nesta knew she had no right to push, not when color stole over Gwyn's cheeks and her head bowed slightly. Shame—it was shame and fear.

Something in Nesta's chest tightened as she began to walk away. "All right. Let me know if you learn anything regarding the Trove."

Nesta mulled the conversation over during the hours she worked. When she checked the sign-up sheet as she left the library at sundown, no names had been added.

She felt Clotho's eyes on her as she surveyed the empty page. Nesta at last turned toward the priestess, seated at her desk with her hands folded before her. Silence stretched between them, but Nesta said nothing as she left.

She went to the stairwell rather than to her room or the dining room, and stared down into the curving redness of the steps.

Nesta began the descent, slower this time, contemplating each placement of her foot. Let each step downward be a thought, a piece of one of Amren's puzzles, that she sifted through.

Down and down she went, turning over each word and glance from Gwyn during the time Nesta had worked in the library. *Step to step*, she told herself with each burning, trembling movement of her legs. *Step to step to step*.

Again, she replayed the conversation. Each step was a different word, or motion, or scent.

Nesta was on step two thousand when she halted.

She knew what she had to do.

CHAPTER 24

Five days later, Cassian sat before the desk of the library's high priestess and watched her enchanted pen move. He'd met Clotho a few times over the centuries—found she had a dry, wicked sense of humor and a soothing presence. He'd made a point not to stare at her hands, or at the face he'd only seen once, when Mor had brought her in so long ago. It had been so battered and bloody it hadn't looked like a face at all.

He had no idea how it had healed beneath the hood. If Madja had been able to save it in a way she hadn't been able to save Clotho's hands. He supposed it didn't matter what she looked like, not when she had accomplished and built so much with Rhys and Mor within this library. A sanctuary for females who'd endured such unspeakable horrors that he was always happy to carry out justice on their behalf.

His mother had needed a place like this. But Rhys had established it long after she'd left this world. He wondered if Azriel's mother had ever considered coming here, or if he'd ever pushed her to.

"Well, Clotho," he said, leaning back in the chair, surrounded by the sounds of rustling parchment and the robes of the priestesses like fluttering wings, "you asked for an audience?"

Her pen made a flourish as it finished what she'd been writing.

I have asked Nesta twice now not to practice in the library, and she has disregarded my request. For five days, she has blatantly ignored my commands to stop.

Cassian's brows rose. "She's practicing down here?"

Again, the pen scraped over the paper. He glanced to the open pit to his left, as if he'd spot Nesta down there. A week had passed since that madness in her bedroom, and they had not spoken of it, done nothing further. He wasn't entirely sure it would be wise to continue.

In addition to the grueling set of exercises to hone her body, Cassian had walked her through the minutiae of hand-to-hand combat, individual steps and movements that could be assembled in endless combinations. Learning each of those steps required not just strength but focus—to remember which movement correlated with the numbered step, to let her body start to remember all on its own: a jab, a hook, a high kick . . . He'd lost count of how many times he'd caught her muttering at her body to remember so she didn't need to *think* so hard.

But he knew she liked the punches. The kicks. A light shone in her face as her body flowed through the motions, a slingshot of strength all narrowing to a point of impact. He'd always felt that way when he did the movements correctly, like his body and mind and soul had lined up and begun singing.

Clotho wrote, *Nesta has practiced constantly of late.*

"Has she done any damage?"

No. But I asked her to stop, and she has not.

He suppressed his smile. Perhaps the morning lessons weren't demanding enough. "Is her work suffering for it?"

No. That's beside the point.

His mouth twisted to the side.

Clotho wrote, *I need you to put a stop to this.*

"Does it bother the others?"

It distracts them, to see someone kicking and punching at shadows.

Cassian had to duck his head so she wouldn't read the amusement in his eyes. "I'll talk to her. Is she down there now?" He nodded to the sloping ramp. "With your permission, of course."

This was their safe harbor. It didn't matter if he was a member of Rhys's court, or that he'd come here before. Every time, he asked permission. He'd only ever failed to do so once: when Hybern's Ravens had attacked.

Yes. I give you permission to enter. Nesta is on Level Five. Perhaps you shall manage to get through to her.

Taking that as his cue, Cassian rose. "You do know this is Nesta Archeron we're talking about? She does nothing unless she wishes to. And she's the least likely to listen to me."

Clotho huffed a laugh. *She has a will of iron.*

"Of steel." He smiled. "Good seeing you, Clotho."

You as well, Lord Cassian.

"Just Cassian," he said, as he had said so many times now.

You are a lord in good deeds. It is not a title born, but earned.

He bowed his head as he said thickly, "Thank you."

It took him until he reached the section where Clotho had said Nesta would be to shake off the high priestess's words. What they meant to him.

The scuffing steps greeted him first, then the steady, rhythmic breathing he'd come to know so intimately. Cassian made his breathing match it, turned his own steps silent, and peered into the next row of stacks.

Anyone walking along the ramp would only have to look to the right to see Nesta standing there, in a near-perfect fighting stance, throwing punches toward the shelf. She'd picked five books as targets and worked through each punch toward them as if they were the parts on a body he'd shown her where to strike.

Then she halted, blew out a breath and brushed back a strand of errant hair, and straightened the books before returning to the metal cart behind her.

"You're still dropping your elbow," he said, and she whirled, falling back against the cart with enough surprise that he swallowed his laugh. He'd never seen Nesta Archeron so . . . ruffled.

She lifted her chin as she stalked toward him. He watched every movement of her legs. She'd stopped throwing her weight onto her right leg so much, and muscles shifted in her thighs, sleek and strong. Three weeks might not be much time for a human body to pack on muscle, but she was High Fae now. "I'm not dropping my elbow," she challenged, emerging from the row of stacks and into the flat area before the slope of the ramp.

"I just saw you do it twice with that right hook."

She leaned against the end of a long shelf. "I assume Clotho sent you to reprimand me."

He shrugged. "I didn't know you were so invested in the training that you kept at it down here."

Her eyes practically glowed in the dimness. "I'm tired of being weak. Of depending on others to defend me."

Fair enough. "Before I dispense with the lecture about ignoring Clotho's requests, let me just say that—"

"Show me." Nesta stepped away from the shelf and squared off against him. "Show me where I'm dropping my elbow."

He blinked at the rippling intensity in her face. Then he swallowed.

Swallowed, because there she was: a glimpse of that person he'd known before the war with Hybern had ended. A glimmer of her, like a mirage—like if he looked at it too long, she'd slip away and vanish.

So Cassian said, "Get into your stance."

Nesta obeyed.

Hoping Clotho wouldn't come shove him over the railing for disobeying her orders, he said, "All right. Throw the right hook."

Nesta did so. And dropped her damn elbow.

"Get back into position." She did, and he asked, "May I?"

Nesta nodded, and kept perfectly still as he made minute adjustments to the angle of her arm. "Punch again. Slowly."

She heeded him, and his hand wrapped around her elbow as it began to dip. "See? Keep this up." He maneuvered her arm back into starting position. "Don't forget to flow the weight through your hips." He took her arm, keeping a good foot of distance between their bodies, and moved it through the punch. "Like this."

"All right." Nesta reset herself, and he took a step away. Without his order, she did the punch again. Perfectly.

Cassian whistled.

"Do that with more force and you'll shatter a male's jaw," he said with a crooked grin. "Give me a combination one-two, then four-five-three, then one-one-two."

Nesta's brows bunched as she reset herself. Her feet shifted into position, grounding her weight into the stone floor.

And then she moved, and it was like watching a river, like watching the wind cut through a mountain. Not perfect, but close.

"If you did that against an opponent," Cassian said, "they'd be on the ground, gasping for air."

"And then I'd make the kill."

"Yes, a sword through the heart would finish the job. But if you struck their chest hard enough with that final punch, you might make one of their lungs collapse. On a battlefield, you'd opt for either the killing blow with a sword or just leave them there, unable to move, for someone else to finish off while you face the next opponent."

She nodded, as if this all seemed like perfectly normal conversation. Like he was giving her gardening tips.

"All right." Cassian cleared his throat and tucked back his wings, "so, no more practicing in the library. The next person Clotho asks to scold you probably won't be someone you feel like talking to."

Nesta's eyes darkened as she considered which of her least favorite people it would be, and she nodded again.

His task done, he said, "Give me one more combination." He rattled off the order.

Her smile was nothing short of feline as she did just that. And her right hook didn't so much as bob downward.

"Good," he said, and turned toward the ramp that would lead him out.

He startled at what he beheld: priestesses stopped along the railings on several different levels, staring toward them. Toward Nesta.

At his attention, they instantly began walking or working or shelving books. But a young priestess with coppery-brown hair—the only one of them with no hood or stone—lingered at the rail the longest. Even from a level below and across the pit, he could see that her large eyes were the color of shallow, warm water. They were wide for a moment before she, too, quickly vanished.

Cassian looked back to Nesta, who met his stare with near-simmering eyes.

"Your right hook was perfect this morning," he murmured.

"Yes."

"But not when I watched you in the stacks."

"I figured you'd correct me."

Shock and delight slammed into him. She'd moved out of the stacks before she let him do so. Into plain view. So they would all see him teaching her.

He gaped at her.

"You can tell Clotho I won't need to practice in the library anymore," Nesta said mildly, and turned back down the row.

She'd known Clotho and the others would never invite him, and never go up to the ring to see what he could do. How he'd teach them. So she'd shown the priestesses what she was learning, day after day.

More than that, she'd pissed off Clotho enough that the priestess had ordered him down here.

Where Nesta had used him in a demonstration. Not for herself, but for the priestesses who'd drifted over to watch.

Cassian let out a soft laugh. "Crafty, Archeron."

Nesta lifted a hand over a shoulder in farewell as she reached her cart.

✣

They'd needed to see it, Nesta realized. What Cassian was like when he taught her. That there was touching, but it was always with her permission, and always professional. Needed to see how he never mocked her, only gently corrected. And needed to see what he'd taught her. Hear him say precisely what she could do with all those punching and kicking combinations.

What the priestesses might learn to do.

But that evening, as Nesta left, the sign-up sheet remained blank.

She looked back at Clotho, who sat at her desk, as she always did, from dawn until dusk.

If the priestess gathered that she'd been played, she didn't let on. But there was something like sorrow leaking from Clotho, as if she, too, had wanted to see that sheet filled today.

Nesta didn't know why it mattered. Why Clotho's sorrow knocked the wind from her, but then Nesta was moving, up through the House to the ten thousand steps.

Perhaps she was good for nothing after all. Perhaps she'd been a fool to think that this trick might convince them. Maybe physical training wasn't what they required to overcome their demons, and she'd been arrogant enough to assume she knew what they needed.

Down and down the stairs Nesta walked, the walls pressing in.

She only made it to stair nine hundred before she turned around, her steps as heavy as if they'd been weighed with lead blocks.

Nesta was still sweating and breathing hard when she stumbled into her room and found a book on the nightstand. She raised a brow at the title. "This isn't your usual sort of romance," she said to the room.

It wasn't a romance at all. It was an old bound manuscript called *The Dance of Battle*.

Nesta said, "You can take this one back, thank you." The last thing she wanted to read at night was some dreary old text about war strategy. The House did no such thing, and Nesta sighed and picked up the manuscript, the black leather binding so age-worn it was butter soft.

A familiar smell drifted to her from the pages. "You didn't leave this for me, did you?"

The House replied by plopping down a stack of romances, as if to say, *This is what I would have chosen.*

Nesta peered at the manuscript, full of Cassian's scent, as if he'd read it a thousand times.

He'd left it for her. Deemed her worthy of whatever lay inside.

Nesta perched on the edge of the bed and thumbed open the text.

✢

It was midnight when she took a break from reading *The Dance of Battle* and rubbed her temples. She hadn't put it down, not even to eat dinner at her desk, holding it with one hand while she devoured her stew with the other.

It was astonishing how much of the art of warfare was like the social manipulation her mother had insisted she learn: picking battlegrounds, finding allies amongst the enemies of one's enemies . . . Some of it was wholly new, of course, and such a precise way of thinking that she knew she'd have to read the manuscript many times to fully grasp its lessons.

She'd been aware that Cassian knew how to lead armies. Had watched him do so with unflinching precision and cleverness. But reading the manuscript, she realized she had never understood just how much advanced thinking went into planning battles and wars.

Nesta set the manuscript on her nightstand and lay back against her pillows.

She pictured Cassian on a battlefield, as he'd been that day he'd gone up against a Hybern commander and thrown a spear so hard the male had been hurled from his horse upon impact.

He departed from the manuscript's advice in only one way: he fought on the front lines with his soldiers, rather than commanding from the rear.

She let her thoughts drift for a time, until they snared upon another tangle of thorns.

Did it matter if the priestesses didn't show up for training? Beyond her own reluctance to concede failure, did it matter?

It did. Somehow, it did.

She had failed in every aspect of her life. Utterly and spectacularly failed, and keeping others from realizing it had been her main purpose. She had shut them out, had shut herself out, because the weight of all those failures threatened to shatter her into a thousand pieces.

Nesta rubbed her face with her hands.

Sleep was a long time coming.

✠

Sweat was still running down her body when Nesta entered the library the next afternoon, aiming for the ramp to take her down to where she'd left her cart.

She didn't have the courage to look at the empty sign-up sheet. To rip it down.

She didn't have the courage to look at Clotho and admit her defeat. She kept walking.

But Clotho halted her with an upraised hand. Nesta swallowed. "What?"

Clotho pointed behind Nesta, her gnarled finger indicating the doorway. No, the pillar.

And it was not sorrow leaking from the priestess, but something like buzzing excitement. Something that made Nesta whirl on her heel and stride for the pillar.

A name had been scrawled on the sheet.

One name, in bold letters. One name, ready for tomorrow's lesson.

GWYN

PART TWO

BLADE

CHAPTER 25

"Stop looking so nervous," Cassian muttered out of the corner of his mouth.

"I'm not nervous," Nesta muttered back, even as she bounced on her feet, trying not to stare toward the open archway as the clock ticked toward nine.

"Just relax." He straightened his jacket.

"You're the one fidgeting," she hissed.

"Because *you're* making me fidget."

Steps scuffed on the stone beyond the archway, and Nesta's breath rushed from her in a wave she didn't realize she was holding back as Gwyn's coppery-brown hair appeared. In the sunlight, the color of her hair was extraordinary, strands of gold glinting, and her teal eyes were a near-perfect match to the stones the other priestesses wore.

Gwyn beheld them standing in the center of the ring and stopped short.

The tang of her fear set Nesta approaching. "Hello."

Gwyn's hands were shaking as she took another step into the ring and peered into the open bowl of the sky.

The first time she'd been outside—truly outside—in years.

Cassian, to his credit, moved to the rack of wooden practice weapons that he'd claimed they wouldn't be using for months, and pretended to adjust them.

Gwyn swallowed. "I, um—I realized on the way up here that I don't have proper clothes." She gestured to her pale robes. "I suspect these will not be ideal."

Cassian said without looking over, "I can teach you in the robes, if you wish. Whatever's most comfortable."

Gwyn offered him a tight smile. "I'll see how today's lesson goes and then decide. We wear the robes mostly from tradition, not strict rules." She met Nesta's gaze again as she smiled. "I forgot how it feels to have the full sun upon my head." She peered up again. "Forgive me if I spend some time gawking at the sky."

"Of course," Nesta said. She hadn't encountered Gwyn yesterday after seeing that she'd signed up for this morning's lesson, but she'd been almost afraid to—worried that one accidentally uttered sour remark would make Gwyn reconsider.

Words stalled in Nesta's throat, but Cassian seemed to anticipate that. "All right. No more chitchat. Nes, show our new friend—Gwyn, is it? I'm Cassian. Nes, show her your feet."

"Feet?" Gwyn's copper brows rose.

Nesta rolled her eyes. "You'll see."

⁜

Gwyn grasped the concept of grounding through her feet better than Nesta had, and certainly had no issues with dropping her weight into her right hip and other things Nesta had worked to correct for three weeks. Even with the robes, it was clear that Gwyn was built lithe and lean, accustomed to the casual grace of the Fae that Nesta was only learning.

She'd expected to have to coax her friend, but once Gwyn overcame her initial trepidation, she was a willing participant, and a merry companion. The priestess laughed at her own mistakes, and did not bristle at corrections from Cassian.

By the end of the lesson, though, Gwyn's robe was damp with sweat, tendrils of hair curling around her flushed face. Cassian ordered them to drink some water before their cooldown.

As Gwyn poured herself a glass, she said, "At the temple in Sangravah, we had a set of ancient movements that we would go through every sunrise. Not for battle training, but for calming the mind. We did cooldowns after those, too, though we called them groundings. The movements took us out of our bodies, in a way. Let us commune with the Mother. The groundings settled us back into the present world."

"Why did you sign up for this, then?" Nesta drank the glass Gwyn extended. "If you already have mind-calming exercises you're accustomed to?"

"Because I don't ever want to feel powerless again," Gwyn said softly, and all those easy smiles and bright laughs were gone. Only stark, pained honesty shone in her remarkable eyes.

Nesta swallowed, and though instinct told her to pull away, she said quietly, "Me too."

✣

The bell above the shop door jangled as Nesta entered, brushing off the snowflakes that had stuck to the shoulders of her cloak. Cassian had needed to go up to the Illyrian Mountains after their second lesson with Gwyn, and to her surprise, he had asked Nesta to join him. He'd already cleared it with Clotho that she'd be a few hours late for her work at the library. He hadn't explained why beyond a casual comment about getting her out of the House and into the fresh air.

But she'd accepted, and hadn't told him why, either. Cassian hadn't even seemed curious when she requested he leave her at Windhaven so she could go shopping. Perhaps a spark had gleamed in his eye, as if he'd guessed, but he'd been distant, quiet.

Given that Cassian was up here to meet with Eris, she didn't blame him. He'd left Nesta by the fountain in the center of the freezing village, making sure she knew that if she needed to warm up, Rhys's mother's house was unlocked.

Velaris was still gripped in summer's hand, autumn just barely tugging it away, but Windhaven had already yielded completely to winter's embrace. Nesta wasted little time in entering the shop.

"Nesta," Emerie said by way of greeting, peering over a young-looking male's broad shoulder and wings from where she stood helping him at the counter. "It's good to see you."

Was that relief in her voice? Nesta made sure the door behind her was firmly latched before striding in, the snow on her boots leaving muddy tracks alongside those left by Emerie's customer.

The male half-turned toward Nesta, revealing a blandly handsome face, dark hair tied back at the nape of his neck, and glassy brown eyes. The asshole was drunk. *Asshole* seemed to be the correct term, since Emerie's rigid posture revealed distaste and wariness.

Nesta sauntered up to the counter, giving the male a once-over that she knew usually made people want to throttle her. From the way he stiffened, swaying slightly on his booted feet, she knew it'd worked. "Good morning," she said cheerfully to Emerie. Another thing males seemed to detest: being ignored by a female.

"Wait your turn, witch," the male grumbled, turning back to the counter and Emerie.

Emerie crossed her arms. "I think we're done here, Bellius."

"We're done when I say we're done." The words were half-slurred.

"I have an appointment," Nesta said, leveling a cool glance at him. She sniffed at the male. Her nose crinkled. "And you seem to need an appointment with a bath."

He turned fully to her, muscled shoulders pushing back. Even with the glazed expression, ire boiled in his stare. "Do you know who I am?"

"A drunk fool wasting my time," Nesta said. Two Siphons—a blue darker than Azriel's—sat atop the backs of his large hands. "Get out."

Emerie stilled, as if bracing herself for the retaliation. But she said before the male could reply, "We'll discuss this later, Bellius."

"My father sent me to convey a message."

"Message received," Emerie said, chin lifting. "And my answer is the same: this store is mine. If he wants one so badly, he can open his own."

"Hateful bitch," Bellius bit out, swaying back a step.

Nesta laughed, cold and hollow. Fae and humans had more in common than she'd realized. How many times had she witnessed her father's debtors darkening their doorstep to shake him down for money he didn't have? And then there had been the time when they had gone beyond threats. When they'd left her father's leg shattered. Any sense of safety shattered with it.

"Get out," Nesta said again, pointing to the door as Bellius bristled at her fading laughter. "Do yourself a favor and get out."

Bellius rose to his full height, wings flaring. "Or what?"

Nesta picked at her nails. "I don't think you want to find out the *or what* part."

Bellius opened his mouth, but Emerie said, "Your father now has my answer, Bellius. I suggest you get some water from the fountain before you fly home."

Bellius only spat onto the floorboards and stalked for the exit, throwing Nesta a hazy glare as he slammed the door behind himself.

In silence, Nesta and Emerie watched him stagger into the snow-swept street and spread his wings. Nesta frowned as he shot into the sky.

"Friend of yours?" Nesta asked, facing Emerie at the counter again.

"My cousin." Emerie cringed. "His father is my uncle. On my father's side." She added before Nesta could ask, "Bellius is a young, arrogant idiot. He's due to participate in the Blood Rite this spring, and his arrogance has only grown these past months as he anticipates becoming a true warrior. He's skilled enough that he got placed on a scouting unit to the continent—and just returned to celebrate his accomplishment, apparently." Emerie wiped at an invisible speck of dirt on the counter. "I didn't expect him to be drunk midday, though. That's a new low for him." Color stained her cheeks. "I'm sorry you had to witness it."

Nesta shrugged. "Dealing with drunk fools is my specialty."

Emerie kept fiddling with the imaginary spot on the counter. "Our fathers were two of a kind. They believed children should be harshly disciplined for any infraction. There was little room for mercy or understanding."

Nesta pursed her lips. "I know the type." Her mother's mother had been the same way before she'd died of a deep-rooted cough that had turned into a deadly infection. Nesta had been seven when the stern-faced dame who had insisted on being called Grandmamma had beaten her palms raw with a ruler for missteps in her dancing lessons. *Worthless, clumsy girl. You're a waste of my time. Maybe this will help you remember to pay attention to my orders.*

Nesta had only felt relief when the old beast had died. Elain, who'd been spared the cruelties of Grandmamma's tutelage, had wept and dutifully laid flowers at her grave—one soon joined by their mother's stone marker. Feyre had been too young to understand, but Nesta had never bothered to lay flowers for her grandmamma. Not when Nesta bore a scar near her left thumb from one of the woman's nastier punishments. Nesta had only left flowers for her mother, whose grave she had visited more often than she cared to admit.

She hadn't once visited her father's grave outside Velaris.

"Are you all right?" Nesta asked Emerie at last. "Will Bellius return?"

"No," Emerie said, shaking her head. "I mean, I'm fine. But no—he's a member of the Ironcrest war-band. Their lands are a few hours' flight from here. He won't return anytime soon." She shrugged. "I get these little visits from my uncle's family every now and then. Nothing I can't handle. Though Bellius was a new one. I guess they think he's adult enough now to bully me." Nesta opened her mouth, but Emerie offered her another half smile and changed the subject. "You look well. Far healthier than when I saw you . . . What was it now? Almost three weeks ago." She gave Nesta an assessing glance. "You never came back."

"We moved our training to Velaris," Nesta explained.

"I was about to write to you before Bellius interrupted me. I asked about making leathers with fleece inside." Emerie leaned her forearms on the immaculate counter. "It can be done, but it's not cheap."

"Then it's beyond my means, but thank you for finding out anyway."

"I could order it and let you pay it off as you're able."

It was a generous offer. Far beyond the kindness anyone had ever shown Nesta in the human realm, when her father had been trying to sell his wood carvings for a few pitiful coppers.

Only Feyre had kept them fed and clothed, earning scant amounts for the pelts and meat she hunted. She'd kept them alive. The last time she'd hunted for them, the food had run out the day before. If Feyre hadn't returned home with meat that night, they either would have had to starve to death or beg in the village.

Nesta had told herself that day that Tomas would take her in, if necessary. Maybe even Elain, too. But his family had been hateful, with too many mouths to feed already. His father would have refused to feed her, without question. She'd been prepared to offer the only thing she had to barter to Tomas, if it would have kept Elain from starving. Would have sold her body on the street to anyone who'd pay her enough to feed her sister. Her body had meant nothing to her—nothing, she'd told herself as she'd felt her options closing in. Elain meant everything.

But Feyre had come back with that food. And then vanished over the wall.

Three days afterward, Nesta broke it off with Tomas. Enraged, he'd launched himself at her, pinning her against the enormous woodpile stacked along the barn wall. *Spiteful whore*, he'd growled. *You think you're better than me? Acting like a queen when you haven't got shit*. She'd never forget the sound of her dress tearing, the greed in his eyes as his hands pawed at her skirts, trying to raise them as he fumbled with the buckle on his belt.

Only pure, undiluted terror and survival instinct had saved her. She'd let him get close, let him think her strength had failed, and then clamped her teeth down on his ear. And ripped.

He'd screamed, but he'd loosened his grip on her—just enough that she'd broken free and scrambled through the snow, spitting his blood out of her mouth, and did not stop running until she'd reached the cottage.

And then word had come of their father's ships: found, with all the wealth intact.

Nesta knew it was a lie. The trunks of jewels and gold had not come from that doomed shipment, but from Tamlin, payment for the human woman he'd stolen away. To help the family he'd doomed to die without Feyre's hunting.

Nesta shook off the memory. "It's all right. But thank you."

Emerie rubbed her long, slender hands together. "It's freezing, and I'm about to take my lunch break. Would you like to join me?"

Beyond Cassian, no one had invited her to dine in a long time. She'd given them no reason to. But there it was: an honest, simple offer. From someone who had no idea how terrible she was.

Having lunch with Emerie was an indulgence; it was only a matter of time until the female learned more about Nesta. Until she heard every horrible thing, and then the invitations would stop. Had she been any better than Bellius, drunk and simmering with hatred for months? If Emerie knew, she'd kick her out of this shop, too.

But for now, neither rumor nor truth had reached Emerie.

"I would like that," Nesta said, and meant it.

✠

The back room of Emerie's shop was as immaculate as the front, though crates of extra stock were stacked against one wall. Two windows looked out onto a snow-covered garden, and beyond that, the nearest mountain peak squatted, blocking the gray sky with its rocky bulk.

A small kitchen lay to the right, little more than a hearth and a counter and a small worktable. A few wooden chairs sat around it, and Nesta realized the table was also the dining area. A place setting had been laid there for one person.

"Just you?" Nesta asked as Emerie went to the wood counter and gathered a platter of roast beef and a dish of roasted carrots. She set them on the table before Nesta and grabbed a loaf of bread, along with a bowl of butter.

"Just me." Emerie opened a cabinet to retrieve a second place setting. "No mate or husband to bother me."

She spoke a bit tensely, like there was more to it than that, but Nesta said, "Me neither."

Emerie threw her a wry look. "What about that handsome General Cassian?"

Nesta blocked out the memory of his head between her thighs, his tongue at her entrance, sliding into her. "Not a chance," Nesta said, but Emerie's eyes glimmered with knowing.

"Well, it's nice to meet another female who's not obsessed with marriage and baby-making," Emerie said, sitting at the table and gesturing for Nesta to do the same. She'd put some roast beef, carrots, and bread onto Nesta's plate, and slid the bowl of butter to her. "It's cold, but it's meant to be eaten that way. I usually stop for lunch only long enough to feed myself."

Nesta dug in and grunted. "It's delicious." She took another bite. "Did you make this?"

"Who else would? We don't have any sort of food shops here except the butcher." Emerie pointed with her fork to the garden beyond the building. "I grow my own vegetables. These carrots came from that garden."

Nesta took a bite. "They have a lovely flavor." Butter and thyme and something bright . . .

"It's all in the spices. Which are in short supply around here, unfortunately. Illyrians don't particularly know or care about them."

"My father used to be a merchant," Nesta said, a chasm yawning open in her at the words. She cleared her throat. "He traded spices from all over the world. I can still remember the smell in his offices—it was like a thousand different personalities all crammed into one space."

Feyre had loved to hang about their father's office, more fascinated in the trade than what Nesta had been taught was acceptable for a wealthy girl. Feyre had always been that way: completely uninterested in the rules that governed their lives, uninterested in becoming a true lady who would help advance their family's fortunes through an advantageous marriage.

They had rarely agreed on anything. And those visits to their father's offices had resulted in a simmering resentment between them. Feyre had tried to get her interested, had shown her so many rarities to tempt her. But Nesta had barely listened to her sister's explanations, mostly eyeing up their father's business partners for whether their sons might be a good match. Feyre had been disgusted. It had made Nesta even more determined.

"Did you travel with him?"

"No, my two sisters and I remained home. It wasn't appropriate for us to travel the world."

"I always forget how similar human ideas of propriety are to the

Illyrians'." Emerie took another bite. "Would you have wanted to see the world, if you could?"

"It was half a world, wasn't it? With the wall in place."

"Still better than nothing."

Nesta chuckled. "You're right." She considered Emerie's question. If her father had offered to bring them on one of his ships, to let them see strange and distant shores, would they have gone? Elain had always wanted to visit the continent to study the tulips and other famed flowers, but her imagination had stretched no further. Feyre had talked once about the glorious art in the continent's museums and private estates. But that was all the western edge of it. Beyond that, the continent was vast. And to the south, another continent sprawled. Would she have gone?

"I would have put up a fight," Nesta said at last, "but in the end, I'd have yielded to curiosity."

"Do you still have any family in the human lands?"

"My mother died when I was twelve, and my father . . . He did not survive the most recent war. Their parents died during my childhood. I have no kin on my father's side, and my mother had one cousin, who lives on the continent and conveniently forgot about us when we fell on hard times."

Nesta had written letter after letter when they'd fallen into poverty, begging her cousin Urstin to take them in. They'd gone unanswered, and then the money for postage had run out. Nesta still wondered if their cousin had ever learned what had become of the relatives she'd ignored and left to die.

Nesta asked carefully, "What about your family?" She'd seen and heard enough from Bellius to have a general idea, but she couldn't help asking.

"Mother died giving birth to me, and my elder brother died in a skirmish between war-bands ten years before I was born. My father died during the war with Hybern." The words were stiff, cold. "I do not bother with the rest of my kin, though my father's family makes it a point to try to claim this store and his wealth as their own."

"They're not entitled to it, are they?"

"No. Rhysand changed the inheritance laws centuries ago to include females, but my uncles don't seem to care. They still show up every now and then to bother me like Bellius did. They believe a woman should not run her own business, that I should wed a male in this village and leave the store to them." She grimaced. "They're vultures."

Emerie had finished her lunch and poured some tea for each of them. "It's a shame that you won't be coming up here very often. I could use another sensible person to talk to."

Nesta blinked at the compliment, the bit of truth it revealed about Emerie: she was unhappy in this place. All those questions about traveling . . . "Would you ever move away?"

Emerie choked on a laugh. "And go where? At least here I know people. I've never left this village. Never even been up to that mountaintop over there." She gestured to the window, and Nesta made it a point not to look at her wings.

Nesta sipped from her tea. It was a strong brew, with a bit of a bite. She must have made a face because Emerie explained quietly, "Tea is in short supply here—a luxury that I indulge. But to spread it out, I add a little willow bark to it. It also helps with some of my . . . pains."

"What pains?"

"My wings sometimes hurt. The scars, I mean. Like an old wound."

Nesta kept her pity tamped down. She finished her tea right as Emerie did, and said, "Thank you for the food." Rising, she picked up her plate.

"I'll get it." Emerie hustled around the table. "Don't trouble yourself."

She moved with an easy grace, like someone confident in her body.

Nesta drifted to the front of the shop, but then said, at last voicing her reason for visiting, "The training I'm doing with Cassian in the House of Wind is open to anyone—any female, I mean. Females who have experienced . . . hardship." Emerie's wings, her horrible family, were not the same as what Gwyn had endured, but everyone's traumas wore different masks. "We train each morning, from nine to eleven, though we sometimes run until noon. You're welcome to come."

Emerie stiffened. "I have no way of getting there, but I appreciate the offer."

"Someone could come retrieve you, and bring you back." Nesta didn't know who, but if she had to ask Rhys himself, she would.

"It's a generous offer, but I have my shop to run." Emerie's face yielded nothing, as battle-hardened as Azriel's. "I'm not interested in a warrior's training. I doubt it would win me patrons in this town to have them know I'm doing such a thing."

"You don't seem like a coward."

The words rang between them.

Emerie bit her lip. But Nesta shrugged. "Send word if you wish to join us. The offer stands."

✠

Cassian hated to admit it, but for a spoiled, soulless asshole, Eris had his uses. Mostly one: the bubble of heat that warmed them against the chill winds wending through the pines of the Illyrian Steppes. Some fire magic to warm their bones.

"The Dread Trove," Eris mused, surveying the heavy gray sky that threatened snow. "I've never heard of such items. Though it does not surprise me."

"Does your father know of them?" The Steppes weren't neutral ground, but they were empty enough that Eris had finally deigned to accept Cassian's request to meet here. After taking days to reply to his message.

"No, thank the Mother," Eris said, crossing his arms. "He would have told me if he did. But if the Trove has a sentience like you suggested, if it *wants* to be found . . . I fear that it might also be reaching out to others as well. Not just Briallyn and Koschei."

Beron in possession of the Trove would be a disaster. He'd join the ranks of the King of Hybern. Could become something terrible and deathless like Lanthys. "So Briallyn failed to inform Beron about her quest for the Trove when he visited her?"

"Apparently, she doesn't trust him, either," Eris said, face full of contemplation. "I'll need to think on that."

"Don't tell him about it," Cassian warned.

Eris shook his head. "You misunderstand me. I'm not going to tell him a damned thing. But the fact that Briallyn is actively hiding her larger plans from him . . ." He nodded, more to himself. "Is this why Morrigan is back in Vallahan? To learn if they know about the Trove?"

"Maybe," Cassian lied. She was still trying to convince them to sign the new treaty. But Eris didn't need to know that.

"Here I was," Eris said, "thinking Morrigan was going there so often to hide from me."

"Don't flatter yourself. It's only coincidence." He wasn't sure if the lie held.

"Why shouldn't I flatter myself with such thoughts? You flatter yourself, thinking you're more than a mongrel bastard."

Cassian's Siphons glinted atop his hands, and Eris smirked at the evidence that he'd landed the blow. But Cassian forced himself to say calmly, "That's all the information I have."

"You've given me a great deal to consider."

"Make sure you keep it *quiet*," Cassian warned again.

Eris winked before winnowing away.

Alone in the howling wild, Cassian blew out a breath. Embraced the chill winds, the pine-fresh scent, and willed it to wash away his irritation and discomfort.

But it lingered. For some reason, it lingered.

CHAPTER 26

Without doing extra training between the stacks, Nesta found herself less exhausted when she left the library. Cassian had retrieved her from Windhaven after two and a half hours, and she'd already been so bored sitting in Rhys's mother's house that she'd nearly smiled to see him. But Cassian's face had been tight, his eyes cold and distant, and he'd barely spoken to her when Rhys had appeared. Rhys had barely spoken to her, either, but that was to be expected. It was better if they didn't speak at all.

Yet Cassian hadn't said more than "I'll see you later" before leaving again with Rhys after the High Lord had brought them back to the House of Wind, his face still tight and angry.

With the extra energy buzzing through her that night, wondering incessantly why Cassian had been so upset, Nesta didn't feel like eating in her room and falling asleep. So she found herself in the doorway of the dining room.

Cassian was lounging in his chair, a glass of wine in his hand, staring at nothing. A brooding warrior-prince, contemplating the death of his enemies. She took a step into the room, and the wineglass vanished.

She snorted. "I'm not so wine-addled that I'd steal it from your hand."

"The House is under specific orders—no wine when you're in the room." He flexed his fingers as he sat up. "It took it from me."

"Ah." She claimed the seat across from him as a place setting and a plate of food appeared, along with water for both of them.

Cassian returned to staring at his half-eaten food. She hadn't seen his face this grave since the war.

"Did something happen with the queens or the Trove?"

He blinked. "What?" Then gave a one-shouldered shrug. "No, just . . . Eris was his usual charming self today." He pushed around the roast chicken with his fork.

Nesta picked up her own fork, hungry enough that she let the subject drop as she devoured her food. When she'd taken the edge off her hunger, she said, "I asked Emerie to join training."

"I'm assuming she said no." His words were flat, his face distant.

"Indeed. But if she changes her mind, I thought maybe someone could winnow her here."

"Sure." She could tell he wasn't just being short with her—he was so preoccupied with whatever was eating at him that he could barely talk.

It bothered her more than it should have. Bothered her enough that she asked, "What happened?" She made herself eat more, acting as casual as possible, trying to coax him into opening up. To talk about what had brought that bruised look to his eyes.

His gaze lowering to his plate, Cassian told her about the meeting with Eris.

"So Eris is set on helping us find the Trove—and making sure his father doesn't get his hands on it, or hear about it," Nesta said when he'd finished. "Isn't that a good thing? Why are you riled?" *Why do you look so battered?*

"It's the ugliness of his fucking *soul* that riles me. I don't care if he calls me a mongrel bastard." Eris had called him such things today, she realized. Rage rippled through her. "It's just that, ally or not, I *hate* him. He's so slick and unruffled and . . . I can't stand him." He set down his fork and stared toward the window behind her. "Eris and his twisted word games and politics are an enemy I don't know how to handle. Every time I meet with him, I feel like he's got the upper hand. Like I can only catch up to him, and he sees through my every fumbling attempt at being clever. Maybe that makes me a stupid brute after all."

True sorrow filled his face—and enough self-loathing that Nesta rose from her seat. He went still as she rounded the table, only lifting his head when she leaned against the edge of the table beside his plate. "Rhys should kill him and be done with it."

"If anyone is going to kill Eris, it will be Mor or me." His hazel eyes were nearly pleading. Not with her, she knew, but with fate. "But killing him would prove him and his ilk right about me. And regardless of how I feel about Eris, he would be a better High Lord than Beron. No matter what I want, there's still the well-being of the Autumn Court to consider."

Cassian was good. In his soul, in his warrior's heart, Cassian was good in a way Nesta knew most people were not. In a way she knew she was not and would never be.

He was not a warrior who killed on a whim, but a male who carefully considered every life he had to take. Who'd defend what he loved until death.

And Eris . . . He'd hurt Cassian. With what he'd done to Morrigan, yes, but also with the words so similar to ones that Nesta herself had wielded. The wound lay in Cassian's eyes, as raw as any injury.

Shame rushed through her. Shame, and anger, and a wild sort of desperation. She couldn't abide the pain in his eyes, teetering on the brink of despair. Couldn't stand the absence of the grinning and winking and swaggering she knew so well.

She'd do anything to get rid of that look in his eyes. Even for a few moments.

So Nesta braced her hands on the arms of his chair as she brushed a kiss to his neck.

Cassian's breath caught. But she pressed another kiss to the soft, warm skin of his neck, just beneath his ear. Another, lower now, closer to the collar of his dark shirt.

He trembled, and she kissed the hard knot in the center of his throat. Licked it.

Cassian shifted in his chair, groaning softly. His hand rose to clasp her hip, as if he'd push her away, but she removed him. "Let me," she said against his neck. "Please."

He swallowed, and that hard knot moved against her mouth. But he didn't stop her, and so Nesta kissed him again, moving to the other side of his neck. Reaching that spot just beneath his ear as she laid a hand on his chest and felt his heartbeat hammering into her palm.

She didn't kiss his mouth. She didn't want that distraction. Not as she slid between him and the table and dropped to her knees.

His eyes went wide. "Nesta."

She reached for the top of his pants, the bulge already pressing through. "Please," she said again, and met his stare. From where she knelt between Cassian's legs, he towered over her, but the edge in his eyes softened almost imperceptibly before he nodded. He reached to help her with the buttons and stays, but she lightly laid a hand atop his.

Her fingers were steady, sure, as she unfastened his pants. Her head wholly clear.

The muscles in his thighs shifted against her as she pulled him free and nearly gasped.

His cock was enormous. Beautiful, and hard, and absolutely enormous. Her mouth dried out, every plan she'd had requiring sudden reassessment. There was no way he'd fit entirely in her mouth. Perhaps no way he'd even fit in her *body*.

But she sure as hell wanted to try.

Her fingers shook a little as she stroked them down the thick, long shaft. The skin was so soft—softer than silk or velvet. And he was hard as steel beneath. He shuddered, and she lifted her eyes to find his gaze fixed on her hand.

"How do you like it?" she asked, her voice breathy as hot need washed through her. She wrapped her hand around his cock—her fingers barely able to reach around him completely. "Gentle?" She made a feather-soft pass over him, squeezing lightly.

Cassian shook his head, as if beyond words.

She stroked him again, slightly harder. "Like this?"

His chest heaved, his teeth shining as he gritted them. But he shook his head.

Nesta smiled, and when she pumped him a third time, she squeezed hard, letting her nails graze the sensitive underside of his shaft.

His hips arced off the chair, and she pinned a hand to them. "I see," she murmured, and did it again. Harder still, twisting her fist as she reached the round head.

He tried to arch into her hand, but she pinned him again with that other hand.

"And this?" she purred, head lowering. "Do you like this?"

Nesta licked across his broad head, tongue sliding into the small slit across its tip. She licked up the small bead of moisture already gathered there.

Everything in her body turned molten; a surge of wetness slicked between her thighs as the taste of him filled her mouth, salt and something more, something vital.

"Oh, gods," Cassian panted. And the words, the groan they were borne on, were so delicious that Nesta sucked his tip into her mouth and grazed her tongue along its underside.

He leaned his head back against the chair, hissing.

She licked up his shaft in one long motion. Rubbed her thighs together as she tasted him, felt all that hot, proud steel against her mouth. She licked down the other side, coating him, making it easier for herself as she put her mouth around him again and slid him between her lips.

He filled her almost immediately, and she glanced down to discover there was enough of him still exposed that she needed to add her hand. "Nesta," he pleaded, and she made another pass at him, pulling him out nearly all the way before swallowing him again, letting her throat relax, desperate for as much of him in her mouth as could fit.

Cassian's hand speared into her hair, gripping, and she realized he was holding himself back. Didn't want to ram himself into her, hurt her, displease her.

And that wouldn't do. Not at all.

She wanted him undone, wanted him grabbing her head and fucking her mouth as hard as he wished.

So when Nesta took him into her mouth again, hand working in unison, she dragged her teeth. Lightly enough to hurt—just a bit.

Cassian bucked, and she let him, swallowing him down greedily, squeezing him with her hand enough to tell him she wanted this, wanted him to let himself go. She withdrew her lips to the tip of him, rolling her tongue around him, and gazed at him from under her lashes.

His eyes were on her, wide and glazed with lust.

And when Cassian met her stare, beheld her looking up at him—

He unleashed himself.

✢

He couldn't take it. It was torture, a special kind of torture, to have Nesta kneeling before him with his cock in her mouth and hand and not be able to roar with pleasure. But then she stared at him through her lashes, and the sight of her with his cock between her lips snapped something.

He didn't care that they were in the dining room, that a wall of windows and doors lined half the space and anyone flying by might see.

Cassian slid his other hand into her hair, fingers twining into her braided coronet, and he thrust up into her mouth.

She took him deep, and moaned so loudly it reverberated along his cock and straight into his balls. They tightened further, and release gathered in his spine, a scorching knot that had him arcing into her mouth again. He was utterly at her mercy.

Nesta moaned once more, a soft encouragement, and Cassian needed nothing else. Gripping her hair, her scalp, holding her in place, he thrust his hips. She met him with each stroke, mouth and hand working in unison, until the slick heat of her, the teeth that sometimes grazed him, teased him, the tightness of her fist—they were unbearable, were all he cared about.

Cassian fucked her mouth, and her moaning had him deciding he'd fuck the rest of her, too. Strip those pants off her and drive into her so hard she'd be screaming his name to the ceiling.

He made to pull out, but Nesta refused to move. He growled, his fingers clamping on her head to still her. "I want to be inside you," he managed to say, his voice like gravel.

But Nesta looked up at him again from under her lashes, and he watched his length disappear into her mouth. His tip bumped against the back of her throat.

Oh, gods. He clenched his teeth. "I want to finish inside you."

Nesta only huffed a laugh, and sucked him down so deep that he couldn't stop it. Couldn't stop the release as she slid her other hand into his pants and cupped his balls, squeezing softly.

Cassian came with a roar that shook the glasses on the table, arcing up into her as he spilled himself down her throat.

She weathered it, weathered him, and when he'd stopped shuddering, she smoothly, gracefully, slid her mouth off him.

Nesta held his stare while she swallowed. Swallowed down every ounce of what he'd spilled into her mouth. And then her lips curved upward, a queen triumphant.

Cassian panted, not caring that his cock was still out, slick and leaking, only that she was mere inches away and he was going to return this particular favor she'd given him.

Nesta rose to her feet, eyes flicking to his cock. The heat in her gaze threatened to burn him, and the scent of her arousal wrapped itself around him and dug its claws in deep.

"Take off your pants," he growled.

Nesta's smile only grew, pure feline amusement.

He'd fuck her on this table. Right now. He didn't care about anything else, about the common space they were in or Eris or Briallyn or Koschei or the Dread Trove. He needed to be inside her, to feel that hot tightness around him and claim her as she had claimed him.

Nesta's fingers slid to the buttons and laces of her pants, and he shook as he watched them free the top button—

Steps scuffed down the hall. A warning. From someone who knew how to remain silent.

Cassian stiffened, then shoved his aching cock into his pants. Nesta heard the sound and moved a few feet away, refastening that top button. Cassian had just finished setting himself to rights when Azriel strode in.

"Good evening," his brother said with a grating level of calm, striding toward the table.

"Az." Cassian wasn't able to keep the bite out of his tone. He met his brother's too-aware stare and silently conveyed every bit of annoyance he felt at his timing. Azriel only shrugged, surveying the food the House had brought him. As if he knew exactly what he'd interrupted and took his chaperone duties *very* seriously.

Nesta was watching them, but as soon as Cassian turned to her, she launched into movement, pushing off the table and aiming for the door. "Good night." She didn't wait for him to respond before she was gone.

Cassian leveled a glare at Az. "Thanks for that."

"I don't know what you're talking about," Az said, even as he smiled down at his food.

"Asshole."

Az chuckled. "Don't show your hand all at once, Cass."

"What's that supposed to mean?"

Az nodded toward the doorway. "Save something for later."

"Busybody."

Az took a bite. "You let her suck your cock in the middle of the dining room. At a table I'm currently using to eat my dinner. I'd say that entitles me to an opinion."

Cassian laughed, his earlier gloom chased away. By her. All by her. "Fair enough."

CHAPTER 27

Nesta hadn't the faintest idea how she'd look Cassian in the face the next morning, but Gwyn provided a buffer she was all too eager to use. She met the priestess on the steps up to the training pit, and Gwyn offered her a bright smile. "Morning."

"Morning," Nesta said, falling into step with her. "Anything on the Trove?"

Gwyn shook her head. She still wore her robes, though she'd taken to tying back her hair in a tight braid. "I even asked Merrill last night. She broke through that glamour, but beyond a few mentions in old texts, she couldn't find anything more than what you already know. Not a hint about when or where they were lost, or who lost them. We can't even uncover who last possessed them, since it's information that goes back at least ten thousand years."

It was always a shock to remember just how old the Fae were. How old Amren must be, to have remembered the Dread Trove objects when they were still free in the world. But apparently even Amren had no memory of who'd last used them.

Nesta shoved away the thought of the female, and the accompanying cold slice of pain.

"It might prove an impossible task," Gwyn said, mouth twisting to one side. "Is there no other way of finding it?"

There was. It involved bones and stones. Nesta's body locked up. "No," she lied. "There's no other way."

⁜

"You're going up to Windhaven?" Nesta found herself asking Cassian as Gwyn bade them farewell at the end of their lesson. Gwyn had started on fighting stances that morning, and it had taken enough focus from all of them that Nesta hadn't had a moment to really speak to him alone. There had been one slightly overlong glance when she'd appeared, and that had been it.

She had no regrets about what she'd done in the dining room. Even if it had been glaringly obvious that Azriel had known what he was interrupting.

But standing here alone with Cassian . . . The taste of him lingered in her mouth, as if he'd branded himself onto her tongue.

She'd lain awake in bed last night thinking of every stroke, every sound he'd made, still feeling the press of his fingers into her head as he'd thrust into her mouth. The memory alone had made her slide a hand between her legs, and she'd needed to find release twice before her body calmed enough to sleep.

Cassian plucked his jacket from where he'd left it, shrugging into the black leather and scales. "I need to inspect the legions again. Make sure they're preparing for possible conflict and that the recruits are in good shape."

"Ah." Their eyes met, and she could have sworn his darkened, as if remembering every delicious moment from the night before. But she shook her head, clearing away the cobwebs.

"Gwyn's doing well," Cassian said, nodding to the archway where the priestess had disappeared. "She's a nice girl."

Nesta had learned that Gwyn was twenty-eight—indeed, just a girl to him.

"I like her," Nesta admitted.

Cassian blinked. "I don't think I've ever heard you say that about anyone." She rolled her eyes, but he added, "It's too bad the other priestesses won't come."

Nesta checked the sign-up sheet every day, but no one else had added their name. Gwyn told Nesta that she'd personally invited a few of the priestesses, but they were too scared, too unsure.

"I don't know what I can do to encourage them," Nesta said.

"Keep doing what you're doing." He finished fastening his jacket.

A brisk autumn breeze flowed past, bringing with it scents from the city below: bread and cinnamon and oranges; roast meats and salt. Nesta inhaled, identifying each one, wondering how they could all somehow combine to create a singular sense of autumn.

Nesta angled her head as an idea struck her. "If you're stopping by Windhaven, can you do me a favor?"

⁜

Cassian stood in Emerie's shop and made his best attempt at a nonthreatening smile as he laid out the contents of the sack he'd carried.

Emerie peered at what he placed onto her pristine counter. "Nesta gave you this?"

Technically, Nesta had informed him, the House had given it to her. But she'd asked the House for these items, intending them to be brought here. "She said it's a gift."

Emerie picked up a brass tin, pried open the top, and inhaled. The smoky, velvety scent of tea leaves floated out. "Oh, this is good stuff." She lifted a glass vial of finely ground powder. When she twisted the lid off, a nutty, spicy scent filled the shop. "Cumin." Her sigh was like a lover's. She moved to another and another, six glass containers in total. "Turmeric, cinnamon, allspice, cloves, and . . ." She peered at the label. "Black pepper."

Cassian laid the last container on the table, a large marble box that weighed at least two pounds. Emerie yanked off the lid and let out a laugh. "Salt." She pinched the flaky crystals between her fingers. "A lot of salt."

Her eyes shone as a rare smile flitted across her face. It made her look younger, wiped away the weight and scars of all those years with her father. "Please tell her I say thank you."

He cleared his throat, remembering the speech Nesta had drilled into him. "Nesta says you can thank her by showing up to training tomorrow morning."

Emerie's smile wavered. "I told her the other day: I have no means to attend."

"She thought you'd say that. If you want to come, send word, and one of us will bring you." It'd have to be Rhys, but he doubted his brother would object. "If you can't stay the full time, that's fine. Come for an hour, before your shop opens."

Emerie's fingers fell away from the spices and tea. "It's not the right time."

Cassian knew better than to push. "If you ever change your mind, let us know." He turned from the counter, aiming for the door.

He knew Nesta had given the gift in part to tempt Emerie to join, but also from the kindness of her heart. He'd asked why she was sending these items, and she'd said, "Emerie needs spices and good tea." It had stunned him, just as it had stunned him earlier to hear her admit that she liked Gwyn.

Nesta around Gwyn was a wholly different creature than who she was with the court. They didn't tease or laugh with each other, but an easiness lay between them that he'd never witnessed, even when Nesta was with Elain. She'd always been Elain's guardian, or Feyre's sister, or Cauldron-Made.

With Gwyn . . . he wondered whether Nesta liked the girl because with her, she was simply Nesta. Perhaps she felt that way around Emerie, too.

Had she gone into Velaris, night after night, not only to distract and numb herself, but to be around people who didn't know the weight of all she carried?

Cassian reached the door, blowing out a soft breath. He'd refused to think of what she'd done to him in the dining room while they'd been training, especially with Gwyn there, but seeing Nesta's tentative smile as she'd shoved the tea and spices into a bag had him suppressing the urge to push her against the wall and kiss her.

He had no idea where things stood with them. If they were back to a favor for a favor. She'd given him no inkling about whether she'd let him into her bed, or if she'd gotten on her knees to knock him out of the brooding he'd fallen into.

If she had, it implied some level of caring about his well-being, didn't it? And pity. Fuck, if she'd sucked him because she pitied him—

No. It hadn't been that. He'd seen the desire in her eyes, felt the softness of her mouth on his neck in those initial touches. It had been comfort, given in the only way she knew how.

Cassian opened the door and looked back, finding Emerie still at the counter, her hand resting on the array of spices and tea. Her eyes were solemn, her lips a tight line. She didn't seem aware of his presence, so he took that as his cue to leave and leaped into the skies.

⸸

Nesta climbed the steps to the training ring, pondering the Dread Trove. She assumed the others had met with no better luck than she had, and if things were indeed as urgent as Azriel had claimed, then perhaps library research wasn't the best route.

But her stomach clenched to weigh the other option, to recall what had occurred the first and only time she'd scried. Her hands shook as she climbed the last of the steps. She squeezed her fingers into fists, blowing out a steady breath through her nose.

Cassian already stood in the center of the ring. He grinned as she emerged.

It was a wider grin than his usual ones, excited and—pleased.

Nesta's eyes narrowed as she stepped into the brightness of the ring. Gwyn was already waiting a few feet from Cassian, a smile lighting her own face.

And before them, drinking a glass at the water station, stood Emerie.

CHAPTER 28

As graceful as Gwyn had been, Emerie proved to be equally awkward and unbalanced.

"It has to do with your wings," Cassian said with such gentleness that Nesta, balancing on one leg and sweeping the other up behind her, nearly fell into the dirt next to Emerie. "Without full use of your wings, your body compensates for its off-kilter balance in ways like that." He nodded toward the ground-eating spill she'd taken.

Gwyn halted her own balancing. "Why?"

"The wings usually act as a counterweight." He offered a hand to help Emerie rise. "They're full of delicate muscles that constantly adjust and steady without us so much as thinking about it." Emerie ignored his hand and stood herself. Cassian explained carefully, "Many of the key muscles can be impacted when someone's wings are clipped."

Gwyn glanced to Nesta, who tensed, frowning. Gwyn and Emerie had fallen into an easy camaraderie within minutes. That could have been due to Gwyn peppering Emerie with questions about her shop as they'd gone through the opening exercises.

Emerie dusted the dirt off the legs of her leathers, looser than the ones Nesta wore, as if she were uncomfortable with the skintight norm.

Cassian's eyes softened. "Which of the healers clipped you?"

Emerie's chin lifted, color stealing across her face. She met his eyes, though—with a level of directness that Nesta could only admire. "My father did it himself."

Cassian swore, low and nasty.

Emerie said, voice cold, "I fought him, so his work became even sloppier."

Gwyn and Nesta kept quiet as Emerie stretched out her right wing nearly all the way before it bunched and shuddered. So did Emerie's face. "I can't extend this one past here." She stretched out the left wing—to barely half its length. "This is all I can get on this side."

Cassian looked like he'd be sick. "He deserved to die in that battle. Deserved to die a long time before that, Emerie." His Siphons glared in answer, and something wild and wicked heated in Nesta's blood at the pure rage in his face, his growling words.

Emerie folded back her wings. "He deserved to die for far more than what he did to my wings."

"If you're going to come to Velaris every day, I can get Madja up here. She's the court's private healer." Rhys had brought Emerie, Nesta had learned. And would return her in an hour.

Emerie only went stiffer. "I appreciate the offer, but it's unnecessary."

Cassian opened his mouth, but Nesta interrupted, "Enough chit-chat. If we only get Emerie for an hour today, then walk us through the punching, Cassian. Let her see what she'll need to catch up to."

Emerie threw her a grateful look, and Nesta offered her a slight smile in return.

Cassian nodded, and from the gleam in his eye, she knew he was well aware of why she'd interrupted.

Gwyn asked Emerie, "Do you have libraries in Illyria?" Another lifeline thrown.

"No. I've never been in one." The stiffness faded from Emerie's posture, word by word.

Gwyn retied her shining hair at the nape of her neck. "Do you like to read?"

Emerie's mouth curled upward. "I live alone, up in the mountains. I have nothing to do with my spare time except work in my garden and read whatever books I order through the mail service. And in the winter, I don't even have the distraction of my gardening. So, yes. I like to read. I cannot survive without reading."

Nesta grunted her agreement.

"What manner of books?" Gwyn asked.

"Romances," Emerie said, adjusting her own hair, the thick black braid full of reds and browns in the sunlight. Nesta started. Emerie's eyes lit. "You too? Which ones?"

Nesta rattled off her top five, and Emerie grinned, so broadly it was like seeing another person. "Have you read Sellyn Drake's novels?"

Nesta shook her head. Emerie gasped, so dramatically that Cassian muttered something about sparing him from smut-obsessed females before heading farther into the ring. "You *must* read her books. You *must*. I'll bring the first one tomorrow. You'll stay up all night reading it, I swear."

"Smut?" Gwyn asked, catching Cassian's muttered words. There was enough hesitation in her voice to make Nesta draw up straight.

Nesta glanced at Emerie, realizing the female didn't know about Gwyn—her history, or why the priestesses lived in the library. But Emerie asked, "What do you read?"

"Adventure, sometimes mysteries. But mostly I have to read whatever Merrill, the priestess I work with, has written that day. Not as exciting as romance, not by a long shot."

Emerie said casually, "I can bring one of Drake's books for you, too—one of her milder ones. An introduction to the wonders of romance." Emerie winked at Nesta.

Nesta waited for Gwyn to refuse, but the priestess smiled. "I'd like that."

✥

Rhys appeared in the ring precisely when he said he would. One hour—no more, no less.

Red dirt and sweat covered Emerie, but her gaze shone bright as she bowed to the High Lord.

Gwyn, however, stilled, those large teal eyes looking even more unearthly as they widened. No fear tinged her scent, but rather something like surprise—awe.

Rhys threw her an easy smile, one Nesta would have bet was crafted to put people at ease in his oh-so-magnificent presence. The casual smile of a male used to people either fleeing in terror or falling to their knees in worship. "Hello, Gwyn," he said warmly. "Good to see you again."

Gwyn blushed, shaking herself out of her stupor, and bowed low. "My lord."

Nesta rolled her eyes, and found Rhys watching her. That casual smile sharpened as he met her stare. "Nesta."

"Rhysand."

The other two women were glancing between them, the bouncing of their stares almost comical. Cassian just strode to Nesta's side and slung an arm around her shoulders before drawling to Rhys, "These ladies are going to hand your ass to you in combat soon enough."

Nesta made to step out from under the heavy, sweaty weight of his arm, but Cassian clamped a too-friendly hand on her shoulder, his grin unfaltering. Rhys's gaze slid between them, little warmth to be found in his eyes. But plenty of wariness.

Little princeling didn't like her with his friend.

Nesta leaned into Cassian. Not much, but enough for a trained warrior like Rhysand to note.

A dark, silken hand brushed inside her mind. A request.

She debated ignoring it, but found herself opening a small door through the steel, spiked barrier she kept around herself day and night. The door was essentially a peephole, and she allowed what she supposed was the equivalent of her mental face to peer through it to the dark, sparkling plane beyond. *What?*

You are to treat Gwyn with kindness and respect.

The thing that stood beyond the fortress of her mind was a creature of claws, scales, and teeth. It was veiled from sight beneath writhing shadows and the occasional passing star glinting in the darkness, but every now and then, a glimpse of a wing or a talon shone.

Mind your own business. Nesta slammed that small viewing hole shut.

She blinked, slowly registering Emerie asking Cassian about tomorrow morning's lesson, and what she'd miss today by leaving an hour early.

Rhysand's eyes glittered.

Cassian's arm remained around Nesta, and his thumb moved over her shoulder in an idle, reassuring caress. Whether he knew of or sensed her silent conversation with his High Lord, he didn't let on.

"Ready?" Rhys asked Emerie, that kind, lovely smile appearing again. Emerie might have blushed. Rhysand had that effect on people.

Nesta often wondered how Feyre could stand it—all the people lusting after her mate. Nesta pushed out of Cassian's arm again, and this time he let her. She followed Emerie to where she was gathering her heavy cloak. "So you'll come back tomorrow?" Nesta asked. A glance over her shoulder revealed Gwyn walking to the water station, either to give the two males privacy or from discomfort at being left with them.

Guilt pricked at Nesta for that abandonment, and she made a mental note not to allow it to happen again. Gwyn had been fine with Cassian these past days: she did not touch him, and he did not touch her, but she hadn't shied from him as she did now. Nesta didn't want to think about why that was, what scars had been etched so deeply in Gwyn that two of the most trustworthy males in this entire land couldn't put her at ease.

Rhysand might be an arrogant, vain bastard, but he was honorable. He fought like hell to protect innocents. Her dislike of him had nothing to do with what he'd proved so many times: he was a fair, just ruler, who put his people before himself. No, she just found his personality—that slick smugness—grating.

Emerie answered, "I'll come back tomorrow."

Nesta angled her head. "I had no idea tea and spices were that convincing."

Emerie smiled slightly. "It wasn't only the gift, but the reminder of what they mean."

"What's that?"

Emerie gazed skyward, closing her eyes as an autumn breeze rippled past. "That there is a world beyond Windhaven. That I am too much of a coward to see it."

"You're not a coward."

"You said I was the other day."

Nesta winced. "I spoke in anger."

"You spoke truth. I stayed awake that night thinking of it. And then you had Cassian deliver the spices and tea and I realized that there *is* a world out there. A vast, vibrant world. Maybe these lessons will make me a little less scared of it."

Nesta offered a tentative smile. "Sounds like a good enough reason to me."

⁜

Cassian watched Rhys's face carefully as Nesta and Emerie spoke, and Gwyn drifted over to join them. Promises of books to be swapped filled the air.

Rhys said to him, *This is an interesting development.*

Cassian didn't bother to make his face look pleasant. *I could have done without you giving Nesta a mental warning.*

Rhys's brows narrowed. *How did you know I did that?*

The bastard didn't even try to deny it.

I noticed the way she tensed. And I know you well, brother. You saw Gwyn and thought the worst of Nesta. She's treated her—and Emerie—with kindness.

That's what pissed you off?

I'm pissed off that you can't seem to believe even one good thing about her. That you refuse *to fucking believe one good thing about her. Was it necessary to bait her like that?*

Regret glimmered in Rhys's eyes.

Cassian went on, *You're not making it easier. Let her build these bonds, and stay the hell out of it.*

Rhys blinked. *I'm sorry. I will.*

Cassian blew out a breath. Rhys added, *Did you really feel you had to put your arm around her shoulders to restrain her?*

I don't want the two of you within three feet of each other. You have a pregnant mate, Rhys. You'll kill anyone that presents a threat to Feyre. You're a danger to all of us right now.

I'd never harm someone Feyre loves. You know that.

There was enough tension in the words that Cassian clapped his brother on the shoulder, squeezing the hard muscle beneath. *Maybe drop Emerie off on the other side of the House tomorrow. Give Nesta some time to sort her shit out.*

All right.

The three females approached them. Rhys opened his wings and said to Emerie, "Shall we?"

Emerie took the hand Rhys extended. "Yes." She looked to Cassian, then to Nesta, and said, "Thank you."

Damn if it didn't hit him in the heart, that gratitude and hope in Emerie's eyes.

Rhys gathered her to him, careful of the intimate press of her wings against his body, and shot into the sky.

As Rhys soared above the House's wards, just before he winnowed to Windhaven, he said to Cassian, *I don't know what the fuck the two of you have been doing in this House, but it reeks of sex.*

Cassian snorted. *A polite male never tells.*

Rhys's laughter rumbled in his mind. *I don't think you know what the word* polite *means.*

Thank the gods for that.

His brother laughed again. *I told Az playing chaperone would be useless.*

CHAPTER 29

Nesta's legs gave out on step three thousand.

Panting, sweat running down her back, down her stomach, she braced her hands on her trembling thighs and closed her eyes.

The dream had been the same. Her father's face, filled with love and fear, then with nothing as he died. The crack of his neck. Hybern's sly, cruel smile.

Cassian and Azriel hadn't been at dinner, and she'd received no explanation for it. They were probably either at the river house or out in the city, and she'd been surprised to find herself wishing for the company. Surprised to find that the silence of the dining room pressed on her.

Of course she wouldn't be invited out. She'd made a point to be as unpleasant as possible for well over a year now. And more than that, they had no obligation to include her in everything.

No one had any obligation to include her at all. Or the desire to, apparently.

Her panting echoed off the red stone. She'd awoken from the

nightmare in a cold sweat, and had been halfway here before she realized where she was going. If she even made it to the bottom, where would she go? Especially in her nightgown.

She could still see her father behind her closed eyes. Felt every flash of horror and pain and fear she'd endured during those months surrounding the war.

She had to find the Dread Trove—somehow.

She'd failed every task they'd ever given her. Had failed to stop the wall from being blasted apart, failed to save the Illyrian legion from the Cauldron's incinerating blow—

Nesta shut down that train of thought.

Something thudded on the step beside her, and she blinked to find a glass of water.

"Thank you," she said, drinking deep, letting its coolness settle her further. She asked into the dimness, "Have you read any books by Sellyn Drake?"

The House didn't answer, which she assumed amounted to a no. "A friend is bringing me one of her novels tomorrow. I'll share it with you when I'm done."

Nothing. Then a cool breeze ran down the stairwell, soothing her sweaty brow. "Thank you," she said again, leaning into the breeze.

Something else clinked beside her on the step, and she found two flat oval stones and three chunks of age-browned bone—anklebones of some ovine beast. Her mouth dried out. Bones and stones—for scrying. "I can't," she rasped.

That breeze knocked the bones together, their clicking like a question thrown into the stairwell. *Why?*

"Bad things happened the last time. The Cauldron *looked* at me. And took Elain." She couldn't stop her body from locking up. "I can't endure it, risk it. Not even for this."

The bones and stones vanished, along with that cooling breeze.

Nesta began the ascent, groaning softly. With each step, she could have sworn she tasted disappointment in the air.

⸸

"Nesta has to start looking for the Trove," Amren said, swirling her wine in its glass as she sat across from Cassian at the river house's massive dining table. Their monthly court dinner, as usual, had turned into hours of talking around this table, and multiple bottles of wine later, as the clock ticked toward one in the morning, none of them showed any signs of moving.

Only Feyre had gone to bed. Being pregnant made her unbearably sleepy, she'd groused. So tired that she needed naps throughout the day, and was asleep most nights by nine.

Cassian met Amren's gray stare. "Nesta's been looking. Don't push her."

Rhys said from where he lounged at the head of the table, "She's had the priestesses researching for her. I'd hardly call that looking."

Varian, seated beside Amren, his arm draped over the back of her seat, asked, "You still haven't asked Helion to research the Trove in his libraries?" Varian was the only person outside of the Night Court—and Eris—whom Rhys had allowed to know of their search. But it had come with a risk: Varian served Tarquin, High Lord of the Summer Court. Though he had promised Rhys not to say anything about it to Tarquin without prompting, if Tarquin asked Varian about it, he'd find his allegiances held in a precarious balance.

Tarquin and Rhys's relationship had healed since the war, but not enough for Rhys to trust the male with knowledge of the Trove. And Cassian, who'd gotten into one tiny little fight that might have resulted in one tiny little building being destroyed the last time he'd been in the Summer Court, was inclined to agree. Not about Tarquin. No, he liked the male. And liked Varian a great deal. But there were wicked people in the Summer Court—in every court—and he did not trust that they were as kind as their ruler.

"Helion is a last resort," Rhys said, sipping his wine. "Which we may come to in a matter of days if Nesta does not at least attempt a scrying." The last words were directed toward Cassian. "I'd have Elain try her hand before we approach him, though."

Elain had already departed with Feyre, claiming she had to be up with the dawn to tend to an elderly faerie's garden. Cassian didn't exactly know why he suspected this wasn't true. There had been some tightness in Elain's face as she'd said it. Normally when she made such excuses, Lucien was around, but the male remained in the human lands with Jurian and Vassa.

Cassian countered, "Nesta will do it, if only to keep Elain from putting herself at risk. But you have to understand that Nesta was deeply affected by what happened during the war—Elain was taken by the Cauldron after she scried. You can't blame her for hesitating."

Amren said, "We do not have the time to wait for Nesta to decide. I say we approach Elain tomorrow. Better to have both of them working on it."

Azriel stiffened, an outright sign of temper from him as he said quietly, "There is an innate darkness to the Dread Trove that Elain should not be exposed to."

"But Nesta should?" Cassian growled.

Everyone stared at him.

He swallowed, offering an apologetic glance to Az, who shrugged it off.

Amren drained her wine and said to Cassian, "Nesta has a week. One more week to find the Trove with her own methods. Then we seek out other routes." She threw a nod toward Azriel. "Including Elain, who is more than capable of defending herself against the darkness of the Trove, if she chooses to. Don't underestimate her."

Cassian and Azriel looked to Rhys, who merely sipped from his own wine. Amren's order held. As Rhys's Second in this court, short of Rhys overruling her, her word was law.

Cassian glowered at Amren. "It's not right to wield Elain as a threat to manipulate Nesta into scrying."

"There are harsher ways to convince Nesta, boy."

Cassian leaned back in his chair. "You're a fool if you think threats will make her obey you."

Everyone tensed again. Even Varian.

Amren's lips spread in a sharp grin. "We are on the cusp of another war. We let the Cauldron slip from our hands in the last one and it nearly cost us everything." Amren's new Fae form was proof of that—she'd yielded her immortal, otherworldly self to remain in this body. No gray fire glowed in her eyes. She was mortal, in the way that High Fae were mortal. Varian's fingers tangled in the blunt ends of her hair, as if to reassure himself that she was here, she'd remained with him. "We must head off this potential disaster before we lose the advantage. If we need to manipulate Nesta into scrying, even by using Elain against her, then we'll do what is necessary."

His stomach tightened. "I don't like it."

"You don't have to like it," Amren said. "You just have to shut up and do as you're told."

"Amren," Rhys said, the word laced with reprimand and warning.

Amren didn't so much as blink in remorse, but Varian frowned at her. "What?" she snapped.

The Prince of Adriata gave her an exasperated smile. "Haven't we talked about this? About . . . being nice?"

Amren rolled her eyes. But her face softened—ever so slightly—as she met Cassian's stare again. "A week. Nesta gets a week."

⁜

Three days passed. Emerie came to each lesson, and while Gwyn had mostly caught up to Nesta's progress, Emerie would need more work. So Nesta and Gwyn partnered with each other, going through the sets of exercises that Cassian showed them before he worked one-on-one with Emerie on her balance and mobility.

None of them minded, not when Emerie had been right about the Sellyn Drake books. Nesta had stayed up two nights in a row reading the author's first novel, which was as toe-curlingly erotic as she could have wished. And, as promised, Emerie had brought a copy of one of Drake's tamer novels for Gwyn, who had arrived blushing the next morning and told Emerie that if the book was considered tame, then she could only imagine the content of the others.

After that first day, Emerie stayed for the entire length of their lessons, which had now officially stretched into a full three hours, deciding that her morning business traffic was slow enough to risk it. So they trained, and between their exercises they talked about books, and Nesta woke on the fourth morning and found herself . . . excited to see them again.

She was shelving a tome in the library that afternoon when Gwyn found her. Thanks to Gwyn's lesson each morning, she'd been busier in the afternoons, which meant that Nesta rarely saw her in the library save for when Gwyn was running through the stacks, hunting for some book or another for Merrill. Occasionally, Nesta heard a lovely, soaring snippet of song from some distant corner of the library—the sole indicator that Gwyn was near.

But that afternoon, it was Gwyn's panting that announced her presence seconds before she appeared, her eyes wide enough that Nesta went on alert, scanning the dimness behind the priestess. "What?" Had the darkness below chased her?

Gwyn mastered herself enough to say, "I don't know how, but Merrill learned you swapped the book out." She gasped for air as she pointed up to a level high above. "You should go."

Nesta frowned. "Who cares? I'm not going to let her scare me off like some errant child."

Gwyn blanched. "When she's in a fury, it is—"

"It is what, Gwyneth Berdara?" crooned a female voice from the stacks. "When I'm in a fury, it is *what*?"

Gwyn winced, turning slowly as the white-haired beauty appeared from the gloom. Her pale robes flowed behind her as if on a phantom wind, and the blue stone atop her hood flickered with light. Gwyn bowed her head, face paling. "I meant nothing by it, Merrill."

Nesta ground her teeth at the bow, the fear on Gwyn's face, in her soft words.

Priestesses halted along the railings above them.

Merrill turned her remarkable eyes to Nesta. "I do not appreciate thieves and liars."

"Neither do I," Nesta said coolly, lifting her chin.

Merrill hissed. "You tried to play me for a fool in my very own office." She didn't so much as look at Gwyn, who cringed away.

"I don't know what you're talking about."

"Oh? You mean when I went to see the book that my inane assistant had *incorrectly* given me—oh, yes, I knew about that from the start—and found the proper volume instead, with *your* scent upon it, it wasn't you who did it?" Merrill looked between Gwyn and Nesta. "It is inexcusable to ask others to make up for your own stupidity and carelessness."

Gwyn's fear grated against her senses. Nesta said, voice dropping, "Gwyn did no such thing. And who cares? Are you so bored down here that you have to invent these dramas to entertain yourself?" She waved a hand to the open walkway behind Merrill. "We're both busy. Clear off and let us work in peace."

Someone gasped on a level above.

Merrill laughed, that phantom wind around her whispering. "Do you not know who I am, girl?"

"I know that you are keeping us from our work," Nesta said with that flat calm she knew made people irate. "And I know that this is a library, but you hoard books like it is your own personal collection."

Merrill bared her teeth. "You think I do not know *you*? The human girl who was shoved into the Cauldron and came out High Fae. The female who slew the King of Hybern and held up his head like a trophy as his blood rained upon her."

Surprise lit Gwyn's face at the graphic description.

Nesta didn't allow herself to so much as swallow.

"The wind whispers to me even here, under so much stone," Merrill said. "It finds its way in through the cracks and murmurs the goings-on of the world in my ear." Merrill snorted. "Do you think you are entitled to do as you please now?"

Nesta's power rumbled in her veins. She stomped on it, shoved it down and strangled it. "I think you like to hear yourself talk too much."

"I am descended from Rabath, Lord of the Western Wind," Merrill seethed. "Unlike Gwyneth Berdara, I am no lackey to be dismissed."

To hell with this witch. To hell with restraint and hiding.

Nesta let enough of her power simmer to the surface that she knew her own eyes glowed. Let it crackle, even as she ignored its wild, unholy bellowing.

Gwyn had backed away a step. Even Merrill blinked as Nesta said, "With a fancy title like that, surely such a petty grudge should be beneath you."

Nesta smiled, savage and cruel. Merrill only glanced between her and Gwyn before saying, "Get back to your work, nymph."

Wind snapping at her heels, Merrill stalked into the gloom.

Nesta dropped the thread of her power, quelling its music and roaring with an iron hand.

But it wasn't until Merrill's brisk wind faded that Gwyn leaned against a stack, rubbing her hands over her face. The priestesses who'd been watching launched into movement again, their whispering filling the library.

Nesta asked into the rustling quiet, "Nymph?"

Gwyn lowered her hands, noted the lack of glowing power in Nesta's eyes, and sighed in relief. But her voice remained casual. "My grandmother was a river-nymph who seduced a High Fae male from the Autumn Court. So I'm a quarter nymph, but it's enough for this." Gwyn gestured to her large eyes—blue so clear it could have been the shallow sea—and her lithe body. "My bones are slightly more pliant than ordinary High Fae's, but who cares about that?"

Perhaps that was why Gwyn was so good at the balancing and movement.

Gwyn went on, "My mother was unwanted by either of their people. She could not dwell in the rivers of the Spring Court, but was too untamed to endure the confinement of the forest house of Autumn. So she was given in her childhood to the temple at Sangravah, where she was raised. She partook in the Great Rite when she was of age, and I, we—my sister and I, I mean—were the result of that sacred union with a male stranger. She never found out who he was, for the magic chose him that night, and no one ever showed up to ask about twin girls. We were raised in the temple as well. I never left its grounds until . . . until I came here."

Such pain filled Gwyn's eyes then. Such terrible pain that Nesta knew not to ask about her mother, or the twin sister.

Gwyn shook her head, as if dispelling the memory. She spread her fingers. "My twin had the webbed fingers of the nymphs—I don't."

Had.

Again, Gwyn sighed. "Merrill will make your life a living hell, you know."

"She can try," Nesta said mildly. "It'd be difficult to make it any worse."

"Well, now we have a common enemy. Merrill will never forget this." She nodded toward the railings where the priestesses had been. "Though I suppose they won't, either. It's not every day someone stands up to her. Only Clotho can really make her fall in line, but Clotho lets her have her way, mostly because Merrill throws those windy tantrums that can send everyone's manuscripts scattering."

"Anytime you need someone to knock Merrill down a few pegs, let me know."

Gwyn smiled slightly. "Next time, perhaps I'll have the courage to do it myself."

⊹

It seemed the priestesses didn't forget what Nesta had done.

Nesta, Gwyn, and Emerie were going through their opening stretches, Cassian stone-faced and eagle-eyed to catch any mistake, when footsteps scuffed in the archway beyond the pit.

They all paused at the three hooded figures who emerged, hands clasped so tightly that their knuckles were white.

But the priestesses stepped into the sunlight, the open air. Blinked up at it, as if remembering what such things were.

Gwyn nimbly rolled to her feet, grinning so broadly that Nesta was momentarily taken aback by it. The priestess had been pretty in the library, but with that joy, that confidence as she aimed for the three priestesses, she had emerged into a beauty to rival Merrill or Mor.

Or maybe nothing had changed at all beyond that confidence, the way Gwyn's shoulders were pushed back, her head high, her smile free as she said, "Roslin. Deirdre. Ananke. I was hoping you'd come."

Nesta hadn't checked the sign-up sheet that morning. Had stopped believing anyone except Gwyn would ever come to training.

But the three of them huddled together as Cassian offered a casual smile that was nearly a replica of Rhys's. Designed to put people at ease and lessen the threat of his power, his body. "Ladies," he said, gesturing to the ring. "Welcome."

Roslin and Ananke said nothing, but the one in the middle, Deirdre, tugged back her hood.

Nesta clamped down on every instinct that would have had her gasping. Emerie, on the mat beside her, seemed to be trying to do the same.

A long, vicious scar cut across Deirdre's face, narrowly missing her left eye. It was raised, stark white against her brown skin, and flowed from her tightly curling black hair to her slender, lovely jaw. Her round dark eyes, framed by a thick sweep of lashes that made them seem even rounder, were wide but determined as she said, "We hope we are not too late."

All of them looked to Nesta. But she wasn't the leader here.

She threw Cassian a glance, and he gave her a shrug as if to say, *I'm just the instructor.*

Another scar flowed down Deirdre's neck, disappearing beneath her robe. For such scars to exist on a High Fae at all suggested an event of such violence, such horror, that Nesta's stomach clenched. But she stepped toward the priestess. "We were just starting."

⸸

"Give me those stones and bones, please," Nesta said quietly to the House as she sat in the private library, a map of all seven courts before her, Cassian a step behind her.

A small earthenware bowl appeared beside the map, filled with them.

Nesta swallowed against the dryness in her mouth.

Cassian whistled. "It really does listen to you."

She peered over a shoulder. She'd invited him here after she'd returned from working in the library out of pure caution, she told herself. If she lost control, if she wasn't able to witness where her finger landed on the map, someone had to be here. That person just so happened to be him.

Never mind that he'd once stood beside her, his hand upon her back as it was now, and let her lean into his warmth and strength.

Cassian glanced between the bowl of scrying instruments and the map. "Why did you change your mind?"

Nesta didn't give herself time to hesitate before she slid her fingers into the bowl and scooped up the handful of stones and bones. They clinked against each other, hollow and ancient.

"I couldn't stop thinking about those priestesses who came to practice today. Roslin said she hadn't set foot outside in sixty years. And Deirdre, with those scars . . ." She took a long breath. "I am asking them to be brave, to work hard, to face their fears. Yet I'm not doing the same."

"No one accused you of that."

"I don't need anyone to say it. I know it. And I might fear this scrying, but I fear being a cowardly hypocrite even more."

The priestesses had been novices in every sense of the word: Ananke had such terrible balance she'd fallen over trying to plant her toes in the dirt. Roslin had been only a fraction better. Neither had removed their hoods, not as Deirdre had done, but Nesta had caught glimpses of wine-red hair on Roslin and golden hair on Ananke, their skin pale as cream.

Cassian said, "You sure you don't want to do this with Rhys and Amren around?"

Nesta squeezed the bones and stones in her fist. "I don't need them."

He fell silent, letting her concentrate.

It had taken a few moments the first and only time she'd done it. To let her mind go empty, to wait for that tug through her body that had hauled her toward an unseen force. She'd been whipped across the earth, and when she'd opened her eyes, she'd been standing in a war-tent, the King of Hybern before her, the Cauldron a squatting, dark mass beyond.

Nesta closed her eyes, willing her mind to quiet as she lifted her tight fist over the map. She focused upon her breathing, upon the rhythm of Cassian's breathing.

Her swallow was loud to her ears.

She'd failed at everything. But she could do this.

She'd failed her father, failed Feyre for years before that. Failed her mother, she supposed. And with Elain, she'd failed as well: first in letting her get taken by Hybern that night they'd been stolen from their beds; then by letting her go into that Cauldron. Then when the Cauldron had taken her into the heart of Hybern's camp.

She'd failed and failed and failed, and there was no end to it, no end—

"Anything?"

"Don't talk."

Cassian grunted, but sidled closer, his warmth now solidly at her side.

Nesta willed her mind to empty. But it couldn't. It was like being in that damned stairwell—she just circled around and around and around, down and down.

The Dread Trove. She had to find the Dread Trove.

The Mask, the Harp, the Crown.

But the other thoughts pressed in. Too many.

The Mask, she strained to think. *Where is the Mask of the Dread Trove?*

Her palm slickened with sweat, the stones and bones shifting in her fist. If the Mask was aware like the Cauldron had been . . . She couldn't let it see her. Find what she loved most.

Couldn't let it see her, find her, hurt her.

The Mask, she willed the stones and bones. *Find the Mask.*

Nothing answered. No tug, no whisper of power. She exhaled through her nostrils. *The Mask*, she willed them.

There was nothing.

Her heart thundered, but she tried again. A different route.

Thought of their common origin—the one she and the Trove shared. The Cauldron.

Yawning emptiness answered.

Nesta furrowed her brow, clenching the items harder. Pictured the Cauldron: the vast bowl of darkest iron, so large multiple people could have used it as a bathtub. It had a physical shape, yet when that icy water had swallowed her, there had been no bottom. Just a chasm of freezing water that had soon become utter darkness. The thing that had existed before light; the cradle from which all life had come.

Sweat beaded on her brow, as if her very body rebelled against the memory, but she made herself recall how it had sat in the King of Hybern's war-tent, squatting atop the reeds and rugs, a primordial beast that had been half-asleep when she'd entered.

And then it had opened an eye. Not one she could see, but one that she could feel fixed on her. It had widened as it realized who stood there: the female who had taken so much, too much. It had narrowed all of its depthless power, its rage, upon her, a cat trapping a mouse with its paw.

Her hand shook.

"Nesta?"

She couldn't breathe.

"Nesta."

She couldn't endure it, the memory of that ancient horror and fury—

She opened her eyes. "I can't," she rasped. "I can't. The power—I don't think I have it anymore."

"It's there. I've seen it in your eyes, felt it in my bones. Try again."

She couldn't summon it. Couldn't face it. "I can't." She dropped the stones and bones into their dish.

She couldn't endure the disappointment in Cassian's voice, either, as he said, "All right."

She didn't eat dinner with him. Didn't do anything except crawl into her bed and stare up at the darkness, and free-fall into it.

✠

It was searching for her.

Winding through the hallways of the House, wending like a dark snake, it searched and sniffed and hunted for her.

She couldn't move from her bed. Couldn't open her eyes to sound the alarm, to flee.

She felt it come closer, crawling up the stairs. Down her hallway.

She couldn't move her body. Couldn't open her eyes.

Darkness slid through the crack between her door and the stone floor.

No—it couldn't have found her. It would catch her this time, hold her down on this bed and rip from her everything she had taken from it.

The darkness slithered to her bed, and she forced her eyes open to see it gather over her, a cloud with no shape, no form, but such wicked presence that she knew its name before it leaped.

She screamed as the Cauldron's darkness pinned her to the bed, and then there was nothing but the horrible weight of it filling her body, tearing her apart from the inside out—

And then nothing.

✠

Cassian jolted awake and reached for the knife on his nightstand.

He didn't know why. He'd had no nightmare, heard no sound.

Yet terror and dread sluiced through him, ratcheting up his heartbeat. The lone Siphon on his hand glowed like fresh blood, as if also seeking an enemy to strike.

Nothing.

But the air had gone cold as ice. So cold his breath clouded, and then the lamps flared to life. Flared and flickered, flashing, as if desperately signaling to him.

As if the House were begging him to run.

He vaulted from the bed, and the door opened before he could careen into it. Launching into the hall, knife in hand, he didn't care that he was in his undershorts, or that he only had one Siphon. Az's door flung open a heartbeat later, and his brother's steps closed in behind him as Cassian hit the stairs and raced down them.

He'd reached the landing of Nesta's level when she screamed.

Not a scream of rage, but of pure terror.

His body distilled at that scream, as if it were no more than the knife in his hand, a weapon to be used to eliminate and destroy any threats to her, to kill and kill and not stop until every last enemy was dead or bleeding.

Her door was open, and light blazed from within. Silvery, cold light.

"Cassian," Az warned, but Cassian pushed himself faster, running as swiftly as he ever had in his life. He slammed into the archway of her door, rebounding off it and into the room, and came up short at what he beheld.

Nesta lay in her bed, body arched. Bathed in silver fire.

She was screaming, hands ripping at the sheets, and that fire burned and burned without destroying the blankets, the room. Burned and writhed, as if devouring her.

"Holy gods," Azriel breathed.

The fire radiated cold. Cassian had never heard of such a power amongst the High Fae. Fire, yes—but fire with *warmth.* Not this icy, terrible twin.

Nesta arched again, sobbing through her teeth.

Cassian lunged for her, but Azriel grabbed him around the middle. He snarled, debating whether he could rip out of Azriel's arms, but the hold Az had on him was too clever.

Nesta screamed again, and a word appeared in it. *No.*

She began shouting it, pleading, *No, no, no.*

Nesta arched once more, and that fire sucked in, as if a great inhale had been made, and was about to be exhaled, rupturing through the world—

The windows of the room blew out.

Night burst in, full of shadows and wind and stars.

And as Nesta erupted, silver fire blasting outward, Rhys pounced.

He smothered her fire with his darkness, as if he'd dropped a blanket on it. Nesta screamed, and this time it was a sound of pain.

The night cleared enough that Cassian could see Rhys at the bed, roaring something that the wind and fire and stars drowned out. But from his lips, Cassian knew it was her name. "Nesta!" Rhys shouted. The wind cleared enough for Cassian to hear this time. "*Nesta! This is a dream!*"

Nesta's fire reared again, and Rhys shoved a wave of blackness upon her. The entire House shook.

Cassian thrashed against Azriel, bellowing at Rhys to stop it, stop hurting her—

Rhys's darkness pushed down, and Nesta's flame battled upward, as if their two powers were swords clashing in battle, fighting for the advantage.

Dominance thundered in Rhys's words this time. "Wake up. It's a dream. *Wake up.*"

Nesta still fought, and Rhys gritted his teeth, power gathering again.

"Let me go," Cassian said to Azriel. "Az, let me go right now." Azriel, to his surprise, did.

Cassian knew the odds were against him. He had a knife and one Siphon. To get caught in the magic between Nesta and Rhys would be akin to entering a lion's den unarmed.

But he walked to where silver fire and darkest night battled.

And he said with steady calm, "Nesta."

The silver fire flickered.

"Nesta."

He could have sworn her consciousness, that power, shifted toward him. Just long enough.

The wave of Rhys's power that hit her wasn't the brute attack of earlier, but a soft wave that washed over that flame. Banked it.

Rhys went still in a way that told Cassian his brother was no longer fully present, but rather in the mind of the female who had gone unmoving upon the bed. He'd rarely thought twice about Rhys's gifts as a daemati—Feyre's gift, too—but he'd never been more grateful for it.

Cassian barely dared to breathe. Azriel hovered behind him as Rhys stood before the bed.

Slowly, that flame receded. Vanished like smoke.

Slowly, Nesta's body relaxed.

And then her breathing evened out, her body going limp. Blissfully unconscious.

Cassian swallowed, his heart pounding so hard he knew Azriel could hear it as his brother came up beside him.

Then Rhys inhaled sharply, his body full of movement again. Azriel asked, his own shadows gathering at his shoulders, "What happened?"

But Rhys just walked to the little sitting area and slumped into a chair. The High Lord's hands were shaking—trembling so wildly that Cassian had no idea what to do. From the worry etched on Azriel's face, neither did his brother.

Cassian asked, "Should we send for Feyre?"

"No." The word was a snarl. Rhys's eyes flared like violet stars. "She doesn't come near here."

"Was that . . ." Azriel glanced to the bed and the unconscious female atop it. "That was Nesta's true power? That silver fire?"

"Only the surface of it," Rhys whispered, hands still shaking as he ran them down his face. "Fuck."

Cassian braced his feet, as if he could physically intercept whatever Rhys was about to say.

"I went into her nightmare." Rhys peered up at Cassian. "Why didn't you tell me you attempted a scrying today?"

"It didn't work." And Nesta's fear and guilt had been so heavy in the room that his chest had ached. He'd left her alone afterward, knowing she'd want privacy.

Rhys blew out a shuddering breath. "The scrying was a trip wire. For the memories. I caught that as I went in." His throat worked, as if he'd heave, but he held it down. "She was dreaming of the Cauldron. Of . . . of when she went in." Cassian had never seen Rhys at such a loss for words.

"I saw it," Rhys whispered. "Felt it. Everything that happened within the Cauldron. Saw her take its power with her teeth and claws and rage. And I saw . . . *felt* . . . what it took from her."

Rhys rubbed his face, and slowly straightened. He met Cassian's stare unflinchingly, his eyes full of remorse and agony. "Her trauma is . . ." Rhys's throat bobbed.

"I know," Cassian whispered.

"I guessed," Rhys breathed, "but it was different to *feel* it."

"What is her power?" Azriel asked.

"Death," Rhys whispered, hands trembling again as he got to his feet and aimed toward the window, which was now repairing itself shard by shard, as if a careful, patient hand worked upon it. He gazed at the female sleeping in the bed, and fear clouded the face of the High Lord of the Night Court. "Pure death."

CHAPTER 30

The dream had been real and not real, and there had been no end to it, no escape.

Until a familiar male voice had said her name.

And the terror had stopped, as if the axis of the world had shifted toward that voice. That voice, which became a doorway, full of light and strength.

Nesta had reached a hand toward it.

And then there had been another male voice in her mind, and this one had been familiar as well, and full of power. But it had been kind, in a way she had never heard the voice be to her, and it had eased her from the black pit of the dream, leading her with a star-flecked hand back to a land of drifting clouds and rolling hills under a bright moon.

She had curled up on one of those hills, safe and guarded in the moonlight, and slept.

Nesta dozed, heavy and dreamless, and did not open her eyes until sunlight, not moonlight, kissed her face.

She was in her room, the sheets askew and half-spilled on the floor, but . . .

Cassian was sleeping in a chair beside her bed.

His head was at an awkward angle, and his wings drooped onto the stone—and he was wearing only his undershorts and a blanket that looked as if someone had draped it over his lap.

It had been a nightmare, she realized with a cold splash of awareness. She'd dreamed of the Cauldron; she'd been lost in it, screaming and screaming.

And it had been his voice she'd heard. His voice and . . .

There was no sign of Rhysand. Just Cassian.

She stared at him for long minutes, the unusual paleness of his face, the brows still scrunched with worry, as if he fretted for her even in his sleep. The sun gilded his dark hair and shone through his wings, bringing out the undertones of reds and golds in both.

Like a knight guarding his lady. She couldn't stop the image, sprung from the pages of her childhood books. Like a warrior-prince, with those tattoos and that muscle-bound chest.

Her throat tightened unbearably, her eyes stinging.

She would not let herself cry, not for herself or for the sight of him keeping watch beside her bed all night.

But it was as if her furious blinking woke him, as if he could hear the flutter of her lashes.

His hazel eyes shot to hers, like he always knew precisely where she was. And they were so full of worry, of that unrelenting goodness, that she had to fight like hell to keep the tears from falling.

Cassian said gently, "Hey."

She clamped down on herself. "Hello."

"Are you all right?"

"Yes." No. Though not for the reason he believed.

"Good." He groaned, stretching, first his arms and then his wings. Muscles rippled. "You want to talk about it?"

"No."

"That's fine."

And that was that.

But Cassian threw her a half smile, and it was so normal, so *him* in a way that no one else was or would ever be, that her throat tightened again. "You want breakfast?"

Nesta managed to answer his half smile with one of her own. "I like your priorities, General."

✢

"What happened to you?" Emerie asked as they panted through their abdominal exercises. "You look white as death."

"Bad dreams," Nesta said, willing herself not to look to where Cassian stood, instructing Roslin from a respectful distance on how to do a proper squat. They'd had a quiet breakfast, but it hadn't been awkward. It had been comfortable—easy. Pleasant.

Gwyn asked, on Nesta's other side, "Do you have them often?"

"Yes." Nesta finished a sit-up, grunting through the weakness in her middle.

"Me too," Gwyn said quietly. "Some nights, I need a sleeping potion from our healer to knock me out."

Emerie gave Gwyn an assessing look. Emerie never asked about Gwyn's past, or the histories of the other priestesses, but she was a cunning female. Surely she'd seen the way they kept a healthy distance from Cassian, scented their hesitation and fear, and put a few things together. Emerie asked Nesta, "What did you dream about?"

Nesta's body locked up, but she launched back into motion, refusing to let the memories master her. "I dreamed of the Cauldron. What it did to me."

Gwyn said, playing with her hair, "I dream of my past, too."

But Gwyn's admission, Nesta's own, didn't weigh them down. Nesta's head had cleared slightly. And somehow, she found she could push herself harder.

Perhaps in voicing those truths, they'd given them wings. And sent them soaring into the open sky above.

⁜

"How are you holding up?"

Cassian sat across from Rhys's desk at the river house, an ankle resting on a knee, and asked, "Me? How about you? You look like hell."

"Yesterday was a rough day, followed by a rough night." Rhys rested his head atop a propped fist on his desk.

Cassian angled his head. "What happened before the disaster that was last night?"

Gods, he'd nearly wept this morning to open his eyes and find Nesta staring at him, her face clear and free of pain. The shadows still lingered, yes, but he'd take anything over her screaming. Over that magic Rhys could only explain as *pure death*.

When Rhys didn't answer, Cassian said, "Rhys."

Rhys didn't look at him as he whispered, "The baby has wings."

Joy sparked through Cassian—even as the broken whisper and what those words meant made his blood go cold. "You're sure?"

"We had an appointment with Madja yesterday morning."

"But he's only a quarter Illyrian." It was possible, of course, for the baby to have inherited wings, but unlikely, given that Rhys himself had been born without them, and only conjured them through whatever strange, unearthly magic he possessed.

"He is. But Feyre was in an Illyrian form when he was conceived."

"That can make a difference? I thought she only made the wings—nothing else."

"She shape-shifts. She transforms her entire self into the form she takes. When she grants herself wings, she essentially alters her body at its most intrinsic level. So she was fully Illyrian that night."

"She doesn't have the wings now."

"No, she shifted back before we knew."

"So let her change back into an Illyrian to bear the babe."

Rhys's face was stark. "Madja has put a ban on any more shape-shifting. She says that to alter Feyre's body in any way right now could put the baby at risk. On the chance that it could be bad for the baby, Feyre is forbidden to so much as change the color of her hair until after the birth."

Cassian raked a hand through his hair. "I see. But, Rhys—it'll be all right. It's not that bad."

Rhys snarled. "It *is* bad. For so many gods-damned reasons, it is fucking *bad*."

Rhys was as close to being beside himself as Cassian had seen him since he'd returned from Amarantha's court. "Breathe," Cassian said calmly.

Rhys's eyes simmered; the stars within them winked out. "Fuck you."

"Take a breath, Rhysand." Cassian gestured to the window behind him, the lawn sloping down to the river. "You want to go fight it out, I've got energy to burn."

The study doors opened, and Azriel walked in. From the grim expression etched on his face, he already knew.

Azriel claimed the seat beside Cassian. "Tell us what you need, Rhys."

"Nothing. I need to not fall apart so my mate doesn't pick up a whiff of this when she comes home for lunch." Rhys narrowed his eyes, and power rumbled in the room. "*No one* says a word about this to Feyre. *No one*."

"Didn't Madja warn her?" Azriel asked.

"Not strongly. She only mentioned an elevated risk during labor." Rhys let out a harsh laugh. "An elevated risk."

Cassian's stomach twisted.

Azriel said, "I know this is bad timing, but there is another thing to consider, Rhys."

Rhys lifted his head again.

Azriel's face was like stone. "Feyre won't show for another few weeks, but someone will notice soon enough. People will learn of her pregnancy."

"I know."

"Eris will learn."

"He's our ally. I suspect he'll be focused more on dealing with his father and finding his missing soldiers than on this."

Then Az went for the throat. "And Tamlin will learn."

Rhys's snarl set the lights guttering. "And?"

Cassian shot Azriel a warning glare, but Az said, unafraid and unbowed, "We need to be prepared for any fallout."

"Like I give a fuck about Tamlin right now."

That Rhys couldn't understand what Az meant told Cassian how distraught and terrified he was.

Cassian tried to mimic Az's calm tone. "He may react badly."

"He sets foot over this border and he dies."

"I don't doubt that," Cassian said. "But Tamlin is already hanging by a thread. You and Lucien have made it clear that he's barely improved this past year. Learning of Feyre's pregnancy might make him crumble again. With a new war possible and Briallyn up to her bullshit with Koschei, we need a strong ally. We need the Spring Court's forces."

"So we're to hide her pregnancy from him?"

"No. But we need to summon Lucien," Azriel said, just a shade tightly, as if he didn't like it one bit. "We need to tell him the news, and permanently station him at the Spring Court to contain any damage and to be our eyes and ears."

Silence. They let the words sink in for Rhys.

"The idea of coddling Tamlin makes me want to shatter that window," Rhys said, but it was with enough of a grumble that Cassian nearly sagged in relief. At least that sharp edge of violence had been dulled. Just a fraction.

"I'll contact Lucien," Azriel offered.

Fear still lingered in Rhys's eyes, so Cassian walked around the desk and hauled his High Lord to his feet. Rhys let him.

Cassian slung an arm around Rhys's shoulders. "Let's go get bloodied up."

CHAPTER 31

Nesta was just settling herself at the dining table, stomach gurgling with hunger, when Cassian entered.

Limped in was more like it.

She couldn't stop a near-silent gasp from escaping her as she took in the black eye, the split lip, the bruised jaw.

"What happened?" she demanded.

Cassian shuffle-hopped to his chair and then dropped into it. "I sparred with Rhys."

"You look like a tenderized piece of meat."

"You should see him." He laughed hoarsely.

"Why did you fight like that?" If it had something to do with her nightmare—

"Rhys needed to get it out of his system." Cassian sighed at the bowl of roast chicken and rice soup that appeared before him. "Despite that smooth exterior my brother presents to the world, he needs to let loose every now and then."

"Your idea of letting loose and mine appear to be very different."

He snorted, sipping a spoonful of soup. "It wasn't for fun. Just to release some tension."

"About what?" She knew she had no business inquiring.

But Cassian set down the spoon, his face turning grave. "The baby has wings."

She needed to blink a few times to process that. "How can they know already?"

"Madja's magic allows her to glean a general shape of a babe within the womb, to check that all is well. He's large enough now for her to detect that all the limbs are in order . . . and that he has wings."

Utterly incredible, the way their magic could work. To actually be able to see within the womb itself.

Nesta couldn't stop the small voice in her mind from wondering what her own power might do, if she untethered her leash on it. And couldn't stop the bolt of panic that answered. As if thinking about it would allow it to roam free.

Nesta made herself ask, "So Rhysand didn't want the baby to have wings?"

Cassian kept eating. "It's not that. It will be a joy for him, for me and Az and Feyre, too, I suppose, to teach the baby how to fly, to love the wind and sky as we do. The problem is the birth."

"I don't understand."

"How many half-Illyrians have you met?"

"Only Rhys, I suppose."

"That's because they're extremely uncommon. But Rhys's mother was Illyrian herself. And Illyrian women hardly ever marry and reproduce outside their communities. Illyrian males do so far more often, or at least fuck around, but you rarely see the offspring."

"Why?"

"Illyrian females have a pelvis shaped specifically for children with wings to pass through. High Fae females do not. And when a child has wings, they can get stuck during labor." His face had gone pale beneath the bruises. "Most females die, the babes with them. There's no way for magic to help, short of fracturing a female's pelvis to widen it for the birthing. Which might kill the babe anyway."

"Feyre is going to die?" Her words were a whisper. For a heartbeat, every bit of spite, of anger, of bitterness faded away. Pure, clear panic replaced it.

"A few do survive." Cassian made to rub his face, then stopped before he could press the bruises. "But the labor is so brutal that many of them either come close to death or are so altered by it that they can't have another child."

"Even with a healer to repair them?" Her heart was pounding, so sickeningly fast she had to set down her utensils.

"Honestly, I don't know. And any attempts in the past to cut the child out of the mother's womb have been . . ." He shuddered. "No mother has ever survived." Nesta's blood turned to acid. Cassian rolled his shoulders. "So we won't even try that route. Madja will be there each step of the way, though, doing whatever she can. And we don't yet know how Feyre's own magic will impact the birth."

"Is Feyre distraught?"

"She doesn't know the full scope of it. But all of us who have grown up here know what it means for a High Fae female to bear a baby with wings."

Nesta willed herself to settle the fear leaching through her. "And Rhys needed to fight out his fear."

"Yes. Along with his guilt and pain."

"Perhaps another court has a healer who knows more than Madja. Maybe one with a winged people. The Dawn Court has the Peregryns—Drakon's people are Seraphim. Miryam doesn't have wings and yet she's given birth to Drakon's children."

"Rhys is heading to their island tomorrow. And Mor is making discreet inquiries at the Fae courts on the continent." He ran a hand through his hair, Siphon catching the light. "If there is a way to save

Feyre from a death sentence, Rhys will find it. He will stop at nothing until he figures out a way to spare her."

Silence fell, and the weight upon her chest was nearly unbearable. Rhys would do that, she knew without a doubt. The High Lord would go to the ends of the world for a way to save Feyre.

She said quietly, "I'll try scrying again."

Cassian's black eye was stark in the light as he lowered his brows in warning. "After last night—"

She lifted her chin. If that babe survived . . . Nesta would not allow him to be born into a world once more plunged into war. But she didn't say that, couldn't open herself up like that. "I need to regain my strength after yesterday's attempt. We'll do it tomorrow night."

"I want Rhys and Amren there. And Az."

"Fine."

Cassian leaned back in his chair. It was almost comical, his heavy stare combined with his split lip and black eye. He said after a moment, "Why haven't you sought me out?"

Nesta knew what he meant solely from the way his voice had dropped an octave.

She could play this game of distraction. He had no idea how well she'd learned to play it. So she let her own voice drop, too. "Why haven't you sought *me*?"

"I'm taking my cues from you. You seemed to have no interest in me after . . ." He nodded to the table between them, the floor where she'd knelt between his legs. "I didn't hurt you, did I?"

Nesta let out a rough laugh. "No, you didn't hurt me." She reached across the table, tracing a finger down his arm before meeting his eyes. "I loved it when you fucked my mouth, Cassian."

His eyes darkened. She rose, and he went wholly still as she rounded the table and came to a stop beside his chair. "Do you want to fuck me on this table?" she asked softly, running a hand over the smooth surface. He shuddered, as if he imagined that touch on his skin.

"Yes," he said, voice guttural. "On this table, on this chair, on every surface in the House."

"I don't think the House would appreciate such filthy behavior. Even if it's a romance reader as well."

"I . . . What?" His breath had turned uneven.

She leaned in to press a kiss against his torn mouth. It wasn't a loving gesture. Wasn't even a sweet one. It was a challenge and a wicked taunt to forget their fear and pain and come tangle with her. "I have no interest in bedding a male who looks like he's been in a tavern brawl," she said onto his lips.

"We can dim the lights."

Nesta chuckled. Desire had fogged his eyes, and she knew if she looked down, she'd see the evidence of how affected he was. But she wouldn't give herself that temptation.

He'd be her reward—but only after she'd accomplished the scrying.

Her lips curved. "When you're healed and looking pretty again," she said, pulling away, "then I'll let you fuck me wherever you please in this House."

Cassian's hands dug into the arms of his chair, as if restraining himself from leaping upon her. But his mouth parted in a savage grin. "Deal."

+

No one asked about Nesta's change of heart when she and Cassian entered the study in the river house late the next afternoon and found Rhys, Feyre, Azriel, and Amren waiting before a giant map of the faerie realms. A bowl of stones and bones sat beside it.

They all stared, weighed and judged her. But her eyes went to Feyre, who stood across the room, a hand resting idly on the slight swell of her belly.

Nesta refused to let anything show on her face as she offered her sister a small nod of greeting. She hated herself when Feyre's eyes softened—hated the raw emotion there as Feyre nodded back, smiling tentatively.

She couldn't stand the relief and happiness in Feyre's eyes. That merely acknowledging her sister politely had caused it. Unable to stomach it, Nesta glanced to where Rhysand stood at Feyre's side. One look into his eyes and Nesta allowed her mind to open—just a crack.

I will not say a word to Feyre, she swore.

She didn't do it for any particular kindness, but to wipe that cautious look from Rhys's eyes before it grated further. He'd no doubt either heard or guessed that Cassian had told her about the baby's wings.

Rhys only said, his voice wary, *Thank you*.

Nesta didn't ask about his visit to Miryam and Drakon—if he'd learned anything at all. She reached the table, Cassian keeping close. But she forgot about him as she faced Amren, who was watching her with cool distaste.

The words from months ago that Nesta had tried so hard to forget swarmed from the darkest pit of her memory, each one stinging. *You have become a pathetic waste of life*.

Nesta dropped Amren's stare, focusing on the map. "Let's be quick about this."

Azriel asked from beside Amren, "When you attempted it two days ago, you felt nothing?"

"Nothing." Nesta's fingers hovered over the bowl of tools. "My mind circled itself."

"What did you think of?" Amren asked.

How much she hated herself. Her father. How much she feared the Cauldron.

Nesta said, "The Trove. And what happened the last time I scried."

Feyre said, "We won't allow any harm to come to Elain. Rhys warded her this morning, and we have eyes on her at all times."

"Eyes can be blinded," Nesta said.

"Not the ones under my command," Azriel said with soft menace. Nesta met his stare, knowing he was the only one aside from Feyre who could truly understand her hesitation. He'd gone with Feyre into the heart of Hybern's camp to save Elain—he knew the risk. "We won't make the same mistake twice."

She believed him. "All right." She scooped up the stones and bones. They were ice-cold against her fingers.

Clenching them tight, Nesta closed her eyes and held her arm over the map spread across the table. No one spoke, though the weight of their gazes pressed on her.

Cassian's warmth seeped into her side, his wings rustling near her back.

She let that warmth, the rustle anchor her.

He had come to save her from her nightmare, had stayed with her while she slept. Had guarded and fought for her. He would let no harm come to her now.

No harm

No harm

No harm

What had been an endless spiral of thoughts vanished. A gaping hole yawned open in her mind.

No harm

No harm

No harm

Nesta eased into that darkness, as if slowly submerging herself in a pool.

Cassian's arm brushed hers, and she let that anchor her, too. A lifeline out. She took his hand with her free one and interlaced their fingers. Let the touch ground her as she allowed the last of her mind to slip beneath the black surface.

And then nothing.

Falling slowly. Drifting, like a small stone fluttering to the bottom of a pond.

The Mask, she whispered, casting her mind into the eternity. *Where is the Mask of the Dread Trove?*

Still she drifted in liquid night.

In the beginning, and in the end, there was Darkness and nothing more. She had first heard that truth, understood it, during her battle with the Cauldron. And understood it again now as she floated into that same strange place, both full and empty, forever cold.

Where is the Mask? she asked the void.

Distantly, like a candle in a window, she felt Cassian's hand tighten on hers. That was the way back. Nothing could trap her, hold her, if she had that way home.

Where is the Mask?

⁜

For long minutes, only the ticking of the grandfather clock in the corner filled the study.

Nesta stood beside Cassian, her fingers now loose in his hand, her other hand extended over the map, bones and stones bulging within.

Cassian swapped glances with Feyre. He'd barely been able to look at her when he'd entered, to see the slight swelling in her lower belly. But he'd made himself grin, the portrait of casual, arrogant ease.

Now a chilled, phantom breeze drifted past him. The hair on the back of his neck stood.

Amren let out a soft hiss. "Where is she wandering to?"

Nesta's hand remained over the map. But her fingers in his had gone cold as ice.

Cassian squeezed her hand, willing warmth into it.

Across the table, Azriel's breath clouded. Rhys stepped closer to Feyre, positioning himself to intercept any unexpected threats.

"This didn't happen that time during the war with Hybern," Azriel murmured.

Before any of them could answer, Nesta's eyelids shifted—like she was seeing something. Her brows bunched, just a quiver toward each other. Her fingers tightened on the stones and bones, knuckles going white. Still the air grew colder.

"If you see the Mask, girl, then now would be the time to let go," Amren ordered, her voice wary.

Nesta's hand remained shut. But her eyes still moved rapidly behind their lids, searching, seeking.

"Nesta," Feyre commanded. "Open your hand." Feyre had gone into Nesta's mind the last time—had pulled her out, thanks to the daemati power she'd inherited from Rhys. Feyre swore softly. "She never lowered her shields. Her shields are . . ."

"A fortress of solid iron," Rhys murmured, eyes on Nesta.

"I can't get in," Feyre breathed. "Can you?"

"Her mind is guarded with something that no faerie magic can break," Amren said. The essence of the Cauldron itself.

But Nesta showed no sign of fear, no scent of it.

"Give her time," Cassian murmured. Gods, it was cold. Nesta's eyelids fluttered again.

"I don't like this," Feyre said. "Wherever she is, it feels deadly."

The cold kept dropping. Nesta's hand tightened in his—a hard squeeze.

A warning.

"Get her out, Rhys," Cassian demanded. "Get her out now."

"I can't," he said softly, his power a cloak of stars and night around him. "I— The doors to her mind were open the other night. They're shut now."

"She doesn't want it seeing her. Or us," Feyre said, her face tight. "She's locked it out, but also locked herself in."

Cassian's stomach twisted. "Nesta," he said into her ear. "Nesta, open your hand and come back."

Her breathing sharpened. The cold deepened.

"*Nesta*," he snarled—

And the cold halted. It didn't vanish, but rather . . . stopped. Nesta's eyes flicked open.

Silver fire burned within. Nothing Fae looked out through them.

Rhys shoved Feyre behind him. She shoved her way back to his side. But Nesta's hand continued to squeeze Cassian's. He squeezed back, let his Siphons send a bite of power into her skin.

She turned her head so slowly it was like watching a puppet move. Her eyes met his.

Death watched him.

But Death had walked beside him every day of his life. So Cassian stroked his thumb along her palm and said, "Hello, Nes."

Nesta blinked, and he let his Siphons bite her with his power again. The fire flickered.

He nodded to the map. "Let go of the stones and bones." He didn't let her scent his fear. Here was the being the Bone Carver had whispered about, exalted and feared.

Her eyes flamed. No one dared breathe.

"Let go of the stones and bones, and then you and I can play," Cassian said, letting her sense his heat and need, forcing himself to remember that taunting kiss at dinner and her promise to let him fuck her wherever he wished in the House; what it had done to him, how much he'd ached. He let it all blaze in his eyes, let the scent of his arousal wrap around her.

Everyone tensed as he leaned in, head dipping, and kissed her.

Nesta's lips were chips of ice.

But he let their coldness sting his own, and brushed his mouth against hers. Nipped at her bottom lip until he felt it drop a fraction. He slid his tongue into that opening, and found the inside of her mouth, usually so soft and warm, crusted with hoarfrost.

Nesta didn't kiss him back, but didn't shove him away. So Cassian sent his heat into it, fusing their mouths together, his free hand bracing her hip as his Siphons nipped at her hand once more.

Her mouth opened wider, and he slid his tongue over every inch—over her frozen teeth, over the roof of her mouth. Warming, softening, freeing.

Her tongue lifted to meet his in a single stroke that cracked the ice in her mouth.

He slanted his mouth over hers, tugging her against his chest, and tasted her as he'd wanted to taste her the other night, deep and thorough and claiming. Her tongue again brushed against his, and then her body was warming, and Cassian pulled back enough to say against her lips, "Let go, Nesta."

He drove his mouth into hers again, daring her to unleash that cold fire upon him.

Something thunked and clinked beside them.

And when Nesta's other hand gripped his shoulder, fingers now free of stones and bones, when she arched her neck, granting him better, deeper access, he nearly shuddered with relief.

She broke the kiss first, as if sliding into her body and remembering who kissed her, where they were, who watched.

Cassian opened his eyes to find her so close that they shared breath. Normal, unclouded breath. Her eyes had returned to the blue-gray he knew so well. Stunned surprise and a little fear lit her face. As if she'd never seen him before.

"Interesting," Amren observed, and he found the female studying the map.

Feyre gaped, though, Rhys's hand gripped tight in her own. Caution blazed on Rhys's face. On Azriel's, too.

What the hell did you do to pull her out of that? Rhys asked.

Cassian didn't really know. *The only thing I could think of.*

You warmed the entire room.

I didn't mean to.

Nesta pulled away—not harshly, but with enough intent that Cassian peered at where she and Amren focused on the map.

"The Bog of Oorid?" Feyre frowned at the spot in the Middle. "The Mask is in a bog?"

"Oorid was once a sacred place," Amren said. "Warriors were laid to rest in its night-black waters. But Oorid changed to a place of darkness—don't give me that look, Rhysand, you know what I mean—a long time ago. Filled with such evil that no one will venture there, and only the worst of the faeries are drawn to it. They say the water there flows to Under the Mountain, and the creatures who live in the bog have long used its underground waterways to travel through the Middle, even into the mountains of the surrounding courts."

Feyre frowned. "It can't be more specific, though?" She asked Rhys, "Do we have a detailed map of the Middle?"

Rhys shook his head. "It's forbidden to map the Middle beyond vague landmarks." He pointed to the sacred mountain in its center, where he'd been held for nearly fifty years. "The Mountain, the woods, the bog . . . All can be seen from land and air. But its secrets, those discovered on foot—those are forbidden."

Feyre's frown didn't lighten. "By whom?"

"An ancient council of the High Lords. The Middle is a place where wild magic still dwells and thrives and feeds. We respect it as its own entity, and do not wish to provoke its wrath by revealing its mysteries."

Feyre faced Nesta, who was staring blankly at where the stones and bones had fallen in a neat little pile atop the bog. "The Middle is where the Weaver of the Wood dwelled," Feyre said, voice tight. "If you go to the bog, you'll need to be armed."

"We'll both be armed," Cassian declared. "To the teeth."

When Nesta didn't respond, they all looked at her. None of them dared ask about that power, the being that had looked out at him. The one he'd melted away with his kiss. He could still taste that ice on his tongue, smell the scent similar to hers yet wholly different.

Nesta said, "We go tomorrow."

Feyre started, "You need time to prepare—"

"We go tomorrow," Nesta repeated. Cassian gleaned everything she wouldn't say. She wanted to go tomorrow so she didn't have the chance to think better of it. To learn more about the peril she'd be facing.

His fingers brushed against the small of her back, savoring her warmth after all that cold. "We'll leave after breakfast."

CHAPTER 32

"I should go with you," Rhys said to Cassian as they gathered in the foyer of the river house the next morning.

"*I* should go with you," Feyre countered, leaning against the stair railing, frowning at her mate and Cassian.

Nesta watched them in silence, the weight of the weapons she carried like phantom hands pushing on her back, her thighs, her hips. *You're still as likely to hurt yourself as you are an opponent*, Cassian had said as he laid his weapons on the dining table this morning, *but it's better than going into Oorid unarmed*. She'd selected a dagger and he'd grinned. *Pointy end goes into your enemy.*

She'd given him a withering look, but had allowed him to assist her with the straps and buckles of the various sheaths, focusing upon his strong hands whispering over her skin and not the task at hand.

"We both should go with you," Rhys amended. "But at least Azriel will be there."

"Thanks for your confidence," Cassian said wryly, and kissed Feyre's cheek. Rhys must have lowered her shield—for the moment.

"You two aren't even parents yet and your mother-henning has reached an unbearable level."

"*Mother-henning?*" Feyre choked on a laugh.

"It's a word," Cassian said, so casually that Nesta wondered if he comprehended the danger they were walking into.

Nesta slid her gaze to Azriel, who shrugged subtly in confirmation. Yes, they were about to venture into a lethal, ancient bog. No, Cassian didn't seem as disturbed as the two of them were.

Nesta scowled, and Az offered her a slight smile. They could be allies, that smile seemed to say. Against Cassian's utter insanity. She found herself answering Azriel with a slight smile of her own.

Rhys sighed to the ceiling. "Shall we?"

Nesta glanced up the stairs past Feyre. Elain had again opted to remain in her room when Nesta was present, which was just fine. Absolutely, utterly fine. Elain could make her own choices. And had chosen to thoroughly shut the door on Nesta. Even as she fully embraced Feyre and her world. Nesta's chest tightened, but she refused to think of it, acknowledge it. Elain was like a dog, loyal to whatever master kept her fed and in comfort.

Nesta wrenched her attention from the stairs, cursing herself for a fool for even looking.

"I don't like this," Feyre blurted, stepping toward her. "You haven't had enough training."

Cassian smirked. "She has two Illyrian warriors guarding her. What could go wrong?"

"Don't answer that," Rhys said drily to his mate. He met Nesta's gaze. Stars were born and died in his eyes. "If you don't want to go—"

"You need me," Nesta said, chin lifting. "The bog is large enough that you won't be able to find the Mask without my . . . gifts." She had no idea how *she'd* find the Mask in Oorid, but they could at least begin exploring the area today. Or so Cassian had said this morning.

Feyre seemed poised to object, but Azriel extended his scarred hands to Cassian and Nesta. Feyre stepped forward again. "The Middle is like nothing you have experienced before, Nesta. Don't let your guard down for a moment."

Nesta nodded, not bothering to say that she'd operated by that principle for a long time.

Azriel didn't give them a chance to exchange another word before murmuring shadows swept around them. Nesta couldn't help clinging to Azriel, gleaning on some innate level that if she let go, she would tumble through this space between places and be lost forever.

But then gray, watery light hit her. And the air—the air was heavy, full of slow-running water and mold and loamy earth. No wind moved around them; not even a breeze.

Cassian whistled. "Look at this hellhole." Dropping Azriel's hand, Nesta did just that.

Oorid stretched before them. She had never seen a place so dead. A place that made the still-human part of her recoil, whispering that it was *wrong wrong wrong* to be here.

Azriel winced. The shadowsinger of the Night Court *winced* as the full brunt of Oorid's oppressive air and scent and stillness hit him.

The three of them surveyed the wasteland.

Even the Cauldron's water hadn't been as solidly black as the water here, as if it were made of ink. In the shallows mere feet away, where the water met the grass, not one blade was visible where the surface touched it.

Dead trees, gray with age and weather, jutted like the broken lances of a thousand soldiers, some draped with curtains of moss. No leaves clung to their branches. Most of the branches had been cracked off, leaving jagged spears extending from the trunks.

"Not one insect," Azriel observed. "Not one bird."

Nesta strained to listen. Only silence answered. Empty of even a whistle of a breeze. "Who would bury their dead here?"

"They didn't put them in the earth," Cassian said, his voice oddly muffled, as if that thick air gobbled up any echo. "These were water burials."

Nesta said, "I'd rather be burned to ashes and cast to the wind than be left here."

"Noted," Cassian said.

"This is an evil place," Azriel whispered. True fear shone in the shadowsinger's hazel eyes.

The hair on Nesta's arms rose. "What manner of creature dwells here?"

"You're asking this now?" Cassian said, brows high. He and Azriel had both worn their thicker armor, summoned by tapping the Siphons atop the backs of their hands.

"I was scared to ask before," Nesta admitted. "I didn't want to lose my nerve."

Cassian opened his mouth, but Azriel said, "Things that hunt in the water and feast on flesh."

"No one's seen a kelpie in a damn long time," Cassian countered.

"That doesn't mean they're gone."

"What's a kelpie?" Nesta asked, heart pounding at the tension etched into their faces.

"An ancient creature—one of the first true monsters of the faeries," Cassian said. "Humans called them by other names: water-horses, nixies. They were shape-shifters who dwelled in the lakes and rivers and lured unwitting people into their arms. And after they drowned them, they feasted. Only the entrails would make it back to shore."

Nesta stared toward the bog's black surface. "And they live in there?"

"They vanished hundreds of years before we were born," Cassian said firmly. "They're a myth whispered around fires, and a warning for children not to play near the water. But no one knows where they went. Most were hunted, but the survivors . . ." He conceded with a nod to Azriel, "It's possible that they fled to the Middle. The one place that could protect them." Nesta grimaced. Cassian threw her a grin that didn't meet his eyes. "Just don't go running after a beautiful white horse or a pretty-faced young man and you'll be fine."

"And stay out of the water," Azriel added solemnly.

"What if the Mask is in the water?" She gestured to the vast bog. They'd fly over it, they'd decided, and let her sense whatever lay here.

"Then Az and I will draw straws like the tough warriors we are and the loser goes in."

Azriel rolled his eyes, but chuckled. Cassian's grin at last glowed in his gaze as he opened his arms. "Oorid's beauty awaits, my lady."

✠

Cassian had been to some horrible places in his five centuries of existence.

The Bog of Oorid was by far the worst. Its very essence spoke of death and decay.

The oppressive air muffled even the sound of their wings, like Oorid would abide no sound disturbing its ancient slumber.

Nesta clung to him as he flew, Az at his side, and Cassian peered at the dead forest that spread below, the black water that had flooded it like an obsidian mirror. It was so still that he could see their reflections perfectly.

The wind whipping her braided hair, Nesta said, "I'm not sure what I'm looking for."

"Just keep all your senses open and see if anything sparks." Cassian began a wide circle to the west. The air seemed to press on his wings, as if it would cast them down to the earth.

But to enter that black water would be a last resort.

Islands of grass dotted the expanse, some so crowded with brambles that he could find no safe place to land. The tangles of thorns were a mockery of what might have been—as if Oorid had ever produced roses. Not a single flower bloomed.

"It's unbearable." Nesta shivered.

"We'll stay only as long as we can stomach it," Cassian said, "and if we don't find anything, we'll return tomorrow and pick up where we left off."

He had two swords, four knives, an Illyrian bow, and a quiver of arrows, plus all seven Siphons. Yet he couldn't shake the feeling of flying naked.

"What else dwells here other than kelpies?"

"Some say witches," he murmured. "Not the human kind," he added when she raised a brow. "The kind that used to be something else and then their thirst for magic and power turned them into wretched creatures, banished here by various High Lords."

"They don't sound so bad."

"They drink young blood to fill the coldness the magic left in them."

Nesta winced. Cassian went on as she scanned the bog, "There are lightsingers: lovely, ethereal beings who will lure you, appearing as friendly faces when you are lost. Only when you're in their arms will you see their true faces, and they aren't fair at all. The horror of it is the last thing you see before they drown you in the bog. But they kill for sport, not food."

"And all these horrible creatures are just *left* here, untended?"

"The Middle lies under no High Lord's jurisdiction. It's long been the dumping ground for any unwanteds."

"Not the Prison?"

"Their crimes are ones of nature. A kelpie is designed to lure and kill, just as a wolf is designed to hunt its prey. The Middle keeps them separate from us without punishing them for what they were made to be."

"But no one will come rid the world of them?"

"The Middle is full of primal magic. It has its own rules and laws.

Hunt the kelpies or lightsingers without provocation and you might find yourself trapped here."

She shuddered. "How would the Mask have wound up in the bog?"

"I don't know." He nodded toward the ground. "You feel anything?"

"No. Nothing."

Cassian glanced over a shoulder to Az before they entered a cloud of mist hovering above the northern section of the bog. It was so thick that Cassian rose higher, not wanting to impale them on a tall tree. The mist was chill enough to run icy fingers down his wings, his face.

Nesta jolted, then breathed, "Cassian."

He cleared the mist, banking to the left. "You sensed something?"

"I don't know what I sensed." She swallowed. "Something is here."

He looked over his shoulder again to signal Azriel.

But Az wasn't there.

CHAPTER 33

"Azriel!"

Cassian's shout didn't even echo.

Clinging to his neck, Nesta scanned the mist. Cassian hung back from it, wings beating in place as he searched for his brother. "Hold on," he hissed before he launched into a drop, using the momentum to swoop into the mist.

Blue light flared below—ahead. Azriel's Siphons.

"Fuck," Cassian spat, and shot lower.

Trees thrust upward, sharp as swords, and he swerved around them, wings within an inch of shredding on those spikes. Nesta's heart thundered, but she wouldn't shut her eyes against the death all around, not as Cassian dropped beneath the mist's curtain and they beheld what Azriel faced.

Cassian turned so swiftly Nesta barely had time to brace herself, and then he was flying back the way he'd come, through the mist. "Where are you going?" she demanded. "There are two dozen soldiers there!"

"Autumn Court soldiers," Cassian clarified, wings pumping so hard the wind ripped at her eyes. "I don't know what the fuck they're doing here, or if Eris has royally fucked us over, but one of them shot an ash arrow through Az's wing."

"Then why are we flying *away*?"

"Because I'm not landing with you in the middle of that."

"Put me down!" she shouted. "Put me down wherever and go back to him!" He didn't, surveying the bog below for the right place. She slammed a hand on his muscled chest. "Cassian!"

"I know what each second costs me, Nesta," he said quietly.

"Put me down in a fucking tree, then!" She pointed to one that they narrowly avoided.

He spotted an area he deemed safe enough: a solid stretch of grassy land, the remnants of a tree rising from its midst. He set her in the tree, as she'd suggested, perching her on the highest, sturdiest branch. It groaned and swayed beneath their weight. "Stay here," he commanded, waiting until she'd wrapped her hands around the branch and was clinging like a child who'd climbed too high. "I'll be back soon. Do *not* climb down. No matter what you may see or hear."

"Go." She was utterly useless in a fight, she knew. She would only distract him.

"Be careful," he warned, as if he weren't the one about to head into danger, and then he was gone. Nesta clung to the tree branch so hard her entire body trembled, the silence of the bog wrapping around her like a leaden blanket.

Oorid devoured Cassian's swift wingbeats within seconds, so she couldn't even hear him as he disappeared into the mist.

✠

Cassian aimed toward where his senses told him Az still fought. His eyesight sure as fuck didn't help him—the mist seemed thicker now.

The Autumn Court was here. Were these Eris's missing soldiers, or had he played them all for fools? Had Beron somehow learned of their plans?

He flew, swift as he could, praying Az had held them off, even with that ash bolt through his wing. The restraint of the ash bolt on Az's power was the only reason the soldiers weren't already dead—why Azriel's Siphons had been a flicker and not an incinerating wall against soldiers who were far less skilled.

Cassian descended into cool calm, willing each of his Siphons awake. He fed his power into them, and they refracted it back, confirming that they were ready, he was ready, for the bloodletting to begin.

Azriel's blue Siphons flared ahead, a smear of cobalt in the mist, and Cassian shot higher into the sky, until that blue was a flutter beneath him.

He stopped flapping entirely so the warriors wouldn't hear any wingbeats.

Then he spread his wings silently and slid into a free fall. Mist bit at him, the heavy air slapped his face, but he drew a blade and the knife at his thigh in silence.

The mist broke five feet above the skirmish.

The soldiers didn't have time to look up before Cassian was upon them.

Blood sprayed and males screamed, power bouncing off the red of Cassian's Siphons. Az battled it out with six soldiers at once, left wing limp and bleeding, his own Siphons blazing. The ash bolt had rendered Az's power nearly useless. But the Siphons had been blazing as a signal—for Cassian.

The sight of Az's injured wing made his head begin roaring.

Cassian killed and killed and did not stop.

⁜

Too long.

Cassian and Azriel had been gone for too long.

Nesta's limbs were beginning to lock up from the effort of clinging like a bear cub to the tree. She knew she had scant minutes until her body rebelled and let go.

There was no sound, no flash of light. Only the silent bog and the mist and the dead tree.

Every breath echoed her thoughts. Every breath was gobbled up by Oorid's oppression.

She'd seen Cassian face Hybern soldiers. Two dozen from the Autumn Court should be nothing. But why were they here?

Her legs shook so badly she nearly lost her grip on the branch. She knew she presented an utterly pathetic picture, laid out along the branch precisely as Cassian had left her, legs wrapped around it, ankles crossed over each other, fingers digging into the dry, silvery wood.

Carefully, she pushed herself up, her arms tingling with the numbness of clenching tight for so long. Her legs buckled with relief, too, as she released their grip, letting them hang in the air. She scanned the general direction Cassian had gone. Nothing.

He'd fallen in battle before—she'd seen him gravely injured. The first time in Hybern, when he'd tried to crawl toward her as she went into the Cauldron. The second time against Hybern's forces, when he'd been gutted and Azriel had held his entrails in with his bare hands. And the third time against the King of Hybern himself, when she had asked him, ordered him, to use her as bait, the distraction while she drew the king away from Feyre and the Cauldron.

After so many brushes with death, it was only a matter of time until it stuck.

Her mouth dried out. Azriel had been struck with an ash arrow. What if the soldiers had injured Cassian similarly? What if they were both in need of help?

She could do nothing against two dozen soldiers—against a single soldier, if she was being honest—but she couldn't endure sitting in a tree like a coward. Not knowing if he lived. And she had magic. Had no idea how to use it, but . . . she had that, at least. Maybe it would help.

She told herself she was concerned for Azriel, too. Told herself she cared about the shadowsinger's fate as much as Cassian's. But it was Cassian's dead face that she couldn't bear to imagine.

Nesta didn't let herself reconsider as she again laid herself out on the branch, wrapping her arms around it as she blindly lowered her leg, seeking the branch just beneath—

There. Her foot found purchase, but she didn't let it bear her full weight. Still clinging to the branch, fingernails digging into the dead wood hard enough that splinters sliced beneath them, she lowered herself onto the one below. Panting, she knelt again, and once more lowered her foot, finding another branch. But it was too far. Grunting, she brought her leg back up and carefully placed her hands on either side of her knees, focusing upon her balance, just as Cassian had taught her, thinking through every motion of her body, her feet, her breathing.

Fingertips screaming at the splinters piercing the sensitive flesh beneath her nails, she dropped her legs until they hit the branch below. The branch under it was closer but thinner—wobblier. She had to lay herself flat on it to keep from teetering off.

Branch by branch, Nesta descended until her boots sank into the mossy ground, and the tree loomed like a giant above her.

The bog stretched all around, miles of black water and dead trees and grass.

She'd have to wade through the water to reach him. Nesta focused on her breathing—or tried to. Each inhale remained shallow, sharp.

Cassian could be hurt and dying. To sit idle wasn't an option.

She scanned the shoreline five feet ahead for any hint of shallower water to wade through to the nearest mossy island, covered in flesh-shredding thorns, but the water was so black it was impossible to determine if it was shallow or if it dropped to a bottomless pit.

Nesta focused on her breathing again. She knew how to swim. Her mother had made sure of it, thanks to a cousin who had drowned in childhood. *Murdered by faeries*, her mother had claimed. *I saw her dragged into the river.*

Had it been a kelpie? Or her mother's own fears warped into something monstrous?

Nesta made herself approach the edge of the black water.

Run, a small voice whispered. *Run and run, and do not look back.*

The voice was female, gentle. Wise and serene.

Run.

She couldn't. If she were to run, it would be toward him, not away.

Nesta stepped to the water's edge, where grass disappeared into blackness.

Her face stared back at her from the stillness. Pale and wide-eyed with terror.

Run. Was that voice merely all that remained of her human instincts, or something more? She gazed at her reflection as if it would tell her.

Something rustled in the thorns of the island, and she snapped up her head, heart thundering as she scanned for that familiar male face and wings. But there was no sign of Cassian. And whatever was in that bramble . . . She should find another island to head for.

Nesta surveyed her reflection again.

And found a pair of night-dark eyes looking back through it.

CHAPTER 34

Nesta stumbled away so fast she landed on her backside, the mossy ground cushioning the impact. A face broke through the black water where her reflection had been.

It was whiter than bone and humanoid. Male. Bit by bit, inch by inch, the head rose above the black water, obsidian hair drifting in the water around the creature, so silken it might as well have been the surface.

His black eyes were enormous—no whites to be seen—his cheekbones so sharp they could have sliced the air. His nose was narrow and long, like a blade, and water dripped from its tip over a mouth . . . a mouth . . .

It was too large, that mouth. Sensuous lips, but too wide.

Then his arms slid from the water.

In stiff, jolting movements they jerked onto the moss, white and thin, ending in fingers as long as her forearm. Fingers that dug into the grass, revealing four joints and dagger-sharp nails. They cracked and popped as he stretched and dug them into the grass, grappling for purchase.

Nesta's breath sawed out of her, terror a roaring in her mind as she crawled backward.

He heaved himself out of the water, revealing a bony torso, his black hair dragging behind him like a net.

She lurched back again as he slowly lifted his head.

That too-wide mouth parted. Twin rows of rotted teeth, jagged as shards of glass, filled his mouth as he smiled.

Her bladder loosened, her lap becoming wet and warm.

He scented it, saw it, and that mouth widened further, fingers twitching as they hauled more and more of him from the water. His narrow, bare hips—

He pushed himself onto his arms as he slid a long, white leg from the blackness. Another. And then he knelt on all fours, smiling at her.

She couldn't move. Couldn't do anything but stare into that white face, the black eyes as dark as the bog, the twitching, too-long fingers and that mouth, those eel's teeth—

He spoke then, and it was not a language she recognized. His voice rasped, deep and hoarse, full of terrible hunger and cruel amusement.

The gentle female voice in her head pleaded, *Run, run, run.*

His head cocked, sodden black hair sloshing with the movement, full of what seemed to be bog weeds. As if he'd heard that female voice, too. He spoke again, and it was like rock grating on rock—his tone more demanding.

Kelpie. This was a kelpie, and he would kill her.

Run, the voice shouted. *Run!*

Nesta's legs had become distant, numb. She couldn't remember how to use them.

The kelpie's head twitched, fingers convulsing in the grass. His smile grew again. So wide she spied the long, black tongue writhing in his mouth, as if he could already taste her flesh.

Nesta couldn't recall how to scream as he lunged for her.

Couldn't do anything at all as those long fingers wrapped around her legs, claws ripping through her skin, and yanked her toward him.

Pain ripped Nesta from her stupor, and she fought, fingers grabbing at the grass. It came free in clumps, as if it had no roots at all. As if the bog would do nothing to help her.

The kelpie towed her along as he slithered back into the frigid water.

And dragged her under the surface.

✠

The two soldiers were on their knees.

Their light leather armor bore Eris's insignia of two baying hounds on the breast. It didn't confirm anything. They might have been ordered here by Eris, or Beron, or both of them. Until Azriel or Rhys could get answers out of them, Cassian wouldn't waste time theorizing. Not that the soldiers offered any explanations.

Their faces were vacant. Not a trace of fear in them, or in their scents.

Azriel panted, wing bleeding freely from where he'd ripped away the ash arrow. Cassian, covered in blood that was not his own, assessed the two surviving soldiers, their fallen companions around them. Many in pieces.

"Bind them," Cassian said to Azriel, who had already healed enough to summon his Siphons' power. Blue light speared from his brother, wrapping around the two males' wrists, their ankles, their mouths—and then chained them together.

Cassian had dealt with enough assassins and prisoners to know keeping two prisoners alive would allow him to confirm information, to play them off each other.

The soldiers had fought viciously with sword and flame, yet they hadn't spoken to their opponents or to one another. These two seemed as unfocused and blank as their comrades.

"Something is wrong with them," Azriel murmured as the two soldiers simply stared up at them with violence in their eyes. Violence, but no recognition or awareness that they were now at the mercy of the

Night Court, and would soon learn how that court got answers out of their enemies.

Cassian sniffed. "They smell like they haven't had a bath in weeks."

Az sniffed as well, grimacing. "Do you think these are Eris's missing soldiers? He said they'd been acting strange before they vanished. I'd certainly consider this strange behavior."

"I don't know." Cassian wiped the blood from his face with the back of his hand. "I suppose we'll find out soon enough." He surveyed his brother from head to toe. "You all right?"

"Fine." But Az's voice was tight enough to indicate that his wing hurt like hell. "We need to get out of here. There might be more."

Cassian stiffened. He'd left Nesta in a tree. A high tree, granted, but—

He launched skyward, not waiting to see if Az could follow before he was flapping toward that sprawl of land. Better than an island, he'd decided. On an island she'd have been trapped. But the swath of grass he'd left her in had looked as if it had once been a meadow, and the tree was so tall it would have taken a giant to reach. Or something else with wings.

The air parted, and Azriel appeared at his heels, unsteady and bobbing, but flying. Darkness rose behind them, confirmation that Az wielded his shadows to hide their captives.

Cassian tracked Nesta by scent back to that tree, the mist lightening only as its uppermost branches appeared. But Nesta wasn't in it.

He hovered in place as he scanned the tree, the ground. "Nesta!" She wasn't in the grass, or in the next tree. He dropped to the earth, tracking her scent all around the area, but it went no farther. Went right up to the water and vanished.

Azriel landed, whirling in place. "I don't see her."

The water remained still as black glass. Not a ripple. The island fifteen feet across the water—had she gone that way?

Cassian couldn't breathe right, couldn't think right—

"NESTA!"

Oorid devoured his roar before it could echo across the black water.

CHAPTER 35

There was no light, nothing but frigid water and clawed hands hauling her through it.

She had been here before. It was just like the Cauldron, being hurled into the icy dark—

This was how she would die, and there was nothing to do about it, no one to save her. She'd taken her last breath and hadn't even made it a good one, so focused on her terror she had forgotten that she had weapons, and she had magic—

Weapons. Blind in the darkness, Nesta grabbed the dagger at her side. She'd fought back against the Cauldron. She'd do so now.

Her bones groaned where the kelpie clutched her, its grip informing her where to strike. Working against the rush of the water as it sped along, Nesta sliced her dagger down, praying she didn't cut off her own leg.

Bone reverberated against the blade. The grip on her leg splayed, and she shoved the tip of her dagger in farther as the arm ripped away.

She flailed in spinning darkness. Up and down blurred and warped, and she was drowning—

Spindly hands slammed into her chest, one wrapping around her throat as her back hit something soft and silty. The bottom.

No, she wouldn't end like this, helpless as she'd been that day against the Cauldron—

Lips and teeth collided with her mouth, and she screamed as the kelpie kissed her. His black tongue shoved into her mouth, tasting of foul meat.

For a heartbeat, she wasn't beneath the water, but against a woodpile in the human lands, Tomas's hard mouth crushing into hers, his hands pawing at her—

Nesta struggled to pull her head away, to free her mouth, but air filled her lungs. As if the kelpie had breathed it into her. As if he wanted her alive a little longer, to prolong her pain.

The kelpie withdrew, and Nesta had enough sense to shut her aching, brutalized mouth, to trap in that breath he had given her. To not question how such a thing was even possible.

The kelpie's hands ripped at her body, tearing away every weapon with unerring aim, as if he did not need to see in this darkness, as if those large black eyes could pick up any trickle of light like some deep-sea creature. Her entire body went stiff and unmoving, each brutal touch entitled and furious and delighting in her fear.

When he had disarmed her, her lungs were burning again, and she felt that thin male body pushing her into the bottom once more as he shoved his mouth to hers.

She gagged, but opened for him, letting him fill her mouth with another life-giving breath that had nothing to do with kindness. His tongue wriggled like a worm against hers, and his spindly, too-large hands ran down her breasts, her waist, and when she gagged again, fighting against her sob, his laugh puffed through her lips.

He pulled away, rows of teeth ripping at her mouth as he did, and she shook when he lingered, stroking at her hair. His little prize—that was what the touch said. How he would make her suffer and beg before the end. She had escaped the monsters of the human realm only to find the same ones above the wall. Had escaped from Tomas only to wind up here, raging as she had then.

That pleading female voice had faded. As if whatever she was, whoever she was, she knew no hope existed now.

Nesta fumbled internally for her power while the kelpie began to swim again, a hand around her wrist, lugging her behind him.

Her legs bumped into metallic objects and bones, somehow preserved within the bog.

Some of the bones still felt fleshy.

Please, she begged that power within her, slumbering and ancient and terrible. *Please.* Nesta cast for it, seeking it in the chasm inside herself.

She could see it glowing ahead, golden and shining. Her fingers strained for it.

The kelpie swam faster through the darkness, wending between the objects in the water as if they were the roots of a tree.

The golden thing drew nearer, and it was a round disk, her power, growing closer and closer and closer. As Nesta was dragged along, that golden disk rushed toward her splayed fingers. The kelpie didn't seem to see it; he didn't veer away as it shot toward her outstretched hand.

It was not her power that shone ahead.

The golden disk connected with her fingers, and Nesta knew what it was as she gripped it tight. Like called to like. Power to power.

The kelpie pulled her along, unaware. Nesta's breath again became short. Her feet and legs sliced into dagger-sharp objects, ripping open on a few.

Power lay in her hand. Death gripped her by the other.

She knew what she had to do with the sort of clarity only pure desperation and terror could bring. Knew what she had to risk. Her fingers tightened on the thing in her hand.

The kelpie slowed, as if sensing her shift. But not fast enough.

He couldn't stop her from slamming the Mask onto her face.

CHAPTER 36

Her lungs stopped hurting. Her body stopped aching.

She did not require air. She did not feel pain.

She could see dimly through the eyeholes of the Mask. The kelpie was a lean white thing—a creature of pure hate and hunger.

He dropped her, as if in shock and fear. As if he hesitated when he beheld what she now wore.

It was all Nesta needed.

She could feel them around her. The dead.

Feel their long-rotted bodies, some mere bones and others preserved, half-eaten beneath their ancient armor. Their weapons lay nearby, discarded and ignored by the creatures of the bog, who had been more interested in feeding on decaying flesh, even long-rotted.

Thousands and thousands of bodies.

But she would not call thousands. Not yet.

Her blood was a cold song, the Mask a slithering echo to it, whispering of all she might do. *Home*, it seemed to sigh. *Home*.

Nesta did not refuse it. Only embraced it, letting its magic—colder than her own and as old—flow into her veins.

The kelpie mastered himself, and bared his twin sets of teeth before he sprang.

A skeletal hand wrapped around his ankle.

The kelpie whirled, peering downward. Just as another bony hand, covered in a gauntlet cracked with age, wrapped around the other ankle.

A hand with flesh falling from its fingers gripped his mane of black hair.

The kelpie twisted toward her again, black eyes wide.

Drifting in the water, the power of the Mask an icy song through her, Nesta summoned the dead. To do what her own body could not.

Though she had fought back against Tomas, against the Cauldron, against the King of Hybern, they had all *happened* to her. She had survived, but she had been helpless and afraid.

Not today.

Today, she would happen to *him*.

The kelpie thrashed, freeing himself from one skeletal hand as ten others, at the ends of long, bony arms, extended. Their bodies rose with them. He tried to swim out of their grip, but a towering skeleton half-clad in rusted armor appeared behind him. Wrapped its arms around him. A face that was only bone peered over the kelpie's shoulder, jaws opening to reveal pointed teeth—not High Fae, then—that gleamed before they buried themselves in the kelpie's white flesh.

He screamed, but it was soundless. Just as the dead were soundless, surging from the murky bottom, some in marching formation, and converging on him.

Nesta let the power flow through her, allowing the Mask to do as it wished, raising the honored dead who had once been buried here and had suffered the sacrilege of serving as an endless meal to the kelpie and his ilk.

The kelpie bucked against the dead, his eyes pleading now. But Nesta looked upon him without an ounce of mercy, still tasting his foulness in her mouth.

She knew he could see her teeth gleaming. Knew the kelpie could see her cold smile as she bade the dead to rip him to shreds.

✠

"NESTA!"

Up to his waist in the black water, so inky he couldn't see his own hips beneath it, Cassian roared her name as Az soared overhead, scanning, scanning—

He'd caught her scent at the water's edge—her scent and urine, gods damn him to hell. She'd seen something, been attacked by something so awful she'd wet herself, and now she was gone, under this water—

"NESTA!"

He didn't know where to start in this blackness. If he continued to make much more noise, other things would come looking, but he had to find her, or else he'd crumple up and die, he'd—

"NESTA!"

Azriel landed in the water beside him. "I don't see anything," he panted, eyes as frantic as Cassian knew his own were. "We need Rhys—"

"He's not answering."

As if the bog swallowed their messages the same way it swallowed sound.

Cassian waded up to his chest, hands blindly grappling for any sort of clue, a body—

He bellowed at the thought, and even Oorid couldn't muffle the sound.

He hurled himself forward, and only Azriel's hand at the collar of his armor halted him. Az snarled, "*Look.*"

Cassian gazed where Azriel pointed at the deeper water. The surface was rippling. Golden light shone beneath. Cassian splashed toward it, but Az halted him again, his Siphons flaring blue.

Then the spears broke the surface.

Like a forest rising from the water, spear after spear after spear appeared. Then the helmets, dripping water, some rusted, some shining as if freshly forged. And beneath those helmets: skulls.

"Mother save us," Azriel whispered, and it was undiluted terror, not awe, hushing his voice as the dead rose from Oorid's depths.

A line of them; a legion. Some mere collections of upright bones, jaws hanging and eyes unseeing. Some half-preserved, decaying flesh flapping over exposed ribs. Judging by their fine armor, they were warriors and kings and princes and lords.

They rose from the water, standing in the shallows near the thorny island. And as that golden light broke the surface before them, the dead knelt.

Every word emptied from Cassian's head as Nesta, too, emerged from the water, as if lifted on a pillar from beneath. A golden mask sat upon her face, primitive but embossed with whorls and patterns so ancient they'd lost all meaning.

Water sluiced down her clothes, her hair had been ripped from its braid, and in her hand, clenched there . . .

A kelpie's head dangled by its sheet of black hair, torn-up face frozen in a scream. Exactly as the King of Hybern's head had hung from her hand.

Only silver fire burned behind the eyes of the Mask.

"Holy gods," Azriel breathed.The dead stood motionless, a legion poised to strike. Her will was their will; her command their only reason for being. They had no self left—only her, only Nesta, flowing through them.

"Nesta," Cassian whispered.

Nesta released the kelpie's head. The black water at her feet swallowed it whole.

Cold power rippled toward them, and as it hit, Cassian let it surge past him, around him, yielded himself to it. Because to stand against it would be to provoke the Mask's wrath. To stand against it would be to stand against Death itself.

Death *herself*.

Azriel shook, weathering that primal power.

But they were both Illyrian, whether Az liked it or not. And so they did what their people had always done before Death's beautiful face. They bowed.

Chest-deep in the water, they couldn't bow far, but they lowered their heads until their faces nearly touched the surface. Cassian lifted his eyes as he held the position, and watched the gold of the Mask's reflection dance upon the water. Then that gold shifted.

He raised his head in time to see Nesta peel away the Mask.

The dead collapsed. Fell under the black surface in splashes and ripples and vanished entirely. Not one spear remained.

Nesta sank as if dropped, too. Cassian lunged for her, icy water biting at his face. He grabbed her just as she went under.

She was nearly boneless as he hauled her back to Az, who had his sword out against anything that might come crawling from that water. When they reached the shore and the grass and the tree, Cassian surveyed her pale face, ripped and scratched around her mouth and jaw—

Nesta blinked, and her eyes were again blue-gray, and then she was clutching the Mask to her chest like a child with a doll and shaking, shaking, shaking.

It was all Cassian could do to put his arms around her and hold her close, until the trembling stopped and unconsciousness offered her the mercy of oblivion.

CHAPTER 37

There was a place in the Court of Nightmares where even Keir and his elite squadron of Darkbringers did not dare tread.

Once the Night Court's enemies entered that place, they did not come out. Not alive, anyway.

Most of what remained of their bodies didn't leave, either. Those went through the hatch in the center of the circular room—and into the pit of writhing beasts below. To their scales and claws and merciless hunger. The beasts did not feed often; they could receive a body every ten years and make it last, going into hibernation between meals.

The trickling blood of the two Autumn Court males through the black stone floor's grate woke them.

Their snarls and hisses, their snapping tails and scraping claws should have incentivized the males chained to the chairs to talk.

Azriel leaned against the wall by the lone door, Truth-Teller bloody in his hand. Cassian, a step beside him, and Feyre, on Az's other side, watched as Rhys and Amren approached the two males.

"Are you feeling more inclined to explain yourselves?" Rhys said, hands sliding into his pockets.

Only the knowledge that Nesta slept safely in a bedroom in Rhys's palace above this mountain, warded by his High Lord's power, allowed Cassian to remain in this room. The Mask, covered with a black velvet cloth, lay on a table in another room of the palace, equally warded and bespelled. Azriel had winnowed them away from the bog moments after Nesta had passed out, and had brought them to Rhys's residence atop the Hewn City. Cassian knew, when Rhys had vanished a heartbeat later, that he'd gone to the bog for the Autumn Court soldiers, and would bring them here.

Nesta had been unconscious ever since.

The two males were similar-looking, in the way that people from individual courts tended to share characteristics: the Autumn Court skewed toward hair of varying shades of red, brown or gold eyes—sometimes green, and mostly pale skin. The male on the left had auburn hair that was browner; the hair of the one on the right shone like bright copper. Both remained vacant-faced.

"They must be under some sort of an enchantment," Amren observed, circling the males. "Their only drive seems to be to harm without reason, without context."

"Why did you attack members of my court in the Bog of Oorid?" Rhys asked with that same mild calm that so many had heard right before being ripped to bloody ribbons.

Rhys had agreed that the soldiers who attacked were likely the Autumn Court soldiers who had gone missing, but how they had ended up in the Bog of Oorid . . . Well, that was what they intended to uncover. Rhys had tried to get into their heads, but found nothing but fog and mist.

The males only stared toward Cassian, toward Azriel, and bristled with violence.

Feyre observed from the wall, "They're like rabid dogs, lost to sanity."

"They fought like them, too," Cassian said. "No intelligence—just a desire to kill."

Rhys extended a hand toward the one with the brownish hair, the male bleeding from places Azriel knew would hurt but not kill. Az knew where to slice up a male without letting him bleed out. Knew how to make this last for days.

"If they're under a spell from Briallyn or Koschei," Feyre asked, "then is it right to harm them like this?"

The question echoed through the chamber, over the snarling of the hungry beasts.

Rhys said after a moment, "No. It isn't."

Amren said to Feyre, "The fog around their minds and the fact that they endured Azriel's ministrations without showing an understanding of anything beyond basic pain at least confirms our suspicions."

"If that's how you wish to justify it," Feyre said a tad coldly, "then fine."

All of them, Feyre included, had been tortured at one point or another.

Feyre turned to Rhys. "We need to ask Helion to visit. Not for the—you know," she said, glancing to the two soldiers, who might very well still be aware of everything, even trapped within their heads, "but to break the spell upon them."

"Yes," Rhys said, eyes shining with something like guilt and shame. Some silent conversation passed between him and his mate, and Cassian knew Rhys was asking about the torture—apologizing for making Feyre witness even the ten minutes Azriel had worked.

But Feyre, Cassian knew, had been aware of what she'd see before entering. And well aware that these ten minutes had only been the opening movements in a symphony of pain that Azriel could conduct with brutal efficiency.

Feyre's face softened after a moment, and she offered Rhys a slight smile that made his eyes brighten. Rhys declared, "They stay here, under guard. I'll contact Helion immediately."

Cassian asked, "And Eris? When do we tell him we found his soldiers? Or what we did to most of them?"

"You acted in self-defense," Feyre said, arms crossing. "As far as I'm concerned, whoever was controlling the soldiers is to blame for their deaths, not you."

Amren added, "We'll tell Eris once we verify everything. There's still a possibility that he's somehow behind this."

Feyre nodded her approval, but her mouth tightened. "These two males have families who are surely worried about them. We should be as quick as possible."

Cassian shut out the thought of all the males whom he hadn't left standing—who all had worried families as well. Every death had a weight, sent a ripple into the world, into time. It was too easy to forget that. He glanced to Az, but his brother's face was stone-cold. If Az regretted what they'd done, he revealed no hint of it. Cassian tucked in his wings. "We'll be as fast as we can."

They left the males in the room, blood still trickling down to the writhing beasts.

⁜

Up they walked, out of the dungeons of the Hewn City, out of the wretched place itself, until they stood amongst the moonstone pillars of the beautiful palace above it. Rhys aimed for the room with the Mask. He opened the door and went stiff.

Nesta sat at the table, staring at the cloth-covered Mask.

"How did you get in here?" Rhys asked, night swirling at his fingertips. Cassian knew his brother had made the wards on the door impenetrable. Or they should have been.

"The door was open," Nesta said numbly, and scanned their faces as if looking for someone. Cassian stepped into the room, and her eyes settled on him.

He offered her a grim smile.

"The Mask opened the door for you?" Amren demanded.

"I found myself beckoned here," Nesta said, even as she looked Cassian over.

Checking for injuries, he realized. She was looking to see if *he* was harmed. As if he were the one with a brutalized mouth, neck marked by claws, calves and shins lacerated. Her wounds had stopped bleeding, already scabbing, but—Cauldron damn him, he couldn't stand the sight of one bruise on her.

"Does it speak to you?" Feyre asked, angling her head.

Cassian had told them everything—as far as he'd been able to gather. Nesta had been attacked by a kelpie, dragged under the water, and had somehow found the Mask. Summoned the dead of Oorid to her to slay the kelpie. And emerged triumphant.

"Only a desperate fool would don that Mask," Amren said, keeping well away from the table. Whether it was to put distance between herself and Nesta or to avoid the Mask, he had no idea. "You're lucky to have been able to pry it from your face. Most of those who have worn it could never remove it. In order to sever it, they had to be beheaded. It's the cost of the power: you can raise an army of the dead to conquer the world, but you can never be free of the Mask."

"I wished it to let go, and it did," Nesta said, surveying Amren with cool disdain.

"Like calls to like," Rhys said. "Others could not free themselves because the Mask did not recognize their power. The Mask rode them, not the other way around. Only one Made from the same dark source can wear the Mask and not be ruled by it."

"So Queen Briallyn could use it," Azriel said. "Perhaps that's why the Autumn Court soldiers were in Oorid: she can't yet risk setting foot here, but she found a unit to go in for her."

The words rippled through the room.

Nesta again stared at the Mask. "It should be destroyed."

"That's not possible," Amren said. "Perhaps if the Cauldron had been truly destroyed, the Mask might have been weakened enough for the High Lords and Feyre to join their power and do it."

"If the Cauldron had been destroyed," Feyre said with a shiver, "then life would have ceased to exist."

"So the Mask remains," Amren said wryly. "It can only be dealt with. Not eliminated."

"We should dump it in the sea, then," Nesta said.

"No taste for the living dead, girl?" Amren asked.

Nesta slid her eyes toward Amren in a way that had Cassian bracing for the worst. "No good can come of its power."

"If we dump it in the sea," Azriel said, "some wicked creature might find it. It's safer to keep it locked up with us."

"Even if it can open doors and undo spells?" Rhys asked.

"Like calls to like," Feyre said into the puzzled quiet. "Perhaps Nesta could ward it and lock the room. Contain it."

"I don't know how to do those spells," Nesta said. "I failed at the most basic of them while training with Amren, remember?"

Feyre's head tilted to one side. "Is that what you think, Nesta? That you failed?"

Nesta straightened, and Cassian's chest tightened at the wall that rose in her eyes, brick by brick. At the truth Nesta had let slip with that one word. "It doesn't matter," she said, her old self rearing its head as her chin lifted. "Tell me how to do the spells, and I'll try." She directed the last part to Amren, to Rhys.

"When Helion comes," Rhys said gently, as if he, too, understood what Nesta had revealed, "I'll have him show you. He knows spells for warding that even I don't."

The silence became tense enough that Cassian made himself grin. "Considering that Nesta brushed off Helion's smoldering advances during the war, he might not be so inclined to help her."

"He'll help," Rhys said, stars shimmering in his gaze. "If only for another shot at her."

Nesta rolled her eyes, and the gesture was so normal that Cassian's smile became more genuine, edged now with relief.

You wear your heart for all to see, brother, Rhys said without turning Cassian's way.

Cassian only shrugged. He was past caring.

Feyre said to Nesta, "We should get Madja to tend to your wounds."

"They're already healing," Nesta said, and Cassian wondered if she had any idea how awful she looked.

Indeed, Amren said, "You look like a cat tried to eat your face off." She sniffed. "And you smell like a swamp."

"Being dragged through a bog will do that to you," Cassian said to Amren, earning a surprised look from Nesta. He asked her, "How did the kelpie snare you?"

Nesta's scratched-up throat bobbed. "I grew . . . nervous when you—both of you—didn't come back." The silence in the room was palpable. "I went to find you."

Cassian didn't dare say that he'd only been gone thirty minutes. Thirty minutes, and she'd been in a panic like that? "We wouldn't have left you," he said carefully.

"I wasn't afraid of being left. I was afraid both of you were dead."

That she kept emphasizing *both of you* tightened his chest. He knew what she was carefully avoiding saying. She'd been worried enough that she'd ventured into Oorid's perils for him.

Nesta turned from his stare. "I was about to go into the water when the kelpie appeared. It crawled onto the bank, spoke to me, and then dragged me in."

"It spoke to you?" Rhys asked.

"Not in a language I knew."

Rhys's mouth quirked to the side. "Can you show me?"

Nesta frowned, as if unwilling to relive the memory, but nodded. Both of their gazes went vacant, and then Rhys pulled back.

"That thing . . ." He surveyed Nesta with blatant shock that she had survived. Rhys turned to Amren. "Have a listen."

Their eyes became glazed, and none of them spoke as Rhys showed Amren.

Even Amren's face paled at whatever Rhys showed her, and then she was shaking her head, her black bob of hair swaying. "That is a dialect of our tongue that has not been spoken in fifteen thousand years."

"I could only pick up every other word," Rhys said.

Feyre arched a brow. "You speak the language of the ancient Fae?"

Rhys shrugged. "My education was thorough." He waved an idle, graceful hand. "For exactly these situations."

Azriel asked, "What'd the kelpie say?"

Amren shot an alarmed glance at Nesta, then answered, "He said: *Are you my sacrifice, sweet flesh? How pale and young you are. Tell me, are they resuming the sacrifices to the waters once more?* And when she didn't respond, the kelpie said, *No gods can save you. I shall take you, little beauty, and you shall be my bride before you are my supper.*"

Nesta's hand drifted to the marks on her face, then recoiled.

Horror slid through Cassian—then molten rage.

"People used to sacrifice to kelpies?" Feyre asked, nose crinkling with disgust and dread.

"Yes," Amren said, scowling. "The most ancient Fae and humans believed kelpies to be river and lake gods, though I always wondered if the sacrifices started as a way to prevent the kelpies from hunting them. Keep them fed and happy, control the deaths, and they wouldn't crawl out of the water to snatch the children." Her teeth flashed. "For this one to still be speaking that ancient dialect . . . He must have retreated to Oorid a long time ago."

"Or been raised by parents who spoke that dialect," Azriel countered.

"No," Amren said. "The kelpies do not breed. They rape and

torment, but they do not reproduce. They were made, legend says, by the hand of a cruel god—and deposited throughout the waters of this land. The kelpie you slew, girl, was perhaps one of the last."

Nesta gazed at the Mask again.

Rhys said, "It flew to you. The Mask." He must have seen it in her head.

"I was trying to reach for my power," Nesta murmured, and they all stilled—she'd never spoken of her power so explicitly. "This answered instead."

"Like calls to like," Feyre repeated. "Your power and the Mask's are similar enough that to reach for one was to reach for the other."

"So you admit your powers remain, then," Amren said drily.

Nesta met her stare. "You already knew that."

Cassian stepped in before things went south. "All right. Let Lady Death get some rest."

"That's not funny," Nesta hissed.

Cassian winked, even as the others tensed. "I think it's catchy."

Nesta glowered, but it was a human expression, and he'd take that any day over that silver fire. Over the being who had walked on water and commanded a legion of the dead.

He wondered if Nesta would agree.

✣

Nesta stayed at the moonstone palace atop the Hewn City. Feyre had suggested that the bright openness would be better than the dim, red halls of the House of Wind. At least for tonight.

Nesta had been too tired to disagree, to explain that the House was her friend, and would have pampered and fussed like an old nursemaid.

She barely noted the opulent bedroom—overhanging the side of the mountain, snowcapped peaks gleaming in the sunshine all around, a bed piled with glowingly white linens and pillows, and . . . Well, she *did* notice the sunken bathing pool, open to the air beyond, water spilling over the lip that projected above the drop and trickling into the endless fall below.

Ribbons of steam snaked along its surface, inviting and scented with lavender, and she had enough presence of mind to strip off her clothes and climb in before sullying the sheets again. They'd already been changed since she'd slept earlier—she knew because she'd left a great, muddy imprint on the bed when she'd arisen, and now it was pristine.

Nesta eased into the bath, grimacing as the water stung her wounds. Beyond the peaks, the sun shifted from white gold to yellow, sinking toward the earth's embrace. Fat, fluffy clouds drifted by, filled with peach-colored light, lovely against the purpling sky. Her fingers rose to her hair, and as she dragged her hands through the tangled, still-sodden mess, she watched the sky transform itself into the most beautiful sunset she'd ever beheld. Bits of bog weed and mud cracked out of her hair, whisked away by the water over the edge of the pool.

Sighing, Nesta slid under, her face stinging, and scrubbed at her scalp. She emerged, her hair still thick and gritty, and scanned the wall next to the pool—there. Vials of what had to be concoctions for washing one's body and hair.

She poured a dollop into her hands, her nose filling with the scent of mint and rosemary, and scrubbed it through her hair. She let the heady scent pull the tension from her as much as it could, and lathered her heavy locks. Another dunk under the water had her rinsing out the bubbles. When she emerged, she reached for the bar of soap that smelled of sweet almonds.

Nesta washed every part of herself twice. And only when she finished did she let herself take in the view again. The sunset was at its peak, the sky ablaze with pink and blue and gold and purple, and she willed it to fill her, to clear away any lingering trace of Oorid's darkness.

She had never experienced anything like the Mask's power. The kelpie, at least, had felt real—her terror and anger and desperation had all been human, ordinary feelings. As soon as she'd donned the Mask, those feelings had vanished. She had become more, had become something that did not need air to breathe, something that did not understand hate or love or fear or grief.

It had scared her more than anything else. That utter lack of feeling. How good it had felt, to be so removed.

Nesta swallowed. She hadn't confessed it to any of them. She'd been contemplating the Mask when they'd found her in its room, contemplating that void. Wondering whether anyone had ever donned the Mask not to raise the dead, but to simply stop being inside their own minds.

She had been aware, yes. Had killed the kelpie because she wished it dead. But all the weight, the echoing thoughts, the hatred and guilt that sliced her like knives—they had vanished.

And it had been so seductive, so freeing and lovely, that she'd known the Mask had to be destroyed. If only to save herself from it.

But it could not be destroyed. And she was the sole person who might contain it.

Never mind that, for the same reason, she'd be the sole person with access to it. Everyone else would be safe from its temptation and power—except for her. The one who most needed to be barred from it.

A knock sounded on her door, and Nesta dropped below the dark surface of the pool, letting her long hair cover her breasts, before she said, "Yes?"

Cassian strode in, a tray of food in hand, and halted when he didn't see her on the bed. His eyes shot to the sunken pool, and she could have sworn he almost dropped the tray onto the white carpet. "I . . . You."

His loss of words was enough to pull her from her thoughts, to curve the corners of her mouth upward. "Me?"

He shook his head like a wet dog. "I brought some food. I assumed you'd want dinner."

"There's no dining room?"

"There is, but I thought you might need to unwind."

She surveyed him, surprised that he knew her well enough to guess that the thought of speaking to everyone again, of dressing in suitable clothes, was draining—miserable. Knew her well enough to grasp that she'd rather eat in her room and piece herself together.

Cassian cleared his throat. "I'll put it over there." He jerked his chin to the desk next to the bathtub's far edge, where the water tumbled off the mountain.

Nesta pivoted as he strode a shade stiffly to the desk and set down the tray.

"Right." He cleared his throat again. "Enjoy your bath. And the meal."

Seeing Cassian so flustered pushed away the shadows in her heart. Thoughts of the Mask became a distant rumble. "Do you want to get in?"

He sucked in a breath, but something like pain washed over his features. "You're hurt."

Nesta stood, water sluicing off her, her hair plastering to her breasts and doing nothing to hide her peaked nipples beneath. "Do I look injured to you?"

He nodded toward the scabbed cuts all over her body, her face. "Yes?"

She snorted. "It looks worse than it feels by now."

Cassian didn't reply, his chest rising and falling in a sharp rhythm. With each uneven lift, she began to throb between her legs, as if her body answered his own.

Yes, her body seemed to say. *This—him. Life to drive away the Mask; life to drive away the horror of Oorid.* The need to touch him, feel his warmth and strength, pounded through her.

If he wouldn't climb into the bath, then she'd have to go to him.

Nesta waded toward the steps of the sunken tub, and Cassian went rigid.

He whispered, "I thought you were dead today."

Nesta reached the stairs. "So did I." She stepped upward, exposing her midriff. "I thought you were dead, too."

"You must have been happy."

She smiled, watching his gaze drop with every piece of her revealed. Another step upward had her sex bared to him. "It did not make me happy." She reached the floor of the room.

Through what Nesta knew was five hundred years of will, Cassian lifted his focus to her face as she walked to him, water dripping off her body. "You want to do this?" he breathed.

"Yes." She stopped a foot away, her wet hair draped along her torso, and stared up into his face. His eyes burned like hazel stars. Nesta gave him a smile that was pure Fae. "Just sex."

The words seemed to spark something, because Cassian blinked. "Right. Just sex." He didn't say it as lightly as she did. And still didn't reach for her.

So she said, "There can be nothing more than sex, Cassian."

His jaw tightened, and he seemed to struggle with some internal battle before he said darkly, "Then I'll take whatever you offer me." He leaned in, his body still not touching hers, and said against her ear, "And I'll take you however you wish me to."

Her toes curled on the stones, her hair dripping. "And if I wish to take *you*?"

He smiled against her ear. "Then I'll beg you to ride me into oblivion."

She went molten, and from the way his wings tucked in, she knew he could scent the wetness building between her thighs.

Cassian gently pulled her wet hair from her breasts. Her breathing came in sharp pants as he traced the tip of a finger around her nipple. Then did it again.

Words eluded her. She couldn't remember any of them, couldn't remember anything except that one finger, circling her nipple, her entire body throbbing with need.

Cassian flicked her nipple, a hard, sharp bite that made her whimper.

Desperate for more of him, for all of him, Nesta said, "Do what you want."

He circled her nipple again, a predator playing with its dinner. "That doesn't sound very exciting, *do what you want.*" He clamped her nipple between his thumb and forefinger, the demand in it enough that she looked up at his face. He was the portrait of male arrogance, a warrior poised to conquer, and she nearly climaxed at the sight of it. His eyes darkened. "The way you sometimes look at me makes me think such filthy things, Nesta."

"Do them. Do all of them."

He pinched her nipple just short of drawing pain, and she arched into the touch, a silent plea for more, for him to unleash himself. "We don't have time in one night for all the things I want to do to you, with you. Every place I want to touch and fill you."

She rubbed her thighs together, desperate for any friction. "Then do your best."

Cassian laughed darkly, but his other hand came up to her untouched breast, circling as well. She watched his light brown fingers play against her pale skin, watched him touch her like he wanted to map every inch of her body and had all the time in the world to do it. Below his waist, she could just make out his hardness.

"Do you want to suck me again?" he whispered against her ear. "Do you want me down your throat again?"

Nesta let out a confirming whimper.

"Did you still taste me days later?"

She couldn't answer, couldn't reveal the truth.

His fingers clamped on her nipples, drawing just enough pain that she went wholly wet. "Did you?"

"Yes. I tasted you for days." The words tumbled out, and with them, clarity and hunger sharpened her focus. Ripped her from that needy daze. "I've thought about your cock in my mouth every night since, while I had my hand between my legs."

He growled, and she skimmed a hand against his hardness, squeezing. She lifted her head and met his darkened stare, baring her teeth. "I thought about your head between my legs, too," she said, heart thundering, "and how your tongue slid into me." She squeezed him again.

Cassian groaned, and his thumbs caressed her too-sensitive nipples.

Nesta put her other hand on his chest, backing him toward the bed, and he went willingly, letting her set the pace, the location. "I promised that you could fuck me wherever you wanted in the House," she said, her voice a deep, rolling purr that she barely recognized. The backs of his thighs hit the bed, and he halted her, one hand dropping to her waist to steady them. "But this isn't the House." His breathing rasped around them as she smiled up at his drawn, taut features. "So I think that means we'll fuck wherever *I* want."

Cassian grinned, and the hand at her waist swept down to cup her bare ass. He squeezed one cheek. "As long as I still get to fuck you in the House."

She met his savage grin. "Good."

His hand drifted further south, between her legs, feeling her from behind. His fingers brushed against the wetness pooled there, and he swore, drawing his hand back, holding it between them. Her wetness gleamed on his two fingers, and his eyes glittered with predatory intent as he lifted them to his mouth and licked them, one by one.

Her body ached, clamping around emptiness, desperate for something to fill it. For him to fill it. She stroked her fingers down the length of his cock, still trapped within his pants. And as she made a second pass, he slanted his mouth over hers.

It was a grazing, taunting kiss.

She bit his lower lip. And then he was grabbing her to him, crushing their bodies together, both hands now gripping her ass as he pressed her against his length. Their open mouths clashed and met, and she tasted herself on his tongue, her fingers grappling in his silken hair, dragging against his scalp.

Cassian twisted, flipping them, and then she was lying flat against the mattress as he stood before her.

He tore his mouth away as he propped her legs on the bed, folding them at the knees. As he tugged her to the mattress's edge, so that her sex was on display for him.

He knelt, wings rising above him, and dragged his tongue clean up her center.

Nesta moaned at the same moment he did, and he let her writhe, as if he knew it'd torment her more to undulate, but to have nothing to fill her, not until he wished it. He gave her another savoring lick, lingering at the apex of her thighs, sucking the bundle of nerves into his mouth, nipping with his teeth, before he began again.

Again. Again.

He was devouring her, melting her body like a piece of chocolate on his tongue.

She couldn't endure it, and she clasped her own breast, desperate for more touch, more sensation. He looked up from between her legs and marked her hand kneading her breast. Marked it and smiled, his teeth flashing white against the flushed gleam of her. "Do you like seeing me kneel before you?" he asked, the words rumbling into her very core. He dipped his tongue into her. "You taste like you do."

Nesta arched, thrusting herself further onto his tongue, but Cassian only laughed against her and denied her what she wished. He gave her another slow, slow lick from base to top, and as he reached that bundle of nerves, he slid two fingers into her.

Two, not one, because he seemed to know she was already waiting for him, that she wanted him unbound and rough and wild. She bowed off the bed, and he thrust his fingers in again, his breathing uneven as he said, "How do you want it?"

He pumped his hand into her again, wringing out her reply. "Hard," she gasped.

"Thank the Mother," he swore, and she heard metal clicking and leather whispering, and then his tongue caressed her again, past that bundle of nerves, up her stomach, to her breasts, until he was over her.

Cassian moved her further onto the bed. She didn't care that her legs fell open for him, only cared that he was now naked, and all that rippling muscle and golden skin gleamed above her.

He lowered himself to the cradle of her thighs, and his eyes were so wide she could see the whites around them. He opened his mouth, but she didn't want to hear the words, didn't want to know whatever he'd been about to say. She framed his face in her hands and kissed him savagely, her tongue scraping over his teeth as she ground their mouths together.

The broad tip of his cock nudged at her entrance, slipping in the slickness there, and he reached down to guide himself in.

At Cassian's first prod into her body, fire erupted within her. She panted into his mouth, nipping at his bottom lip as he eased himself in. Just an inch.

He halted. He was large enough that the stretching was edged in sweetest pain—large enough that she wondered if she'd be able to fit all of him. He trembled, holding himself barely inside her, as if he were now wondering the same.

His hesitation, his care, melted some ice-cold shard within her. And made her snap free of any restraint.

Nesta gripped his ass, muscles flexing beneath her fingertips, and hauled him into her.

Only another inch. Only another inch, because Cassian braced his arms against the bed, hips pulling against her hold. "I'll hurt you."

"I don't care." She ran her tongue over his jaw.

"I do," he ground out, body straining as she attempted to pull him into her. "Nesta."

Her fingers dug in again, her very blood and bones crying out for more of him, but he refused to move.

"Nesta. Look at me."

Fighting the roaring of her body, she obeyed. Heat blazed in his eyes, and something more than that. "Look at me," Cassian breathed.

Gods spare her, but she did. She couldn't take her gaze off him. Found herself free-falling into his darkened eyes, his beautiful face.

His hips flexed, and he slid in another inch—then retreated nearly to her edge.

Their breathing synced, and Nesta stilled beneath him, a feeling of utter calm, utter fullness spreading through her as his hips moved again, and he pushed back in, a little farther this time.

Cassian held her gaze through each small thrust, each retreat. He stretched her, filling her inch by inch, and Nesta knew he'd been right to go slow for this first joining.

Retreating and advancing, Cassian filled her. They said nothing, only shared breath, their eyes wide as they gazed at each other.

He pulled outward again, the movement long enough this time that she knew he was nearly all the way in. He halted, his cock barely inside her, and studied her face. A conquering warrior-god. He had called her Lady Death, and he was her sword.

Cassian leaned down to kiss her. And as his tongue slid into her mouth, he thrust home in a mighty, final push.

Nesta moaned as he slammed to the hilt, and the full impact of him hit her, stretched her, and she couldn't breathe fast enough. Cassian withdrew again, and slammed back into her, propelling their bodies farther onto the bed.

He groaned this time, and the sound was her undoing. She wrapped her legs around his back, careful of his wings, and lifted her hips to meet his. He sank even deeper, and she dug her nails into his shoulders.

Gods—nothing had ever felt so good, so full, so burning with pleasure. Nothing had ever felt like this, nothing.

Cassian set the pace, smooth and deep, and for a moment, it was all Nesta could do to match him stroke for stroke. For a moment, she looked between their bodies to where his cock plunged into her, so thick and long and gleaming with her that she tightened around him, her release already building.

He felt her inner muscles squeeze him harder and growled, "Fuck, Nesta."

And she liked seeing him undone enough that she did it again, clenching on him just as he seated himself fully. He arched into it, fingers digging into the bed. "Fuck," he repeated.

It wasn't enough, though. Wasn't close to enough. She wanted Cassian roaring, wanted him so lost that he couldn't remember his own name.

Nesta halted him with a hand on his chest. Just one hand, and he stopped, utterly at her command. If she wanted it to end here, it would.

It softened her enough that she couldn't quite keep the tremor out of her voice as she said, "I want you deeper."

Cassian panted, eyes wild, as she crawled out of his arms. As she turned onto her stomach and lifted her backside for him, offering herself.

He made a low sound of need. She arched her hips higher, inviting him to take, to feast.

His restraint shattered. He was on her in an instant, lifting her hips higher as he sheathed himself in a single thrust. Nesta screamed then, a sound of such pleasure she knew it echoed off the mountains, feeling him hit the deepest spot of her.

Cassian pounded into her, a hand moving from her hip to her hair, tugging her head back, baring her throat. She gave herself over to it, to him, and the lack of control was heady, so pleasurable that she could barely stand it. He thrust harder, so deep with this angle that she might have been screaming again, might have been sobbing.

His other hand drifted between her legs, his cock pounding into her, her hair gripped like reins in one hand, her pleasure in his other. She was utterly at his mercy, and he knew it—he was snarling with desire, slamming home so hard his balls slapped against her.

The silken touch had her erupting.

Her climax crashed upon her, out of her, her inner muscles clenching him tight.

Cassian roared, the sound echoing through the room, and he became utterly wild as release found him and he spilled into her with such force that his seed ran down her thighs.

And then his weight fell upon her back, and only an arm that he threw out to brace them kept them from collapsing.

Reeling, Nesta could only breathe, breathe, breathe.

Cassian lay buried in her, and it felt so good, so right, that she wanted him always this deep in her, his seed spilling down her legs, forever.

"Oh, gods," he whispered against her spine, over the tattoo inked along it. "That was . . ."

"I know," she panted. "I know."

It was as much as she'd confess. As much as she'd let herself admit.

Too good. It had felt too good, and nothing and no one would ever compare to it.

He said, voice shaking, "I've made a mess of you."

She buried her face in the blanket. "I like it."

Cassian went still, but he gently extracted himself from her in a long, long pull. He dragged his seed with him, and another rush of it tickled down her thighs, dripping on the blanket, as he pulled out fully. She didn't move. Couldn't move. Didn't want to move.

She felt him kneeling behind her, staring at the ass she still held upward, the view it presented.

"I shouldn't enjoy seeing that so much," he growled.

Her breasts tightened. But she asked coyly, "Seeing what?"

"You. Covered in me. That beautiful sex of yours."

She blushed and lowered her body to the mattress. "No one has ever called it beautiful."

"It is. It's the most beautiful I've ever seen."

She smiled into the blanket. "Liar."

"I'm beyond lies right now, Nesta."

His voice was so rough she looked over a shoulder. Cassian still knelt, and his face . . . It was utterly devastated, as if she'd taken him apart and left him in ruin. "What is it?" she asked, but he moved off the bed and reached for his fallen clothes.

Nesta twisted, her legs and core drenched in his essence and hers, but he donned his pants, gathering up his shirt and jacket, and the weapons she hadn't realized he'd carried. When he lifted his head, he threw her a wicked smile. "Just sex, right?"

It was a trap, somehow. She couldn't discern in what way, but the words were dangerous. She'd meant them, though. Or had wanted to, at least. So Nesta said, "Right."

His eyes flickered, and he grinned again, aiming for the door. "Thanks for the ride, Nes." He winked, and was gone.

She stared at the door, puzzling over his exit, so swift that his seed still leaked out of her.

Was it punishment? Had he not enjoyed it? She had the proof of his enjoyment between her legs, but males could find their pleasure and still not deem it good.

Was he trying to demonstrate what she'd done to all those males? Bedded them and then kicked them out?

She'd said just sex, but had thought it might at least come with some . . . cuddling. A few minutes to enjoy the feel of his body against hers before pride made her order him to leave.

Nesta knelt in the bed, and stared at the door, the silence her only answer.

CHAPTER 38

"You took him to your bed, didn't you?"

Emerie's whispered question had Nesta whipping her head toward her, stomach muscles quivering as she held the upward positioning of her curl. Emerie, a mirror image to her left, simply smirked at the shock on Nesta's face. Gwyn, on Emerie's other side, was just wide-eyed.

Nesta schooled her features into neutrality and uncurled to the ground, making sure to hold her abdominal muscles tight until her back was flat against the stone once more. "Why would you say that?"

"Because you and Cassian have been exchanging sultry looks all morning."

Nesta scowled at Emerie. "We have not."

It was an effort not to look across the ring, to where Cassian was now walking the newest group of priestesses—two this time, Ilana and Lorelei—through foot positioning and balance. Nesta *had*, in fact, caught him staring her way twice since the lesson had begun two hours ago, but she'd made a point not to engage in lingering eye contact.

"You have," Gwyn whispered, low enough that Cassian's Fae hearing wouldn't pick up her words. Nesta rolled her eyes.

"Well, if you won't talk about that," Emerie said with equal quiet, "then at least tell us what happened yesterday—why there was no lesson, and where you were in the afternoon."

"I was asked to keep it secret," Nesta said. Her wounds had healed and vanished already, making it easy to do so.

"It has something to do with the Trove," Gwyn said, those teal eyes noticing too much.

Nesta didn't reply, and that was answer enough. Emerie knew the basics—as much as Gwyn had been told—and frowned. But she kept her voice whisper-soft. "So you really didn't sleep with him?"

Nesta did another curl, torso rising to her knees. "I didn't say that."

Emerie let out a *hmmm*.

Nesta's cheeks flushed. Emerie and Gwyn swapped glances. And it was Gwyn who said, "Was it good?"

Nesta did another curl, and Cassian barked from across the ring, "Emerie! Gwyn! If you can do those curls as well as you run your mouths, you'd be done by now."

Emerie and Gwyn grinned fiendishly. "Sorry!" they shouted, and launched into motion.

Nesta grew still as Cassian's gaze met hers. The space between them went taut, the sounds of the exercising priestesses fading into nothing, the sky an azure blur above, the wind a distant caress on her cheeks—

"You too, Archeron," he ordered, pointing to where Emerie and Gwyn now exercised, apparently doing their best not to laugh. "Do another fifteen." Nesta threw a scowl at all of them and began her curls again. *That* was why she'd been avoiding eye contact with him.

Cassian's attention slid elsewhere, but with each curl upward, Nesta found herself reining in the urge to gaze his way. She lost count three times. Bastard.

Between curls, Gwyn said, "You know, Nesta, if you're having trouble concentrating . . ."

"Oh, please," Nesta muttered.

Gwyn let out a breathy laugh. "I mean it. I learned about a new Valkyrie technique last night. It's called Mind-Stilling."

Nesta managed to ask, body screeching with the effort of the curls, "What is it?"

"They used it to steady their minds and emotions. Some of them did it three or four times a day. But it's basically the act of sitting and letting your mind go quiet. It might help with your . . . concentration."

Emerie snickered, but Nesta paused, ignoring Gwyn's implication. "Such a thing is possible? To train the mind?"

Gwyn halted her exercising, too. Her teasing smile turned contemplative. "Well, yes. It requires constant practice, but there's a whole chapter in this book I summarized for Merrill about how they did it. It involved deep breathing and becoming aware of one's body, then learning to let go. They used it to remain calm in the face of their fears, to settle themselves after a hard battle, and to fight whatever inner demons they possessed."

"Illyrian warriors do no such thing," Emerie murmured. "Their heads are full of rage and battle. It's only gotten worse since the last war. Now that they're rebuilding their ranks."

"The Valkyries found heightened emotions distracting in the face of an opponent," Gwyn said. "They trained their minds to be weapons as sharp as any blade. To be able to keep their composure, to know how to access that place of calm in the midst of battle, made them unshakable opponents."

Nesta's heart pounded with every word. Quieting her mind . . . "Can you get a scribe to make copies of the chapter?"

Gwyn grinned. "I already did."

Cassian barked, "Do you three want to gossip or train?"

Nesta threw him a scathing look. "Don't tell him of this," she warned them. "It's our secret." And wouldn't Cassian be surprised when *she* became the unflappable one?

Emerie and Gwyn nodded their agreement as Cassian sauntered over. Every muscle, every bit of blood and bone in Nesta's body went on alert. She'd returned to the House this morning, winnowed in by a too-neutral Rhys. Cassian had been nowhere in sight.

She'd had all of thirty minutes to eat breakfast and change into her spare leathers, since the ones she'd worn in the bog were still soaked. The pair she'd donned were bigger—not baggy, but just slightly larger. She hadn't noticed how tight her usual set was until she slid into the far more comfortable ones. Hadn't noticed how much muscle she'd packed onto her thighs and arms this month until she realized her movements had been restricted by the old pair.

Cassian paused before them, hands on his hips. "Is there something more interesting today than your training?"

He knew. The bastard knew they'd been discussing him. The spark in his eye, the half grin, told her.

Emerie's lips quivered with the effort to keep from smiling. "Not at all."

Gwyn's attention bounced between Nesta and Cassian.

Cassian said to the priestess, "Yes?"

Gwyn shook her head too quickly to be innocent and began her abdominal curls again, sweat gleaming on her freckled face. Emerie joined her, the two of them working so diligently that it was laughable. Nesta peered up at Cassian. "What?"

His eyes danced with wicked amusement. "Did you finish your set?"

"Yes."

"And the push-ups?"

"Yes."

He stepped closer, and she couldn't help but think of how he'd approached last night, the way those hands had grasped her hips as he'd pounded into her from behind. Something must have shown on her face, because he said in a low voice, "You've certainly been productive, Nes."

She swallowed, and knew the two females beside her were eating up every word. But she lifted her chin. "When do we get to do something of use? When do we start on archery or swords?"

"You think you're ready to handle a sword?"

Emerie let out a fizzing noise, but kept working.

Nesta refused to smile, to blush, and said without breaking Cassian's stare, "Only you can tell me that."

His nostrils flared. "Get up."

✢

Cassian had told himself two dozen times since walking out of that bedroom that the sex had been a mistake. But watching Nesta challenge him, the innuendo like a sizzling flame, he couldn't for the life of him remember why.

Something to do with her only wanting sex, something to do with the sex being the best damn sex he'd ever had, and how it had left him in veritable pieces.

Nesta blinked. "What?"

He nodded toward the center of the pit. "You heard me. You think you're ready to handle a sword, then prove it."

Her friends were clearly aware of what they'd done last night. Emerie couldn't even hide her laughing, and Gwyn kept sneaking looks at them.

He barked at the two females, "Finish your exercises now or do double."

They stopped their gawking.

Nesta was still staring up at him, sweat and exertion filling that beautiful face of hers with color. A bead of perspiration slid down her temple, and he had to clench his fists to keep from leaning in to lick it away. She asked, "We're going to learn swords?"

He aimed for the rack across the ring and she followed. "We're going to start with wooden practice swords. Over my rotting corpse am I putting actual steel into the hands of novices."

She snickered, and he stiffened. He tossed over a shoulder, "If you're too childish to talk of blades without giggling, then you're not ready for swordplay."

She scowled. But Cassian said, "These are weapons of death." He let his voice lift so all the females could hear him, though he spoke only to her. "They need to be treated with a healthy dose of respect. I didn't even touch a real sword for the first seven years."

"Seven *years*?" Gwyn demanded behind them.

He reached the rack and drew out a long blade, a near-replica of the Illyrian one down his back. "You think children should be swinging around a real sword?"

"No," Gwyn sputtered. "I just meant—do you plan for us to practice with wooden swords for seven years?"

"If you three keep giggling, then yes."

Nesta said to Gwyn and Emerie, "Don't let him bully you."

Cassian snorted. "Dangerous words for a female about to go head-to-head with me."

She rolled her eyes, but hesitated when he extended the practice sword to her hilt-first. "It's heavy," she observed as she took its full weight.

"The real sword weighs more."

Nesta glanced to his shoulder, where the hilt of his blade peeked over. "Really?"

"Yes." He nodded to her hands. "Double-handed grip on the hilt. Don't choke up too close to the shaft."

Emerie began coughing, and Nesta's mouth twitched, but she held it—fought it. Even Cassian had to tamp down a laugh before he cleared his throat.

But Nesta did as he bade.

"Feet where I showed you," he said, well aware of every eye on them. From the way Nesta's face turned grave, Cassian knew she was aware, too. That this moment, with these priestesses watching, was pivotal, somehow.

Vital.

⁜

Nesta met Cassian's stare. And every thought of sex, of how good it had felt, eddied from her head as she lifted the blade before her.

It was like a key sliding into a lock at last.

It was a wooden sword, and yet it wasn't. It was a part of practice, and yet it wasn't.

Cassian walked her through eight different cuts and blocks. Each was an individual move, he'd explained, and like the punches, they could be combined. The most difficult thing was to remember to lead with the hilt of the sword—and to use her entire body, not just her arms.

"Block one," he ordered, and she lifted the sword perpendicular to her body, raising upward against an invisible enemy. "Slice three." She rotated the blade, reminding herself to lead with the stupid hilt, and slashed downward at an angle. "Thrust one." Another pivot and she lunged forward, slamming the blade through the breastplate of an imaginary enemy.

Everyone had stopped to watch.

"Block three," Cassian commanded. Nesta switched to a one-handed grip, her left hand coming up to her chest, where he'd told her to hold it. That would be her shield hand, he'd said, and learning to keep it tucked close would be key to her survival. "Slice two." She dragged the sword in a straight line upward, splitting that enemy from groin to sternum. "Block two." She pivoted on one foot, dragging the sword from that enemy's chest to intercept another invisible blow.

None of her movements possessed any semblance of his elegance or power. They were stilted and it took her a second to remember each of the steps, but she told herself that would take more than thirty minutes of instruction. Cassian had reminded her of that often enough.

"Good." He crossed his arms. "Block one, slice three, thrust two."

She did so. The movements flowed faster, surer. Her breath clicked into sync with her body with each thrust.

"*Good*, Nesta. Again."

She could see the muddy battlefield, and hear the screams of friend and foe alike. Each movement was a fight for survival, for victory.

"Again."

She could see the King of Hybern, and the Cauldron, and the Ravens—see the kelpie and Tomas and all those people who had sneered at the Archerons' poverty and desperation, the friends who had walked away with smiles on their faces.

Her arm was a distant ache, secondary to that building song in her blood.

It felt good. It felt so, so good.

Cassian threw out different combinations, and she obeyed, let them flow through her.

Every hated enemy, every moment she'd been powerless against them simmered to the surface. And with each movement of the sword, each breath, a thought formed. It echoed with every inhale, every thrust and block.

Never again.

Never again would she be weak.

Never again would she be at someone's mercy.

Never again would she fail.

Never again, never again, never again.

Cassian's voice stopped, and then the world paused, and all that existed was him, his fierce smile, as if he knew what song roared in her blood, as if he alone understood that the blade was an instrument to channel this raging fire in her.

The other females were utterly silent. Their hesitation and shock shimmered in the air.

Slowly, Nesta broke her stare from Cassian and looked to Emerie and Gwyn, already moving across the ring. Cassian had the wooden swords ready by the time they arrived.

No fear shone in their eyes. As if they, too, saw what Cassian did. As if they, too, heard those words within Nesta's head.

Never again.

CHAPTER 39

The fire inside her didn't stop.

Nesta could barely get through her work in the library that afternoon thanks to that fire, that bouncing energy. By the time the clock chimed six, she bade Clotho farewell and went straight to the outside stairwell.

Down and down, around and around and around.

Step to step to step.

She didn't stop. Couldn't stop.

As if she had been freed from a cage she hadn't realized she'd been held in.

Every step downward, she heard the words. *Never again*.

She had escaped the kelpie by pure luck. But she had been terrified. As terrified as when she'd been hauled into the depths of the Cauldron, as terrified as she'd been with Tomas. At least with Tomas, she had fought. With the kelpie, she had barely done anything until the Mask had spared her.

She had become so afraid. So meek and trembling. It was unacceptable. Unacceptable that she had let herself balk and cower and curl inward.

Down and down, around and around and around.

Step to step to step.

Never again. Never, ever again.

Nesta reached the six thousandth step and began the ascent.

✠

The first of the autumnal rains arrived the next day, and Cassian half-expected the priestesses not to show up for practice, but they were already waiting in the cold and wet when he entered the training ring. None bothered to use magic to keep dry.

As if they wanted the grit, the extra effort.

In the center of the group stood Nesta, her eyes already focused.

Cassian's blood heated, unable to keep his desire contained at the sight of that fierceness in her face, the eagerness to learn more, push harder.

He hadn't sought her out last night, deciding to sleep at the river house rather than risk temptation. The sex had been that good—and he knew if he didn't put up some semblance of a barrier, it'd consume him entirely. *She'd* consume him entirely.

Nesta, Emerie, and Gwyn stood together, and—there were three new priestesses today.

"Ladies," he said by way of greeting, surveying the eleven soaked females waiting like troops to be commanded on a battlefield. Roslin had removed her hood, revealing a head of deep red hair and pale skin over delicate features. Her eyes were the color of caramel, and if she was afraid to be revealing her face at last, she did not let on. Cassian surveyed the rest of the lineup, and—well, that was new. Gwyn was in Illyrian leathers. Nesta's old ones, from the scent of them.

Cassian observed them, all clear-eyed and eager. "I think we need another tutor."

✠

The next morning, though the females were hesitant around a newcomer, Azriel kept so aloof and quiet that they quickly relaxed around him. Az had readily agreed to squeeze in the lessons before heading out to keep an eye on Briallyn.

Cassian continued to train Nesta, Emerie, and Gwyn. The rain didn't let up, and they were all soaked, but the exertion kept the bite of the cold away.

"So this can really down a male in one move?" Gwyn asked Cassian as he stood before Nesta. They'd taken a break from the swords to stretch their hands, but rather than sit idle and have their bodies go stiff with inactivity, he'd shown them a few techniques to get out of a pinch.

Gwyn had been distracted today—one eye on the other side of the ring. Cassian could only assume she was watching his brother, who had given Gwyn a small smile of greeting upon arrival. Gwyn hadn't returned it. Cassian cursed himself for a fool. He should have asked her if she'd be comfortable with Azriel here. Perhaps he should have asked all the priestesses about including another male, but especially Gwyn—whom Azriel had found that day in Sangravah.

She'd said nothing about it during the lesson. Only glanced every now and then toward Az, who remained dutifully focused on his charges. Cassian couldn't read the expression on her face.

He concentrated on the females in front of him. "This move will knock anyone unconscious if you hit the right spot." Cassian took Nesta's hand, placing it on his neck. Her fingers were so small against his, and freezing cold. He might have run his thumb over the back of her hand before he positioned her fingers. "You want to go for this pressure point. Hit it hard enough, you'll make them drop like a stone."

Nesta's fingers tightened, and he grabbed her hand. But she smirked, as if knowing she'd caught him. He squeezed her chilled fingers. "I know you were thinking of it."

"I'd never do such a thing," she said mildly, her eyes dancing.

Cassian winked, and Nesta slid her hand from his neck. "All right," he said. "Back to swords. Who wants to show me the eight points again?"

✢

Despite changing their clothes, Nesta and Gwyn remained chilled to the bone an hour after their lesson had finished. Nestled in a warm, comfortable nook in a rarely visited part of the library, Nesta sipped at her peppermint tea, letting its warmth soak through her body as she read through the chapter Gwyn had copied. She'd given one to Emerie before their friend had left, getting a promise from the Illyrian that she'd practice tonight and they'd compare notes tomorrow.

"So it's really that easy?" Nesta asked, setting down the papers on the worn couch cushion.

Gwyn, seated on the opposite end of the couch, stretched her feet toward the fire, robes rustling. "It certainly *seems* easy, but according to everything I've read, it's not."

"This says you just sit somewhere comfortable and quiet, close your eyes, breathe a whole lot, and let your mind go."

"I'm telling you: it took the Valkyries months to learn the basics, and mastering it required doing these exercises *multiple* times a day. But let's try it. It says at the end of this chapter that if we're doing this for the first time, we might grow sleepy—or even fall asleep during it—but learning to fight the urge to sleep is for further down the road."

"I could use a nap after today's training," Nesta muttered, and Gwyn chuckled her agreement. Nesta set her tea on the low table before the couch. "All right. Let's try it."

"I memorized the steps, so I'll lead us through it," Gwyn offered.

Nesta snorted. "Of course you did."

Gwyn playfully smacked her on the shoulder. "Learning this is my job, you know."

"You'd have memorized this information anyway."

"Fair enough." Gwyn laughed, finishing her own tea and then sitting up straight. "Get into a comfortable seated position—alert, but at ease."

"I don't even know what that means."

Gwyn demonstrated, scooting until her spine touched the back cushions, feet flat on the floor, hands lightly resting on her knees. Nesta copied the position. Gwyn surveyed her, then nodded. "Now take three deep breaths, in through your nose for a count of six, out through your mouth for a count of six. After you finish the third breath, close your eyes, and keep breathing."

Nesta obeyed. Inhaling and exhaling for that long required more concentration and effort than she expected. Her breathing was too loud to her ears; each breath seemed out of sync with Gwyn's. Had she taken two breaths, or three? Or four?

"I can feel you overthinking this," Gwyn murmured. "Close your eyes and keep breathing. Take five breaths."

Nesta did. Without anything to visually distract her, she figured her breathing would be easier to track.

It wasn't. Somehow, her mind just wanted to wander off. She *told* herself to focus on the count, on timing each breath and keeping a tally of how many she'd taken, and yet she found herself thinking of the couch cushions, her cooling tea, her still-damp hair—

How many breaths had it been? "I think I'm losing my mind," Nesta muttered.

Gwyn shushed her. "Now let your breathing steady, and focus on the sounds around you. Acknowledge them, then let them fade away."

Nesta did. To her left, she could make out shuffling feet and whispering robes. Who was walking through the stacks? What book were they—

Focus. Let the sounds go. Someone was walking nearby. She marked it, and with an exhale, sent the thought floating away. To her right, Gwyn's breathing remained steady.

Gwyn was probably good at this. Gwyn was good at everything, actually. It didn't irk her, though. For whatever reason, Nesta wanted to crow about her friend to anyone who'd listen.

Her friend. That was what Gwyn was. It had been—

Focus. Let go. Nesta noted Gwyn's breathing, released the thought, and moved on to the next sound. Then the next.

"Now survey your body," Gwyn said softly. "Starting at your head, slowly working down to your toes, assess how you're feeling. If there are sore spots—"

"Everything is sore after that sword lesson," Nesta hissed.

Gwyn choked on another laugh. "I mean it. Note if there are sore spots, if there are spots that feel good . . ." Papers rustled. "Oh, and the instructions also say that when you're done, you should assess how *you* are feeling. Don't dwell on it, but just acknowledge it."

Nesta didn't particularly like the sound of the last bit, but she obeyed. Every part of her body ached, from a stiffness in her neck to a soreness along her left foot. She hadn't realized how many little pieces of herself existed, all constantly blaring their pains or status. How much noise it produced in her head. But she acknowledged each of those things. Let them drift away.

Assessing her emotions, however . . . How *was* she feeling? Right now, tired yet . . . content to be here with Gwyn. Laughing. Doing this. If she went deeper . . .

"Now we're going to work on focused breathing. In through the nose, out through the mouth. Do ten of them, then start over. If a thought pops up, acknowledge it, then send it on its way. Tell yourself, *I am the rock against which the surf crashes*. Your thoughts are the surf. Let them crash over you."

Easy enough.

It wasn't. The first few times Nesta counted ten breaths, no thoughts plagued her at all. But when she began the next set . . .

What would Elain think, to see Nesta here with a friend? The thought bubbled up from nowhere. As if in opening her mind, it had rushed toward her. Would Elain be pleased, or would she feel the need to warn Gwyn about Nesta's true self?

She'd been on breath five. No, six. Wait—maybe it had only been three.

"Start over if you lose count," Gwyn said, as if she'd heard the halt of Nesta's steady breathing.

Nesta did so, focusing on the breaths and not Elain. *I acknowledge this thought about my sister, and I am letting it go.*

She was on her seventh breath when her sister appeared again. *And yet somehow all you think of is what* my *trauma did to* you.

Had Elain been right? Feyre had admitted she was guilty of it, too, but—Feyre hadn't known Elain as Nesta did. Or, it hadn't been that way before. Before Elain had chosen Feyre.

Before Amren had chosen Feyre.

Before—

I acknowledge these thoughts and I am letting them go.

Nesta inhaled an eighth time. *I am focusing on my breathing. These thoughts exist, and I am letting them pass me by.*

Nesta took another breath. Forced her mind to think only of her breathing.

"When you finish your next set of ten," Gwyn said, near and yet far away, "stop counting your breaths and just let your mind do as it wishes. We'll do that for a few heartbeats, then stop. The goal is to work up to longer and longer periods of this."

Nesta did so, counting each of the ten remaining breaths. Feeling that moment of halting like a looming wave. She finished the tenth breath.

Do as you want, mind. Go drift into those dark, horrible places.

It didn't, though. Her mind lingered. Didn't wander. It just . . . sat there. Contented. Resting. Like a cat curled at her feet.

Stilled.

Only a few moments passed before Gwyn whispered, "Begin to sink back into your body. Mark the sounds around us. Mark the feeling in your fingers, your toes."

Strange—so strange to find her body suddenly . . . calmed. Distant. Like she'd somehow indeed been able to step back. Let it rest. And her mind . . .

"Open your eyes," Gwyn breathed.

Nesta did. And for the first time in her life, she felt utterly settled into her own skin.

CHAPTER 40

The rain kept falling for two days, the temperatures plummeting with it. Leaves lay scattered around Velaris, and the Sidra was now a silver snake, sometimes hidden by the drifting mists. The females showed up every damn day without fail.

But only Nesta stood at his side as he knocked on the door of the small blacksmith's shop on the western outskirts of Velaris.

The gray-stoned, thatched-roof shop hadn't changed in the five centuries he'd been patronizing it—he bought all his non-Illyrian weapons there. He'd have taken her to an Illyrian blacksmith, but they were mostly backward, superstitious males who wanted females nowhere near their shops. The ruddy-skinned High Fae male who opened the door for them was skilled and kind, if gruff.

"General," the male said, wiping his sooty hands on his stained leather apron. He opened the door wider, delicious heat blasting out to meet them in the chilled rain. The blacksmith's dark eyes swept over Nesta, noting her soaked hair and leathers, the calm intensity of her features despite the awful weather.

She'd had that same look on her face, in every line of her body, while training this morning. And when Cassian had issued the invitation to join him here during the lunch hour. He'd invited all of the females, but Emerie had to return to Windhaven, and the priestesses had been unwilling to leave the mountain. So only Nesta had come with him to the small village, with the city looming on its eastern side and broad, flat plains stretching away toward the sea to the west.

"How can I assist you?"

Cassian nudged Nesta forward with a hand to the small of her back, and grinned at the male. "I want Lady Nesta to learn how a blade is made. Before she picks up a real one."

The blacksmith surveyed her again. "I don't need an apprentice, I'm afraid."

"Just a quick demonstration," Cassian said, keeping his smile in place as he glanced to Nesta, who was staring over the blacksmith's broad shoulder into the workshop behind him. The blacksmith frowned deeply, so Cassian added, "I want her to learn how much work and skill goes into the process. To show her that a blade is not merely a tool for killing, but a piece of art as well." Flattery always helped smooth the way. Rhys had taught him that.

Nesta's gaze shifted to the blacksmith's face, and for a moment, they stared at each other. Then Nesta said, "Whatever you can show me, in whatever free time you have, would be much appreciated."

Cassian tried not to show his surprise at her polite words. The hint of deference.

It seemed to do the trick, as the blacksmith waved them in.

Nesta listened while the dark-haired male explained the various stages of forging a blade, from the quality of the ore to the proving. Cassian kept near her, asking questions of his own, since she said little herself. One of the few times she'd spoken had been to request to move away from the roaring fires of the forge room to the quieter, cooler dark of the workshop proper. But as the blacksmith finished going over the design process for more ornate blades, Nesta asked, "Can I try it?" At the blacksmith's hesitation, Nesta stepped forward, eyes on the doorway beyond them, filled with the bellowing of the forge. "Hammering the blades, I mean. If you have any to spare." She glanced at Cassian. "You'll be compensated, of course."

Cassian nodded. "We'll pay for the blades if they're damaged."

The blacksmith surveyed Nesta again, as if testing the ore in her, then nodded. "I've got a few you could try your hand at."

He led them back into the heat and flame and light, and Cassian could have sworn Nesta was inhaling and exhaling in a perfect, controlled rhythm. She kept her gaze only on the blacksmith, however, as he carried over a half-made sword and laid it upon the anvil. Pretty, but ordinary. A common, everyday sword, the blacksmith said. After a swift, flawless demonstration, he handed her the hammer. "Brace your feet like so," the blacksmith said, and Nesta followed his instructions until she lifted the hammer above one shoulder and swung down.

A clanking thunk sounded, and the sword clattered. A clumsy near-miss. Nesta gritted her teeth. "That's not as easy as it looks."

The blacksmith pointed to the sword. "Try again. It takes a while to grow accustomed to it." Cassian had never heard the male speak so . . . gently. Normally their conversations were swift and to the point, free of formalities or personal tidbits.

Nesta struck the sword again. A better hit this time, but still a sorry blow. Coals popped in the forge behind them, and Nesta flinched. Before Cassian could ask why, she'd gritted her teeth again and struck the sword a third time. Fourth. Fifth.

By the time the blacksmith brought out a dagger, she'd gotten the hang of it. Was even smiling slightly. "Daggers require a different technique," the blacksmith explained, again demonstrating. So much work and skill and dedication, all for an ordinary blade. Cassian shook his head. When had he last stopped to appreciate the craftsmanship and labor that went into his weapons?

Sweat beaded Nesta's brow as she hammered at the dagger, blows and body surer now. Pride wended through his chest. Here she was, that female who'd been forged during the war with Hybern. But different—more focused. Stronger.

Cassian was only half-listening when the blacksmith brought out a great sword.

But he snapped to attention as Nesta fell upon it in one smooth movement, the hammer striking clear and true.

Strike after strike, and Cassian could have sworn the world paused as she unleashed herself with the same intensity she brought to training.

The blacksmith smiled at her. The first time Cassian had ever seen the male do so.

Nesta's arm arched above her, the hammer gripped in her clenched fingers. It was a dance, each of her movements timed to the ringing echo of the hammer on the blade. She pounded the sword to a music no one but she could hear.

Cassian let her keep at it, the rain and wind rustling the thatched roof a distant counter-beat above them, and began to wonder what would emerge from the heat and shadows.

✢

Learning swordplay was no easy task—it required repetition and muscle memory and patience—but Nesta, Emerie, and Gwyn were game.

No, Cassian realized as he watched them put away their swords in the icy rain that continued the next day. They were more than game: they trained with a newfound, steady focus. No one more so than Nesta, who now shelved her sword and took up a length of linen. She began wrapping her hands, rolling her neck as she did so.

They hadn't spoken after the blacksmith lesson yesterday afternoon, though she'd thanked him quietly upon returning to the House of Wind. She'd had that intensity upon her face again, eyes distant—as if focusing on some invisible target. So he hadn't sought her out last night, even though every part of him had screamed to do so. But he'd give her time. Let her initiate when she was ready. If she wanted him again.

Cassian shut down the thought. Allowed the icy rain to cool his desire, his dread.

In silence, Nesta approached the punching block, a fallen tree trunk that had been wrapped in thick blankets. She approached it as if she were facing an opponent.

She glanced over her shoulder to Cassian as she stopped before it, a question in her eyes.

He nodded. "You want to use the last fifteen minutes to spar, go ahead."

That was all she needed, and he was too pleased to say more as Nesta took up her fighting stance and began punching.

✣

The first impact of her knuckles against the padded wood hurt. But she hit where she was supposed to, and her thumb remained where she'd made it learn to stay, and when she pulled her arm back, the pain became a song. She threw another punch, eliciting a satisfying *thunk* from the wood.

Good—it felt *good*. To get it out, to channel it this way.

Her breathing was sharp as a blade, but she threw a left hook, then two jabs of her right fist.

She didn't feel the rain, didn't feel the cold.

Every punch carried her fear, her rage, her hate out of her body and into that wood.

For three days, she'd had fire in her blood. For three days, she had dreamed of swords and stairs and combat. She couldn't stop it. Had fallen into bed so tired that she had no chance to even read before she was unconscious. There certainly had been no sex with Cassian. Not even a smoldering glance over the dining table.

Azriel's presence helped. He now trained the newest recruits, quiet and gentle yet unfaltering, and if she didn't know better, she'd swear at least two of the priestesses—Roslin and Ilana—sighed every time he walked past.

Some small, awful part of her was glad they didn't sigh over Cassian. She punched that thought out of herself, too. That pathetic, selfish thought.

Just as all of her was pathetic, and selfish, and hateful.

One-two, two-one-one; she punched and punched, throwing all of herself into the wood.

✢

"By the Cauldron," a familiar male voice said beside Cassian, and he turned to find Lucien in the archway to the training area. The rest of the priestesses and Azriel had left ten minutes earlier. Nesta hadn't even noticed. "Feyre said she was training, but I hadn't realized she was . . . well, *training*."

Cassian nodded his hello, keeping his eyes on Nesta where she punched the padded wood over and over, just as she had for the last twenty-five minutes straight. She'd gone into a place Cassian knew too well—where thought and body became one, where the world faded to nothing. Working something out from deep inside of herself. "Did you think she was filing her nails?"

Lucien's mechanical eye clicked. His face tightened as Nesta threw a spectacular left hook into the wood beam. It shuddered with the impact. "I wonder if there are some things that should not be awoken," he murmured.

Cassian cut him a glare. "Mind your own business, fireling."

Lucien just watched Nesta attack, his golden skin a little pale.

"Why are you here?" Cassian asked, unable to help the sharpness. "Where's Elain?"

"I am not always in this city to see my mate." The last two words dripped with discomfort. "And I came up here because Feyre said

I should. I need to kill a few hours before I'm to meet with her and Rhys. She thought I might enjoy seeing Nesta at work."

"She's not a carnival attraction," Cassian said through his teeth.

"It's not for entertainment." Lucien's red hair gleamed in the dimness of the rainy day. "I think Feyre wanted a progress assessment from someone who hasn't seen her in a while."

"And?" Cassian bit out.

Lucien threw him a withering look. "I'm not your enemy, you know. You can drop the aggressive brute act."

Cassian gave him a grin that didn't meet his eyes. "Who says it's an act?"

Lucien let out a long sigh. "Very well, then."

Nesta threw another series of punches, and Cassian knew she was leading up to the knockout blow. Two left jabs and a right hook that slammed into the wood so hard it splintered.

And then she stopped, her fist pressed against the wood.

Her panting breath swirled from her mouth in the frigid rain.

Slowly, she straightened, fist lowering, steam rippling through her teeth as she turned. He caught a flicker of silver fire in her eyes, then it vanished. Lucien had gone still.

Nesta stalked toward the two males. She met Lucien's stare as she approached the archway, and said nothing before continuing into the House. As if words were beyond her.

Only when her footsteps vanished did Lucien say, "Mother spare you all."

Cassian was already walking to the wooden beam.

A small disc of impact lay in its center, through the padding, all the way to the wood itself. It glowed. Cassian raised shaking fingers to it.

To the burn mark, still sparking like an ember.

The entire wood block was smoldering from within. He touched his palm to it. The wood was cold as ice.

The block dissolved into a pile of cinders.

Cassian stared in stunned silence, the smoking wood hissing in the rain.

Lucien came up beside him. He only said again, voice solemn, "Mother spare you all."

CHAPTER 41

Helion, High Lord of the Day Court, arrived at the Hewn City the next afternoon on a flying horse.

He'd wanted to enter the dark city in a golden chariot led by four snow-white horses with manes of golden fire, Rhys had told Cassian, but Rhys had forbidden the chariot and horses, and let Helion know that he could winnow in or not come at all.

Hence the pegasus. Helion's idea of a compromise.

Cassian had heard the rumors of Helion's rare pegasuses. Myth claimed his prized stallion had flown so high the sun had scorched him black, but beholding the beast now . . . Well, Cassian might have been envious, if he didn't have wings himself.

The winged horses were rare—so rare that it was said Helion's seven breeding pairs of flying horses were the only ones left. Lore held that there had once been far more of them before recorded history, and that most had just vanished, as if they'd been devoured by the sky itself. Their population had dwindled further in the last thousand years, for reasons no one could explain.

This hadn't been helped by Amarantha, who had butchered three dozen of Helion's pegasuses in addition to burning so many of his libraries. The seven pegasus pairs that remained had survived thanks to being set free before Amarantha's cronies could reach their pens in the highest tower of Helion's palace.

Helion's most beloved pair—this black stallion, Meallan, and his mate—hadn't produced offspring in three hundred years, and that last foal hadn't made it out of weaning before he'd succumbed to an illness no healer could remedy.

According to legend, the pegasuses had come from the island the Prison sat upon—had once fed in fair meadows that had long given way to moss and mist. Perhaps that was part of the decline: their homeland had vanished, and whatever had sustained them there was no longer.

Cassian let himself admire the sight of Meallan alighting on the black stones of the courtyard before the towering gates into the mountain, the stallion's mane blowing in the wind off his jet-black wings. Few things remained in the faerie realms that could summon any sort of wonder from Cassian, but that magnificent stallion, proud and haughty and only half-tamed, snatched the breath from his chest.

"Incredible," Rhys murmured, similar admiration shining in his face.

Feyre beamed with delight, and Cassian knew from that look that she'd be painting this beast—and possibly its stunning master as well. Azriel, too, blinked in awe as the stallion pawed at the ground, huffing, and Helion patted the pegasus's thick, muscular neck before dismounting.

"Well met," Rhys said, striding forward.

"It's not the parade I wished," Helion said, clasping Rhys's hand, "but Meallan knows how to make an entrance." He let out a whistle, and the pegasus pivoted gracefully despite his size, flapped those mighty wings, and leaped back into the skies to wait elsewhere for his master.

Helion grinned at Feyre, who'd watched the stallion soar into the clouds with wide eyes. He said, "I'll take you on a ride if you wish."

Feyre smiled. "I would ordinarily take you up on that offer, but I'm afraid I can't risk it."

Helion's brows lifted. For a heartbeat, Rhys and Feyre conferred silently, and then Rhys nodded.

Rhys's voice filled Cassian's head a second later. *We're telling him.*

Cassian kept his face neutral. *Why risk it?*

Rhys said solemnly, *Because we need his libraries.* To find any way to save Feyre, Rhys didn't say. His High Lord went on, *And because you and Azriel were right: it's only a matter of time until Feyre is showing. She's indulged my request for a shield, but she'll have my balls if I suggest glamouring her to hide the pregnancy.* Rhys grimaced. *So here we go.*

Cassian nodded. *I've got your back, brother.*

Rhys threw him a grateful glance, and then must have lifted his shield on his mate because Feyre's scent—that wonderful, lovely scent—filled the air. Helion's eyes widened, going right to her middle, where her hand now rested against the small swelling. He let out a laugh. "So this is why you needed to learn about impenetrable shields, Rhysand." Helion leaned in to kiss Feyre's cheek. "My congratulations to you both."

Feyre beamed, but Rhys's smile was less open. If Helion noted it, he said nothing. The High Lord of Day considered Cassian and Azriel, then frowned. "Where's my beautiful Mor?"

Az said tightly, "Away."

"Pity. She's far nicer to look at than either of you."

Cassian rolled his eyes.

Helion smirked, picking an invisible fleck of lint from his draped white robe, then faced Rhys. His dark brown skin gleamed over the strong muscles of his bare thighs and legs, the golden sandals that laced up his calves useless in the snowcapped terrain around them. The High Lord carried no weapons—the only metal on him was the golden armband around one muscled biceps, fashioned after a snake, and the spiked golden crown atop his shoulder-length black hair. There would never be any mistaking Helion for anything but a High Lord, yet Cassian had always rather liked his casual, irreverent air. The male drawled to Rhys, "Well? You wanted me to do some digging into a spell? Or was that an excuse to get me to your twisted pleasure palace under this mountain?"

Rhys sighed. "Please don't make me regret bringing you here, Helion."

Helion's golden eyes lit. "Where would the fun be if I didn't?"

Feyre linked her arm through his. "I missed you, my friend."

Helion patted her hand. "I'll deny it to the grave if you tell anyone, but I missed you too, Cursebreaker."

⁂

"I like this palace *much* more than the one beneath," Helion said an hour later, surveying the moonstone pillars and gauzy curtains blowing in a mild breeze that belied the snow-crusted mountain range around them. Beyond the palace's shields, Cassian knew that breeze became a howling, bitter wind that could flay the flesh from one's bones.

Helion flung himself into a low-lying chair before one of the endless views, sighing. "All right. Do you want my assessment now that we're out of the Hewn City?"

Feyre slid into the seat beside his, but Cassian, Rhys, and Az remained standing, the shadowsinger leaning against a pillar, half-hidden from sight. Feyre asked, "Are the soldiers enchanted?"

Helion had spoken to and briefly touched the hands of the two Autumn Court soldiers chained in that room, kept alive and fed by Rhys's magic. Helion's face had tensed when he'd touched their hands—and he'd then murmured that he'd seen enough.

Nothing in the Hewn City had seemed to disturb him until that moment. Not the towering black pillars and their carvings, not the wicked people who occupied it, not the utter darkness of the place. If it reminded Helion of his time Under the Mountain, he did not let on.

Amarantha had modeled her court there after this one, apparently—a sorry replica, Rhys had said.

"*Enchanted* isn't the right word," Helion said, frowning. "Their bodies and actions are indeed not their own, but no spell lies upon them. I can feel spells—like threads. Ones that can enchant feel like bindings around an individual. I sensed none of that."

"So what ails them?" Rhys asked.

"I don't know," Helion admitted with unusual gravity. "Rather than a thread, it was more like a mist. A fog, exactly as you described it, Rhysand. There was nothing to grasp on to, nothing tangible to break, yet it was *there*."

Rhys asked, "Does it feel less like a spell and more like . . . an influence?"

Shit. *Shit*.

Helion rubbed his jaw. "I can't explain how, but it's as if this fog around their mind sways them." He noted their expressions. "What is it?"

Feyre's mouth tightened. "The Crown—part of the Dread Trove."

And then it all came out, Queen Briallyn and her hunt for the Trove, Koschei's involvement, the Mask that Nesta had retrieved. Only Eris's secrets regarding the depths of Beron's treachery remained unspoken. When Feyre finished, Helion shook his head slowly. "I thought we'd at least have a break from trying to avoid disasters like this."

"Just the Harp remains at large, then," Azriel said. He remained leaning against the pillar, swathed in shadows. "If Briallyn has the Crown, it's possible she's had it for a while—and it's why the other queens fled to their own territories. Maybe they thought she'd use it on them, and ran. Maybe she even found it here during the war, while we were all distracted with fighting Hybern, and used it to pull her forces back, to bide her time. It could be what brought her to Koschei's attention—that it's what he wants from her."

"I can buy that," Feyre said, "but why use it on Eris's soldiers to attack our people in Oorid? What's the motive?"

"Perhaps it was to let us know she's aware that *we* know of her plans," Rhys suggested.

"But how did she know we'd be in the bog?" Cassian asked. "Those soldiers didn't have the power to winnow—they would have had to travel on foot for weeks before they got there."

"They've been missing for more than a month," Feyre pointed out.

Helion said, "Remember that Briallyn is Made, too. She might not be able to scry for the Cauldron, but she can scry for the Dread Trove as well as Nesta Archeron can. She could have learned the Mask was in Oorid, but did not dare to venture into its darkness. It's possible that she planted the soldiers to take the Mask from you once you found it."

"Or trick us into killing them, thus making an enemy of the Autumn Court," Cassian said.

"But Briallyn has to be stupid," Feyre said, "if she thinks those soldiers would be enough to overpower any of us."

Helion nodded to Feyre. "You said the Mask is here now? May I see it?"

"We need your help with it, actually," Feyre said. "Rhys warded and locked the room where the Mask lies, but it opened the locks to let my sister in, likely because she's Made. And if she can get in, it's possible Briallyn could as well." Feyre slid her tattooed hands into her pockets. "Can you show Nesta how to ward it herself? Something perhaps with a bit more . . . oomph?"

"Oomph?" Rhys asked, lifting an eyebrow.

"Oomph," Feyre said, throwing him a glare. "We can't all be silver-tongued like you."

Rhys winked. "Good thing you benefit from it, Feyre darling."

Cassian chose to ignore the innuendo, and the flicker of arousal from both of them. Helion, however, snickered.

Azriel cleared his throat. "Nesta's waiting."

"She's here?" Helion practically shimmered with golden light.

"Yes," Feyre said simply, rising from the chair. Cassian didn't miss the sultry look his High Lady gave Rhys as she passed by, aiming for the rooms at the northern end of the palace. And he didn't miss the deep laugh Rhys gave her in return, full of sensual promise.

He couldn't help the pang in his chest at the casual intimacy, the blatant affection and love. A far cry from *just sex*.

Helion trailed, commenting on the palace's beauty. Cassian blocked him out, too busy mulling over how Nesta hadn't so much as bothered to object when he'd left her bed. And hadn't so much as approached him for more since.

He'd held himself back, especially since she seemed to drive herself into the ground during practice, working out whatever she needed to in her heart, her mind. But he hadn't been able to stop remembering it—the sex, and that image of her, her backside still upraised as she lay on the bed, her beautiful sex swollen and gleaming, wet with his seed.

"What are *you* thinking about?" Helion drawled as they approached a shut wooden door.

Cassian straightened. He hadn't realized his thoughts had dragged such a scent from him. He grinned. "Your mother."

Helion chuckled. "I always forget how much I like you."

"Happy to remind you." Cassian winked.

Feyre reached the door, knocked, and then there she was—Nesta.

She sat at the table where the Mask rested, a book open before her. From the speed with which she shut the volume, Cassian knew she'd been reading one of the romances she, Emerie, and Gwyn traded amongst them.

Cassian found himself tensing as Helion stepped into the room, and Nesta rose. She'd worn a dark blue dress today—the first time in a month he'd seen her in one. No longer did it hang off her. She'd packed on enough weight that the bodice was again formfitting, and those lush breasts swelled gracefully above the scooped neckline.

Helion offered a bow of his head, the epitome of courtly grace. "Lady Nesta."

Nesta bobbed a curtsy, but her eyes cut to Feyre. "Lady?"

Feyre shrugged. "He's being polite."

Nesta slid her eyes to Cassian's. "Now I understand why you find the title grating."

He smiled, and Helion blinked—as if shocked she'd forgotten a High Lord stood before her.

But Nesta had blown past Helion the first time they'd met, too, utterly unimpressed.

Cassian said to her, "It never gets easier."

Nesta faced Helion again, taking in that spiked golden crown and the draped white robe. "Was that your winged horse that flew over earlier?"

Helion's smile was a thing of cultivated beauty. "He is my finest stallion."

"He's lovely."

"As are you."

Nesta angled her head as Cassian found himself near-breathless, waiting for her reply. Feyre and Rhys seemed to be trying not to laugh, and Azriel was the portrait of cool boredom.

Nesta surveyed Helion for long enough that he shifted on his feet. A High Lord *shifted on his feet* under her gaze. She said at last, "I appreciate the compliment," and that was that.

That pause while she'd surveyed Helion had been a courtier's pause. Assessing how best to strike.

Helion frowned slightly.

Rhys cleared his throat, amusement glittering in his eyes. "Well, there it is." He pointed to the black velvet mound on the table. "Nesta?"

She pulled away the cloth. Ancient, beaten gold gleamed, and Helion hissed as a cold, strange power filled the room, whispering like a chill breeze.

Helion whirled to Nesta, all sensuality vanished. "You truly wore this and lived?" It wasn't a question meant to be answered. "Cover it again, please. I can't stand it."

Rhys tucked in his wings. "It affects you that much?"

"Doesn't it rake its cold claws down your senses?" Helion asked.

"Not as much as all that," Feyre said. "We can sense its power, but it didn't bother any of us so seriously."

Helion shuddered, and Nesta threw the cloth over the Mask. As if the cloth somehow blinded it to their presence. "Perhaps an ancestor of mine once used it, and the warning of its cost is imprinted upon my blood." Helion shook out a breath. "All right, not-Lady Nesta. Allow me to show you some warding tricks even clever Rhysand doesn't know."

⁜

In the end, Helion created the wards and keyed them to Nesta's blood. A pinprick of it, courtesy of Truth-Teller, had done the job, and Cassian had found himself tensing at the sight of that little bead of red. Its scent.

It was an effort of will to tell his body there was no threat, that the blood was willing, that she was fine. But it didn't stop him from grinding his teeth loudly enough that Feyre whispered to him beneath Nesta and Helion's conversation, "What's wrong with you?"

Cassian muttered back, "Nothing. Stop being such a busybody, Cursebreaker."

Feyre shot him a sidelong glance. "You're acting like a caged animal." Her lips curved upward. "Are you jealous?"

Cassian kept his voice neutral. "Of Helion?"

"I don't see anyone else in this room who's currently holding my sister's hand and smiling at her."

The bastard was indeed doing that, though Nesta remained stone-faced. "Why would I be jealous?"

Feyre's laugh was a rustle of air.

Cassian couldn't stop his answering grin, earning a confused glance from Azriel. Cassian shook his head, just as Nesta pulled her hand from Helion's grip and asked, "So it's done?"

"Once we leave this room, no one shall be able to enter it. Even you, if you do not unlock my wards, cannot enter."

Nesta loosed a little sigh. "Good."

"I'll show you the unlocking spell," Helion said, but she stepped away from him.

"No," Nesta said abruptly. "No, I don't want to know it."

Silence fell.

Nesta declared to none of them in particular, "If Briallyn is hunting for the Mask, if she apprehends me, I don't want to have any knowledge of how to free it." It was wise, even if it made him sick to consider, but he could have sworn it was a lie. Could have sworn that Nesta didn't want to have access to the information—for herself.

As if she might be tempted by the Mask.

Rhys said, "That's fine. Helion can show me, and if we need the knowledge, I'll show you." Rhys held out a hand to Helion, indicating how he'd prefer to be shown the spell. Their fingers interlaced, their eyes going vacant, and then Rhys blinked. "Thank you."

Azriel said, "We have to notify Eris about his soldiers' reappearance. And what we did to them."

Cassian surveyed his family, his friends. "How much do we tell Eris? Do we let him know we have the Mask?"

The question hung there. Then Rhys said, "Not yet." He nodded to Cassian. "Pay Eris a visit tomorrow." Rhys gestured to Nesta. "You go with him."

Nesta stiffened, and Cassian tried not to gape. "Why?" she asked.

"Because you savor playing the game," Rhys said. He'd undoubtedly noticed how smoothly she dealt with Helion's attempts to flirt earlier. Rhys knew how to wield a tool at his disposal. "But it's your choice," he added.

Cassian cleared his throat. "Sounds fine to me." Nesta, to his surprise, didn't object.

"I want to confirm that Briallyn has the Crown," Azriel said. "I'll travel to the human lands tomorrow."

"No," Feyre and Rhys said at the same time, in the same breath.

Azriel's eyes shuttered. "I wasn't asking for permission."

Rhys smirked. "Doesn't matter."

Az opened his mouth to object, but Feyre said, "You're not going, Azriel. If Briallyn has the Crown and catches you, even if she just suspects you're nearby, who knows what she could do to you?"

"Give me some credit, Feyre," Az said. "I can keep hidden well enough."

"We take no risks," Feyre said, voice flat with command. "Pull all your spies out."

"Like hell I will."

Cassian braced himself, but Feyre didn't back down. "Information from your spies—*any* spies—can't be trusted with the Crown in play. Amren said it needs close contact to sink its claws into someone's mind. We stay far away from Briallyn."

Azriel bristled and turned to Rhys. "And you agree with her?"

"She's your High Lady," Rhys said coldly. "What she says is law."

Az eyed him, eyed Feyre. Determined that they were an immovable unit, an impenetrable wall against which his fury would only break again and again.

In the taut silence, Helion nodded to the bright hall beyond the room. "I would like to remove myself from the Mask's odious presence, and perhaps enjoy your palace, Rhysand. It's been a long while since I was in a place of such quiet. If you'll allow it, I'll stay here for an hour or two."

"Something bothering you at home?" Rhys inquired, falling into step beside the High Lord.

Cassian caught Nesta's stare as he left the room, and she grabbed her book before following them out. Feyre exited with Azriel, murmuring with a tattooed hand on his shoulder.

Cassian asked Nesta, "What are you reading today?"

"*A Brief History of the Great Sieges* by Osian."

He almost stumbled a step. "Not a romance?"

"I realized after you left me *The Dance of Battle* that there's a great deal left for me to learn. Last night I asked the House to give me something you might read."

"Why?"

Nesta tucked the book under an arm. "What's the point in learning fighting techniques if I don't know their true purpose and uses? You'd train me into a weapon, and I'd be just that: someone else's weapon. I want to know how to wield it—myself, I mean. And others."

Cassian was stunned into silence as they ascended the steps, following Helion and Rhys, who chatted away at the head of their group. "You plan on leading an army, Nes?"

"Not an army." She glanced sidelong at him. "But perhaps a small unit of females."

She was dead serious. "The priestesses?"

"I don't know if they'd join, but . . . There are others out there, I'm sure, who might. I'm immortal now, or as close to it as possible. I have nothing but time to plan far into the future."

His chest tightened. Planning for the future. It was a hell of a good sign.

⁜

Cassian knocked on Nesta's bedroom door at the House after dinner. She hadn't joined him and Azriel, though perhaps it had been for the best.

The High Lord and High Lady of the Night Court had faced off against the shadowsinger this afternoon, and emerged triumphant.

Perhaps *triumphant* wasn't the right word, but the argument had ended with Azriel grudgingly agreeing not to spy on Briallyn for the time being—and brooding all through dinner.

Nesta's voice echoed through the wood. "Enter."

He found her in bed, a book propped up against her knees. It appeared she'd gone back to romance. "No more war books?" He held up the three he had brought with him—his reason for being here. His excuse.

"Only during the day." She sat up, gathering the blankets around her waist. "What are those?"

"More texts I thought you might be interested in." He set them on the desk.

Nesta dipped her chin in a shallow nod, her long braid bobbing over her chest with the movement. She wore a long-sleeved nightgown, and, though there was no fire in the hearth, the room stayed warm. As if the House had noted her dislike for fires and heated it another way.

He forced himself to move from the desk, to aim for her door again.

She said before he'd reached the archway, "Was it not good for you?"

Cassian turned slowly. "What?"

A flush stained her cheeks as she lifted her chin. "Was the sex not good for you?"

He swallowed. "Why would you ask that?"

Nesta's throat bobbed. She was . . . Fuck, was she really that unsure of him? "You left quickly. And didn't seek me out again."

I left quickly because I needed to keep some pieces of myself intact. "You've been focused on training."

Her eyes flickered with something like hurt. "All right. Well, good night."

"I didn't mean it like that. Fuck, Nesta." He stalked toward the bed, and she straightened again, peering at him as he towered over her. "How could I be so selfish—to demand more sex from you when you're so invested in training?"

"It's not a demand if both sides want it," she said. "And I just worried you . . . didn't enjoy it as much as I did."

"You think I haven't sought you out because I didn't *enjoy* myself?" When she said nothing, he braced his hands on either side of her and leaned in to whisper in her ear, breathing in her scent, "I enjoyed myself *too* much. I've thought about it for days and days." She shivered, and he smiled against the soft shell of her ear. He loved this—seeing that icy exterior crumble, seeing how he affected her. "Have you been touching yourself at night, thinking about it like I do?"

Nesta's chin dipped in the barest of nods, and from the corner of his eye, he spied a flash of her teeth as she bit her bottom lip. "Have those sweet little fingers felt as good as mine?"

Her breathing hitched, but she wouldn't answer. He knew she didn't want to give him the satisfaction. He nipped at her earlobe, drawing a gasp from her. "Well?"

"I don't know," she whispered. "I'd have to see again."

"Hmm." Cassian lowered his mouth, pressing a kiss beneath her ear. His cock hardened, already aching against his pants. "Shall we do a little side-by-side comparison?"

She whimpered, and he crawled onto the bed, straddling her legs. His blood pounded through every inch of him, in time to the pulse in his cock, and he pulled away from her neck to find her eyes bright with desire.

The world quieted, and she stared and stared at him as he slowly pulled the blankets down to her waist. Her nightgown was rucked up her thighs, and he ran a hand over one of them, thumb stroking the sleek muscles building there. "Why don't you show me how you touch yourself, Nesta? And then I'll remind you how I touch you." He bared his teeth in a wicked grin. "You can tell me what feels better."

Her chest heaved, her pebbled breasts peeking through the nightgown. His mouth watered, body trembling with the restraint needed to keep from putting his mouth over them.

She seemed to read every line of his body, his desire. Her eyes glinted with molten fire. "While I . . . touch myself, you are forbidden to touch me." A feral smile. "And forbidden to touch yourself."

His skin heated, stretching too tight over his bones. "All right."

Cassian waited for her to nestle into the pillows, but she grabbed the hem of her nightgown to pull it over herself, bunching it into a ball before chucking it to the floor.

Every thought eddied from his mind as she half-reclined there, utterly naked, those beautiful breasts peaked and waiting for him, her silken flesh near-glowing. And between her legs . . . She drew her knees up slightly, spreading them. Baring herself.

Cassian made a low, pained sound. Her pink sex gleamed—its heady, seductive scent beckoning. He needed to taste it, to feel her on his tongue, on his cock—

"No touching," Nesta purred, because his hand had been drifting toward his cock, desperate for any sort of relief from the sight of her open and bare, the faelights gilding her.

His breath rasped in his throat—and then vanished entirely as Nesta slid two delicate fingers down her body. They stopped atop that bundle of nerves, circling slowly.

Her breathing turned uneven, but she watched him observe her as she made another circle, and then moved lower. A slow, torturous slide down her center before her wrist curved, and she dipped her fingers into herself.

Cassian groaned, hips bucking a bit where he knelt, and she cut him a reprimanding look. He stilled, unable to think about anything other than her two fingers as she slid them into herself again, and moaned.

They emerged shining with her wetness, and he might have been panting as she plunged them into herself a third time, deep and slow.

"This," she breathed, her fingers beginning a slow, steady pump, "is what I do when I think of you every night."

If she so much as touched him, he'd come. But he growled, "Do it harder."

She shivered as if his words were a physical touch, and obeyed. They both groaned this time, and he found himself saying, "Please."

He didn't know what it meant—only that he needed to touch her.

Nesta smiled at him with feline amusement. "Not yet."

She drove her hand between her legs again. "I imagine you taking me, over and over again. Rough, like we did before." He couldn't breathe, couldn't do anything but stare at her hand, her pleasure-hazed face. "I imagine you less patient than you were the first time, just thrusting into me, all the way." She echoed her words with a swift plunge of her fingers.

"I don't want to hurt you," he got out, praying to the Mother and the Cauldron to maintain his sanity.

"You won't hurt me." Her other hand teased that bundle of nerves. "I want you unleashed."

Cassian made a low noise of need.

She huffed a wicked laugh. "Do you want to watch me come? Or do you want to taste it?"

"Taste." He'd beg on hot coals for one lick of her.

She spread her legs wider. "Then have at me, Cassian."

His name on her lips was his undoing. He gripped her thighs and spread them wide, and then his mouth was on her, licking her from base to apex in a long, luxurious slide.

She moaned, louder than the first time, and he only grabbed her legs again, hooking them over his shoulders as he buried his face against her.

There was nothing gentle in it, nothing teasing. He feasted with tongue and lips and teeth, and every taste of her made the roaring in his blood rise like a mighty wave within him. Nesta ground against him, toes tickling his wings so much he had to pause for a moment to keep from coming at that mere touch. He'd teach her wingplay later. Because he wanted her to touch his wings, to learn where to stroke while he fucked her so that he'd come hard enough to see stars, to learn what places to stroke even while he wasn't fucking her so he'd come in her hand, her mouth.

He slid his tongue into her core, release already building under his skin, in his spine. Too soon—he didn't want to go too soon.

He made himself take a breath. Made himself pull back, pull away. The sight of her on the pillows, naked and open for him, nearly made him come.

But he removed his shirt. His pants.

Only when he was naked, kneeling between her legs, his cock jutting forward, did he say, "Do you want my fingers, my tongue, or my cock, Nesta?" He fisted the last item for her, pumping himself in a slow, nearly painful squeeze. She watched, eyes widening, as if remembering the size of him inside her.

"What of a side-by-side comparison?" she managed to say, but the haughtiness wasn't in her eyes, not as he pumped himself again, savoring how it made her breath catch.

"Whatever you want. Whatever you need from me." He knew those were a fool's words, knew he offered up too much.

But she only looked at his cock. "I want that. Now."

He muttered a prayer of thanks to the Mother and lay over her, bracing himself on his arms. "Put me inside you."

When Nesta's hand wrapped around him, he arched, gritting his teeth. She smiled at that, and pumped him as hard as he'd pumped himself, just this side of pain. Then she fitted him to her drenched entrance.

He didn't wait this time. Didn't go tenderly, not when she'd told him she wanted it otherwise.

Cassian plunged into her, driving right to the hilt.

Nesta let out a sound somewhere between a moan and a scream, and he found himself echoing it as all her silken, blazing heat gripped him. She was so perfectly, mind-meltingly tight. As if she'd been made for him, and he'd been made for her.

Cassian drew out in a long slide, and thrust back, seating himself fully. Her fingernails dug into his shoulders, the pain of it secondary, the pain of it a pleasure as she marked him.

He withdrew again, lowering his head to watch his cock slide out of her, gleaming with her wetness—and then enter her anew. Every inch into that tight, blazing core of her was paradise and torment, and he needed more, needed to be deeper, needed to crawl so far inside her that there would be no disentangling them.

Her nails sliced through his skin, and the tang of his blood filled the air. He just leaned down to kiss her. She parted for him instantly, and he let her taste herself on his tongue, moving his own in time to his thrusts.

Nesta wrapped her lips around his tongue and sucked on it as she had his cock, and any sane thought faded away. Gathering her to him, Cassian knelt, her legs locking around his waist as he thrust up and up and up into her. She tipped her head back, baring her throat, and he bit down on the center of it, hard enough to leave a mark.

Nesta moved on his cock, and he drove deeper into her. Scraped his teeth over her neck.

She let go of his shoulder to cup her breast, and he nearly climaxed as he found her lifting it up toward him in silent command.

Cassian licked her nipple, and she ground onto him, those delicate inner muscles clenching tight. "*Fuck*," he said around her breast. She laughed breathily and did it again.

Then there was only his tongue and teeth at her breast, the near-savage pounding of his cock into her tight warmth, the rhythm of her hips as she met him for each stroke, as if trying to work him even deeper. He dragged his mouth from her breast to bite her neck, her shoulder, sealing their bodies together, fusing them into one being as he thrust deeper still, harder still.

And then her fingers found his wings. The touch wasn't slicing, but gentle—such a gentle, tentative, wondrous stroke that he roared.

Release barreled into him, and he rammed up into her in such a mighty thrust that she screamed, climaxing with him. She clamped around him, pulsing and milking, and he bucked, frenzied, reduced to this need to be in her, to spill into her, to spill as much of himself as he could.

Nesta rode him until he'd stopped spurting, until her pleasure had her draped over his chest, an arm still outstretched toward his wing.

They clung to each other, and he tried to piece himself back together, to remember what the fuck his name was and where they were.

But there was only her. Only this female in his arms.

And the only name he could remember was hers.

✠

Nesta couldn't move.

Wrapped around Cassian where he knelt in the center of the bed, his hands still digging into her ass to hold her in place, his cock buried deeply inside her, she didn't *want* to move.

She'd never been this way with anyone, where one look from her lover brought her a heartbeat away from release; one look from him and she was taking off her clothes and pleasuring herself in front of him.

She didn't have it in herself to be embarrassed. Not when it had felt so good, so right.

He was trembling, his wings twitching as his cock at last finished spending itself.

She told herself she shouldn't enjoy it so much—seeing him undone, feeling his seed inside her, leaking out of her. And the fact that she did had her climbing away at last, moaning softly as she slid off his cock.

She knelt before him, nearly knee to knee. "I still need more."

Cassian's head lifted, eyes flashing. "I know."

She couldn't breathe under that stare, that beautiful face. "How can I need you again so soon?" It wasn't a coy, courtier's question—it was voiced out of sheer desperation. Because she did need more. She needed him back inside her, needed his weight, his mouth and teeth on her. She had no explanation for it, that rising, unquenchable thirst.

His eyes flickered. "I've needed you from the moment I first met you. And now that I get to have you, I don't want to stop."

"Yes," she breathed, about as much of the truth as she'd admit. "Yes."

They stared at each other for a long minute, for eternity. And then, to her shock and delight, Cassian hardened before her eyes. "Do you see what you do to me?" he asked. "Do you see what happens every time I look at you, all fucking day?"

She smirked. "I vaguely recall you boasting weeks ago that *I* would be the one to crawl into your bed. It seems like you did the crawling."

His lips twitched upward. "It would seem so." Her heart thundered as he held her stare. "Get on your hands and knees," he ordered, his voice so low she could barely understand him. But her blood heated, and an ache that had nothing to do with how hard he'd just taken her began to build between her legs once more.

So Nesta did as he bade, baring herself, still wet and gleaming with both of their releases.

He snarled in satisfaction. "Beautiful." She whimpered a bit—because beneath the praise, pure lust simmered. He growled, "Put your hands on the headboard."

Her breath began sawing out of her again, but she obeyed, already thrumming with need.

Cassian rose behind her, gripping her hips. He knocked a knee against each of her own, spreading her legs wider. Callused fingertips brushed down the length of her spine, over the tattoo there, the ink binding them.

He leaned to whisper in her ear, "Hold on tight."

CHAPTER 42

Cassian got the summons to the river house just after dawn.

He hadn't slept in Nesta's room—no, after that second time, when his entire body had been turned to sated, content jelly, he'd rolled off her and returned to his own suite. She hadn't said anything. The understanding had been there, though: just sex, but they needn't wait so long again.

Sleep had been elusive as he'd thought of what they'd done, what he'd done to her. The second time had been even rougher than the first, and she'd taken everything he'd thrown at her, met his demanding pace and depth, and had held that headboard until her body had collapsed with pleasure. Gods, sex with Nesta was like . . .

He didn't let himself dwell on comparisons as he sat in Rhys's office next to Amren and Azriel, facing their High Lord across his desk. Those thoughts had not done him any favors last night. Or this morning, when he woke hard and aching, and realized that the scent of her was all over him.

He knew his friends smelled it. Neither Rhys nor Az had commented, but Amren's eyes had narrowed. Yet she said nothing, and he wondered if Rhys had given her a silent command. Cassian filed away his curiosity about why Rhys might have felt the need to do such a thing.

"All right, Rhysand," Amren said, tucking one foot under her thigh. "Tell me why I'm here before breakfast while Varian is still sleeping soundly in my bed."

Rhys pulled back a canvas tarp that had been over part of his desk. "We're here because I got a visit at dawn from a blacksmith out by the western edge of the city."

Cassian went still as he saw what lay there: a sword, a dagger, and a longer great sword, all sheathed in black leather. "What blacksmith?"

Rhys leaned back in his chair, crossing his arms. "The one you and Nesta visited several days ago."

Cassian's brow furrowed. "Why did he bring you these weapons? As a gift?"

Azriel leaned forward, a scarred hand reaching for the closest sword.

"I wouldn't do that," Rhys warned, and Az halted.

Rhys said to Cassian, "The blacksmith dumped them here in an absolute panic. He said the blades were cursed."

Cassian's blood chilled.

Amren asked, "Cursed in what way?"

"He just said cursed," Rhys replied, motioning to the weapons. "Said he wanted nothing to do with them and they were our problem now."

Amren slid her eyes to Cassian. "What happened in the shop?"

"Nothing," he said. "He let her hammer at the metal for a bit, so she could get a sense of the hard work that went into making weapons. But there was no *cursing*."

Rhys straightened. "Nesta hammered the blades?"

"All three," Cassian said. "First the sword, then the dagger, and then the great sword."

Rhys and Amren exchanged a look.

Cassian demanded, "What?"

Rhys asked Amren, "Is it possible?"

Amren gazed at the blades. "It has been . . . It has been such a long time, but . . . yes."

"Someone please explain," Azriel said, peering at the three blades from a safe distance.

Cassian forced himself to sit perfectly still as Rhys dragged a hand through his black hair. "Once, the High Fae were more elemental, more given to reading the stars and crafting masterpieces of art and jewelry and weaponry. Their gifts were rawer, more connected to nature, and they could imbue objects with that power."

Cassian instantly knew where this was headed. "Nesta put her power in those swords?"

"No one has been able to create a magic sword in more than ten thousand years," Amren said. "The last one Made, the great blade Gwydion, vanished around the time the last of the Trove went missing."

"This sword isn't Gwydion," Cassian said, well aware of the myths regarding the sword. It had belonged to a true Fae High King in Prythian, as there had been in Hybern. He had united the lands, its people—and for a while, with that sword, peace had reigned. Until he had been betrayed by his own queen and his fiercest general, and lost the sword to them, and the lands fell into darkness once more. Never again to see another High King—only High Lords, who ruled the territories that had once answered to the king.

"Gwydion is gone," Amren said, a shade sadly, "or has been gladly missing for millennia." She nodded toward the great sword. "This is something new."

Azriel said, "Nesta created a new magic sword."

"Yes," Amren said. "Only the Great Powers could do that—Gwydion was given its powers when the High Priestess Oleanna dipped it into the Cauldron during its crafting."

Cassian's blood chilled, waves rippling over his skin. "One touch from Nesta's magic while the blade was still hot . . ."

"And the blade was infused with it."

"Nesta didn't know what she was doing," Cassian said. "She was letting off some steam."

"Which might be worse," Amren said. "Who knows what emotions she poured into the blades with her power? It might have shaped them into instruments of such feelings—or it might have been the catalyst to release her power. There is no way of knowing."

"So we use the sword," Cassian said, "and figure it out."

"No," Amren countered sharply. "I wouldn't dare draw these blades. Especially not the great sword. I can feel power clustering there. Did she work on that one longest?"

"Yes."

"Then it is to be treated as an object of the Dread Trove. A *new* Trove."

"You can't be serious."

Amren's brows flattened. "The Dread Trove was forged by the Cauldron. Nesta possesses the Cauldron's powers. So anything she crafts and imbues with her power becomes a new Trove. At this point, I wouldn't so much as eat a piece of bread if she'd toasted it."

They all stared at the three blades atop the desk.

Azriel said, "People will kill for this power. Either kill her to stop it, or kill us to capture her."

"Nesta forged a new Trove," Cassian said, reining in his rage at the truth of Azriel's words. "She could create *anything*." He nodded to Rhys. "She could fill our arsenals with weapons that would win us any war." Briallyn, Koschei, and Beron wouldn't stand a chance.

"Which is why Nesta must not learn about it," Amren said.

Cassian demanded, "What?"

Amren's gray eyes held steady. "She cannot know."

Rhys said, "That seems like a risk. What if, unaware, she creates more?"

"What if, in one of her moods," Amren challenged, "Nesta creates what she pleases just to spite us?"

"She'd *never* do that," Cassian said hotly. He pointed at her. "You fucking know it, too."

"Nesta would create not a Dread Trove," Amren said, unfazed by his snarling, "but a Trove of Nightmares."

"I can't lie to her," Cassian said, looking to Rhys. "I can't."

"You don't need to lie," Amren answered. "Simply don't volunteer the information."

He appealed to Rhys, "You're all right with this? Because I'm sure as hell not."

"Amren's order holds," Rhys said, and for a heartbeat, Cassian hated him. Hated the mistrust and wariness he beheld on Rhys's face.

"I'd be careful when you're fucking her," Amren added, lips curling in a sneer. "Who knows what she might transform you into when her emotions are high?"

"That's enough," Azriel said, and Cassian turned grateful eyes to his brother. Az continued, "I'm with Cassian on this. It's not right to keep the knowledge from Nesta."

Rhys considered, then gazed long and hard at Cassian. Cassian weathered the look, kept his back straight and face grave. Rhys said at last, "When Feyre returns from her studio, I'll ask her. She'll be the deciding vote."

It was a compromise, and even Amren could agree with that. Cassian nodded, uneasy but willing to let the decision lie in Feyre's hands.

Amren nestled back into her chair. "That sword shall be known by history." Her eyes darkened as she looked at the great sword, her words echoing. "It remains to be seen whether it shall be known for good or evil."

Cassian shook off the shiver that slithered down his spine, as if fate itself heard her words and shuddered. He threw her a grin. "You do love to be dramatic, don't you?"

Amren scowled, then rose. "I'm going back to bed." She pointed at

Rhysand. "Put those weapons somewhere no one will find them. And Mother damn you if you dare unsheathe one."

Rhys waved her off, bored and tired. "Of course."

"I mean it, boy," Amren said. "Do *not* unsheathe those blades." She surveyed all three of them before she left. "Any of you."

For a moment, only the ticking grandfather clock made a sound.

Rhys looked toward it. Then he said, eyes distant, "I can't find anything to help Feyre with the baby—with the labor."

Cassian's chest tightened. "Drakon and Miryam?"

Rhys shook his head. "The Seraphim's wings are as flexible and rounded as the Illyrians' are bony. That's what will kill Feyre. Miryam's children were able to pass through her birth canal because their wings bent easily—and nearly every one of her human people who's mixed with Drakon's has had similar success." Rhys's throat bobbed. His next words cracked Cassian's heart. "I didn't realize how much hope I'd been holding on to until I saw the pity and fear in their faces. Until Drakon had to embrace me to keep me from falling apart."

Cassian crossed to his brother in a few steps. He clasped Rhys's shoulder, leaning against the edge of the desk. "We'll keep looking. What about Thesan?"

Rhys loosened the uppermost buttons on his black jacket, revealing a hint of the tattooed chest beneath. "The Dawn Court had nothing of use. The Peregryns are similar to the Seraphim—they're related, though distantly. Their healers know how to get a breech baby with wings to turn, how to get it out of the mother, but again: their wings are flexible."

Azriel appeared on Rhys's other side, a hand on his shoulder as well.

The clock ticked on, a brutal reminder of every second racing toward sure doom. What they needed, Cassian realized with each tick of that clock, was a miracle.

Azriel asked, "And Feyre still doesn't know?"

"No. She knows the labor will be difficult, but I haven't told her yet that it might very well claim her life." Rhys spoke into their minds, as if he couldn't say it aloud, *I haven't told her that the nightmares that now send me lurching from sleep aren't ones of the past, but of the future.*

Cassian squeezed Rhys's shoulder. "Why won't you tell her?"

Rhys's throat worked. "Because I can't bring myself to give her that fear. To take away one bit of the joy in her eyes every time she puts a hand on her belly." His voice shook. "It is fucking eating me alive, this terror. I keep myself busy, but . . . there is no one to bargain with for her life, no amount of wealth to buy it, *nothing* that I can do to save her."

"Helion?" Azriel asked, eyes pained.

"I told him before he left yesterday. Pulled him aside when Feyre had winnowed home, and begged him on my knees to find something in his thousand libraries to save her. He said every head librarian and researcher who can be spared will be put on it. Somewhere in history, someone must have studied this. Found a way to deliver a baby with wings to a mother whose body was not equipped for it."

"We'll hold on to our hope, then," Cassian said. Rhys shuddered, hanging his head, his silken black hair obscuring his eyes.

Cassian lifted his stare to Azriel, whose face conveyed everything: hope wouldn't keep Feyre alive.

Cassian swallowed hard, and shifted his gaze to the three blades on the desk.

Their hilts were ordinary—as might be expected from a blacksmith in a small village. He made fine weapons, yes, but not artistic masterpieces. The great sword's hilt was a simple cross guard, the pommel a rounded bit of metal.

Gwydion, the last of the magic swords, had been dark as night and as beautiful.

How many games had Cassian played as a child with Rhys and Azriel, where a long stick had been a stand-in for Gwydion? How many adventures had they imagined, sharing that mythical sword between them as they slew wyrms and rescued damsels?

Never mind that Rhys's particular damsel had slain a wyrm herself and rescued him instead.

But if Amren was right . . . Cassian couldn't think of another place in the world that held three magic blades, let alone one.

These might very well be the only ones in existence.

Cassian drummed his fingers on the desk, curiosity biting deep. "Let's have a look."

"Amren said not to," Azriel warned.

"Amren's not here," Cassian said, smirking. "And we don't need to *touch* them." He clapped Rhys on the shoulder. "Use that fancy magic to unsheathe them."

Rhys lifted his head. "This is a bad idea."

Cassian winked. "That should be written on the Night Court crest."

A few stars blinked into existence in Rhys's eyes. Azriel muttered a prayer.

But Rhys took two steadying breaths and unspooled his power toward the massive sword, letting it lift the blade in star-flecked hands.

"It's heavy," Rhys observed, brows bunched in concentration. "In a way it should not be. Like it's fighting against my magic." He kept the sword floating above his desk, perpendicular to it, as if it were held in a stand.

Cassian braced himself as Rhys angled his head, his magic probing the hilt, the scabbard. Rhys mused, "The blacksmith never said anything about *what* had seemed cursed, and he must have touched it several times—to feel the power and to bring it here, at least. So it can't be a death-sword to slay any careless hand."

Azriel grunted. "I'd still be careful."

With a wicked smile toward Az, Rhys used his power to draw away the black scabbard.

It did not go easily, as if the sword did not wish to be revealed—or not by Rhysand.

But inch by inch, the scabbard slid from the blade. And inch by inch, fresh steel glowed—truly *glowed*, like moonlight lay within the metal.

Even Az didn't school his features into anything but gaping awe as the scabbard fell away at last.

Cassian stumbled back, gawking.

Iridescent sparks danced along the blade. Pure, crackling magic. The light danced and spurted as if an invisible hammer still struck it.

The hair on Cassian's body rose.

Rhys inhaled, rallying his magic, then floated and unsheathed the other sword and the dagger.

They did not spark with raw power, but Cassian could feel them. The dagger radiated cold, its blade gleaming so bright it looked like an icicle in the sun. The second sword seemed hot—angry and willful.

But the great sword between the two others . . . The sparks faded, as if sucked into the blade itself.

None of them dared touch it. Something deep and primal within Cassian warned him not to. That to be impaled or sliced by that blade would be no ordinary wound.

A soft, female laugh rippled from the door, and Cassian didn't need to turn to know Amren stood there. "I knew you idiots wouldn't be able to resist."

Rhys murmured, "I have never seen anything like this." His magic set the three blades to rotating, allowing them to observe every facet. Az's face was still slack with awe.

"Amarantha destroyed one," Amren said.

Cassian started. "I never heard that."

Amren amended, "Rumor claimed she dumped one into the sea. It would not come to Amarantha's hand, nor the hands of any of her commanders, and rather than let the King of Hybern attain it, she disposed of it."

Azriel asked, "Which sword?"

"Narben." Amren's red lips quirked downward. "At least that's what rumor said. You were Under the Mountain then, Rhys. She would have kept it secret. I only heard from a fleeing water-nymph that it had been done."

"Narben was even older than Gwydion," Rhys said. "Where the hell was it?"

"I don't know, but she found it, and when it would not bend to her, she destroyed it. As she did all good things." It was as much as Amren would say about that terrible time. "It was perhaps in our favor. Had the King of Hybern possessed Narben, I fear we would have lost the war."

Narben's powers had not been the holy, savior's light of Gwydion, but ones far darker. "I can't believe that witch threw it into the sea," Cassian said.

"Again, it was a rumor, heard from someone who heard it from someone. Who knows if she actually found Narben? Even if it would not obey her, she'd have been a fool to throw it away."

"Amarantha could be shortsighted," Rhys said. Cassian hated the sound of her name on his brother's tongue. From the flare of rage on Azriel's face, so did the shadowsinger.

"But you, Rhysand, are not." Amren nodded to the still-rotating weapons. "With these three blades, you could make yourself High King."

The words clanged through the room. Cassian slowly blinked.

Rhys said tightly, "I don't wish to be High King. I only wish to be here, with my mate and my people."

Amren countered, "All seven courts united under one ruler would give us far better odds of survival in any upcoming conflict. No bickering and politicking required to dispatch our armies. Malcontents like Beron would have no ability to threaten our plans by allying with our enemies."

"We would have to fight an internal war first. I would be branded a traitor by my friends in other courts—I'd be forced to make them kneel."

Azriel stepped forward, shadows trailing from his shoulders. "Kallias, Tarquin, and Helion might be willing to kneel. Thesan will kneel if the others do."

Cassian nodded. Rhys as High King: he could think of no other male he'd trust more. No other male who would be a fairer ruler than Rhys. And with Feyre as High Queen . . . Prythian would be blessed to have such leaders. So Cassian said, "Tamlin would probably fight, and lose. Beron would be the only one standing in your way."

Rhys's teeth flashed. "Beron is already standing in my way, and doing a damn good job of it. I have no interest in justifying his behavior." He gave Cassian a withering look. "Don't we have to leave soon to winnow you and Nesta down to the Spring Court to meet with Eris?"

"Don't change the subject," Cassian drawled.

Rhys's power rumbled in the room. "I do not want to be High King. There is no need to discuss it."

"Yours is a terrible and beautiful power, Rhysand," Amren said, sighing. "You have three magic blades before you, each a kingmaker in its own right, and yet you would rather share that power. Keep to your borders. Why?"

Rhys demanded, "Why do you want me to turn conqueror?"

Amren shot back, "Why do you shy from the power that is your birthright?"

"I did nothing to earn that power," Rhys said. "I was born with it. It is a tool to defend my people, not to attack others." He surveyed them. "Where is this talk coming from?"

Azriel said quietly, "We are weakened—all seven courts. Even more at odds with each other and with the rest of the world since the war. If Montesere and Vallahan march on us, if Rask joins with them, we will not withstand it. Not with Beron already turned against us and allied with

Briallyn. Not if Tamlin cannot master his guilt and grief and become what he once was."

Cassian picked up the thread, tucking in his wings. "But a land united under one king and queen, armed with such power and objects . . . Our enemies would hesitate."

Rhys snarled, "If you think for one moment that Feyre would be remotely interested in being High Queen, you're delusional."

Amren said, "Feyre would see it as a necessary evil. To protect your child from being born into war, she would do what is necessary."

"And I won't?" Rhys demanded, standing. "I will not be High King. I will not consider it, not today and not in a century."

Amren looked to the great sword, still slowly rotating above them. "Then explain to me why, after thousands of years, objects that once crowned and aided the old Fae have returned. The last time a High King ruled Prythian, it was with a *magic sword* in his hand. Look at that great sword before you, Rhysand, and tell me that it is not a sign from the Cauldron itself."

Cassian's breath caught in his throat. "It was a fluke, Amren. Nesta didn't make it on purpose."

Amren shook her head, hair swaying. "Nothing is a fluke. The Cauldron's power flows through Nesta, and could use her as a puppet without her knowledge. It wanted those weapons Made, and thus they were Made. It wanted Rhysand to have them and thus the blacksmith brought them to you. To you, Rhysand, not to Nesta. And do not forget that Nesta herself—and Elain, with whatever powers she has—is here. Feyre is here. All three sisters blessed by fate and gifted with powers to match your own. Feyre alone doubles your strength. Nesta makes you unstoppable. Especially if she were to march into battle wearing the Mask. No enemy could stand against her. She'd slay Beron's soldiers, then raise them from the dead and turn them on him."

Cassian's blood chilled. Yes, Nesta would be unstoppable. But at what cost to her soul?

Rhys leveled a cool stare at Amren. "I will not entertain this ridiculous notion for another moment."

Cassian knew they'd been dismissed. He nodded to Az, who followed him toward the doors. They paused, however, right before the threshold. Looked back at their brother, their High Lord, now seated alone at his desk. The weight of so many choices pressing heavy on his broad shoulders, drooping his wings.

"Very well then, Rhysand." Amren also turned from the desk and the blades Rhys's magic now sheathed and set upon the surface. "But know that the Cauldron's benevolence will be extended to you only for so long before it is offered to another."

CHAPTER 43

Breathing in the heady, sweet scent of the purple lilac bush blooming behind them, Nesta glanced sidelong at Cassian. She could have sworn he was subtly scratching himself whenever she turned away to admire the sheer beauty and peace of the Spring Court forest.

Rhys had winnowed them here, silent and stone-faced, then vanished. Cassian hadn't seemed disturbed by it, though, so Nesta hadn't asked. Especially not as they waited for Eris to appear at any moment.

Nesta feigned gazing toward a bramble of roses, then whipped her head back to Cassian to find him indeed scratching at his arms. "What is wrong with you?"

"I hate this place," he muttered, flushing. "Allergies."

Nesta swallowed a laugh. "You don't need to hide it from me. In the human realm, I used to get so itchy I had to take two baths a day to get rid of all the pollen." Well, before they'd gone to the cottage. After that, Nesta had been lucky to bathe once a week, thanks to the hassle of heating and hauling so much water to the lone tub in a corner of their bedroom. Sometimes, she and Elain had even shared the same bathwater, drawing straws for who went in second.

Nesta's throat constricted, and she surveyed the swaying cherry blossoms overhead. Elain would love this place. So many flowers, all in bloom, so much green—the light, vibrant green of new grass—so many birds singing and such warm, buttery sunshine. Nesta felt like a storm cloud standing amid it all. But Elain . . . The Spring Court had been made for someone like her.

Too bad her sister refused to see her. Nesta would have told Elain to visit this place.

And too bad the lord who ruled these lands was a piece of shit.

"Eris is late," Nesta said to Cassian. They'd been waiting ten minutes. "Do you think he's coming?"

"He's likely sipping some tea, enjoying the fact that we're here, waiting for him." Cassian considered. "Well, he only knows I'm coming. But he'll enjoy the thought of making me wait."

"He's a bastard." The few times she'd met the High Lord of Autumn's son, Nesta had detested the preening, cold-faced male. Exactly the sort of person who would abandon an injured Morrigan in the woods.

"Are you talking about me, or the brute beside you?" a deep, smooth voice said from the shadows of a budding dogwood.

And there he was, as if her thoughts had conjured him. Eris dressed as immaculately as Rhysand, not a strand of his long red hair out of place. But though Eris's angular features were handsome, no light shone in his eyes. No joy.

Those eyes landed on Nesta, raking from her braided hair to her leathers to her boots. "Hello, Nesta Archeron."

Nesta met the male's stare. She said nothing, letting cool contempt freeze over her gaze.

Eris's mouth quirked upward. But the expression vanished as he turned to Cassian. "I hear you have something to tell me regarding my soldiers."

Cassian crossed his arms. "Good news and bad news, Eris. Take your pick."

"Bad. Always the bad first." Eris's smile was full of poison.

"Most of your soldiers are dead."

Eris only blinked. "And the good news?"

"Two of them survived."

Nesta studied every minute shift on Eris's face: rage glimmering in his eyes, displeasure in his pursed lips, annoyance in the fluttering of a muscle in his jaw. As if countless questions were racing through his mind. Eris's voice remained flat, though. "And who did this?"

Cassian grimaced. "Technically, Azriel and I did. Your soldiers were enchanted by Queen Briallyn and Koschei to be mindless killers. They attacked us in the Bog of Oorid, and we were left with no choice but to kill them."

"And yet two survived. How convenient. I assume they received Azriel's particular brand of interrogation?" Eris's voice dripped disdain.

"We could only manage to contain two," Cassian said tightly. "Under Briallyn's influence, they were practically rabid."

"Let's not lie to ourselves. You *only* bothered to contain two, by the time your brute bloodlust ebbed away."

Nesta saw red at the words, and Cassian sucked in a breath. "We did what we could. There were two dozen of them."

Eris snorted. "There were certainly more than that, and you could have easily spared more than two. But I don't know why I'd expect someone like you to have done any better."

"Do you want me to apologize?" Cassian snarled. Nesta's heart began to pound wildly at the anger darkening his voice, the pain brightening his eyes. He regretted it—he hadn't liked killing those soldiers.

"Did you even try to spare the others, or did you just launch right into a massacre?" Eris seethed.

Cassian hesitated. Nesta could have sworn she saw the words land their blow. No, Cassian had not hesitated. Nesta knew he hadn't. He would never hesitate to save someone he loved from an enemy. No matter what it cost him.

Nesta took one step closer to Eris. "Your soldiers shot an ash arrow through one of Azriel's wings."

Eris's teeth flashed. "And did you join in this massacre, too?"

"No," she said frankly. "But I wonder: Did Briallyn arm the soldiers with those ash arrows, or did they come from your private armory?"

Eris blinked, the only confirmation required. "Such weapons are banned, aren't they?" she asked Cassian, whose features remained taut. The conflagration within her burned hotter, higher. She returned her attention to Eris. If he could toy with Cassian, then she'd return the favor. "Who were you storing those arrows for?" she mused. "Enemies abroad?" She smiled slightly. "Or an enemy at home?"

Eris held her stare. "I don't know what you're talking about."

Nesta's smile didn't waver. "Would an ash arrow through the heart kill a High Lord?"

Eris's face paled. "You're wasting my time."

Nesta shrugged. "And you're wasting ours. For all we know, you bespelled your soldiers to kill us. Claimed your hounds found scents at the site of their disappearance that linked it to Briallyn, and then lied about Beron's alliance. Perhaps you even got Morrigan's father to delay his visit to Velaris as a piece in a grand scheme to gain our trust. All part of your game."

Cassian's gaze was a physical touch on her face, but she kept her attention on the stiff-backed Eris. "If you want to play warmonger, go right ahead, Eris." Her smile widened. "I like an interesting opponent."

"I am not your enemy," Eris spat, and Nesta knew she'd won. From the brush of Cassian's fingers at the small of her back, he knew, too.

Cassian said, "I regret that I couldn't save more of your soldiers, Eris. I really do. The remaining two will be sent back to you today, though they remain in the Crown's thrall. But I'm not your enemy, either. Briallyn and Koschei are our enemies—both of ours. If the families of those soldiers need anything, I will gladly give what I can to help them."

Something like pride bloomed in her at Cassian's earnest words. He'd give all he had to those families, if it would right this wrong.

Eris glanced between them. Noted the hand on her back. What Cassian had left exposed.

Eris said to Nesta with a smirk, "You're a pretty little treat. I'd be happy to play any manner of game with you, Nesta Archeron."

Cassian's fingers tightened on her back. Eris seemed to sense that, too. Did Cassian have any idea of the things he left vulnerable for people like Eris to strike at? He lived too honestly, too boldly, to notice or care. She couldn't help but admire it.

"When you get tired of the animal," Eris said to her, jerking his chin toward Cassian, "come find me. I'll show you how a future High Lord plays."

Cassian growled, opening his mouth, but halted.

Eris went still as well.

Nesta felt it a heartbeat later. The presence creeping toward them on soft paws.

Cassian shoved her behind him just as a golden-furred beast with curling horns leaped from behind the brambles, landing in the forest clearing.

She'd never forget that beast. How it had broken down the door of their cottage and terrified her to her bones. How all she'd been able to think of was shielding Elain while Feyre had grabbed that knife to face it. Face him.

Tamlin.

Green eyes assessed them. Marked Eris. Then Cassian. Then her.

Tamlin snarled, low and deep, and Cassian's Siphons flared. "We were just leaving," Cassian said with steady calm, hand reaching for

Nesta's. He'd launch them into the air. But would he be fast enough to avoid Tamlin's claws? Or power?

Tamlin's gaze remained on her. Raging and hateful.

This was the male, the beast, her sister had once loved. Had given up everything, including her mortal life, to save. Who had then taken her love and twisted it, nearly breaking Feyre in the process. Until Rhys. Until Cassian and the others had helped bring her back. Helped her learn to love herself once more.

Nesta didn't care if he'd come to help during the final battle with Hybern. Tamlin had hurt Feyre. Unforgivably.

It had never concerned her before. Irked her, yes, but . . . Nesta found her fingers curling. Found her lips peeling back from her teeth as she snarled.

Her youngest sister had been taken by this male because Nesta herself hadn't been able to face him. Tamlin had even looked at her and *asked* if she'd go in Feyre's place. And she had said no, because she was a hateful, horrible coward.

She would not be a coward now.

Nesta let an ember of her power glow in her eyes. Let Tamlin see it as she said, "You will not touch us."

"I have every right to kill trespassers on my lands." The words were guttural, nearly impossible to understand. As if Tamlin had not spoken in a long while.

"Are these still your lands?" Nesta asked coolly, stepping out from behind Cassian. "Last I heard, you don't bother to rule them anymore."

Eris remained utterly still. He'd been caught meeting with them, she realized. If Tamlin told anyone—

Nesta said, "I suggest you keep your maw shut about this."

Tamlin bristled, hackles rising. "You're exactly as nasty as your sister said you were."

Nesta laughed. "I'd hate to disappoint."

She held his emerald stare, knowing silver flames flickered in her own. "I went into the Cauldron because of you," she said softly, and could have sworn thunder grumbled in the distance. Cassian and Eris faded away into nothing. There was only Tamlin, only this beast, and what he had done to her and her family.

"Elain went into the Cauldron because of you," Nesta went on. Her fingertips heated, and she knew if she looked down, she'd find silver embers flaring there. "I don't care how much you apologize or try to atone for it or claim you didn't know the King of Hybern would do such a thing or that you begged him not to do it. You colluded with him. Because you thought Feyre was your *property*."

Nesta pointed at Tamlin. The ground shook.

Cassian swore behind her.

Tamlin shrank from her outstretched finger, claws digging into the earth. "Put that finger down, you witch."

Nesta smiled. "I'm glad you remember what happened to the last person I pointed at." She lowered her arm. "We're going now."

She stepped back to where Cassian was already waiting, arms open. He wrapped them around her waist. Nesta glanced to Eris, who gave her a shallow, approving nod, then vanished.

Nesta said to Tamlin before they shot into the skies, "Tell anyone you saw us, High Lord, and I'll rip your head from your body, too."

⁜

Nesta stared into the pit of darkness at the bottom of the library.

She'd been unable to sleep, barely able to keep from returning to the encounter with Tamlin all day. Cassian had flown to the river house, and had not returned. Perhaps Rhys had gone to ensure Tamlin's silence about their scheming with Eris. Maybe Rhys would do them all a favor and turn Tamlin's mind into jelly.

Nesta rested her arms on the railing of Level Five, letting her head hang. This late, no one was up, and she didn't know where the dormitories were, so she couldn't seek out Gwyn. Not that she'd want to wake her friend. She doubted Gwyn would want to hear her problems anyway.

A glass of warm milk appeared on the railing beside her.

Nesta peered at the dim library. "Thank you," she said to the House.

The Spring Court had felt stagnant. Hollow. Empty despite its growing life. But this House was alive. It welcomed her, wanted her to grow and thrive. It was a place where she might rest or explore, where she could be whoever and whatever she wished.

Was that what home was? She had never learned. But this place . . . Yes, *home* might be a good name for it. Perhaps that was what Feyre had felt, too, when she'd left the Spring Court and come to these lands. Perhaps Feyre had fallen in love with this court as much as she had its ruler.

Something stirred in the darkness below. Nesta straightened, milk forgotten.

There. In the heart of the black pit, like a tendril of smoke . . . something moved.

It seemed to expand and contract, throbbing a wild beat—

"I thought I'd find you here. Well, either here or the stairs to the city."

Cassian's voice sounded behind her, and Nesta whirled.

He went on alert, but Nesta glanced over a shoulder toward the darkness. Nothing.

It was gone. Or she'd imagined it.

"It's nothing," she said as he peered over the railing. "Just shadows."

Cassian blew out a breath, leaning against the railing. "Can't sleep?"

"I keep thinking about Tamlin."

"You did well with him. And you did well against Eris, too. I don't think he'll forget that anytime soon."

"He's a snake."

"Glad we agree on something."

Nesta huffed a laugh. "I didn't appreciate him speaking to you like that."

"It's how a lot of people speak to me."

"That doesn't make it right." She had spoken to him like that. She had said far worse things to Cassian than Eris had. Her throat tightened.

But she said, "I can't believe Feyre ever loved Tamlin."

"Tamlin never deserved her." Cassian rested a hand on her back.

"No." Nesta again peered into the darkness below. "He didn't."

CHAPTER 44

"Someone remind me why this was a good idea?" Gwyn panted beside Nesta, sweat running along her face as they went over their basic sword-work.

"Remind me, too," Emerie grunted. Nesta, too winded to speak, simply grunted with her.

Cassian chuckled, and the sound raked itself down her body. He'd taken her hand in the library last night, leading her up to her room, his eyes still soft. But that had faded when he'd spied a copy of Gwyn's chapters about the Valkyries on Nesta's desk. She'd been reading about them, she'd explained when he'd picked up the pages and leafed through them.

His only answer had been to kiss her deeply before lying on the bed, positioning her above his face so he could feast on her leisurely. Nesta endured all of a minute until she'd needed to touch him, and had pivoted, letting him continue devouring her while she'd stretched down his body and taken him into her mouth.

She'd never done that—feasted and been feasted upon—and he'd come on her tongue just before she'd come on his. They'd waited only a short time, panting in silence on her bed, before she climbed over him, stroking him with her hand, then her mouth, and when he was ready, she'd sunk onto him, taking in each marvelous, thick inch. With him stretching and filling her so deliciously, she'd climaxed swiftly. He'd chased her pleasure with his own, gripping her hips and bucking into her, hitting that perfect spot and sending her climaxing again.

She'd been slightly, pleasantly sore this morning, and he'd winked at her across the breakfast table, as if aware of how tender certain areas were while sitting.

There was no trace of that smug satisfaction now as Cassian said to them, "I'd thought today would be a good day to integrate the eight-pointed star, but if you're already complaining, we can wait until next week."

"We're not complaining," Gwyn said, sucking in air. "You're just running us ragged."

The newest priestesses working with Az were already wobbling on exhausted legs.

Cassian caught Nesta's stare. "Some Valkyrie unit you have."

Gwyn whirled on Nesta. "You told him?"

"No," Nesta and Cassian said together. Cassian added, "You think I haven't noticed the breathing techniques that let you get that calm, steady look even when me and Az are pissing you off? I sure as hell didn't teach you that. I can recognize Mind-Stilling a mile off."

They just gawked at him. Then Gwyn asked, "You know the technique?"

"Of course I do. I fought beside the Valkyries in the War."

Stunned silence rippled. Nesta had forgotten how old these Fae were, how much Cassian had seen and lived through. She cleared her throat. "You knew the Valkyries personally?"

Gwyn let out a high-pitched noise that was nothing but pure excitement. Azriel, on the other side of the ring with the rest of the priestesses, half-turned at the sound, brows high.

Cassian flashed a grin. "I fought beside the Valkyries for five battles. But that stopped at the Battle of Meinir Pass." His smile faded. "When most of them died to save it. The Valkyries knew it was a suicide mission from the start."

Azriel returned to his charges, but Nesta had a feeling the shadowsinger monitored every word, every gesture from his brother.

Even Gwyn stopped smiling. "Why did they fight, then? Everyone there knew it would be a slaughter. But I've never been able to find anything on the politics behind it."

"I don't know. I was a grunt for an Illyrian legion; I wasn't privy to any of the leaders' discussions." He looked to Nesta, who was gaping at him. "But I had . . . friends who fell that day." The way he hesitated on *friends* made her wonder if any had been more than that. And even though they were honorable, fallen dead, something ugly twisted in her chest. "The Valkyries fought when even the bravest males would not. The Illyrians tried to forget that. I fought against males who were my superiors, arguing to help the Valkyries. They beat me senseless, chained me to a supply wagon, and left me there. When I came to, the battle was over, the Valkyries slain."

This was the male she'd taken to her bed, who'd left again last night without kissing her good-bye. "Why didn't you mention this when you saw the pages about them on my desk?"

"You didn't ask." He unsheathed his Illyrian blade. "Enough history." He drew four lines in the dirt, all intersecting to form an eight-pointed star. "This is your map for striking with a sword. These eight maneuvers. You've learned six of them. You'll learn the other two today, and we'll start on the combinations."

Gwyn asked, "Why don't we use the Valkyrie techniques, if you admired them so much?"

"Because I don't know them."

Nesta smirked. "If we are to be Valkyries born again," she said, "maybe we should combine the Illyrian and Valkyrie techniques."

She'd meant it in jest, but the words rumbled through the space, as if she'd spoken some great truth, something that made fate sit up. Azriel turned to them fully this time, eyes narrowed. Like those shadows had whispered something to him.

A chill breathed down Nesta's spine.

Cassian stared into their faces. Like he beheld something he hadn't seen there before.

At last, he said thickly, "Today, we learn Illyrian techniques." He nodded to Gwyn. "Tomorrow, you bring me whatever information you have on the Valkyries' style."

"It's an enormous amount," Gwyn said. "Merrill is writing a book on it. I could get you a copy of the current manuscript, since it has most of the information in one place."

Cassian seemed to gain control of whatever emotion had taken hold of him, for he rubbed his jaw. Nesta's blood thrummed in response. "Something new," he said more to himself than to them. "Something old becoming something new."

He grinned again, and Nesta found her mouth twitching to answer with a grin of her own.

Especially as Cassian's eyes brightened. "All right, ladies. First lesson about Valkyries: they don't whine about being sweaty."

✢

"Valkyries?" Feyre asked from across the dining table in the river house, fork half-raised to her lips. "Truly?"

"Truly," Cassian said, sipping from his wine at dinner that evening. He'd come down to the manor to discuss what to do with the weapons Nesta had Made—to learn what Feyre's vote would be. She hadn't hesitated before saying that Nesta should be informed. But when she'd volunteered to tell her, Cassian had stepped in. He'd tell Nesta, when the moment was right.

The only one who hadn't voted was Mor, who remained in Vallahan to keep coaxing its rulers to sign the new treaty, her absence marked by a place of honor set for her at the table.

"We never heard of them in the human lands," Elain said. She'd been as riveted as Feyre to hear Cassian tell of it: first of Nesta and the others' interest, then of the brief history of the female fighters. "They must have been fearsome creatures."

"Some were as lovely as you, Elain," Rhys said from beside Feyre, "from the outside. But once they set foot into the arena of battle, they became as bloodthirsty as Amren."

Amren lifted her glass in salute. "I liked those females. Never let a male boss them around—though I could have done without their foolish king. He is as much to blame for their deaths as the Illyrians who walked away during that battle."

"I can't argue with that," Cassian said. It had taken him a long, long time to get over that battle. He'd never been back to that pass in the Gollian Mountains, but rumor claimed its rocks remained barren, as if the earth still mourned the females who'd given their lives with no hesitation, who had laughed at death and embraced life so fully. His first lover beyond the Night Court's borders had been from the Valkyries' ranks—a bold-hearted female named Tanwyn with a smile like a storm. She'd ridden into that battle at the head of the Valkyries and had never come out of the pass. Cassian added after a moment, "Nesta would have fit in well with them."

"I always thought she was born on the wrong side of the wall," Elain admitted. "She made ballrooms into battlefields and plotted like any general. Like you two," she said, nodding to Cassian, and then, a bit more shyly, to Azriel.

Azriel offered her a small smile that Elain quickly looked away from. Cassian tucked away his puzzlement. Lucien was certainly not here to snarl at any male who looked at her for too long.

Feyre at last took her hearty bite of food. "Nesta is a wolf who has been locked in a cage her whole life."

"I know," Cassian said. She was a wolf who had never learned how to *be* a wolf, thanks to that cage humans called propriety and society. And like any maltreated animal, she bit anyone who came near. Good thing he liked being bitten. Good thing he savored the bruises and scratches she left on his body every night, and that her unleashing when he was buried in her made him want to answer it with his own.

Elain leaned forward. "You only think you know—you haven't seen her on the dance floor. That's when Nesta truly lets the wolf roam free. When there's music."

"Really?" Nesta *had* told him once, when he'd dragged her out of a particular seedy tavern, that she'd been there for the music. He'd ignored her, thinking it an excuse.

"Yes," Elain said. "She was trained in dance from a very young age. She loves it, and music. Not in the way I enjoy a waltz or gavotte, but in the way that performers make an art of it. Nesta could bring an entire ballroom to a halt when she danced with someone."

Cassian set down his wine. "She mentioned dance lessons to me a few weeks ago." He'd assumed those lessons were why Nesta had quickly mastered her footwork and balance, despite her initial difficulty. The muscle memory must have remained intact. But if dance had been drilled into her as ruthlessly as he'd learned to fight—

"She wouldn't have gone into much detail about it," Elain said. "Nesta was only fourteen at the last ball we went to before—well, before we were poor . . ." Elain shook her head. "Another young heiress was at the ball, and she positively *hated* me. She was several years older, and I'd never done anything to provoke her hatred, but I think . . ."

"She was jealous of your beauty," Amren said, an amused smile on her red lips.

Elain blushed. "Perhaps."

It was definitely that. Even though Elain would have been barely thirteen at the time.

"Well, Nesta saw how she treated me, her casual cruelties and snubs, and bided her time. Waited until that ball, when a handsome duke from the continent was there to find a bride. His family had run out of money, which was why he'd deigned to come over at all—to nab a rich bride to refill their estate's coffers. Nesta knew the heiress had her sights set on him. The girl had bragged about it to all of us in the powder room at every ball for weeks leading up to it.

"Nesta spent a small fortune on her gown and jewels for that night. Our father was always too scared of her to say no, and that night . . . Well, she truly looked the part of the daughter of the Prince of Merchants. An amethyst silk gown with gold thread, diamonds and pearls at her neck and ears . . ." Elain sighed. Such wealth. Cassian had never realized what wealth they'd possessed and lost.

"The entire ball stopped when Nesta entered," Elain said. "She made an entrance of it, perfectly cool and aloof, even at fourteen. She barely glanced the duke's way. Because she'd learned about him as well. Knew he grew bored of anyone that chased him. And knew that the wealth on her that night dwarfed anything that heiress was wearing."

Amren was grinning now. "Nesta tried to win a duke out of spite? At *fourteen*?"

Elain didn't smile. "She lured him into asking her for a dance with a few well-placed looks across the ballroom. The same waltz that heiress wanted for herself, had boasted would be all she needed to secure his marriage bid. Nesta *took* that dance from her. And then took the duke from her, too. Nesta danced that night like she was one of you."

"If you've seen Cassian's dancing," Rhys muttered, "that's not saying much."

Cassian flipped off his High Lord as Feyre and Az chuckled.

Elain continued, voice hushed with near-reverence, "The duke was vain, and Nesta played into that. The entire room came to a standstill. Their dancing was that good; she was that beautiful. And when it ended . . . I knew she was an artist then. The same way Feyre is. But what Feyre does with paint, that's what Nesta did with music and dance.

Our mother saw it when we were children, and honed it into a weapon. All so Nesta might one day marry a prince."

Cassian froze. A prince—was that what Nesta wanted? His stomach clenched.

"What happened to the duke?" Azriel asked.

Elain grimaced. "He proposed marriage the next morning."

Rhys choked on his wine. "She was fourteen."

"I told you: Nesta is a *very* good dancer. But that was what my father said—she was too young. It was a graceful exit, since my father, despite his faults, knew Nesta well. He knew she had taunted that duke into making a marriage offer just to punish the heiress for her cruelty toward me. Nesta had no interest in him—knew she was far too young. Even if the duke seemed more interested in just . . . reserving her until she was old enough." Elain shuddered with distaste. "But I think some part of Nesta believed she would indeed marry a prince one day. So the duke went home with no bride, and that heiress . . . Well, she was one of the people who delighted in our misfortunes."

"I'd forgotten," Feyre murmured. "About this, and about her dancing."

"Nesta never spoke of it afterward," Elain said. "I just observed."

Nesta was wrong, Cassian realized, to think Elain as loyal and loving as a dog. Elain saw every single thing Nesta had done, and understood why.

Amren asked pointedly, "So your mother twisted Nesta's creative joys into a social climber's arsenal?"

Feyre cut in, "Our mother was not what one would call a pleasant person. Nesta has made her own choices, but our mother laid the groundwork."

Elain nodded, folding her hands in her lap. "So I'm very pleased to hear of this Valkyrie business. I'm happy that Nesta finds interest in something again. And might channel all of . . . *that* into it." *That*,

Cassian knew, meant her rage, her fierce and unyielding loyalty to those she loved, her wolf's instincts and ability to kill.

They moved on to far merrier subjects, but Cassian mulled it over throughout the evening. The fighting was only one part of it. The training would sustain her, funnel that rage, but there had to be more. There had to be joy.

There had to be music.

CHAPTER 45

"I think the Valkyries were even more sadistic than the Illyrians," Gwyn grunted, and Nesta could see the priestess's legs shaking as she held the pose that had been illustrated in one of her many research volumes. "No amount of Mind-Stilling will get me through these exercises. What was that phrase they used? *I am the rock against which the surf crashes.* A rock never had to hold a lunge, though."

"This is outrageous," Emerie agreed, teeth gritted.

Cassian idly flipped a long dagger in his hand. "I warned you that they were stone-cold warriors."

Nesta panted through her teeth in a steady rhythm. "My legs might break."

"You three still have . . . twenty seconds." Cassian looked to the clock Azriel had dragged up from the House and left on the water station table. The shadowsinger was away today, but the priestesses he usually trained had been left with a strict lesson plan.

Nesta's legs wobbled and burned, but she rooted her strength through her toes, focusing on her breathing, her breathing, her breathing, as the Mind-Stilling had bade her to do. She sought that place of calm, where she might be beyond her thoughts of pain and her shaking body, and it was so close, so near, if she could just concentrate, breathe more deeply—

"Time," Cassian declared, and the three of them collapsed onto the dirt. He laughed again. "Pathetic."

"You try it," Gwyn panted, lying prone on the earth. "I don't think even you could survive that."

"Thanks to the passages you sent me last night, I was here at dawn doing the exercises myself," he said. Nesta raised her brows. He hadn't been at dinner, and hadn't sought her out, but she'd been tired enough after a few nights of little sleep that she hadn't minded. "I figured if I'm going to torture you three, I should at least be able to back it up." He winked. "For exactly the moment when you groused that I should suffer alongside you."

"No wonder you look like that," Emerie muttered, turning over to lie on her back and gaze at the crisp autumn sky. The days had given up any attempt at being warm, though true cold had not yet set in. The sun offered a kernel of heat against the chill breeze, a buttery, bone-heating warmth that Nesta savored as she, too, lay on her back.

"I'll take that as a compliment." His grin tightened something low in Nesta's gut.

He caught her staring and that grin became a little more knowing. But he just said to her, "If you were to name a sword, what would you call it?"

Gwyn answered, though she hadn't been asked, "Silver Majesty."

Emerie snorted. "Really?"

Gwyn demanded, "What would *you* call it?"

Emerie considered. "Foe Slayer, or something. Something intimidating."

"That's no better!"

Nesta's mouth tugged upward at their teasing. Gwyn looked to her, teal eyes bright. "Which one is worse: Foe Slayer or Silver Majesty?"

"Silver Majesty," Nesta said, and Emerie crowed with triumph. Gwyn waved a hand, booing.

"What would you call it?" Cassian asked Nesta again.

"Why do you want to know?"

"Humor me."

She lifted a brow. But then said with all sincerity. "Killer."

His brows flattened.

Nesta shrugged. "I don't know. Is it necessary to name a sword?"

"Just tell me: If you had to name a sword, what would you call it?"

"Are you getting her one as a Winter Solstice present?" Emerie asked.

"No."

Nesta hid her smile. She loved this—when the three of them ganged up on him, like lionesses around a very muscled, very attractive carcass.

"Then why keep asking?" Gwyn said.

Cassian scowled. "Curiosity."

But his jaw tightened. It wasn't that. There was something else. Why would he want her to name a sword?

"Back to work," he said, clapping his hands. "For all that sass, you're doing double time on the Valkyrie lunge hold."

Emerie and Gwyn groaned, but Nesta surveyed Cassian for another moment before following their lead.

She was still mulling it over when they finished two hours later, drenched in sweat, legs wobbling. Emerie and Gwyn picked up their earlier conversation and aimed for the water station.

Nesta watched the two of them go, then turned to Cassian. "Why were you pestering me about naming a sword?"

His eyes remained on Gwyn and Emerie. "I just wanted to know what you'd name one."

"That's not an answer. Why do you want to know?"

He crossed his arms, then uncrossed them. "Do you remember when we went to the blacksmith?"

"Yes. *He's* giving me a blade for Winter Solstice?"

"He's given you three. The ones you touched."

She arched an eyebrow.

He tapped his foot on the ground. "When you hammered those blades, you imbued them—the two swords and the dagger—with your power. The Cauldron's power. They're now magic blades. And I'm not talking nice, pretty magic. I'm talking big, ancient magic that hasn't been seen in a long, long time. There are no magic weapons left. None. They were either lost or destroyed or dumped in the sea. But you just Made three of them. You created a new Dread Trove. You could create even more objects, if you wished."

Her brows rose higher with each absurd word. "I Made three magic weapons?"

"We don't know yet what manner of magic they have, but yes."

She angled her head. Emerie and Gwyn halted their chatting at the water station, as if they could see or sense the shift in her. And it wasn't the fact that she'd Made these weapons that hit her like a blow.

"Who is 'we'?"

"What?"

"You said 'We don't know what manner of magic they have.' Who is 'we'?"

"Rhys and Feyre and the others."

"And how long have all of you known about this?"

He winced as he realized his error. "I . . . Nesta . . ."

"*How long?*" Her voice became sharp as glass. The priestesses were watching, and she didn't care.

He did, apparently. "This isn't the place to talk about it."

"You're the one trying to coax a name out of me in the middle of training!" She gestured to the ring.

Her blood pounded in her ears, and Cassian's face grew pained. "This isn't coming out the way it should. We argued about whether to tell you, but we took a vote and it went in your favor. Because we trust you. I just . . . hadn't gotten a chance to bring it up yet."

"There was a possibility you wouldn't even *tell* me? You all sat around and judged me, and then you *voted*?" Something deep in her chest cracked to know that every horrible thing about her had been analyzed.

"It . . . Fuck." Cassian reached for her, but she stepped back. Everyone was staring now. "Nesta, this isn't . . ."

"Who. Voted. Against me."

"Rhys and Amren."

It landed like a physical blow. Rhys came as no surprise. But Amren, who had always understood her more than the others; Amren who'd been unafraid of her; Amren with whom she'd quarreled so badly . . . Some small part of her had hoped Amren wouldn't hate her forever.

Her head went quiet. Her body went quiet.

Cassian's eyes widened. "Nesta—"

"I'm fine," she said coldly. "I don't care."

She let him see her fortify those steel walls within her mind. Used every bit of Mind-Stilling she'd practiced with Gwyn to become calm, focused, steady. Breathing in through her nose, out through her mouth.

She made a show of rolling her shoulders, of approaching Emerie and Gwyn, whose faces bunched with concern in a way Nesta knew she didn't deserve, in a way that she knew would one day vanish, when they, too, realized what a wretch she was. When Amren told them what a pathetic waste of life she was, or they heard it from someone else, and they ceased being her friends. She wondered if they'd even say it to her face, or if they'd just disappear.

"Nesta," Cassian said again. But she left the ring without looking back at him.

Emerie was on her heels instantly, trailing her down the stairs. "What's wrong?"

"Nothing," Nesta said, her own voice foreign to her ears. "Court business."

"Are you all right?" Gwyn asked, a step behind Emerie.

No. She couldn't stop the roaring in her head, the cracking in her chest. "Yes," she lied, and didn't look back as she hit the landing and vanished down the hall.

Nesta made it to her bedroom, where she ran the bath. She knew Cassian would come by. So she stood by the tub, the water gushing from the spout, while he knocked on her door. She waited until she sensed him leave, giving up on her as everyone else had done, and then shut off the flow.

She asked the House, "Is he gone?"

The door opened in answer.

"Thank you." She strode into the empty hallway. Perhaps the House hid her from sight, for she saw and scented no glimpse of Cassian as she hurried down the short flight of stairs near her room. Down the hall. Right through the archway into that long stairwell.

Then and only then did she let her fury out. Then and only then did she drop that coldness and give herself over to the raging of her heart.

Amren had deemed her so untrustworthy, so awful, that knowing she had this world-altering gift would be dangerous. Amren had spoken to the others about it, and they had *voted* on it.

Down and down and down.

Step to step to step.

Around and around and around.

She didn't count the stairs. Didn't feel her legs moving. There was only the roaring of her blood and the roaring in her head and the crack down the center of her chest. No amount of Mind-Stilling could calm it, smother it.

The ground grew nearer.

She couldn't think around her fury, that pain. Couldn't *think*, only move.

The stairwell turned warmer, farther away from the cold wind above.

Amren had entirely given up on her. The debate about sending her up here had been different—Nesta knew that debate had been out of a desire to help her. She could acknowledge that now.

This debate had been out of hatred and fear of her.

The tiled rooftops became clear. Her legs were shaking. She didn't feel them.

Didn't feel anything but that molten rage as the stairs suddenly stopped and she found herself before a door.

It opened before her fingers could touch the handle. Sunlight flooded the stairwell, revealing cobblestones beyond.

Rage rippling like a storm around her, Nesta stepped back into Velaris at last.

CHAPTER 46

She didn't note the city around her, the people who either beheld her face and kept well away or simply went about their business. Didn't note the vibrant oranges and reds and yellows of the autumn trees or the sparkling blue of the Sidra as she crossed one of the countless bridges spanning its winding body, aiming for its western bank.

Nesta yielded to her fury. Later, she would have no memory of racing up the steps to the loft. No memory of the walk over before she slammed a hand into the wooden door. It shattered beneath her palm, wards fracturing like glass.

Amren and Varian were in bed, the petite female naked as she rode the Prince of Adriata. Both of them halted, Amren twisting toward the door, Varian bolting upright, a shield of water coming around them as Nesta stepped into the room and growled, "*You*. You thought I shouldn't even be *told* what my power can do."

Amren moved with the swiftness of the High Fae, leaping off Varian, who grabbed a sheet to cover himself as she slung a silk robe around her body. That shimmering wall of water made it seem as if they were beneath the ocean's surface. Amren shot Varian a look. "Drop it."

He obeyed, sliding from the bed and shoving his long, muscled legs into his pants.

Nesta snarled at him, "Get out."

But the Summer Court prince watched Amren, his face tight with concern. He'd stay, go down defending her. Nesta snorted, bitterness coating her tongue. Once, Amren had been that person for her—the person she knew would defend her in a fight, would speak for her. Amren nodded to him, and Varian threw Nesta a warning glare before hurrying from the room.

Presumably to tell the others, but Nesta didn't care.

Not as Amren said, "I suppose that loudmouthed bastard told you more than was necessary."

"You voted against me," she said, her cold voice belying the crack in her chest.

"You have done nothing to prove you are able to handle such a terrible power," Amren said with equal iciness. "On that barge, you told me as much when you walked away from any attempt at mastering it. I offered to teach you more, and you walked away."

"I walked away because you chose my sister." Just as Elain had done. Amren had been *her* friend, *her* ally, and yet in the end, it hadn't mattered one bit. She'd picked Feyre.

"I didn't choose anyone, you spoiled girl," Amren snapped. "I told you that Feyre had requested you and I work together again, and you somehow twist that into me *siding* with her?" Nesta said nothing. "I told them to leave you alone for months. I refused to speak about you with them. And then the moment I realized my behavior was not helping you, that maybe your sister was right, *I* somehow betrayed you?"

Nesta shook. "You know how I feel about Feyre."

"Yes, poor Nesta, with a younger sister who loves her so dearly she's willing to do anything to get her help."

Nesta blocked out the memory of Tamlin in his beast form, how she had wanted to rip him limb from limb. She was no better than him, in the end. "Feyre doesn't love me." She didn't deserve Feyre's love. Just as Tamlin hadn't.

Amren barked out a laugh. "That you believe Feyre doesn't only proves you're unworthy of your power. Anyone that willfully blind cannot be trusted. You would be a walking nightmare with those weapons."

"It's different now." The words rang hollow. Was it any different? Was *she* any different than she'd been this summer, when she and Amren had fought on the barge, and Amren's utter disappointment in her failure to *be* anything had surfaced at last?

Amren smiled, as if she knew that, too. "You can train as hard as you want, fuck Cassian as often as you want, but it isn't going to fix what's broken if you don't start reflecting."

"Don't preach at me. *You—*" She pointed at Amren, and could have sworn the female stepped out of the line of fire. Just as Tamlin had done. As if Amren also remembered that the last time Nesta had pointed at an enemy, it had ended with his severed head in her hands. A joyless laugh broke from her. "You think I'd mark you with a death-promise?"

"You nearly did with Tamlin the other day." So Cassian had told them all about that, too. "But I'll say to you again what I said on that barge: I think you have powers that you still do not understand, respect, or control."

"How dare you assume you know what is best for me?"

When Amren didn't answer, Nesta hissed, "You were my *friend*."

Amren's teeth flashed. "Was I? I don't think you know what that word means."

Her chest ached, as if that invisible fist had punched her once again. Steps thudded beyond the shattered door, and she braced for Cassian to come roaring in—

But it was Feyre.

Paint splattered her casual clothes; a smear of white graced her freckled cheekbone. Varian must have run half-naked through the streets to reach her studio. Feyre panted, "Stop this."

Whether Feyre noted or cared about the splinters and debris on the floor, she didn't let on as she moved closer. Feyre pleaded, "Nesta, it should not have come out as it did."

"Did Cassian tell you that?" He'd gone to Feyre, rather than here?

"No, but I can guess as much. He didn't want to keep anything from you."

"My issue isn't with Cassian." Nesta leveled her stare at Amren. "I trusted you to have my back."

"I stopped having your back the moment you decided to use that loyalty as a shield against everyone else."

Nesta snarled, but Feyre stepped between them, hands raised. "This conversation ends now. Nesta, go back to the House. Amren, you . . ." She hesitated, as if considering the wisdom of ordering Amren around. Feyre finished carefully, "You stay here."

Nesta let out a low laugh. "You are her High Lady. You don't need to cater to her. Not when she now has less power than any of you."

Feyre's eyes blazed. "Amren is my friend, and has been a member of this court for centuries. I offer her *respect.*"

"Is it respect that she offers you?" Nesta spat. "Is it respect that your *mate* offers you?"

Feyre went still.

Amren warned, "Don't you say one more fucking *word*, Nesta Archeron."

Feyre asked, "What do you mean?"

And Nesta didn't care. Couldn't think around the roaring. "Have any of them told you, their *respected* High Lady, that the babe in your womb will kill you?"

Amren barked, "*Shut your mouth!*"

But her order was confirmation enough. Face paling, Feyre whispered again, "What do you mean?"

"The wings," Nesta seethed. "The boy's Illyrian wings will get stuck in your Fae body during the labor, and it will kill you both."

Silence rippled through the room, the world.

Feyre breathed, "Madja just said the labor would be risky. But the Bone Carver . . . The son he showed me didn't have wings." Her voice broke. "Did he only show me what I wanted to see?"

"I don't know," Nesta said. "But I do know that your mate ordered everyone not to inform you of the truth." She turned to Amren. "Did you all vote on that, too? Did you talk about her, judge her, and deem her unworthy of the truth? What was *your* vote, Amren? To let Feyre die in ignorance?" Before Amren could reply, Nesta turned back to her sister. "Didn't you question why your precious, perfect Rhysand has been a moody bastard for weeks? Because he *knows* you will die. He knows, and yet he still didn't tell you."

Feyre began shaking. "If I die . . ." Her gaze drifted to one of her tattooed arms. She lifted her head, eyes bright with tears as she asked Amren, "You . . . all of you knew this?"

Amren threw a withering glare in Nesta's direction, but said, "We did not wish to alarm you. Fear can be as deadly as any physical threat."

"Rhys knew?" Tears spilled down Feyre's cheeks, smearing the paint splattered there. "About the threat to our lives?" She peered down at herself, at the tattooed hand cradling her abdomen.

And Nesta knew then that she had not once in her life been loved by her mother as much as Feyre already loved the boy growing within her.

It broke something in Nesta—broke that rage, that roaring—seeing those tears begin to fall, the fear crumpling Feyre's paint-smeared face.

She had gone too far. She . . . Oh, gods.

Amren said, "I think it is best, girl, if you speak to Rhysand about this."

Nesta couldn't bear it—the pain and fear and love on Feyre's face as she caressed her stomach.

Amren growled at Nesta, "I hope you're content now."

Nesta didn't respond. Didn't know what to say or do with herself. She simply turned on her heel and ran from the apartment.

✢

Cassian had gone to the river house. That had been his third mistake of the day.

The first had been how clumsy he'd been in asking about a sword name, prompting Nesta's suspicion. He hadn't been able to lie to her, so he'd told her everything.

The second mistake had been letting Nesta hide in her room and not barging in to speak to her. Letting her take a bath, thinking it'd cool her off. He'd done the same, and when he'd emerged, he'd followed her scent to the floor with the exterior stairs, where the door stood open.

He had no idea if she had made it out or if she'd collapsed within, so he'd taken the steps, too. All ten thousand of them, her scent fresh and furious.

She'd made it to the bottom. The door had been left open.

He'd launched skyward, knowing he'd have trouble tracking her scent in the bustling city, hoping to spot her from the air. He assumed Amren was working at the river house, so that was where he'd gone.

Only Amren wasn't there. And neither was Nesta.

He'd reached Rhys's study when word came. Not from a messenger, but from Feyre—mind to mind with her mate.

Rhys was at his desk, face tight as he silently spoke to her. Cassian saw that look, knew who he spoke to, and went still. Neither was here, which meant they were probably at Amren's apartment, and if Feyre was giving a report . . .

Cassian whirled for the doors, knowing he could be there in a two-minute flight, praying he'd be fast enough—

"Cassian."

Rhys's voice was a thing of nightmares, of the darkness between the stars.

Cassian froze at that voice he'd so rarely heard, and never once directed at himself. "What happened?"

Rhys's face was wholly calm. But death—black, raging death—lay in his eyes. Not a star or shimmer of violet remained.

Rhys said in that voice that was like hell embodied, "Nesta saw fit to inform Feyre of the risk to her and the babe."

Cassian's heart began thundering, even as it splintered.

Rhys held his stare, and it was all Cassian could do to weather it as his brother, his High Lord said, "Get Nesta out of this city. Right now." Rhys's power rumbled in the room like a rising storm. "Before I fucking kill her."

CHAPTER 47

Cassian found Nesta sprinting down a side street, as if she suspected that Rhysand was about to set out on a hunt that only her spilled blood could halt. But he knew she only ran from what she had done, ran from herself. Ran toward one of the taverns she favored so much.

Cassian didn't give Nesta the chance to see him as he soared down the alley, snatched her around the waist and beneath the knees, and swept them into the sky.

She didn't fight him, didn't say a word. Just lay in his arms, her face cold against his chest.

Cassian soared over the House of Wind to find Azriel there, hovering in place, a heavy pack in his hand. Whether that had been from a separate warning from Rhys, or Az's own shadows whispering, he didn't know.

Cassian grabbed the pack, looping it around a wrist and grunting against its weight as he kept hold of Nesta. Az didn't say anything as Cassian careened past, into the autumn skies.

And did not dare look back at the city behind him.

⸸

There were no sounds in her head, her body. She knew Cassian held her, knew they flew for hours and hours, and she didn't care.

She had done an unforgivable thing.

She deserved to be turned into bloody mist by Rhysand. Wished Cassian had not come to save her.

They flew into the mountains until the sun sank behind them. By the time they landed, their surroundings were veiled in darkness. Cassian grimaced as he alit, as if every part of him hurt, and dumped the pack Azriel had given them at his feet.

"We'll camp here tonight," he said quietly—coldly.

She didn't want to speak. Resolved not to say another word for the rest of her life.

"I'll make a fire," he went on, and there was nothing kind in his face.

She couldn't stand it. So she turned away, surveying the small area where he'd landed—a flat bit of dry earth just under the overhang of a black boulder.

In silence, she walked to the deepest part of the overhang. In silence, she lay down upon the hard, dusty earth, using her arm for a pillow, and curled herself toward the rock wall.

She closed her eyes and willed herself to ignore the snapping and cracking of the wood as the fire consumed it, willed herself to melt into the earth, into the mountain, and disappear forever.

Cassian.

Feyre's voice filled Cassian's mind, pulling him from where he'd been watching the stars appear over the sprawling view. He'd flown Nesta to the Sleeping Mountains, the range that separated Illyria from Velaris. They were smaller peaks, not yet in winter's grasp, with plenty of rivers and game to hunt.

Cassian.

I forgot you can mind-speak.

Her laugh sounded. *I can't decide whether I should be insulted or not. Perhaps I should be using the daemati gifts more often.* She paused before saying, *Are you all right?*

I should be asking you that.

Rhysand overreacted. He completely and utterly overreacted.

Cassian shook his head, though Feyre couldn't see it. *I'm sorry you had to learn of it.*

I'm not. I'm furious with all of you. I understand why you didn't tell me, but I'm furious.

Well, we're furious with Nesta.

She had the courage to tell me the truth.

She told you the truth to hurt you.

Perhaps. But she was the only one who said anything.

Cassian sighed through his nose. *She . . .* He thought it over. *I think she saw the parallels between your situations and, in her own way, decided to avenge both of you.*

That's my feeling, too. Rhys disagrees.

I wish you'd found out a different way.

Well, I didn't. But we'll face it together. All of us.

How can you be so calm about this?

The alternative is fear and panic. I will not let my son feel those things. I will fight for him, for us, until I no longer can.

Cassian's throat tightened. *We'll fight for you, too.*

I know. Feyre paused again. *Rhys had no right to chase you from the city, or to threaten Nesta. He has realized that, and apologized. I want you to come back home. Both of you. Where did you even head off to?*

The wilderness. Cassian looked over a shoulder, to where Nesta had been asleep for the past few hours, curled into a tight ball against the wall of rock. *I think we'll stay out here for a few days. We're going to hike.*

Nesta has never been on a hike in her life. I guarantee she will hate it.

Then tell Rhys this is her punishment. Because Rhys, despite apologizing for his threats, would still be furious. *Tell him that Nesta and I are going to hike, and she's going to hate it, but she comes home when I decide she's ready to come home.*

Feyre was quiet for a long minute. *He says that he knows he's supposed to say that's unnecessary, but to tell you he's secretly delighted.*

Good. I am secretly glad to hear that.

Feyre laughed, and the sound was proof that she might have been hurt, startled by the news, but she was indeed adapting to it. Would not let it make her cower and cry. He didn't know why he'd expected any less of her.

Feyre said, *Please take care of her, Cassian. And yourself.*

Cassian glanced to the sleeping female nearly hidden in the shadows of the rock.

I will.

CHAPTER 48

"Get up."

Nesta tensed, cracking open an eye against the blinding brightness of dawn. Cassian stood above her, a plate of what looked like mushrooms and toast in one hand. Her entire body ached from the hardness of the ground and the chill of the night. She'd barely slept, had mostly lain there, staring at the rock, willing herself to ignore the sounds of the fire, wishing to disappear into nothing.

She eased into a sitting position, and he shoved the plate toward her. "Eat. We've got a long day ahead."

She lifted her eyes, heavy and aching, to his face.

There was nothing warm in it. No challenge or light. Just solid, stone-cold warrior.

Cassian said, "We'll be hiking from dawn until dusk, only two stops throughout the day. So eat."

It didn't matter. Whether she ate or slept or hiked. Any of it.

But Nesta forced herself to eat the food he'd prepared, not speaking as he doused the fire he'd built, focusing on anything but the *crack* of the logs. Cassian swiftly packed the few cooking supplies, along with the rest of the food, into the canvas bag.

He picked it up, muscles shifting in his forearm with the weight, and walked to her before dumping it between her feet. "I can't fit a pack that big on my back with the wings. So you'll be carrying it."

Had Azriel known that? From the icy, amused gleam in Cassian's eye, she thought yes.

Nesta finished her food and had nothing to wash her plate with, so she shoved it into the pack.

He said, "You can wash the dishes when we get to the Gerthys River at lunch. It's a six-hour trek from here."

She didn't care. Let him drive her into the ground, let him make her walk and act the servant. It wouldn't fix anything.

Wouldn't fix her.

Nesta stood, joints popping and body stiff. She didn't bother to reweave her braid.

"You can see to your needs around the corner." He nodded toward the slight curve in the cliff face. "No one is out here."

She did as he said. When she returned, he only nodded toward the pack. "Pick it up."

Nesta grunted as she did. It had to be at least a third of her weight. Her back nearly bowed as she hefted it onto her shoulders, but she got it on, wriggling to adjust it. She fiddled with the straps and buckles until it was snug to her spine, the weight balanced across her chest and hips.

Cassian apparently decided that she'd done a decent job. "Let's go."

✠

Nesta let him lead the way, and within ten minutes, her breathing became labored, her legs burning as Cassian stalked up the hillside, cutting along the mountain's face. He didn't speak to her, and she didn't speak to him.

The day was as crisp as one could ever wish, the mountains around them vibrant green, the teal rivers so clear that even from high above, she could see the white stones lining their beds.

Nesta gave herself over to it, the aching of her body, the panting of her breath—so sharp it was like glass—the roaring thoughts.

The sun arced across the sky, wringing the sweat from her brow, her neck. Her hair became soaked with it. Still she walked, trailing Cassian farther up the peak. He reached a rocky outcropping, glanced over a shoulder once to make sure she was behind, then disappeared—presumably going downward.

She reached the outcropping and beheld just how downward it was.

He'd mentioned stopping at a river. Well, far below and ahead lay a broad band of a river, half-shrouded in trees. It didn't look like it would take hours to reach, yet . . . Cassian was walking across the mountain, rather than going straight down. No one would be able to directly descend without tumbling to their death.

An entirely different set of muscles soon began to protest at the descent. It was worse than going upward, she realized—now it felt as if the pack were determined to tip her forward and send her falling into the valley and river.

Cassian didn't bother to carefully pick his steps amongst the grasses and small stones like she did. He, at least, had the reassurance of wings. This high up, the clouds drifted past like idle watchers, none merciful enough to offer shade against the blazing sun.

Nesta's legs shook, but she kept moving. Gripped the straps of the pack where they rested against her chest, and used her arms to ballast its weight. She followed Cassian, down the mountain, step to step, hour by hour.

She walked, one foot after another, and did not say anything at all.

✠

They halted for lunch at the river. If hard cheese and bread could be considered lunch.

Nesta only cared that it filled her aching belly. Only cared that the river before them was clear and clean, and she was parched. She collapsed on its grassy bank, kneeling to bury her face in it. She gasped into the shock of cold, then rose, lifting water to her mouth with a cupped palm again and again, swallowing and swallowing.

She pulled back from the river to lie on her side, her breathing still heavy.

"You have thirty minutes," Cassian said from where he sat in the tall, swaying grass, sipping from his canteen. "Use it however you wish."

She said nothing. Even nodding felt like too much.

He opened the pack and chucked a canteen to her. "Fill this. If you faint, you might fall off the mountain and break every bone in your body."

She didn't look at him. Didn't let him see the word in her eyes. *Good.*

He went still, though. His next words were gentler—and she resented them, too. "Rest up."

✢

Cassian knew that Nesta often hated herself.

But he'd never known she hated herself enough to want to . . . not exist anymore.

He'd seen her expression when he mentioned the threat of falling. And he knew going back to Velaris wouldn't save her from that look. He couldn't save her from that look, either.

Only Nesta could save herself from that feeling.

He let her rest for the thirty minutes he'd promised, and perhaps he was a little pissed at her still, because he merely said, "Let's go," before starting off again.

She followed in that heavy, brimming silence. As quiet as a trailing packhorse.

He knew these mountains well enough from flying over them for centuries: shepherds lived here, usually ordinary faeries who preferred the solitude of the towering green and brownish-black stones to more populated areas.

The peaks weren't as brutal and sharp as those in Illyria, but there was a presence to them that he couldn't quite explain. Mor had once told him that long ago, these lands had been used for healing. That people injured in body and spirit had ventured to these hills, the lake they were now two and a half days from reaching, to recover.

Perhaps that was why he'd come. Some instinct had remembered the healing, felt this land's slumbering heart, and decided to bring Nesta here.

Mile after mile, her silence like a looming wraith behind him, Cassian wondered if it would be enough.

CHAPTER 49

They were halfway up a mountain that had looked like a mere hill from a distance when Cassian said from ahead, "We camp here for the night."

He'd stopped at an outlook over the mountainside, the nearest peak so close she could have hit it with a stone, separated only by another river snaking far below. The ground was pale and dusty, and most of all, it was flat.

Nesta said nothing as she staggered up to level ground, legs giving out at last, and sprawled onto the dirt.

It bit into her cheek, but she didn't care, not as she breathed and breathed, her body trembling. She wouldn't move until dawn. Not even to use the bathroom. She'd rather wet herself than have to move another muscle.

Cassian said from across the small site, "Take off the pack before you pass out so I can at least cook myself dinner."

His words were cold, distant. He'd barely spoken to her all day.

She deserved it—deserved worse.

The thought had her unclipping the straps from where they lay across her hips and chest. The pack thudded to the earth, and she twisted to nudge it toward him with a foot. Her leg trembled with the movement. But she made herself back up, until she was leaning against a small boulder.

He grabbed the pack with only a grunt, as if she hadn't been sweating and shaking under its weight all day. Then he strode off into the nearby brush, the knee-high grasses and bushes rustling.

The wind murmured, wending between the peaks. Shadows slowly crept over the craggy sides of the mountains, the lingering sun casting their upper limits in gold, the chill deepening with each inch yielded to the rising dark.

The river roared down the mountainside, a constant rushing that she'd heard throughout the day as they walked, its many rapids just barely visible from the outlook. Even here, with the light fading, the river's colors shifted from slate to jade to pine as it wandered between the peaks along the valley floor.

It was all so still, yet watchful, somehow. As if she were surrounded by something ancient and half-awake. As if each peak had its own moods and preferences, like whether the clouds clung to or avoided them, or trees lined their sides or left them bare. Their shapes were so odd and long that they looked as if behemoths had once lain down beside the rivers, pulled a rumpled blanket over themselves, and fallen asleep forever.

The thought of sleep must have lured her into it, for the next thing she knew, the world was dark, save for the stars and the nearly full moon, so bright that a fire hadn't been needed. Though she could have used its warmth. Cassian lay a few feet away, his back to her, the moonlight gilding his wings.

He'd left her a plate of food—bread and hard cheese and some sort of dried meat. She didn't touch it, though. Ignored the grumble in her stomach.

She just cracked her stiff neck, wrapped a blanket around herself, and lay upon the ground. She slid her arm again beneath her head and closed her eyes against the cold.

✣

For the next two days, she stared at the back of Cassian's head.

For the next two days, she did not speak.

Every pebble and stone seemed to be on a quest to trip her or twist her ankle or work its way inside her boots.

Afternoon was approaching on the following day, clouds drifting just above the peaks on a swift wind, when her head began pounding. The sunlight turned too bright; her sweat stung.

Despite days of walking, they had only cleared a few of the peaks. Mountains that Cassian sailed over when flying were endless on foot. How he selected the right path, she didn't ask. Where they were going, she didn't ask, either. She just followed him, eyes fixed on his back.

That sight blurred as her head, her whole body swayed a little.

She tried to swallow and found her throat so dry her tongue had stuck to the roof of her mouth. She peeled it free. Water—when had she last had a sip of water? Her canteen was at the top of her pack, but to halt, to pull it out . . . She didn't feel like unbuckling her straps to drop the bag. Like signaling to him that she needed to pause.

Last night had been the same as the previous one: she had reached their camp, collapsed, and barely been able to remove the pack before falling asleep. She woke later to find a plate of cold food beside her, covered with a thin cloth against the elements. She ate while he slept, then closed her eyes again.

Only sheer exhaustion could summon the oblivion she craved. Every time they stopped throughout the day, she was so tired she fell to her knees and dumped the pack. And during the pause in motion, she was so weary she couldn't think about the ruin she'd made of herself, the ruin she'd always been, deep down. No training, no learning about the Valkyries and their Mind-Stilling would help. Nothing would help.

So she could wait for the water. Because to stop was to allow those thoughts in, even if they trailed behind her like leaden shadows, heavier than the pack.

Her ankle twisted on a loose stone, and she gritted her teeth against the lash of pain, but continued. Cassian hadn't so much as stumbled once. She would know: she watched him all day long. But he stumbled now. Nesta lurched forward, but—

No. That was her. She was the one falling.

✣

Cassian was halfway up the dried riverbed when stones crunched and clacked behind him.

He whirled to find Nesta facedown. Not moving.

He swore, rushing down the stony path, and slid to his knees before her. The sharp stones bit his legs through his pants, but he didn't care, not as he turned her over, his heart thundering.

She'd fainted. His relief was a primal thing in him, settling, but—

He hadn't looked back at her in hours. Filmy white crusted her lips; her skin was flushed and sweaty. He grabbed for the canteen at his belt, unscrewing the cap, and pulled her head into his lap. "Drink," he ordered, opening her mouth for her, his blood roaring in his ears.

Nesta stirred, but didn't fight him when he poured a little water down her throat. It was enough to have her opening her eyes. They were glazed.

Cassian demanded, "When was the last time you had water?"

Her eyes sharpened. The first time she'd really looked at him in three solid days. But she only took the canteen and drank deep, draining it.

When she'd finished, she groaned, pushing herself from his lap, but only onto her side.

He snapped, "You should have been drinking water throughout the day."

She stared at the rocks around them.

He couldn't stand that look—the vacancy, the indifference, as if she no longer really cared whether she lived or died here in the wild.

His stomach twisted. Instinct bellowed at him to wrap himself around her, to comfort and soothe, but another voice, an ancient and wise voice, whispered to keep going. One more mountain, that voice said. Just one more mountain.

He trusted that voice. "We'll camp here tonight."

Nesta didn't try to rise, and Cassian scanned for a flatter expanse of ground. There—twenty feet up the riverbed and to the left. Flat enough. "Come on," he coaxed. "A few more feet and you can sleep."

She didn't move. As if she couldn't.

He told himself it was because she'd fainted and might not be sturdy, but he walked back to her. Crouched and picked her up in his arms, pack and all.

She said nothing. Absolutely nothing.

But he knew it was coming—that storm. Knew that Nesta would speak again, and when she did, he'd better be ready to weather it.

✠

Nesta found another plate waiting when she awoke to darkness. The full moon had shown her face, so bright the mountains, the rivers, the valley were illuminated enough that even the leaves on the trees far below were visible. She'd never seen such a view. It seemed like a secret, slumbering land that time had forgotten.

She was nothing before that view, these mountains. As insignificant to any of it as one of the stones that still rattled in her boot. It was a blessed relief, to be nothing and no one.

She didn't remember falling asleep, but dawn broke, and they were again moving. Heading north, he said—showing her, in a rare moment of civility, that the mossy sides of trees always faced that way, helping him stay on course.

There was a lake, he told her during lunch. They'd reach it tonight, and stay there a day or two.

She barely heard. One foot after another, mile after mile, up and down. The mountains watched her, the river sang to her, as if guiding her onward to that lake.

No amount of driving her body into the earth would make her good. She knew it. Wondered if he did, too. Wondered if he thought he was trekking out here with her on a fool's errand.

Or maybe it was like one of the ancient stories she'd heard as a child: he a wicked queen's huntsman, leading her into the deep wild before carving out her heart.

She wished he would. Wished someone would cut the damned thing from her chest. Wished someone would smother the voice that whispered of every horrible thing she had ever done, every awful thought she'd had, every person she'd failed.

She had been born wrong. Had been born with claws and fangs and had never been able to keep from using them, never been able to quell the part of her that roared at betrayal, that could hate and love more violently than anyone ever understood. Elain had been the only one who perhaps grasped it, but now her sister loathed her.

She didn't know how to fix it. How to make any of it right. How to stop being this way.

She didn't remember a time when she hadn't been angry. Maybe before her mother had died, but even then her mother herself had been bitter, disdainful of their father, and her mother's disdain had become her own.

She couldn't quell that relentless, churning anger. Couldn't stop herself from lashing out before she could be wounded.

She was no better than a rabid dog. She had been a rabid dog with Amren and Feyre. A beast, exactly like Tamlin. She hadn't even cared that she'd made it down the House stairs at last—did it count, when it was driven by fury?

Did *she* count—was she worth being counted?

It was the question that sent everything crumpling inside her.

Nesta cleared the hill Cassian had mounted ahead, and a sparkling, turquoise lake spread before them. It lay slightly sunken between two peaks, as if a pair of green hands had been cupped to hold the water within them. Gray stones lined its shore.

Nesta didn't see the lake, or the stones, or the sunlight and green.

Her vision blurred, and her eyes stung as if they had been sliced—cleaved open to allow the tears to pass.

She made it to the stones before she fell to her knees, so hard the rock bit into her bones. Was she worth being counted?

She knew the answer. Had always known it.

Cassian whirled toward her, but Nesta didn't see him, either, or hear his words.

Not as she buried her face in her hands and wept.

CHAPTER 50

Once the wrenching, gasping sounds came out of her, Nesta knew she could not stop.

She knelt on the shore of that mountain lake and let go entirely.

She allowed every horrible thought to hit her, wash through her. Let herself see Feyre's pale, devastated face as Nesta had revealed the truth, as she'd let her own anger and pain ride her.

She could never outlive it, her guilt. There was no point in trying. She sobbed into the darkness of her hands.

And then the stones clicked, and a warm, steady presence appeared beside her. He didn't touch her, but his voice was nearby as he said, "I'm here."

She sobbed harder at that. She couldn't stop. As if a dam had burst and only letting the water run its course, raging through her, would suffice.

"Nesta." His fingers grazed her shoulder.

She couldn't bear that touch. The kindness in it.

"Please," she said.

Her first word in five days.

He stilled. "Please what?"

She leaned from him. "Don't touch me. Don't—don't be *kind* to me." The words were a sobbing, rippling jumble.

"Why?"

The list of reasons surged, fighting to get out, to voice themselves, and she let them decide. Let them flow through her, as she whispered, "I let him die."

He went quiet.

Through her hands on her face, she continued to whisper. "He came to save me, and fought for me, and I let him die with hate in my heart. Hate for him. He died because I didn't stop it." Her voice broke, and she wept harder. "And I was so horrid to him, until the very end. I was so, so horrid to him all my life—and still he somehow loved me. I didn't deserve it, but he did. And I let him die."

She bowed over her knees, saying into her palms, "I can't undo it. I can't fix it. I can't fix that he is dead, I can't fix what I said to Feyre, I can't fix any of the horrible things I've done. I can't fix *me*."

She sobbed so hard she thought her body would break with it. Wanted her body to come apart like a cracked egg, wanted what was left of her soul to drift away on the mountain wind.

She whispered, "I can't bear it."

Cassian said quietly, "It isn't your fault."

She shook her head, face still in her hands, as if it'd shield her from him, but he said, "Your father's death is not your fault. I was there, Nesta. I looked for a way out of it, too. And there was nothing that could have been done."

"I could have used my power, I could have *tried*—"

"Nesta." Her name was a sigh—as if he were pained. Then his arms were around her, and she was being pulled into his lap. She didn't fight it, not as he tucked her against his chest. Into his strength and warmth.

"I could have found a way. I should have found a way."

His hand began stroking her hair.

Her entire body, right down to her bones, trembled. “My father’s death, it’s—it’s the reason I can’t stand fires.”

His hand stilled, then resumed. “Why?”

“The logs . . .” She shuddered. “They *crack*. It sounds like breaking bone.”

“Like your father’s neck.”

“Yes,” she breathed. “That’s what I hear. I don’t know how I’ll ever *not* hear his neck snapping when I’m near a fire. It’s . . . it’s *torture*.”

He continued to stroke her head.

A wave of words pushed themselves out of her. “I should have found a way to save us before then. Save Elain and Feyre when we were poor. But I was so *angry*, and I wanted him to try, to fight for us, but he didn’t, and I would have let us all starve to prove what a wretch he was. It consumed me so much that . . . that I let Feyre go into that forest and told myself I didn’t care, that she was half-wild, and it didn’t matter, and yet . . .” She let out a wrenching cry. “I close my eyes and I see her that day she went out to hunt the first time. I see Elain going into the Cauldron. I see her taken by it during the war. I see my father dead. And now I will see Feyre’s face when I told her that the baby would kill her.” She shook and shook, her tears burning hot down her cheeks.

Cassian kept stroking her hair, her back, as he held her by the lake.

“I hate it,” she said. “Every part of me that . . . *does* these things. And yet I can’t stop it. I can’t let down that barrier, because to let it fall, to let everything in . . .” This was what would happen. This shrieking, weeping mess she’d become. “I can’t bear to be in my head. I can’t bear to hear and see everything, over and over. That is all I hear—the snapping of his neck. His last words to me. That he loved me.” She whispered, “I didn’t deserve that love. I deserve *nothing*.”

Cassian’s hands tightened on her, her own hands falling away as she buried her face against his jacket and wept into his chest.

He said after a moment, “I can tell you more about my mother, and how her death nearly destroyed me. I can tell you in detail about what I did afterward, and what that cost me. I can tell you about the decade it took me to work through it. I can tell you how many days and nights I suffered during the forty-nine years Amarantha held Rhys captive, the guilt tearing me apart that I wasn't there to help him, that I couldn't save him. I can tell you how I still look at him and know I'm not worthy of him, that I failed him when he needed me—that fact drags me from sleep sometimes. I can tell you I've killed so many people I've lost count, but I remember most of their faces. I can tell you how I hear Eris and Devlon and the others talk and, deep down, I still believe that I am a worthless bastard brute. That it doesn't matter how many Siphons I have or how many battles I've won, because I failed the two people dearest to me when it mattered the most."

She couldn't find the words to tell him that he was wrong. That he was good, and brave, and—

"But I'm not going to tell you all of that," he said, pressing a kiss to the top of her head.

The wind seemed to pause, the sunlight on the lake brightening.

He said, "I am going to tell you that you will get through it. That you will face all of this, and you will get through it. That these tears are *good*, Nesta. These tears mean you care. I am going to tell you that it is not too late, not for any of it. And I can't tell you when, or how, but it will get better. What you feel, this guilt and pain and self-loathing—you will get through it. But only if you are willing to fight. Only if you are willing to face it, and embrace it, and walk through it, to emerge on the other side of it. And maybe you will still feel that tinge of pain, but there *is* another side. A better side."

She pulled back from his chest then. Found his gaze lined with silver. "I don't know how to get there. I don't think I'm capable of it."

His eyes glimmered with pain for her. "You are. I've seen it—I've seen what you can do when you are willing to fight for the people you love. Why not apply that same bravery and loyalty to yourself? Don't say you don't deserve it." He gripped her chin. "Everyone deserves happiness. The road there isn't easy. It is long, and hard, and often traveled utterly blind. But you keep going." He nodded to the mountains, the lake. "Because you know the destination will be worthwhile."

She stared up at him, this male who had walked with her for five days in near-silence, waiting, she knew, for this moment.

She blurted, "All the things I've done before—"

"Leave them in the past. Apologize to who you feel the need to, but leave those things behind."

"Forgiveness is not that easy."

"Forgiveness is something we also grant ourselves. And I can talk to you until these mountains crumble around us, but if you don't wish to be forgiven, if you don't want to stop feeling this way . . . it won't happen." He cupped her cheek, calluses scraping across her overheated skin. "You don't need to become some impossible ideal. You don't need to become sweet and simpering. You can give everyone that *I Will Slay My Enemies* look—which is my favorite look, by the way. You can keep that sharpness I like so much, that boldness and fearlessness. I don't want you to ever lose those things, to cage yourself."

"But I still don't know how to fix myself."

"There's nothing broken to be fixed," he said fiercely. "You are *helping* yourself. Healing the parts of you that hurt too much—and perhaps hurt others, too."

Nesta knew he wouldn't have ever said it, but she saw it in his gaze—that she had hurt him. Many times. She'd known she had, but to see it again in his face . . . She lifted her hand to his cheek and laid it there, too drained to care about the gentleness of the touch.

Cassian nuzzled into her hand, closing his eyes. "I'll be with you every step of the way," he whispered into her palm. "Just don't lock me out. You want to walk in silence for a week, I'm fine with that. So long as you talk to me at the end of it."

She stroked a thumb over his cheekbone, marveling at him—the words and his beauty. Some essential piece of herself clicked into place. Some piece that whispered, *Try*.

Cassian opened his eyes, and they were so lovely they nearly stole the breath from her. Nesta leaned forward until their brows touched. And despite all that brimmed in her heart, all that flowed through her body, sure and true, she merely whispered, "Thank you."

✠

The storm had broken, and it was not what Cassian had expected. He had expected rage capable of bringing down mountains. Not tears enough to fill this lake.

Every sob had broken his heart.

Every shake of her body as the words worked themselves out of her had torn him to shreds. Until he hadn't been able to keep from wrapping himself around her, comforting her.

She hadn't heard wood cracking in a fire, but breaking bone. He should have known.

How many fires had Nesta flinched from, hearing not the wood but her father's snapping neck? At last year's Winter Solstice party, she'd been pale and withdrawn—far worse than usual. And they'd had a massive, crackling fire in that room with them. Had kept it burning hot and loud all night.

Every snap would have reminded her of her father. Each one would have been brutal. Unbearable. And when she'd suddenly rushed from the town house at the end of the party . . . Had it been to get away from them, or to get free of the sound? Possibly both, but . . . He wished she'd said something. He wished he'd at least known.

And fuck, how many fires had he built these last few days? That first night, she'd curled as far from the flame as she could get. Had slept with an arm over her head. Blocking her ears, Mother damn him. And at the blacksmith, when she'd requested to move to a cooler, quieter room—one *without* the crackle of the forge . . . It had taken more courage than he'd understood for her to ask to return to the workshop, to the flames, to hammer at those blades.

She'd been suffering, and he'd had no idea how much it consumed every facet of her life. He'd seen her self-loathing and anger—but hadn't realized how much she had been aware of it. How much it had eaten her up. He couldn't stomach it. To know she'd hurt this much, for so long.

Cassian held her on the shores of the lake until the sun set, until the moon rose, and they remained there, listening to each other breathe, as if the world had been flooded by her tears, as if they were both waiting to see what emerged once the floodwaters receded.

The lake gleamed like a silver mirror in the moonlight, so bright it could have been dusk.

His stomach grumbled with hunger, but as the moon drifted higher, he pressed a kiss to her head. "Get up."

She stirred against him, but obeyed. He groaned, legs stiff from sitting for so long, and rose with her. Her arms wrapped around herself. As if she'd retreat behind that steel wall within her mind, her heart.

Cassian drew the Illyrian blade from down his back.

It gleamed with moonlight as he extended it to her hilt-first. "Take it."

Blinking, eyes still puffy with tears, she did. The blade dipped as she wrapped her hands around it, as if she didn't expect its weight after so long with the wooden practice swords.

Cassian stepped back. Then said, "Show me the eight-pointed star."

She studied the blade, then swallowed. Her features were open, fearful but so trusting that he nearly went to his knees. He nodded toward the blade. "Show me, Nesta."

Whatever she sought in his face, she found it. She widened her stance, bracing her feet on the stones. Cassian held his breath as she took up the first position.

Nesta lifted the sword and executed a perfect arcing slash. Her weight shifted to her legs just as she flipped the blade, leading with the hilt, and brought up her arm against an invisible blow. Another shift and the sword swept down, a brutal slash that would have sliced an opponent in half.

Each slice was perfect. Like that eight-pointed star was stamped on her very heart.

The sword was an extension of her arm, a part of her as much as her hair or breath. Every movement bloomed with purpose and precision. In the moonlight, before the silvered lake, she was the most beautiful thing he'd ever seen.

Nesta finished the eighth maneuver, and returned the sword to center.

The light in her eyes shone brighter than the moon overhead.

Such light, and clarity, that he could only whisper, "Again."

With a soft smile that Cassian had never seen before, standing on the moon-washed shores of the lake, Nesta began.

PART THREE

VALKYRIE

CHAPTER 51

"So you mean to tell me," Emerie muttered from the side of her mouth as they stood in the training ring two days later, "that you got into a fight with your family, disappeared for a week with Cassian, and came back able to use an *actual* sword, but I'm supposed to believe you when you say *nothing happened*?"

Gwyn snickered, her attention fixed on tying a length of white silk ribbon to a wood beam jutting from the side of the pit. Neither the ribbon nor the beam had been there a week ago, and Nesta had no idea how they'd even anchored the wood into the stone, but there it was.

The crisp morning wind ruffled Nesta's hair. "That's exactly what I'm telling you."

"Tell me you at least had a week's worth of sex," Emerie muttered.

Nesta choked on a laugh as Cassian stiffened across the ring—but he didn't turn. "There might have been some." After that night beside the lake, she and Cassian had lingered there for two entire days, either training with his sword or fucking like animals on the shore, in the water, bent over a boulder as she moaned his name so loudly it echoed off the peaks around them. He'd taken her over and over, and she'd clawed at him and torn his skin every time, as if she could climb into him and fuse their souls.

They'd returned last night, and she'd been too tired to venture to his room. She assumed he'd been called to the river house, because he hadn't been at dinner, nor had he sought her out.

She wasn't ready to see Feyre, though. For all she'd confessed to Cassian, that step . . . She'd face it soon.

"Done," Gwyn declared, the white ribbon fluttering in the wind where it hung from the beam. Behind them, a few of the priestesses working with Azriel had turned to see what the ribbon business was about. The shadowsinger crossed his arms, angling his head, but remained in his half of the ring.

Cassian, however, approached Gwyn's handiwork and ran the white silk between two fingers. Nesta couldn't stop her blush.

He'd done that by the lake: after he'd fucked her with his fingers, he'd held her gaze while he rubbed them together, testing the slide of her wetness against his skin the same way he was touching that ribbon. From the way his hazel eyes darkened, she knew he was recalling the same.

But Cassian cleared his throat. "Explain," he ordered Gwyn.

Gwyn squared her shoulders. "This is the Valkyrie test for whether your training is complete and you're ready for battle: cut the ribbon in half."

Emerie snorted. "What?"

But Cassian made a contemplative noise, gesturing to the other half of the ring. "Az told me you also started preliminary work with the steel blades while we were gone." He nodded to Gwyn and Emerie, the former glancing toward Azriel, who watched in silence. "So show me what you learned. Cut the ribbon in two."

"We slice the ribbon in two," Emerie asked Gwyn warily, "and our training is complete?"

Gwyn again glanced to Azriel, who drifted closer. She said, "I'm not entirely sure."

Cassian released the ribbon. "A warrior's training is never complete, but if you're able to slice this ribbon in two—with one cut—then I'd say you can hold your own against most enemies. Even if you've only been training for a little while." At their silence, he looked between them. "Who's first?"

Again, the three of them swapped glances. Nesta frowned. Whoever went first would get the brunt of the humiliation. Gwyn shook her head. No way in hell.

Emerie's mouth popped open. "Why me?" she demanded.

"What?" Cassian asked, and Nesta realized they hadn't been speaking.

"You're oldest," Gwyn said, nudging Emerie toward the ribbon.

Emerie groused, but stepped up to the dangling ribbon, grudgingly taking the sword Cassian extended. Azriel murmured over a shoulder to the priestesses under his charge as they watched. They instantly began moving again. But Azriel's attention remained on the ribbon.

"Should we bet?" Gwyn asked Nesta.

"Shut up," Emerie hissed, though amusement lit her eyes.

Nesta smirked. "Go ahead, Emerie."

Cursing under her breath, wings tucking in tight, Emerie lifted the blade in near-perfect form and sliced at the ribbon.

The white silk fluttered and bent around the blade. And absolutely did not slice in two.

"Let's all admit we knew that would happen," Emerie said, teeth bared as she slashed the sword again. The ribbon danced harmlessly away.

Cassian clapped her shoulder. "Looks like I'll see you at training tomorrow."

"Asshole," Nesta muttered.

Cassian laughed and took the sword from Emerie, and—in the same breath—spun, swiping low and even.

The bottom half of the ribbon fluttered to the ground. A perfect slice.

He grinned. "At least I can cut the ribbon."

✦

Nesta didn't forget that parting shot. Not as they finished training for the day, and certainly not when she dragged Cassian down the stairs, straight to his bedroom, need bellowing in her veins.

Cassian apparently felt the same, as he'd scarcely spoken these last few minutes, his eyes blazing bright. They only made it as far as his desk against the wall before she'd grabbed him—right as he'd pushed her down onto the wooden surface and stripped off her pants.

Bent over the desk, her bottom half entirely exposed, Nesta ground her aching nipples into the wood surface, savoring the brutal crush. Her jacket, her shirt, her boots—all stayed on. In fact, her pants were only pushed down to her ankles, restricting her movement further. Leaving her utterly at his mercy.

And as his cock at last sank deep into her, the two of them groaned. He stood behind her, one hand braced on the desk, the other clenching her hip as he pulled out nearly to the tip, then pushed back in slowly. Nesta writhed.

"I could fuck you for days," he said against her sweaty neck. She moaned into a pile of papers. "I'm fucking soaked with you," he growled, and the hand at her hip slid around to tease the apex of her thighs.

At the first taunting stroke, she breathed, "Cassian."

He pounded into her at a steady, deep pace. The liquid slide of his cock into her sounded obscenely through his otherwise silent bedroom. His balls brushed against her, tickling her with each powerful thrust. "Harder." She wanted him imprinted on her very bones. "*Harder.*"

"*Fuck*," he exploded on a breath, and pulled back from where he'd braced himself. "Hold on to the desk," he ordered, and Nesta stretched to grip the edges just as his hands landed on her hips. His thighs pushed into her own, spreading her further—as wide as she could go—and he gave no warning before his hands tightened and he unleashed himself.

Exquisite, punishing thrusts slammed so deep he hit her innermost wall, and her eyes rolled back into her head at the sheer bliss of it. He became savage, unrelenting. She might have been sobbing at the pleasure, the sheer size of him, so large there would never be any getting used to it. Every unrelenting push had her inching against the desk, the wood and papers teasing her breasts, and she nearly wept at that, too.

Cassian's fingers dug into her hips so hard Nesta knew she'd bruise, loved that she'd bruise. He shifted his stance, and his cock plunged even deeper, rubbing against that spot, and the sounds that came from her weren't human or Fae, but something far more primal.

"Fuck, yes," he snarled at her abandon. "That's it, Nesta." He accentuated each word with a savage thrust. "Do I feel good to you?"

She whimpered her confirmation, then managed to say, "I like it when you ride me hard. Every time I move and my body is sore . . ." She had to fight for words. For control. "I think of you. Of your cock."

"Good. I want my cock to be the only thing you think about." His pace faltered as he licked up the column of her neck. She could hear the taunting smile in his words as he whispered, "Because your pretty little cunt is the only thing I think about."

At the words, his foul language, her toes curled. But she wouldn't let him win this one, not when this had somehow become a competition for who could make the other come first, so she whispered, "I love being so covered in your seed that it leaks out of me for ages afterward. I love feeling it slide down my thighs and knowing you left your mark in me."

"Fuck," he blew out, his pounding wild now, so unchecked only her hold on the desk kept her feet on the ground. "*Fuck!*"

Cassian came with a roar, and at the first pulse of his cock spurting deep into her, she climaxed, screaming loud enough that he clamped a hand over her mouth. She bit down on his fingers, and he kept moving in her, spilling himself over and over. Until his seed was again running down her thighs, until he slid his fingers through a stream of it and brought it up to that spot at the apex of her sex. "You have no idea what you just started," he whispered in her ear, smearing his wetness there, rubbing into her sensitive flesh with idle circles.

Nesta didn't reply as his fingers flicked against her, and she came again.

⁜

Nesta did not venture down to the city to see Feyre. Or Amren.

But she kept going to the stairs. She hadn't been able to reach the bottom again. Part of her knew that if she wanted to, she might accomplish it—just as she might open her mouth and ask Cassian to take her to the river house. But she didn't.

So she kept trying the stairs for another week straight, always getting about halfway down before turning back, her legs absolute jelly by the time she returned to the hallway.

It was fitting, given that her arms were jelly, too. Yes, she wielded the sword with her entire body, but her arms hurt most of all. And it didn't help that they'd started on shields now.

No one had managed to slice Gwyn's ribbon in two.

They all tried at the start and end of every lesson, and all failed. Nesta had begun to resent the sight of a ribbon anywhere—tying back Roslin's red hair, folded in the accessory drawer of her dressing table, even bound for place-keeping into the latest romance Emerie had loaned her. They all laughed at her. Taunted her.

So Nesta ran the steps, and practiced, and failed. She took Cassian to her bed every night and sometimes during the day, though they never slept in each other's rooms. Not once. They fucked, they savaged each other, and then they parted.

No matter that there were some nights when she wanted him to stay. Wanted to roll off him and snuggle into his warmth and fall asleep to the sound of his breathing. But he always left before she mustered the courage to ask.

Nesta was leafing through a tome of military history in the library—that had *one* paragraph on Valkyrie ambush strategies—when Gwyn appeared. "Tell me you found their secret to cutting the ribbon."

"You and that ribbon," Nesta muttered, shutting the tome. Of all of them, Gwyn had become the most relentless about succeeding.

Gwyn crossed her arms, pale robes rustling. She winced and rubbed her shoulder. "Did you know shields weighed so much? I certainly didn't. No wonder the Valkyries learned to use them as weapons as deadly as their swords." She sighed. "They'd have been quite a sight in battle: cracking open enemy skulls with blows from their shields, throwing them to knock an opponent onto their backs before skewering them . . ." She rubbed her shoulder again. "Their arm muscles must have been as hard as steel."

Nesta snorted. "Indeed." She cocked her head. "Now that you're here, I want to ask a favor."

Gwyn arched a brow. "About the Trove?"

"No." Nesta knew she had to scry—soon—for the Harp. She'd lost a good week in the mountains, and if Queen Briallyn already had the Crown . . . Time was not on their side. But she said, "You mentioned a while ago that you have evening services—with music, right?"

Gwyn smiled. "Oh, yes. You want to join us? I promise, it's not all religious stuff. I mean, it is, but it's beautiful. And the cave we have the service in is beautiful, too. It was carved by the underground river that flows beneath the mountain, so the walls are smooth as glass. And it's acoustically perfect—the shape and size of the space amplifies and clarifies each voice within."

"It sounds heavenly," Nesta admitted.

"It is." Gwyn smiled again, eyes lighting with pride. "Some of the songs you'll hear are so ancient they predate the written word. Some of them are so old we didn't even have them in Sangravah. Clotho found them in books shelved below Level Seven. Hana—she'll be the one who plays the lute—figured out how to read the music."

"I'll be there." Nesta shifted on her feet. "I think I need something like that." At Gwyn's quizzical look, Nesta said, "I . . ." She fumbled for the smoothest way to say it. "I . . ."

Gwyn slid her hands into the robe's pockets, her face open—waiting.

Nesta finally said, letting herself voice the words, "After the war, I was in a bad place. I still am, I suppose, but for more than a year after the war . . ." She couldn't look Gwyn in the eye. "I did a lot of things I regret. Hurt people I regret harming. And I hurt myself. I drank day and night and I . . ." She didn't want to say the word to Gwyn—*fucked*—so she said, "I took strangers to my bed. To punish myself, to drown myself." She shrugged a shoulder. "It's a long story, and not one worth telling, but through it all, I picked taverns and pleasure halls to frequent because of the music. I've always loved music." She braced herself for the damning judgment. But only sorrow filled Gwyn's face.

"You've probably guessed that my residency in the House, my training, my work in the library is my sister's attempt to help me." Her sister whom she had still not apologized to, whom she still didn't have the courage to face. "And I . . . I think I might be glad Feyre did this for me. The drinking, the males—I don't miss any of it. But the music . . . that I miss." Nesta waved a hand, as if she could banish the vulnerability she'd offered up. But she went on, "And since I'm not particularly welcome in the city, I was hoping you meant it when you said I could come to one of your services. Just so I can hear some music again."

Gwyn's eyes shone, like the sunlight on a warm sea. Nesta's heart thundered, waiting for her reply. But Gwyn said, "Your story is worth telling, you know."

Nesta began to object, but Gwyn insisted, "It is. But yes—if you want music, then come to the services. We will be glad to have you. *I* will be glad to have you."

Until Gwyn learned how horrible she'd been.

"No," Gwyn said, apparently reading the thought on her face. She grabbed Nesta's hand. "You . . . I understand." Nesta heard Gwyn's own heart begin thundering. "I understand," Gwyn repeated, "what it is to . . . fail the people who mean the most. To live in fear of people finding out. I dread you and Emerie learning my history. I know that once you do, you'll never look at me the same again." Gwyn squeezed Nesta's hand.

Her story would come later. Nesta let her see it in her face, that when Gwyn was ready, nothing she could reveal would make her walk away.

"Come to the service this evening," Gwyn said. "Listen to the music." She squeezed her hand again. "You'll always be welcome to join me, Nesta."

Nesta hadn't realized how badly she'd needed to hear it. She squeezed Gwyn's hand back.

CHAPTER 52

The wooden pews that filled the massive, red-stoned cavern were packed with pale-hooded figures, their blue gems glimmering in the torchlight as they waited for the sunset service to begin. Nesta claimed a spot on a pew in the rear, earning a few curious looks from the hooded females who filed past, but no one spoke to her.

A dais lay at the far end of the space, though no altar sat upon it. A natural stone pillar rose from the ground, the top flattened into something like a podium. Nothing else. No effigies or idols, no gilded furniture.

A silver-haired figure stalked down the aisle, a cold wind at her heels, and the others gave her a wide berth. Nesta stiffened as Merrill's twilight-colored eyes settled upon her and narrowed with recognition—and hatred. But the female kept moving, taking her place atop the dais, where Clotho had appeared. Still no Gwyn.

The last of the priestesses found whatever seat was available, and silence fell as a group of seven females stepped onto the dais beside Merrill and Clotho. Some were hooded; others were bareheaded. And one of those bareheaded priestesses—

Gwyn. Her eyes glowed with mischief and delight as they found Nesta's, as if to say, *Surprise*.

Nesta couldn't help but smile back.

A bell rang seven times somewhere nearby, echoing through the stones, through Nesta's feet. Each peal was a summons, a call to focus. Everyone rose at the seventh peal. Nesta gazed at the sea of pale robes and blue stones as the entire room seemed to suck in a breath.

As that seventh bell finished pealing, music erupted.

Not from any instruments, but from all around. As if they were one voice, the priestesses began to sing, a wave of sparkling sound.

Nesta could only gape at the lovely melody, the voices from the front of the cavern leading it, lifting higher than the others. Gwyn sang, chin high, a faint glow seeming to radiate from her.

The music was pure, ancient, by turns whispering and bold, one moment like a tendril of mist, the next like a gilded ray of light. It finished, and Merrill spoke about the Mother and the Cauldron and the land and sun and water. She spoke of blessings and dreams and hope. Of mercy and love and growth.

Nesta half-heard it, waiting for the sound, the perfect, beautiful sound, to begin again. Gwyn seemed to be shimmering with pride and contentedness.

Merrill finished the prayer, and the group began another song.

It was like a braid, the song—a plait of seven voices, weaving in and out, individual strands that together formed a pattern. Halfway through it, a drum appeared in the hand of the singer on the far left. A harp began strumming in the hands of one on the far right. A lute sounded from the center.

She'd never heard such music. Like a spell, a dream given form. The entire room sang, each voice resonating through the stone.

But Gwyn's voice rose above them all, clear and powerful and yet husky on some notes. A mezzo-soprano. The word floated from the depths of Nesta's memory, voiced by a watery-eyed music tutor who'd quickly declared Nesta hopeless at singing or playing, but in possession of an unusually fine ear.

The song ended, and more prayers and words flowed from Merrill, Clotho silent beside her. Then another song started—this one merrier, faster than the other. As if the songs were a progression. This one was a lilting chant, the words tumbling over each other like water dancing down a mountainside, and Nesta's foot tapped on the ground in time to the beat. Nesta could have sworn that beneath the hem of Gwyn's robe, the priestess's foot was doing the same. The words and the counter-melodies danced around and around, until the walls hummed with the music, until the stone seemed to be singing it back.

They finished, and started another song—led into it by a rolling drumbeat, then a single voice. Then the harp joined, a second voice with it. Then the lute, along with a third. The three sang around and into each other, another braid of voices and melodies. They reached the second verse, and the other four joined in, the room with them.

Gwyn's voice soared like a bird through the cavern as she started the third song with a solo, and Nesta closed her eyes, leaning into the music, shutting out one sense in order to luxuriate in the sound of her friend. Something beckoned in Gwyn's song, in a way the others' hadn't. Like Gwyn was calling only to her, her voice full of sunshine and joy and unshakable determination. Nesta had never heard a voice like Gwyn's—by turns trained and wild, as if there was so much sound fighting to break free of Gwyn that she couldn't quite contain it all. As if the sound *needed* to be loose in the world.

The others joined Gwyn for the second verse, and the harp's harmonies rose above their song, archways of wordless notes.

With her eyes closed, only the music mattered—the song, the voices, the harp. It wrapped around her, as if she'd been dropped into a bottomless pool of sound. Gwyn's voice rose again, holding such a high note it was like a ray of pure light, piercing and summoning. Two other voices rolled in to join, pulsing around that repeated high note, the harp still strumming, voices whispering and flowing, lulling Nesta down, down, down into a pure, ancient place where no outside world existed, no time, nothing but the music in her bones, the stones at her feet, her side, overhead.

The music took form behind Nesta's eyes as the priestesses sang lyrics in languages so old, no one voiced them anymore. She saw what the song spoke of: mossy earth and golden sun, clear rivers and the deep shadows of an ancient forest. The harp strummed, and mountains rolled ahead, as if a veil had been cleared with the stroke of those strings, and she was flying toward it—toward a massive, mist-veiled mountain, the land barren save for moss and stones and a gray, stormy sea around it. The mountain itself held two peaks at its very top, and the stones jutting from its sides were carved in strange, ancient symbols, as old as the song itself.

Nesta's body melted away, her bones and the stones of the cavern a distant memory as she flowed into the mountain, beheld towering, carved gates, and passed through them into a darkness so complete it was primordial; darkness that was full of living things, terrible things.

A path led into the dark, and she followed it, past doors with no handles, sealed forever. She felt horrors lurk behind those doors, one horror greater than the others—a being of mist and hatred—but the song led her past them all, invisible and unmarked.

This place was utterly lethal. A place of suffering and rage and death. Her very soul quaked to wander its halls. And even though she had passed by the door keeping her safe from that one being more horrible than all the rest . . . she knew it watched her. She refused to look back, to acknowledge it.

So Nesta drifted down and down, the harp and the voices pulsing and guiding, until she stopped before a rock. She laid a hand on it to find it was only an illusion, and she passed through it, down another long hall, beneath the mountain itself, and then she stood in a cavern, almost the twin to the one the priestesses sang in, as if they were linked in song and dreaming.

But rather than red stone, it was carved of black rock. Symbols had been etched into the smooth floor, into the curving walls, rising toward a ceiling so high it faded into gloom. Spells and wards pulsed around the room, but there, in the center of the space, set upon the floor as if it had been laid there by someone who'd merely walked away and forgotten it . . .

There, in the center of the chamber, sat a small, golden harp.

Cold leached through Nesta, clarifying her thoughts enough to realize where she stood. That the music of the priestesses had lulled her into a trance, that her own bones and the stone of the mountain surrounding her had been her scrying tools, and she had drifted to this place . . .

The Harp gleamed in the darkness, as if it possessed its own sun within the metal and strings. *Play me*, it seemed to whisper. *Let me sing again. Join your voice with mine.*

Her hand reached toward the strings. *Yes.*

The Harp sighed, a low purr rolling off it as Nesta's hand neared. *We shall open doors and pathways; we shall move through space and eons together. Our music will free us of earthly rules and borders.*

Yes. She'd play the Harp, and there would be nothing but music until the stars died out.

Play. I have so long wished to play, it said, and she could have sworn she heard a smile within the sound. *What might my song unlock in here?* A cold, humorless laugh skittered along Nesta's bones. It sang again, *Play, play—*

The song halted, and the vision shattered.

Nesta's knees gave out as the room swept in, and she collapsed onto the pew, earning an alarmed look from Gwyn through the crowd. Her heart thundered, her mouth was dry as sand, and she forced herself to rise to her feet again. To listen to the end of the service as she pieced it all together, realized what she had discovered in her unwitting scrying.

ᚐ

"You're sure of this?"

Cassian leaned a hip against Rhys's desk. "Nesta said the Harp is beneath the Prison."

"She's never been to the Prison," Rhys said, frowning.

Cassian had honestly thought Nesta might be drunk when she'd burst into the dining room an hour earlier, breathless, and told him her wild story. He'd hardly been able to follow what she'd said, except for the fact that she believed the Harp was at the Prison.

Worse, that she'd *woken up* the Harp in the Prison. What havoc might it wreak unchecked? The thought chilled Cassian to the core.

So he'd flown down here and found Rhys in his study. Again poring over old healers' volumes, trying to find some way to save his mate.

Rhys leaned back against his seat. Considered.

Az had winnowed to a meeting point on the eastern coast to get a report from Mor about the Vallahan situation, and Feyre was out to dinner with Amren, so it was just the two of them tonight. Cassian had suggested that Nesta come tell Rhys herself, but she'd refused. She'd been shaken—had needed some time to pull herself back together. He'd check in on her later. Make sure she hadn't withdrawn too far into her head.

Rhys drummed his fingers on his biceps. Stared at his desk for a long moment. "When we heard about Beron's treachery, I had Helion show me how to apply a shield like the one I had around Feyre to the Prison itself."

"You guessed this would happen?"

"No." A muscle ticked in Rhys's jaw. "Feyre and I were concerned that Beron would try to free the inmates to use in a conflict—just as we used the Bone Carver in the war. Give me tonight, and I'll get the shield untangled and open for you tomorrow."

"It takes that long to undo a shield?"

Rhys dragged a hand through his hair. Worries etched deep lines into his brow. "It's a combination of magic and spell work, so yes. And I'll admit I'm distracted enough these days that I might need some extra time to make sure it's done correctly."

Cassian's stomach bottomed out at the bleakness in Rhys's face. But he only said, "All right."

A blade appeared on the desk, summoned from wherever Rhys kept it. The great sword Nesta had Made.

"Take it with you," his High Lord said quietly. "I want to see what happens if Nesta uses it."

"A visit to the Prison isn't the time for one of your experiments," Cassian countered.

The stars in Rhys's eyes winked out. "Then let's hope she doesn't need to draw it."

CHAPTER 53

"Rhysand really gave this sword to me of his own free will?" Nesta asked Cassian the next morning as they hiked the mossy, rock-strewn side of the towering mountain known as the Prison. It was exactly as she'd pictured it in her trance—and even more horrible in person. The very land seemed abandoned. Like something great had once existed here and then vanished. Like the land still waited for it to return.

"Rhys said if we're going into the Prison, we should be well armed," Cassian said, his dark hair tossed by the cold, wet wind off the thrashing gray sea beyond the plain to their right. "And this is the best place he can think of for us to try out the sword you Made."

"So if it goes badly, at least it will kill me, not anyone else?" Nesta couldn't keep the sharpness from her tone. Rhys had winnowed them here, depositing them at the base of the mountain, as no magic could pierce its heavy wards. Nesta hadn't been able to look him in the eye.

"You're not going to be killed. Either by that blade or anything in there." His jaw tightened as he surveyed the towering gates far above. He'd put many of the current inmates inside, and Nesta had heard Feyre's harrowing tales of visiting the Prison on several occasions.

Little frightened her sister—that Feyre found it to be petrifying didn't help the twisting sensation in Nesta's gut.

"You remember the rules?" Cassian asked as they neared the gates of bone, intricately carved with every manner of creature.

"Yes." Hold Cassian's hand the entire time, don't speak of Amren, don't speak of *anything* regarding the Trove or the court or Feyre's pregnancy, don't speak of the creatures he put in here, don't do anything except walk and stay on high alert. And get that Harp out before it could unleash chaos.

The bone gates groaned open. Cassian tensed, but kept climbing upward. "Looks like we're expected."

Down into the darkness, into hell itself, they walked.

Nesta clutched Cassian's hand, her rope to life in this lightless place. One of Cassian's Siphons flared with red light, bloodying the black walls, the doors they sometimes passed.

Cassian moved with the fluidity of a trained warrior, but she noted his gaze darting around the path they walked, which plunged into the earth. The entrance to the hidden hall she'd seen in her scrying had been far, far below—between an iron door with a single rune upon it and a little alcove in the stone.

Soft noises whispered through the rock. She could have sworn nails scraped behind one door. When she glanced at Cassian, his face paled. He noticed her stare and patted his left pectoral—right above the thick scar there. Indication of who was imprisoned behind that door. Who ran their nails over it.

Her blood chilled. Blue Annis.

Cobalt skin and iron claws, he'd said. Annis savored eating her prey.

Nesta swallowed, squeezing Cassian's hand, and they continued downward.

Minutes or hours passed, she didn't know. In the gloom, the heavy, whispering air, time had ceased to matter.

Nausea roiled through her. Amren had been in this place for thousands of years, thrown in by fools who had feared her in her true form, that being of flame and light who had laid waste to Hybern's army.

Nesta couldn't imagine spending a day in this place. A year.

She didn't know how Amren hadn't gone mad. How she'd found the strength to survive.

She'd treated Amren badly. The small thought wedged into her mind. She had used her, exactly as Amren said, as a shield against everyone. And Amren, who had survived millennia in this awful place, alongside the worst monsters in the land . . . Amren found *her* abhorrent.

Misery burned like acid.

Something pounded through the rock to their left, and Nesta flinched. Cassian squeezed her hand. "Ignore it," he murmured.

Down and down, into a place worse than hell. And then she spied an alcove burned into her memory, behind her eyelids. And—yes, beside it was that iron door with the sole rune on its surface.

"Here." Nesta jerked her chin toward the bald stone. "Through the rock."

When Cassian didn't reply, she twisted to him.

His focus lay fixed on the iron door. His golden-brown skin had gone ashen.

His lips mouthed the name of the being behind it.

Lanthys.

"You're sure . . ." Cassian swallowed. "You're sure this is the place?"

"Yes." Nesta didn't grant them time to reconsider as she outstretched her free hand and stepped up to the stone.

Her fingers passed through the rock. As if it didn't exist.

Cassian yanked her back, but she pushed forward, and her hand, then her wrist, then her arm vanished. And then they were through.

"I had no idea there was anything else in the Prison," Cassian breathed as they continued down another hallway. No doors lined it, just smooth stone. "I thought there were only cells."

"I told you," she answered. "I saw a chamber here."

The light of the Siphon atop Cassian's hand revealed an archway and openness—and there it was. Raised symbols carved into the floor cast shadows against the crimson light. The entire round chamber was full of them. And in its center—the golden Harp, covered in intricate embossing, set with silver strings.

It didn't sing, didn't speak. It might as well have been an ordinary instrument.

Which was exactly why Nesta tugged Cassian into a halt beneath the archway, not daring to step onto the carved floor. "We need to be careful." Nesta peered into the vast, empty chamber. "There are wards and spells here."

Cassian rubbed his jaw with his free hand. "My magic doesn't skew toward spells. I can blast apart magical shields and wards, but if it's a trap like Feyre and Amren faced at the Summer Court, I can't sense it."

Nesta tapped her foot in a swift beat. "Rhysand's wards on the Mask couldn't keep me out. The Mask wished for me to come, so it allowed me through. Maybe the Harp will do the same. Like calls to like, as you all enjoy saying."

"I'm not letting you go into that room alone. Not if that thing wants to *play*."

"I don't think we have a choice."

He squeezed her hand, calluses rubbing against her own. "You lead, I'll follow."

"What if my presence would go unnoticed, but yours sets off a trap? We can't risk that."

His throat bobbed. "I can't risk you."

The words slammed into her heart. "I . . . You can. You have to." Before he could further object, she said, "You are training me to be a warrior. Yet you'd keep me from danger? How is that any better than a caged animal?"

The words must have struck something in him. "All right." Cassian unbuckled the great sword he'd carried for her. He looped it around her middle, its weight considerable. She adjusted her balance. "We try it your way. And at the first sign of something wrong, we leave."

"Fine." She swallowed the dryness in her mouth.

His eyes glittered, noting her hesitation. "Not too late to change your mind."

Nesta bristled. "I'm not allowing anyone but us to get their hands on the Harp."

With that, she stepped to the demarcation line between the hall and the chamber. Bracing herself, she pushed a foot forward.

It was like stepping through mud.

But the wards allowed her through. Nesta took another step, arm extended behind her to hold Cassian's hand. The pressure of the spells pushed against her calves, her hips, her body, squeezing her lungs. "These are like no wards I've felt before," she whispered, standing still as she waited for any hint of a triggered trap. "They feel old. Incredibly old."

"They probably predate this place being used as a prison."

"What was it before?"

"No one knows. It's always been here. But this chamber . . ." He surveyed the space beyond her. "I didn't know places like this existed here. Maybe . . ." He frowned. "Part of me wonders if the Prison was either built or stocked with its inmates to hide the Harp's presence. There are so many terrible powers here, and the wards on the mountain itself . . . I wonder if someone hid the Harp knowing that it'd never be noticed with so much awful magic around it."

Her mouth had dried again. "But who put it here?"

"Your guess is as good as mine. Someone who existed before the High Lords ruled. Rhys told me once that this island might have even been an eighth court."

"You don't recognize these markings on the ground?"

"Not at all."

She loosed a long breath. "I don't think any traps were triggered."

He nodded. "Be quick."

Their gazes held, and Nesta turned from the raw worry in his eyes as she pulled her hand from his and entered the chamber.

✣

The wards lay heavy against Nesta's skin with each step across the stone floor to the shining Harp.

"It looks newly polished," she observed to Cassian, who watched from the archway. "How is that possible?"

"It exists outside the bindings of time, just as the Cauldron does."

Nesta studied the carvings in the floor. They all seemed to spiral toward one point. "I think these are stars," she breathed. "Constellations." And like a golden sun, the Harp lay at the center of the system.

"This *is* the Night Court," Cassian said drily.

But it felt . . . different from Night Court magic somehow. Nesta paused before the Harp, the wards pressing into her skin as she surveyed its golden frame and silver strings. The Harp sat atop a large rendering of an eight-pointed star. Its cardinal points stretched longer than the other four, with the Harp situated directly in the heart of the star.

The hair on the back of her neck stood. She could have sworn the blood in her body reversed course.

She had the creeping feeling she'd been brought here.

Not by the Cauldron or the Mother or the Harp. By something vaster. Something that stretched into the stars carved all around them.

Its cool, light hands guided her wrists as she picked up the Harp.

Her fingers brushed the icy metal. The Harp hummed against her skin, as if it still held its final note, from the last time it had been used—

Fae screamed, pounding on stone that hadn't been there a moment before, pleading for their children's sakes, begging to be let out let out let out—

Nesta had the sensation of falling, tumbling through air and stars and time—

It was a trap, and our people were too blind to see it—

Eons and stars and darkness plunged around her—

The Fae clawed at stone, tearing their nails on rock where there had once been a door. But the way back was now forever sealed, and they begged as they tried to pass their children through the solid wall, if only their children could be spared—

Light flashed, blinding. When it cleared, she stood in a white-stoned palace.

A great hall, where five thrones graced a dais. The sixth throne, in the center, was occupied by a pointy-eared crone. A golden, spiked crown rested on her head, blazing like the hate in her black eyes.

The Fae crone stiffened, blue velvet robes shifting with the movement. Her eyes, clear despite her wrinkled face, sharpened. Right on Nesta.

"You have the Harp," the queen said, voice like crinkling paper. And Nesta knew who she stood frozen before, what crown lay on her thin, white hair. Briallyn's gnarled fingers curled on the arms of her throne, and her gaze narrowed. The queen smiled, revealing a mouth of half-rotted teeth.

Nesta backed up a step—or tried to. She couldn't move.

Briallyn's horrible smile deepened and she said conversationally, "My spies have told me who your friends are. The half-breed and the broken Illyrian. Such lovely girls."

Nesta's blood churned, and she knew her eyes were blazing with her power as she snarled, "You come near them and I'll rip out your throat. I will hunt you down and gut *you."*

Briallyn tutted. "Such bonds are foolish. As foolish as you still holding on to the Harp, which sings answers to all my questions. I know where you are, Nesta Archeron—"

Darkness erupted.

Unmoving, solid darkness, slamming into Nesta as hard as a wall.

Screams still echoed.

No—no, that was a male bellowing her name.

And she had not slammed into the darkness. She'd collided with the stone, and now lay upon the floor, the Harp in her hands.

"*NESTA!*" Red light flared, washing like a bloody tide upon the stones, her face, the ceiling. But Cassian's Siphons could not break through the wards. He could not reach her.

Nesta clutched the Harp to her chest, the last of its reverberations echoing through her. She had to let go. Somehow, in touching the Harp while Briallyn was wearing the Crown, she had opened a pathway between their minds, their eyes. She could see Briallyn, and Briallyn could see her, could sense where she was. She had to let go—

She couldn't do more than twitch her fingertips as invisible, oppressive weight bore into her, like it'd flatten her into dust upon the ground. *Let go*, she silently bade it, gritting her teeth, fingers brushing over the nearest string. *Free me, you blasted thing.*

A beautiful, haughty voice answered, full of music so lovely it broke her heart to hear it. *I do not appreciate your tone.*

With that the Harp pushed into her harder, and Nesta roared silently.

Her nail scraped over the string again. *Let me go!*

Shall I open a door for you, then? Release that which is caught?

Yes! Damn you, yes!

It has been a long while, sister, since I played. I shall need time to remember the right combinations . . .

Don't play games. Nesta chilled at the word it had used. *Sister.* Like she and this thing were one and the same.

The small strings are for games—light movement and leaping—but the longer, the final ones . . . Such deep wonders and horrors we could strum into being. Such great and monstrous magic I wrought with my last minstrel. Shall I show you?

No. Just open up these wards.

As you wish. Pluck the first string, then.

Nesta didn't hesitate as her fingertip curled over the first string, grasping and then releasing it. A musical laugh filled her mind, but the weight lifted. Vanished.

Nesta heaved a breath, shoving upward, and found herself free to move as she wished. The Harp lay still in her hands, dormant. The very air seemed lighter. Looser. Like opening another doorway had shut the one to Briallyn.

"NESTA!" Cassian thundered from across the chamber.

"I'm fine," she called out, shaking off her lingering tremors. "But I think someone very wicked used this last." She stared into the darkness above. "I think they used it to . . . to trap their enemies and their enemies' children into the stone itself." Was that what had been happening to her just now? The Harp had been pushing her into the rock, fusing her soul with it? She shivered.

Cassian demanded, "Are you hurt? What happened?"

She groaned, rising slowly. "No. I . . . I touched it and it held a memory. A bad one." One she'd never forget. "And we need to leave. It showed me Briallyn, wearing the Crown. She *saw* me here." The words tumbled out as Nesta waded back through the ward-heavy cavern, feeling that center spot, the star at its heart, like a physical presence at her back. Those vast, light hands seemed to pull at her, trying to make her return, but she ignored them, explaining to Cassian what she'd heard from the Harp, and what she'd seen in the vision with Briallyn.

Cassian's breathing remained uneven. He didn't relax one muscle until she stepped back into the tunnel hallway. Until his hand was again around hers. He didn't even bother to look at the Harp, or comment on Briallyn. He only surveyed her for any sign of harm.

It was as intimate as any look he'd ever given her. Even when he was buried deep inside her, moving in her, his gaze had never been so openly raw.

She tucked the Harp into her side and couldn't stop the hand she lifted to his cheek. "I'm fine."

He pressed a kiss into the heart of her palm. "I don't know why I doubted you." He pulled from her touch. "Let's get the hell out of here." Dark promise laced the words—and she knew what they'd be doing as soon as they dumped the Harp off to become Rhysand's problem.

Her cheeks heated, something like pleasure going through her. That he would pick her, them—that he wanted the reassurance of her body that much.

She interlaced her fingers through his, squeezing as tightly as their hands could be pressed together. He squeezed back, and tugged her down the passageway, away from the site of pain and long-forgotten memory. The sword bounced against her thigh, and she said, breaking the silence, "I named it Ataraxia."

He glanced over his shoulder at her. "That sword? What's it mean?"

"It's from the Old Language. I found it in a book the other day in the library. I liked the sound of it."

"Ataraxia," he said as though he were trying out the weapon itself. "I like it."

"I'm so glad you approve."

"It's better than Killer or Silver Majesty," he threw back. His grin was brighter than the glowing Siphon atop his left hand. Her pulse raced. "Ataraxia," he said again, and Nesta could have sworn the blade hanging from her belt hummed in answer. As if it liked the sound of his voice as much as she did.

They neared the end of the tunnel, but Nesta paused him with a tug on his hand. "What?" he asked, scanning the cavern. But she rose onto her toes and kissed him lightly. He blinked with almost comic shock as she pulled away. "What was that for?"

Nesta shrugged, her cheeks heating. "Gwyn and Emerie are my friends," she said quietly. She tucked away her horror that Briallyn had eyes on them. "But . . ." She swallowed. "I think you might be, too, Cassian."

Cassian's silence was palpable, and she cursed herself for laying bare that wish, that realization. Wished she could wipe away the words, the stupidity—

"I've always been your friend, Nesta," he said hoarsely. "Always."

She couldn't bear to see what was in his eyes. "I know."

Cassian brushed his mouth over her temple, and they exited the tunnel at last, entering the main path of the Prison, its heavy gloom.

Nesta whispered, finally daring to say it, "And I've always—"

Cassian threw her behind him so fast the rest of the words died in her throat.

"Run." His heartbeat—his pure terror—filled the air. "Nesta, *run*."

She whirled toward what he faced, his Illyrian blade gleaming ruby in the light of his Siphon. As if a blade could do anything.

The door to Lanthys's cell lay open.

CHAPTER 54

Cassian beheld the open door to Lanthys's cell and knew two things.

The first, and most obvious, was that he was about to die.

The second was that he would do anything in the world to prevent Nesta from meeting the same fate.

The second clarified his mind, cooled and sharpened his fear into another weapon. By the time the voice slithered from the darkness around them, he was ready.

"I wondered when you and I would meet again, Lord of Bastards."

Cassian had never, not once, forgotten the timbre and iciness of that voice, how it made his very blood bristle with hoarfrost. But Cassian answered, "All these centuries in here and you haven't invented a more creative name for me?"

Lanthys's laugh twined around them like a snake. Cassian gripped Nesta's hand, though his order to run still hung between them. It was too late for running. At least for him. All that remained was buying her enough time to escape.

"You thought yourself so clever with the ash mirror," Lanthys seethed, voice echoing from all around them. The light of Cassian's left

Siphon revealed only red-washed, misty darkness. "Thought you could best *me*." Another laugh. "I am immortal, boy. A true immortal, as you might never hope to be. Two centuries in here is nothing. I knew I'd only need to bide my time before I found a way to escape."

"You found a way?" Cassian drawled to the mist that was Lanthys. "It seems like someone helped you out." He clicked his tongue.

He just had to wait—wait until the attack came. Then Nesta could run. She was rigid beside him, utterly frozen. He nudged her with a foot, trying to knock her from her stupor. He needed her primed to run, not rooted to the spot like a deer.

"The door opened of my will alone," Lanthys purred.

"Liar. Someone opened it for you."

Lanthys's mist thickened, rumbling with ire.

Nesta swallowed audibly, and Cassian knew. When she'd ordered the Harp to let her go . . . The Harp had also released Lanthys. *Just open up these wards*, she'd instructed it. So it had: the wards on her, and the wards nearby—on Lanthys's cell. It had said it wanted to play. And here it was: playing with their lives.

What if the Harp had extended its reach beyond Lanthys's door? If every single cell door here was open . . .

Fuck.

But Cassian said to the monster he feared above all others, "So you plan to swirl around me like a rain cloud? What of that handsome form I saw in the mirror?"

"Is that what your companion prefers?" Lanthys whispered from too close—far too close. Nesta cringed away. Lanthys inhaled. "What *are* you?"

"A witch," she breathed. "From Oorid's dark heart."

"There is a name I have not heard in a long while." Lanthys's voice sounded mere feet from Nesta. Cassian gritted his teeth. He needed the monster gathered on the other side of her—so the path upward was clear. Had to draw Lanthys over toward him. "But you do not smell of

Oorid's heaviness, its despair." An inhale, still behind them, blocking the way out. "Your scent . . ." He sighed. "A pity you've marred such a scent with Cassian's stink. I can barely distinguish anything on you besides his essence."

That alone, Cassian realized, kept Lanthys from realizing what she was. Being interested, as the Bone Carver had been. But it revealed another dangerous truth: where to strike first.

"What is it you are obscuring behind you?" Lanthys asked, and Nesta turned, as if tracking him, keeping the Harp hidden at her back. Lanthys chuckled, though. "Ah. I see it now. Long have I wondered who would come to claim it. I could hear its music, you know. Its final note, like an echo in the stone. I was surprised to find it down here, hidden beneath the Prison, after all that time."

The mist swirled and Lanthys drawled, "Such exquisite music it makes. What wonder it spins. Everything pays fealty to that Harp: seasons, kingdoms, the order of time and worlds. These are of no consequence to it. And its last string . . ." He laughed. "Even Death bows to that string."

Nesta swallowed again. Cassian squeezed her hand tighter and said casually, "You true immortals are all the same: arrogant windbags who love to hear yourselves talk."

"And you faeries are all blind to your own selves." Lanthys crooned, circling again, and Cassian readied his blade. "Based upon scent alone, I would say that you two are—"

Cassian released Nesta's hand and lunged forward, spearing his blade into the mist before Lanthys could say one more damning word.

Lanthys screamed in rage as Cassian's Siphons flared, and Cassian roared, "*RUN!*" before he struck again. Lanthys retreated, and Cassian used the breath to free the Siphon from his left hand before chucking it to her, willing it to light. "*Go!*" he commanded as he tossed the stone to her. Red splashed across her fear-tight face as she caught his Siphon, but Cassian was already pivoting to Lanthys.

The crunching, fading steps told him Nesta obeyed.

Good.

Lanthys gathered in the darkness, a cobra readying to strike.

Cassian just prayed Nesta made it out of the gates before he died.

⳩

Nesta ran from the voice that was hate and cruelty and hunger entwined. The voice that robbed her of joy, of warmth, of anything but primal, basic fear.

Her thighs protested at the path's steepness, but she sprinted up toward the gates, obeying Cassian's command, the roaring from the warrior and the monster echoing off the stones. Red light flashed behind her. The doors of the Prison's cells rattled. Beasts screamed behind them, as if realizing one of them had gotten out. Wanting out themselves.

She clenched the Harp in one hand, Cassian's Siphon blazing in the other. She had to reach the gates. Then make it down the mountain. And then holler for Rhysand, and pray he had some sort of spell to sense his name on the wind. Then he'd have to race back up the mountain, down the path, and . . .

Cassian might be dead by the time she reached the gates so high above. He might be dying now.

A cold bolt shot through her heart.

She had run from him. *Left* him.

The Harp warmed in her hand, humming. The gold gleamed as if molten.

We shall open doors and pathways; we shall move through space and eons together, it had sung during her unintentional scrying. *Our music will free us of earthly rules and borders.*

Open doors . . . She had opened a door with it—to Lanthys's cell. Opened a door through its own power pressing on her. But to move through space . . .

The small strings are for games—light movement and leaping—but the longer, the final ones . . . Such deep wonders and horrors we could strum into being.

Nesta counted the strings. Twenty-six. She'd touched the first, the smallest, to free herself from the Harp's power, but what did the others do?

Twenty-six, twenty-six, twenty-six . . .

Gwyn's voice floated from far away, recounting Merrill's earlier research on dimensions. The possibility of *twenty-six* dimensions.

We shall move through space and eons together . . . The small strings are for games—light movement and leaping . . . Could the Harp . . . Nesta's breath caught in her throat. Could the Harp transplant her from one place to another? Not only open a door, but create one she might walk through?

Free us of earthly rules and borders . . .

She had to try it. For Cassian.

Motion stirred in the gloom above, rushing steps headed her way. Someone had entered the Prison through the gates. Nesta angled Cassian's Siphon toward the sound, bracing for whatever monster might come barreling down—

Fae males in worn, dirty armor charged toward her. At least ten Autumn Court soldiers.

She knew who'd sent them, winnowing them on Koschei's power. Who controlled them, even from across the sea.

I know where you are, Nesta Archeron.

And since Rhys had lowered the shields around the Prison . . . they'd walked right in.

Nesta didn't think. She seized that silver fire within her. Let it wreathe her hands.

"Take me to Cassian," she whispered, and plucked the first silver string of the Harp.

The world and oncoming soldiers vanished, and she had the sense of being thrown, even as she stood still, and she prayed and prayed—

Metal flashed, and red light flared, and there was Cassian, bleeding on the ground, Siphons blazing, fighting the mist in front of him.

There was nowhere to strike a fatal blow. The mist scattered at every thrust of Cassian's sword, and Lanthys shrieked at each one, but Lanthys could not be killed. Only contained, Cassian had said.

And the Harp could open doorways—but not slay people. She ran for Cassian, finger readying on the Harp's string to haul them out of there.

But Cassian's eyes flared, and he yelled, "*GET*—"

The mist wrapped around his throat and hurled him.

Her scream shattered through the tunnel as he hit the rock wall, wings crunching, and fell to the floor. He didn't move.

A laugh like a knife scraping over stone filled the tunnel and then Nesta was thrown, too, slamming into the wall so hard her teeth clacked and her head spun, breath whooshing from her as her fingers splayed on the Harp before she hit the floor.

But she'd landed near Cassian, and she hurried to turn him over, praying his neck hadn't snapped, that she hadn't doomed him by coming here—

Cassian's chest rose and fell, and the mighty, primal thing inside her body breathed a sigh of relief. Short-lived, as Lanthys laughed again.

"You shall wish the blow killed him before I'm through with you both," the creature said. "You shall wish you kept running." But Nesta refused to hear another word, not as she knelt over Cassian, the only thing between him and Lanthys.

She had been here before.

Had been in this exact position, his head on her lap, Death laughing at them.

Then, she had curled over him and waited to die. Then, she had stopped fighting.

She would not fail this time. The mist pressed in, and she could have sworn she felt a hand reach for her.

It was enough to set her moving.

Drawing her sword in the same movement with which she shot to her feet, Nesta slashed a perfect combination.

Lanthys screamed, and it was nothing like what she'd heard before—this was an earsplitting sound of pure shock and fury.

Nesta hefted Ataraxia, settling her weight between her feet, making sure her stance was even. Unshakable. The blade began to glow.

The mist contorted, shrinking and writhing as if it fought an invisible enemy, and then it became solid, blooming with color.

A naked, golden-haired male stood before her. He was of average height, his golden skin sculpted with muscle, his sharp-boned face simmering with hate. Not a repulsive, awful creature, but one of beauty.

His black eyes narrowed upon the blade as he hissed, "*That is not Narben.*" The name meant nothing to her.

Nesta lunged, thrusting Ataraxia into eighth position. Lanthys leaped back.

Cassian groaned, stirring to consciousness as she held the ground in front of her.

"Which death-god are you?" Lanthys demanded, glancing between the blade and her. The silver fire sizzling in her eyes.

Nesta swung Ataraxia again, and Lanthys cringed away. Afraid of the blade.

That which could not be killed was afraid of her blade. Not her, but Ataraxia. Her Made weapon.

"Get in your cell." Nesta advanced a step, Ataraxia pointed before her. Lanthys backed slowly toward his cell.

"What *is* that blade?" His golden hair swayed down to his waist as he backed away again.

"Its name is Ataraxia," Nesta spat. "And it shall be the last thing you see."

Lanthys burst out laughing, the sound like a crow's cawing. Hideous, compared to his beautiful form. "You named a death-sword *Ataraxia*?" He howled, and the very mountain shook.

"It shall slay you whether you like its name or not."

"Oh, I do not think so," Lanthys seethed. "I rode in the Wild Hunt before you were even a scrap of existence, *witch from Oorid*. I summoned the hounds and the world cowered at their baying. I galloped at the head of the Hunt, and Fae and beast bowed before us."

Nesta flipped Ataraxia in her hand, a movement she'd taken to doing with the Illyrian blades in idle moments during training. She'd seen Cassian do it often, and found that it dispelled any extra energy.

She hadn't realized it was such an effective intimidation technique. Lanthys shrank back.

She prayed the Autumn Court soldiers coming down the path any moment would hesitate before the blade, too. Knew they wouldn't. Not with Briallyn and the Crown controlling them.

"Which death-god are you?" Lanthys asked again. "*Who are you beneath that flesh?*"

"I am nobody," she snapped.

"Whose fire burns silver in your gaze?"

"You know whose fire," she stalled.

But it struck true, somehow. Lanthys's skin drained of color. "It is not possible." He looked to the Harp beside a stirring Cassian, and his eyes widened again. "We heard about you down here. You are the one the sea and the wind and the earth whispered of." He shuddered. "*Nesta*." He grinned, showing teeth slightly too long. "You took from the Cauldron itself."

Lanthys halted his retreat. And extended a broad, graceful hand. "You do not even know what you could *do*. Come. I shall show you." He smiled again with those too-long teeth, turning his face from beauty to horror with a quirk of his lips. "Come with me, Queen of Queens, and we shall return what was once lost." The words were a lullaby, a honeyed promise. "We shall rebuild to what we were before the golden legions of the Fae cast off their chains and overthrew us. We shall resurrect the Wild Hunt and ride rampant through the night. We shall build palaces of ice and flame, palaces of darkness and starlight. Magic shall flow untethered again."

Nesta could see the portrait Lanthys wove into the air around them. She saw herself on a black throne, a matching crown in her unbound hair. Enormous onyx beasts—scaled, like those she'd seen on the Hewn City's pillars—lay at the foot of the dais. Ataraxia leaned against her throne, and on her other side . . . Lanthys sat there, his hand laced through hers. Their kingdom was endless; their palace built of pure magic that lived and thrived around them. The Harp sat behind them on an altar, the Mask, too, but the golden Crown wasn't there.

It rested atop Lanthys's head.

And that was the snarled thread that pulled her out—the naked gleam of his greed. He'd seen the Harp, known she was after the Trove, and revealed what he'd do with it. The Crown he'd claim for himself. It would have no influence over her, but their rule would be one of coercion. Enslavement.

A fourth object lay on the altar, veiled in shadow. But she couldn't make out more than a gleam of age-worn bone—

The vision shifted, and they writhed on a great black bed, the golden skin of Lanthys's back shining as he moved inside her. Such pleasure—she had never known such pleasure with anyone. Only he could fuck her like this, driving so deep, her body warm and supple and wet for him, and soon, soon his seed would take root in her womb and the child she would bear him would rule entire universes—

Another snarled thread that led outward. Past the illusion.

Her body was not his to touch, to fill with life. And she *had* known pleasure richer than what he'd shown her.

Nesta blinked, and it was gone.

Lanthys growled. He now stood only as far away as her reach. Ataraxia's reach. "I can take care of *that* problem," he snarled toward Cassian. "And you will forget those ties soon enough."

She hefted Ataraxia higher. "Go back into your cell and shut the door."

"I shall just escape again." Lanthys chuckled. "And when I do, I will find you, Nesta Archeron, and you shall be my queen."

"No. I don't think I will." Nesta let her power ripple down the blade. Ataraxia sang, blazing like the moon.

Lanthys paled. "What are you doing?"

"Finishing the job."

And his eyes were so fixed upon the glowing blade that he didn't spare a sideways glance to Cassian. Did not see the dagger drawn. The one Cassian threw with impeccable aim.

It embedded to the hilt in Lanthys's chest.

Lanthys screamed, arching, and Nesta leaped. She sliced a two-three combination, slashing straight across, letting the power of her breath, her legs, and her core carry the blade through.

Ataraxia sang the heartsong of the wind as it whipped through the air.

Lanthys's head and corpse fell in different directions, thumping upon the stones.

Strange black blood spurted from his form, and then Cassian was there, groaning as he wrapped a hand around hers again. "The Harp," he panted, his face the portrait of pain. Blood leaked down his temple. "Pick it up and let's go. We have to get out of here."

"Can you even stand?"

He swayed on his feet. He wouldn't make it three steps.

"Yes," he grunted. To get her out of here, she knew he'd try. Just as she knew that Lanthys was dead. Had it been the sword, or her power? Since she'd Made the sword, she supposed it technically counted *as* her power, but . . . What could not be killed had been slain. Somehow. A small part of her delighted in it, even as the rest of her trembled.

Now the scrape and thud of footsteps rushed toward them. "Autumn Court soldiers," she breathed, pointing to the dark path upward. "More of them. Briallyn sent them to get the Harp."

"More—"

Screaming began throughout the mountain. Petrified, pleading screaming, fists pounding. Not on the rock or the doors that held them, but on the opposite walls of their cells. As if they were begging the Prison to spare them from her and that sword.

Lanthys had fallen. And the occupants of the Prison had felt it.

Even the footsteps of the Autumn Court soldiers seemed to slow at the sound.

Nesta smiled darkly, and picked up the Harp. "We're not running out of here. And we leave the Autumn Court soldiers untouched." If only to prove Eris wrong. But Cassian's wounds . . . Yes, they needed to leave. Quickly. "Hold on to me," she commanded, and whispered, "The front lawn of Feyre's house along the Sidra River in Velaris."

Cassian barked a warning, but she plucked three strings this time. Only pulling one had carried her down here, so she supposed that two would take them perhaps a bit farther than that, and Velaris . . . Well, it seemed like it'd take three strings. She didn't want to know where all twenty-six strings might take her if strummed. Or if someone made a melody.

The world vanished; again she had the sensation of falling while standing still, and then—

Sun and grass and a crisp autumn breeze. A massive, lovely estate behind them, the river before them, and not a trace of the Prison or Lanthys. Nesta let go of Cassian as Rhysand burst out of the house's glass doors. He gaped at his friend, and when Nesta beheld Cassian in the daylight . . . Blood trickled from his hair down his cheek. His lip was split; his arm hung at an odd angle—

That was all Nesta saw before Cassian collapsed to the grass.

CHAPTER 55

"It's a small cut. Stop fussing."

"Your skull was cracked, and your arm was broken. You're grounded for a few days."

"You can't be serious."

"Oh, I most certainly am."

Nesta might have smiled at Cassian and Rhysand's standoff had she not agreed with the High Lord. Feyre stood beside her mate, concern tightening her features.

Ataraxia still weighed heavy in Nesta's hand. The Harp in the other.

Her sister's eyes slid to her. Nesta swallowed, holding Feyre's gaze. She prayed that her sister could read the silent words on her face. *I am sorry for what I said to you in Amren's apartment. I am truly sorry.*

Feyre's eyes softened. And then, to Nesta's shock, Feyre answered into her mind, *Don't worry about it.*

Nesta steeled herself, shaking off her surprise. She'd forgotten that her sister was . . . What was the word? Daemati. Able to mind-speak, as Rhys could. Nesta said, heart thundering, *I spoke in anger, and I'm sorry.*

Feyre's pause was considerable. Then she said, the words like the first rays of dawn, *I forgive you.*

Nesta tried not to sag. She intended to ask about the baby, but Rhys turned to her and said, "Put the Harp on the desk, Nesta."

Nesta did, careful not to touch any of the twenty-six silver strings.

"It allowed you to winnow within and outside of the Prison," Feyre said, peering at the Harp. "I suppose because it is Made, and exists beyond the rules of ordinary magic?" She glanced to Rhys, who shrugged. Feyre's mouth pursed. "If any of our enemies got their hands on this, they'd use it against us in a heartbeat. No wards around this house, the House of Wind, around any of our caches and hiding places would be safe. Not to mention that the Harp seems to have a will of its own—a desire to stir up trouble. We can't plant it back in the Prison, not now that it's been awakened."

Rhys rubbed his jaw. "So we lock it up with the Mask, warded and spelled so it can't act out again."

"I'd keep them separate," Feyre advised. "Remember what happened when the halves of the Book were near each other? And why make it easier for an enemy to get both of them?"

"Good point," Cassian said, wincing as if the words made his skull ache. Madja had healed the hairline fracture just above his temple, but he'd be in pain for a few days. And his broken arm was healed, but still delicate enough to require care. The sight of all the bandages was enough to make Nesta wish she could kill Lanthys again.

Rhys drummed his fingers on the desk, surveying the Harp. Then he asked Nesta, "Beyond seeing Briallyn, you said you also saw something when you first touched the Harp?"

Nesta had briefly explained it when they'd arrived. "I think whoever used it last did something horrible with it. Maybe trapped the people who once lived on the Prison's island in the walls, somehow. Is that possible?"

Doubt shone in Rhys's eyes.

Nesta asked, "What is the Wild Hunt?" She'd also told him of their encounter with Lanthys, and the presence of the Autumn Court soldiers. Cassian had convinced Rhys not to engage with them, at least until they could deal with Briallyn. When Rhys had raised his shield around the Prison once more, they'd already vanished.

Rhys blew out a breath, leaning back in his chair. "Honestly, I thought it mere myth. That Lanthys remembers such a thing . . . Well, there's always room for lying, I suppose, but on the off chance he was telling the truth, that'd make him more than fifteen thousand years old."

Feyre asked, "So what is it, then?"

Rhys lifted a hand, and a book of legends from a shelf behind him floated to his fingers. He laid it upon the desk. He flipped it open to a page, revealing an image of a group of tall, strange-looking beings with crowns atop their heads.

"The Fae were not the first masters of this world. According to our oldest legends, most now forgotten, we were created by beings who were near-gods—and monsters. The Daglan. They ruled for millennia, and enslaved us and the humans. They were petty and cruel and drank the magic of the land like wine."

Rhys's eyes flicked to Ataraxia, then to Cassian. "Some strains of the mythology claim that one of the Fae heroes who rose up to overthrow them was Fionn, who was given the great sword Gwydion by the High Priestess Oleanna, who had dipped it into the Cauldron itself. Fionn and Gwydion overthrew the Daglan. A millennium of peace followed, and the lands were divided into rough territories that were the precursors to the courts—but at the end of those thousand years, they were at each other's throats, on the brink of war." His face tightened. "Fionn unified them and set himself above them as High King. The first and only High King this land has ever had."

Nesta could have sworn the last words were spoken with a sharp look toward Cassian. But Cassian only winked at Rhys.

"What happened to the High King?" Feyre asked.

Rhys ran a hand over a page of the book. "Fionn was betrayed by his queen, who had been leader of her own territory, and by his dearest friend, who was his general. They killed him, taking some of his bloodline's most powerful and precious weapons, and then out of the chaos that followed, the seven High Lords rose, and the courts have been in place ever since."

Feyre asked, "Does Amren remember this?"

Rhys shook his head. "Only vaguely now. From what I've gleaned, she arrived during those years before Fionn and Gwydion rose, and went into the Prison during the Age of Legends—the time when this land was full of heroic figures who were keen to hunt down the last members of their former masters' race. They feared Amren, believing her one of their enemies, and threw her into the Prison. When she emerged again, she'd missed Fionn's fall and the loss of Gwydion, and found the High Lords ruling."

Nesta considered all Lanthys had said. "And what is Narben?"

"Lanthys asked about it?"

"He said my sword isn't Narben. He sounded surprised."

Rhys studied her blade. "Narben is a death-sword. It's lost, possibly destroyed, but stories say it can slay even monsters like Lanthys."

"So can Nesta's sword, apparently," Feyre said, studying the blade as well.

"Beheading him with it killed him," Rhys mused.

"A slice from it seemed to bind him into a physical form," Nesta corrected. "Cassian's dagger struck true only after Lanthys had been forced to give up his mist."

"Interesting," Rhys murmured.

Cassian said, "You still haven't explained the Wild Hunt."

Rhys turned a few pages in the book, to an illustration of a host of riders on horses and all manner of beasts. "The Daglan delighted in terrorizing the Fae and humans under their control. The Wild Hunt was a way to keep all of us in line. They'd gather a host of their fiercest, most merciless warriors and grant them free rein to kill as they pleased. The Daglan possessed mighty, monstrous beasts—hounds, they called them, though they didn't look like the hounds we know—that they used to run prey to ground before they tortured and killed them. It's a terrible history, and much of it might be elaborated myths."

"The hounds looked like the beasts in the Hewn City," Nesta said quietly.

They all looked at her.

She admitted, "Lanthys showed me a vision. Of . . . what he and I might be. Together. We ruled in a palace, king and queen with the Trove, and at our feet sat those hounds. They looked like the scaled beasts carved into the Hewn City's pillars."

Even Rhys had no answer to that.

Cassian's jaw tightened. "So even while he tried to kill you, he was trying to seduce you?"

Nesta's stomach churned, but she refrained from mentioning how graphic that vision had been. "There was a fourth object in the vision, but it was in shadow—was there ever a fourth part of the Trove? All I could make out was a bit of ancient bone."

Rhys ran a hand through his dark hair. "As far as history has confirmed, there are only three objects in the Trove."

Feyre asked, "What if it's protected by a spell, like the one to shield all thought of the Trove, to keep people from ever knowing about the fourth object?"

Rhys's eyes shadowed. "Then the Mother spare us, because even Amren only vaguely remembers a rumor of it."

The words hung there. Nesta asked, "So. Now I go after the Crown."

"No," Cassian said, his pain-hazed eyes sharpening.

Feyre nodded in agreement. "Briallyn knows we have the other two items. She sent those soldiers to get the Harp."

Cassian growled. "I thought Eris was being an asshole, but when I told him about the two dozen soldiers in Oorid, he said there had been more in the unit that disappeared." He rubbed his jaw. "I should have listened. Should have looked into it. Briallyn had another dozen waiting to attack." Self-loathing filled his face, and Nesta suppressed the urge to reach for his hand.

Feyre countered, "Eris spews enough bullshit on a good day that anyone might miss an offhanded comment like that, Cass. At least we can now tell Eris where the rest of his soldiers are." Nesta could have hugged her sister for the relief that bowed Cassian's shoulders upon hearing her words. For all his arrogance, the opinions of his friends, his family, mattered deeply. None of them would ever chide him for failure, but he'd punish himself for it.

Nesta brushed her fingers against Cassian's in silent understanding. His own curled against hers, meeting her stare as if to say, *See? We're the same after all.*

Feyre went on, "If Briallyn wants the Mask and the Harp badly enough that she acted so swiftly today, she'll keep coming to us. And we'll be waiting for her." A fierce light entered her eyes.

Rhys frowned. "Even with just the Crown, though, Briallyn can do a great deal of damage. For all we know, Beron is under her control, as in thrall to her as Eris's soldiers are. We need to put an end to her and retrieve the Crown. Before war truly erupts."

"It's too risky," Feyre countered. "We pursued the Cauldron in Hybern and it went badly."

"Then we learn from our mistakes," Rhys challenged.

"She'll have set a trap," Feyre said. "We don't go after it."

Silence fell before Rhysand said, "Then we need to secure wartime alliances again—and fast. And do some damage control on the ones we already have that might be strained."

Cassian arched a brow, worry shining in his eyes. "You sound as if you have an idea."

"Eris is coming to the Winter Solstice celebration at the Hewn City," Rhys said. It was fast approaching, Nesta realized. "He's shaken by Tamlin catching you two meeting with him, and wondering if we'll balk from the alliance now that there's the slim chance Tamlin might reveal it. Or decide to sell him out first. We need to remind Eris of our continued commitment, and that he is . . . important to us. That we have his back."

Cassian snarled with disgust; Feyre echoed the expression.

"So buy him a present," Feyre said, waving a hand, "and tell him we all send our love."

"He'll want more than that," Rhys said, mouth twitching, and his eyes fell upon Nesta.

Cassian straightened before Rhys could even speak. "You're not going to use her."

Feyre glanced between them, and after a second, as if her mate had spoken into her mind, she demanded, "Really, Rhys?"

Rhys leaned back, and Nesta frowned, the only one of them apparently not aware of what this meant. Rhys said to her, "You don't have to do anything you don't wish to. But Elain mentioned that you have particular skill on the dance floor. Skill that once won you the hand of a duke in a single waltz."

She'd forgotten that night, the blur of jewels and silks and that duke's handsome face. All she'd felt then was wild, savage triumph.

"Over my dead fucking body," Cassian exploded.

Nesta asked, "You want me to dance with Eris?" Her heart began to pound, not entirely with fear.

"I want you to seduce him," Rhys said. "Not into bed, but to make him realize what he might attain once he understands that we have no plans to break this alliance. To weigh the benefits more strongly than the risks."

Nesta crossed her arms, ignoring Cassian's pointed glare, silently demanding that she dismiss this notion entirely. "You really think my dancing with Eris will solidify his loyalty?"

"I think Eris is our ally, and will expect to dance with a lady of this court at the ball no matter what. I won't let Feyre within five feet of him, Mor might kill him, and Amren is more likely to scare him off than win him over, so you and Elain are the only options."

"Elain doesn't go near him," Feyre said. "And you won't *let* me near him?"

Rhys threw her a charming smile. "You know what I mean."

Feyre rolled her eyes. "You're becoming insufferable." She turned to Nesta. "Eris isn't . . . He's not good. He's not like Beron, but he . . ."

"I know what he did to Morrigan," Nesta said. Or rather, what he didn't do: help her, when her family had brutalized her and dumped her over the Autumn Court border as punishment for ruining their marriage alliance. Eris had found her, and then merely walked away. "I dealt with him the other day. I know what I'd be getting into with him."

"Mor," Rhys went on, "can teach you the dances. She had to learn all of them, and since she still presides over the Court of Nightmares, she's the best one to instruct you."

"Nesta hasn't agreed to anything," Cassian snapped. "Even one dance with that prick is too much—"

"I'll do it," Nesta cut in, if only to spite him for being so . . . territorial. She glanced to the sword still in her hand. "I just killed an immortal being. Eris is nothing. And if it will make him remember why he wants to be allied with us, make him think he might attain me if he holds up his end, then fine."

"He's already our ally," Cassian countered. "One dance is really going to secure his continued cooperation?"

"We need to show Eris that we respect and trust him," Feyre conceded with a defeated sigh. "Even if we don't. And letting him dance with one of our family is proof of that—at least for someone from the Autumn

Court. If he winds up eating out of Nesta's hand, fantastic. If it just makes him remember that we're on his side, good. But these bonds have to be maintained."

"I don't like it," Cassian growled.

"You don't have to like it," Feyre said, head lifting, full of that High Lady's authority. "You just have to watch from the sidelines and not look like you want to rip his head off."

Nesta cut in, "Tell Morrigan I'll meet with her for dancing lessons whenever she's available."

Feyre and Cassian, still bristling at each other, silently turned toward her.

Nesta approached the desk, laying Ataraxia there. "Here," she said to Rhys. "You can take it back."

Rhys said nothing, but Feyre's brows rose. "Why don't you keep it?"

Cassian's curious stare seared her like a brand, but Nesta only said, "I have no interest in more death."

✠

Nesta inhaled through her nose for a count of six, held her breath for a few seconds, then exhaled through her mouth for another six beats. In the quiet of her bedroom that night, settled in the chair, she focused on her breath, nothing more.

Any thoughts that came in, she acknowledged and let pass. Even if some kept returning.

She didn't care where they hid the Harp. If they needed her blood to ward it as they had for the Mask, they'd let her know. But the thought of what came next—

Breathe. Count.

Nesta inhaled again, attention fixing on her expanding ribs, the feeling of the breath in her body. Even weeks into it, some days' Mind-Stilling exercises were harder than others. But she kept at it, ten minutes in the morning and ten minutes at night.

Nesta exhaled, counting. Kept going.

That was all she supposed she could do: just keep going. One day, one breath at a time.

She let that thought go, too. Breathed and breathed, and then stopped the counting altogether. Let her mind wander.

But her mind did not shoot in every direction. It remained calm. Resting.

Content right where it was.

✢

War had left the cottage untouched. But the harsh winters since Nesta had last seen it had not been so kind.

Azriel had winnowed her and Cassian here after training, but hadn't lingered. Apparently, Gwyn wanted him to go over dagger handling, so he'd left them with a promise to return in an hour.

Nesta had no idea if an hour would be too much, or too little. Had no idea why she'd asked Cassian to come here with her, really. But she'd gotten it into her head that she needed to visit. To see this place.

The midday autumn sun made the disrepair all the more stark: the thatched roof that had molded or balded in spots, the overgrown weeds already turning brown before the winter, rising up to the small windows in the stone walls. Nesta's throat tightened, but she forced herself to walk toward the entry.

Cassian remained silent behind her, footsteps so quiet he could have been the brisk wind through the too-tall grasses. His head and arm had been fully healed by this morning, two days after Nesta had agreed to bewitch Eris. Cassian had even exercised alongside her earlier, though at a slower pace than usual. Like he was indeed heeding Rhys and Madja's warning to go easy. That he'd gone through the exercises without grimacing had caused some intrinsic part of her to sigh with relief—and dare ask him to join her today. She'd never have invited him along if he'd still been injured.

Not that there was much of an enemy here to pose a threat. No humans wandered the leaf-strewn road beyond the cottage; only a few birds chirped a halfhearted melody from the almost barren trees.

Muted, drab, and empty. That was how this land felt, even with autumn upon it. As if even the sun couldn't be bothered to shine properly here.

Nesta's heart thundered as she laid a hand against the cold wooden door. Claw marks still gouged it.

"Tamlin's handiwork, I take it?" Cassian asked behind her.

Nesta shrugged, unable to find the words. She and Elain had rehung the door after Tamlin had broken it. Their father, his leg wrecked beyond repair and unable to bear weight, had watched them, offering unhelpful advice.

Her fingers curled into a fist and she shouldered the door open. Its rusted hinges objected, creaking, and a dusty, half-rotten scent swarmed her nose.

Her cheeks heated. For Cassian to be here, to see this—

"Just a brute, remember?" He stepped to her side. "I've lived in far worse. At least you had walls and a roof."

Nesta hadn't realized how much she needed to hear those words, and her shoulders loosened as she stepped into the cottage proper. In the chill dimness, broken only by rays of sunlight, she frowned at the ceiling. "This house *used* to have a roof." The damage had let in all manner of creatures and weather—the former had made themselves comfortable, judging by the nests and various scattered droppings.

Nesta's mouth turned dry. This horrible, awful, dark place.

She couldn't stop her shaking.

Cassian laid a hand on her shoulder. "Walk me through it."

She couldn't. Couldn't find the words.

He pointed to a long worktable. One leg had collapsed, and the whole thing lay at a slant. "You ate here?"

She nodded. They'd eaten here, some meals in silence, some with her and Elain trying to fill the quiet with their idle chatter, some with her and Feyre at each other's throats. Like those last meals they'd had with her in this house.

Nesta's stare drifted to the paint flaking off the walls. The intricate little designs. Cassian followed her stare. "Did Feyre paint that?"

Nesta swallowed, and managed to get out, "She painted every chance she got. Any extra coin she managed to save went toward paints."

"Have you ever seen what she's done to the cabin up in the mountains?"

"No." She'd never been there.

"Feyre painted the whole thing. Just like this. She told me once that there's a dresser here . . ."

Nesta aimed for the bedroom. "This one?" Cassian followed her, and gods, it was so cramped and dark and smelly. The bed was still covered with its stained linens. The three of them had slept here for years.

Cassian ran a hand over the painted dresser, marveling. "She really did paint stars for herself before she knew Rhys was her mate. Before she knew he existed." His fingers traced the twining vines of flowers on the second drawer. "Elain's drawer." They drifted lower, curling over a lick of flame. "And yours."

Nesta managed a grunt of confirmation, her chest tight to the point of pain. There in the corner sat a pair of worn, half-rotted shoes. Her shoes. One of them was bursting at the toe's seam. She'd worn those shoes—in public. Could still remember mud and stones creeping in.

Her heart thundered, and she walked out of the room, back into the main space.

She didn't mean to, but she looked toward the dark fireplace. Toward the mantel.

Her father's wood figurines lay atop it, thickly coated with dust and cobwebs. Some had been knocked over, presumably by whatever creatures now lived here.

That familiar roaring filled her ears, and Nesta's steps thudded too loudly on the dusty floorboards as she approached the fireplace.

A carving of a rearing bear—no bigger than her fist—sat in the center. Nesta's fingers shook as she picked it up and blew off the dust.

"He had some skill," Cassian said quietly.

"Not enough," Nesta said, setting the bear back onto the stone mantel. She was going to vomit.

No. She could master this. Master herself. And face what lay before her.

She inhaled through her nose. Exhaled through her mouth. Counted the breaths.

Cassian stood beside her through all of it. Not speaking, not touching. Just there, should she need him. Her friend—whom she'd asked to come here with her not because he was sharing her bed, but because she *wanted* him here. His steadiness and kindness and understanding.

She plucked another figurine from the mantel: a rose carved from a dark sort of wood. She held it in her palm, its solid weight surprising, and traced a finger over one of the petals. "He made this one for Elain. Since it was winter and she missed the flowers."

"Did he ever make any for you?"

"He knew better than to do that." She inhaled a shuddering breath, held it, released it. Let her mind calm. "I think he would have, if I'd given him the smallest bit of encouragement, but . . . I never did. I was too angry."

"You'd had your life overturned. You were allowed to be angry."

"That's not what you told me the first time we met." She pivoted to find him arching a brow. "You told me I was a piece of shit for letting my younger sister go into the woods to hunt while I did nothing."

"I didn't say it like that."

"The message was the same." She squared her shoulders, turning to the small, broken cot in the shadows beyond the fireplace. "And you were right." He didn't reply as she strode to the cot. "My father slept here for years, letting us have the bedroom. That bed in there . . . I was born in that bed. My mother died in that bed. I hate that bed." She ran a hand over the cracking wood of the cot's frame. Splinters snagged at her fingertips. "But I hate this cot even more. He'd drag it in front of the fire every night and curl up there, huddling under the blankets. I always thought he looked so . . . so *weak*. Like a cowering animal. It enraged me."

"Does it enrage you now?" A casual, but careful question.

"It . . ." Her throat worked. "I thought him sleeping here was a fitting punishment while we got the bed. It never occurred to me that he *wanted* us to have the bed, to keep warm and be as comfortable as we could. That we'd only been able to take a few items of furniture from our former home and he'd chosen that bed as one of them. For our comfort. So we didn't have to sleep on cots, or on the floor." She rubbed at her chest. "I wouldn't even let him sleep in the bed when the debtors shattered his leg. I was so lost in my grief and rage and . . . and sorrow, that I wanted him to feel a fraction of what I did." Her stomach churned.

He squeezed her shoulder, but said nothing.

"He had to have known that," she said hoarsely. "He *had* to have known how awful I was, and yet . . . he never yelled. That enraged me, too. And then he named a ship after me. Sailed it into battle. I just . . . I don't understand why."

"You were his daughter."

"And that's an explanation?" She scanned his face, the sadness etched there. Sadness—for her. For the ache in her chest and the stinging in her eyes.

"Love is complicated."

She dropped his stare at that. She was a coward for avoiding his gaze. But she lifted her chin. "I never once considered what it was like for him. To go from this man who had made his own fortune, become known as the Prince of Merchants, and then lose everything. I don't think losing my mother broke him the same way as losing his fleet. He'd been so sure the venture would gain him even more wealth—an obscene amount of wealth. People told him he was mad, but he refused to listen. When they were proved right . . . I think that humiliation broke him as much as the financial loss."

She studied the calluses already building across her fingers and palms. "The debtors seemed gleeful when they came here—like they'd resented him all this time and were more than happy to take it out on his leg. I spent the entire time more terrified for what they'd do to me and Elain. Feyre . . . She tried to get them to stop. Stayed here with him while we hid in the bedroom." She made herself meet Cassian's gaze again. "I didn't just fail Feyre by letting her go into the woods. There were plenty of other times."

"Have you ever told her this?"

Nesta snorted. "No. I don't know how."

He studied her, and she resisted the urge to squirm under the scrutiny. "You'll learn how. When you're ready."

"How very wise of you."

Cassian sketched a bow.

Despite this house, the history all around her, Nesta smiled. She pocketed the carved rose. "I've seen enough."

He arched a brow. "Really?"

She clenched the wooden rose in her pocket. "I think I just needed to see this place. One last time. To know we got out. That there's nothing left here except dust and bad memories."

He slid an arm around her waist as they walked for the door, again surveying all the little paintings Feyre had squeezed into the cottage. "Az won't be back for a little while. Let's go flying."

"What about the humans?" They'd run screaming in terror.

Cassian gave her a wicked smile, opening that half-broken door for her. Leading her into the sunlight and clean air. "It'll add a little spice to their days."

CHAPTER 56

A month passed, and winter crept upon Velaris like hoarfrost over a windowpane.

Morning training became a chilled affair, their breath clouding the frosted air as they worked with swords and knives, the metal so cold it bit into their palms. Even their shields sometimes became crusted with frost. Valkyries learned to fight in all kinds of weather, Gwyn told them. Especially the cold. So when snow fell occasionally, Nesta and the others trained, too.

Nesta had to switch into another size of leathers, and when she looked in the mirror each morning to braid her hair, the face that stared back had lost its gauntness, the shadows beneath the eyes. Even with Cassian fucking her on every surface of the House, sometimes until the early hours of the morning, the exhaustion, the purple bruises under her eyes, had vanished.

She told herself it didn't matter that he never stayed in her bed afterward to hold her. She wondered when he'd grow tired of it—of her. Surely he'd get bored and move on. Even if he feasted on her each night as if he were starving. Gripped her thighs in his powerful hands and licked and suckled at her until she writhed. Sometimes she straddled his face, hands clenching the headboard, and rode his tongue until she came on it. Sometimes it was her tongue on him, around him, and she swallowed down every drop he spilled into her mouth. Sometimes he spilled on her chest, her stomach, her back, and she came at the first splash of him on her skin.

She couldn't imagine tiring of him. Having him over and over only made her need grow.

She'd been practicing dances with Morrigan in the House study twice a week, the two of them barely swapping more than a few words as Nesta learned waltz after waltz, some particular to the Hewn City, others to the Autumn Court, others to the Fae in general.

Rhys had given them the Veritas orb so Morrigan might share with Nesta her memories of the dances—and the music that accompanied them.

Nesta had watched the steps, the balls and parties that were sometimes full of light and others that had darkness and sorrow around the edges. Morrigan had offered no explanation beyond comments about a dancer's technique.

The music, though . . . It was brilliant. So full of life and motion that she always found herself wishing she had another hour or two of lessons just to hear it again and again and again.

No one ever showed up to watch them, not even Cassian. If Morrigan reported on their progress, she never let on.

Now, with Winter Solstice three days away, Morrigan was wrapping up her lesson as snow drifted past the wall of windows. She asked Nesta suddenly, "What are you wearing to the ball, anyway?"

Nesta, leaning against the worktable to catch her breath and listening to the strains of the violin through the Veritas orb's shimmering mirage, shrugged. "One of my dresses."

"Oh, no." Sweat beaded on Morrigan's brow, and her braided golden hair curled slightly with the moisture. "Eris . . ." She searched for the words. "He's all about appearances. You have to wear the right thing."

Nesta considered what Morrigan usually wore, and frowned. "I can't wear something that revealing." Both Morrigan and Feyre opted for *less is more* when it came to their Hewn City attire. Nesta had no issues with nudity before her bedroom partners, but in public . . . The human had not been ripped from her entirely.

"I'll look around." Morrigan pushed off the windowsill. "See what we have."

"Thank you, Morrigan."

It was the first normal conversation they'd had. The first time Nesta had even uttered those words to Morrigan. Ever said her name.

Morrigan blinked, realizing it, too. "It's just Mor, you know. Amren is the only person in this court who calls me Morrigan, and that's because she's a cranky old bastard."

Nesta's lips twitched upward. "Very well, then." She added, trying it out, "Mor."

The clock chimed one, and Nesta began walking out the door, leaving the orb and its soaring music where it lay on the desk. "I need to head to the library." She was already going to be late, but the music had been so enthralling she hadn't wanted to stop.

"So do I, actually," Morrigan—Mor—said, and they fell into step in the hall. "The work I'm doing for Rhys and Feyre in Vallahan requires some research, and Clotho has been looking into it for me."

"Ah."

Stilted silence fell as they strode down the stairs, then into another hall.

The towering doors to the library appeared before Nesta asked, "Does it bother you that I'll be dancing with Eris?"

Mor considered. "No. Because I know you're going to make him crawl before the end of it."

It wasn't a compliment. Not really.

They found Clotho at her usual desk. She rose, greeting Mor with an embrace that left Nesta speechless.

"My old friend," Mor said, her face lit with warmth. The face she showed everyone in this court except for Nesta. And those in the Hewn City.

Shame tightened Nesta's gut. But she said nothing as Clotho's enchanted pen and paper wrote, *You look well, Mor.*

"Eh." Mor lifted a shoulder. "Nesta's been running me ragged with dancing lessons, but I've been fine."

I found the books you requested. Clotho placed a crooked hand atop a pile of books on her desk.

Nesta took that as her cue to leave, and nodded to the females as they fell into a discussion about the material. Gwyn was waiting a level below, watching them—with Emerie in the stacks behind her.

"What are you doing here?" Nesta asked Emerie. She'd still been in the training ring when Nesta had hurried off to her dancing lesson. But that had been hours ago.

"I wanted to see where you two work," Emerie said, eyes upon Clotho and Mor a level above. She sighed, nodding toward Mor. "I always forget how beautiful she is. "She never comes to Windhaven these days." Nesta could have sworn pink stole over Emerie's brown cheeks.

Indeed, in the library's deep gloom, Mor shone like a ray of sunshine. Even the darkness at its bottom seemed to slither away.

"I was showing Emerie the wonders of Merrill's office while she's off at a meeting," Gwyn said. "I've got to go work, but I thought you could bring her around while you shelve." Gwyn threw her a wry glance. "And dance."

Nesta rolled her eyes. She might have been caught practicing her waltzes in the stacks once or twice. Or ten times.

Nesta nodded to Emerie, drawing the female's gaze away from Mor's animated hand gestures. "Come on."

But Gwyn said, "Actually, before you two go, I wanted to give you something. Since it's probably the last time we'll see each other until Winter Solstice is over."

Nesta and Emerie swapped confused looks. The latter asked, "You got us presents?"

Gwyn only said, "I'll meet you down at your cart." With that, she dashed into the gloom.

Emerie and Nesta aimed for Level Five, where Nesta had left her cart. It had been replenished with books needing to be shelved. She explained what she did, but Emerie seemed to be half-listening. Her face had gone pale.

"What?" Nesta asked.

Emerie's brows bunched. "I . . . I must not have drunk enough water during training." They'd tried out two new Valkyrie techniques that Gwyn had found the night before, and both had been particularly brutal, ordering them to use shields as springboards for launching a fellow Valkyrie into the skies, and to do their abdominal curls bearing the weights of those shields.

No one had managed to cut the ribbon, though Emerie had nicked an edge two days ago.

"What's wrong?" Nesta pressed.

Emerie's eyes turned bleak. "It's . . . I swear, I can hear my father yelling down here." Her hands trembled as she lifted one to brush a strand of hair behind an ear. "I can hear him screaming at me, can hear the furniture breaking . . ."

Nesta's blood went cold. She whipped her head to the downward slope to their right. No darkness lurked there, but they were low enough . . . "This place is ancient and strange," she said, even as she processed what Emerie had admitted. She had never spoken of her father beyond the wing clipping. But Nesta had gathered enough: the man had been a beast like Tomas Mandray's father.

"Let's go up a level, where the darkness doesn't whisper so loudly.

I'm sure Gwyn will find us easily enough." She linked her arm with Emerie's, pressing her body close, letting some of her warmth leak into her friend.

Emerie nodded, though she remained wan.

Nesta wondered if Emerie heard her father's bellowing every step of the way.

Gwyn did find them, the priestess panting and flushed as she handed out two rectangular parcels, each roughly the size of a large, thin book. "One for each of you."

Nesta opened the brown paper and beheld a stack of pages filled with writing. At the top of the first page, it merely said, *Chapter Twenty-One*. She read the first few lines beneath it, then nearly dropped the pages. "This—this is about *us*."

Gwyn beamed. "I convinced Merrill to add us into the penultimate chapter. She even let me write it—with her own annotations, of course. But it's about the rebirth of the Valkyries. About what we're doing."

Nesta had no words. Emerie's hands were once more shaking as she leafed through the pages. "You had *this* much to say about us?" Emerie said, choking on a laugh.

Gwyn rubbed her hands together. "With more to come."

Nesta read a line at random on the fifth page. *Whether the sun beat hot on their brows or freezing rain turned their bones to ice, Nesta, Emerie, and Gwyneth arrived at practice each morning, ready to . . .*

The back of her throat ached; her eyes stung. "We're in a book."

Gwyn's fingers slid into hers, squeezing tight. Nesta looked up to find her holding Emerie's free hand as well. Gwyn smiled again, her eyes bright. "Our stories are worth telling."

⸸

Nesta was still reeling from the generosity of Gwyn's gift that evening when she found a note from Cassian, telling her he needed to stay overnight in one of the Illyrian outposts to deal with some petty squabble between war-bands. With the Blood Rite mere months away, he'd said, tensions were always high, but this year seemed particularly bad. New feuds popping up every few days, old grudges resurfacing . . . Nesta, despite the note's contents, had smiled to herself, picturing Cassian's take-no-bullshit face as he laid down the law.

But her amusement had soon faded, and though she tried Mind-Stilling twice after dinner, she couldn't get herself to settle. Kept thinking of Gwyn's gift, of Emerie's terrified face as she sensed whatever was in the darkness.

Sitting at her desk, staring at nothing, Nesta cupped her forehead in her palm.

A mug of hot chocolate appeared beside her, along with a handful of shortbread. Nesta chuckled. "Thank you."

She sipped from her drink, nearly sighing at the richness of the cocoa. "I'd like to try a fire," she said quietly. "A small one."

Instantly, the House had a tiny blaze going in the fireplace. A log popped, and Nesta straightened, stomach twisting.

It was a fire. Not her father's neck. Her gaze shifted to the carved wooden rose she'd placed upon the mantel, half-hidden in the shadows beside a figurine of a supple-bodied female, her upraised arms clasping a full moon between them. Some sort of primal goddess—perhaps even the Mother herself. Nesta hadn't let herself dwell on why she'd felt the need to set the rose there. Why she hadn't just thrown it in a drawer.

Another log cracked, and Nesta flinched. But she remained sitting there. Staring at that carved rose.

Would she live the rest of her life like Emerie, always glancing over a shoulder for the shadow of the past to haunt her? Did she appear as Emerie had this afternoon, terrified and pained?

She owed herself more than that. Emerie, too, deserved more. A chance to live a life without fear and dread.

So Nesta could try. Right now. She'd face this fire.

Another log cracked. Nesta ground her teeth. *Breathe. Inhale for six, hold, exhale for six.*

She did just that.

This is a fire. It reminds you of your father, of something horrible happening. But this is not him, and while you are feeling uncomfortable, you can get through it.

Nesta focused on her breathing. Made herself unclench each of her too-tight muscles, starting with her face and working all the way down to her toes.

All while she told herself, over and over, *This is a fire. It makes you uncomfortable. This is why you react as you do. You can breathe through this. Work through this.*

Her body didn't loosen, but she was able to sit there. Endure the fire until it dimmed to embers, and then went out entirely.

She didn't know why she found herself on the verge of tears as the cinders smoldered. Didn't know why the rush of pride that filled her chest made her want to laugh and whoop and dance around the room. She hadn't done anything more than sit by a fire, but . . . she had sat. Stayed.

She had not failed. She had faced it and survived.

She might not have saved the world or led armies, but she had made this small, initial step.

Nesta wiped at her eyes, and when she looked around her quiet room, she startled to find a trail of evergreen twigs leading to her now-open door.

Cocking a brow, she rose. "What's all this about?" she asked the House, following the trail it had left.

Down the hall, along the stairs, all the way down to the library itself. "Where are we going?" Nesta asked the warm air. Mercifully, even the night owls amongst the priestesses had gone to sleep, leaving no one to see her hurrying after the trail of branches. Around the levels of the library they twined, deeper and deeper, until they reached the seventh level.

Nesta drew up short as the trail stopped at the edge of the wall of darkness.

A light flickered beyond it. Several lights.

As if to say, *Come. Don't be afraid.*

So Nesta sucked in a breath as she stepped into the gloom.

Little tea lights wended into a familiar darkness. She and Feyre had once ventured down here—had faced horrors here. No evidence remained of that day. Only the firelit dimness, the candles leading her to the lowest levels of the library.

To the pit itself.

Nesta followed them, spiraling to the bottom of the pit, where one small lantern glowed, faintly illuminating the rows of books veiled in permanent shadow around it.

Heart racing, Nesta lifted the lantern in one hand and gazed at the darkness, untouched by the light from the library high, high above. The heart of the world, of existence. Of self.

The heart of the House.

"This . . ." Her fingers tightened on the lantern. "This darkness is *your* heart."

As if in answer, the House laid a little evergreen sprig at her feet.

"A Winter Solstice present. For me."

She could have sworn a warm hand brushed her neck in answer. "But your darkness . . ." Wonder softened her voice. "You were trying to show me. Show others. Who you are, down deep. What haunts you. You were trying to show them all those dark, broken pieces because the priestesses, and Emerie, and I . . . We're the same as you."

Her throat constricted at what the House had gifted her. This knowledge.

She lifted the lantern higher and blew out its flame.

Let the darkness sweep in. Embraced it.

"I'm not afraid," she whispered into it. "You are my friend, and my home. Thank you for sharing this with me."

Again, Nesta could have sworn that phantom touch caressed her neck, her cheek, her brow.

"Happy Solstice," she said into the beautiful, fractured darkness.

CHAPTER 57

Cassian normally looked forward to Winter Solstice for a host of reasons, starting with the usual three days of drinking with his family and ending with the riotous fun of his annual snowball fight with his brothers. Followed by a steam in the birchin and more drinking, usually until all three of them passed out in variously stupid positions. One year, he'd awoken wearing a blond wig and nothing but an evergreen garland around his groin like a loincloth. It had itched and scratched awfully—though it was nothing compared to his pounding hangover.

He supposed, at its root, he loved the Winter Solstice because it was uninterrupted time with the people he treasured most.

This year, just as it had last year, it filled him with nothing but churning acid.

The Court of Nightmares was decorated as it usually was, adorned for the celebration that lasted three whole days surrounding the longest night of the year. Each night held a different ball, and at the first of them, Nesta would dance with Eris.

Tonight. In a matter of moments.

He'd had a month to prepare for this. A month of being in Nesta's bed—or at least fucking her in it. The Cauldron knew she hadn't ever asked him to stay after he pulled out of her.

He stood at the foot of the black dais, staring out at the glittering throng with a face that promised death. Az stood on the other side of the dais, wearing a similar expression.

Each and every one of the people here could fucking burn in hell.

Starting with Keir, at the head of the gathered crowd. Ending with Eris, standing proud and tall—wearing Night Court black—beside him.

Mor stood by Feyre's and Rhysand's thrones, representing them until they arrived.

The entire throne room was bedecked in black candles, evergreen wreaths and garlands, and holly berries. The twin banquet tables flanking either side of the massive space overflowed with food, but it was forbidden to all until Feyre and Rhys allowed it.

He'd lightened some of his Night Triumphant demeanor with the people of the Hewn City lately, but not by much. Cassian didn't envy Rhys his juggling act. They couldn't isolate Keir, not if they were to need his Darkbringers again. Hence the nicer tone. But they couldn't let him forget the ass-kicking he'd receive if he stepped out of line. Hence the only *slightly* nicer tone.

They'd heard nothing of the Crown, nothing from Briallyn. She had not come for the Trove. Cassian wasn't stupid enough to believe it was over. None of them were.

The towering doors to the throne room at last yawned open.

Dark power rumbled through the mountain, warning of their approach. The mountain sang with it. Everyone turned as the High Lord and High Lady appeared, crowned and garbed in black.

Rhys looked his usual handsome self, but Feyre . . .

The room gasped.

Tonight also served another purpose: to tell the world of Feyre's pregnancy.

She wore a dress of sparkling black panels, much like the one she'd first worn here—and it did nothing to hide her swelling belly.

No, it showed off her pregnant womb, gleaming in the candlelight.

Rhys's face was a portrait of smug, male pride. Cassian knew he'd shred anyone who so much as blinked wrong at Feyre into a million bloody ribbons. Indeed, cold violence rippled off Rhys as they walked toward the dais, Feyre's baby-rich scent filling the air. He'd let everyone here smell it, further confirming that she was with child.

Feyre might as well have been a goddess of old, crowned and glowing, her belly swollen with life. Her serene face was lovely, and her full red lips parted in a smile at Rhys as they aimed for their thrones. Keir looked torn between anger and shock; Eris's face was carefully neutral.

Motion at the back of the room tugged Cassian's stare from his enemies, and then—

Both sisters wore black. Both walked behind Rhys and Feyre, a silent indicator that they were a part of the royal family. Had mighty powers of their own. They'd planned it that way, wanting Eris to see for himself how valuable Nesta was. Cassian wondered if Elain and Nesta had broken their silence while waiting for their entrance. They hadn't spoken to each other for months now.

Elain in black was ridiculous. Yes, she was beautiful, but the color of her long-sleeved, modest gown leeched the brightness from her face. It wore her, rather than the other way around. And he knew the cruelty of the Hewn City troubled her. But she hadn't hesitated to come. When Feyre had offered to let her remain home, Elain had squared her shoulders and declared that she was a part of this court—and would do whatever was needed. So Elain had let her golden-brown hair down tonight, and pinned it back with twin combs of pearl. He'd never once in the two years he'd known her found Elain to be plain, but wearing black, no matter how much she claimed to be part of this court . . . It sucked the life from her.

Nesta in Night Court black threatened to bring him to his knees.

She'd braided her hair over her head in her usual style, but atop it, a delicate tiara of glinting black stone rested, slender spikes jutting upward in a dark corona. Each spike was topped with a tiny sapphire, as if the spikes were so sharp they'd pierced the sky and drawn cobalt blood.

And the dress . . .

Silver thread embroidered the skintight velvet bodice, the straps so narrow they might as well have been nothing against her moon-white skin. The neckline plunged nearly to her navel, where the silver thread gathered to hold a small sapphire that matched the ones on her crown. The full skirts brushed the dark floor, rustling in the rippling silence.

Nesta's chin remained high, accentuating her long, lovely neck. Her red-painted lips cocked in a feline smirk as her kohl-lined eyes took in the room watching her every breath.

Nesta seemed to glow with the attention. Owned it. Commanded it.

Feyre and Rhys took their thrones, and Nesta and Elain came to stand at the foot of the dais, between him and Azriel. Cassian didn't dare say a word to Nesta, or even glance at her, at the body on display—the body he'd tasted so many times now it was a miracle no imprint of his lips lay against her neck.

He didn't dare look at Eris, either. One glance and it'd give away their entire game. Even her scent—*his* scent, Cassian knew with no small amount of satisfaction—had been carefully glamoured to hide any trace of him.

Feyre declared to the assembled crowd, "May the blessings of the Winter Solstice be upon you."

Keir scuttled forward, bowing low. "Allow me to extend my congratulations." Cassian knew the bastard didn't mean a word of it.

Eris stalked to his side, their honored guest. "And allow me to extend mine as well, on behalf of my father and the entire Autumn Court." He flashed Feyre a pretty, cultivated smile. "He shall be thrilled by this news."

Rhys's mouth curled in a cruel half smile, the stars winking out in his eyes. "I'm sure he will."

There was no pretending tonight: Rhys truly was the High Lord of the Court of Nightmares while Feyre and their babe were here. He'd slaughter anyone who threatened them. And enjoy it.

Rhys said to no one in particular, "Music."

An orchestra hidden in a screened-in mezzanine began playing.

Feyre raised her voice and said, "Go—eat." The crowd undulated as people aimed for the tables.

Only Eris and Keir remained before them. Neither spared Mor so much as a glance, though she smirked down at them, her red dress like a flame in the gloom of the hall.

Cassian, in his black armor, felt more like the beasts carved into the towering pillars beneath this mountain. He'd brushed his hair and left it loose, and that had been the extent of his grooming for tonight. He'd spent most of his time thinking about how he'd like to peel Eris's skin off in tiny strips, how Rhys and Feyre had crossed a line by asking this of Nesta. He loved them both, but they could have found another way to ensure Eris's allegiance. Not that Cassian had come up with a better alternative.

At least Briallyn and Koschei had not yet acted further. Though he had no doubt they'd be making their next move soon.

Feyre commanded the crowd, her voice like thunder at midnight, "Dance."

People paired off and fell seamlessly into the music. Keir went with them this time.

"Before you join the merriment, Eris," Rhys drawled, a long black box appearing in his hands, "I'd like to present you with your Solstice gift."

Cassian kept his face blank. Rhys had gotten the bastard a *gift*?

Rhys floated the box over to Eris on a night-kissed wind. Let enough of that wind remain, wrapping behind Eris, for Cassian to know it blocked him from sight. From Keir's sight, specifically.

Eris lifted his brows, flipping open the carved lid. He stiffened, voice going low. "What is this?"

"A present," Rhys said, and Cassian caught a glimpse of a familiar hilt in the box.

The dagger Nesta had Made. Cassian refrained from whirling on Rhys and Feyre, demanding to know what the hell they were thinking.

Eris sucked in a breath. Feyre said, "You can sense its power."

"There's flame in it," Eris said, not touching the dagger. As if his own magic warned him. He shut the lid, face slightly pale. "Why give this to me?"

"You're our ally," Feyre said, a hand resting on her belly. "You face enemies that exist outside of the usual rules of magic. It seemed only fair to give you a weapon that operates outside those rules, too."

"This is truly Made, then."

Cassian braced himself for the truth, the damning, dangerous truth to be revealed about Nesta. But Rhys said, "From my personal collection. A family heirloom."

"You possessed a Made item and kept it hidden all these years? During the war?"

"Don't take our generosity for granted," Feyre warned Eris quietly.

Eris stilled, but nodded. He extended the box back to Rhys. "I'll leave it in your keeping while I dance, then." He added with what Cassian could have sworn was sincerity, "Thank you."

Feyre nodded as Rhys took the box and set it beside his throne. "Use it well." She smiled softly at Eris. "Ordinarily I would ask you to dance, but my condition has left me unwell enough that I worry about what so much spinning would do to my stomach." It was the truth. Feyre had bolted from dinner three nights ago to find the nearest toilet. Now she made a show of looking between her two sisters. Elain gave a passable impression of appearing interested. Nesta just looked bored. Like they hadn't just given away the dagger she'd Made.

Perhaps it was because Nesta's eyes had drifted toward the dancing, shimmering throng. As if she couldn't help herself when the music swelled. She seemed to be half-listening. Maybe music meant more to her than the dagger—more than magic and power.

Feyre noted the direction of Nesta's stare. "My oldest sister shall take my place."

Nesta barely glanced to Eris, who pulled his assessing gaze from Elain to stare at the eldest Archeron sister with a mix of wariness and intent that set Cassian's jaw grinding. Or it would have been grinding, if he hadn't mastered himself in time to keep his face blank as Nesta began walking toward Eris.

Eris offered an arm, and Nesta took it, her face neutral, her chin high, each step gliding. They halted at the edge of the dance floor, pulling apart to face each other.

Others watched from the sidelines as the dance finished and the introductory strains of the next began, a harp strumming high and sweet. Eris extended a hand, a half smile on his mouth.

As if those harp strings wrapped around Nesta's arm, she raised it, and placed her hand in his precisely as the last, swift pluck of the harp sounded.

Percussion and horns blasted; low stringed instruments started a rushing stroke of music. A summons to the dance in a countdown to movement. Cassian reminded himself to breathe as Eris slid his broad hand over Nesta's waist, tucking her in close. She lifted her chin, looking up into his face as a deep-bellied drum thumped.

And as the violins began their sweeping song, a beckoning back-and-forth, Nesta moved as if her very breath were timed to the music.

Eris went with her, and it was clear that he knew the dance's nuances and exact notes, but Nesta . . .

She gathered her skirts in her other hand, and as Eris led her into the waltz's opening movements, her body went loose and taut in so many different places Cassian didn't know where to look: she was bent and shaped and directed by the sound.

Even Eris's eyes widened at it—the sheer skill and grace, each movement of her body precisely tuned to each note and flutter of music, from her fingertips to the extension of her neck as she turned, the arch of her back into a held note. Cassian dared a glance at Feyre and Rhys and found even their normally composed faces had gone a bit slack.

By the time Nesta and Eris finished their first rotation through the dance floor, Cassian had the growing feeling that Elain had rather undersold her sister's abilities.

⸸

The music burned through Nesta.

Had there ever been such a perfect, half-wild sound in the world? Mor's memories on the Veritas were nothing compared to this, hearing it performed live, dancing through it. It flowed and swam around her, filling her blood, and if she could have done so, she would have melted into the melody, become the rolling drums, the soaring violins, the clashing cymbals with the counter-beat, the horns and reeds with their high-arcing song.

There wasn't enough space inside her for the sound, for all it made her feel—not enough space in her mind, her heart, her body; and all she could do to honor it, worship it, was dance.

Eris, to his credit, kept up.

She held his eyes throughout each step, let him feel her supple body, how pliant it was as she arched into a cluster of notes. His hand tightened on her, fingers digging into the groove of her spine, and she let a small smile rise to her red-painted lips.

She had never worn such a color on her mouth. It looked like sin personified. But Mor had done it, along with the swoop of liquid kohl over her upper eyelids. And when Nesta had looked in the mirror at last, she hadn't seen herself staring back.

She'd seen a Queen of the Night. As merciless and cold and beautiful as the god Lanthys had wanted to make her. Death's Consort.

Death herself.

Eris released her waist to spin her, and it was no effort to time her rotation to the flutter of notes, her gaze locking back to his exactly as the music returned to the melody. Flame simmered in his eyes, and he spun her again—not a prescribed move in the dance, but she followed through, snapping her head around to meet his gaze once more, her skirts twirling.

His lips curled with approval, his test passed.

Nesta smirked back at him, letting her eyes glitter. *Make him crawl*, Mor had said. And she would.

But first she would dance.

✠

Cassian knew the waltz. Had watched and danced it for centuries. Knew its last half minute was a swift frenzy of notes and rising, grand sound. Knew most dancers would keep waltzing through it, but the brave ones, the skilled ones would do the twelve spins, the female blindly turning with one arm above her head, rotated again and again and again by her partner as they moved across the dance floor. To spin was to risk looking the fool at best, to eat marble at worst.

Nesta went for it.

And Eris went with her, eyes blazing with feral delight.

The music stomped into its crashing finale, drums striking, violins whirring, and the entire room straightened, eyes upon Nesta.

Upon Nesta, this once-human female who had conquered death, who now glowed as if she had devoured the moon, too.

Between one beat and the next, Eris lifted Nesta's arm above her head and whipped her around with such force her heels rose off the ground. She'd barely finished the rotation when he spun her again, her head turning with such precision it took Cassian's breath away.

And her feet . . .

One spin after another after another, moving across the now-empty dance floor like a night storm, Nesta's slipper-clad feet danced so fast they were a near blur. He knew that Eris turned her arm, but her feet held her, propelled them. It was she who led this dance. On the seventh spin, she twirled so swiftly she rose fully onto her toes.

On the ninth spin, Eris released her fingers. And Nesta, arm still stretched above her head, rotated thrice more. Each one of the sapphires atop her tiara glimmered as if lit with an inner fire. Someone gasped nearby. It might have been Feyre.

And as Nesta spun solo—on the toes of one perfect foot—she smiled. Not a courtier's slick smile, not a coy one, but one of pure, wild joy, brought by the music and the dance and her wholehearted yield to it.

It was like seeing someone being born. Like seeing someone come alive.

By the time Nesta finished the last rotation, that absurd defiance of basic laws of movement and space, Eris had her hand again, spinning her three more times, his red hair glinting like fire as if in echo to the unchecked, dark joy bursting from her.

Nesta's mother had wanted a prince for her. Cassian now thought she'd undervalued her daughter. Only a king or an emperor would do for someone with that level of skill.

She was seducing Eris within an inch of his life. The murmuring of the Hewn City confirmed that Cassian wasn't the only one noting it.

Eris's eyes gleamed with wanton desire as he drank in Nesta's smile, the glow about her. He knew what Nesta might become with a little ambition. The right guidance.

If he learned that the Dread Trove answered to her, that she'd Made his new dagger . . .

It was a mistake, to bring her here. To dangle her before Eris, the world.

Emerging from her cocoon of grief and rage, this new Nesta might very well send entire courts to their knees. Kingdoms.

The music rose and rose and rose, faster and faster and faster, and as its last few notes sounded, Eris again released her. Nesta spun solo once more, three more precise, perfect rotations as Eris dropped to a knee before her and held up a hand.

The final note blasted and held, and Nesta halted with preternatural ease, taking Eris's hand in the same movement that her back arched and she flung up her other arm, the portrait of triumph.

✠

The next dance began, and Nesta did not hesitate when Eris led her into it. It was a lighter, easier dance than the first, whose music had been a song in her blood.

Her partner might be a monster, but he knew how to dance. Had known how her body screamed to do those extra, solo turns, and let her go free not once but twice, and even then it had not been enough. If she hadn't been wearing the heavy dress, she might have begged the orchestra to play the song again so she could just execute spin after spin after spin by herself, knowing when to throw in doubles and triples by instinct and ear alone.

She was drunk on the music. But the second dance required no wild spinning or excess of emotion. As if the conductor of the orchestra hidden in this room wanted her to have a breather. Or at least talk to her partner.

Eris's amber eyes studied hers. "Trust Rhysand to keep you hidden away."

Right. She was to flatter him, keep him on their side. "I just saw you the other week."

Eris chuckled. "And as riveting as it was to see you send Tamlin scrambling off with his tail between his legs, I didn't see *this* side of you. The time since the war has changed you."

She didn't smile, but she met his stare directly as she said, "For the better, I hope."

"Certainly for the more interesting. It seems you came to play the game tonight after all." Eris spun her, and when she returned to him, he murmured in her ear, "Don't believe the lies they tell you about me."

She pulled back just enough to meet his gaze. "Oh?"

Eris nodded to where Mor watched them from beside Feyre and Rhys, her face neutral and aloof. "She knows the truth but has never revealed it."

"Why?"

"Because she is afraid of it."

"You don't win yourself any favors with your behavior."

"Don't I? Do I not ally myself with this court under constant threat of being discovered and killed by my father? Do I not offer aid whenever Rhysand wishes?" He spun her again. "They believe a version of events that is easier to swallow. I always thought Rhysand wiser than that, but he tends to be blind where those he loves are concerned."

Nesta's mouth twitched to one side. "And you? Who do you love?"

His smile sharpened. "Are you inquiring after my eligibility?"

"I'm merely saying it's hard to find a good dance partner these days."

Eris laughed, the sound like silk over her skin. She shivered. "Indeed it is. Especially one who can both dance and tear the King of Hybern's head from his shoulders."

She let him see a bit of that person—see the savage rage and silver fire he'd witnessed before Tamlin. Then she blinked and it was gone. Eris's face tightened, and not from fear.

He twirled her again, the waltz already coming to a close. He whispered in her ear, "They say your sister Elain is the beauty, but you outshine her tonight." His hand stroked down the bare skin of her back, and she arched slightly into the touch.

Nesta made her throat bob, let a hint of color rise to her cheeks.

The waltz finished, and they seamlessly fell into the next dance, a little more demanding this time. She remembered this one from her lessons with Mor—it was lovely and sweeping and like being in a dream, until its final minute became so grand it always knocked the breath from her. Anticipation thrummed through her, brightening her eyes.

"You're wasted at the Night Court," Eris murmured as she twirled, skirts enveloping the two of them. "Absolutely wasted."

"I'm not sure that's a compliment."

Another chuckle. Motion lurked at the corner of her eye, but she didn't break her stare from Eris's, didn't halt her steps until—

"Move."

Cassian's cold voice cracked through the spell of the music, halting her. He stood before them, amid the sea of people twirling around and around, and even though most wore black, his armor and blades made him seem . . . different. Like a true piece of the night.

Eris looked down his straight nose at Cassian. "I don't take orders from brutes."

Nesta stifled her snarl and said coolly to Cassian, "Am I to understand that you would like to dance with me?"

"Yes." His hazel eyes were burning with violence. Had he really believed what he'd seen on this dance floor?

Eris bared his teeth at Cassian. "Go sit at your master's feet, dog."

It took all her concentration, every moment of Mind-Stilling, to keep from ripping out Eris's throat. But Nesta shoved her fury down, to the place where she'd stifled her power. "No one likes a selfish partner, Eris." She didn't so much as look at Cassian. Didn't trust what she'd do if she beheld pain in his eyes at Eris's insult. Feyre and Rhysand had given Eris one of her blades just to ensure his continued alliance. She wouldn't jeopardize it. So she added with a croon, "Time to share."

Eris threw her a mocking smile. "We'll play later, Nesta Archeron." He ignored Cassian as he aimed for the dais again.

Alone with Cassian, the packed dance floor teeming around them, Nesta demanded, "Are you happy now?"

His face was like stone. "No." A glance over his shoulder showed her a tight-faced Rhys and Feyre, who were undoubtedly shouting at him mind to mind. But if she and Cassian lingered like this for too long, the spell she'd woven around Eris might be disrupted, and . . .

Cassian offered up his hand. Swallowed once.

He was *nervous*. This male who had faced down enemy armies, who had battled to the brink of death more times than she cared to count, who had fought so many dangers it was a miracle he lived . . . he was nervous.

It softened some crucial piece of her, and Nesta slipped her hand into his, their calluses rasping against each other. His hand slid around her waist, so large it spanned nearly halfway across. She gathered her skirts, and lifted her gaze to his.

Nesta fell back a step, leading him, them, into the dance, and Cassian went with her.

He was not graceful like Eris. He did not instinctively move to each beat like she did. But he kept up, willing to follow her into the music, into the sound and the movement, and his eyes did not, would not, leave her face.

Their steps quickened, and Cassian found his rhythm.

He spun her, and she whipped herself around, his arms waiting to catch her.

His hand on her waist tightened, his only warning as he launched them further, faster into the music. Cassian smiled at her, and the world faded away.

The music was no longer the most beautiful thing in existence. He was.

Nesta couldn't stop it then.

The answering smile that bloomed through her at last, stealing across her face, bright as the dawn.

✣

Cassian would only yield Nesta to Azriel, who swept her into a waltz as easily as breathing.

Wandering over to the wine table to pour himself a goblet, Cassian met the eyes of a few courtiers gawking at Nesta and let them see what would happen if they so much as approached her. They quickly fell away, and he leaned against a pillar, content to watch Nesta dance with his brother.

Mor was at his side a moment later, her lips curving upward. "Looks like our lessons paid off."

Cassian kissed her cheek. "I owe you one." They'd been training in secret these past weeks. Mor had been positively giddy when he'd asked for her help.

But her eyes were dark now, her face wan.

"How are you doing?" he asked neutrally, well aware of the people around them. What Mor had been and was now to them.

Mor lifted one shoulder, then let it drop. "Fine." She nodded to Nesta. "I enjoyed seeing what she did." She elbowed him in the ribs. "Though I suppose you didn't. You just *had* to cut in, didn't you?"

He crossed his arms. "Rhys can deal with it."

"It seems like Rhys is," Mor said, and Cassian followed her stare toward the dais, where Eris stood beside the thrones, speaking with Rhys and Feyre.

Without Rhys so much as blinking in their direction, Cassian found that Rhys had let him in on the conversation—he was inside Rhys's mind, seeing and hearing the conversation through Rhys's eyes. From Mor's sudden stillness, he knew she'd been brought in, too.

"All right," Eris was saying to Rhys, sliding his hands into his pockets. "You showed me what I can have, Rhysand. I'm intrigued enough to ask what you'd want in return."

Feyre blurted into Rhys's thoughts, *What?!*

Cassian wanted to echo the same, his entire body tightening. But Rhys didn't move from where he lounged on his throne. "What do you mean by that?"

Lust glazed Eris's eyes. Covetous, calculating lust. Cassian swallowed his growl. "I mean that whatever you want, I'll give it to you in exchange for her. As my bride." He jerked his chin to the box with the dagger at Rhys's feet. "I'd rather have her than that."

He danced three dances with her! Feyre squawked. Rhys's lips seemed to be fighting a losing battle not to smile.

Cassian could only stare at Eris's throat, pondering whether to strangle him or slit the skin wide open. Let him bleed out on the floor.

"That's not my decision," Rhys said calmly to Eris. "And it seems foolish for you to offer me anything I want in exchange for her, anyway."

His jaw tightened. "I have my reasons."

From the shadows in his eyes, Cassian knew something more lay beneath the rash offer. Something that even Az's spies hadn't picked up on at the Autumn Court. All it would take was one push of Rhys's power into his mind and they'd know, but . . . it went against everything they stood for, at least amongst their allies. Rhys demanded their trust; he had to give it in return. Cassian couldn't fault his brother for that.

Eris added, "It is a bonus, of course, that in doing so, I would be repaying Cassian for ruining my betrothal to Morrigan."

Asshole. Cassian's hands curled into fists, but Mor's fingers landed on his arm. Gentle and reassuring.

Can't we throw him to the beasts under the cell and be done with him? Feyre seethed to Rhys.

Again, Rhys's lips twitched. *So bloodthirsty*, Cassian heard his High Lord croon to his mate. But Rhys said, "Anything I want, whether it be armies from the Autumn Court or your firstborn, you would grant me in exchange for Nesta Archeron as your wife?"

Cassian growled low in his throat. His brother was letting this carry on too far.

Eris glared. "Not as far as the firstborn, but yes, Rhysand. You want armies against Briallyn and my father, you'll have them." His lips curved upward. "I couldn't very well let my wife's sister go into battle unaided, could I?"

You can return every Solstice present in exchange for letting me tear him apart, Feyre said. Cassian clamped his mouth shut to avoid shouting his agreement toward them.

But Rhys, the bastard, silently laughed. His face remained stone-cold as he said, "I'll consider it, and talk to Nesta. Keep the dagger, though. You might need it."

Cassian glanced to Azriel and Nesta, still beautifully waltzing.

It didn't spark one ember of his temper.

But Eris . . . Ally or not, he'd make sure the prick got what was coming to him.

CHAPTER 58

Nesta had stood here once before. A year before, actually.

A different house, in a different part of this city, but she had stood outside while the others celebrated the Winter Solstice within, and felt like a ghost looking in through a window.

Ice crusted the Sidra behind the house, the lawn sloping down to it winter white. But evergreen garlands and wreaths decorated the river house—the epitome of merry warmth.

"Stop scowling," Cassian said. "It's a party, not a funeral."

She glared, but he opened the front door to a riot of music and laughter.

She hadn't slept with him after the ball, or since. He'd looked inclined when they'd returned to the House of Wind, but she'd simply said she was tired and had gone to her own room.

Because as soon as that music had faded and the dance had stopped, she'd realized how stupidly she'd been smiling at him, how low those walls in her mind had dropped. Eris had danced with her twice more after Azriel, and he'd had such intent in his eyes she knew she'd woven her spell around him well. He'd bid for her, she'd learned with no small amount of smugness.

Nesta left it to Rhysand and Feyre to decide how to wield that offer.

Instead, she'd focused on training. Gave herself over to it. The sessions had been halted through the holiday, but she'd gone up to the ring the next morning to practice anyway, punching the wood beam vigorously to work out her roaring thoughts.

Now, she followed Cassian into the river house, where he immediately aimed for the family room, shucking off his snow-crusted cloak and dropping it onto a bench in the grand foyer on the way. Nesta frowned at the dripping snow on the brocaded material and picked it up, eager for anything to do with herself to avoid going into that room. She unfastened her own cloak, scanning the hall for a coat closet or rack, and found the former tucked under the stair archway. She hung both garments there, and heaved a long breath as she shut the door.

"You came," Elain said behind her, and Nesta started, not having heard her sister approach. She scanned Elain from head to toe, wondering if she'd been taking lessons in stealth either from Azriel or the two half-wraiths she called friends. Gone was the ill-suited black dress from the ball, replaced by a gown of amethyst velvet, her hair half-up and curling down to her waist. She glowed with good health. Except . . .

Her brown eyes were wary. Usually, that look was reserved for Lucien. The male *was* definitely in the family room, since Nesta knew Feyre and Rhys had invited him, but for that look to be directed at her . . .

They hadn't spoken of their argument in the few minutes they'd had together before the ball's procession, and then she'd avoided Elain entirely until the event was over. She didn't know what she'd say. How to make it right.

Nesta cleared her throat. "Cassian said it might be . . . good if I came."

Elain's eyes flickered. "Did Feyre pay you, like last year?"

"No." Shame washed through her.

Elain sighed, glancing over Nesta's shoulder to the open doorway across the entry. The party within, only for their small inner circle. "Please don't upset Feyre. It's her birthday, first of all. And in her state—"

"Oh, *fuck you*," Nesta snapped, and then choked.

Elain blinked. Nesta blinked back, horror lurching through her.

And then Elain burst out laughing.

Howling, half-sobbing laughs that sent her bending over at the waist, gasping for breath. Nesta just stared, torn between questions and wanting to throw herself into the icy Sidra. "I— I'm so sorry—"

Elain held up a hand, wiping her eyes with the other. "You've *never* said such a thing to me!" She laughed again. "I think that's a good sign, isn't it?"

Nesta shook her head slowly, not understanding. Elain just linked her arm through Nesta's and led her toward the family room, where Azriel stood in the doorway, monitoring them. As if he'd heard Elain's sharp laugh and wondered what had caused it.

"I was just checking on dessert," Elain explained as they approached the doorway and Azriel. Nesta met the shadowsinger's stare and he gave her a nod. Then his gaze shifted to Elain, and though it was utterly neutral, something charged went through it. Between them. Elain's breath caught slightly, and she gave him a shallow nod of greeting before brushing past, leading Nesta into the room.

Mor lounged on a green velvet couch before the fireplace; Amren sat in Varian's lap on the matching couch opposite her, Feyre beside them, a hand on her belly. Rhys sprawled in an armchair, and Cassian occupied a second armchair with Lucien leaning against it, arguing with them about something that seemed related to a sporting event.

Nesta had tried to convince Emerie and Gwyn to join her, but both had refused. Emerie had said she was obligated to visit her horrible family, and Gwyn merely said she wasn't ready to leave the library to go farther than the training ring. So here Nesta was, alone with the same group she'd dealt with last year.

When they'd watched her sit sullen as a child in the back of the town house living room, then storm out.

Feyre smiled at her, glowing with health and life. But Nesta's gaze snagged on Amren.

The female did not so much as look her way.

Varian did, and he threw her a wary glance that said enough: No, Amren wouldn't speak to her.

Her chest tightened. But Cassian beckoned her over. He rose from his seat, offering it to her, even though there were a dozen more in the room. "Sit," he said. "Do you want some peppermint tea?"

She knew they all watched her, hated that they did, and understood why, too. But she nodded at Cassian and sat, saying to Feyre, "Happy birthday."

Feyre smiled again. "Thank you."

And that was that. Nesta ignored the collective sense of relief that filled the room and pivoted, finding herself peering up at Lucien, who greeted her with a wary dip of his chin. Elain, the wretch, had taken the seat between Feyre and Varian, about as far from Lucien as she could get. Azriel remained in the doorway. "How's the Spring Court?" Nesta asked. The fire crackled merrily to her right, and she let the sound ripple through and past her. Acknowledged the crack and what it did to her, and released it. Even as she concentrated on the male she'd addressed.

Lucien's jaw tightened. "How you'd expect."

Tension rippled through the room, confirmation that Tamlin had heard the news of Feyre's pregnancy. From Lucien's grim face, she knew he hadn't reacted well. Nesta said, "And Jurian and Vassa?"

"At each other's throats, as they like to be," he said, a tad sharply. She wondered what that was about—and for the life of her couldn't read it. Lucien asked, sipping his tea, "How's the training?"

She gave him a smile—a true one. "Good. We're learning how to disembowel a male."

Lucien choked on his drink, nearly spewing it onto her head. Cassian appeared, a cup of tea steaming in his hands, and passed it to her before he declared proudly to Lucien, "As you'd expect, Nes excels at it."

Mor lifted her glass in a mockery of a toast. "My favorite part of training."

Nesta frowned. "We haven't cut the ribbon yet, though."

Mor's brows bunched. "So you really are learning Valkyrie techniques."

Nesta nodded. They'd been so busy during their dancing lessons that the details of training hadn't come up.

Mor grinned. "You mind if I start joining you once this business with Vallahan is over? I never got to train with the Valkyries before the first War, and after it, they were all gone."

"I think the priestesses would like to see you," Nesta said, and glanced to Cassian to make sure he didn't mind. He waved a hand.

Mor's grin turned fiendish. "Good. I also want to make sure Cassian actually wears his present to practice."

"Gods spare me," Cassian groaned, and Nesta's stomach twisted. She hadn't bought them anything—hadn't bought *him* anything. She'd said as much before he'd flown her down here, and he hadn't cared, but . . . she cared.

She cradled her tea, and the conversation wended around her. But she managed to tuck that dread away, at least for now. Managed to participate.

Azriel lingered near the door, quiet enough that when Feyre and Mor began talking about some of her paintings, Nesta went over to him.

"Why don't you sit?" She leaned against the doorway beside the shadowsinger.

"My shadows don't like the flames so much." A pretty lie. She'd seen Azriel before the fire plenty. But she looked at who sat close to it and knew the answer.

"Why did you come if it torments you so much?"

"Because Rhys wants me here. It'd hurt him if I didn't come."

"Well, I think holidays are stupid."

"I don't."

She arched a brow. He explained, "They pull people together. And bring them joy. They are a time to pause and reflect and gather, and those are never bad things." Shadows darkened his eyes, full of enough pain that she couldn't stop herself from touching his shoulder. Letting him see that she understood why he stood in the doorway, why he wouldn't go near the fire.

His secret to tell, never hers.

Azriel's face remained neutral.

So Nesta gave him a small nod and walked back into the fray, taking a seat on the rolled arm of the nearest couch.

⸸

An hour passed before Mor began grousing about opening presents. Rhys snapped his fingers and a heap of them appeared.

Cassian braced himself for whatever awful gift Mor had gotten him—and glanced to Nesta. He'd kept her present in his pocket, saving it to give to her in private later. He'd done the same last year, and the damn thing had ended up at the bottom of the Sidra. Probably swept out to sea.

He'd spent months tracking down the book, so tiny it would fit in a doll's hands, but so precious it had cost him an indecent amount of money. A miniature illuminated manuscript, crafted by the skilled hands of the smallest of the lesser Fae—one of the first printed books in existence. It hadn't been meant for reading—but he'd figured that someone who adored books as much as Nesta would savor this piece of history. Even if she resented all things Fae. He'd regretted throwing it into the river the moment it had vanished under the ice, but . . . he'd been foolish that night.

This year, he prayed it was different. It felt different.

Nesta had been better tonight than last year. Another person entirely. She didn't laugh freely like Mor and Feyre, or smile sweetly like Elain, but she spoke, and engaged, and sometimes smirked. She saw everything, heard everything. Even the fire, which she seemed to ignore. Pride filled his chest at that—and relief. It had only increased when he'd noticed that she'd cared enough about Az's aloofness to go up to him to chat.

Only Amren ignored her, and Nesta ignored Amren. The tension between them was a living band of lightning. But no one said anything, and they seemed content to pretend the other didn't exist.

No one offered gifts for the baby, as it went against Fae tradition to do so before a babe was born, fearful of calling bad luck by counting one's blessings too soon. But Feyre's birthday gifts were bountiful—perhaps glaringly so.

Cassian's gifts were the usual odd medley: an ancient manuscript on warfare from Rhys, a bag of beef jerky from Azriel—*I literally couldn't think of anything you'd enjoy more*, Az had said when Cassian had laughed—and a hideously ugly green sweater from Mor that made his skin look jaundiced. Amren had given him a travel set of spices—*so you don't have to suffer whenever you're in Illyria*—and Elain gave him a specially designed ceramic mug with a lid that he could travel with, bespelled against breaking, to keep tea warm for hours.

Feyre gave him a painting, which he opened in private, and had to fight back tears before he hid it behind the chair. A portrait of him, Azriel, and Rhys, standing atop Ramiel after the Blood Rite. Bloody and bruised and filthy, faces filled with grim triumph, their hands linked as they touched them to the monolith at its peak. She must have looked into Rhys's mind for the image.

Cassian had kissed her cheek, her shield down for the moment, and murmured his thanks—as if that would ever cover it. He'd cherish the painting for the rest of his life.

He and Lucien did not exchange gifts, though the male had brought a gift for Feyre and one for his mate, who barely thanked him after opening the pearl earrings. Cassian's heart strained at the pain etching deep into Lucien's face as he tried to hide his disappointment and longing. Elain only shrank further into herself, no trace of that newfound boldness to be seen.

Cassian could feel Nesta watching him, but when he looked, her face was unreadable. No one had gotten her presents except for Feyre and Elain, who had together given her a year's worth of book-buying credit to her favorite bookshop in the city. It was capped at around three hundred books, which they seemed to think would be more than she could read in a year. Five hundred books' worth would have been a safer bet, he knew.

But then Azriel approached her. Nesta had blinked at the gift the shadowsinger set in her lap. "I didn't get you anything," she murmured to Az, her cheeks turning rosy.

"I know," he said, smiling. "I don't mind."

Cassian tried to focus on the present in his hands—the silver comb and brush set he'd gotten Mor, engraved with her name—but his gaze snagged on Nesta's fingers as she opened the small box. She peered at what was inside, then looked at Azriel in confusion. "What is it?"

Azriel plucked up the small folded silver wand within and unfurled it. One end held a clip, the other a small glass sphere. "You can attach this to whatever book you're reading, and the little ball of faelight will shine. So you don't have to squint when you're reading at night."

Nesta touched the glass ball, no bigger than her thumbnail, and faelight flickered within, casting a bright, easy glow upon her lap. She tapped it again and it turned off. And then she jumped to her feet and flung her arms around Azriel.

The room went silent for a beat.

But Azriel chuckled and squeezed her gently. Cassian smiled to see it—to see them. "Thank you," Nesta said, quickly pulling away to marvel at the device. "It's brilliant."

Azriel blushed and stepped back, shadows swirling.

Nesta looked over to Cassian, and that light was once more in her eyes. Enough that he almost gave her his gift there and then.

But considering how last year's attempt had gone, considering that since the ball she'd stayed out of his bed . . . he held back.

In case she shattered his heart all over again.

⸸

By one in the morning, Nesta's eyes ached with exhaustion. The others were still drinking, but as she hadn't been offered any wine—or wanted any, for that matter—she had not joined them in their singing and dancing. Though she had helped herself to thirds of Feyre's ridiculously large pink birthday cake.

Cassian had said they were going to stay here tonight, as he'd be too drunk to fly them back to the House of Wind, and Mor and Azriel would be too drunk to winnow them, not to mention that he'd still have to fly them the last bit of the way. Rhys and Feyre would likely be enjoying each other by the time they were all ready to leave.

The door Feyre had directed her to was already open, faelights glowing inside the opulent bedroom bedecked in whites and creams and tans. Candles flickered in glass jars on the marble mantel. The curtains were already down for the night, heavy swaths of blue velvet—the only pop of color in the room, along with a few blue trinkets. It was soothing and smelled of jasmine, precisely the sort of room she'd have designed for herself if she'd been given the chance.

She *had* been given the chance, she realized. Feyre had asked, and she'd refused. Apparently, Feyre had done it herself, somehow knowing what she'd like.

Nesta sat at the small vanity, staring at her reflection in the quiet.

Her door opened with a creak, and then Cassian was there, leaning against her doorway, gazing at her in the mirror. "You didn't want to say good night?"

Her heart began thundering. "I was tired."

"You've been tired for a few nights now." He crossed his arms. "What's going on?"

"Nothing." She twisted on the cushioned stool of the vanity. "Why aren't you downstairs?"

"You never asked about your present."

"I assumed I wasn't getting one from you."

He pushed off the door frame and shut the door behind him. He took up all the air in the room just by standing there. "Why?"

She shrugged. "I just did."

He pulled a small box from his jacket and set it on the bed between them. "Surprise." Cassian swallowed as she approached, the only sign that this meant something to him.

Nesta's hands turned sweaty as she picked the box up, examining it. She didn't open it yet, though. "I am sorry for how I behaved last Solstice. For how awful I was."

He'd gotten her a present then, too. And she hadn't cared, had been so wretched she'd wanted to hurt him for it. For caring.

"I know," he said thickly. "I forgave you a long time ago." She still couldn't look at him, even as he said, "Open it."

Her hands shook a little as she did, finding a silver ball nestled in the black velvet box. It was the size of a chicken egg, round save for one area that had been flattened so it might be set upon a surface and not roll. "What is it?"

"Touch the top. Just a tap."

Throwing a puzzled glance at him, she did so.

Music exploded into the room.

Nesta leaped back, a hand at her chest as he laughed.

But—*music* was playing from the silver orb. And not just any music, but the waltzes from the ball the other night, pure and free of any crowd chattering, as if she were sitting in a theater to hear them. "This isn't the Veritas orb," she managed to say as the waltz poured out of the ball, so clear and perfect her blood sang again.

"No, it's a Symphonia, a rare device from Helion's court. It can trap music within itself, and play it back for you. It was originally invented to help compose music, but it never caught on, for some reason."

"How did you get the crowd noise out when you trapped the sound the other night?" she marveled.

His cheeks stained with color. "I went back the next day. Asked the musicians at the Hewn City to play it all again for me, plus some of their favorites." He nodded to the ball. "And then I went to some of your favorite taverns and found those musicians and had them play . . ."

He trailed off at her bowed head. The tears she couldn't stop. She didn't try to fight them as the music poured into the room.

He had done all of this for her. Had found a way for her to have music—always.

"Nesta," he breathed.

She shut her eyes against the realization rising within her like a tidal wave. It would sweep away everything in its path once she admitted it. Consume her entirely. The thought was enough for her to straighten and wipe away her tears. "I can't accept this."

"It was made for you." He smiled softly.

She couldn't bear that smile, his kindness and joy, as she corrected, "I will not accept it." She placed the orb back in its box and handed it to him. "Return it."

His eyes shuttered. "It's a gift, not a fucking wedding ring."

She stiffened. "No, I'll look to Eris for that."

He went still. "Say that again."

She made her face cold, the only shield she had against him. "Rhys says Eris wants me as his bride. He'll do anything we want in exchange for my hand."

The Siphons atop Cassian's hands flickered. "You aren't considering saying yes."

She said nothing. Let him believe the worst.

He snarled. "I see. I get a little too close and you shove me away again. Back to where it's safe. Better to marry a viper like Eris than be with me."

"I am not *with* you," she snapped. "I am *fucking* you."

"The only thing fit for a bastard-born brute, right?"

"I didn't say that."

"You don't need to. You've said it a thousand times before."

"Then why did you bother to cut in at the ball?"

"Because I was fucking jealous!" he roared, wings splaying. "You looked like a *queen*, and it was painfully obvious that you should be with a princeling like Eris and not a low-born nothing like me! Because I couldn't stand the sight of it, right down to my gods-damned bones! But go ahead, Nesta. Go ahead and fucking *marry* him and good fucking luck to you!"

"*Eris* is the brute," she shot back. "He is a brute and a piece of *shit*. And I *would* marry him, because I am *just* like him!"

The words echoed through the room.

His pained face gutted her. "I deserve Eris." Her voice cracked.

Cassian panted, his eyes still lit with fury—and now with shock.

Nesta said hoarsely, "You are good, Cassian. And you are *brave*, and brilliant, and kind. I could kill anyone who has ever made you feel less than that—less than what you are. And I know I'm a part of that group, and I hate it." Her eyes burned, but she fought past it. "You are *everything* I have never been, and will never be good enough for. Your friends know it, and I have carried it around with me all this time—that I do not deserve you."

The fury slid from his face.

Nesta didn't stop the tears that flowed, or the words that tumbled out. "I didn't deserve you before the war, or afterward, and I certainly don't now." She let out a low, broken laugh. "Why do you think I shoved you away? Why do you think I wouldn't speak to you?" She put a hand on her aching chest. "After my father died, after I failed in so many ways—denying myself of you . . ." She sobbed. "It was my punishment. Don't you understand that?" She could barely see him through her tears. "From the moment I met you, I wanted you more than reason. From the moment I saw you in my house, you were all I could think about. And it *terrified* me. No one had ever held such power over me. And I am still terrified that if I let myself have you . . . it will be taken away. Someone will take it away, and if you're dead . . ." She buried her face in her hands. "It doesn't matter," she whispered. "I do not deserve you, and I never, ever will."

Utter silence filled the room. Such silence that she wondered if he'd left, and lowered her hands to see if he was there.

Cassian stood before her. Tears streaming down his beautiful, perfect face.

She didn't balk from it, letting him see her like this: her most raw, most base self. He'd always seen all of her, anyway.

He opened his mouth and tried to speak. Had to swallow and try again.

Nesta saw all the words in his eyes, though. The same ones she knew lay in her own.

So he stopped trying to speak, and closed the distance between them. Slid a hand into her hair, the other going around her waist and tugging her against him. He said nothing as he dipped his head, mouth brushing the tears sliding along one of her cheeks. Then the other.

She closed her eyes, letting herself savor his lips on her over-hot skin, the way his breath caressed her cheek. Each gentle kiss echoed those words she'd seen in his eyes.

Cassian pulled back, and remained that way long enough that she opened her eyes again to find his face inches from her own. "You're not going to marry Eris," he said roughly.

"No," she breathed.

His eyes blazed. "There will be no one else. For either of us."

"Yes," she whispered.

"Ever," he promised.

Nesta laid a hand on his muscled chest, letting the thunderous beating of the heart beneath echo into her palm. Let it travel down her arm, into her own chest, her own heart. "Ever," she swore.

It was all he needed. All she needed.

Cassian's mouth met hers, and the world ceased to exist.

The kiss was punishing and exalting, thorough and frenzied, a claiming and a yielding. She had no words for it. She flung her arms around him, pressing as close as she could get, meeting his tongue stroke for stroke.

He growled and nudged her back toward the bed, his mouth devouring and tasting and saying everything she couldn't yet voice, but one day, maybe soon, she could. For him, she'd fight to find the courage to say it.

The backs of her legs hit the mattress, and he broke their kiss to attend to their clothes.

She expected tearing and rending. But he gently removed her dress, fingers trembling as they unhooked each button down the back of her gown. Her own trembled as she removed his shirt.

Then they were naked, and staring at each other again with those unspoken words in their eyes, and she let him lay her upon the bed. Let him climb atop her.

There was nothing rough or wild about what followed.

She didn't want his head between her legs. Didn't even want his fingers. When he slid one down the center of her, she let him feel that she was ready and then took his hand, interlacing their fingers as her other wrapped around his cock and guided him toward her.

He nudged at her entrance, and then halted. His eyes met hers.

And then Cassian kissed her deeply as he slid home.

She gasped. Not at the fullness of having him inside her—but at that thing in her chest. The thing that thundered and beat wildly as he looked at her again, slid out nearly to the tip, and thrust back in.

On that second thrust, the thing in her chest—her heart . . . On that second thrust, it yielded entirely to him.

On his third, he kissed her again.

On the fourth, Nesta twined her arms around his head and neck and held him there as she kissed and kissed and kissed him.

On the fifth, the walls of that inner fortress of ancient iron came down. Cassian pulled away, as if sensing it, and his eyes flared as they met her own.

But he kept moving in her, making love to her thoroughly, unhurriedly. So Nesta let all that lay beyond those iron walls unspool toward him. Thread after thread of pure golden light flowed into him, and he met it with his own. Where those threads wove together, life glowed like starfire, and she had never seen anything more beautiful, felt anything more beautiful.

She was crying, and she didn't know why—only that she never wanted it to end, this binding between them, the feeling of him moving so deep in her that she wanted him imprinted beneath her skin. His tears dripped onto her face, and she reached up to brush them away. He leaned his head into her hand, nuzzling her palm.

"Say it," Cassian whispered against her skin.

She knew what he meant. Somehow, she knew what he meant.

Nesta waited until he'd thrust again, driving as deep into her as he'd ever gone, and whispered, "You're mine."

He groaned, thrusting hard.

She whispered, "And I am yours." Those golden threads between their very souls shone with the words, as if they formed a harp strummed by a heavenly hand.

For it was music between their souls. Always had been. And his voice was her favorite melody.

"Nesta." She heard the plea in her name. He was close, and wanted her to go with him. Wanted to tumble into ecstasy together. It was important to him, for some reason, that for this joining, this moment, they went as one.

Cassian lowered his head to her breast, teeth clamping around her nipple as his tongue flicked against it.

It was all Nesta needed to spur her toward climax. She moaned, and he did it again, timing his tongue to the hard thrust of his cock. Again, again.

The golden threads shimmered and sang, and she couldn't take it, the music between their souls, the feel of his body on her and in her, and—

Release blasted through her, obliterating every last bit of that inner wall, razing mountains and forests, wiping the world clean with light and pleasure, stars crashing down from the heavens in a never-ending rain.

Cassian roared as he came, and the sound was the summons of a hunt, a symphony, a single clear horn playing as dawn broke over the world.

There was only this moment, this thing shared between them, and it lasted for an eternity. Time was of no consequence. Time had always stood still around him, around them.

He spilled and spilled himself into her, longer than ever before, as if he'd been holding himself back all the times before now, as if he had let his own inner wall come crumbling down.

Forever, forever, forever.

The word was echoed in their every breath, every pounding of their hearts, so in sync that they seemed to beat as one.

Then silence fell, exquisite and serene, and Cassian remained buried in her, staring down at her with wonder and joy in his face.

Nesta reached up to kiss him.

One kiss led to another and another, and hunger rose like the tide within her, between them. And then Cassian was moving in her again, faster and harder, and time ceased to exist once more.

Hours later, days and weeks and months and millennia later, when they were both finally spent, when their souls had cleaved together entirely, Cassian pulled out of her and collapsed against the bed.

Nesta could hardly remember words. But she found them when she whispered into the darkness, "Stay with me."

A shudder rocked through him, but he only smiled as he tucked her into his side.

And warm and safe and home at last in Cassian's arms, Nesta slept.

CHAPTER 59

Nesta opened her eyes.

She knew she was warm and content, though it took her a moment to remember the reason. To realize she was still in Cassian's arms. She reveled in it. Savored each breath that brushed against her temple, felt the press of his fingers along her lower back. A calm settled over her, strikingly similar to what she felt when she did her daily Mind-Stilling.

Cassian awoke soon after, giving her a sleepy, sated smile. It softened into something tender, and for long minutes, they lay there, staring at each other, Cassian idly brushing his hand down her back. Caressing soon turned to more fervent touching, and as the dawn broke, they tangled again, their lovemaking thorough and unhurried.

When she again lay sweating and panting beside him, running a finger down the groove of his muscled stomach, Nesta murmured, "Good morning."

Cassian's fingers idly smoothed her hair. "Good morning to you, too." He glanced toward the mantel—the small wooden clock in its center, then lurched upright. "Shit."

Nesta frowned. "You have somewhere to be?" He was already

hopping into his pants, scanning the floor for the rest of his clothes. Nesta silently pointed to the other side of the bed, where his shirt lay atop her dress.

"Snowball fight. I'll be late."

Nesta had to unload each word of his statement. But she could only ask, "What?"

"Annual tradition, with Rhys and Az. We go up to the mountain cabin—remind me to take you there one day—and . . . Well, it's a long story, but we've done it pretty much every year for centuries, and I haven't won in years. If I don't win this year, I will *never* hear the end of it." All of this was said while shoving himself into his shirt, leather jacket, and boots.

Nesta just laughed. "You three—the most feared warriors in all the land—have an annual *snowball* fight?"

Cassian reached the door, throwing her a wicked grin. "Did I mention we take a steam in the birchin attached to the cabin afterward?"

From that wicked grin, she knew he meant *completely naked*. Nesta sat up, hair sliding over her breasts. His eyes dipped lower, a muscle pounding in his neck. For a heartbeat she hoped he'd lunge for her again. Indeed, his nostrils flared, scenting the need that boiled in her just at the sight of his gaze roving freely over her body, the way every part of him tensed.

But Cassian swallowed, grin and wickedness fading as he cleared his throat. "After the fight, I need to do a comprehensive inspection of the legions in Illyria for a few days. I'll be back after that."

Without so much as a farewell kiss, he vanished.

✢

Three days passed with no word from Cassian. He'd been replaced in training by a stone-faced Azriel, who was more aloof than usual and wouldn't even give her a smile. But he didn't object when she brought her Symphonia to the ring each morning for some extra motivation while exercising. The priestesses had marveled at the gift, a few of them dancing to the music, but Nesta had only been able to think about how much time and effort Cassian had put into it. How he had known what such a present would mean to her.

Her entire body ached with need, setting her teeth on edge. Three days without him might as well have been three months. She'd become desperate enough for him that her hand now slid between her legs in the bath, in bed, even during lunch in her room. But release left her empty, as if her body knew it needed him in her, filling her. She'd asked Azriel every day when he'd be back, and Azriel had only said, *Soon*, before conducting their lessons.

Maybe she'd gone mad. Maybe that was what that iron wall around her mind had been—the thing that kept her sanity in check. Surely it wasn't normal to think of a person this much, need them *this* much.

It was that worry that hounded her as they wrapped up lessons, panting and sweating despite the frigid morning thanks to the Valkyrie sprints they'd been practicing: ten seconds at a full sprint, thirty seconds trotting, another ten seconds sprinting . . . For fifteen minutes straight. Once they could get through it, they'd add in their shields. Then swords. All of it designed to build their stamina and focus on controlling their breathing between bursts of attack and retreat. All of it utter insanity that couldn't quite dull the edge of Nesta's fretting as she asked Emerie and Gwyn, "Do you want to stay over at the House with me tonight?" She motioned to the archway. "Have a read-in or something?"

Gwyn blinked, considering. She had not set foot outside of the library save to come to these lessons or to use the practice ring to hack at that ribbon. But she said, "I'll ask Clotho."

Emerie smirked at Nesta, as if aware of why she needed company. "Sure."

That evening, Nesta and Emerie read in companionable silence in the private library, waiting for Gwyn. Emerie had sprawled across the armchair, legs dangling over an arm, her back against the other. Without looking up from the book in her lap, she said, "Cassian must be *really* good at sex, if you're so tied up in knots while he's gone."

Nesta cleared her throat, dispelling the memories of his mouth, his strong body, the way his silken black hair fell on either side of his face as he lay over her, swaying as he pounded into her. "He's . . ." She made a low noise in her throat.

"I figured," Emerie said, chuckling. "He's got the Walk."

"The Walk?"

Emerie smirked. "You know, when a male knows how to use his cock well and struts around with that swagger that basically declares it to everyone."

Nesta rolled her eyes. "I'd hope he knows how to use it well after being alive for five hundred years." She snorted. "Though I've met plenty who proved that wrong."

Emerie arched a brow for her to continue, but a knock sounded on the library door. Gwyn's head popped in, and she scanned the room before entering. She bore a small bag, presumably of what she'd need for the night. Nesta had already asked the House to prepare a bedroom for all three of them to share, and she'd entered the private library to find it transformed: by the window against the far wall, a worktable and chairs had been swapped for three cots, each laden with blankets and pillows.

Gwyn smiled, though her pulse pounded wildly against the column of her throat. "Sorry I'm late. Merrill made me go over a paragraph with her *ten times*." Gwyn sighed. "Please tell me all the chocolate is for us."

The House had stocked the table between the armchairs with piles of chocolate: truffles and confections and bars of it. Along with cookies and small finger cakes. And a platter of cheeses and fruit. And carafes of water and various juices.

Gwyn surveyed the table. "Did you go to all this trouble?"

"Oh, no," Emerie said, eyes glowing. "Nesta's been holding out on us."

Nesta scoffed, but Emerie said, "The House will get you *anything you want*. Just say it aloud." At Gwyn's raised brows, Emerie said, "I'd like a slice of pistachio cake, please."

A plateful of one appeared before her. As well as a bowl of whipped cream topped with raspberries.

Gwyn blinked. "You live in a magic house."

"It likes to read," Nesta admitted, patting a stack of the romances. "We've bonded over that."

Gwyn whispered to the room, "What's your favorite book?"

One thumped on the table beside Emerie's cake, and Gwyn squawked in surprise. But then rubbed her hands together. "Oh, this is delightful."

"That smile means trouble," Emerie said.

Gwyn's grin just widened.

⁜

Two hours later, Nesta found herself fully clothed in a bathtub in the middle of the private library, the entire thing filled with bubbles. No water, just bubbles. In matching tubs on either side of her, Emerie and Gwyn were giggling. "This is ridiculous," Nesta said, even as her mouth curved upward.

Each one of their requests had gotten more and more absurd, and Nesta might have felt like they were exploiting the House had it not been so . . . exuberant in answering their commands. Adding creative flourishes.

Like the fact that each bubble held a tiny bird fluttering about inside.

Silent fireworks still exploded in the far corner of the room, and a miniature pegasus—Nesta's request, made only when her friends goaded her into submitting one—fed on a small patch of grass by the shelf, content to ignore them. A cake taller than Cassian stood in the center of the room, lit with a thousand candles. Six frogs danced circles around a red-and-white-spotted toadstool, the waltzes provided by Nesta's Symphonia.

Emerie wore a diamond crown and six strings of pearls. Gwyn sported a broad-brimmed hat fit for any fine lady, perched at a rakish angle on her head. A lace parasol leaned against her other shoulder, and she twirled it idly as she surveyed the windows, the world beyond, and said in a hushed voice, "I sometimes wonder if I shall ever have the courage to go out there again. I fear every day that I won't."

Nesta's smile slid away. She considered her words before she said, "I feel the same."

Because this existence, living in the House, training, working in the library . . . It wasn't real life. Not entirely. When she was allowed to return to the city proper, then she'd face life again. See if she was worthy of it. The thought made her stomach twist.

Dispelling the gloom, Gwyn leaped out of her tub, bubbles spraying, and padded for her bag. "Now, don't you two dare laugh at me, but I brought something for us to do. I didn't realize we'd have a magic house to keep us occupied." She pulled out a bundle of various colored threads. "My sister and I used to braid bracelets and put these little charms on them full of wishes for each other." She lifted a sack, dumping a few silver coins into her palm. They were no larger than her pinkie nail, and as thin as a wafer. Her voice grew soft. "We believed that the wish would come true once the bracelet fell off."

Emerie asked gently, "What was her name?"

"Catrin." Gwyn's voice held so much pain and longing. "We were fraternal twins. Her hair was dark as onyx, her skin pale as the moon. And she was as moody as the sea." She laughed quietly. "Despite her faults—and mine—we loved each other dearly. We were all each other had while growing up. She was the only one I could truly rely on. I miss her every day."

Nesta couldn't stop herself from thinking of Feyre.

Gwyn said, "I wish I could just have one more moment with her.

Just one, to tell her that I love her and say good-bye." She wiped at her eyes, lifting her head. Looked right at Nesta. "It's what really mattered in the end, you know. Not our petty fights or differences. I forgot all of that the moment she . . ." Gwyn shook her head. "It's all that matters."

Nesta nodded slowly. Perhaps it wasn't just her and Feyre, then. Perhaps *all* sisters had difficulties, fights, chasms between them. She wasn't perfect, but . . . neither was Feyre. They had both made mistakes. And both had long, long lives ahead of them. What had occurred in the past did not have to dictate the future.

So Nesta nodded again, letting Gwyn see her understanding. "It's all that matters," Nesta agreed.

Gwyn smiled, and then straightened, clearing her throat. "I managed to track the thread and charms down before Solstice, thinking I'd make them for you as little presents, but they took longer to arrive than I thought they would. So I figured we could make the bracelets tonight." She carefully set the materials upon the nearest table.

Nesta and Emerie rose to survey the variety of threads: all colors and hues, all carefully bundled. "Show me how to do it," Emerie said softly. Nesta wondered if Gwyn's words had resonated with her, too—what pain and hope Emerie might be holding within her.

But Gwyn grinned, beginning her demonstration by selecting three colors that she thought matched Emerie's spirit, she claimed. Green, purple, and gold. Nesta refrained from snickering and selected colors for Gwyn: blue, white, and teal. Emerie, in turn, selected Nesta's colors: navy blue, crimson, and silver. Nesta and Emerie dutifully tried to copy Gwyn's "easy" steps: doubling up the thread, knotting it, cutting the looped bits, then pinning the top of the bracelet beneath a heavy book as they separated each length by color. And then began a process of looping and pulling, back and forth. Emerie's knots were flawless. Nesta's . . .

"Your bracelet is going to be an eyesore, Gwyn." Nesta scowled at the wobbly, bunched-up mess that was her first ten rows.

"Keep going," Gwyn said, leagues ahead on her own bracelet and beginning to add pretty patterns within the rows. "The knots will get better-looking with practice. Just tell me when you've gotten to the halfway point and then we'll add the charm."

They worked in music-filled companionship, idle chatter bouncing between them, Emerie and Gwyn occasionally laughing at Nesta's awful workmanship. "Now," Gwyn said when they were halfway through, "we make wishes for each other." She reached for one of the tiny coins. "I'll just hold this in my hand, think of something for Emerie, and—"

"Wait," Nesta said, catching Gwyn's hand before it could touch the charm. "Let me."

Her friends regarded her curiously, and Nesta swallowed. "Let me make a wish for all of us," she explained, gathering the three charms. A small gift—for the friends who had become like sisters.

A chosen family. Like the one Feyre had found for herself.

Nesta squeezed the charms in her palm, closing her eyes, and said: "I wish for us to have the courage to go out into the world when we are ready, but to always be able to find our way back to each other. No matter what."

Gwyn and Emerie cheered at that. And when Nesta opened her eyes, palm unfurling, she could have sworn the coins glowed faintly.

CHAPTER 60

Cassian had been gone for five days. Five days, to inspect every single one of the Illyrian legions, and remember how to behave like a normal, sane male rather than a lovesick puppy. But somehow, by the time he returned, a shift had occurred.

Not just the world-altering shift that had happened on Winter Solstice between him and Nesta. But a shift between Nesta and Emerie and Gwyn.

He emerged into the frigid morning to find the three of them already in the practice ring. They stood around the beam, the ribbon drifting gracefully on the icy wind. Gwyn held a blade in her hand, and Emerie and Nesta stood a few feet away. All three wore braided, colorful bracelets with silver charms dangling from them.

Cassian lingered at the doorway as Nesta murmured to Gwyn, "You've got this." Azriel came up beside him, silent as the shadows that wreathed his wings.

Gwyn stared the ribbon down like an enemy on a battlefield. It rippled in the wind, dancing away, its motions unpredictable as any foe.

"Do it for the miniature pegasus," Emerie said. Cassian had no idea what it meant, but Gwyn's lips twitched upward.

Nesta laughed.

The sound might as well have been a lightning strike to his head for how much it rocked him, that laugh. Free and light and so unlike anything he'd ever heard from her that even Azriel blinked. A true laugh. "The miniature pegasus," Nesta said, "was an illusion. And is now back in his make-believe meadow."

"He loved Gwyn most," Emerie teased. "Despite your efforts to woo him."

They fell silent again as Gwyn shifted her feet, angling the blade. The wind waggled the ribbon again, as if taunting her.

Cassian glanced over at Az, but his attention was fixed on the young priestess, admiration and quiet encouragement shining from his face.

Gwyn whispered, "I am the rock against which the surf crashes." Nesta straightened at the words, as if they were a prayer and a summons. Gwyn lifted the blade. "Nothing can break me."

Cassian's throat tightened, and even from across the ring, he could see Nesta's eyes gleaming with pride and pain.

Emerie said, "Nothing can break *us*."

The world seemed to pause at the words. As if it had been following one path and now branched off in another direction. In a hundred years, a thousand, this moment would still be etched in his mind. That he would tell his children, his grandchildren, *Right then and there. That was when it all changed.*

Azriel went wholly still, as if he, too, had felt the shift. As if he, too, were aware that far larger forces peered into that training ring as Gwyn moved.

Smooth as the Sidra, swift as the wind off the Illyrian Mountains, her entire body working in singing harmony, Gwyn lunged toward the ribbon, twirled, and as she spun, her arm opened up, executing a perfect backhanded slice that cut the winter morning itself.

Half the ribbon fluttered to the red stone.

A flawless, precise slice. Not one frayed strand rippled in the wind as the severed ribbon hanging from the beam flapped.

Nesta bent down, picked up the fallen half of the ribbon, and solemnly tied it around Gwyn's brow. A makeshift version of what the priestesses wore atop their heads with their stones. But Cassian had never seen Gwyn display her Invoking Stone.

Gwyn lifted trembling fingers to her brow, touching the ribbon with which Nesta had crowned her.

Nesta's voice was thick as she declared, "Valkyrie."

⸸

It became the ritual: to cut that ribbon, to be crowned with its severed half and anointed Valkyrie.

Gwyn was the first. Emerie the second. By the end of training that morning, Nesta became the third.

It made facing Cassian only slightly easier. Even if the need within her had only grown worse, clawing at the underside of her skin, begging to get out. To get to him.

Every time she met his stare, or got within a few feet of him, it roared at her to strip off her clothes and offer herself to him. She focused on the white ribbon around her brow, focused on what the three of them had accomplished.

The lesson finished, and she might have dragged Cassian down to her bedroom had he not simply taken to the skies and left. He didn't come back until the following morning.

He was avoiding her.

But the next morning, she understood why—or at least he had a reason for his vanishing act.

The training ring had been transformed again.

An obstacle course lay all around it, coiled like a snake throughout. Nesta was one of the last to arrive, and joined the crowd of females who lingered by the door, murmuring about it as Cassian and Azriel turned to them all. Cassian said, "Valkyries were fearless and brilliant warriors on their own. But their true strength came from being a highly trained unit." He motioned to the obstacle course. "Alone, none of you will be able to get through that course. Together, you can find a way."

Emerie snorted.

Cassian leveled a grin at her. "Looks simple, doesn't it?"

Emerie had the good sense to look nervous.

Azriel clapped his hands, and all the females straightened. "You'll work in groups of three."

Gwyn asked Az, her teal eyes bright, "What do we get if we finish the course?"

Az's shadows danced around him. "Since there's no chance in hell any of you will finish the course, we didn't bother to get a prize."

Boos sounded. Gwyn lifted her chin in challenge. "We look forward to proving you wrong."

✠

Proving Azriel and Cassian wrong would take a while, it seemed.

Gwyn, Emerie, and Nesta made it the farthest in three hours: a grand, whopping halfway.

Roslin, Deirdre, and Ananke made it to the obstacle behind them before time was up, and Ananke's golden hair was matted with blood from the blow she'd taken to the head from a spinning, many-armed wooden *thing*.

"Sadistic monsters," Gwyn hissed as the three friends limped toward the water station, defeat heavy on their shoulders.

"We try again tomorrow," Emerie swore, sporting a black eye thanks to the swinging log that had knocked her on her ass before Nesta could grab her. "We keep trying until we wipe that smug look off their stupid perfect faces."

Indeed, Azriel and Cassian had just leaned against the wall, arms crossed, and smiled at them the entire time.

Gwyn threw Azriel a withering stare as she strode past him. "See you tomorrow, Shadowsinger," she tossed over a shoulder.

Az stared after her, brows high with amusement. When he turned back, Nesta grinned. "You have no idea what you just started," she said. Az angled his head, hazel eyes narrowing as Gwyn reached the archway.

"Remember how Gwyn was with the ribbon?" Nesta winked and clapped the shadowsinger on the shoulder. "You're the new ribbon, Az."

✢

The obstacle course remained impossible.

The bastards changed it every night. Each new morning was a different, harder challenge. But one that had an overall pattern: it usually began with some array of footwork, whether doing a swift run of knee-to-chest steps through a ladder on the ground or balancing on a suspended beam. Then came mental testing—puzzles that required them to think together, and then rely on each other to get through. And when they were thoroughly exhausted, the feats of strength came in.

The three of them made it to the third stage only once in the next two weeks.

Roslin, Ananke, and Deirdre were close on their heels, propelling Gwyn to push her group harder. She wanted to be the first. Wanted Nesta and Emerie and her to be the ones who wiped the smirks from Azriel's and Cassian's faces. Especially Azriel's.

Never mind that, after the first day, they only had an hour to get through the course. The other two hours were spent as a group, working on military training: marching in formation (harder and stupider than it looked), fighting side by side (more dangerous than it seemed), and learning how to move, think, breathe as a unit.

But they kept at it. Marched in Valkyrie phalanxes. Fought as one, with Cassian and Azriel playing their opponents. Learned to hold their shields in place against the onslaught of the Illyrians' Siphons, their towering male forms. Every bit of Valkyrie endurance training paid off: every infernal squat or lunge now allowed them to brace their shields with little effort. To hold steady against an enemy attack.

They exercised as one, in precise lines as they did their abdominal curls to the same beat. Did push-ups together. If one collapsed, they all had to start over again.

But they kept going. Through sweat and breath and blood, they forged themselves together.

And sometimes, when the evening services were over, the three of them would gather in the library and read about military strategy. About Valkyrie lore. About the techniques of the ancients.

More of the priestesses cut the ribbon—Roslin. Deirdre. Ananke. Ilana. Lorelei.

Everything Azriel and Cassian threw at them, they took and threw right back.

And every night, Nesta ran the stairs of the House. Farther and farther and farther. She hadn't been able to reach the bottom again since that fight with Amren, but she kept trying.

No longer did memories and words send her rushing down it. Now she was driven by pure, unrelenting purpose.

Nesta, Gwyn, and Emerie defeated the obstacle course two months to the day after it had been brought in. Of course, it was on a day when all the priestesses had been summoned away by Clotho for some special ceremony, so there was no one to witness it other than Cassian and Azriel. Only Gwyn had been exempted from the ceremony, apparently.

And when Gwyn reached the finish line, bloody and panting and grinning so wildly her teal eyes glowed like a sunlit sea, she only extended her battered hand to Azriel. "Well?"

"You already have your prize," Azriel said simply. "You just passed the Blood Rite Qualifier. Congratulations."

Gwyn gaped. Nesta and Emerie halted. But Gwyn said to him, "*That* was why you invited them?"

Nesta had no idea what the priestess was talking about, but followed her gaze upward, to the lip of the pit, where a stone-faced Lord Devlon and another male peered in, scowling.

No doubt this was the reason the other priestesses had been occupied today.

Cassian murmured to Nesta, "I had a feeling today might be the day."

Devlon seemed ready to erupt, his face purple with rage, but he looked to Cassian and nodded tersely.

"You told the priestesses not to come?" Nesta asked Cassian and Azriel.

"We informed Clotho that we might have some observers today," Azriel answered, eyes full of ice and death as he stared down Devlon. The male looked away from the shadowsinger before grunting to his crony and flying eastward toward Illyria. Azriel went on, watching them vanish, "Clotho explained it to the others—and they chose to find other ways to fulfill their day."

Nesta asked Gwyn, "But it seemed like you didn't know what we were doing."

"Cassian and Azriel warned me that we'd be watched by males today, but didn't specify why. I had no idea it was the Blood Rite Qualifier." Her eyes shone bright above the dirt smudged on her face.

Emerie had blanched, though. She asked Cassian, "We're not entering the Blood Rite, are we?"

"Only if you want to," Cassian assured her. She alone of all the females here would understand the true horrors of the Blood Rite, Nesta knew. "But we wanted Devlon—and whoever he tells—to understand that you're as talented as any Illyrian unit. This was the only way they'd get it. Being a Valkyrie means nothing to them, and you certainly don't need their approval, but . . ." He glanced to Emerie again. "I wanted them to know. What you've accomplished. That even though Valkyries don't have something akin to the Blood Rite, you're as trained as any warrior in Illyria."

"The courses?" Gwyn asked.

"Different routes," Azriel said, "from various Qualifiers over the centuries."

Cassian grinned. "Short of partaking in the Blood Rite, you're now as close to being Illyrian warriors as you can be."

Silence fell. Then Nesta said, wiping the blood from the corner of her bruised mouth, "I'd rather be a Valkyrie." The females murmured their agreement.

Cassian laughed. "Gods help us."

CHAPTER
61

One test remained.

Not any Cassian had given her, or any decreed by Illyrians or Valkyries, but one she'd set for herself.

Nesta figured today was as good as any to push herself on those last few hundred steps.

Down and down and down she went.

Around and around and around.

They had sliced the Valkyrie ribbon, and had passed the Blood Rite Qualifier. But they would keep training. So much remained to be learned, so much remained that she looked forward to learning with all of them. With her friends.

With Cassian.

They alternated bedrooms, sleeping wherever was closest to their love-making. Or fucking. There was a difference, she'd realized. Lovemaking usually happened late at night or first thing in the morning, when he was lazy and thorough and smiling. Fucking usually happened at lunch or random times, against a wall or bent over a desk or straddling his lap, impaling herself on him again and again. Sometimes it started off as fucking and became the tender, intense thing she called lovemaking. Sometimes the lovemaking dissolved into frantic fucking. She could never tell what would happen, which was part of why she could never get enough.

She passed one hundred steps. Two hundred. A thousand.

Her head was clear. It burned with purpose, with direction and focus. She woke up each morning glad to be there, to throw herself against the world and see what it did. She had music each night at the evening services, where she had learned most of the songs and sang with the priestesses, letting her voice ring out alongside Gwyn's. She had music from Cassian's Symphonia, which she played whenever she could.

And she had music in her heart. A song made up of Cassian's voice, of Gwyn's and Emerie's laughter, of her own breathing as she went down and down and down the stairs.

Two thousand. Three thousand.

Nesta's feet flew, her steps unfaltering, even as her muscles burned.

She fought through it. Gritted her teeth in a feral grin.

She gave herself to the burning, the exhaustion and the pain. She did not let them consume her, but allowed them to wash over her. Through her. Did not permit them to bend or deter her.

She was the rock against which such things crashed. With each step, each breath, she yielded to the Mind-Stilling. It was the next phase in the Valkyrie mind-training: to go from seated calm to active soothing. To be able to steady the mind, focus it, while in the midst of chaos.

Four thousand. Five thousand. Six thousand. The Mind-Stilling became as easy as breathing.

She would not be mastered by anything again. She was the master of herself.

Seven thousand. Eight thousand. Nine thousand.

And this person she was becoming, emerging into day by day . . .

She might even like her.

The stairs vanished. And then there was only a door before her.

Nesta swayed, body still seeming to think it had to keep going around and around, but she took hold of the knob. Opened the door to the dusk and city beyond.

The lights had all been dimmed, but merry voices filled the streets. No one would prevent her from venturing into the city, to a tavern, and drinking herself silly. No one would come to haul her back. She'd made it down the stairs. Life lay before her.

Only, she found herself looking up. Toward the House where a Starfall party would be held in an hour. The male who would be there, who'd encouraged her to come.

She faced the city—the lovely, vibrant city. None of it seemed as vibrant as what waited above. The climb would be brutal, and almost without end, but at the top . . . Cassian would be waiting. As he had waited for her for years now.

Nesta smiled. And began the climb.

⸸

Cassian, clad in his courtly finery, was standing at the door to the stairs when she returned.

He was so exquisite that if Nesta hadn't already been panting from the climb, she'd have found herself unable to breathe.

Five steps had Nesta across the hall. Her arms around his neck. Her mouth on his.

She kissed him, and he opened for her, letting those silent words pass between them, holding her so tight their heartbeats echoed into each other.

When she pulled away, breathless from the kiss and all that filled her heart, Cassian only smiled. "The party already started," he said, kissing her brow and stepping away. "But it's still nearing its peak." Indeed, music and laughter trickled down from levels above.

Cassian extended a hand, and Nesta wordlessly took it, letting him lead her down the hall. When she looked at the steps upward and her legs buckled, he scooped her into his arms and carried her. She leaned her head against his chest, closing her eyes, savoring the sound of his heart thumping. All the world was a song, and this heartbeat its core melody.

Open air and music flowed around her, glasses clinking and clothing rustling, and she opened her eyes again as Cassian set her down.

Stars flowed overhead. Thousands and thousands of stars. She barely remembered last year's Starfall. Had been too drunk to care.

But this, so high up . . .

Nesta didn't care that she was covered in sweat, wearing her leathers amongst a bejeweled crowd. Not as she staggered onto the veranda at the top of the House and gaped at the stars raining across the bowl of the sky. They zoomed by, so close some sparked against the stones, leaving glowing dust in their wake.

She had a vague sense of Cassian and Mor and Azriel nearby, of Feyre and Rhys and Lucien, of Elain and Varian and Helion. Of Kallias and Viviane, also swollen with child and glowing with joy and strength. Nesta smiled in greeting and left them blinking, but she forgot them within a moment because the stars, the stars, the stars . . .

She hadn't realized that such beauty existed in the world. That she might feel so full from wonder it could hurt, like her body couldn't contain all of it. And she didn't know why she cried then, but the tears began rolling down her face.

The world was beautiful, and she was so grateful to be in it. To be alive, to be here, to see this. She stuck out a hand over the railing, grazing a star as it shot past, and her fingers came away glowing with blue and green dust. She laughed, a sound of pure joy, and she cried more, because that joy was a miracle.

"That's a sound I never thought to hear from you, girl," Amren said beside her.

The delicate female was regal in a gown of light gray, diamonds at her throat and wrists, her usual black bob silvered with the starlight.

Nesta wiped away her tears, smearing the stardust upon her cheeks and not caring. For a long moment, her throat worked, trying to sort through all that sought to rise from her chest. Amren just held her stare, waiting.

Nesta fell to one knee and bowed her head. "I am sorry."

Amren made a sound of surprise, and Nesta knew others were watching, but she didn't care. She kept her head lowered and let the words flow from her heart. "You gave me kindness, and respect, and your time, and I treated them like garbage. You told me the truth, and I did not want to hear it. I was jealous, and scared, and too proud to admit it. But losing your friendship is a loss I can't endure."

Amren said nothing, and Nesta lifted her head to find the female smiling, something like wonder on her face. Amren's eyes became lined with silver, a hint of how they had once been. "I went poking about the House when we arrived an hour ago. I saw what you did to this place."

Nesta's brow furrowed. She hadn't changed anything.

Amren grabbed Nesta under the shoulder, hauling her up. "The House sings. I can hear it in the stone. And when I spoke to it, it answered. Granted, it gave me a pile of romance novels by the end of it, but . . . you caused this House to come alive, girl."

"I didn't do anything."

"You Made the House," Amren said, smiling again, a slash of red and white in the glowing dark. "When you arrived here, what did you wish for most?"

Nesta considered, watching a few stars whiz past. "A friend. Deep down, I wanted a friend."

"So you Made one. Your power brought the House to life with a silent wish born from loneliness and desperate need."

"But my power only creates terrible things. The House is good," Nesta breathed.

"Is it?"

Nesta considered. "The darkness in the pit of the library—it's the heart of the House."

Amren nodded. "And where is it now?"

"It hasn't made an appearance in weeks. But it's still there. I think it's just . . . being managed. Maybe the House's knowledge that I'm aware of it, and didn't judge it, makes it easier to keep in check."

Amren put a hand above Nesta's heart. "That's the key, isn't it? To know the darkness will always remain, but how you choose to face it, handle it . . . that's the important part. To not let it consume. To focus upon the good, the things that fill you with wonder." She gestured to the stars zooming past. "The struggle with that darkness is worth it, just to see such things."

But Nesta's gaze had slid from the stars—finding a familiar face in the crowd, dancing with Mor. Laughing, his head thrown back. So beautiful she had no words for it.

Amren chuckled gently. "And worth it for that, too."

Nesta looked back at her friend. Amren smiled, and her face became as lovely as Cassian's, as the stars arching past. "Welcome back to the Night Court, Nesta Archeron."

CHAPTER 62

Spring dawned on Velaris. Nesta welcomed the sun into her bones, her heart, letting it warm her.

They had made it through the winter with no movement from Briallyn or Beron, no armies unleashing. But Cassian warned that many armies did not attack in the winter, and Briallyn might have been amassing them in secret. Azriel was forbidden from getting within a few miles of her, thanks to the threat of the Crown, and any reports had to be verified by multiple sources. In short: they knew nothing, and could only wait.

The mood hadn't been helped by a rare red star blasting across the sky one day—an ill omen, Nesta had heard the priestesses muttering. Cassian reported that even Rhys had been rattled by it, seeming unusually contemplative afterward. But Nesta suspected that the omen wasn't the only thing contributing to Rhys's solemnity. Feyre was only two months from giving birth, and they still knew nothing about how to save her.

She channeled that growing worry into her training with the

priestesses. Azriel and Cassian devised more training simulations, and they moved through them as a unit, thought and battled as a unit.

Nesta sometimes wondered if they would ever see battle. If these priestesses would ever be willing to leave here to fight, to face violence that might summon the devouring demons of their pasts. Did she wish to move beyond simulations to actual combat? What would it do to her, to see her friends killing or being killed?

It was a final test, she supposed. One they might not ever be taking.

Perhaps the Blood Rite, which Cassian had told her was only a few days away, had started as just that: a way to introduce young Illyrian warriors to killing in a contained environment, a stepping-stone to the full mercilessness of battle.

But Nesta's first foray into merciless battle came in the form of a letter. An impatient, demanding letter that requested her presence immediately. And Cassian's.

Eris was waiting for Nesta and Cassian when they arrived in a forest clearing nestled in the Middle. But Nesta didn't bother to do more than glance at the High Lord's son—not with the sight rising above the trees. The sacred mountain—*the* mountain under which Feyre, Rhys, and all the other High Lords had been trapped by Amarantha. It rose like a wave on the horizon, bleak and barren and somehow thrumming with presence.

"Have you never seen it?" Eris asked by way of greeting, tracking her stare.

"No." She looked away from the unnerving peak. "Why is it sacred to you?"

Eris shrugged, and Nesta knew Cassian monitored his every breath. "There are three of them, you know. Sister peaks. This one, the mountain called the Prison, and the one the Illyrian brutes call Ramiel. All bald, barren mountains at odds with those around them."

"We didn't come for a history lesson," Cassian muttered.

Nesta cut him a look. "I asked. I want to know."

Cassian snorted, and jerked his chin to Eris in a silent order to go on.

"We don't know why they exist, but do you not find it strange that two out of the three have underground palaces carved into them?"

"I'd hardly call the Prison a palace," Cassian cut in. "Just ask the inmates."

Eris gave him a mocking smile, but continued, "Unsurprisingly, the Illyrians were never curious enough to see what secrets lie beneath Ramiel. If it, too, was carved up like the others by ancient hands."

"I thought Amarantha made the court Under the Mountain herself," Nesta said.

"Oh, she decorated it and made us act like a sorry imitation of your Court of Nightmares, but the tunnels and halls were carved long before. By who, we don't know."

"That's all the history I can take," Cassian said, earning a withering glare from Eris. Nesta followed suit. Cassian only gave her an amused wink before continuing, "Your letter seemed to imply that your father was making a move. Out with it."

"My father went to the continent again last week. He came back seeming normal, without the glassy-eyed aloofness my soldiers displayed. He did not invite me to accompany him, or explain what he discussed with Briallyn. I can only assume the fallout is approaching, though, and wanted to warn you. It was not something I could risk putting in writing. But for now . . . for now, it seems as if the world is holding its breath."

"For what?" Nesta asked.

"For you to find the Harp."

Nesta blinked. And realized too late, too slowly, that they had not told Eris they'd found it. And her blink had given it away.

Eris demanded, "You have it?"

"Does it make a difference?" Cassian said casually.

"The Night Court possesses two objects of the Trove. I'd say yes." Eris straightened. "Is that what all these delays have been about? Biding your time so you can learn the Trove's secrets and use the power for your own gains?"

"That's absurd," Nesta snapped. "What do we have to gain?"

Red flame sizzled in Eris's eyes. "What did the King of Hybern have to gain by attaining the Cauldron and invading our lands?"

"We have no interest in conquest, Eris," Cassian said, crossing his arms. "You know that. And we're not going to use the Trove."

Eris barked a laugh. Nesta could see that he didn't believe them—that he was so used to the twisted politics and scheming of his court that even when the simple, easy truth was offered, he could not see it. "I find myself not entirely comfortable with your court possessing two items in the Trove." His gaze shifted to Nesta. "Especially when you have so many other weapons in your arsenal."

Nesta stiffened, but Cassian didn't so much as shift on his feet. "Rhys has his own plans, Eris. You can't be foolish enough to think we'd tell you *all* of them, but I can assure you they don't involve using the Trove."

Nesta tried not to gape at the cool, amused voice that had come out of Cassian. A courtier's voice. As if he'd been listening to her and Rhysand, and had perfectly replicated that combination of boredom and cruelty. Nesta couldn't help the thrill that shot down her spine. She wanted him to use that voice in the bedroom. Wanted him to whisper like that in her ear while he—

"So you claim," Eris said. "I suppose you're going after the Crown now." His hair shone like embers in the dappled light.

Cassian smirked. "We'll tell you when you need to know. And we'll try not to forget this time."

Eris picked at a piece of lint on his jacket. At his side hung the dagger Rhys and Feyre had gifted him, simple and plain compared to the finery on him. *Her* dagger. "You'd be truly stupid to go after Briallyn directly."

"Leave the heroics to the brutes, Eris," Cassian said. "Wouldn't want to risk cutting up those pretty hands."

Eris's fingers curled slightly on his biceps. Nesta reined in her smile. Cassian's words had found their mark.

"And what will you do when you have all three objects in the Trove?" Eris's brows flattened. "You can't destroy them; and I doubt hiding them would work. Considering the danger that gathers around us, I don't see why you wouldn't use them."

Nesta kept silent, content to let Cassian take the lead.

Cassian let out a soft laugh, and Nesta's blood again sang at the mastery of it. He'd toy with Eris a bit longer. Indeed, Cassian asked coolly, "And what are you going to do to stop us?"

Eris only said, "If you fail in retrieving the Crown, you risk Briallyn using it upon you. She could turn you on each other. Make you do unspeakable things. Even reveal to her where the other two objects are. And you'd have no choice but to tell her everything." He worried about them revealing their alliance—for his own sake. "You threaten to expose us. Do *not* pursue the Crown."

"We'll see," Cassian said, the portrait of unruffled calm. Nesta nearly snickered as he nodded toward the dagger at Eris's side. "We have our own ways to protect ourselves against the Crown." Nesta hid her surprise. The weapons she Made shielded against the Trove? No one had told her such a thing.

Eris glowered. "Has this been the plan the whole time? To string me along, make me an enemy of my father, then use the Trove against all of us?"

"You made yourself an enemy of your father," Cassian said, smiling faintly. "When he finds out, I wonder if he'll let your hounds rip you to shreds, or if he'll do it himself."

Eris paled slightly. "Don't you mean *if* he finds out?"

Cassian said nothing. Kept his face neutral. Nesta stifled her smugness and did the same.

Eris observed them. For the first time since Nesta had known the male, uncertainty banked the fire in his gaze.

And then he turned toward the other subject in his letter, facing Nesta before he asked, "And my offer for you?" Not one ounce of affection or longing laced his words.

Nesta lifted her chin, smirking at last. "I suppose once we have the Crown in our hands, the Night Court won't need you after all. Neither will I."

She could have sworn Cassian was repressing a laugh, but she kept her gaze on Eris, who went rigid, rippling with rage. "I do not appreciate being toyed with, Nesta Archeron. My offer was sincere. Stay with the Night Court and you risk your ruin."

Cassian cut in smoothly, "Try to fuck us over, Eris, and you risk yours."

Eris's upper lip curled. "Do whatever you want." He straightened, as if shaking off any emotion, face going cold and cruel again. "It's your lives you gamble with, not mine." He chuckled, nodding to Cassian. "So what if the world loses another brute to war? Good riddance."

Cassian smiled slowly. "Thanks for your well-wishes, Eris."

And with that, Cassian swept Nesta into his arms and shot into the sky, the trees passing in a green blur, the sacred mountain lurking at their backs.

Nesta peered into his face as they flew northward, and found Cassian grinning.

"You did well," she said, brushing a hand down his neck.

"I pretended I was you," he admitted. "I think I got the *I Will Slay My Enemies* look down, didn't I?"

Nesta laughed, leaning her head against his chest. "You did."

⸸

They flew for hours, content to be alone, soaring over the land. They flew and flew, Cassian tireless and unfaltering, and Nesta let herself revel in the feeling of his arms. In just being with him. And even though the cold sank into her skin, by the time the lights of Velaris appeared on the darkening horizon, she was sorry to see them.

But he brought them to the city proper, landing on one of the bridges spanning the Sidra. "I thought we'd walk for a little," he said, interlacing his fingers with hers.

After so long in the empty skies, the people all around them seemed to press in. But Nesta nodded, falling into step beside him, savoring his calluses against her own, the rub of the thread that kept his Siphon in place atop his hand, the warmth that leaked from him.

"What do you think Eris will do?" They hadn't spoken of it during the flight.

"Sulk, then come up with his next way to insult me," Cassian said, and Nesta laughed. He gave her a sidelong glance. "You liked seeing me play courtier?"

Nesta's mouth quirked upward. "I wouldn't want you to be that way forever, but it was . . . enticing. It gave me some ideas."

His eyes glowed, and though they were within view of the entire city, he laid a hand against her cheek. Brushed a kiss to her mouth. "It gave me some ideas as well, Nes." He pressed against her, and she understood his meaning entirely.

She laughed and pulled away, aiming for the end of the bridge. "People are watching."

"I don't care." He fell into step beside her again, slinging an arm over her shoulder for emphasis. "I have nothing to hide with you. I want them to know we share a bed." He kissed her temple, tucking her into his side as they walked through the bustling city.

Such a simple, lovely claim, and yet . . . She found herself asking, "Does it undermine my image as a warrior to be with you?"

"No. Does it undermine Feyre's when she's seen with Rhys?"

Her stomach tightened. Her heartbeat pulsed in her arms, her gut. "It's different for them," she made herself say as they reached the end of the bridge and turned to walk along the quay flanking the river.

Cassian asked carefully, "Why?"

Nesta kept her focus on the glittering river, vibrant with the hues of sunset. "Because they're mates."

At his utter silence, she knew what he'd say. Halted again, bracing for it.

Cassian's face was a void. Completely empty as he said, "And we're not?"

Nesta said nothing.

He huffed a laugh. "Because they're mates and you don't want us to be."

"That word means nothing to me, Cassian," she said, voice thick as she tried to keep the people who strode past from overhearing. "It means something to all of you, but for most of my life, husband and wife was as good as it got. *Mate* is just a word."

"That's bullshit."

When she only began walking along the river again, he asked, "Why are you frightened?"

"I'm not frightened."

"What spooked you? Just being seen publicly with me like this?"

Yes. Having him kiss her and realizing that soon she'd have to return to this world humming around them, and leave the House, and she didn't know what she would do then. What it would mean for them. If she would plunge back into that dark place she'd occupied before.

Drag him down with her.

"Nesta. Talk to me."

She met his stare, but wouldn't open her mouth.

Cassian's eyes blazed. "Say it." She refused. "*Say it, Nesta.*"

"I don't know what you're talking about."

"Ask me why I vanished for nearly a week after Solstice. Why I suddenly had to do an inspection *right* after a holiday."

Nesta kept her mouth shut.

"It was because I woke up the next morning and all I wanted to do was fuck you for a week straight. And I knew what that meant, what had happened, even though you didn't, and I didn't want to scare you. You weren't ready for the truth—not yet."

Her mouth went dry.

"*Say it*," Cassian snarled. People gave them a wide berth. Some outright turned back toward the direction they'd come from.

"No."

His face shuttered with rage even as his voice became calm. "Say it."

She couldn't. Not before he'd ordered her to, and certainly not now. She wouldn't let him win like that.

"Say what I've guessed from the moment we met," he breathed. "What I knew the first time I kissed you. What became unbreakable between us on Solstice night."

She wouldn't.

"I am your *mate*, for fuck's sake!" Cassian shouted, loud enough for people across the river to hear. "You are *my* mate! Why are you still fighting it?"

She let the truth, voiced at last, wash over her.

"You promised me forever on Solstice," he said, voice breaking. "Why is one word somehow throwing you off that?"

"Because with that one word, the last scrap of my humanity goes away!" She didn't care who saw them, who heard. "With that one stupid word, I am no longer human in any way. I'm one of *you*!"

He blinked. "I thought you wanted to be one of us."

"I don't know what I want. I didn't have a *choice*."

"Well, I didn't have a choice in being shackled to you, either."

The declaration slammed into her. *Shackled*.

He sucked in a breath. "That was an incredibly poor choice of words."

"But the truth, right?"

"No. I was angry—it's not true."

"Why? Your friends saw me for what I was. What I am. The mating bond made you stupidly blind to it. How many times did they warn you away from me, Cassian?" She barked a cold laugh.

Shackled.

Words beckoned, sharp as knives, begging for her to grab one and plunge it into his chest. Make him hurt as much as that one word hurt her. Make him bleed.

But if she did that, if she ripped into him . . . She couldn't. Wouldn't let herself do it.

He pleaded, "I didn't mean it like—"

"I'm calling in my favor," she said.

He went still, brows bunching. And then his eyes widened. "Whatever you're—"

"I want you to leave. Go up to the House of Wind for the night. Do not speak to me until I come talk to *you*, or until a week has passed. Whichever comes first. I don't care."

Until she'd mastered herself enough to not hurt him, to stop feeling the old urge to strike and maim before she could be wounded.

Cassian lurched toward her, but winced, back arching. Like the bargain tattoo on his back had burned him.

"Go away," she ordered.

His throat worked, eyes bulging. Fighting the power of the bargain with his every breath.

But then he whirled, wingbeats booming as he leaped into the skies above the river.

Nesta remained on the quay as her spine tingled, and she knew her tattoo had vanished.

⁜

Emerie was at her kitchen table when Nesta appeared at the back door. Mor had winnowed her here without a question, without so much as a glance of disapproval. Nesta had been beyond caring about it, though.

Was only grateful the female had appeared—likely sent by Cassian. She didn't care about that, either.

Nesta made it two steps into Emerie's shop before she collapsed and cried.

She barely noticed what happened. How Emerie helped her into a chair, how the words tumbled out, explaining what she and Cassian had said, what she'd done to him.

A knock sounded on the door an hour later, and Nesta stopped crying when she saw who stood there.

Gwyn threw her arms around Nesta. "I heard you might need us." Nesta was so stunned to see the priestess that she returned the hug.

Mor, a step behind, gave her a concerned nod, and then winnowed away.

Emerie was the one to say to Gwyn, "I can't believe you left the library."

Gwyn stroked Nesta's head. "Some things are more important than fear." She cleared her throat. "But please don't remind me too much. I'm so nervous I really might vomit."

Even Nesta smiled at that.

Her two friends fussed over her, sitting at the kitchen table and drinking hot cocoa—a belated Solstice gift to Emerie from Nesta, pilfered from the House's larder. They ate dinner, and then dessert, and discussed their latest reads. They spoke about everything and nothing long into the night.

Only when Nesta's eyes burned with exhaustion, her body a limp weight, did they go upstairs. There were three bedrooms above the shop, all pristine and simple, and Nesta changed into the nightgown Emerie offered without a second thought.

She'd talk to him tomorrow. Sleep now, safe with her friends around her, and talk to him tomorrow.

She'd explain everything—why she'd balked, why it frightened her, this next step into the unknown. The life beyond it. She'd apologize for using their bargain to send him away, and not stop apologizing until he smiled again.

Perhaps the future did not need to be so planned—she could just take it one day at a time. As long as she had Cassian at her side, her friends with her, she could do it. Face it. They wouldn't let her fall back into that pit. Cassian would never let her fall again.

But if she did fall . . . he'd be waiting for her at the top again. Hand outstretched. She didn't deserve it, but she'd endeavor to be worthy of him.

Nesta fell asleep with that thought ringing, a weight lifted from her chest.

Tomorrow, she'd tell Cassian everything. Tomorrow, her life would begin.

✢

A male scent filled her room. It wasn't Cassian. And it wasn't Rhys or Azriel.

It was full of hate, and Nesta lurched upward just as a rough laugh sounded. Down the hall, Gwyn screamed—then fell silent.

In the dark, she could make out nothing, and she fumbled for the power within her, for the knife next to the bed—

Something cold and wet pressed into her face.

It burned her nostrils, flaying open her mind.

Darkness swept in, and she was gone.

CHAPTER 63

Nesta's bargain had required that he go to the House of Wind for the night.

And that he could speak to her only once she spoke to him, or after a week had passed.

Easy enough rules to maneuver around. He made a mental note to teach her to word her bargains a little more cleverly.

Cassian waited until the required night had passed and then found Rhys at dawn, asking his brother to winnow him into Windhaven. Mor had reluctantly informed him she'd brought Nesta there the day before. He'd finish this fight with Nesta, one way or another. It had never frightened him. The mating bond, or that Nesta was his. He'd guessed it well before the Cauldron had turned her.

The only thing that frightened him was that she might reject it. Hate him for it. Chafe against it. He'd beheld the truth in her eyes on Solstice, when the mating bond had been like so much gold thread between their souls, but she'd still hesitated. And yesterday his temper had gotten the better of him, and . . . he'd start off round two by getting her to say just one word to him, so he'd be free to speak the rest.

The apology, the declaration he still needed to make—all of it.

He scented both Nesta and Gwyn at Emerie's back door when he knocked. It moved him beyond words, that Gwyn had braved the world beyond the library to comfort Nesta. Even as it shamed him that he'd been the cause of it.

But at his side, Rhys's face was suddenly pale. "They're not here."

Cassian didn't wait before he shoved into the shop, breaking the lock on Emerie's door. If someone had hurt them, taken them—

No one was in the cozy room in the back. But—suddenly there were *male* scents in this room, as if they'd winnowed right in.

Illyrians had no magic like that.

Except on one night, when Illyrians possessed an ancient, wild power.

"No." He charged up the stairs, the steps rank with those male scents, and that of the females' fear. He found Nesta's room first.

She'd fought. The bed was shoved across the room, the nightstand turned over, and blood—male blood, from the scent of it—lay in a puddle on the floor. But the acrid scent of the sleeping ointment, enough to knock out a horse, lingered.

His head went quiet. Emerie's and Gwyn's rooms were the same. Signs of a struggle, but not of the females themselves.

Fear bloomed, so vast and broad he could barely breathe. It was a message—to the females for thinking themselves warriors, and to *him* for teaching them, for defying the Illyrians' archaic hierarchies and rules.

Rhys came up beside him, his face white with that same dread. "Devlon just confirmed everything. The Blood Rite began at midnight."

And Gwyn, Emerie, and Nesta had been snatched from their beds. To participate in it.

PART FOUR

ATARAXIA

CHAPTER 64

Someone had poured sand into her mouth. And taken a hammer to her head.

Was still pounding on it, apparently.

Nesta pried her tongue from her teeth, swallowing a few times to work some moisture back into her mouth. Her aching head—

Scents hit her. Male, varied, and so many—

Hard, cold ground lay beneath her bare legs, pine needles poking through the thin material of her nightgown. Chill, blood-icing wind carried all those male scents above a tide of snow and pine and dirt—

Nesta's eyes flew open. A broad male back filled her vision, most of it obscured by a pair of wings. Bound wings.

Images of last night pelted her: the males who'd grabbed her, how she'd fought until they'd pushed something against her face that had her blacking out, hearing Gwyn and Emerie screaming—

Nesta jolted upright.

The view was worse than she'd expected. Far, far worse.

Slowly, silently, she twisted in place. Unconscious Illyrian warriors were strewn around her. At her back, at her head. At her bare feet. More surrounded her, at least two hundred, stretching between the towering pines.

The Blood Rite.

She must have awoken before the others because she was Made. Different.

Nesta reached inward, toward that place where the ancient, awful power rested, and found nothing. As if the well had been drained, as if the sea had receded.

The Blood Rite's spells bound magic. Her powers had been rendered useless.

She knew her shaking wasn't entirely from the cold. Whatever time she had wouldn't last long. The others would soon stir.

And find her standing among them, in nothing but a nightgown. Without weapons.

She had to move. Had to find Emerie and Gwyn in this endless sprawl of bodies. Unless they had been dumped elsewhere.

Cassian, Rhysand, and Azriel had all been left in different places, she remembered. They'd spent days killing their way to each other amid the bloodthirsty warriors and beasts who roamed these lands. But they had somehow found each other and scaled Ramiel, the sacred mountain, and won the Rite.

She'd be lucky to clear this general area.

Her breath catching, Nesta eased to her feet. Away from the shield of the warriors' bodies, the cold slammed into her, nearly robbing her of breath. Her shaking deepened.

She needed something warmer. Needed shoes. Needed to make a weapon.

Nesta peered at the watery sun, as if it'd tell her what direction to go to find her friends. But the light seared her eyes, worsening the pounding in her head. Trees—she could find the mossy side of the trees, Cassian had said. North would lie that way.

The nearest tree rose about twenty feet and ten bodies away. From what she could see, no moss grew anywhere on it.

So she'd find higher ground and survey the land. See where Ramiel loomed and if she could spot the other dumping grounds.

But she needed clothes and weapons and food and to find Gwyn and Emerie, and oh, gods—

Nesta pressed a hand over her mouth to keep her trembling exhale to near-silence. Move. She had to *move*.

But someone already had.

The rustle of his wings gave him away. Nesta whirled.

A hundred feet off, separated from her by the sea of sleeping bodies, stood a beast of a male.

She didn't know him, but she recognized that gleam in his eye. The predatory intent and cruel amusement. Knew what it meant when his stare dipped to her nightgown, her breasts peaked against the frigid cold, her bare legs.

Fear burned like acid through her entire body.

None of the others stirred. At least she had that. But this male . . .

He glanced to his left—just for a blink. Nesta followed his stare, and her breath caught. Embedded in the trunk of a tree, gleaming faintly, was a knife.

Impossible. Having weapons in the Blood Rite went against its rules. Had the male known it would be there, or had he just spied it before she had?

It didn't matter. It only mattered that the knife existed. And it was the sole weapon in sight.

She could run. Let him lunge at the knife and flee in the opposite direction and pray he didn't follow.

Or she could go for the blade. Beat him to it and then . . . she didn't know what she'd do then. But she stood in a field of sleeping warriors who would all soon awaken, and if they found her weaponless, defenseless—

Nesta ran.

⁜

Cassian couldn't breathe.

Hadn't been able to breathe or speak for long minutes now. His family had arrived, and they all surrounded him in the wrecked bedroom of Emerie's house. They were speaking, Azriel with some urgency, but Cassian didn't hear him, heard nothing but the roaring in his head before he said to no one in particular, "I'm going after them."

Silence fell, and he turned to find them all staring at him, pale and wide-eyed.

Cassian tapped the Siphons on the backs of his hands, and his remaining Siphons appeared at his shoulders, knees, and chest. He nodded to Rhys. "Winnow me to her. Az, you find Emerie and Gwyn."

Rhys didn't move an inch. "You know the laws, Cass."

"Fuck the laws."

"What laws?" Feyre demanded.

"Tell her," Rhys ordered him, night swirling around his wings. Cassian bristled. "*Tell her, Cassian.*"

The asshole had used that inherent dominance on him. Cassian gritted out, "Anyone who pulls a warrior from the Blood Rite will be hunted down and executed. Along with the warrior who is dishonorably removed from the Rite."

Feyre rubbed at her face. "So Nesta, Emerie, and Gwyn have to stay in the Rite."

"Even I can't break those rules," Rhys said, a shade softer. "No matter how much I might want to," he added, clasping Cassian's shoulder.

Cassian's stomach turned over. Nesta and her friends—*his* friends—were in the Rite. And he could do nothing to interfere, not without damning them all. His hands shook. "So, what—we just sit on our asses for a week and wait?" The idea was abhorrent.

Feyre gripped his trembling fingers, squeezing tight. "Did you—Cassian, weren't you listening at all when we got here?"

No. He'd barely heard anything.

Azriel said tightly, "My spies got word that Eris has been captured by Briallyn. She sent his remaining soldiers after him while he was out hunting with his hounds. They grabbed him and somehow, they were all winnowed back to her palace. I'm guessing using Koschei's power."

"I don't care." Cassian aimed for the doorway. Even if . . . Fuck. Hadn't he been the one to tell Rhys not to go after those soldiers? To leave them be? He was a fool. He'd left an armed enemy in his blind spot and forgotten about it. But Eris could rot for all he cared.

Az said, "We have to get him out."

Cassian drew up short. "*We?*"

Rhys stepped up next to Azriel, Feyre beside him. A formidable wall. "We can't go," Feyre said, nodding to Rhys. It needed no explanation: with the babe less than two months away, Feyre wasn't risking anything. But Rhys . . .

Cassian challenged his High Lord, "You can be in and out in an hour."

"I can't go." Midnight storms swirled in Rhys's eyes.

"Yes, you fucking can," Cassian said, rage rising like a tidal wave that would sweep away all in its path. "You—"

"I can't."

It was agony—pure, undiluted agony that filled Rhys's face. And fear. Feyre slipped her tattooed fingers through Rhys's.

Amren asked sharply, "Why?"

Rhys stared at the tattoo on Feyre's fingers, interlaced with his. His throat bobbed. Feyre answered for him. "We made a bargain. After the war. To . . . only leave this world together."

Amren began massaging her temples, muttering a prayer for sanity.

Azriel asked, "You made a bargain to die together?"

"Fools," Amren hissed. "Romantic, idealistic *fools*." Rhys turned bleak eyes to her.

Cassian couldn't get a breath down. Az stood still as a statue.

"If Rhys dies," Feyre said thickly, fear bright in her own eyes, "I die." Her fingers grazed her swollen belly. The babe would die, too.

"And if *you* die, Feyre," Azriel said softly, "then Rhys dies."

The words rang hollow and cold like a death knell. If Feyre didn't survive the labor . . .

Cassian's knees threatened to buckle. Rhy's face was tight with pleading and pain. "I never thought it'd turn out like this," Rhys said quietly.

Amren massaged her temples again. "We can discuss the idiocy of this bargain later." Feyre glared at her, and Amren glared right back before saying to Cassian, "You and Azriel need to retrieve Eris."

"Why not you?"

Feyre pinched the bridge of her nose. "Because Amren is . . ."

"Powerless," Amren snarled. "You can say it, girl."

Feyre winced. "Mor left for Vallahan this morning and is out of our daemati magic's range. Az can't go in alone. We need you, Cassian."

Cassian stilled. They just waited.

For Nesta to participate in the Blood Rite, to risk every horror and misery while he went off to save fucking *Eris* . . . "Let him die."

"As tempting as that is," Feyre said, "he poses a great danger to us in Briallyn's hands. If he's under the Crown's influence, he'll reveal everything he knows." She asked Cassian, "What *does* he know about us, exactly?"

"Too much." Cassian cleared his throat. Through their own bickering, through his need to goad Eris, he'd revealed too much. "He was worried about what we'd do with Nesta as a Night Court power, and with all three objects of the Dread Trove at our disposal. He thought the Night Court might turn around and attempt some sort of power grab."

Feyre said hopefully, "Maybe the Made dagger we gave him will grant him immunity from the Crown. If he's carrying the dagger, if they haven't unarmed him, it might shield him against another Made object."

"But we don't know that," Rhys countered. "And he'll still be in Briallyn's clutches. She might be able to sense the dagger herself—and it might respond to her."

Az added darkly, "And there are plenty of other methods to get him to talk."

Amren cut in, "You need to go now." She turned to Feyre and Rhys. "We will return to Velaris and have a nice, long talk about this bargain of yours."

Cassian didn't bother to read Feyre's and Rhys's expressions as he gazed toward the small window, the wilderness beyond. As if he could see Nesta there.

He summoned his armor, the intricate scales and plates clamping with reassuring familiarity over his body. "I trained Nesta well. Trained them all well," he said, his throat working. He added into the silence as Az tapped his Siphons and his own armor appeared, "If anyone can survive the Blood Rite, it's them."

If they could find each other.

⁜

Nesta broke into a flat-out sprint toward the tree with the knife, the male launching into movement only a heartbeat afterward.

He tripped over the scattered bodies, but Nesta kept her knees up. A mirror of every footwork exercise they'd done with the ladder on the ground, as if those bodies were the rope rungs to avoid. Muscle memory kicked in; she barely glanced at the tangle of limbs as she aimed for the tree. But the male had found his footing and closed in fast.

Someone had to have planted the weapon, either under the cover of darkness last night or weeks ago. The Blood Rite was savage enough without true weapons—only the weapons they made—but with actual steel thrown in . . .

The male had a good six inches and a hundred pounds on her. In physical combat, he'd possess every advantage. But if she could get that knife—

Nesta broke free of the bodies, legs flying as she ran the last few feet to the tree trunk with her hand outstretched. She brushed the knife's handle—

The male barreled into her with all the force of a full-grown Illyrian warrior.

The breath whooshed out of her at the impact as they went down—and over the hill's edge on the other side of the tree.

They tumbled toward the streambed a hundred feet below, flipping as they careened down the side of the hill. Rocks and leaves cracked and scratched against her, wings snapped above and below her, her hair lashed her face as her hands grappled—

Nesta slammed into the streambed so hard her spine groaned, the male landing atop her, sending every remaining scrap of breath exploding from her lungs.

His wings twitched. But he did not move.

Nesta opened her eyes to find herself staring into his unseeing gaze. To find her hand clenching the dagger she'd buried in his throat soaked in warm blood.

Grunting, Nesta rolled him off. Left the dagger sticking out of his throat, blood still leaking from the wound. The knife had pierced all the way through to the nape of his neck.

Nesta spat a mouthful of blood onto the dry stones. Her nightgown was covered in blood and dirt, her skin raw and stinging. But she was alive. And the male was not.

Nesta allowed herself to inhale slowly through her nose for a count of six. She held the breath, then slowly loosed it. Did the breathing exercise twice more. Assessed the state of her body, from her pounding head to her torn feet. Breathed again.

When her mind had stilled, Nesta pulled the knife from the male's throat. Then stripped off his clothes, item by item, including his boots. She dressed herself with cold efficiency, shucking off the bloody nightgown and dropping it onto the male's face in a mockery of a funeral shroud, then tucked the knife into the belt she cinched as tight as it would go. The clothes hung off her, and the too-big boots might be a liability, but it was better than the nightgown.

And then she went to find her friends.

CHAPTER 65

Nesta scaled the other side of the valley to find the land beyond empty of warriors. Behind her, across the small ravine, the others still slept. No sign of Emerie or Gwyn amongst them. No sign of where they might be, either.

Cassian had told her while lying in bed one night, sweaty and spent, that there were three dumping grounds for the Rite—one in the north, one in the west, and one in the south. Her friends had to be in the others, either together or one in each. They'd be terrified when they awoke.

Gwyn—

Nesta refused to consider it as she hurried through the pines, putting distance between herself and the sleeping warriors before she found a towering tree. She climbed, sap quickly coating her fingers, and when she cleared the canopy . . .

Ramiel might as well have been across an ocean. It loomed straight ahead, with two mountains and a sea of forest and the gods knew what else between her and its barren slopes. It looked identical to Feyre's painting. She peered at the sun, then at the trunk below her, searching for moss. There—just below her left foot.

Ramiel was east. So she'd been dumped in the west, and the others . . .

She had to pick either north or south. Or would she be better off heading for the mountain and hoping she found them along the way?

She scoured her memory for any advice Cassian might have offhandedly given her. Cassian . . . Maybe he was already on his way to save her.

The bubble of hope in her chest ruptured. He couldn't rescue her. He'd informed her himself about the laws forbidding such a thing. He'd be executed, and so would she. Even Rhysand or Feyre couldn't stop it.

Cassian wasn't coming to save her. No one was coming to save her, or Emerie, or Gwyn.

Nesta flexed her fingers, working some movement back into them after sitting still for so long. She swore softly at the blood that dribbled from the few small cuts on her hands.

They should have healed by now. But the magic that bound the Rite also suppressed any healing magic within a faerie's blood, apparently. Including her own.

Any wounds could be fatal. Would heal at a human, mortal pace. Nesta allowed herself to take another few slow, steadying breaths. She could do this. *Would* do this.

She'd save her friends. And herself.

Shouting echoed from far behind her. The others were waking. Cursing, Nesta hurried down the tree, bark and pine needles sticking to her sap-crusted hands. She had to pick a direction, and be running by the time she hit the bottom.

The shouting behind her became accented by screams.

She glanced back, making sure no one was gaining on her. And as she did, she caught a flash of light from the woven bracelet on her left wrist. From the little silver charm in the middle, glinting in the light.

No—it was *glowing*.

Nesta brushed a fingertip over the charm. It buzzed against her skin. Dread sluiced through her—a pricking at her nape, as if a soft voice whispered, *Hurry*.

Nesta twisted to better see it against the sun, but the light within the charm vanished. Nesta pivoted northward. The charm shone again.

Brows rising, she angled her arm to the east: nothing. South: only a faint glow. No sense of urgency, of pure panic. But north . . . The charm blazed, and again that dread filled her.

Nesta sucked in a breath, remembering that night in the House when they'd made the bracelets. Remembering her wish for them: *the courage to go out into the world when we are ready, but to always be able to find our way back to each other. No matter what.*

She'd Made the charms. Into beacons. And whichever of her friends lay to the south wasn't in nearly as much danger as the one to the north.

The land that way was uphill. A small blessing. The other warriors would likely choose the fastest and easiest way to Ramiel and avoid a route that involved climbing.

But how could the charms work here? The Rite banned magic, both from a wielder and from any objects. Unless the power surrounding the Rite didn't stifle Made items. Fae spells had to be carefully worded—perhaps whoever had woven this spell for the Illyrians had never considered the possibility of a Made item winding up in the Rite.

Her own power lay dormant, though. She strained inward, reaching for it, but only emptiness met her.

Her throat tightened. She was herself a Made thing—and yet she was a person, too. The magic recognized her as a *person* and not a thing.

She hadn't realized how badly she'd needed to be shown that distinction. She inhaled the pine and distant promise of snow. *Alive*. Even in this hellscape, she was alive.

And she'd make sure her friends were, too.

Exhaling slowly, mastering her breath, Nesta lowered her arm and began moving.

Her too-big boots hit the ground, her toes shifting within them.

By the time Nesta straightened, checking the knife at her side, she was already heading north.

✢

It occurred to Nesta after ten minutes of running uphill, the glimmering charm still urging her along, her feet in those infernal boots slipping this way and that, that she needed water. And food. And would need shelter before sunset. And would have to decide whether to risk a fire, or possibly die from cold just to avoid being found.

The clothes she'd swiped off the male weren't thick enough to help her survive the night. And if the gray sky was any indication, snow or rain might be imminent.

But no warriors were on her tail. At least she had that. Unless they were as stealthy as Cassian and Azriel.

The thought had her checking her frantic pace, silencing her steps. Tucking the bracelet and glowing charm into her sleeve to hide its gleam in the dimness. Trying to leave scant evidence of her passing as she scaled a particularly steep hill and surveyed the terrain beyond.

More trees and rocks and—

Nesta dropped to the ground as an arrow whizzed past. A fucking *arrow*—

The knife hadn't been a fluke. Someone had dumped weapons in the Blood Rite. Nesta scanned the terrain behind her for the arrow. There—stuck in the base of a tree.

She slid back down the hill until she reached it, pried it free, and tucked it into her belt. Then climbed the hill again, keeping low, as she peered over the crest once more.

And came face-to-face with a razor-sharp arrowhead.

"Get up," the warrior growled.

✢

With every league Cassian flew around the queens' once-shared castle, Cassian cursed Eris for being stupid enough to get captured. Now this was Briallyn's stronghold, he supposed. Patches of snow still crusted the hilly, open land, though the first buds and sprouts of spring poked through. He kept high enough that breathing was difficult, so high that he'd appear no more than a very large bird to any human on the ground. But with his Fae eyesight, he could clearly make out what crossed the land.

He saw nothing of Eris, though. No red hair, no lick of fire, no hint of his soldiers. Azriel, circling in the opposite direction, signaled that he hadn't seen anything, either.

It was an effort to stay focused. To keep flying, circling like vultures, when his mind drifted to the northwest. To the Illyrian Mountains and the Blood Rite and Nesta.

Had she survived the initial surge? The warriors would be waking by now.

Fucking Eris. How could he have been reckless enough to let those soldiers get close?

Cassian again scanned the terrain below, fighting to keep his breathing steady in the thin air. He'd find Eris swiftly. Kick his ass, if he had time.

And what then? He couldn't do anything to help Nesta. But at least he could be closer to the Rite. Should the worst happen . . .

He shut down the thought. Nesta would survive. Gwyn and Emerie would survive.

He'd allow no other alternative.

CHAPTER 66

The Illyrian warrior was smaller than the one Nesta had killed, but this male had gotten his hands on a bow and arrow.

"Give me your weapons," he ordered, eyes darting over her, noting the blood coating her face, crusting her chin and neck.

Nesta didn't move. Didn't so much as lower her chin.

"Give me your *fucking* weapons," the male warned, voice sharpening.

"Where did you come from?" she demanded, as if he didn't have an arrow pointed at her face. And then, before he had time to answer, "Was another female there?"

The male blinked—and it was the only confirmation Nesta needed before she handed over the arrow. Slowly, slowly reached for the knife. "Did you kill her, too?" Her voice had dropped to pure ice.

"The crippled bitch? I left her to the others." He grinned. "You're better prey anyway."

Emerie. She couldn't be far off, if this male had already seen her. Nesta pulled the knife free.

The male kept the arrow pointed. "Drop it and back up ten paces."

Emerie was alive. And nearby. And in danger.

And this motherfucker wouldn't stop Nesta from saving her.

Nesta bowed her head, shoulders slumping in what she hoped the male believed was a show of resignation. Indeed, he smiled.

He didn't stand a chance.

Nesta lowered the knife. And flicked her wrist, fingers splaying as she let it soar toward the male.

Right into his groin.

He screamed, and she charged as his hand loosed on the bow. She slammed into him and the weapon, the string slapping her face hard enough to draw tears, but they crashed down, and he was shrieking—

No one would stand between her and her friends.

Her mind slid to a place of cold and calm. She grabbed the bow, flung it away. As the male writhed on the ground, trying to wrench out the knife piercing his balls, she leaped upon it, shoving it in harder. His scream sent birds scattering from the pines.

Nesta twisted the blade free, leaving him lying there. She grabbed the two arrows but didn't bother freeing the quiver pinned beneath his back. She retrieved the Illyrian bow, snatched her knife, and ran in the direction from which he'd come.

His howls followed her for miles.

⸸

A river announced its presence well before Nesta reached it. So did the warriors on its near bank, tentatively speaking with each other—feeling each other out, she guessed—as they filled what seemed to be canteens. Like someone had left those, too.

No sign of Emerie.

She kept behind a tree, downwind, and listened.

Not a whisper about Emerie or another female. Just tense rule-making about the alliances they were forming, how to reach Ramiel, who had left the weapons and canteens for them . . .

She was about to hunt for an easy spot to cross the river, away from the males, when she heard, "Pity that bitch escaped. She'd have made for good entertainment on the cold nights."

Everything in Nesta's body went still. Emerie had made it to this river. Alive.

Another said, drinking from the rushing water, "She's probably washed halfway down the mountain. If she isn't dead from the rapids, the beasts will get her before dawn."

Emerie must have jumped into the river to get away from these males.

Nesta ran her fingers across the bow slung over her shoulder. The arrows in her belt hung like weights. She should kill them for this. Fire these two arrows into two of them and *kill* them for hurting her friend—

But if Emerie had survived . . .

She pushed off the tree. Slipped to the next. And the next. Followed the river, her steps barely more than the whisper of water over stone.

Through the pines, down the hills. The rapids increased, the rocks rising like black spears. A waterfall roared ahead. If Emerie had gone over it . . .

The rapids hurtled over the edge, to the bottom a hundred feet below. No surviving that.

Nesta's throat dried out.

And dried out further as she beheld what lay across the river, caught on a fallen tree jutting from the rocky bank directly before the plunge to the falls.

Emerie.

Nesta rushed to the edge of the water, but snatched her foot back from its icy fingers. Emerie appeared unconscious, but Nesta didn't dare risk shouting her name. A glance at the sky revealed the sun at its midafternoon point, but it offered no heat, no salvation.

How long had Emerie been in the frigid water?

"Think," Nesta murmured. "Think, think."

Each minute in the water risked killing Emerie. She lay too far away to discern any injuries, but she didn't stir against the branch. Only her twitching wings showed any sign of life.

Nesta peeled off her clothes. Wished she'd taken the nightgown to tie her knife and two arrows around her leg, rather than leave them on the shore, but she had no choice. She took the Illyrian bow, though, strapping it across her chest, the string digging into her bare skin.

Naked, she eyed the distance between the falls, the rapids, the rocks, and Emerie.

"Rock to rock," she told herself. Braced for the cold.

And leaped into the water.

Nesta gasped and sputtered at the icy shock, hands shaking so hard she feared she'd lose her grip on the slick rocks and be hurtled over the falls. But she kept going. Aiming for Emerie. Closer and closer, until finally she swam frantically between the last rock and the riverbank—and Emerie draped over the half-submerged tree beyond it.

Shaking, teeth chattering, Nesta dragged Emerie free of the branches and farther up the bank, then crouched over her.

Emerie's face was battered, her arm bleeding from a gash in her biceps. But she breathed.

Nesta reined in her sob of relief and gently shook her friend. "Emerie, wake up."

The female didn't so much as moan in pain. Nesta searched through Emerie's dark hair, and her fingers came away bloody.

She had to get her across the river. Find shelter. Make a fire and get them warm. The bow she'd carried wasn't enough to protect them. Not nearly.

"All right, Emerie." Nesta's teeth chattered so hard her face ached. "Sorry about this."

She gripped her friend's nightgown and ripped it down the middle, baring Emerie's thin, toned body to the elements. Nesta peeled off the nightgown and twisted it into a long rope, then unshouldered the bow.

"You're not going to enjoy this part," Nesta said through her clacking teeth, hauling Emerie back to the water. "Neither am I," she muttered, the icy water biting into her numbed feet.

Cold as the Cauldron. Cold as—

Nesta let the thought pass, willing it to drift by like a cloud. Focused.

She managed to get Emerie into the water up to their waists, holding her as tightly as her shaking fingers would allow. Then she hoisted her friend onto her back and hooked the Illyrian bow around them both, letting the near-unbreakable string dig into her own chest so the wood rested against Emerie's spine, tethering them together.

"Better than nothing." She looped Emerie's limp arms around her shoulders, then took Emerie's nightgown and wrapped it around her wrists, tying them in place. "Hold on," she warned, even though Emerie remained an unmoving weight across her back.

Rock to rock. Just as she'd done before. Rock to rock and then back to the shore.

Rock to rock. Step to step.

She'd done ten thousand steps in the House of Wind. Had done more than that over these months. She could do this.

Nesta moved deeper into the water, biting back her cry at its cold.

Emerie swayed and banged into her, and the Illyrian bow's string dug into Nesta's chest hard enough to slice the skin. But it held.

Step to step to step.

By the time Nesta returned to the far bank, shaking, near sobbing, the bowstring had drawn blood. But they were on solid land, and her clothes and weapons were there, and—and now to find warmth and shelter.

Nesta laid Emerie on the pine needles, covering her friend with the dry clothes she'd left behind, and gathered what wood she could carry. Naked, shaking, she could barely hold on to the sticks in her arms as she piled them near Emerie. Her trembling fingers struggled to twist the sticks long enough to ignite a spark, to coax the kindling to a flame, but—there. Fire. She raided the area for fallen logs, praying they weren't too wet from the mists off the rapids to catch flame.

When the fire was crackling steadily, Nesta slithered under her pile of clothes beside Emerie and wrapped her arms around her friend, their skin pressing close. They were both freezing, but the fire was warm, and beneath the male's large clothes the chill from the water began to fade.

But they were utterly exposed to the world. If someone came by, they'd be dead.

Nesta held Emerie, feeling her body warm by increments. Watching her breathing ease. Feeling her own chattering teeth calm.

Soon it would be night. And what would emerge in the dark . . .

Nesta remembered Cassian's tales of the monsters that prowled these woods. She swallowed, wrapping her arms more tightly around Emerie. She glanced at her arm, the charm still glowing faintly, only pointing southward now. A sole glimmer of hope, of direction. What had happened to Gwyn? Was she enduring her worst nightmares again? Was she—

Nesta focused on her breathing. Stilled her mind.

She'd survive the night. Help Emerie. Then find Gwyn.

Around a river, she'd learned on her hike with Cassian, cave systems were often carved out by the water. But to find one, she'd have to leave Emerie . . .

Nesta glanced at the vanishing sun, then slipped out from under the pile of clothes. She covered Emerie with leaves and twigs, added another log to the fire, and risked taking the male's jacket to wrap around herself.

Nesta wore the boots, even though her blistered feet objected, and made a careful circle around the campsite, listening for anything. Anyone. Scanning every rock and cleft boulder.

Nothing.

The sky darkened. There had to be caves around here somewhere. Where the *fuck* were they? Where—

"The entrance is here."

Nesta whirled, dagger out, to find an Illyrian male standing ten feet away. How he'd crept up, how he'd survived given the gash running down the side of his face—

He noted her own wounds, her nakedness beneath the coat, the bare legs and the boots. The knife.

Yet no lust or hatred clouded his brown eyes.

The male carefully pointed to what she'd mistaken for a leaf-covered boulder. "That's a cave. Big enough to fit inside."

Nesta drew herself up to her full height. Let him see the cold violence in her eyes.

"You won't survive an hour on the ground once night falls," the male said, his boyishly charming face neutral. "And if you're not already scaling a tree, then I'm going to guess you've got someone hurt with you."

She revealed nothing.

He lifted his hands. No weapons, no blood on him save the gash leaking down his face. "I came from the landing site to the west." Where she'd come from. "I saw the body in the gulch—you did that to Novius, didn't you? He was naked. You're in a male's clothes. And that must be the knife that pierced his throat. Do you know who the hell dumped weapons here?"

Nesta kept her silence. Night deepened around them.

The male shrugged when she didn't reply. "I decided to head northward, hoping to reach Ramiel by a less traveled path, avoiding conflict with the others entirely, if I can. I have no quarrel with you. But I am going into that cave now, and if you're smart, you'll bring whoever is with you and come inside, too."

"And have you take my weapons and kill me in my sleep?"

The male's brown eyes flickered. "I know who you are. I'm not stupid enough to go after you."

"It's the Blood Rite. You'd be forgiven."

"Feyre Cursebreaker would not forgive me for killing her sister."

"So you do this to gain her favor?"

"Does it matter? I swear an oath on Enalius himself not to kill you or whoever is with you. Take it or leave it."

"Not to kill us or harm us in any way. Or have anyone you know do so, either."

A slight smile. "You adapted to the rules of the Fae quickly. But yes. I swear that, too."

Nesta's throat bobbed as she weighed the male's expression. Glanced to the hidden cave entrance behind him.

"I need help carrying her."

⁜

They didn't risk a fire in the cave, but the male, whose name was Balthazar, offered his thick wool cloak to cover Emerie. Nesta slid Emerie into the dead male's clothing, leaving herself wearing only the leather jacket, and though it went against every instinct, she allowed Balthazar to sit on her other side, his warmth leaking into her chilled body.

"When dawn comes, be gone," Nesta said into the dark of the musty, leaf-filled cave as night fell.

"If we survive the night, I'll be glad to go," Balthazar said. "The beasts of the woods might smell your friend's blood and track us right to this cave."

Nesta slid her gaze to the young warrior. "Why aren't you out there killing everyone?"

"Because I want to reach the mountain and become Oristian. But if I meet someone I'd like to kill, I won't hesitate."

Silence fell, and remained.

Within moments, branches snapped.

Balthazar's body tightened, his breath becoming impossibly quiet. In the pitch-black of the cave, the only sounds were the rustle of their clothes and the leaves beneath them.

A howl rent the night, and Nesta flinched, clutching Emerie closer to her side.

But the snapping branches and howling moved off, and Balthazar's body relaxed. "It's just the first," he whispered into the blackness. "They'll prowl until dawn." She didn't want to know what was out there. Not as screaming began in the distance. "Some can climb trees," Balthazar murmured. "The dumb warriors forget that."

Nesta stayed silent.

"I'll take first watch," the warrior said. "Rest."

"Fine." But she did not dare close her eyes.

✠

Nesta remained awake the entire night. If Balthazar knew she hadn't been sleeping during his watch, he didn't say. She'd used the time to do her Mind-Stilling exercises, which kept the edge off, but not entirely.

The crackle of brush under the paws and talons of stalking beasts and the screaming of the Illyrians continued for hours.

When Balthazar nudged her with a knee and she feigned waking, he only murmured that he was going to sleep and tucked himself against her. Nesta let herself soak up his warmth against the frigid cave air. Whether his deep breaths were true sleep or faked, as hers had been, she didn't care.

Nesta kept her eyes open, even when they became unbearably sore and heavy. Even when the warmth from her two companions threatened to lull her to sleep.

She would not sleep. Wouldn't lower her guard for one moment.

Dawn eventually leaked through the lattice of branches, and the screams and howling faded, then vanished. A quick inspection in the dim light revealed that though her friend remained unconscious, the wound on Emerie's head had stopped bleeding. But—

"You'll find plenty of clothes today," Balthazar said, seeming to read her mind. He stepped into the daylight and peered around, then cursed under his breath. "Plenty of clothes."

The words sent Nesta scrambling out of the cave.

Winged bodies lay everywhere, many half-eaten.

A brisk wind ruffled Balthazar's dark hair as he walked away. "Good luck, Archeron."

⸸

Eris was nowhere to be found in the lands surrounding the queens' castle. But Azriel had encountered a passing human merchant on the road from the palace, who hadn't hesitated when he'd been asked whether a Fae male had recently arrived. He readily supplied that a red-haired Fae male had been dragged into the castle the night before last. He'd heard in the tavern that the male was to be taken soon to another site.

"We'll wait here until they leave the castle. Then trail them from the cloud cover," Azriel said, face dark.

Cassian grunted his agreement and dragged a hand through his hair. He'd barely slept, thinking of Nesta, and of Feyre and Rhys.

Cassian and Azriel hadn't discussed their brother's bargain, which would doom Rhys should Feyre not survive the labor. To lose her would be unbearable, but to also lose Rhys . . . Cassian couldn't think of it without feeling sick. Perhaps Amren was working on some way to undo the bargain—if anyone could think of a way, it would be her. Or Helion, he supposed.

Cassian and Azriel were beyond Rhys's and Feyre's daemati range, though. They'd have no news of anything.

But he'd know if Nesta were dead. In his heart, his soul, he'd sense it. Would feel it.

A mate always did.

Even if she'd rejected that bond.

⸸

Nesta had lived through the night, thanks to dumb luck and an Illyrian more interested in politics than killing.

Exhaustion slowed every movement as Nesta picked her way through the dismembered bodies, peeling off whatever clothes were intact and not stained by blood or bodily fluids. Many of the warriors had pissed or shit themselves when the beasts of the forest had found them. Finding a clean pair of pants was a tall order.

But Nesta gathered enough, including a smaller pair of boots for herself and one set for Emerie, and picked up another dagger, two canteens of water, and what seemed to be someone's half-eaten rabbit dinner.

By the time she returned to the cave—dressed, watered, and with half a leg of rabbit in hand—Emerie was awake. Weak, but awake. She said nothing as Nesta handed her the meat and the water, then helped her dress.

Only when Nesta eased her out of the cave and Emerie surveyed the carnage did she rasp, "Gwyn?"

Nesta, her arm looped around Emerie's middle, lifted her free hand—the one with the bracelet on her wrist. She slowly pointed her arm in each direction. "South," she said when the charm gleamed. Gwyn's general location hadn't changed since yesterday.

Emerie sucked in a breath. Lifted her own bracelet to the south. The charm glittered almost frantically now, emitting an urgent sense of needing to move, to act, to be swift.

Wonder flashed in Emerie's eyes before sharpening to grim focus. "Let's hurry."

CHAPTER 67

Emerie confirmed that she'd been attacked and chased by the males Nesta had spied at the river. She'd leaped in as a final shot at survival, hit her head on a rock, and remembered nothing until the cave.

Nesta gave her a swift, brutal rundown of her own encounters as they picked their way southward, mostly keeping silent to listen for any passing Illyrians. A few solo warriors ignored them as they trudged past, covered in blood, all heading east; a few packs battled each other; and many more bodies lay on the cold earth.

They scanned for any gleam of copper hair. But they saw and heard no sign of Gwyn. They did not speak of whether their charms might be leading them toward a body.

The day passed, and they found another cave as night fell, huddling together for warmth. Emerie insisted on taking the first watch, and Nesta slept at last. When her friend woke her, Nesta had the feeling that Emerie had let her doze for longer than she should have.

In the morning, they emerged to find blood mixed with the snow on the ground. The animal tracks around the mouth of the cave were large enough to roil Nesta's stomach.

Soon, snow began falling in earnest. Enough to veil the world ahead and behind, and any enemies with it. They shivered with each step southward, though they'd piled on extra jackets from fallen warriors, and as the morning crept toward midday, Nesta flexed her fingers to keep her hands from freezing through.

If she survived, she'd never again complain about the summer heat; never again take for granted her coat and hat and gloves and that stupid scarf Cassian had made her wear out of her apartment all those months earlier.

"I smell fire," Emerie murmured. They'd last spoken hours ago, concentrating instead on staving off the cold that was so deep it made their teeth ache.

They halted behind two pines, surveying the terrain, the snow-heavy sky. Nesta consulted her charm. "That way," she said, inclining her head to the left. "The fire is also in that direction—the wind's carrying the smoke down from that ridge."

"It could be Gwyn's fire," Emerie suggested hopefully.

Nesta nodded, calming her pounding heart. They inched along, darting from tree to tree, listening for any danger around them, any hint of Gwyn ahead. They'd been moving for several minutes when the laughter reached them. Male laughter.

Emerie's face paled as she held her bracelet toward the source of the laughter. Its charm glowed, glinting even in the sun's weak winter light.

"Keep downwind," Nesta said grimly. "We'll take the ridge from the southern side."

⸸

A nightgown hung on a branch near the camp's edge.

Nesta's stomach rose, her meager breakfast burning her throat. A soft inhale of breath from Emerie was her friend's only sign of dread and pain as they climbed the last of the ridge toward the warriors camped atop it. They were boasting about the males they'd killed, the remaining trek toward Ramiel. Nesta strained to hear any hint of a female amongst them. If Gwyn's nightgown was hanging from a tree, then Gwyn—

To hell with reaching Ramiel. She'd spend the rest of the week here, killing them all slowly.

The crest of the ridge lay ten feet above.

Nesta controlled her breathing, keeping it silent and shallow, as the Valkyries had done. A glance at Emerie told her the female was doing the same, even as rage kindled in her dark eyes.

They'd decided before they ascended the slope that, as Emerie's wings arced too high above her head, Nesta would assess what lay beyond the ridge. Emerie held two knives; Nesta had one dagger and the Illyrian bow and two arrows. Nesta would have to use her peek to gather information about what weapons the males had, too.

They swapped one final look, just as the males burst into laughter, and Nesta rose. Only high enough for her vision to clear the ridge's edge.

Ten males sat around a fire, eating. Some had axes, some had swords, some had knives. Nesta picked out the male in the middle, laughing and talking the loudest, as the leader. His face—she'd seen his face before. Somewhere.

No sign of Gwyn. Nesta ducked back down, pivoting toward Emerie.

But Emerie was gone. Dragged halfway down the slope, and held between two grinning males.

⸸

No one went in or out of the towering, gray-stoned castle. Azriel and Cassian took turns circling it from high above, waiting for any sign of a departing group, but the gates did not open. Nobody even came or departed from the walled city surrounding it. As if the gates had been locked, its people kept within. No villages dotted the hills around it, either.

The castle seemed to have risen out of the earth and settled there, squatting like some enormous beast over the land.

"Briallyn has to know we're here," Cassian said as he alit, his latest aerial survey completed. "You think she's waiting for us to make a move?"

"I think the better question is if Eris is still alive," Azriel murmured, shadows whispering in his ear. "I can't get a read on it."

"Waiting is pointless. We should break in. Keep out of sight, so she won't even know we're there and be tempted to use the Crown on us."

"I told you: the place is guarded with as many wards as the House of Wind. If Briallyn is moving Eris, we'll be better off catching him then."

"Maybe the merchant was wrong."

"Maybe. We'll continue surveillance through tomorrow." Azriel crossed his arms. "I know you want to help Nesta. Maybe Amren can find some loophole in the laws . . ."

Cassian swallowed hard. "There's no loophole. If I interfere, we're both dead. And even if I did, Nesta would kill me if I jumped in to save her. She'd never forgive me for it."

He'd had nothing else to do except contemplate it these past days. Nesta's fate was her own. She was strong enough to forge her own path, even through the horrors of the Blood Rite. He'd taught her the skills to do so himself.

And even if the laws had allowed it, he would never take that away from her: the chance to save herself.

✣

"I didn't think you'd be stupid enough to fall for the nightgown, but I suppose that's the difference between a female thinking she's a warrior and the real thing," the cold-faced leader said as Nesta and Emerie were hurled at his booted feet. He chuckled, eyes glassy enough that Nesta wondered if someone had smuggled in a case of wine along with the weapons. "Hello Emerie."

Nesta recognized the male then. Bellius, Emerie's hateful cousin.

Emerie only spat, "Where the *fuck* is she?"

Bellius shrugged. "Found the nightgown a few miles ago. Perhaps some other warrior fucked and killed her." His smile held nothing but evil. "You shouldn't have come here, cousin."

Emerie retorted, "I was brought here against my will, *cousin*. But now I'll enjoy proving you and your father wrong.

His teeth shone in the dim, snowy light through the forest canopy. "You've disgraced your father. Disgraced our family."

Nesta eyed her weapons at the male's feet, all ceded upon Emerie's capture.

"Was it you who sabotaged the Rite with these weapons?" Nesta seethed.

Bellius chuckled again, though his eyes remained hazy. Flakes of snow gathered in his dark hair. "I wouldn't call it sabotage. And neither did she."

Nesta froze. She'd seen that glassy-eyed look before—on the faces of Eris's soldiers.

And that word—*she*. Had Briallyn somehow ensnared Bellius with the Crown? He'd looked glassy-eyed when she'd seen him in Emerie's shop months ago. When he'd recently come back from a scouting trip to the continent. Briallyn must have intercepted him then. Perhaps used the Crown to influence the Illyrians to break their sacred rules of the Rite, to plant the weapons here. But why?

Bellius said to Emerie as the female shook with rage, "You know I can't let you leave here alive. Our family would never recover from the shame."

"Fuck you," Emerie snarled. "Fuck your family."

Bellius just eyed Nesta, smiling faintly. He brushed the snow from the shoulders of his jacket. "I get first crack at the High Fae bitch," he said to his warriors.

Nesta's gut churned, acid burning through her. She had to find some way out of this, even outnumbered, unarmed, with no magic—

The pure panic and rage in Emerie's face told her that her friend, too, was coming up short on any solution.

Bellius stepped toward them.

And then blood splattered across the side of his face as the guts of one of his cronies spilled onto the snow before him.

✠

The thing that crawled over the ridge had been crafted of nightmares. Part cat, part serpent, all black fur and sharp claws and hooked teeth. It halted at the edge of the camp. Didn't look down at the gutted corpse of the warrior whose abdomen it had sliced open with a single swipe. Blood stained the snow around him in a wide circle.

The warriors, Bellius with them, readied themselves. Bellius drew his sword.

The creature leaped. Warriors screamed, weapons flashing in the bloodied, shrieking fray.

"*Run*," Nesta ordered Emerie, surging to her feet. She snatched her weapons, and Emerie lunged to grab a sword as it flew from a warrior's hand and into the snow.

A female voice rang out from the other side of the ridge. "*Here!*"

Nesta nearly sobbed at the voice, at the coppery head of hair that popped up, the hand beckoning as Bellius and his males squared off against the thing tearing into them. Nesta and Emerie reached the hilltop's edge and slid down, snow spraying. Gwyn waited on its other side, bloodied and in a warrior's clothes, face filthy and torn, but eyes clear.

"Follow me," Gwyn breathed, and they wasted no effort arguing as they half-fell down the hillside and sprinted through the trees, aiming to the southeast.

They ran until the warriors' screams, the beast's roars, were distant. Until they faded away entirely.

They stopped near a trickle of a stream through the snow, panting so hard Nesta had to lean against a tree.

"How?" Emerie gasped out.

"I woke up before the others," Gwyn said between breaths, a hand on her chest.

"So did I," Nesta said. "I thought it was because I'm Made, but maybe it's because you and I aren't Illyrian."

Gwyn nodded. "I started running, and found a cache of weapons almost immediately." She gestured to the blood on her Illyrian leathers. "I changed from the nightgown into someone else's clothes. From a body, I mean." She held up her wrist. "Did you know this thing glows? I remembered your wish for us: that we'd always be able to find our way back to each other. No matter what. I figured it would lead me to you. It must be somehow immune to the magic ban in the Rite."

She smiled crookedly at Nesta. "I kept to the trees the first two nights, watching the beasts, and I spotted that horrible male and his companions this morning. Saw they'd found my nightgown and displayed it, and I knew they were hunting for you. I thought I'd take them out before they could find you."

"You led the beast right to them."

"I learned where the beasts sleep during the day," Gwyn said. "And that they get *very* angry when awoken." She pointed to the cuts on her face, her hands. "I barely outran that one as I led it toward the camp. My timing was just good luck, though."

Emerie shuddered. "The Mother watched over us."

Nesta could have sworn the charms on their bracelets let out a soft, singing hum at that.

But Gwyn winced. "He's really your cousin?"

"I hope I can refer to that sad fact in the past tense after this," Emerie said coolly.

Nesta offered her a savage smile. "We need to keep moving. If Bellius or any of his friends survive, they'll want to kill us even more now."

Four more days. They had to last four more days.

Gwyn said hoarsely as they moved into the wilderness, the snow mercifully lightening, "You two came looking for me."

"Of course we did," Emerie said, interlacing her hand with Gwyn's, then Nesta's, and squeezing tightly. "It's what sisters do."

CHAPTER 68

Nesta far preferred caves to trees. But as night fell and no caves revealed themselves, she found herself with no other option but to scale one behind Emerie and Gwyn, the latter revealing how she'd managed to rest while up one: a long stretch of rope. It must have been one of the items Queen Briallyn had the Illyrians leave, presumably for trussing captives or stringing them up or strangling them, and Gwyn had used it to bind herself to the trunk of a tree each night. It was long enough that the three of them, sitting side by side on a massive branch, were able to tie themselves together and to the tree itself.

"How'd you avoid the creatures climbing up to eat you?" Emerie asked Gwyn, who was wedged between her and Nesta. "They were pulling Illyrians off the branches like apples."

"Maybe because I don't smell like an Illyrian," Gwyn said, frowning at her clothes. "Despite these." She nodded to Nesta. "You don't, either. If we're lucky, our scents will mask Emerie's."

"Perhaps," Nesta said, voice quieting as the night deepened. The snow had finally stopped hours ago, and even the whipping wind had eased. A small miracle.

Gwyn peered forward to look at Emerie. "How much do you know about the Rite?"

Emerie tucked her hands under her armpits for warmth. "A good amount. My father and brother—and my horrid cousins—talked about it endlessly. Any family gathering, all the males told and retold their oh-so-glorious tales from their own Rites. How many they killed, the beasts they escaped. None of them ever made it to Ramiel, though." Emerie nodded to Nesta. "They always hated that about Cassian. And Rhysand and Azriel. They *hated* that the three of them made it to the very top and won the whole thing."

"The mountain is that hard to climb?" Gwyn asked, voice hushed.

Emerie grunted. "Hard to reach; harder to climb. It's covered in jagged rock that slices you up like a cheese grater."

Nesta shuddered.

"And with our healing slowed to a human rate thanks to the rules of the Rite," Emerie went on, "we'll be lucky to make it to the Pass of Enalius in one piece."

"What's that?" Nesta asked.

Emerie's eyes shone. "Long ago—so long ago they don't even have a precise date for it—a great war was fought between the Fae and the ancient beings who oppressed them. One of its key battles was here, in these mountains. Our forces were battered and outnumbered, and for some reason, the enemy was desperate to reach the stone at the top of Ramiel. We were never taught the reason why; I think it's been forgotten. But a young Illyrian warrior named Enalius held the line against the enemy soldiers for days. He found a natural archway of stone amongst the tangle of boulders and made that his bottleneck. He died in the end, but he held off the enemy long enough for our allies to reach us. This Rite is all to honor him. So much of the history has been lost, but the memory of his bravery remains."

As Cassian's name would last through history, Nesta thought. Would her own? Some small part of her wished for it.

"There are a few different paths to the top of Ramiel," Emerie went on. "But the hardest one, the most infamous, is the one that takes you through the Pass of Enalius. Through the archway of stone. They call that path the Breaking."

"Why am I not surprised that's the one Cassian and his brothers took?" Nesta grumbled.

Emerie and Gwyn chuckled, but when a beast roared in the distance, they instantly fell quiet.

Nesta murmured, "We should take watches."

They divvied them up, Nesta taking first watch, Emerie second, and Gwyn third, and when that was decided, they sat in silence for a long moment. They'd eaten a meager meal of some roast squirrel Gwyn had managed to pilfer from an unsuspecting Illyrian, but hunger remained a vocal knot in their bellies.

Nesta leaned into Gwyn's warmth, let it seep through her bones. And prayed to whatever god might be listening that the rumbling of their stomachs wouldn't reveal them to the beasts below.

✢

The fourth day brought sun, bright enough to make the snow blinding, even in the shadows of the pines. Gwyn had climbed their tree to its summit, then estimated that Ramiel lay days away to the northeast. Leaving them, should they make it, a day to climb its barren face.

"I couldn't see if anyone else was ahead," Gwyn announced, "but there's a massive ravine nearby with a small wooden bridge. We must be the first to find it—if anyone else had, they would have destroyed the bridge to prevent further use. We need to reach it before the others do."

"How far ahead?" Nesta asked, checking the knife at her side, the rope she'd coiled over a shoulder and the Illyrian bow there. Emerie had the sword she'd snatched from Bellius's camp, and Gwyn bore a shield and a knife of her own.

"Several hours, if we can run it," Gwyn said.

"Running risks attention," Emerie warned.

"Walking risks losing the bridge," Nesta countered.

The three of them looked at each other. "Run, then," Gwyn said, and they nodded.

They set a light pace, meant to keep their steps silent and easy even with the snow underfoot, but running after days of exhaustion, limbs stiff with cold and belly mostly empty, made Nesta's head pound.

"We've got company," Emerie panted, and the three of them halted. Not five hundred yards away stood six males.

"Do you think they know about the bridge?" Gwyn breathed.

As soon as she said it, the males burst into a sprint. Not toward them, but toward the ravine.

Swearing, Nesta launched into movement with Gwyn and Emerie close behind, snow flying at their feet. "Hurry!" she shouted.

Through the trees ahead, the world lightened—as if the forest had stopped. It had, she realized. At the ravine's edge, now equidistant between them and the males. Whoever made it first would cut the bridge behind them.

And if they both reached the bridge at the same time . . .

"We have to intercept them," Nesta panted. "Well before they reach the bridge." She altered her trajectory abruptly, and Emerie and Gwyn moved with her as one. The males aiming for the bridge seemed to realize their enemy was now coming right at them. They slowed, reaching for their weapons.

Nesta found her target, a male with a good foot on her, and swiped with her dagger as she careened into him. He'd been running fast enough that he lost his balance and went down as he dodged her blow. Precisely where she wanted him: right in front of Emerie. Nesta pivoted to the next male as her friend drove her sword into the first male's chest.

The next male Nesta attacked was ready, swiping with a short sword. She ducked, twirling away—allowing him to land the blow on Gwyn's shield. Just as Gwyn ducked, slashing across his shins with a dagger.

The four others—

Nesta weaved and bobbed against another male, dagger to dagger. Each movement sang in perfect harmony with her breath; each pivot of her body, her limbs, was part of a symphony.

The male swung broadly at Nesta, and she glimpsed her opening. She let his blow go wide before slamming her elbow into his nose. Bone met bone with a crunch that rang through her.

He went down with a grunt and Nesta's blade slashed silver and red across his throat. She didn't let herself feel the warm slickness of his blood.

Another male already charged at her, and Gwyn shouted Nesta's name—grabbing her attention just before the priestess chucked a shield to her.

Nesta caught it, spinning in the snow on one knee as she absorbed the impact of its weight. Expelling her breath in a mighty exhale, she lifted the shield high as the male brought down a sword meant for her head. Nesta met the blow, thrusting the shield upward and knocking the male off balance. She slammed her knife into his boot.

He screamed, falling backward, and Nesta leaped to her feet, swinging the shield so hard it dented as it slammed into his head. The reverberations bit into her hand and forearm, but she kept her grip on the shield.

Nesta whirled to the next opponent, but her friends had halted. The males around them were down.

Utter silence filled the snowy forest. Even the birds in the pines had stopped chirping.

"Valkyries," Emerie said, eyes blazing bright.

Nesta grinned through the blood she knew was splattered on her face. "Hell yes."

⁜

"Four fucking days," Cassian hissed from where he and Azriel monitored the castle. "We've been sitting on our asses for four fucking days."

Azriel sharpened Truth-Teller. The black blade absorbed the dim sunlight trickling through the forest canopy above. "It seems you've forgotten how much of spying is waiting for the right moment. People don't engage in their evil deeds when it's convenient to you."

Cassian rolled his eyes. "I stopped spying because it bored me to death. I don't know how you put up with this all the time."

"It suits me." Azriel didn't halt his sharpening, though shadows gathered around his feet.

Cassian blew out a breath. "I know I'm being impatient. I *know* that. But you really think we shouldn't go up to that damned castle and peek inside?"

"I told you: their castle is too heavily warded, and full of magical traps that would trip up even Helion. Beyond that, Briallyn has the Crown. I have no interest in explaining to Rhys and Feyre why you died on my watch. And even less interest in explaining it to Nesta."

Cassian stared toward the castle. "You think she's alive?" The question haunted him with every breath these last few days.

"You'd know if she'd died," Azriel said, pausing his work and looking up at Cassian. He tapped his brother's chest with a scarred hand. "Right here—you'd know, Cass."

"There are plenty of other unspeakable things that could be happening to her," Cassian said, voice thickening. "To Emerie and Gwyn."

The shadows deepened around Azriel, his Siphons gleaming like cobalt fire. "You—we—trained them well, Cassian. Trust in that. It's all we can do."

Cassian's throat tightened, but a motion drew Azriel's gaze away. Cassian shot to his feet. "Someone's leaving the castle." The two of them wordlessly launched into the skies, entering the cloud cover within moments. In the chill, thin air, Cassian glimpsed only what the gaps in the clouds offered.

But it was enough.

A small caravan had left the eastern city gates, departing down the bare road that led through the hills.

"I don't see a prison wagon," Cassian said over the wind.

Azriel's gaze remained on the earth below. "They don't need one," he said with quiet venom.

Cassian had to wait until the next gap in the clouds to see.

No, they hadn't needed a prison wagon. Because riding atop a white horse at the front of the party, side by side with a hunched, small figure, was Eris.

"Stupid asshole," Cassian snarled. "She snared him with the Crown."

"No," Az said quietly. "Look at his left. He's still got the dagger at his side. If he was in her thrall, he'd have already handed it over."

"So possessing another Made object does protect him against the Crown." Which meant . . . "Traitor." Cassian spat. "I don't know why I'm surprised." His hands curled into fists. "Let's get him, drag his ass home, and tear him apart." He'd been drawn away from Nesta for this? For Eris's games?

Azriel's voice cut through the howling wind. "We follow them. Capture Eris now and we might not get anything out of him. At least not quickly. We trail them and learn just how far this betrayal goes. See who they're meeting with. It has to be important, for them to leave the safety of the castle."

There was no arguing with the logic of it, even if Cassian's heart screamed at him with every flap of his wings to fly back home.

⸸

Nesta, Emerie, and Gwyn hadn't even reached the bridge when a new group of males closed in, armed with bows and arrows.

"We can make it," Emerie panted, sprinting at the head of their pack toward the bridge, now visible through the snow-crusted trees. "We can outrun them."

Arrows whizzed past.

Emerie hit the bridge first, the rickety contraption bouncing with her weight as she practically flew across it. Arrows thudded into the trees, the ground, the bridge posts, and Nesta didn't hesitate as she raced over the slats, not daring to look at the plunge below to a barren riverbed, only at Emerie as she cleared the bridge—

A scream of pain blasted behind them, and Nesta whirled at the end of the bridge to find Gwyn still on the other side with an arrow through her thigh. Down. Too close to the males closing in—

"*CUT IT!*" Gwyn roared.

"Get up," Nesta ground out. "*Get up.*"

The priestess tried. She made it to her feet, but she'd never cross the bridge in time.

So Nesta took the Illyrian bow off her shoulder. Took the coil of rope off, too, and handed it blindly to Emerie. "Tie one end to that tree, and then around yourself." Nesta didn't wait to see if she was obeyed before she knotted the other end to the arrow. Fitted the arrow into the bow.

"We didn't learn archery," Emerie breathed.

But Nesta nocked the arrow in place. Took aim. Right at Gwyn, who eyed the rope tied to the arrow, the other end around the tree and Emerie, and understood.

"My sister taught me." Nesta's arms trembled as she drew back the string. "A long time ago."

Teeth gritted, grunting, Nesta strained for every inch. Aimed for Gwyn as her friend ran toward the bridge, hobbling, face white with pain, leaving a trail of blood in the snow behind her.

Nesta let the arrow soar as the first of the males broke through the trees.

It flew true. Landed in the snow at Gwyn's feet.

The priestess grabbed the arrow and wrapped the rope around her middle, over and over again as she ran for the bridge—

Nesta dropped the bow. Gwyn had reached the bridge's far side and was yelling, "*CUT IT CUT IT CUT IT!*"

The males cleared the trees. They raced toward the bridge and the limping Gwyn, gaining on her fast. Nesta had only to throw out a hand before Emerie tossed the sword to her.

Gwyn, limping halfway down the bridge, didn't stop moving. The males were only a few feet behind, crowding onto the rickety structure.

Nesta brought the blade down upon the bridge's ropes. Even as the wood fell out from beneath her, Gwyn still seemed to be running, then leaping into the open air, only that rope around her middle to keep her from death as she began to plunge—

But Nesta had grabbed on to the rope, dropping before the bridge post and wrapping her legs around it, holding on tightly as inch after inch of rough fiber ripped through her hands. Behind her, braced against the pine tree, Emerie held on just as tightly.

Gwyn fell toward the ravine floor, Illyrian males shrieking as they tumbled, untethered, with her.

Nesta screamed, her palms on fire. Red coated the rope, but she clamped her torn hands tighter and breathed through the ripping, tearing sensation.

Until Gwyn halted her plunge, yanked to a stop. The entire world seemed to suck in a breath as Nesta waited for the snap of the rope.

But Gwyn only careened toward the rock face, grunting in pain as she hit.

The Illyrians who had fallen had carried the only bows, thankfully, and the males on the other side cursed and spat.

But Nesta and Emerie paid them no heed as they hauled Gwyn upward, bloodied hands turning the rope redder still. Each pull had Nesta panting against the pain until Gwyn cleared the cliff edge, grimacing as the arrow through her thigh touched the ground. It had been a clean shot, but blood soaked her leg. Her face was already pale.

"Fucking *bitches*!" one of the males roared.

"Oh, shut up!" Emerie bellowed across the ravine, helping Nesta lead Gwyn into the snowy trees, their breaths puffing out before them. "Find something new to call us!"

⸸

They managed to slide the arrow out of Gwyn's leg and bind it using an extra shirt they'd taken from a dead warrior, but the priestess still limped. Her face had grown ashen, and even propped up between Nesta and Emerie, she kept their pace glacial.

Yet they continued toward Ramiel, now visible ahead of them.

They encountered no one else. It began snowing again around midday, and Gwyn's steps grew staggered. Her breathing too labored. Soon Nesta and Emerie were half-carrying her between them.

By the time evening fell, just getting Gwyn high into a tree took all their remaining strength. They secured themselves to its trunk with the bloodied rope, and Nesta and Emerie idly plucked tiny rope fibers from their torn hands. They had no more food, only water.

The next day was the same: slow walking, snow flurries, ears straining for any hint of other warriors, too many breaks, only water to fill their bellies, and, as night fell, a new tree.

But this tree was the very last before a barren slope rose above them like a black beast.

They'd made it to the foot of Ramiel.

⸸

Nesta awoke before dawn, checked that Gwyn breathed, that her leg hadn't become infected, and stared at the black-and-gray slope ahead.

Far up, too far, lay its peak with the sacred black stone. Three stars glinted above the mountain: Arktos and Oristes to the left and right; Carynth crowning them. Their light flared and waned, as if in invitation and challenge.

"Cassian told me only twelve have made it this far," Nesta murmured to her friends. "We've already earned the title of Oristian just by being here."

Emerie stirred. "We could stay up here today, wait it out overnight, and be done at dawn. To hell with any titles." It was the wise thing to do. The safe thing to do.

"That path," Nesta said, pointing to a small one along Ramiel's base, "could also take us down south. No one would go that way, because it takes you away from the mountain."

"So we'd come all this way and just hide?" Gwyn said, voice hoarse.

"You're hurt," Nesta countered. "And that is a *mountain* in front of us."

"So rather than try and fail," Gwyn demanded, "you would take the safe road?"

"We would live," Emerie said carefully. "I'd love nothing more than to wipe the smirks off the lips of the males in my village, but not at this cost. Not if it costs us you, Gwyn. We need you to live."

Gwyn studied Ramiel's craggy, unforgiving slope. Not much snow graced its sides. Like the wind had whipped it all away. Or the storms had avoided its peak entirely. "Is it living, though? To take the safe road?"

"You're the one who's been in a library for two years," Emerie said.

Gwyn didn't flinch. "I have. And I am tired of it." She surveyed the blood-soaked leather along her thigh. "I don't want to take the safe road." She pointed to the mountain, to the slender path upward. "I want to take *that* road." Her voice thickened. "I want to take the road that no one dares travel, and I want to travel it with you two. No matter what may befall us. Not as Illyrians, not for their titles, but as something *new*. To prove to them, to everyone, that something new and different might triumph over their rules and restrictions."

A cold wind blew off Ramiel's sides. Whispering, murmuring.

"They call this climb the Breaking for a reason," Emerie countered gravely.

Nesta added, "We haven't eaten in days. We're down to the last of our water. To climb that mountain—"

"I have been broken once before," Gwyn said, her voice clear. "I survived it. And I will not be broken again—not even by this mountain."

Nesta and Emerie kept silent as Gwyn released a sharp breath. "A commander from Hybern raped me two years ago. He had his soldiers hold me down on a table. He laughed the entire time."

Tears gleamed in Gwyn's eyes. "Hybern attacked in the dead of night. We were all asleep when they broke into the temple and began the slaughter. I shared a room with my twin, Catrin. We woke at the first of the screaming from the walls. She was . . . Catrin was always the strong one. The smart and charming one. After our mother died, she took care of me. Looked out for me. And that night, she ordered me to go protect Sangravah's children while she ran right for the temple walls."

Gwyn's voice shook. "When I reached the children's dorm, the slaughter was only a few halls away. I gathered the children, and we ran for one of the catacomb tunnels. They were accessible through a trapdoor in the kitchen, and I'd gotten the last child in when I heard the soldiers coming. I . . . I knew they'd find us if I went and left the door uncovered, so I threw a rug over it and then moved the kitchen table atop it. I'd just finished moving the table when the soldiers found me."

Nesta couldn't breathe. Gwyn stared at the mountain rising high above. Even the wind had seemed to quiet to hear her words.

"The screaming had stopped, and they had other priestesses with them. Including Catrin. But their commander walked in, and asked me where the rest of us were. They wanted the children, too. The girls."

Nesta could hear Emerie's thundering heart, its frantic beat echoing her own.

Gwyn swallowed. "I told him the children had taken the mountain road to get help. He didn't believe me. So he grabbed Catrin, because our scents were nearly identical, you see, and told me that if I didn't reveal where the children were, he'd kill her. And when I didn't give the children up . . ." Her mouth shook. "He beheaded Catrin right there, along with two other priestesses. And then he told his soldiers to *go to work* on us. He claimed me. I spat in his face." Tears slid down her cheeks. "And then he . . . went to work."

Nesta's heart cracked.

"I hadn't yet participated in the Great Rite, and we were so remote up there that I never had the chance to lie with a male, and he took that from me, too. And then he called over three of his soldiers and told them to keep going until I revealed where the children had gone."

Nausea roiled Nesta's gut. She couldn't have moved if she'd wanted to.

"The first had just unbuckled his belt when Azriel arrived." Silent, unending tears streamed down Gwyn's face.

"Azriel slaughtered all of them within moments. He didn't hesitate. But I could barely move, and when I tried to get up . . . He gave me his cloak and wrapped me in it. Morrigan arrived a few minutes later, and then Rhysand appeared, and it became clear some of the soldiers had gotten away with the piece of the Cauldron, so Azriel headed after them. Mor healed me as best she could, then brought me to the library. I couldn't . . . I couldn't bear to be at the temple, with the others. To see Catrin's grave and know I failed her, to see that kitchen every day for the rest of my life.

"The first five months I was at the library, I barely spoke. I didn't sing. I went to the priestess who counsels all of us, and sometimes I just sat there and cried, or screamed, or said nothing. And then I began working with Merrill, upon Clotho's request, and the work focused me. Motivated me to get out of bed each morning. I started singing during the evening service. And then you came along, Nesta."

Gwyn's eyes slid to hers, brimming with tears and pain and—hope. Precious, beautiful hope. "And I could tell something bad had happened to you, too. You were fighting it, though. Not letting it master you. I knew Catrin would have been the first to sign up for training, so . . . I did, too. But even training these months hasn't erased the fact that I let my sister die. You asked me once why I don't wear the hood or the Invoking Stone. That stone is a sign of holiness. How can someone like me wear it?"

Gwyn stopped at last, as if waiting for them to damn her.

But tears were running down Emerie's face. They didn't halt as Emerie took Gwyn's hand and said, "You are not alone, Gwyn. Do you hear me? *You are not alone.*"

Nesta took Emerie's other hand as her friend went on, "We have suffered differently, but . . . My father once beat me so badly he broke my back. He kept me in bed for weeks while I healed, telling people I was ill, but I wasn't. It was . . . It was one of the lesser of his evils." She paused. "He beat my mother before that. And she . . . I think she shielded me from him, because he never laid a hand on me until she was gone. Until he beat her so badly she couldn't recover. He made me dig her grave on a night with a new moon, and told people she'd miscarried a babe and died from blood loss."

She angrily wiped a tear away. "Everyone believed him. They always believed him—he was so charming to them, so smart. Whenever people told me how lucky I was to have such a good father, I wondered if I'd imagined all the bad parts. Only my scars, my wings reminded me of the truth. And when he died, I was so happy, yet they expected me to mourn him. I should have told them all what a monster he was, but I didn't. They had turned a blind eye to my wing-clipping while he was alive; why should they bother to believe the truth now that he was among the honored dead?"

Emerie's nose crinkled. "I still feel his fists on me. Still feel the impact of him slamming my head into a wall, or crunching my fingers in a door, or just railing on me until I blacked out." She was shaking, and Nesta squeezed her hand tighter. "He never gave me any money or allowed me to earn my own, never let me eat more than he deemed appropriate, and wormed his way so far into my mind that *I still hear him* when I look in the mirror or make a mistake."

She swallowed. "I came to training because I knew he'd have forbidden it. I came to training to get his voice out of my head. And to know how to stop a male if one ever puts another hand on me again. But none of it will ever bring my mother back, or the fact that I hid while my father took out his rage upon her. Nothing will ever make that right. But this mountain . . ." Emerie pointed to the small dirt path at the base of the peak. "I'll climb it for my mother. For her, I'll face the Breaking and go as far as I can."

The two of them looked to Nesta. But her gaze remained upon the mountain. Its peak. That path leading up to it. The hardest of all the routes.

Finally Nesta said, "I was sent to the House of Wind because I had become such a wretch, drinking and fucking everything in sight. My . . . family couldn't stand it. For more than a year, I abused their kindness and generosity, and I did it because . . ." She exhaled a shuddering breath. "My father died during the war. Before my eyes, but I did nothing to stop it." And then it all came out. She told the two of them every horrible thing she had done and thought and savored. Told them of the Cauldron and its terror and pain and power. Told them the worst of her, so that if they decided to risk climbing that mountain with her, they'd go into it with their eyes open. So that they could choose to pull back now.

And when Nesta finished, she braced herself for the disappointment in their faces, the disgust.

Gwyn's hand slid into hers, though. Emerie tightened her grip on Nesta's other hand, too.

"Neither of you is to blame for what happened," Nesta whispered. "Neither of you failed *anyone*."

"Neither did you," Emerie said softly.

Nesta gazed at her friends. And saw pain and sorrow in their tear-streaked faces, but also the openness of letting each other see the broken places deep inside. The understanding that they would not turn away.

Nesta's eyes stung as Gwyn said, "So we climb Ramiel. We take the Breaking. We win to prove to everyone that something new can be as powerful and unbreakable as the old rules. That something no one has ever seen before, not entirely Valkyrie nor entirely Illyrian, can win the Blood Rite."

"No," Nesta said at last. "We win to prove to *ourselves* that it can be done." She bared her teeth in a feral grin at the mountain. "We win the whole damn thing."

CHAPTER 69

Eris and the small caravan rode eastward for three days, stopping only to eat and sleep. Their pace was leisurely, and from the glimpses Cassian and Azriel got through the clouds, it seemed Eris was unchained. Briallyn's small, hunched figure rode at his side each day. But they caught no sign of the Crown on her—no glint of gold in the sun.

The Blood Rite would end the next day. Cassian had heard nothing of Nesta, felt nothing. But he'd barely slept. Had hardly been able to keep his focus on the party ahead as they entered a low-lying forest beyond the hills, ancient and knotted and full of hanging moss.

"I've never been here before," Azriel murmured over the wind. "It feels like an old place. It reminds me of the Middle."

Cassian kept his silence. Didn't speak as they trailed their quarry deeper into the wood to a small lake in its center. Only when the party halted at its dark shores did Azriel and Cassian land nearby. Begin their silent tracking on foot.

The group must not have been concerned about being overheard, because Cassian could make out their words from well beyond their campsite along the shore. Twenty of them had gathered, a mixture of what looked like human nobility and soldiers. Eris's white stallion had been hitched to a branch. But the male—

"Over here, Cassian," Eris crooned.

Cassian whirled, and found the High Lord's son holding a knife at his ribs.

⁜

By midday, Nesta could barely breathe. Gwyn was dragging, Emerie was panting, and they'd begun to ration their water. No matter how high they climbed, how many boulders they cleared along the narrow path, the peak grew no closer.

They saw no one else. Heard no one else.

A small mercy.

Nesta's breath singed her lungs. Her legs wobbled. There was only the pain in her body and the relentless circling of her thoughts, as if they were vultures gathering to feast.

She just wanted to turn off her *mind*—

Was it possible that the Breaking wasn't merely physical, but mental as well? That this mountain somehow dredged up every bit of her fear and sucked her mind deep into it?

They halted for lunch, if water could be called lunch. Gwyn's leg was bleeding again, her face ghostly white. None of them spoke.

But Nesta noted their haunted eyes—knew they heard their own horrors.

They rested for as long as they dared, then moved again.

Keep going upward. That was the only way. Step to step to step.

⁜

"It looks like we're two-thirds of the way up," Emerie rasped from ahead.

Night had fallen, the moon bright enough to keep the Breaking's path illuminated. To show those three stars above Ramiel's peak. Beckoning. Waiting.

If they reached it by dawn, it'd be a miracle.

"I need to rest," Gwyn said faintly. "Just—just another minute." Her face was gray, her hair limp. The leathers along her leg soaked red.

Emerie had taken a spill on a loose rock two hours earlier and twisted her ankle—she was limping now as well.

They were moving too slowly.

"The Pass of Enalius isn't too far ahead," Emerie insisted. "If we can make it through the archway, then it's a clear shot to the top."

Gwyn breathed, "I'm not sure if I can."

"Let her rest, Emerie," Nesta said, sitting on a small boulder beside Gwyn. Dawn had to be four hours off. And then it would be over. Would it matter if they'd reached the peak by then? If they'd won? They'd gotten this far. They'd—

"How did they get here?" Gwyn asked, swearing.

Nesta went still. From her vantage point, she could see straight down. To where a beam of moonlight illuminated a familiar-looking male and six others climbing the mountain behind them. A good ways back, but closing in.

"Bellius," Emerie whispered.

"We need to go," Nesta said, lurching to her feet. Gwyn followed, wincing.

Nesta sized up the males. Emerie and Gwyn were too injured to fight, too exhausted, and—

"Put your arms around my neck," Nesta said, offering her back to Gwyn.

"What?"

Nesta did it for her. She had climbed the ten thousand stairs of the House of Wind, up and down, over and over and over again. Perhaps for this. This very moment.

"We're winning this fucking thing," Nesta said, bending to grab Gwyn's legs. Teeth gritted, Nesta hoisted Gwyn onto her back.

The muscles in her thighs strained, but held. Her knees did not buckle.

Her gaze lay on the terrain ahead. She would not look behind.

So Nesta began to climb, Emerie limping beside her.

With the wind as their song, Nesta and Emerie found their rhythm. They climbed, squeezing and slithering and hauling their weight. And the males fell behind, like the mountain was silently whispering, *Go, go, go*.

⁜

"I knew you were a lying bastard," Cassian said through his teeth. Azriel, a step away, could do nothing. Not with Eris angling that knife—Nesta's dagger—into Cassian's ribs. He could have sworn flame seared into him where the knife met his leather. "But this is low, even for you."

"Honestly, I'm disappointed in Rhysand," Eris said, digging the tip of the knife through Cassian's leathers enough for him to feel its bite, and that ripple of searing flame. Whether it was Eris's power through the blade or whatever Nesta had Made it into, he didn't care. He just needed to find some way to avoid it piercing his skin. "He's become so bland these days. He didn't even try to look into my mind."

"You can't win this," Azriel warned with quiet menace. "You're a dead male walking, Eris. Have been for a long time."

"Yes, yes, all that old business with the Morrigan. How boring of you to cling to it so."

Cassian blinked. *The* Morrigan.

Eris never referred to her like that.

"Let him go, Briallyn," Cassian growled. "Come play with us instead."

The Made dagger slid away from his ribs, and a withered, reedy voice said from nearby, "I'm already playing with you, Lord of Bastards."

⁜

Nesta's legs shook. Her arms trembled. Gwyn was a half-dead weight at her back. The blood loss had made her so weak it seemed she could barely hold on.

The Breaking flowed through an archway of black stone where the path became broader and easier. The Pass of Enalius. Emerie had paused only long enough to run a bleeding hand over the stone, her dirty face full of wonder and pride. "I am standing where none of my ancestors have been before," she whispered, voice choked.

Nesta wished she could pause alongside her friend. Could marvel with her. But to stop, even for a breath . . . Nesta knew that once she halted, she wouldn't be able to move again.

The flattening of the path around the archway was only a temporary relief. They soon reached a cluster of stones—the last of the impossible climbing before it seemed to become a direct path to the top. Dawn remained a good two hours off. The full moon's light was beginning to fade as it sank toward the west.

The group of males would catch them before the summit.

Nesta's fingers spasmed as she reached for Emerie's outstretched hand where her friend knelt atop one of the sharp boulders. If they could get past this section—

Her knees buckled, and Nesta went down, face smacking into a rock so hard stars burst across her vision, but all she could do was hold on to Gwyn as they tumbled and slammed into rocks and gravel and rolled and rolled downward, Emerie's screams ringing in her ears, and then—

Nesta collided with someone hard.

No—not someone, though she could have sworn she felt warmth and breath. She'd hit the archway of stone. They'd fallen all the way back down to the Pass of Enalius, dangerously close to the males who pursued them.

"Gwyn—"

"Alive," her friend groaned.

Emerie slid to her knees on the path. "Are you hurt?"

Nesta couldn't move as Gwyn untangled herself. The two of them were covered in dirt, debris, and blood. "I can't . . ." Nesta panted. "I can't carry you anymore."

Silence fell.

"So we rest," Gwyn managed to say, "then we continue."

"We'll never make it in time," Nesta said. "Or at least before the males catch up."

Emerie swallowed. "We try anyway." Gwyn nodded. "Rest a minute first. Maybe the dawn will reach us before they do."

"No." Nesta peered down the path. "They're climbing too fast."

Again, silence.

"What are you saying?" Emerie asked carefully.

Nesta marveled at the hope and bravery in their faces. "I can hold them off."

"No," Gwyn said, voice sharpening.

Nesta schooled her features into utter coldness. "You are both injured. You will not survive the fight. But you can manage the climb. Emerie can help—"

"No."

"I can use the bottleneck of the path right there," Nesta plowed ahead, pointing to the space beyond the archway, "to keep them off long enough for you two to reach the top. Or dawn to come. Whichever happens first."

Gwyn bared her teeth. "*I refuse to leave you here.*"

Emerie's pained face told Nesta enough: she understood. Saw the logic.

Nesta said to Gwyn, "It is the only way."

Gwyn screamed, "*IT IS NOT THE ONLY WAY!*" And then she was sobbing. "I will not abandon you to them. They will *kill* you."

"You need to go," Nesta said, even as her hands began shaking. "Now."

"No," Gwyn wept. "No, I won't. I'll face it with you."

Something deep in Nesta's chest cracked. Cracked open completely, and what lay within bloomed, full and bright and pure.

She wrapped her arms around Gwyn. Let her friend sob into her chest. "I'll face it with you," Gwyn whispered, over and over again. "Promise me we'll face it together."

Nesta couldn't stop her tears then. The chill wind froze them on her cheeks. "I promise," she breathed, stroking Gwyn's matted hair. "I promise."

Gwyn sobbed, and Nesta let herself sob with her, squeezing her tightly. Letting her stroking hand come to rest on Gwyn's neck.

A pinch in the right spot, exactly on that pressure point Cassian had shown her, and it was done.

Gwyn went down. Unconscious.

Nesta grunted, carefully lowering Gwyn to the ground as she peered up at Emerie. Her friend's face was grave, but unsurprised.

Nesta only said, "Can you carry her the rest of the way?" It would be a feat in itself. "Or at least keep going until dawn?"

"I will." Nesta knew Emerie would find that strength. She had a soul of steel. Emerie laid her sword before Nesta. Her dagger. The shield.

"Keep the canteens," Nesta said, patting her own. "I've got enough." Another lie.

"She'll never forgive you for this," Emerie said.

"I know." The males had risen higher. She didn't wait for Emerie to speak before she helped ease Gwyn onto Emerie's back, the latter hissing at the weight upon her wings, splaying them at awkward angles. Nesta tied the bloodied rope around them, binding them together. Emerie grimaced, but managed to move a few steps.

"Come with us," Emerie offered, eyes lined with silver.

Nesta shook her head. "Consider it the repayment of a debt."

A tear slipped down Emerie's cheek. "For what?"

"For being my friends. Even when I didn't deserve it."

Emerie's face crumpled. "There is no debt, Nesta."

But Nesta smiled softly. "There is. Let me pay it."

Swallowing back her tears, Emerie nodded. Hefted Gwyn higher and winced, but managed to hobble through the arch. Toward the rocks and the last stretch of the Breaking, all the way up to the peak.

Nesta did not say good-bye. She just inhaled through her nose, held the breath, then exhaled. Repeated her Mind-Stilling again and again, until her breath became the steady crash of waves and her heart became solid stone, and every inch of her body was hers to control.

She was the rock against which the surf broke. These males would break against her, too.

⁜

They had no choice. With Eris in Briallyn's grip, Cassian and Azriel could only follow the hunched, cloaked figure to the lake. Cassian didn't dare consider whether the Crown was being used on him. If it'd be used on Azriel.

The party in which Eris and Briallyn had traveled had dispersed, nowhere to be seen along the lake. Had they even been real? Or just an illusion?

A glance at Az revealed his brother stone-faced, cold fury in his eyes.

The hunched, cloaked figure stopped before the stones of the lake. Eris halted beside her.

"Out with it, then," Cassian said.

Briallyn drew back the hood of her cloak.

There was nothing there. The material fell and pooled on the stones. Eris's face remained blank. Empty.

"Just an animated kernel of magic," a slithering voice drawled from the lake.

Thirty feet from shore, standing atop the surface, floated a shadow. It shifted and warped, its edges fluttering, but it had the vague shape of a tall male.

"Who are you?" Azriel demanded.

But Cassian knew. "Koschei," he whispered.

✠

Nesta stood under the Pass of Enalius for a long minute.

She took out her canteen. Drank the last of the water. Chucked it to the side.

She tucked the dagger into her belt. Picked up the sword. And drew a line in the dirt in front of the archway.

Her final stand. Her last line of defense.

Nesta gathered the shield. Peered over her shoulder to where Emerie had cleared the last cluster of boulders and now struggled up the long, straight path to the peak.

A small, quiet smile passed over Nesta's face.

Then she hefted her shield. Angled her sword.

And stepped beyond the line she'd drawn to meet her enemy.

CHAPTER 70

Bellius sent his warriors through the bottleneck first. A wise move, designed to wear Nesta down.

She had no choice but to meet them.

There were no hateful voices in her head. Only the knowledge that her friends lay behind her, beyond the line she'd drawn in the earth, and she would not cede that line to these males.

She would not fail her friends. She had no room for fear in her heart.

Only calm. Determination.

And love.

Nesta's lips curved in a smile as the first of the warriors ran at her, sword raised. She was still smiling when she lifted her shield to take the full impact of the blow.

Nesta slammed her shield into the first male, sliced the shins of the second, and dispatched the third with a parry that sent him careening into the fourth and both of them tumbling to the ground. One for each breath, a movement for each inhale and exhale. She stilled her mind again, let it root her.

For a heartbeat, she wondered what she might have done with

Ataraxia in her hand. What she might do with this body, these skills trained into her bones. If she was worthy of the sword at last.

She'd opted for a name in the Old Language, a tongue no one had spoken in fifteen thousand years. A name Lanthys had laughed to hear.

Nesta engaged four of the Illyrians at once, then five, then six, and the males started to go down, one after another. Nesta held the line in a storm of unflinching focus and death, guarding the friends at her back.

Ataraxia, she had named that magic sword.

Inner Peace.

CHAPTER 71

The being that stood atop the lake was a shadow. It must be a reflection, Cassian thought. Smoke and mirrors.

"Where is Briallyn?" Azriel demanded, Siphons flaring like cobalt flame.

"I spend so many months preparing for you," Koschei crooned, "and you don't even wish to speak to me?"

Cassian crossed his arms. "Let Eris go, and then we'll talk." He prayed Koschei didn't know of the Made dagger that Eris had again sheathed at his side, that the Crown's aura of power had blinded even Briallyn to its presence. But if the death-lord got his hands on it . . . Fuck. Cassian didn't let himself so much as glance toward the blade.

"You fell for it rather easily," Koschei went on, "though you took your time making contact. I thought you'd rush in for the kill, brute that you are." They could make out nothing of him beyond the shadows of his form. Even Azriel's own shadows kept tucked behind his wings. Koschei laughed, and Azriel stiffened. Like his shadows had murmured a warning.

His Siphons flared again. "Run," Az breathed, and the pure terror on his brother's face had Cassian spreading his wings, readying to launch—

But his wings halted. His entire body halted.

Azriel grabbed Eris and shot into the skies, the Made dagger with them. They had to get it far from Koschei. Yet Cassian could not move.

Cassian's Siphons glowed like fresh blood, then sputtered out. Azriel shouted his name from high above. Koschei drifted closer to the shore. "You can take him now, Briallyn. You have plenty of time before dawn."

A small, hunched figure emerged from behind the trees. A crone. A golden crown sat upon her head, right above her arched ears. Hate burned in her eyes.

Koschei said, "Tell my Vassa I'm waiting." His shadows swirled.

Azriel soared back toward the ground, his Siphons creating a blue orb of power encircling him, but Briallyn had already reached Cassian.

"I have need of you, Lord of Bastards," the ancient-looking queen seethed. Cassian could say nothing. Couldn't move. The Crown glowed like molten iron. Briallyn ordered Koschei, "Winnow us."

The death-lord pointed a long-fingered hand at Briallyn and Cassian. Flicked his fingers once.

And the world vanished, spinning into blackness and wind.

✢

Nesta's shield had become a millstone. Her sword, slick with blood, hung from her hand, a leaden, slippery weight.

Every inch of her body burned. With exhaustion, with her wounds, with the knowledge that behind that line she'd drawn in the dirt, through the archway at her back, Gwyn and Emerie were still breathing, still climbing that final piece of the Breaking to the summit.

So she'd killed the Illyrian males who squeezed through those jagged rocks. Who believed they'd find an untrained, helpless female and found death waiting for them before the archway.

Only one remained.

Some inner part of her quaked at the unseeing, battered faces. The blood running from the corpses.

Valkyrie, she whispered to herself. *You are a Valkyrie, and once again, you are holding the pass. If you fall, it will be to save the friends who saved you, even when they didn't know they were doing so.*

A glance over her shoulder showed Emerie still scaling the last of the summit, so slow, but so close. Dawn neared, but . . . they could make it. Win this thing.

Nesta again faced the archway. Knew who she'd find.

Bellius leaned against a boulder, sword in hand, shield dangling from the other. "Impressive work for a High Fae whore."

The male pushed off the rock of the archway, not sparing a glance at the warriors he'd let die for him. "You know, our god—the first of the Illyrians—held the ground against enemy hordes right where you're standing."

There wasn't a scratch on him. No sign of exhaustion despite the climb.

Bellius smirked. "He drew a line in the dirt as well." He nodded toward it. "Nice little touch."

Nesta hadn't known that tidbit of their history. But she revealed nothing. She became blood and dirt and pure determination.

"It didn't end well for Enalius," Bellius went on. "He died after defending this spot for three days. Climbed with his guts hanging out to the sacred stone at the top and died there. It's why we do this stupid thing. To honor him."

She still didn't speak. But Bellius's eyes drifted to the peak above. Displeasure narrowed them. "My crippled cunt of a cousin and that half-breed disgrace this sacred place."

A flutter of light from the summit washed over Bellius's features.

Nesta's lips curled. Widened into a smile at Bellius's growl.

Gwyn and Emerie had touched the sacred stone and been winnowed away by its magic.

"Seems like you didn't win," Nesta said to Bellius at last.

Hatred darkened Bellius's glassy eyes. As if in answer, snow began falling, great clouds twining around the mountain. Rumbling. The snow clung to the rocks this time.

"I never wanted to win." Bellius's mouth twitched upward. "I just wanted this."

He launched at her.

CHAPTER 72

Emerie and Gwyn had won. They'd made it through the Breaking. It was enough.

Nesta only had to hold this asshole off for a few more minutes—until dawn. Then it'd be over. Her power would return, and she could . . . Nesta didn't know what she'd do. But at least she'd have that weapon.

Bellius lunged, swifter and surer than the others.

Nesta barely had time to lift her shield. The impact shook her to her bones, but he was already pivoting, his own shield swinging for her face—

She twirled out of range. Gods, she was tired. So, so tired, and—

He didn't stop. Didn't give her a moment's reprieve as he attacked, parrying and thrusting, driving her back toward the line, the archway. Hatred burning in his face.

Such blind, driving hatred. Without reason. Without end.

The snow thickened, the wind howling, and the sky rumbled. Bellius struck again, and Nesta lifted her shield, meeting the blow.

Lightning flashed, thunder booming in its wake.

A storm had swept around the mountain, veiling the moon, the stars. Only the lightning arcing across the sky provided illumination to Bellius's onslaught.

She was on the defensive, and if she wanted to survive this, she had to find some way to change that—

But the snow slickened the stones, the dirt, and as lightning lashed across the sky again, blinding them both, he thought faster. Acted faster.

Used her blink to slam his shield into her own, knocking it from her grip.

It clattered onto a stone nearby. Her fool's look toward it had him knocking the sword from her hand, too.

Disarmed like a novice.

Thunder cracked again, and Bellius laughed. "Disappointing." He paused, surveying her. And smiled before he attacked once more.

Nesta dodged assault after assault, but not fast enough to avoid the precise slices Bellius landed to her arms, her legs, her face. She slowed, her feet sliding on the slippery mountainside as the thunder-snow raged.

Another blow and her feet left the ground. The breath slammed out of her as her spine hit something unyielding. A boulder.

Nesta's body refused to move as she panted. Warm blood trickled out of her nose.

Bellius approached, tossing his weapons aside. "Doing this with my bare hands will be so much more satisfying."

Move.

The word rang through Nesta. She had to keep moving.

On shaking hands, as lightning cracked and the snow swirled, Nesta pushed up off the rock. Her legs trembled, begging her to sit, to stop, to just fucking die already.

Bellius advanced, his powerful body sinking into a fighting position. The wild hatred in his gaze seared her.

Her friends had made it . . . but she did not want to die.

She wanted to live, and live well, and live happily.

Wanted to do it with—

Nesta braced her feet apart. Settled her aching, battered body.

Bellius snorted. "You really think you can beat me in hand-to-hand combat?"

Blood flowed from her mouth, her nose. But Nesta smiled anyway, its tang coating her tongue. "I do."

Bellius threw his first punch, putting the entire force of his powerful body into it. Nesta blocked it, driving her fist into his nose. Bone crunched. Bellius howled, falling back a step.

And Nesta hissed, "Because my mate taught me well."

CHAPTER 73

Mate.

The word was a shooting star through Nesta as she and Bellius launched at each other, punching, kicking, dodging. As if voicing the word had given her this final surge of strength—

Bellius slammed his fist into Nesta's jaw, so hard she rocked back a few steps.

She ducked his next move, landing a blow on his ribs. But he kept herding her toward the archway, the line.

Wearing her down. Outlasting her.

She'd keep going. Until the end, she'd fight him.

Bellius's fist connected with her left cheek. Pain cracked through her. Nesta's feet went out from under her. She flew backward, and time slowed.

She landed on the other side of the line in the earth, and could have sworn the mountain shuddered.

Nesta crawled. She didn't care how pathetic it made her appear. She crawled away from Bellius, through the arch, destroying the line she'd drawn.

He advanced, bloodied and sneering. "I'm going to enjoy this."

She'd claimed it would be fine to die for her friends, that it was fine because they had made it, they had won, but to be killed by this *nobody*—

Nesta snarled. She had nothing left. Her body had given up on her. Like so many others had.

Bellius drew a knife from his boot. "I think I'd rather slit your throat."

She was alone.

She had been born alone, and would die alone, and this awful male would be the one to kill her—

Thunder cracked, and the entire mountain shook with its impact. Bellius took one step toward her, knife lifting.

Blood sprayed.

At first, she thought it was lightning that flashed across his throat, opening it so wide that his blood showered the snowy air.

But then she saw the wings. The *other* set of wings.

And when Bellius slumped to the earth, choking on his lifeblood, revealing Cassian standing there, teeth bared, blade in hand, she wondered if the thunder rocking the mountain had been his rage.

Cassian stepped over Bellius's dying body and offered her a hand. Not to sweep her into his arms, but to help her rise. As he had always done.

Nesta gripped his hand and stood, her body bleating in protest.

But she forgot her pain, the death around them, as he folded her into his chest and held her tightly, whispering tenderly into her bloody hair, "And now I'm going to slit your pretty little throat."

⁜

Cassian's words were not his own. His hands were not his own as Nesta—as his *mate*—tried to pull away and he clamped his arms around her. Hard enough that her bones shifted against his hands.

He was screaming. Silently, endlessly. Screaming at her to fight him, to run. Screaming at himself to stop it.

But he couldn't. No matter what he did, he could not stop it.

"Cassian," Nesta said, struggling.

Kill me, he silently begged her. *Kill me before I have to do this.*

"*Cassian.*" Nesta shoved against his chest. But his arms held firm. Squeezed her tighter.

"He can't obey you, Nesta Archeron," rasped an old, withered voice from behind Nesta. "He's mine now."

Cassian could not even widen his eyes in warning. His arms loosened on the queen's silent command, allowing Nesta to turn in his embrace.

Presenting her to Briallyn, who wore the Crown atop her thin, white hair.

CHAPTER 74

Satisfaction flashed in Briallyn's dark eyes, and the three simple spikes of the golden Crown glowed as she lifted a hand.

The storm halted. Cleared away to reveal the pale gray sky before dawn, the last of the stars winking out.

Even nature could be influenced by the Crown.

Horror coiled through Nesta as Cassian's arms slackened. She launched herself a few steps away, whirling, but knew what she'd find. Cassian stood still as a statue. As if he'd been turned to stone. His eyes, normally so bright and alive, had become glassy. Empty.

Briallyn had willed him that way. Had moved people around like chess pieces to ensure that Nesta arrived here. "Why?" Nesta said.

Briallyn's thick fur cloak ruffled in the mountain wind. "Your power is too strong—throwing you into this primitive spectacle wore you down."

"*You* had the Illyrians bring me here?"

"My intent was to grab the maimed one." Nesta's blood boiled at the mention of Emerie. "Bellius fed me the information about your friendship and I saw how much she meant to you when we were linked through the Harp and the Crown. I knew that if I captured her, brought her here, you'd follow, law or no law. You're reckless and conceited enough to think you could save her. But you made it easy for me: you went right to her house in Windhaven. Spared me the trouble of luring you. I let those witless Illyrians take her and the half-breed as an amusing bonus."

Nesta didn't dare look up at Cassian. "All to wear me down?"

"Yes. And without your magic—"

Nesta cut in, demanding, "I was worn down days ago. Why hold off until now?"

Briallyn glowered at the interruption. "I was waiting for *him*." She nodded toward Cassian, who was bristling with rage—something like loathing and fear now pushing through the cloudiness in his eyes. "Days and days, I waited for him to get close enough for me to use the Crown to ensnare him. I had to use that brash princeling Eris to draw him in." A soft laugh. "Eris tried to help his soldiers when they surrounded him during his hunt. *Help* those wretches. He rode right up to them, rather than gallop away as any wise person would. They grabbed him with minimal fuss. Even those infernal hounds of his could do nothing as Koschei winnowed him away."

Was Eris dead? Or now her slave? Cassian's face revealed nothing.

But Briallyn smiled at him. "I was getting worried you'd never approach. Poor Eris would have met a *very* sorry end if that had been the case. His fire wouldn't have withstood Koschei's lake, I don't think."

She glanced toward Bellius's corpse. "He's a hateful brute—just like you, Cassian. Arrogant and brash. He wandered off from his scouting unit to look for *fun* in my lands. So I showed him my idea of fun." Her thin lips twisted in a mockery of a smile.

Briallyn chuckled. "I told him to hunt you down, not kill you, but it seems I wasn't precise enough in my wording. And it's rather satisfying to watch someone kill, especially with tools you've provided for them. I knew the Rite would be so much more entertaining with weapons. I suppose I could have ordered Bellius to stand down, but I was rather enjoying the sight."

Nesta demanded, "Why are you doing this? Why don't you want peace?"

"Peace?" Briallyn laughed. "What peace can I have now?" She waved a hand down at herself. "What I want is retribution. What I want is *power.* What I want is the Trove. So I made sure you knew it, too. Made sure you became my unwitting partner in collecting the items of power from this godsforsaken territory. And I know there's only one way you'll yield them to me. One person for whom you'd do so." A smile toward Cassian. "Your mate."

"I don't have the Trove here."

"You can summon it. The objects will answer to you, no matter the wards on them. And you will hand them over to me."

"And then you'll kill us both?"

"And then I shall Make myself *young* again. I shall leave you both untouched."

Nesta scented the lie.

Cassian grunted out, "*Don't.*"

Briallyn shot him a surprised look, and his mouth shut. He trembled, but remained standing still. Yet the glassiness in his gaze had cleared.

"So," Briallyn said, "you will trade me the Trove for your mate's life. You are so thoroughly Fae now, Nesta Archeron. You would allow the world to turn to ash and ruin before you let your mate die." She frowned with distaste at the bodies around them, the blood. "Summon the Trove, and let us be done with this messy business."

Nesta couldn't stop her shaking. To give Briallyn the Trove, if she could even summon it . . . "No."

"Then I shall have to try to convince you."

Briallyn snapped her fingers at Cassian, and Nesta had half a second to turn before he was upon her.

Panic and rage shone in his eyes, but Nesta could do nothing, absolutely nothing, as he barreled into her, knocking her to the ground. Pinning her there, an arm at her throat, the weight of him, once so intimate and loving, now the thing that would hold her here, hurt her—

Pleading filled his face, utter anguish, as he fought the Crown. Fought it and lost.

"It will destroy him, of course, to kill his own mate," Briallyn said. "You will be dead, and you will die knowing you doom him to a life of misery."

Cassian's free arm shook as he pulled the knife he'd killed Bellius with from his belt. Brought it toward her.

"You kill me," Nesta gasped, "and you don't get the Trove. You'll never find it."

"There are others in your court as delusional as you are. They'll get it for me one way or another, with the right incentive. Granted, I'll need your blood to unlock the wards on the Trove. I saw that, too, you know. When you so foolishly held the Harp in the Prison. But I suppose killing you will provide plenty of the blood required." Briallyn nodded to Cassian. "Get her up."

Nesta didn't fight as he hauled her to her feet. Held the knife against her throat. Pleading shone in his eyes. Pleading and fear and—and love.

Love she did not deserve, had never once deserved, but there it was. Just as it had been there from the instant they'd met.

What was the value of the world, compared to him? To this?

"This is growing tiring," Briallyn said.

Nesta let her mate see the love shining in her face.

The sky filled with soft, gentle light.

"Kill," Briallyn ordered Cassian.

Nesta had loved Cassian since she'd first laid eyes on him. Had loved him even when she did not want to, even when she had been swallowed by despair and fear and hatred. Had loved him and destroyed herself because she didn't believe she deserved him, because he was all that was good, and brave, and kind, and she loved him, she loved him, she loved him—

Cassian's arm shook, and Nesta braced herself for the blow, showing him her forgiveness, her unending, unbreakable love for him—

But Cassian roared.

And then the knife twisted in his hand, angling not toward her, but toward his own heart.

Of his own free will.

Against the Crown's hold, against a gasping Briallyn, he chose to drive the knife into his own heart. *Kill*, she had said. But had not specified who.

And as the sun broke over the horizon, as Cassian's knife plunged for his chest, Nesta erupted with the force of the Cauldron.

⸸

There was nothing in Nesta's head but screaming. Nothing in her heart but love and hatred and fury as she let go of everything inside her and the entire world exploded.

The baying of her magic was a beast with no name. Avalanches cascaded down the cliffs in seas of glittering white. Trees bent and ruptured in the wake of the power that shattered from her. Distant seas drew back from their shores, then raced in waves toward them again. Glasses shook and shattered in Velaris, books tumbled off the shelves in Helion's thousand libraries, and the remnants of a run-down cottage in the human lands crumbled into a pile of rubble.

But all Nesta saw was Briallyn. All she saw was the slack-jawed crone as Nesta leaped upon her, throwing her frail body to the rocky ground. All she knew was screaming as she clutched Briallyn's face, the Crown glowing blindingly white, and roared her fury to the mountains, to the stars, to the dark places between them.

Gnarled hands turned young. A lined face became beautiful and lovely. White hair darkened to raven black.

But Nesta bellowed and bellowed, letting her magic rage, unleashing every ember. Erasing the queen beneath her from existence.

The young hands turned to ash. The pretty face dissolved into nothing. The dark hair withered into dust.

Until all that was left of the queen was the Crown on the ground.

CHAPTER 75

Cassian lay facedown on the earth.

Nesta rushed toward him, praying, sobbing, her magic still echoing through the world.

She turned him over, searching for the knife, the wound, but—

The knife lay beneath him. Unbloodied.

He groaned, cracking his eyes open. "I figured," he rasped, "I should lie low while you did that."

Nesta gaped at him. Then burst into tears.

Cassian sat up, soothing sounds on his tongue, and took her face in his hands. "You Unmade her."

Nesta glanced to the Crown on the earth—the black stain where Briallyn had been. "She had it coming."

He chuckled, leaning his brow against hers. Nesta closed her eyes, breathing in his scent. "You are my mate, Cassian," she said against his lips, and kissed him softly.

"And you're mine," he said, kissing her in turn.

And then his hands slid into her hair. And the kiss . . .

It did not matter, the world around them, or the Crown at her feet, as he kissed her. A mate's kiss. One that set their souls twining, glowing.

She pulled back, letting him see the joy in her eyes, her smile. His awe, his own joy, made her throat tighten.

"Cassian, I—"

But two figures landed beside them, making the mountain shudder, and they whirled to find Mor and Azriel there, faces grave.

"Eris?" Cassian demanded.

"Safe, and the Made dagger is in our possession again," Azriel said, "though Eris is pissed and confused. He's at the Hewn City. But—"

"It's Feyre," Mor said.

CHAPTER 76

The river house was so silent. Like a tomb.

"She started bleeding a few hours ago," Mor said as she led them through the house.

"But she's months away from giving birth," Nesta protested, following close on her heels.

The scent of blood filled the room they entered. So much blood, all over the bed, smeared over Feyre's spread thighs. No babe—and Feyre's face . . . It was white as death. Her eyes were closed, her breathing too shallow.

Rhys crouched at her side, gripping her hand. Panic and terror and pain warred on his face.

Madja, kneeling on the bed between Feyre's legs, blood up to her elbows, said without looking at them, "I turned the babe, but he's not descending. He's wedged in the birth canal."

A small intake of breath from the corner of the room revealed Amren sitting there, her pale face drained of color.

"She's losing too much blood, and I can feel the babe's heart in distress," Madja announced.

"What do we do?" Mor asked as Cassian and Azriel went to stand behind Rhys, hands on his shoulders.

"There is nothing we can do," Madja said. "Cutting the babe out of her will kill her."

"Cutting it out?" Nesta demanded, earning a sharp glare from Rhys.

Madja ignored her tone. "An incision along her abdomen, even one carefully made, is an enormous risk. It's never been successful. And even with Feyre's healing abilities, the blood loss has weakened her—"

"Do it," Feyre managed to say, the words weighted with pain.

"Feyre," Rhys objected.

"The babe likely won't survive," Madja said, voice gentle but no-nonsense. "It's too small yet. We risk both of you."

"All of you," Cassian breathed, eyes on Rhys.

"*Do it*," Feyre said, and her voice was that of the High Lady. No fear. Only determination for the life of the babe within her. Feyre looked up at Rhys. "We have to."

The High Lord nodded slowly, eyes lined with silver.

A hand slid into Nesta's, and she found Elain there, shaking and wide-eyed. Nesta squeezed her sister's fingers. Together, they approached the other side of the bed.

And when Elain began praying to the Fae's foreign gods, to their Mother, Nesta bowed her head, too.

⁜

Feyre was dying. The babe was dying.

And Rhys would die with them.

But Cassian knew it wasn't fear of his own death that had his brother trembling. Cassian's hand tightened on Rhys's shoulder. Night-flecked power leaked from his High Lord, trying to heal Feyre, just as Madja's was, but the blood kept pouring out, faster than any power could stifle.

How had it come to this? A bargain made through love between two mates would now end in three lives lost.

Cassian's body drifted somewhere far away as Madja got off the bed, then returned with a set of knives and tools, blankets and towels.

"Go into her mind to take the pain away," Madja said to Rhys, who blinked in confirmation, then cursed, as if scolding himself for not thinking of it sooner. Cassian looked across the bed, to where Elain was holding Feyre's other hand, and Nesta held Elain's.

Rhys said to his mate, "Feyre darling—"

"No good-byes," Feyre panted. "No good-byes, Rhys."

Whatever Rhys did for the pain had her eyes closing. And Cassian's mind went wholly silent and blank as Madja pulled up Feyre's shift, her knives flashing.

There was no sound when the tiny, winged babe emerged. When Mor stood there, blankets in hand, and took the unmoving boy from Madja's bloody hands.

But Rhys was crying, and tears began pouring down Mor's face as she gazed at the silent babe in her arms.

And then Madja swore, and Rhys—

Rhys began screaming.

Cassian knew, as Rhys lunged for Feyre on the bed, what was about to happen.

Yet no force in the world could stop it.

⳾

The world slowed. Went cold.

There was the silent, too-small babe in Mor's arms.

There was Feyre, sliced open and bleeding out on the bed.

There was Rhysand screaming, as if his soul were being shredded, but Cassian and Azriel were there, hauling him away from the bed as Madja tried to save Feyre—

But Death hovered nearby. Nesta felt it, saw it, a shadow thicker and more permanent than any of Azriel's. Elain sobbed, squeezing Feyre's hand, pleading with her to hold on, and Nesta stood in the midst of it, Death swirling around her, and there was nothing, nothing, nothing to be done as Feyre's breathing thinned, as Madja began shouting at her to fight it—

Feyre.

Feyre, who had gone into the woods for them. Who had saved them so many times.

Feyre. Her sister.

Death lurked near Feyre and her mate, a beast waiting to pounce, to devour them both. Nesta pulled her hand free of Elain's. Stepped back.

She closed her eyes, and opened that place in her soul that had torn free on Ramiel.

✣

Cassian could barely restrain Rhys, even with all seven Siphons blaring along with Azriel's.

He should let Rhys go to her. If they were both about to die, he should let Rhys go to his mate. Be with her in these last seconds, last breaths—

Golden light flickered on the other side of the room, and Amren gasped. Cassian's heart curdled in horror.

Nesta no longer hovered by the side of the bed. She now stood a few feet away.

She wore the Mask. She'd placed the Crown atop her head. And she cradled the Harp in her arms.

No one had ever wielded all three and lived. No one could contain their power, control them—

Nesta's eyes blazed with silver fire behind the Mask. And Cassian knew the being that looked out was neither Fae nor human nor anything that walked the lands of this world.

She began moving toward the bed, and Rhys surged for her.

Nesta held up a hand, and Rhys went still. As still as Cassian had gone under the Crown's control.

Feyre's chest lifted, a death-rattle whispering from her white lips, and Cassian could do nothing but watch as Nesta's fingers, still bloody and filthy from the Rite, drifted to the final string of the Harp. The twenty-sixth string.

And plucked it.

CHAPTER 77

It was Time.

The twenty-sixth string on the Harp was Time itself, and Nesta stopped it as Feyre took her last breath.

Lanthys had said as much. That even Death bowed to the final string. That time was of no consequence to the Harp.

The string made no sound as Nesta plucked it. Only robbed the world of it.

And the death that Nesta felt around her sister, around Rhysand, around the babe in Mor's arms—she bade the Mask to halt that, too. Hold it at bay.

In the beginning
And in the end
There was Darkness
And nothing more

A soft, familiar voice whispered the words. As they had been whispered to her long ago. As it had warned her in Oorid's darkness. A lovely, kind female voice, sage and warm, which had been waiting for her all this time.

The room was a tableau of frozen movement, of shocked and horrified faces twisted toward her, toward Feyre and all that blood. Nesta walked through it. Past Rhys's screaming, straining body, his face the portrait of despair and terror and pain; past grave-faced Azriel; past Cassian, gritting his teeth as he held Rhys back. Past Amren, whose gray eyes were fixed on where Nesta had been, pure dread and something like awe in her face.

Past Mor and that too-small bundle in her arms, Elain at her side, frozen in her crying.

Nesta walked through it all, through Time. To her sister.

Do you see how it might be? that soft female voice whispered, staring out through her eyes. *What you might do?*

I feel nothing, Nesta said silently. Only the sight of Feyre on Death's threshold kept her from forgetting why she was here, what she needed to do.

Is that not what you wanted? To feel nothing?

I thought that was what I wanted. Nesta surveyed the people around her. Her sisters. Cassian, who had been willing to plunge a dagger into his heart rather than harm her. *But no longer.* When the female voice didn't press her, Nesta went on, *I want to feel everything. I want to embrace it with my whole heart.*

Even the things that hurt and hunt you? Only curiosity laced the question.

Nesta allowed herself a breath to ponder it, stilling her mind once more. *We need those things in order to appreciate the good. Some days might be more difficult than others, but . . . I want to experience all of it, live through all of it. With them.*

That wise, soft voice whispered, *So live, Nesta Archeron.*

Nesta needed nothing more as she took her sister's limp hand and knelt upon the floor. Set down the Harp beside her, its silent note still reverberating, holding Time firm in its grasp.

She didn't know what she could offer, beyond this.

Stroking Feyre's cold hand, Nesta spoke into the timeless, frozen room, "You loved me when no one else would. You never stopped. Even when I didn't deserve it, you loved me, and fought for me, and . . ." Nesta looked at Feyre's face, Death a breath away from claiming it. She didn't stop the tears that ran down her cheeks as she squeezed Feyre's slender hand tighter. "I love you, Feyre."

She had never said the words aloud. To anyone.

"I love you," Nesta whispered again. "I love you."

And when the Harp's final string wavered, like a whisper of thunder on the air, Nesta covered Feyre's body with her own. Time would resume soon. She did not have much longer.

She reached inward, toward the power that had made deathless monsters tremble and wicked kings fall to their knees, but . . . she didn't know how to use it. Death flowed through her veins, yet she did not have the knowledge to master it.

One wrong move, one mistake, and Feyre would be lost.

So Nesta held her sister tightly, with Time halted around them, and she whispered, "If you show me how to save her, you can have it back."

The world paused. Worlds beyond their own paused.

Nesta buried her face in the cold sweat of Feyre's neck. She opened that place within herself, and said to the Mother, to the Cauldron, "I'll give back what I took from you. Just show me how to save them—her and Rhysand and the baby." Rhysand—her brother. That's what he was, wasn't he? Her brother, who had offered her kindness even when she knew he wanted to throttle her. And she him. And the baby . . . her nephew. Blood of her blood. She would save him, save them, even if it took everything. "Show me," she pleaded.

No one answered. The Harp stopped its echoing.

As Time resumed, noise and movement roaring into the room,

Nesta whispered to the Cauldron, her promise rising above the din, "I'll give it all back."

And a soft, invisible hand brushed her cheek in answer.

⁜

Cassian blinked, and Nesta had gone from one side of the room to the bed. Had plucked the Harp, and now lay half-atop Feyre, whispering. No silver fire burned in her eyes. Not a cold ember. No sign of the being who'd peered out through her stare, either.

Rhys lunged against his hold, but Amren stepped to their side and hissed, "*Listen.*"

Nesta whispered, "I give it all back." Her shoulders heaved as she wept.

Rhys began shaking his head, his power a palpable, rising wave that could destroy them all, destroy the world if it meant Feyre was no longer in it, even if he only had seconds to live beyond her, but Amren grabbed the nape of his neck. Her red nails dug into his golden skin. "*Look at the light.*"

Iridescent light began flowing from Nesta's body. Into Feyre.

Nesta kept holding her sister. "I give it back. I give it back. I give it back."

Even Rhys stopped fighting. No one moved.

The light glimmered down Feyre's arms. Her legs. It suffused her ashen face. Began to fill the room.

Cassian's Siphons guttered, as if sensing a power far beyond his own, beyond any of theirs.

Tendrils of light drifted between the sisters. And one, delicate and loving, floated toward Mor. To the bundle in her arms, setting the silent babe within glowing bright as the sun.

And Nesta kept whispering, "I give it back. I give it all back."

The iridescence filled her, filled Feyre, filled the bundle in Mor's arms, lighting his friend's face so the shock on it was etched in stark relief.

"I give it back," Nesta said, one more time, and Mask and Crown tumbled from her head. The light exploded, blinding and warm, a wind sweeping past them, as if gathering every shard of itself out of the room.

And as it faded, dark ink splashed upon Nesta's back, visible through her half-shredded shirt, as if it were a wave crashing upon the shore.

A bargain. With the Cauldron itself.

Yet Cassian could have sworn a luminescent, gentle hand prevented the light from leaving her body altogether.

Cassian didn't fight Rhys this time as he raced to the bed. To where Feyre lay, flush with color. No more blood spilling between her legs. Feyre opened her eyes.

She blinked at Rhys, and then turned to Nesta.

"I love you, too," Feyre whispered to her sister, and smiled. Nesta didn't stop her sob as she launched herself onto Feyre and embraced her.

But the gesture was short-lived, hardly the length of a blink before a healthy wail went up from the other side of the room, and—

Mor stammered, weeping, and the babe she brought to the bed was not the small, still thing she'd been holding, but a full-term winged boy. His thick cap of dark hair lay plastered to his head as he mewled for his mother.

Feyre began sobbing then, too, taking her son from Mor, hardly noticing Madja suddenly leaning between her legs, inspecting what was there—the healing. "If I didn't know better, I'd say you'd developed an Illyrian's anatomy," the healer muttered, but no one was listening.

Not as Rhys put his arm around Feyre and together they peered at the boy—their son. Together, they wept, and laughed, and when Madja said, "Let him feed," Feyre obeyed, wonder in her eyes as she brought him to her breast, now swollen with milk.

But Rhys watched in awe for all of a moment before he whirled to Nesta, who had slid off the bed and now stood beside the Mask. Behind her, the Crown and the Harp lay strewn on the floor. Cassian held his breath as the two of them surveyed each other.

Then Rhys fell to his knees and took Nesta's hands in his, pressing his mouth to her fingers. "Thank you," he wept, head bowed. Cassian knew it wasn't in gratitude for Rhys's own life that he knelt upon the sacred tattoos inked upon his knees.

Nesta dropped to the carpet. Lifted Rhys's face in her hands, studied what lay in it. Then she threw her arms around the High Lord of the Night Court and held him tightly.

CHAPTER 78

Gwyn and Emerie were waiting in one of the parlors overlooking the river, healed but still in their torn, bloody clothes. Steam curled off the cups set on the low table before them.

Emerie said thickly as Nesta stopped before their couch, "Two wraiths brought us some tea—"

But Gwyn cut her off, face blazing as she hissed at Nesta, "I should *never* forgive you."

Nesta just leaped onto the couch, hugging Gwyn tightly. She reached out an arm for Emerie, who joined their embrace. "We can talk forgiveness another day," Nesta said through her tears, settling between them. "You won the entire damn thing."

"Thanks to you," Emerie said.

"I got a crown of my own, don't worry," Nesta said, even as she knew Mor was now winnowing all three objects of the Trove back to the place Nesta had taken them from. She'd summoned them, working around Helion's spells. No spell could ever keep them from her—Briallyn had spoken true about that.

"Who healed you?" Nesta pulled back to survey them. "How are you even here?"

"The stone," Emerie explained, features soft with wonder. "It healed every wound on us the moment it brought us out of the Rite. We arrived here, of all places."

"I think it knew where we were needed most," Gwyn said quietly, and Nesta smiled.

Her smile faded, however, as she asked Emerie, "Will your family punish you for what happened to Bellius?" If they so much as thought about doing so, Nesta would pay them a little visit. With the Mask, the Harp, and the Crown.

Which was why the Trove should be kept far away from her.

Emerie shrugged a shoulder. "Deaths happen in the Rite. He fell in combat when one of his fellow warriors turned on him during the hike up Ramiel's slopes. That's as much as they need to know." Her eyes twinkled.

Nesta had a feeling that the truth of what had occurred on that mountain would remain only with them—and the innermost circle of Feyre's court. Cassian had clearly been brought into the Rite against his will. Hopefully no one would ever challenge that fact.

Gwyn laughed hoarsely. "The Illyrians are going to be furious about our winning, you know. Especially because I have no intention of being called Carynthian. I'm content with being a Valkyrie."

"Oh, they'll be in hysterics for decades," Emerie agreed, grinning.

Nesta grinned back, slinging her arms around her friends again and sinking into the deep cushions of the couch. "I can't wait to see it."

And for the first time, with these two friends beside her, with her mate waiting for her . . . it was true.

Nesta couldn't wait to see the future that unfolded. All of it.

The baby, whom Rhys and Feyre named Nyx, was as beautiful as anyone could ever dream a baby to be. Dark hair, with blue eyes that already glowed with his father's and mother's starlight, offsetting the light tan of his skin.

And then there were the tiny wings, which Cassian had never realized were so delicate, so perfect, until he touched their velvet softness. The claws atop them would grow in much later, along with the ability to use the wings themselves, but . . . He stared at the bundle in his arms, his heart full to bursting, and said to where Feyre and Rhys sat on the bed, neatly remade with clean linens, "You have no idea how much trouble this one is going to get into."

Feyre chuckled. "Those pretty eyes will be to blame, I'm sure."

Rhys, still rattled and pale, just smiled.

The door opened, and then Nesta was there, still in her torn, bloody, stolen clothes. She'd held the babe already, and Cassian's chest had swelled, aching, to see her smiling down at Nyx.

But now Nesta's eyes drifted to Cassian, and he saw the quiet request in them.

He silently handed Nyx to Azriel, who winced at the transfer of this most delicate little creature to his scarred hands, and followed Nesta out the door, into the hall, and down the stairs. They didn't speak until they stood on the back lawn of the house, overlooking the river once again awakening in the spring sunshine.

What she'd done, both during the Rite and after it . . . She'd filled them all in briefly. He knew there was more. But perhaps some things would always remain a secret between her and her friends. Her sisters-in-arms.

So Cassian asked, "Is your magic . . . The power's really gone?"

The brisk spring wind whipped her golden-brown hair across her face. "I gave it back to the Cauldron in exchange for the knowledge of how to save them." She swallowed. "But a little remains. I think something else—someone else—stopped the Cauldron from taking all of it. And I made some changes of my own."

The Mother. The only being who would see the sacrifice Nesta had made and give a little back. Perhaps it was she who had peered out at them through the Mask. "What did you change?"

Nesta rested a hand on her abdomen. "I changed myself a little, too. So none of us will have to go through this again."

For a heartbeat, Cassian had no words. "You . . . You're ready for a *baby*?"

Nesta barked a laugh. "No. Gods no. I'll be drinking my contraceptive tea for a while yet." She laughed again. "But I adjusted myself to match what the Cauldron did for Feyre. For when the time is right."

He couldn't tear himself from the quiet joy lighting her face. So he offered her a soft smile. Yes—when the time was right, they would start that journey together.

But what Nesta had done today, what she'd given . . .

"You could have ruled the world with your power," he said carefully.

"I don't want to rule the world." Her eyes were unguarded in a way he had never seen. *Mate*, she had called him.

"What do you want?" Cassian managed to ask, voice rasping.

She smiled, and damn if it wasn't the loveliest thing he'd ever seen. "You."

"You've had me from the moment you met me."

She tucked a strand of hair behind an arched ear. "I know."

He brushed a kiss over her mouth. But Nesta said, "I want a disgustingly ornate mating ceremony."

He laughed, pulling away. "Really?"

"Why not?"

"Because I'll never hear the end of it from Azriel and Mor." Or the Illyrians.

Nesta considered. Then pulled something out of her pocket. A small biscuit, swiped from a tray in the birthing room. "Then here. Food. From me to you, my mate. That's the official ritual, isn't it? The sharing of food from one mate to the other?"

He choked. "These are my two options? A frilly mating ceremony or a stale biscuit?"

Her face filled with such true light, it nearly stole the breath from him. "Yes."

So Cassian laughed again, and folded her fingers around the pathetic biscuit, leaning to whisper in her ear, "We'll make a coronation of it, Nes."

"I already have a crown," she said. "I just want you."

His jaw tightened. Yes, they'd have to figure out what to do with the entire Dread Trove now that they possessed all three objects. How Nesta had summoned it despite the spells Helion had placed on the other two . . . He'd think of that another day. Along with the fact that she'd stopped Time with the Harp. And that she seemed to have some sort of connection—or understanding—with the Mother. *The Mother.*

But Nesta smoothed his bunched brow, as if she could see those worries there. "Later," she promised. "We'll deal with all that later." Including the remaining queens, Koschei, and a still-looming war.

"Later," he agreed, and she slid her arms around his neck.

There were no more words after that. Only the two of them, standing on the riverbank under the sun, letting its warmth seep through their bones.

Nesta pulled away, whispering, "I love you," and it was all Cassian needed before kissing her again, the force of it more powerful and enduring than the Cauldron itself.

CHAPTER 79

Meeting Eris was the last thing Cassian wanted to do, but someone had to check in with the male. Two days after Nyx's birth, Cassian set off to do just that. Eris had been seen to a suite in the Hewn City, and from Keir's stormy expression upon Cassian's arrival, he had a feeling that Eris had told the steward very little.

Eris was reading a book by the roaring fire, an ankle crossed over a knee, as if his presence here were nothing unusual. As if he hadn't been kidnapped, enchanted, and manipulated by a vengeful queen and a death-lord.

Eris lifted his amber eyes as Cassian shut the door. "I can't stay long."

"Good."

Eris closed the book, watching Cassian drop into the seat opposite him. "I suppose you want to know what I told Briallyn."

"Rhys already looked into your mind. Turns out, you didn't know much." He gave the male a slashing grin.

Eris rolled his eyes. "So why am I here?"

Cassian surveyed the male. Eris's clothes remained immaculate, but a muscle ticked on his jaw. "We wanted to know what you told Beron. Since you're sitting here, in one piece, I'm assuming he doesn't know about our involvement in your rescue."

"Oh, he knows that you . . . assisted me."

Cassian straightened, wings shifting.

Eris went on, "Always mix truth and lies, General. Didn't those warrior-brutes teach you about how to withstand an enemy's torture?"

Cassian knew. He'd been tortured and interrogated and never once broken. "Beron tortured you?"

Eris rose, tucking his book under an arm. "Who cares what my father does to me? He believed my story about the shadowsinger's spies informing him that a valuable asset had been kidnapped by Briallyn, and that you lot were disgusted to arrive and find it was me, rather than someone from the Summer or Winter Courts or whoever stoops to associate with you."

Cassian unpacked each word. Beron had tortured his own son for information, rather than thanking the Mother for returning him. But Eris had held out. Fed Beron another lie.

And then there was the way Eris had spoken about the other courts. Something had been off in his words, his tight expression. Was the male jealous?

Cassian opened his mouth, more than ready to launch that question at him and bestow a stinging blow.

Yet he hesitated. Looked into Eris's eyes.

The male had been raised with every luxury and privilege—on paper. But who knew what terrors Beron had inflicted upon him? Cassian knew Beron had murdered Lucien's lover. If the High Lord of Autumn had been willing to do that, what wouldn't he do?

"Get that pitying look off your face," Eris snarled softly. "I know what sort of creature my father is. I don't need your sympathy."

Cassian again studied him. "Why did you leave Mor in the woods that day?" It was the question that would always remain. "Was it just to impress your father?"

Eris barked a laugh, harsh and empty. "Why does it still matter to all of you so much?"

"Because she's my sister, and I love her."

"I didn't realize Illyrians were in the habit of fucking their sisters."

Cassian growled. "It still matters," he ground out, "because it doesn't add up. You know what a monster your father is and want to usurp him; you act against him in the best interests of not only the Autumn Court but also of all of the faerie lands; you risk your life to ally with us . . . and yet you left her in the woods. Is it guilt that motivates all of this? Because you left her to suffer and die?"

Golden flame simmered in Eris's gaze. "I didn't realize I'd be facing another interrogation so soon."

"Give me a damn answer."

Eris crossed his arms, then winced. As if whatever injuries lay beneath his immaculate clothes ached. "You're not the person I want to explain myself to."

"I doubt Mor will want to listen."

"Maybe not." Eris shifted on his feet, and grimaced again. "But you and yours have more important things to think about than ancient history. My father is furious that his ally is dead, but he's not deterred. Koschei remains in play, and Beron might very well be stupid enough to establish an alliance with him, too. I hope that whatever Morrigan is doing in Vallahan will counteract the damage my father will unleash."

Cassian had heard enough. He wanted to return home—to the House, to Nesta. His fierce, beautiful mate, who had saved his High Lord and Lady and their son. He'd never stop being in awe of her, and all she had done. How far she'd come.

And one day, when the time was right . . . They'd take the next steps. They'd walk down whatever road lay ahead of them together.

So Cassian stalked for the door, for the life awaiting him in Velaris.

Eris was still their ally. Was willing to be tortured to keep their secrets. And Cassian didn't need to be a courtier to know his next words would slice deep, but it would be a necessary wound. Perhaps it would be enough to push things in the right direction.

"You know, Eris," he said, a hand wrapping around the doorknob. "I think you might be a decent male, deep down, trapped in a terrible situation." He looked over his shoulder and found Eris's gaze blazing again. But only pity stirred in his chest, pity for a male who had been born into riches, but had been destitute in every way that truly mattered. In every way that Cassian had been blessed—blessings that were now overflowing.

So Cassian said, "I grew up surrounded by monsters. I've spent my existence fighting them. And I see you, Eris. You're not one of them. Not even close. I think you might even be a good male." Cassian opened the door, turning from Eris's curled lip. "You're just too much of a coward to act like one."

CHAPTER 80

Spring bloomed fully around Velaris, and Feyre and Nyx were finally well enough to leave the house each day, going on walks that often lasted hours thanks to the well-wishers who longed to see the child. Someone always accompanied them, usually Rhys or Mor, who was just as protective as the parents of the babe. Cassian and Azriel were hardly better.

But none of the others were present on a warm day a few weeks later, when Nesta joined Feyre and Elain for a walk outside the city. Even a glance at the sky revealed no sign of Cassian, who had been keeping Nesta up until dawn with his lovemaking and had become utterly obnoxious about calling her *mate* any chance he got, except at their continuing morning training with the priestesses.

Succeeding in the Blood Rite didn't mean the training stopped. No, after she and her friends told Cassian and Azriel most of the details of their ordeal, the two commanders had compiled a long list of mistakes that the three of them had made that needed to be corrected, and the others wanted to learn from them, too. So they would keep training, until they were all well and truly Valkyries. Gwyn, despite the Rite, had returned to living in the library.

Gwyn had said she *might* leave for Nesta and Cassian's mating ceremony in three days, which would take place in the small temple on the river house's grounds. Despite Nesta's wishes for an ornate ceremony, she hadn't wanted a giant crowd. The temple was already being bedecked with flowers of every variety, enchanted against wilting, as well as silks and lace and candles and garlands—all of it paid for by Rhys, who could not stop buying her presents. Dresses and jewels and throw pillows and all manner of nonsense had rained down on her until Nesta had to order him to stop, saying that an extravagant mating ceremony would make them even.

So Rhys had ensured that the ceremony would be as outrageous as possible. Nesta had no doubt the temple would be covered in such riches it'd be laughable.

But all that mattered, she realized, was the male who would be standing with her, first as they swore their vows, then as they offered each other food, and then as their friends and family bound their hands together with a length of black ribbon, to remain until the mating was consummated.

Even though the consummating had been going on two or three times a day for weeks now.

But it didn't matter. Nesta could hardly wait for it—the ceremony, the . . . whatever awaited her beyond it. None of it frightened her. None of it left her with that pit of despair. Not with Cassian at her side, her friends at her back, the House of Wind . . .

That had been Rhys's last present before the ceremony: It was theirs. Hers.

Since the House had decided it liked Nesta more than anyone else, Rhys had given it to her and Cassian, with the caveat that the library belonged to the priestesses and that the court still had use of the House for formal occasions. It was good enough for Nesta—better than good.

She'd joined them at the river house one night to find a mating present from Feyre waiting for her. Hanging on the wall in the grand entry.

A portrait of Nesta, holding the line at the Pass of Enalius. She'd let Rhys see some parts of the Rite—but had no idea he'd asked not out of curiosity, but to give his mate ideas for this.

Nesta had stared and stared at her portrait, hung between one of Feyre and one of Elain, and hadn't realized she was crying until Feyre had held her tightly.

A home. The House of Wind, Velaris, this court . . . they were her home. The thought kindled a kernel of light in her chest that had not extinguished, even in the days after the Rite.

That kernel was still flickering as Nesta faced that day's task. The task that was so long overdue.

Feyre left the ornate black carriage at the base of the grassy hill, carrying Nyx as the three of them scaled its soft slope. The city spread before them, glowing in the spring sunshine, but Nesta's eyes remained on the lone stone atop the hill.

Her heart thundered, and she kept a step back as Feyre knelt before the grave marker, showing Nyx to the stone. "Your grandson, Father," she whispered, voice thick. And then Feyre bowed her head, speaking too low for Nesta or Elain, standing at Nesta's side, to hear.

After a few minutes, Feyre rose, letting her tears run, as holding the babe kept her hands occupied. Elain went forward, whispered a few things to their father's grave, and then both sisters looked to Nesta, smiling tentatively.

Feyre had asked this morning if Nesta wanted to come. To show their father the baby.

And there had been no answer in Nesta's heart except one.

So she nodded to her sisters to go on ahead, and they obeyed, easing back down the grassy hill as Nesta lingered by the gravestone.

She searched for the words, for any explanation or apology, but none came.

The sun was a warm hand on her shoulder, like the one that had prevented the last of her power from vanishing, as if telling her that the apology, the begging for forgiveness . . . it was no longer needed.

Her father had died for her, with love in his heart, and though she might not have deserved it then . . . She would do all she could now to earn it. To deserve not just his love, but that of those around her. Of Cassian.

Some days might indeed be difficult, but she'd do it. Fight for it.

Her father had died for her, with love in his heart, and Nesta held love in her own heart as she pulled the small, carved rose from her pocket and set it upon the gravestone. A permanent marker of the beauty and good he'd tried to bring into the world.

Nesta brought her fingers to her lips, pressed a kiss to them, then laid her hand upon the gravestone.

"Thank you," she said, blinking back the stinging in her eyes. "Thank you."

A swift shadow passed overhead, followed by a whisper of wings, and Nesta didn't need to look to know who sailed high above, making sure all was safe. That she was safe.

Busybody. But she blew Cassian a soft kiss, too.

Her mate. Her love. Her friend. The light within her chest brightened to a radiant sun.

She found Feyre and Elain waiting halfway down the hill, Nyx now dozing peacefully in Elain's arms. Her sisters beamed, beckoning her to join.

And Nesta smiled back, her steps light as she hurried down the hill to meet them.

ACKNOWLEDGMENTS

Coming to the end of this book was a journey years in the making in so many ways, from the initial pages that I jotted down while working on *A Court of Wings and Ruin* to the years since then spent drafting, revising, refining. But perhaps most important, this book was a companion during my own journey through the valleys and mountains of mental health, traveling alongside me as I faced all the jagged bits inside myself. While Nesta's story is in no way a direct reflection of my own experiences, there were moments in this book that I very much needed to write—not just for the sake of these characters, but for myself. I hope some of those moments resonate, and will remind you, dear reader, that you are loved, and that you are *worthy* of love, no matter what.

I'm tremendously grateful to be surrounded by people in my professional and personal life who have unflinchingly walked along those hills and valleys with me, especially during such a tumultuous time for our entire world.

To my son, Taran: you bring me joy, and strength, and such love that my heart is overflowing with it every single day. Your laugh is the most beautiful music in the world. (I'm writing that even though you just tried to eat packing peanuts while I wasn't looking.) I'm so honored to be your mom, and I'm so proud of you. I love you, baby bunny.

To my husband, Josh: there are so many pieces of our story scattered throughout all my books, but this one seems to have gotten the lion's share. From the moment I laid eyes on you in our dorm common room sixteen years ago, I knew you'd be The One. Don't ask me how, but you walked in, and I just knew. But I still had no idea what a remarkable, wonderful path we'd walk together—the places we'd see, the life we'd build, and the family we'd create. Thank you for loving me through all of it.

To Annie, my fur-baby and most loyal companion: you are the best sister imaginable to Taran, the best copilot while writing these books, and the best cuddler after a long day of work. I adore your curly tail, your bat ears, your unfailing sass—and your sweet, loving soul.

To my friend and sister Jenn Kelly: I think when you finally read this book, you'll understand the impact your friendship has had on me, and how much good you've brought into my life. You kept reaching out your hand to me, and I will be forever grateful.

To my editor and fellow *New York Times* crossword fanatic, Noa Wheeler: you are a genius. An actual genius, and a lifesaver, and the best damn editor I've ever had the pleasure of working with. Thank you, thank you, thank you for your incredible hard work, your clever and thoughtful ideas, and for pushing me to be a better writer. I wake up every morning truly excited to work with you and learn from you, and I can't begin to tell you how grateful I am for it.

To my agent, Robin Rue: thank you doesn't seem adequate for all you've done for me, and how much I adore working with you. You arrived at the precise moment in my life when I needed you and your expertise the most, and I thank the universe every single day that I have the honor of calling you my agent. Though we've had a million Zoom calls by now, I can't wait to crack open a can of champagne (lol) with you in person one day!

To Jill Gillett: you are my take-no-shit fairy godmother. Thank you for working so tirelessly to make so many of my dreams come true—and for being a brilliant, lovely human being.

To Victoria Cook: you are the epitome of a badass, and I'm so grateful to have you in my corner.

To Maura Wogan: thank you, thank you, thank you for your wisdom, hard work, and generosity.

To Cecilia de la Campa: you are one of the coolest and hardest-working people in this industry. Thank you for championing me and my books!

To Beth Miller: you are an actual ray of sunshine and the most organized person I've ever met. I bow down before your note-taking skills! I'm so grateful for all that you do.

To the Writers House team: while we haven't been working together for very long, you've already surpassed my wildest expectations. I can't imagine my books in better hands—or with better people! I'm so proud to be a part of your family!

To Laura Keefe: thank you for your hard work and the tips on toys to occupy Taran! It's so fun to work with you—thank you for everything!

To the entire global team at Bloomsbury—Nigel Newton, Emma Hopkin, Kathleen Farrar, Rebecca McNally, Cindy Loh, Valentina Rice, Nicola Hill, Amanda Shipp, Marie Coolman, Lucy Mackay-Sim, Nicole Jarvis, Emily Fisher, Emilie Chambeyron, Patti Ratchford, Emma Ewbank, John Candell, Donna Gauthier, Melissa Kavonic, Diane Aronson, Nick Sweeney, Claire Henry, Nicholas Church, Fabia Ma, Daniel O'Connor, Brigid Nelson, Sarah McLean, Sarah Knight, Liz Bray, Genevieve Nelsson, Adam Kirkman, Jennifer Gonzalez, Laura Pennock, Elizabeth Tzetzo, and Valerie Esposito: Thank you for your incredible hard work.

To Kaitlin Severini: thanks so much for your meticulous copyediting!

To Christine Ma: thank you for your eagle-eyed proofing.

To my publishers around the world: I am deeply grateful for all of your support and all the effort you've put into getting these books into the hands of readers around the world.

To Jillian Stein: you are such fun to work with, and one of the most awesome people I know. Thank you for all the hard work—and for being you!

To Tamar Rydzinski: thank you so much for your dedication and kindness.

To Nick Odorisio, actual Jedi master. Thank you for walking me through everything from balance to the importance of the feet to the basics of Jedi master. So much of your wisdom made its way into this book (along with my complaints about crunches and planks and my lack of balance)!

To Jason Chen: thank you for your article on how to throw a punch—and to Aiman Farooq, Keith Horan, Chris Waguespack, and Pete Carvill for the invaluable insight and tips provided in it. If I'm ever in a bar fight, I hope I can at remember at least *some* of your advice! If I've gotten any of the information wrong in this book, the fault is entirely mine.

Thank you to Anna Victoria, whose workout app (Fit Body) helped me experience so much of Nesta's physical transformation firsthand. I never realized how much it would mean to me to be able to do a single push-up (though I could do without those Bulgarian squats!). And thank you to Headspace, for the calm and rest I found through meditating.

To Dr. C: there's so much that I would like to say to you, and I know all of it will fall short in conveying my gratitude. But I'll settle with a thank-you for how much you've helped me.

I would like to extend my deepest thanks to Mahu Whenua in New Zealand. Walking the mountain trails, listening to the roar of the river, watching the sun shift across the land—it all inspired Nesta and Cassian's hike. (Though I nearly snapped my ankle a few times while attempting to write down notes and keep walking!) Your property is my favorite place in the world, where I experienced a level of peace and clarity that I still can't quite explain. Thank you and the Maori people for the healing these lands brought to my weary soul.

To Lynette Noni: thank you for the friendship that brightens my days, and for being the cleverest critique partner on the planet. I don't know what I'd do without you!

To my friend Steph Brown: I love you. That is all. (Okay, it's totally not all, but you know how I feel about you by this point!)

To Louisse Ang and Laura Ashforth: I've said it about a thousand times, but I want you to know how much I adore you and how lucky I am to know both of you.

My wonderful parents and family: it's been so long since we've been able to see each other in person, but I've felt your love even from hundreds of miles away. I don't know what I'd do without you. And to my in-laws, Linda and Dennis: thank you for the chocolate (even when I said I didn't want any!), for being such doting grandparents, and for the unconditional love.

And lastly, to all of my readers: your kindness, generosity, and support mean the world to me. Thank you for taking these characters into your hearts, and for allowing me to do what I love most for a living. I am forever grateful.

BOUND BY BLOOD.
TEMPTED BY DESIRE.
UNLEASHED BY DESTINY.

'Think *Game of Thrones* meets *Buffy the Vampire Slayer* with a drizzle of E.L. James' *Telegraph*

SARAH J. MAAS

HOUSE of EARTH and BLOOD

A CRESCENT CITY NOVEL

BLOOMSBURY

THE FIRST NOVEL
IN THE EPIC SERIES